For Mom and Dad - who have always believed in me.
The Halls for rescuing me that one time.
My Land Lords - they're the best.
And A.

Shinigami Boy

Shinigami Boy

Sophia Hughlette

iUniverse, Inc.
New York Bloomington

Shinigami Boy

Copyright © 2009 Sophia Hughlette

This is a work of fiction. All of the characters, names, incidents,
organizations, and dialogue in this novel are either the products
of the author's imagination or are used fictitiously.

iUniverse books may be ordered through booksellers or by contacting:

iUniverse
1663 Liberty Drive
Bloomington, IN 47403
www.iuniverse.com
1-800-Authors (1-800-288-4677)

ISBN: 978-1-4401-4401-1 (pbk)
ISBN: 978-1-4401-4402-8 (ebk)

Printed in the United States of America

iUniverse rev. date: 6/05/2009

Contents

Chapter 1:
POLTERGEIST

Alec Suzuki was not a normal boy. As far back as he could remember Alec had always been able to see ghosts and evil spirits and was also plagued by them. Some would say he was special, but Alec just wanted to be a normal middle school student. Trouble seemed to follow him wherever he went due to the mischievous and often times dangerous spirits that were attracted to him.

Bitterness left a bad taste in Alec's mouth as he thought about how his 'condition' had already caused him to lose most of his friends. As for the only friends he had left, Alec wondered if they could even be considered human...

Alec was dragging his feet to school when his friends Billy and Jinx literally *popped* up. If passersby on the sidewalk had been paying attention to the young boy and if they also had the ability to see ghosts or magical creatures they would have seen something quite interesting when there was a sudden *pop* and a ghost boy along with a little fairy materialized next to Alec, who didn't act as though anything were out of the ordinary but simply kept walking. He was used to this sort of thing after all.

Billy would have looked like a normal boy of about the same age as Alec if it wasn't for the fact that his body was transparent. Even so, one with Alec's abilities could see that Billy was dressed in a simple t-shirt and shorts along with a baseball cap on his head. And even though the colors were dulled by the transparent nature of his body Alec could see that Billy had yellow blonde hair and sparkling, green eyes.

"Good morning Alec," came Billy's warm voice as he floated next to Alec, his hands behind his head in a casual manner.

"Yo Alec!" came Jinx's small, perky voice next as he flew over and perched right on Alec's shoulder. Jinx was a mischievous, fairy boy with wild, spiky, orange hair that stuck out in all directions and bright blue eyes. He was wearing a strange blue tunic that almost looked like a dress but Jinx wore pants underneath. He held a small wand that had a five-pointed, gold star on the end, carelessly in his hands.

"Hey guys." Alec greeted them in his soft voice as he continued down the busy sidewalk. His middle school happened to be only a few blocks from where he lived. Everything from hospitals, libraries and police stations were all pretty close to each other in a place like New York City. It never ceased to amaze Alec that among so many people he was the only one who could see Billy and Jinx. As the trio continued to walk down the sidewalk people staring could only see and gawk at the young 12 year old boy who was talking to himself.

Alec entered the schoolyard and made his way towards the entrance. He turned to Billy and Jinx. "I'll catch you guys later. Maybe I'll get to eat lunch outside and we can meet up?" Alec told them.

"That would be great Alec!" Jinx nodded enthusiastically.

"We'll be waiting outside for you then." Billy's manner was friendly.

Alec noticed a few of his fellow classmates were staring at him as he said goodbye to Billy and Jinx and that they were beginning to whisper things about him behind their hands to each other and a few of them were outright snickering. Alec sighed. He knew what they thought of him - that he was a crazy weirdo. He didn't want to listen but he couldn't help himself from overhearing bits and pieces of their conversations as he entered the school building.

"Look it's Alec...there he is talking to himself *again.*" "He's *so* weird." "And *creepy.*" "I bet he's talking to his little imaginary friends again." "Imaginary friends? That's *so* lame."

Alec sighed again this time more heavily. This was the norm. He really should be used to it by now but sometimes their words still stung. Everyone thought that Alec was extremely strange since he had been caught talking to himself more than once. Most of the students believed he had a pair of 'imaginary friends', which at the age of 12 was *not* cool. No one had ever believed him when he had tried to tell the truth that he was just talking to his friends - a ghost and a fairy that only he could see. *Well, of course they wouldn't believe me.* Alec shook his head. *If they can't see them why would they believe me that they're there. They're not my friends.*

"Like anyone *would* believe it. Ghosts and fairies. It's no wonder they think I'm crazy. And a weirdo. Man this sucks!" Alec ruffled his shaggy brown hair with his hands in frustration. Then he realized he had just shouted this last part aloud which had earned him a couple more strange looks from his peers. *Aw man*. Alec blushed in embarrassment and quickly rushed inside. He had a feeling it was going to be a *very* bad day.

● ● ● ● ● ● ● ● ● ● ● ● ● ● ●

It started with art class. Alec could feel...*something* in the art room with him and it wasn't his classmates. He shrugged and tried to brush off the annoying feeling of being watched. The hair on the back of his neck were prickling in an irritating fashion as well, so that he kept rubbing his neck absentmindedly. He was just beginning to start his painting when suddenly his paint tubes began to hover in midair. Alec's eyes widened when he realized it had to be a ghost. And the fact that he couldn't see the ghost's material form meant only one thing - it was a poltergeist. *Uh oh.*

They were the worst sort of trickster ghosts Alec had the bad luck to have to deal with occasionally. They seemed to be drawn to Alec for some reason and had lots of fun making mischief around him, and just making his life more difficult than it already was. Before Alec could stop it the paint tubes were suddenly squirted all over him. Alec sighed as the class turned to look at him and then broke out laughing at his expense. Obviously no one would believe that a poltergeist had squirted paint on him so all he could do was apologize to his art teacher for his clumsiness and clean up the mess.

As if the day couldn't get any worse it merely continued to go down hill from there. In math class Alec watched in horror as a poltergeist caused two chalkboard erasers to hover in midair and then go zooming straight for Alec. The math teacher, Mr. Jones, was in the middle of a lecture and hadn't noticed this since his back was turned to the class while he was writing numerical equations on the board. Thinking fast Alec held up his math book and batted the chalkboard erasers away from him before they would have hit him smack in the face. Just when Alec was thinking of giving himself a pat on the back however he realized his mistake - the chalkboard erasers went flying off in Mr. Jones' direction instead!

Oh man. I'm so screwed! Alec thought panicking. "Mr. Jones!" Alec tried to warn him but it was too late.

Mr. Jones took that moment to turn around just as the chalkboard erasers were upon him so that they smacked into his face one by one. They then dropped to the floor to reveal Mr. Jones' red and chalk-covered face along with his angry expression.

"ALEC SUZUKI!"

"Aw man..." Alec moaned as he realized yet another poltergeist's mischief would be blamed on him. He began to hit his head on his desk. His life was cursed. He was definitely doomed.

Alec had been told to stay behind after class to clean all of the chalkboard erasers and then to clean the rest of the classroom as punishment for his bad behavior. He would also be having detention with Mr. Jones everyday that week after school. Alec sighed heavily as he began to mop the floor and then went to work with cleaning the erasers. *Why me?*

Alec was walking to the cafeteria to grab some lunch when he sensed something coming at him from his right. Thinking it was a ghost he turned expecting to see something that may or may not just pass right through him when instead his eyes widened in surprise to see a runaway trash bin. "What the?" Alec exclaimed as he was suddenly knocked into by the trash bin and with such force that he ended up being tipped forward and falling inside of it. The trash bin then continued to roll down the hall at top speed, now with poor Alec inside of it, who was upside down and quite uncomfortable, when finally the trash bin came to a stop. However, this was when it slammed right into the school's principle Mr. Brown bowling him over and covering both Alec and the principle with foul smelling garbage.

"ALEC SUZUKI!"

Today was definitely *not* his day. Alec had to apologize profusely to the principle but he was still getting a phone call to his parents about his conduct. As Alec walked into the cafeteria he wondered if he should just call in sick tomorrow. He looked around for an empty space at a table and saw his classmates giving him a disgusted look, which clearly meant for Alec to stay away. Did he really smell that bad? He thought he had cleaned off most of the garbage. Or was it just because he was a weirdo? Maybe he would go outside and eat lunch with Billy and Jinx after all.

He was about to do so when the captain of their grade's soccer team, Bobby, waved at Alec motioning for him to come over and join his two friends, which were also on the soccer team; their names were John and Luke. Alec looked behind him thinking it must be some kind of mistake and that Bobby must be motioning for someone else that happened to be just behind him. But no one else was there. Alec pointed to himself and mouthed - "Me?" to Bobby confusedly.

Bobby chuckled and nodded as Alec made his way over to their table hurriedly.

"Come and sit with us Alec. We're all on the soccer team after all aren't we? That makes us buddies doesn't it?" Bobby said affably.

Alec nodded vigorously as he quickly took a seat across from the other boy and set his tray down. "Right."

"Oh, darn, I forgot to get something to drink..." Bobby seemed to dig into his pocket for a minute. "Aw man, I must have spent the last of my change.

Hey, Alec if it wouldn't' be too much trouble think you could get me a soda? I'll pay you back." Bobby flashed him a grin.

"Uh sure, no prob." Alec said getting up from the table.

"I'll have a root beer then." Bobby informed him. "What do you guys want?" He asked Luke and John.

"Coke." "Sprite." The two boys chimed at the same time.

Alec felt a trickle of sweat form on his brow in irk that he was now buying not one but three drinks. He shrugged. Oh well, at least boys his age were talking to him and that was a plus from the usual. Alec quickly sped off to get his 'friends' some drinks and was just pushing the button for a sprite when Billy materialized out of nowhere by his side.

"Who are all the drinks for?" Billy asked curiously.

Alec nearly jumped a foot in the air, "Geez! Billy you nearly gave me a heart attack. They're for some of the boys on the soccer team."

Jinx suddenly popped up next to Billy with a flash of gold. "It's not Bobby and those guys again is it? They're always taking advantage of you like this... making you buy them snacks...drinks...food." Jinx began to flick his fingers one by one.

"Those guys are jerks." Billy frowned.

"No they're not." Alec hotly replied. "They're my friends. My *real* friends."

Billy looked hurt but Jinx looked angry as his tiny face turned red and he puffed up his cheeks. "*Real* friends? I don't think you know what real friends are Alec if you think those guys are your friends. Hmph! We're your friends Alec *not* those guys!"

"Yea, well, whatever. I have to get back." Alec ignored his friends as he sped off back towards the cafeteria once more. He was just walking towards Bobby's table when he overheard a bit of their current conversation.

"So are you friends with Alec, Bobby?" Luke was asking him. "You guys sure seem pretty friendly lately."

"Friends? With that weirdo? As if. He's just good for a laugh and he's incredibly easy to boss around. I have that idiot wrapped around my little finger." Bobby chuckled looking quite pleased with himself.

"Thought so." John began with a smirk, "Who in their right mind would actually be friends with that class clown. I mean I hear he still has imaginary friends."

"Man that's lame," Luke shook his head.

"Yea, he's such a freak but at least he's good for something, and that's being our errand boy." Bobby explained.

"Yea," Luke and John nodded in agreement and snickered.

Alec stopped in his tracks as their words sank in. But deep down...he

5

knew they were never his friends to begin with but even though he knew the truth it still hurt to hear it said out loud. Alec shook himself and went to the table with the drinks. "Hey, guys I got your drinks."

"Hey thanks," Bobby was saying as he took a coke can from Alec. "Oh wait, Alec this is coke I wanted a root beer. Mind getting me another?"

Alec sighed. He wished he could just tell Bobby 'No' but for some reason he just couldn't. "Sure thing Bobby, it's no problem." Alec was just turning around to head back to the hallway when the hair on the back of his neck began to prickle. *Uh oh.* He turned around just in time to see his tray of food floating up in the air and heading towards John. *Oh man!* "Hey look out!" Alec called as he tried to grab a hold of his floating tray.

Too late.

The tray was completely emptied over John. John looked livid as the food slopped down his face. And Alec looked completely guilty with his hands up in the air right where the tray had been only seconds before. *Why me?* Alec moaned in his mind.

"Hey, what the hell was that for you little brat!" John cried standing up from his chair.

"I'm so sorry, it was an accident." Alec began to apologize, waving his hands before him.

"I'll show you an accident..." John was saying as he picked up a bowl of pudding from his tray and flung it at Alec, who instantly ducked so that someone behind Alec ended up getting hit in the face with the pudding instead.

"Hey! Who threw that?" The boy cried out indignantly.

Uh oh. Alec could tell where this was going and quickly ducked under the table as the boy, who got hit with the pudding, threw his bowl of spaghetti at John only to miss and have it hit Luke instead.

"FOOD FIGHT!" Someone yelled.

Food began to get flung across the cafeteria from all directions as the students began to go a bit wild as they attacked each other by flinging food from their trays and using it as ammo. The battle had begun. Alec tried to crawl his way towards the door of the cafeteria only to sense that the poltergeist was after him again. *If only it would materialize itself then I could just get rid of the stupid thing.* Alec got up from underneath one of the tables and made a break for the door.

But something suddenly stood in his path-

It looked like a monster made entirely of cafeteria food - it was the poltergeist.

"There you are." Alec smirked as the poltergeist finally showed its true form. Alec leapt forward and aimed for the poltergeist's head and suddenly flicked it right on the forehead using his thumb and index finger. The blow which should have done nothing oddly seemed to be incredibly powerful as the poltergeist was thrown backwards and into the doors of the cafeteria where it then exploded with food flying in all directions as it was exorcized. Alec turned around to see how the food fight was going and watched as Bobby got hit smack on the face with a whole pizza. Two slices of pepperoni seemed to cling to Bobby's eyes as the pizza slid down his face.

Alec couldn't help but smile. That had to be the highlight of his day.

• • • • • • • • • • • • • • • •

Alec was telling Billy and Jinx about the poltergeist that he had ended up having to exorcize while they were walking back home.

"Yea, another one of those poltergeists followed me to school again today. It totally sucked. First it made me look like some kind of clumsy idiot in art class, and then it got my math teacher Mr. Jones as well as the principle Mr. Brown furious with me. My Mom is probably going to be getting a phone call from the principle about my 'bad behavior' tonight. I'm so looking forward to *that.*" Alec's voice was tinged with sarcasm.

Billy looked sympathetic. "Another one? They sure seem to be attracted to you for some reason. Did you manage to exorcize it alright?"

"Yea," Alec ran a hand through his shaggy brown hair, "I had to wait for it to materialize though - that's what I hate about those poltergeists. They're always hiding. It finally showed its true form in the cafeteria after having helped start a food fight. It was a pretty weak one, thank god."

"Well that's good at least." Jinx nodded his head vigorously.

Suddenly, the hair on the back of Alec's neck prickled in warning.

"Look out!" Billy declared as he pushed Alec quickly out of the way from a falling flower pot that had been sitting on a nearby window sill.

"Hey thanks." Alec looked down at the broken flower pot. "Dang, it looks like I've already got another one tailing me..." Alec sighed heavily feeling a bit defeated.

"They just seem to really love you don't they?" Jinx said cheekily.

"Yea, I feel so loved." Alec bit back sarcastically as he continued to stomp down the sidewalk. That's when a car that suddenly got a flat tire began to swerve off the road and strangely enough the car seemed to head in Alec's direction.

"Oh no!" Alec cried as he tried to dodge out of the way only to find that *something* seemed to have a hold of his foot. "Jinx!"

Jinx immediately sprung into action and pointed his wand at Alec. "Levitation!" Jinx's wand glowed with his fairy magic and Alec was immediately lifted off the ground as the car smashed into a telephone pole that had been right behind Alec. Alec looked in shock as the stunned driver began to pull himself together. Luckily, the airbag had inflated and it looked like he was going to be okay.

"Now that was a close one. This poltergeist seems a lot more aggressive than the other ones..." Alec noted as Jinx set him back down. "I wonder what that means? Is this one more powerful? Or is it something else. Great, just great, that would be my luck alright. What do these things even want with me?" Alec hung his head.

Jinx and Billy exchanged worried glances and decided to keep an extra close eye on Alec as he made his way home that day, both tremendously worried for his safety.

⋅ ⋅ ⋅ ⋅ ● ● ● ● ● ● ● ● ● ● ● ● ⋅ ⋅

That night Alec, his mother Laura, and father Mori were all seated at the dinning room table trying to have what Laura would have called 'a nice, normal family dinner'. Key word - 'try' since the lights seemed to be flickering on and off in an eerie manner and the chandelier above the table was swinging back and forth and casting creepy shadows on the walls.

Laura was a typical American housewife with long, blonde hair tied back into a pony tail, crystal blue eyes, and was wearing a stylish and trendy black and white dress, which she had paired off with a nice pair of high-heeled, designer shoes. She was the perfect picture of high style and sophistication. And her make-up and hair were always flawless as far as Alec could remember. Laura had always seemed extremely concerned with outside appearances.

Mori was a middle-aged, Japanese man, who looked a little on the scruffy side when compared to pristine Laura, who was seated right next to him. He was wearing a business suit but his shirt was wrinkled and his tie was partway undone. His hair was slightly shaggy like Alec's and he was in desperate need of a shave.

*Uh oh. I hope it's not a poltergeist. I really wouldn't want to have to deal with it here...not in front of my parents...*Alec sighed as he morosely swirled his mashed potatoes.

"How was your day son?" Mori asked trying to break through the awkwardness.

"Fine." Alec mumbled.

"What did you learn today?" Laura started, trying to be civil.

"Nothing." Alec shrugged.

Laura frowned and was about to tell Alec that there was no way he could have learned 'nothing' when the phone rang. "I'll get it." She said getting up from the table and going over to the phone. "Hello...oh yes, hello Mr. Brown how are you? Alec? Oh I see. I see. I'm so sorry. I understand." Laura hung up the phone and turned towards Alec. "That was your principle Alec. Apparently you've been behaving badly all day...throwing chalkboard erasers at your teachers...rolling a trash can at your principle. You're lucky they didn't decide to expel you! What has gotten into you lately? Well, what do you have to say for yourself?"

"But Mom it wasn't my fault it was..." Alec trailed off biting his lip. He couldn't very well say 'it was the poltergeist Mom' now could he? He knew Laura didn't believe in anything supernatural and got extremely angry when he brought up anything of the sort.

"It was?" Laura prompted, raising an eyebrow.

Alec decided to risk it. "It was a poltergeist Mom."

"A polter-what?" Laura frowned.

"It's a type of ghost, honey." Mori informed her politely.

"I *know* that." Laura spat back at her husband who flinched, "A ghost? You expect me to believe that a ghost made you do all those horrible things at school today? Ghosts aren't real. Don't try and blame your actions on something else Alec. You have to take responsibility for your actions-"

"But it *was* a poltergeist!" Alec stood up from his chair angrily, "I'm not lying! I don't know why I even bothered to tell you the truth. You never believe me!" The lights in the dinning room began to flicker on and off more rapidly. And the cupboards began to rattle, which was causing the plates to begin to slide off the shelves and fall onto the floor where they smashed into pieces.

Laura looked around wide-eyed, "An earthquake?"

"Yea, you just keep on telling yourself that Mom. I know what it really is." Alec gave her a hard stare as the plates began to hover off the floor. "It's a-"

"Don't say it!" Laura covered her ears. "Don't say it's a ghost! Ghosts aren't real!" Laura cried as she suddenly buried her face in her hands so that she wouldn't see the floating plates and sunk to her knees.

Alec shook his head and wondered how she could lie to herself like that when there was a plate floating right by her head...

"Honey!" Mori came to his wife's distraught side and put his arms around her. He then looked up at Alec, "Alec, please just....go to your room."

"You believe me don't you Dad?" Alec insisted, he needed someone to believe him. Someone *alive*. Someone *real*.

Mori looked at his trembling wife and frowned, "I'm sorry Alec...but your mother is right."

"Fine don't believe me! I don't care! I don't need you or anyone! I'll take care of this thing myself! Just like I always do!" Alec yelled as he ran to his room and slammed the door. Alec threw himself on his bed and began to cry into his pillow.

During the night as he lay awake while trying to fall asleep he began to hear footsteps going around the house in rooms that should have been empty and he could hear a chair sliding across the floor of his room.

"You smell yummy...I want to eat you." A voice whispered in his ear causing a chill to go down Alec's spine. Alec quickly shot out of bed and flipped on the nearest light switch. Alec's eyes scanned his bedroom but-

There was nothing there.

• • • • • • • • • • • • • • • •

Something was following him. Something...really powerful. It was the same poltergeist from yesterday, Alec was sure of it. The hair on the back of his neck had been standing on end all day and Alec rubbed the back of his neck irritated. He also couldn't shrug off the feeling that someone was watching him. He kept looking over his shoulder every five seconds and Billy and Jinx were getting very worried about him as they continued to watch his odd behavior.

Somehow he managed to make it through an entire school day without anything bad happening and the poltergeist hadn't tried to make any mischief either. Alec let out a sigh of relief, maybe he had been overreacting and the poltergeist had already decided to leave him alone. Yea, that was it. Sure. Denial was his best friend.

Alec at least hoped that was the case as he headed to soccer practice. A lot of the other boys were doing drills and so Alec decided to do some as well. He dribbled the soccer ball around cones and then went through the same routine again. Soccer - it was the one thing that seemed 'normal' in Alec's crazy, ghost-infested life. It was his one passion. Alec loved soccer. He loved that feeling of making a goal by using nothing but his own skill and talent. It made him feel like he could actually be good at something 'normal' besides exorcizing ghosts. And Alec happened to be quite good at soccer too. He was fast, had good reflexes, and there was no one who could easily steal the ball away from him once he had it. Maybe it was all that running away from poltergeists and ghosts that kept him in shape? Alec wondered and then shrugged. At least something good had come out of all that.

Alec was deep in thought when he suddenly ran straight through a mud puddle. He looked down in surprise to see that he was knee deep in mud. Alec was also equally surprised to see a mud puddle like that on such a bright and sunny day when it hadn't rained in days. *What's a mud puddle even doing here?* He wondered as he raised his eyebrows at it. He began to remove his foot from it when his foot began to sink deeper into the puddle however. *What the?* Alec wondered as his foot seemed to be sinking into the puddle. Beginning to panic, Alec began to push himself forward only to find that his other foot was sinking into the puddle now as well. Something had a hold of his ankle, Alec was sure of it, and 'it' was pulling him down into the puddle. *Uh oh.*

"Billy! Jinx! Where are you guys?" Alec called out to his friends when he realized there was no way he was going to get out of this mess without some help.

Billy and Jinx instantly materialized at Alec's side. Their eyes widened as they saw Alec, who was now waist deep in the mysterious puddle, sinking down rapidly as though he were in a puddle of quick sand.

"Alec!" Jinx exclaimed as he waved his magic wand towards the puddle. A magic bolt hit the puddle but it seemed to have no effect.

"Alec hang on!" Billy urged as he reached his hand out to Alec. Alec reached out and grasped Billy's cold hand and let his friend begin to pull him out of the puddle. Luckily, though Billy had the ability to pass through things, he could also make himself solid if he needed to.

"Something has my ankle." Alec explained to him as Billy couldn't get him further out of the puddle no matter how hard he tried.

"Try wrenching it off with your hand and focus your power like you normally do." Billy directed him.

"You think it's a poltergeist?" Alec's eyes were wide as he followed Billy's instructions and reached his hand down into the mud puddle and wrapped his hand around the 'thing' that had a hold of his ankle. Concentrating his spirit power he began to glow with a blue-tinged aura of light. He then concentrated his spirit energy around his hand until he managed to pry the thing's hold lose, so that it seemed to finally let go of him. But as soon as Alec began to summon more power thinking he could exorcize the 'thing' from the inside out he was suddenly sent flying up and out of the puddle almost as if he had been 'spit out'. Alec could have sworn he had also heard a loud exclamation of - 'BLAH!' Alec landed with a smack, face first on the muddy ground.

"Hey, you alright there Alec?" Jinx asked concernedly poking Alec's back with his wand.

"Peachy," Alec mumbled as he raised his mud-covered face off the ground. He was panting for breath from using his spirit energy and now he was covered from head to toe in mud. A few fellow soccer team members passed Alec by with amused looks on their faces and others were outright laughing at him again.

Alec just sighed and put his face back in the mud wishing he could just disappear or become invisible.

"Hey Alec, you making out with the mud puddle or something?" Bobby laughed with his friends as they ran past, continuing their drills.

Alec just groaned. This was beginning to be a bit too much for him to handle. It was almost as if this latest poltergeist really wanted to kill him...

"Try not to make us look bad at the big game on Saturday, freak." John sneered as he ran past. "Or else."

Billy glared off in their direction, "Want me to haunt their houses?"

Alec shook his head and remembered the big game coming up...if this poltergeist was still after him then...maybe he shouldn't even go. It would probably be a disaster if it showed up at the game but...Alec had been looking forward to this soccer game for weeks. It had been one of the few things keeping him sane with everything else that seemed to be going wrong in his life. Soccer was one of the few things Alec really enjoyed, one of the few things that managed to make him happy despite everything else. He just had to go.

         . . . .

The day of the big game had finally arrived. Alec was more than excited but also a little worried since he didn't know if the poltergeist would decide to make mischief and try and sabotage his game. But things seemed to be going alright as the game was underway. Alec was doing a great job during the game and scoring goals left and right. It was neck and neck though with the opposing middle school's team. And then it happened - if Alec managed to make one more goal his team would win.

Alec managed to get the ball and was dribbling it in front of him as he ran down the field towards the goal. Swerving left and right as he avoided the other soccer players that tried to get in his way and using fancy foot work to keep the ball as they tried to steal it from him. However, just as Alec was reaching the goal and about to try for his shot something caught his attention out of the corner of his eye -

There standing next to the giant scoreboard was a thugish looking, human-like creature made entirely of mud and appearing as though it was wearing a hooded jacket. Alec's eyes widened realizing what it was - the poltergeist. *There you are, you've finally shown yourself!* Alec changed course and started running off in the direction of the poltergeist instead much to the chagrin of his teammates, who frantically yelled after him.

"Aw man, what does he think he's doing?" Luke moaned.

"He's flipped his lid, again." John shook his head.

"That idiot! Where is he going?" Bobby swore.

"The goal is the other way - stupid!" Luke yelled.

But Alec didn't care what they said. Their words could no longer stop him - this was *way* more important. He would not be deterred as he continued to run with the soccer ball towards the poltergeist. A glowing blue aura surrounded Alec as he summoned his spirit energy and it surrounded his soccer ball as he got ready to make his shot. Alec kicked the glowing soccer ball at the mud-poltergeist and watched as the glowing ball flew through the air and hit the poltergeist in its stomach blowing a hole straight through the creature and then the entire creature seemed to explode as it was exorcized.

Alec let out a breath of relief, but couldn't help wondering what the poltergeist had been doing just standing there by the scoreboard like that. *That poltergeist was definitely up to something.* That's when the hair on the back of Alec's neck seemed to prickle in warning and he looked up to see that the scoreboard had become suddenly unstable and looked like it was about to fall over. Alec noticed that one of his teammates wouldn't be able to get out of the way in time and quickly ran towards the boy, who turned out to be John.

"Hey! Look out! Out of the way! It's gonna fall!" Alec yelled as he ran forward. With all his strength Alec pushed John out of the way just as the scoreboard broke off it's two supporting metal legs and fell to the ground -

· ● · ● · ● · ● · ● · ● · ● · ● · ● · ● · ● · ●

Alec blinked and looked up at an unfamiliar white ceiling. He felt stiff and saw that his leg had been propped up on a pillow before him and that it had been set in a cast. He must have broken it. He just hoped that the other boy was alright. He was pretty sure he had managed to push him out of the way in time at any rate. Alec sighed, that poltergeist had really seemed to want to get him for some reason. Like it had really wanted to kill him... which was odd since most of the other poltergeists Alec had encountered had merely wanted to create mischief, but the poltergeists that Alec had been encountering lately seemed much more dangerous. Just what did they want from Alec exactly?

"Alec!" It was his father's voice.

"Alec honey!" It was his mother's voice.

The voices of Alec's parents could be heard as they burst through the hospital room door. Alec looked up in surprise to see his teary-eyed mother and worried looking father. "Oh Alec, honey, thank goodness you're alright." Laura declared as she rushed to Alec's side and hugged him. Alec's eyes widened at this since Laura hardly ever hugged him.

Mori smiled as he watched this exchange between mother and son. "It's good to see you're alright son."

Alec smiled weakly back. He didn't feel alright. Not at all. Because of him being a 'ghost magnet' he had put one of his fellow teammates in danger. If the poltergeists really were trying to kill him now then their attacks would be even more vicious and more dangerous than usual and he couldn't let people get hurt because of him. And so, Alec decided that he would have to give up soccer at least until these poltergeist attacks stopped. If someone were to get hurt or die because of him...he couldn't live with himself. More than ever, that day, Alec wished he were just a normal boy.

Chapter 2:
FAIRY

Alec, Billy, and Jinx were walking to school early one morning when Jinx seemed to remember something.

"Oh! That's right I almost forgot - Alec the Elder Fairy wanted to meet you. He said he was interested in meeting the boy exorcist who could see fairies."

"Elder Fairy?" Alec quirked his head to the side. "Isn't that the guy you take your Fairy Mage lessons from?"

Jinx nodded vigorously, "Yep."

Alec shrugged, "Sure why not."

"Great! Follow me then! The park where the Fairy Tree is isn't too far from here. We should be able to meet with the Elder Fairy and get you back to school before the bell rings!" Jinx excitedly declared as he took off flying in the direction of the park.

Alec shook his head wondering how someone could have so much energy so early in the morning. The trio soon arrived at the park and Alec blinked at it in surprise since he had never noticed that a park was in this area of the city before. He must have passed this area before but never noticed this strange park.

"This park, how odd, I never noticed it here before. It's huge too. Kinda hard to miss..." Alec noted as he made his way into it. He thought that the park itself had to be quite old as he noticed a lot of the trees that were in the park had huge gnarled trunks. And the flowering plants and bushes were huge compared to some of the bushes found in the more recently done modern parks.

Jinx nodded. "This is the oldest park in New York City...one of the last few havens for my kind."

Alec looked at Jinx out of the corner of his eye. "Your...kind?"

"Magical beings like fairies, elves, trolls, brownies, you know." Jinx shrugged.

"Brownies?" Alec's eyebrows raised in surprise. That's when something caught his attention out of the corner of his eye. A squirrel? No – Alec blinked and then did a double take. There were tiny people standing over by an overly large bush and they were smiling and waving enthusiastically at him. Alec blushed at this odd behavior and hesitantly waved and smiled back at them. This seemed to please the little people greatly as they began to hop up and down in excitement. *So little people exist too. Guess it shouldn't come as such a surprise being friends with Jinx and all...*

Jinx grinned, his hands behind his head, and an amused expression on his face, "You see, you're a bit of a celebrity in our world."

Alec blinked in surprise, "Huh? I am...but why?"

Jinx just started whistling a catchy little tune and wouldn't answer - much to Alec's chagrin.

Jinx led them deeper into the park until they finally came to an area where there was a gigantic ancient tree. The tree had knots covering its gnarled trunk which was at least ten feet wide and its roots were big enough that Alec could have sat quite comfortably on one of them. Alec whistled as he looked up, up and up trying to see the top of the tree and his neck began to hurt. There was bright green moss covering parts of the roots and trunk, and Alec saw strange hanging moss draping over some of its branches. The tree was very leafy - its branches filled with tons of silvery green leaves that seemed to sparkle when the sunlight hit them. But the tree itself seemed out of place for a park in the middle of New York and Alec thought it looked like the type of tree one would expect to find in the middle of a rain forest. There was also something 'magical' about the tree. Alec was getting goose bumps just by looking at it.

"Wow." Was all Alec found himself saying.

And then Alec spotted them - the fairies. There they were zooming in circles around the tree and its branches in their brightly colored clothing. Like Jinx they had pointy ears, strange hair and eye colors, and their sparkling wings seemed to catch the sun's rays making their bodies glow. Alec noticed that most of them could be seen holding a small wand in their hands. They seemed to be flying up and into the branches that led deeper and higher into the tree.

"The Fairy Palace is at the top of the tree along with the Elder Fairy. That's where we're going." Jinx informed Alec.

Alec looked up towards the top of the tree again and gulped. "Don't tell me you expect me to climb that!"

Jinx giggled amused. "No silly! We're going to take the elevator of course! After I shrink you down to fairy size first. Now just hold still!" Jinx began to wave his star-topped wand around and around in circles as it began to glow with magical energy.

Alec took a worried step back. Jinx and magic never seemed to mix very well. He had just gotten his wand licence, but was really still a Fairy Mage in training, who had a tendency to botch up the simplest of spells in the most confounding ways. "Whoa wait a minute Jinx, let's discuss this first!" Alec had his arms up before him in a surrendering gesture as he continued to back away from Jinx.

Too late.

"Transfiguration!" Jinx zapped Alec with a lightning bolt of magical energy.

A cloud of purple smoke formed around Alec as he felt himself suddenly changing. His body felt like it had been changed into salt water taffy and it was being stretched and pulled and then rolled into a small ball. The world around him seemed to be turning super sized - the trees, grass, the sky - it all seemed to be very big and very far away all of a sudden. He could feel himself shrinking and then the transformation was finally complete. Alec looked down at this arms and legs and strangely enough saw that he now had eight limbs! Alec reached up his 'hands' to the top of his head and felt two large antenna there. Alec felt a trickle of sweat form on his brow in irk.

"Jinx!!!"

Billy who had simply been able to shift his body into a smaller size tried to hold back a laugh and ended up snorting, "It looks like Jinx turned you into a dung beetle Alec!"

Jinx put a hand behind his head abashed, "Now how did that happen...I was sure he was going to turn into a fairy. Oh well, at least you're small enough to use the elevator now, huh Alec?"

"*Why you...*" Alec's eyebrow twitched in irritation. His attention however was then drawn in front of him as he heard the unmistakable *ping* of an elevator door opening. There in front of him in the trunk of the Fairy Tree - two small elevator doors had suddenly appeared and were opening. Standing on either side of the elevator door were two male fairies that Alec decided had to be guards of some kind due to their uniforms and long staffs held in their hands like weapons. They were watching Jinx, Alec, and Billy with interest.

"Come on, let's go!" Jinx flew into the elevator waiting for Alec and Billy to follow. Alec went inside and he could have sworn the two guard fairies were snickering behind their hands at Alec's form. Alec sighed and then turned to watch as Jinx pushed the button for the one hundred and fiftieth floor. Alec blinked. *Wow, that's a lot of floors.*

During their ride to the one hundred and fiftieth floor the elevator would stop from time to time to let other fairies on or off. Each time the elevator doors opened Alec couldn't help but peak out and see what kinds of rooms were within the trunk of the ancient Fairy Tree. Alec saw that one floor seemed to be completely devoted to fairies that were good at sewing things and saw many hard at work at looms or spinning wheels, brightly colored threads flying through the air.

One floor seemed to be exclusively for carpenter fairies, who were good at building or inventing things. Alec saw many hard at work with their hammers, wood, and metal. Then another floor seemed to be devoted to the Fairy Mages in training, who all seemed to be practicing magic with their tiny wands. With a wave of their wands Alec watched wide-eyed as they turned things into other things, summoned things out of thin air or caused things to lift off the ground all with their fairy magic. And then there was a floor that when the elevator doors opened Alec smelled something absolutely delicious. It smelled just like homemade cookies. And when Alec peaked into this floor he saw that it was entirely devoted to baking fairies.

Alec raised an eyebrow at Jinx, "Hey, wait a minute, I thought elves made cookies."

"That's just what we want you humans to think. You've never had a cookie until you've tried a cookie made by a fairy." Jinx assured him.

The fairies that entered the elevator along with Jinx, Alec and Billy took one look at Jinx and one look at Alec and seemed to realize what had happened - Jinx's reputation for being well, a jinx, preceding him. And so they were smiling this knowing smile or trying to hide a laugh behind their hands during the ride. Alec felt a trickle of sweat form on his brow from this.

"A dung beetle..." One fairy couldn't help but snicker behind his hand.

Alec blushed bright red, he was never going to live this down in the Fairy Kingdom at this rate.

Finally, the elevator doors opened to the one hundred and fiftieth floor and Alec and the others got out. Alec's breath caught in his throat at the view before him. They were in the very center of the branches at the highest point of the ancient Fairy Tree now. On the branches the fairies had made small dwellings that Alec thought looked just like miniature tree houses. Though in his current size they seemed like large tree houses. The insides of the houses were lit with a warm golden light. At the very center Alec could see a palace made of twigs, acorns, grass, colored bird feathers, flowers, sparkling pebbles and other things gathered from nature. Alec was surprised at how grand the palace was able to look having been made out of such things. It simply took his breath away. "Wow."

Jinx smiled, pleased by Alec's reaction. Alec noticed that there were several birds with odd harnesses perched on a platform that was just outside where the elevator had opened, and how small magical creatures and beings that didn't have wings were using these birds to travel towards the center of the tree and the palace. Alec looked over to Jinx and noticed there was a strange gleam in Jinx's eye.

"Oh no, you're not actually thinking...?" Alec gulped. "You don't expect me to ride...a bird!"

"You're the only one of us who can't fly Alec. You'll have to fly to the palace by Sparrow Carrier." Jinx smirked, thoroughly enjoying himself.

"I'm so going to squish you once I get bigger." Alec mumbled as he approached one of the Sparrow Carriers. The bird turned towards Alec as he reached his hand out towards it. "Nice birdie." The bird quirked its head at Alec before reaching forward and taking one of Alec's arms in its beak. Apparently, the bird was hungry. "Ahh! The bird is trying to eat me! Jinx!" Alec cried out as he struggled in the bird's grasp.

"Hang on Alec!" Jinx declared as he went to Alec's aid.

"Everything always does seem to want to eat him." Billy tapped his chin thoughtfully.

"Why me?" Alec sighed while Jinx was trying to pry the bird's beak open with his wand.

* * * * * * * * * * * * * * * *

After Alec finally managed to get on his bird without getting eaten the trio headed towards the Fairy Palace. They landed outside and Alec hopped off his Sparrow Carrier and made sure to stay far away from the bird's beak. Jinx then guided them inside the palace leading them through the front doors and then beyond. They went down several long hallways and then finally they had reached a pair of giant doors made of willow branches that were all twisted into an ornate pattern. Jinx waved his wand at the doors so that they opened and they followed him inside.

The chamber they had just entered turned out to be a spacious study. The entire work area was filled with rolled up parchments, books, and strange artifacts also littered the shelves. There was a large desk at the end of the room and Jinx led them over to it. The chair behind the desk swivelled around to reveal the Elder Fairy. Alec gulped, a bit nervous to be meeting someone so important. The Elder Fairy looked Alec over with a critical eye before breaking out into a warm grin.

Alec blinked surprised at his expression. The Elder Fairy didn't quite seem to be what he had expected and wore bright purple-colored clothing that rivaled even Jinx's bright ensemble and had a friendly expression on his wizened face. He had wild white hair, a matching white beard, and sparkling keen blue eyes much like Jinx's. Alec had expected a much more intimidating figure to be the leader of the Fairy Kingdom. And was that an acorn cap he was wearing on his head...?

"Welcome back Jinx, I see you've brought some interesting friends along with you." The Elder Fairy's eyes drifted over to Billy and then to Alec, "A ghost and a beetle...wait no-" He chuckled. "You must be the boy exorcist that Jinx is always talking about. Alec Suzuki. Jinx, I see you've brought our guest here safely although I see you failed to perform a proper transfiguration. Tisk Tisk. Allow me to set you right." The Elder Fairy stood and waved his wand at Alec with a confident motion.

Alec felt his body changing almost immediately and then Alec looked down at his hands to see that he had human hands again. Alec then reached his hands to the top of his head and let out a breath of relief. No more antenna. Although there seemed to be something rather heavy on his back. Alec looked over his shoulder and his eyes widened - wings. He had wings! "Awesome..."

The Elder Fairy chuckled at Alec's awe. "It's nice when young people are impressed by the little things."

"Thanks." Alec beamed at the Elder Fairy, thoroughly impressed now.

"It is I who should be thanking you, Alec Suzuki." The Elder Fairy's expression was suddenly serious.

"Thanking me?" Alec quirked his head.

The Elder Fairy raised an eyebrow at Alec, "Do you not know? It is not only exorcists that poltergeists and evil spirits target - they also target magical beings or beings with a high spiritual power. You have made this kingdom a safer place for us by being here in New York, boy exorcist. Thank you. From all of us."

The Elder Fairy's voice was very warm as he said this and Alec was caught off guard since in his life he was rarely thanked for anything. He looked away and scratched his cheek bashfully. "Oh no, it's nothing, it's just something I seem to *have* to do..." Then a thought seemed to occur to Alec and he looked back at the Elder Fairy. "Sir, maybe you know." Alec swallowed. "Why exactly do the poltergeists and evil spirits target me like they do? What do they really want from me?"

The Elder Fairy's expression turned grim. "There are two types of poltergeists - mischievous spirits that don't mean any true harm. And poltergeists who are vengeful spirits with one thing on their mind - revenge.

They want the power to fulfill their ends. The reason they're after you Alec is because they want to...eat you."

"Eat me?" Alec squeaked.

The Elder Fairy nodded, "Or rather they wish to eat your spirit. If a poltergeist were to eat the spirit of an exorcist such as yourself they would gain immense power. They would become invincible. They can also gain power from eating the spirits of wandering ghosts that have unfinished business and are simply wandering around the Astral Plane still unable to cross over. Also the spirits of fairies or other magical beings are quite appetizing to a poltergeist."

"They want my spirit." Alec shivered.

The Elder Fairy stroked his chin as he eyed Alec thoughtfully for a moment. "Yes, and there's also another reason why poltergeist and evil spirits keep pursuing you Alec. I'm not sure if you know this but you're really-" The Elder Fairy suddenly shook his head. "A good boy." The Elder Fairy finished and waved his hand dismissively through the air. "But enough about such serious matters. What I'm curious to know is how you've managed to survive being friends with Jinx for so long?"

"I'm a good runner." Alec smirked.

"How about some tea and cookies?" The Elder Fairy suddenly asked Alec. "Children love cookies don't they?"

"Uh, yea, sure, why not." Alec shrugged.

The Elder Fairy clapped his hands and with a *pop* from out of nowhere a tray with a steaming pot of tea, four porcelain cups, and a plate of freshly baked, chocolate chip cookies appeared out of nowhere on the Elder Fairy's desk. "Help yourselves boys."

Alec, Billy and Jinx readily did so, Alec helping to serve the others tea.

The Elder Fairy looked at Alec with a soft expression on his face. "So young to have so much responsibility thrust upon him. Poor boy, I wonder if..." The Elder Fairy shook his head. "No, he's not yet ready to know the truth."

⁎ ⁎ ⁎ ⁎ ⁎ ⁎ ⁎ ⁎ ⁎ ⁎ ⁎ ⁎ ⁎ ⁎

Alec was enjoying his lunch break at school outside with Billy the next day.

"So Alec, what did you think of the Elder Fairy?" Billy asked curiously.

"He seemed really nice. Not really what I expected him to be like. He was way more friendly. And he sure knew how to make delicious chocolate chip cookies! I think I still have a few..." Alec reached into his pocket and pulled out what appeared to be nothing more than crumbs. Alec peered down at his hand, taking a closer look. "Aw man, the cookies stayed small." Alec pouted. "Think Jinx could super size them?" He turned to Billy a hopeful look on his face.

"Maybe, or he could end up blowing them up or turning them into worms or something." Billy chuckled.

Alec was looking a bit green, "Yea, you're probably right." He put the crumbs back into his pocket. "Hey, where is Jinx anyways?"

"Hmm, I dunno actually, he's usually around at lunch time since he always wants to steal your desert. That little guy has such a sweet tooth so it's strange he's not here." Billy tapped his chin. "I wonder where the little guy is."

Alec suddenly noticed Jinx flying towards them at top speed. "Hey, there he is. Hey Jinx!" Alec called over to him. Jinx stopped right in front of Alec's face panting for breath. Alec seemed to notice Jinx's worried expression and frowned. "Hey, is something wrong?"

When Jinx had caught his breath he burst out - "Alec, it's horrible! Fairy Park is in danger. They're going to destroy it! Then we'll have no where else to go...I'll no longer have a home...!"

"Whoa calm down Jinx." Alec started soothingly, "Who's going to destroy Fairy Park?"

"The humans are planning on paving over it and putting up a McDally's!" Jinx choked out, near tears.

"A McDally's?" Alec frowned, "But you said that park is one of the last havens for your kind in all of New York right? We can't let this happen. We'll have to do something. Don't worry Jinx I won't let anything happen to Fairy Park. There must be something I can do to help. At least - I'll do what I can." Alec chewed his lower lip thoughtfully, if only he had a plan. Then Alec's eyes lit up as he suddenly had an idea.

* * * * * * * * * * * * * * * * *

"Save New York's oldest park! Say no to McDally's! Help save New York's oldest park! Say no to McDally's!" Alec chanted as he walked back and forth in front of Fairy Park protesting.

Alec had decided to start his own one-man protest against McDally's paving over Fairy Park. He had made a large sign which read: *Save New York's Oldest Park!* In big green letters and there was a circle with a slash going through it over the McDally's logo which was a goofy dancing burger.

Alec tried to get the attention of the people who were speedily walking by the park but it seemed hopeless. Everyone seemed to be in their own little worlds - they were all on their cell phones, had ipods plugged into their ears, or were playing their handheld gameboys. It was like no one had time for reality any more, and it was just passing them by without them even noticing it. As well as passing Alec by...

Alec sighed, but he wouldn't give up hope. He continued to walk back and forth in front of the park with his sign. The longer he stayed at it the more likely it was that someone would finally stop and listen to what he had to say and if he even got one person to listen to him and his cause...there was hope.

• • • • • • • • • • • • • • • •

Evii Starr, up and coming reporter and her trusty cameraman, Joey, were passing by Fairy Park when Evii spotted Alec. Her eyes seemed to turn into two large hearts as she spotted the lone, middle school boy protesting something about McDally's. "He's just too cute! I wonder what he's up to. Joey, I smell a story! Follow me!"

"Right boss!" Joey obediently ran after his cute, red-headed 'boss'.

Evii went up to Alec and pulled out a microphone from her cleavage causing Alec to blush scarlet as she held the microphone right under his nose, "So tell me little boy, what are you doing here?"

"Oh, I'm trying to save this park." Alec swallowed to get through his nervousness. The reporter who was suddenly talking to him was really pretty. She had short red hair cut into a bob and wore a matching red suit and skirt, which she had paired off with some red high-heeled shoes. "Not a lot of people know this but this is New York's oldest park. And McDally's wants to pave it over and open another one of those fast food burger joints. Isn't that awful?" Alec looked back at the reporter hopefully.

Evii nodded, "Well said, it certainly is! What's your name kid? How old are you? Speak clearly, for the camera now."

Alec blushed awkwardly as he looked up at the camera. "Uh, ah, my name's Alec Suzuki. I'm 12 and am in the 7th grade."

Evii stood in front of Alec and spoke to the camera. "So young and yet so brave to take on a large corporation like McDally's all on his own! Trying to pave over such a lovely park as this one and for what - another fast food restaurant. Do our children really need another burger joint? When they could be playing at a park as nice as this one and getting some heathy exercise? I thought so." Evii nodded as if the home viewers readily agreed with her. "So, you couldn't get any of your little friends to help you with your protesting Alec?" Evii turned back towards Alec and put the microphone once again just under his nose.

Alec looked away and scratched the back of his neck awkwardly, "I don't really have any *real* friends..."

Evii's eyebrows shot up to her hair line. "No friends? That's so...sad! So tragic! It's perfect! This is going to make a great story! Joey cut out that last part."

Alec didn't know if he wanted to laugh or cry at that.

* * * * * * * * * * * * * * * *

Laura and Mori Suzuki were at home having a nice peaceful dinner without even realizing that Alec was missing.

"Ah, isn't this evening so perfect, darling?" Laura smiled to herself at the tranquilness. "How about some TV?" Laura pointed the remote at the TV and it clicked on to a news station. Coming up on screen was a pretty red-haired reporter in a tight, low-cut suit:

Hello folks, this is Evii Starr, reporting to you live from Fairy Park where we are continuing our coverage of Alec Suzuki's one man protest against McDally's. For those of you just tuning in to the story this 12-year-old boy continues his one man demonstration to try and save this park! Apparently, McDally's plans to pave over this historic landmark and build a restaurant. Even though this happens to be New York's oldest park! Evii frowned at the camera and shook her head. *All on his own the boy has been here for the past 5 days! One may wonder where are this poor boy's parents?* Evii wagged her finger at the screen. *Anyways - one may also wonder where are Alec's friends?* Here Evii pouted cutely. *Believe it or not poor Alec Suzuki has no friends, no real ones at least - his only friends are the woodland creatures that reside here in this park.*

The camera shifted to show that Alec was in the background and seemed to be surrounded by squirrels and several pigeons were perched on his arms and shoulders. The camera then shifted back to Evii Starr.

Doesn't that just break your heart? I know it breaks mine. Evii took out a handkerchief from her cleavage and began to dab her eyes with it.

Laura's eyebrow twitched, as her perfect happiness and composure slowly began to crumble.

But seriously like our children need any more fast food when they could be getting some healthy exercise at a park just like this one. As many of you know, Alec has captured the hearts of many Americans and New Yorkers who are now tuning in to this daily evening broadcast. Today I have a special treat of footage from all the days Alec Suzuki has been out here protesting all by himself. Roll the tape Joey!

The tape began to roll and it began to show Alec walking back and forth in front of the park with his hand-made sign in all kinds of weather. First it showed a soaked Alec protesting in the rain, his clothes soaked through, his hair sticking to the sides of his head, completely drenched and shivering from the cold. The next shot of footage showed Alec protesting on an extremely windy day when his sign had suddenly been blown away from him and Alec had been forced to chase it down the sidewalk. Then there was footage of Alec getting caught by surprise during a hail storm and trying to shield himself from the hail stones with his sign. And lastly it showed Alec being buried in a snow fall...

"That's just ridiculous! It's the middle of spring!" Laura scoffed at the footage, as she tucked a stray hair behind her ear.

Mori's jaw had simply dropped at seeing Alec being on TV.

The camera cut back to Evii Starr. She seemed to be wiping away a tear from her face. *So young, so tragic. So adorably cute...a perfect little American hero. Now I ask those of you at home this - isn't there any New Yorker out there among you willing to help this poor, sweet and cute, little boy in his protest?*

Laura had had just about enough and turned the TV off. Just then the phone rang. Laura shrugged as she walked over to get the phone, picking it up. "Hello?" *Hello...hello is this Mr. or Mrs. Suzuki? We'd like to ask you a few questions about your son Alec? Are you proud of his efforts as of late? Hello...?*

Laura's eye twitched in annoyance as she slammed down the phone.

Mori gave her a strange look, quirking his head at her, "Who was it honey?"

Just then, there was a knock at the door.

"Hello! Hello! Is anyone home? We'd like to talk to the parents of Alec Suzuki! Can any of you tell us why you aren't out there with your boy? Why you're letting your boy stay outside day and night on the dangerous streets of New York to protest the destruction of a park - any comments?" Came the voices of several reporters outside.

The phone had begun to ring again and the knocking at the front door continued.

Mori frowned thoughtfully, "I had noticed it had gotten awfully quiet around here."

Laura pulled at her immaculate hairdo, "Alec!!!"

* * * * * * * * * * * * * * * *

Meanwhile, Alec was protesting in front of the park when suddenly he sneezed. "Achoo!" Alec rubbed his nose which was a little red. "Ugh, I think I might be getting a cold."

Billy looked at his friend worriedly. "Hey, you don't look so good Alec." Billy had noticed that Alec was looking rather flushed.

Jinx flew towards Alec and put a tiny hand to his forehead. "He's burning up!"

"Maybe you should take a break." Billy suggested. "You shouldn't push yourself so hard. You've done enough already and with all the publicity that nice reporter lady is giving the park there's a chance now that we'll get to save it."

Alec shook his head weakly. "No, not yet. Just a little while longer. This is all I can really do after all. I'm sorry Jinx. I wish there was something more I could do for you. I'm so pathetic."

Jinx looked moved. *"Alec..."*

Alec was walking forward again when the world started spinning and he began to fall forward. "Alec!" He heard Jinx and Billy cry out in concern. He thought he was going to hit the pavement but someone unexpectedly caught him. Alec looked up to see a lady with kind brown eyes, brown hair tied back into a pony-tail, and who was dressed in a green t-shirt and jeans.

"Whoa, careful there kiddo. You look awful! Here come and sit down and have a nice tofu and alfalfa sandwich. You have a face that says 'feed me!'." The lady guided Alec over to take a seat at a park bench and handed him a strange looking sandwich. Just then however his stomach took that opportunity to rumble.

Alec blushed as he hesitantly took a bite out of the sandwich.

"I'm Rebecca. You're Alec aren't you kiddo?" Rebecca smiled warmly at Alec.

"Yes, but." Alec murmured as he continued to eat the sandwich.

Rebecca ruffled Alec's hair fondly. "You just leave the protesting to us now, kiddo. You're not alone anymore." Rebecca declared as she went to stand over by some friends. Alec noticed that there were a whole bunch of people gathered in front of Fairy Park now and that they were all dressed in the same green t-shirt that Rebecca had on. Upon closer inspection Alec saw that there was something written in yellow letters on the t-shirts: *Save Fairy Park.* Alec raised an eyebrow at this and then he noticed there was the illustration of a fairy on the t-shirt as well. The protestors all had homemade signs in their hands and they began to walk back and forth chanting:

"Save New York's Oldest Park! Down with McDally's! Children need nature! Save New York's Oldest Park!" They continued to chant over and over.

"Who are those guys?" Alec was wide-eyed.

"Environmentalists." Billy informed Alec with a smile.

Alec continued to watch the environmentalists protesting the destruction of the park and couldn't believe that he had actually managed to get the attention of so many people. Hope stirred in his chest. Alec took another bite of his sandwich which was actually pretty good and suddenly felt all choked up. He wasn't alone. Tears began to fall down Alec's face as he ate his sandwich. There was something about eating when he was sad that made his tears fall more easily. The people of New York had come together to help a cause like this one after all.

• • • • • • • • • • • • • • • •

The day of the destruction of Fairy Park had arrived. Construction workers along with their heavy engineering vehicles - bulldozers, excavators, asphalt pavers, a crane and even wrecking ball were all gathered at the location of the park. Alec and the environmentalists were gathered there as well. The environmentalists appeared prepared to protest until the very end.

Alec turned to face the environmentalist group, a serious expression on his face. "Thank you all for coming this far with me but it's time I finished this on my own. You'll only get arrested if you try and stay any longer. And..I have a plan."

Rebecca ruffled Alec's hair with her hand. "You sure kiddo? Well, we trust you so we'll go if you really want us to. Just take care of yourself and don't do anything too drastic. Here's an avocado, alfalfa sprout and carrot sandwich - in case you get hungry. Good luck."

The other members of the environmentalist team said goodbye to Alec and wished him luck as they left the park. Alec, a steely expression in his eyes, turned his attention back towards the park. Now, he had to set his plan into motion. Alec went to the Fairy Tree and had Billy tie him tightly to the trunk of the tree.

The construction team was working their way towards the center of the park sawing down trees when finally they reached Alec. A bulldozer came to a standstill just in front of the Fairy Tree and the man behind the wheel got out to speak with Alec while a few other construction workers with chainsaws in their hands stood nearby.

"Hey, kid, you're going to have to move. We're scheduled to remove that tree today." The construction worker began to explain.

Alec shook his head. "No, I'm not leaving. You'll just have to mow me over along with the tree!"

The construction worker ran a hand through his hair in frustration, "Geez Luis, come on now kid, I don't have anything against you or this park or nuthing but I have a job to do. So are you going to be a good little boy and leave?"

"No." Alec glared back at the man, who sighed heavily and scratched his head.

The construction worker was just about to say more when the sound of the bulldozer's engine starting was heard. The construction worker turned around in surprise. "Huh?" To see that his bulldozer had started up on its own and further more it was now moving towards the construction worker and Alec. "Holy-!" The construction worker was forced to dive out of the way nearly getting mowed over by his own construction vehicle. "Hey, look out kid!" The construction worker tried to warn Alec as the bulldozer was now heading towards Alec and the tree.

"Right on time, poltergeist. You fell for the bait." Alec had a grim smile on his face. "Jinx!" Alec cried out to his fairy friend Jinx who popped out of thin air and waved his wand at Alec's ropes. The ropes instantly turned into saltwater taffy instead of disappearing like they were supposed to.

"Ugh!" Alec had to tug and pull at it along with Billy's help before he managed to break free. As soon as he was free he ran over to the bulldozer and hopped into the driver's seat. The bulldozer was about to hit the Fairy Tree! Alec turned the steering wheel hard left and just barely got the bulldozer to miss the Fairy Tree in time. Whew!

At this point all of the poltergeists that had been drawn to Alec, who tied up to a tree was the perfect, tasty bait to offer up to them, and that had been impossible for them to resist, were making mischief and beginning to possess all of the heavy engineering vehicles causing them to move on their own. All of the bulldozers, excavators, asphalt pavers and the cranes began to chase the construction workers while half of them took off after Alec, who was still driving the bulldozer.

"Epp!" Alec squeaked as he looked behind him and saw the entourage of construction vehicles chasing him.

The construction workers were also beginning to panic:

"G-g-ghosts!" "This park is haunted!" "Run!" "It's the curse of Fairy Park!"

"Jinx a little help!" Alec called out to his friend.

Jinx nodded, "Right. Transfiguration!" Jinx waved his wand towards the group of construction vehicles that were after Alec.

With a sudden *poof* there was a large cloud of purple smoke and all of the construction vehicles had been turned into - a stampede of zoo animals! Alec's eyes widened in disbelief as he saw a rhino, a lion, a zebra, a giraffe, and a monkey. Alec decided it was time to get out of the bulldozer and so jumped out and rolled just as the stampede of animals attacked his bulldozer and mowed it over. Alec felt a trickle of sweat on his brow. That had been close. A little too close.

Alec suddenly noticed a flash of red and watched in disbelief as Evii Starr ran towards the Fairy Tree ready to report on this strange turn of events on the park's scheduled destruction day.

"This is reporter Evii Starr reporting live from Fairy Park. As you can see behind me all of the construction vehicles seem to have become possessed. This park is most definitely haunted folks and the ghosts of Fairy Park don't seem to be too happy that their park is in danger of being mowed over. And over there...? There seems to be a stampede of angry animals and - and they're coming this way! Epp!" Evii began to run. "Joey keep the film rolling! And now it's time for me to run for my life so tune in next time to catch the rest of my show! Cut!"

"I think that was your best show yet, boss!" Joey exclaimed as he ran after Evii.

Evii smirked and yelled back, "I know!"

· · · · · · · · · · · · · · · · ·

And so Fairy Park was saved due to the combined efforts of Alec, Billy, Jinx, a handful of mischievous poltergeists, a bunch of environmentalists, and one feisty reporter.

Meanwhile, at the Fairy Palace Jinx was getting a lecture. The Elder Fairy was pacing in his study, "Jinx! You know humans are not supposed to be witnesses to fairy magic!"

Jinx hung his head, "I'm sorry, Elder."

The Elder Fairy shook his head but then smiled. "Luckily, the humans are blaming this incident on poltergeists and as for the stampede - they're saying it was some kind of camera hoax." The Elder Fairy sighed. "And as for McDally's...it seems they've had a change of heart and have decided to donate the park to New York and make it an official historical landmark. Although the real reason they don't want to put a McDally's there anymore is obviously because no one will want to eat fast food at a haunted restaurant."

Jinx looked up in surprise that the Elder Fairy wasn't mad at him and grinned from ear to ear.

· · · · · · · · · · · · · · · · ·

Meanwhile, at Alec's house. Alec, and his mother and father were eating dinner and watching the news, which happened to be a report about the failed destruction of Fairy Park and its current situation becoming a historical landmark.

"Alec Suzuki," Laura was complaining. "Just what were you thinking? Trying to save some stupid park? What does that even have to do with you anyways? Do you even realize what I've had to put up with lately because of

31

your antics? What with the reporters and telephone calls non-stop! It's been awful for my nerves! I've had to double all my medications - my anti-stress pills, anti-anxiety pills, my anti-anger pills..." Laura continued to list all of the medication she was currently on.

Alec, however, was tuning his mother out until something interesting came up on the news -

McDally's has decided to donate the Fairy Park to the city of New York and it's been named an official historical landmark. They plan to construct a small playground for kids within the park and the park shall be renamed McDally Park... A reporter was informing viewers.

Alec smirked as they showed footage of the park. He could see some of the little people waving at the camera happily, although Alec was sure no one else could probably see them.

"Alec Suzuki? Are you even listening to me!" His mother continued to screech.

Alec sighed. *Well, at least some people even if they're tiny are happy with me.* Alec decided he'd go hide in his room for a while and play some video games, which had always been Alec's favorite escape from reality.

Chapter 3:
ALL HALLOWS NIGHT

Alec, Billy and Jinx were walking home from school together when Bobby, Luke and John caught up to them.

"Hey!" Bobby waved at Alec, "Alec wait up!"

Alec turned around to regard Bobby curiously.

Bobby was panting for breath, bent over slightly with his hands on his knees. "Hey Alec, what are you doing tonight? Me and the boys are going to go trick or treating if you'd like to come with us?"

Alec raised an eyebrow skeptically. "You want *me* the 'cursed boy' to go trick or treating with you guys?"

Bobby ran a hand through his spiky blonde hair, "Yea, well, everyone's been a bit harsh on you after that whole soccer incident but you *did* save John. Ain't that right John?"

John nodded gruffly. "Um, yea, thanks for that by the way."

"No problem..." Alec was surprised to get a 'thank you' out of the usually thick-headed John.

"We'll be meeting up at McDally Park at 8:00 - you know, the park you saved. That was pretty cool how you did that by the way. You should have asked us to come along and protest with you. So coming?" Bobby looked hopeful.

Alec shrugged. "Sure, why not."

Bobby smiled. "Great, see you then! Come on boys lets go."

"Bye Alec." Luke called after him as he caught up to Bobby.

"See ya." John grunted.

Alec blinked after the three boys in shock.

Jinx was throwing them a suspicious look, "They're up to something..."

Alec frowned, turning to Jinx, "What makes you say that?"

Jinx crossed his arms in front of his little chest and frowned right back at Alec. "Why else would they invite *you* to go trick or treating with them? They probably want to trick you into doing something stupid..."

Alec glared back at Jinx angrily. "Maybe they've seen the light and realized just how cool I really am and actually want to be friends with me. I *did* save John after all. He owes me one."

Jinx burst out laughing as if he'd heard the funniest joke on earth. "Yea, sure like that would ever happen!"

Alec felt hurt by this and his face was red from embarrassment. "You're just jealous that the guys want to hang out with me, Jinx. And that they're *real* human boys. They obviously want to let bygones be bygones and become friends, and if that's the case I'm willing to give them a chance."

"Is that wise Alec?" Billy finally butted in to give his own input, "I understand you wanting to have human friends and all but tonight *is* Halloween - the most dangerous night of the year for someone like you. Couldn't you hang out with them some other time?"

A chill went down Alec's spine at Billy's words but he shook his head stubbornly. "I can't go hide under my bed and live my life in fear Billy. I've already made up my mind - I'm going. And you guys can't stop me, so you can either come with me or just stay behind. I won't miss this chance on finally making some *real* friends."

At the word '*real*' both Billy and Jinx flinched. Billy looked hurt and Jinx appeared angry. "Real? What are Billy and I if not your real friends? I thought you were different from other humans Alec but I guess I was wrong. It's like we're not good enough for you or something. And if that's the case then so be it! Who wants to be friends with some human boy exorcist anyways! Hmph! Come on Billy, let's go." Jinx began to fly off, turning around to wait for Billy.

Billy hesitated and then shook his head. "I'm sorry Jinx but one of us needs to stay with Alec tonight. You know as well as I that tonight is the worst night for Alec to be roaming around the streets of New York City alone at night. What if something were to happen to him? He needs us Jinx."

Jinx frowned. "Fine! Stay with Alec for all I care but I'm going. And there's no use begging me to stay!"

Alec crossed his arms across his chest. "Who's begging?"

"You're just being stupid Alec - you'll see!" Jinx glared back angrily but a flash of hurt crossed his features for a moment before it was gone. Though Alec had noticed it and with a tinge of guilt watched as Jinx flew away.

Billy watched thoughtfully as Jinx flew off. "He's just worried about you,

you know. He doesn't want to see you get hurt. He really is your friend Alec and so am I."

Alec's shoulders slumped and he appeared deflated. "I know that...but I've already made up my mind. Maybe I am just being stupid but I can't help myself. You understand don't you Billy?"

Billy smirked, "Don't worry Alec, you know I've always got your back." He raised his fist towards Alec and the two boys bumped fists.

Alec shot Billy a smile, happy knowing he could always count on his best friend.

• • • • • • • • • • • • • • • • • •

Bobby, Luke and John were already waiting at McDally Park when Alec and Billy arrived. Alec looked over the boys' costumes and saw jealously that they were all pretty cool and scary compared to the lame one his mother had picked out for him. He had ended up looking...heaven forbid...the dreaded word...that no twelve-year-old boy wants to be called: *cute.*

Bobby was dressed all in black, he had a black cape with a hood on, and his face had been painted to look like a skull. Bobby was also carrying a fake scythe he had made to complete his 'Grim Reaper' costume. Luke was wearing all yellow and had gelled his hair on either side of his head to look like Wolverine and had fashioned claws out of foil paper. John had decided to dress up like Spiderman, and had painted his face to mimic the Spiderman mask. He was wearing a red sweatshirt and matching blue sweat pants.

"Hey guys, nice costumes." Alec greeted them.

"Yo Alec," Bobby waved him over and then took in the sight of Alec's costume. Alec's mom Laura had dressed him up like a cowboy, with a red cowboy hat and a small plastic pistol, but for some reason Alec looked anything but fearsome. He was also wearing a vest and jeans along with some cowboy boots. Bobby raised an eyebrow at his cowboy ensemble. "Is that a plastic gun?"

"Aw, that's so..." *Here it comes,* Alec bemoaned the dreaded word that would crumble his boyish pride. "Cute!" John laughed.

The word 'BOY' that had been hanging over Alec's head and that had been made of stone crumbled to pieces.

Alec blushed fiercely. "My mom attacked me before I went out and made me wear this. She pretty much thought the same as you John." Alec smirked bashfully.

The three boys snickered at Alec's plight. "Well, she was right, you do look cute." Bobby couldn't resist saying. "Like a little Clint Eastwood or something. Anyways, let's go, we have some tricking to do." A mischievous glint formed in Bobby's eye.

Alec blinked and quirked his head to the side, *Did Bobby just say trick? Didn't he mean 'trick or treating'?*

Why me? Alec bemoaned as he realized the three boys had never really had the intention of going 'trick or treating' for candy all along and instead had a night of mischief planned. Instead of trick or treating the three boys ended up going around vandalizing people's properties and cars. Throwing eggs at people's front doors or windows before running away and teepeeing people's trees, front lawns and cars.

Bobby, Luke, and John were in the process of teepeeing someone's tree on their front lawn by throwing rolls of toilet paper up into its branches when Alec tugged at Bobby's sleeve. "Um, Bobby are you sure we should really be doing this?"

Bobby stopped mid throw and turned to face Alec, frowning at him. "Don't tell me you're a goody two-shoes Alec? You better not be thinking of doing something stupid like telling on us." Bobby stared down at him.

Alec waved his hands frantically in front of him. "Huh? Oh no, of course not!"

Bobby nodded seemingly pleased. "Good. I knew you were cool. Here you do the honors next." Bobby handed Alec a rotten egg to throw at the front door of someone's house. Alec took the egg and stared down at it. Guilt bubbling in his stomach.

Billy, who was floating next to Alec, leaned down to whisper in Alec's ear, "Hey Alec, you're not really going to do it are you?"

Alec kept his voice low as he responded to Billy, "It's not like I really have a choice...If I don't these guys will probably teepee me to a tree! I know it's wrong but..." Alec looked over to where Bobby and the boys were all looking at him expectantly. "Don't worry Billy, I'll come back here later and clean up this mess when we're done 'tricking'. It's the right thing to do after all."

Billy nodded agreeably. "I'll help."

Alec brought his arm back and threw the rotten egg directly at the person's front door where it smashed awfully leaving a trail of green slim. And then someone suddenly burst out from inside the house - from the looks of it it was a little old lady with a cane in her hand and a very angry expression on her lined face. *Uh oh.* The hair on the back of Alec's neck were prickling.

"Hey you little brats! Just what do you think you're doing?" Came the old woman's shrill voice. The old woman turned to see the mess on her front door as well as her teepeed lawn and trees. "Get your butts over here and clean this mess up right now!"

Bobby looked extremely worried. "Run! It's the old hag!" He directed the group as they all took off running. Alec ran with the others, who he noticed had all pulled on sock masks leaving Alec to be the only one with his face exposed. Worry swirled in his gut. He was falling behind the others and it was hard to run in the cowboy boots his mother had made him wear. That's when he suddenly tripped and fell flat on his face.

Alec rubbed his red nose, "Owie..." He then felt an icy grip on his shoulder and turned around to scream.

* * * * * * * * * * * * * * * *

Alec took another sip of his tea as he looked around the inside of the old lady's house. He shook his head ruefully never having thought he'd end up having tea and cookies with some old lady who's house he had tried to vandalize. He really wasn't cut out for this type of thing after all. He made an awful hooligan due to his burning conscience. As soon as the old lady had caught him Alec had apologized profusely and told her he'd be happy to clean up the mess he'd made. He'd also been near tears since he knew that Bobby and the others had simply abandoned him to his fate. Alec flushed to remember it - it was all just so embarrassing. As it turned out as soon as he'd apologized she seemed to forgive him immediately and had invited him in for tea and cookies since as old ladies tend to get - she was a little lonely.

Alec knew that Bobby and the others were probably laughing their heads off right about then about how he'd gotten himself caught - although he was also sure they had no idea that instead of getting some kind of lecture from the old lady he was instead having a surprisingly nice time with her and enjoying the tea and cookies she had given him.

The old lady had gone off to the kitchen to take some fresh chocolate chip cookies out of the oven and came back with a plateful. She set them on the tea table in front of Alec before taking a seat across from Alec in a comfortable looking chair. She pulled a shawl around her bony shoulders as she looked at Alec with a scrutinizing gaze. "What's a nice boy like you doing hanging out with those hooligans anyhow? I remember those naughty three from last year - even with their sock masks. But you're new and they didn't give you a sock mask, which makes me think your new friends tried to set you up." The old woman poured herself some tea and stirred in some sugar thoughtfully.

Billy raised his brows at Alec as if to say - "See, told ya so. She's one smart old lady."

Alec sighed heavily. "Yea, you're probably right. I just...wanted to make some real friends..."

The old lady nodded sagely in understanding as she took a sip of her tea before speaking. "But in life you have to figure out who your *real* friends are.

And real friends stick by you no matter what - they don't run off and abandon you to your fate. You must chose wisely who you put your trust in, boy. And learn to be wise about who you call friend. There are those that are 'friend' in name only and then those that come through for you when you're in a pinch - that's a real friend. People that leave you hanging during the darkest moments of your life aren't really your friends at all."

Alec realized that the old lady must have been speaking from a personal experience. Alec took a bite of a chocolate chip cookie and gave a sidelong glance at Billy. *I've been such an idiot.* Alec then also thought of Jinx and how stupid he'd been towards the little fairy, who was only trying to be his friend. He didn't deserve such friendship. "You're absolutely right." Alec stood up suddenly. "I better get going. Um, ma'am, if you wouldn't mind - may I have a few cookies for the road? I have a friend with a real sweet tooth who I know would just love your cookies."

"Of course." The old lady beamed at him.

His pocket much heavier than before Alec left the old lady's house to see that Bobby, Luke and John were all waiting for him, albeit they were all hiding behind a tree. Alec shrugged and walked up to them.

"So what happened in there? Did the old lady box your ears?" Bobby questioned.

Alec gave him a strange look, "Actually she was really nice - we had tea and cookies together."

Bobby, John, and Luke's jaws all hit the dirt as they looked at Alec in surprise and disbelief. Their little 'plan' hadn't gone quite as they had expected.

"Tea and cookies? You can't be serious dude? That old lady is no easy target. One year when she caught me she hit me over the head with that cane of hers." Bobby informed him while rubbing the back of his head as if he still remembered how that had felt.

"Remember that time she set her dog on us..." Luke shivered.

"And then there was the time she attacked us with her new sprinkler system." John put in.

The three boys looked at Alec with obvious distaste, irked that their little plan hadn't worked out how they wanted. Alec just gave them an innocent look and quirked his head at them, "What?" Alec was beginning to be grateful that Laura had made sure that Alec had looked 'cute' and not 'troublesome' after all.

Bobby ran a hand through his spiky hair, "Anyways, now that you're back we can get going."

Alec quirked an eyebrow, "Go where?"

Bobby and the others exchanged a look. "It's a surprise."

Alec and Billy exchanged their own look of worry. "What do you think they're up to now?" Billy whispered to Alec.

Alec shrugged, "Dunno, but I guess I better just play along in case they plan on picking on any other nice old ladies." Alec also kept his voice down.

· · · · · · · · · · · · · · · · · ·

Bobby led the boys into a more sketchy part of town. In this area of the ghetto there weren't any kids trick or treating and the streets were deserted. Alec could see people looking out from their windows in a very suspicious manner as the foursome walked past. The buildings there were in desperate need of repair and Alec could see that several had broken windows or boarded up doors. Finally, Bobby stopped in front of one old townhouse in particular.

"We're here," Bobby announced.

Alec looked up at the spooky looking townhouse. It was obviously abandoned. Several of the windows were broken and the green paint was peeling off the front door. But there was something else...the hair on the back of Alec's neck prickled in warning. He sensed *something* from within the house...something evil, malevolent. *Uh oh.* It had to be a ghostly presence.

Billy was floating by Alec's side and also looking up at the townhouse thoughtfully when a curious expression formed on his face. "This house seems oddly familiar...I think I know this place..."

Alec turned to Billy in surprise. When Alec had first met Billy and had wanted to help the ghost boy with his unfinished business Billy had told Alec that he mysteriously didn't remember his past. That had left the two at a bit of a dead end but regardless Alec had promised Billy to help him regain his memories and one day help Billy with his unfinished business so that he could cross over. That had been years ago. "Billy, are you remembering something?" Alec had to hide his excitement.

Billy's expression had turned to worry and he still hadn't torn his green eyes away from the townhouse. "Alec I have a bad feeling about this place. I don't think we should go in there."

Alec looked back at the townhouse as well and could still sense that malevolent presence inside - was it a poltergeist perhaps? If so it would indeed be dangerous to go inside, especially since Alec didn't have his soccer ball with him, which he sometimes used when he had to exorcize particularly powerful evil spirits. "Yea, I don't think we should either..." Alec shivered. He then turned around about to leave when Bobby grabbed the back of his jacket.

"Hey now, where do you think you're going?" Bobby started. "Not thinking of running away were you?"

Alec sighed. He was caught. "Maybe..."

"You're not a wimp are you?" Bobby prodded.

Alec frowned. He hated it when people called him a wimp. "No, I'm not a wimp but I'm not stupid either. That house is obviously haunted."

Bobby smirked. "Duh, that's the point silly. This is Halloween! It's the perfect place to try and find a real ghost. Wouldn't it be so frickin cool to get to see a *real* ghost?"

Alec looked over at Billy, who was giggling behind his hand, and shrugged. "It's overrated."

"They say a family was murdered here by a robber..." Bobby began in a spooky voice while holding up a flashlight under his chin for the effect of casting shadows on his skull-painted face. "And that they still haunt this place seeking revenge..." Bobby smirked as his audience all swallowed nervously. "Let's go boys."

Alec gawked, open-mouthed at them. "Hey wait, guys, you're not seriously going in there are you?"

Bobby put his hands on his hips and frowned at Alec, "Yea, we are. We're going to find out if the urban legend is true and this place is really haunted or not. Then at school we'll be heroes for finding out. But if you're too chicken to come along then don't. It's not like your reputation could get any worse what with adding 'coward' to the list. Let's go boys." Bobby, followed by John and Luke, headed towards the door.

Alec sighed heavily.

Billy looked worried. "What are you going to do Alec? You shouldn't let what those boys said get to you. I know you're no coward. You should just stay here."

Alec watched as the three boys entered the house. "I could care less what those losers say but...it's dangerous in there. I sense...something. Something really bad. If it turns out there's a poltergeist or something inside they could really get hurt. I can't just stay here and do nothing. I'm going. You can stay here if you want."

Billy was wide-eyed. "But Alec you don't even have your soccer ball."

Alec frowned and didn't answer as he started forward walking towards the front door. Billy paused a moment before following after him. Alec entered last and the door shut loudly behind him causing all four boys to jump a foot in the air. Alec coughed into his hand. "Wind." He explained, knowing that wasn't true.

Bobby was looking a bit pale, "Yea, of course. We knew that. Let's go." Bobby continued his way deeper into the living room. The first floor had a large, open living room with a large, round, circular rug in the center that had rings of different colors. There were also several chairs and sofas scattered about the room and which had all been covered with white sheets. There was a thin layer of dust covering everything. Bobby noticed there was a staircase to the left leading to the floors above. "Let's go upstairs."

The four boys all decided to check the second floor rooms. Once they were standing in the second floor hallway Bobby turned to the three boys. "Let's all split up - call out if you see something." Bobby smirked and so did John and Luke making Alec think once again that the boys must be up to something.

Alec and Billy headed towards one of the rooms at the end of the hall. Alec sensed something oddly familiar coming from that room in particular. Alec hesitated before reaching out and grasping the doorknob and then turning it to open the door. He entered the dark room and felt along the walls for a light switch and upon finding one he flipped it on. Alec blinked as his eyes adjusted to the flickering light to reveal - a children's bedroom for two kids. There were twin beds and one side of the room was decorated with things that were definitely for a girl while the other side of the room had definitely been decorated by a boy. The room had probably been for a brother and sister, Alec decided.

The girl's side of the room was decorated with ballerina posters above her bed, and there was a small dresser on which sat a dusty jewelry box that, when Alec opened it, revealed a spinning ballerina and a music box song which began to play. There was also a chest of costumes and one of those items of clothing was a pink tutu skirt. Alec decided that whoever this little girl was she wanted to be a ballerina when she grew up. The bed had dusty pink sheets and on it was a mouse in a pink ballerina outfit with a tutu. Alec raised an eyebrow at that until he found a dusty book about a mouse that wanted to be a ballerina and was titled: *Angelina Ballerina*.

Alec then turned his attention towards the boy's side of the room to see that it was mostly decorated with a robot theme. There was a Transformers poster on his wall, and there were several model kits for making robot models set out on a desk with some completed robots and others that had been left unfinished, and Alec noticed there was even a Lego set that was for making robot-like figures out of Legos.

Billy was already floating towards the boy's side of the room, his eyes a bit wide, "This is..." He looked at the robot Lego set and picked up a completed robot model of Optimus Prime, one of the robots from the popular cartoon series about robots called 'Transformers'. "I remember this...this is my room... this is Optimus Prime."

"Your room?" Alec questioned surprised. He then walked over to the desk on the boy's side of the room and picked up a dusty photograph. Alec couldn't see the people in the photograph since it was so dusty so he wiped his hand across the glass. When it cleared he saw a smiley, young girl with bright green eyes and blonde pig-tails, who was standing next to a young boy with matching green eyes and messy blonde hair. Alec recognized the boy almost immediately. "Billy, it's you. But who's...?" Alec was turning to Billy to ask him about the girl in the picture when suddenly the door to the bedroom burst open.

Bobby and his friends, who were all covered up with white sheets, came into the room waving their arms beneath the sheets and moaning: *"Boooo~"*

Alec and Billy both turned towards the doorway, and Alec raised an eyebrow at them. "Was that supposed to scare me?"

"They could have tried a little harder than that." Billy chuckled.

Alec turned to Billy and just laughed with him. "Yea, I know. That was pretty pathetic even for them. They must really think I'm a total wimp or something huh Billy?"

As Billy was laughing his body was shaking from mirth and the Maximus Prime model in his hands was moving up and down so that it appeared to be floating in midair. This seemed to stop Bobby and the boys in their tracks.

"He was just talking to someone..." John's shaky voice started.

"The robot doll...it's like totally floating, dude." Luke was pointing worriedly, with his trembling hand in the direction of the model.

"G-g-ghost!" Bobby declared flinging off his sheet, "Run!"

The other two boys followed suit and flung off their white sheets before taking after their 'leader' down the hallway and screaming their heads off. Alec and Billy broke out into fits of laughter. Alec wiped a tear from his eye since he was laughing so hard. "Man, that was so funny. Hey, Billy, who's this?" Alec handed Billy the photograph he had been looking at earlier.

Billy took the picture from Alec and looked at it. Billy's eyes widened with recognition. "It's...she's...my little sister." He seemed a bit thunderstruck. "I... remember...oh god..." Billy began to look pale - for a ghost.

"What is it?" Alec questioned worriedly.

"It's just that I finally remember what happened to me to make me a ghost. You know that family that Bobby mentioned? The one that was killed by a robber? That was my family. I remember that night...how the robber broke in and my father tried to fight him and was shot. Then my mother was killed next as she tried to protect us. I ran to our room with my sister and shut the door and locked it. I told her to hide under the bed and not to make a sound while I called the police. It took a moment for the robber to break down the door and when he did I was standing there in front of the bed blocking his way to my sister. And that's when he shot me. I didn't cross over because I didn't want to leave my little sister alone...and so I stayed behind as a ghost. Cindy...how could I have forgotten her?"

A dark chuckle suddenly resonated throughout the room. The hair on the back of Alec's neck were standing on end.

Alec looked around the room worriedly, "What was that?"

Billy's eyes widened in fear. "Uh oh. I remember now...he must have never left..."

"Who never left?" Alec had a sinking feeling in his stomach.

"The robber." A lamp suddenly rose off of Cindy's night table and came flying towards Alec. "Look out!" Billy cried as he pushed Alec out of the way. The lamp hit the wall behind where Alec had been standing only seconds before and shattered.

Alec's eyes were wide. "He's become a poltergeist? Oh man! We're so screwed."

Billy nodded, "Let's get out of here."

The boys rushed out of the bedroom just as other objects were beginning to rise up and chase after them. Alec slammed the door shut behind him and could hear several objects knocking into it. Alec knew that they had to get out of the house before the poltergeist decided to show his true form because if that happened Alec knew he would be outmatched without his soccer ball.

The two boys flew down the stairs to the first floor and Alec made a break for the front door - only to have a sofa move into his path. Alec gulped as the sofa suddenly began to skid across the floor towards him. Alec had no choice but to back up and he suddenly found himself backing up into a door which swung open. Windmilling his arms Alec found himself falling backwards and onto his butt in the middle of the kitchen. Alec quickly stood and turned around to see that all of the drawers and cupboards in the kitchen were beginning to open. Then from within the drawers several knives and forks began to rise in the air and zoom towards Alec. The dark chuckle was sounding through the air again. "Epp!" Alec squeaked as he ran back out of the kitchen and quickly slammed the kitchen door shut behind him. He heard the sound of the knives and forks embedding themselves into the other side of the door.

Alec saw that the possessed sofa was still trying to block his way to the door. Alec ran towards the sofa deciding he would try to jump over it when suddenly the rug under his feet was pulled out from under him and Alec found himself once again on his backside. Alec quickly scrambled off the floor and saw that the center of the large, circular rug that was in the living room was beginning to come up off the floor and was taking on the shape of a man. Alec gulped, the poltergeist was beginning to show its material form. He had to get out of there. Then Alec noticed how the poltergeist was maneuvering several more forks and knives to hover in the air in front of Alec and stay pointed at him.

Alec knew that if he even moved an inch for the door those sharp looking forks and knives would soon be flying at him. "Dang, if only I had my soccer ball..."

"*Mmmm* you smell yummy kid. I'm going to eat you all up....your spirit that is..." Came the low throaty voice of the poltergeist. "Now - die! die! die!" The poltergeist waved his hand towards Alec and caused all of the forks and knives to go flying towards him.

Alec threw his arms up, panicking, and did the only thing he could think of doing in a situation as hopeless as that one - "Jinx!"

The small window above the front door suddenly shattered as Jinx broke through. "Alec!" Immediately taking in the scene before him Jinx waved his wand at the forks and knives that were about to impale Alec. "Transfiguration!" The silverware was engulfed in a bright golden light and then with a *poof* of purple smoke the forks and knives began to turn into - kids toys and stuffed animals. Dropping down from the air were suddenly a collection of dolls, bears, and colorful balls.

Alec's gray eyes sparkled as he caught sight of one of the bouncing balls. *Now's my chance!* Alec ran for one of the balls and gathered his spirit energy around him as he began to dribble one of the balls towards the poltergeist. He positioned himself in front of the vengeful ghost and prepared to kick the ball at him. "Take this!" Alec brought his leg back and kicked the ball towards the poltergeist - the ball glowing with a blue tinged light as it sped through the air. The ball hit the poltergeist, who immediately began to melt...

"Oh no...I'm melting...*melting*..." The poltergeist moaned as it began to sink to the floor until- "Just kidding." The poltergeist suddenly sprang back to life from out of the floor still using the carpet as part of its form. Alec blinked in shock. His Spirit Ball had had no effect. He looked crestfallen. Was the poltergeist too powerful?

The poltergeist was laughing maniacally. "Is that the best you've got kid? Too bad. Prepare to die! I'm going to enjoy eating you all up!" Part of the carpet seemed to leap forward towards Alec, who dodged and tried to run for the front door once more.

But as Alec headed for the door something wrapped around his ankle and tripped him up. Alec found himself face first on the floor and rubbing his much injured nose. Alec turned around to see himself being dragged backwards towards the poltergeist who had stretched out a piece of the carpet and was using it like a tentacle to wrap around Alec's ankle and drag him back across the floor. "Epp!"

"I've eaten the spirits of several kids, who have been stupid enough to wander through here on Halloween night and you're next." The poltergeist informed Alec, who gulped.

But then Billy suddenly stood between Alec and the poltergeist with his arms out to his sides. "No! I won't let you hurt my best friend! You're going to have to get through me first!"

"*Billy...*" Alec looked up in surprise at his ghost friend, his voice thick with emotion. He knew how scared Billy really had to be of the poltergeist.

The poltergeist paused to look at Billy. "It's *you*. I remember you - you're the boy of the family I killed. You called the cops on me, you little brat. You know, just after I shot you that's when I heard the police sirens outside. I ran down to the first floor hoping to beat them before they arrived, but as soon as I opened the door I saw that the police already had the place surrounded. I had no choice but to try and fight my way out. I shot at the cops and they shot back. They killed me right there on the front steps. I got killed that night because of you kid. And I've been trapped in this house ever since and do you want to know why? Revenge. I knew I had to pay you back kid. And now that seeing you has jogged my memory I remember my own unfinished business. That night I thought I had killed your entire family but as it turns out I was wrong. You have a sister. I'm going to go and pay your sister a little visit and make you wish you never called the cops, kid!" An evil cackle echoed through the house at the poltergeist's words.

The poltergeist let go of his hold on Alec's leg and suddenly flew towards the front door, which had now opened from the poltergeist's power.

Billy's eyes were wide with fear and worry. "No! Not my sister! You jerk! Don't you dare lay a finger on her!" Billy called after the poltergeist.

"You're not getting away!" Alec declared as he ran towards the fleeing poltergeist and was trying to dribble another ball towards his target. He was just about to kick the ball forward when he suddenly tripped again due to the slippery bottoms of the cowboy boots he was wearing. Alec hit his forehead hard on the floor and looked up in time to see the poltergeist flying through the open door and off into the night. "Dang!" Alec brought his fist down upon the floor. "I let him get away..."

Alec quickly pushed himself off the ground and ignored the aches and pains in his body. "Billy do you have any idea where he's headed?"

Billy nodded, "Yea, the NYC orphanage, it's not too far from here. My sister Cindy has been living there."

Alec put a hand on Billy's shoulder. "Don't worry we'll stop that poltergeist from harming your sister. But first things first, Jinx - I need some proper shoes and a real soccer ball not just some toy. Think you can manage that transfiguration without blowing me up?"

Jinx nodded, "I'll do my best." Jinx waved his wand through the air. "Transfiguration!"

* * * * * * * * * * * * * * * * * *

Alec along with Billy and Jinx all headed over to the NYC orphanage rushing down the deserted street. Alec now had a proper pair of shoes on and a soccer ball in hand. Even if they were both bright pink. Alec sighed. They arrived not much later at the entrance to the orphanage, which really had only been a few blocks away. Thankfully, the place still seemed pretty calm. Only the outside lights were lit since the children inside must have been sleeping at that hour.

Billy and Jinx grabbed onto one of Alec's arms each and lifted him up to a second floor window. Alec kicked it open and jumped from the window sill down into the room. He found himself in a large room with a row of twin-sized beds on either side. Alec noticed that all the children that were asleep in this room were girls so they had luckily come to the right room. "Billy...which one of these girls is Cindy?" Alec asked in a hushed voice.

Billy began to float down the center of the room peering at each bed as he passed and trying to find his sister. That's when he spotted her. He floated towards the bed and as he looked down at the sleeping form of his sister his eyes seemed to soften. "Cindy...peak a boo, I've found you." He smiled.

Alec came over to Billy and looked down at the sleeping girl. "Is this her?" Billy nodded and Alec let out a breath of relief. She appeared to be unharmed. But then where was - ?

A dark chuckle suddenly sounded throughout the room. Uh oh.

"Yo! You dumb brats, I didn't know which one she was. Thank you for leading me straight to her. Now I can gobble little Ms. Ridding Hood all up! Yummy!"

The poltergeist's voice echoed eerily throughout the room. And then the poltergeist suddenly appeared coming out of a long shadow at the foot of Cindy's bed and materializing in front of it. It took the form of a shadowy hooded figure. It's body this time around wasn't made of carpet but made of shadow - dark and translucent.

Billy turned to glare at the poltergeist. "I won't let you lay a finger on my sister!"

Cindy, who had been sound asleep, began to stir in her bed. Her eyes fluttered open and she looked up at Billy so that her matching green eyes widened. "Brother? Am I dreaming?"

Billy looked down at his sister Cindy equally wide-eyed with surprise that she could see him. "Cindy? You can see me?"

Cindy looked past Billy and noticed the dark and hooded figure - there was something horrifyingly familiar about that shadowy man that caused Cindy to start trembling. "Brother, who's that?"

"It's him Cindy, it's the man who killed our parents. But don't worry Cindy I won't let him hurt you. He'll have to get through me first. Besides, my friend Alec is here so everything will okay. He's really strong. You'll see. I promise." Billy reached out his pinky finger towards his sister.

She hesitated before reaching out her own pinky to complete their pinky promise. She wrapped her finger around his ghostly one. "You're so cold..."

"Aw, how sweet. Just kidding!" The poltergeist chuckled. "I think I'll eat your sister first and then eat you, ghost boy. You both have tasty smelling spirits! But also this way you get to watch as you get your just desserts for calling the cops on me kid. Here comes the big bad wolf little girl - I'm going to eat you all up!" The poltergeist suddenly flew towards the brother and sister. Billy wrapped his arms around Cindy and tried to shield her with his body.

Alec dropped his pink and black soccer ball onto the floor. He began to gather his spirit energy around him until a bright blue aura was flaring to life all around him and his soccer ball. "I don't think so. I won't let you hurt my friend's sister. It's time for you to cross over and find peace Mr. Poltergeist. Eat this!"

The poltergeist turned its attention towards Alec now. "That trick again? Don't you realize that your pathetic power isn't enough to stop me boy? I've eaten dozens of spirits to gain this much power and I'll merely be adding all of you to my list. Don't be so impatient to join them in my stomach boy."

"We'll see about that! Have a taste of my full power!" Alec declared as he kicked the soccer ball forward. It was glowing with a light so fierce it hurt Cindy's eyes and she had to cover them with her hands. The aura around Alec was still flaring around him brightly even as he began to stop summoning his power. "Just call me the woodcutter."

The glowing soccer ball shot through the air and hit the poltergeist right in its chest. It seemed to have no effect at first as it kept spinning and the poltergeist laughed uproariously, but then suddenly the ball broke through the poltergeist's chest blowing a hole straight through it. Then Alec's spirit energy seemed to infect the poltergeist like a poison from the inside out.

"What the? Impossible! No!" The poltergeist cried as he was exorcized. The poltergeist's shadowy body exploded and burst into hundreds of tiny dots of red light, which seemed to be sucked down through the floor where they disappeared.

"Alec, you did it! You destroyed him. You've saved us! Thank you!" Billy declared turning his attention back to Alec.

"Good going Alec! That was awesome!" Jinx put in excitedly, but then Jinx's smile faltered as he noticed that Alec's hair had turned completely snow-white. "Alec - your hair!"

Alec was smiling at them weakly before he tried to take a step forward towards Cindy's bed and then he felt himself falling forward as darkness consumed him and he blacked out. He thought he could hear the voices of his friends as he fell calling his name urgently and he wished he had the strength to tell them he was okay before he passed out so that they wouldn't worry.

· · · · · · · · · · · · · · · · · · ·

Alec stirred awake to find an unfamiliar white ceiling above his head, again. Which meant he must be in the hospital. He turned and saw that an IV was stuck in his arm. Blinking he tried to sit up and noticed that Billy, Cindy, and Jinx were all in the room with him.

"Hey, he's waking up." Cindy noticed, breaking out into a grin.

"Alec!" Came Jinx's squeaky voice.

"Alec, how do you feel buddy?" Billy floated by the side of his bed, a worried expression on his face.

Alec struggled to sit up again but felt too weak and so gave up. "I feel fine just...tired and extremely...drained." Alec pouted at his odd condition since he had never really felt that way before.

"That's to be expected with all the spirit energy you used in that attack against the poltergeist!" Jinx explained enthusiastically.

"Spirit...energy." Alec laid his head back on his pillow. "Is that what the blue light is?"

"Yep!" Jinx nodded vigorously, "So you have to be more careful next time. You nearly killed yourself Alec. Spirit energy is the energy that comes directly from your own spirit, your soul, the true essence of who and what you are."

Alec looked over at Billy and Cindy thoughtfully. "The poltergeist?"

"Destroyed." Billy assured him. "Thanks to you, Alec." Billy grasped his friend's hand. "You once promised me you'd help me remember my unfinished business and help me to cross over...well, you've kept your promise Alec."

Alec furrowed his brows together in confusion, "Billy, what are you saying?"

"My unfinished business was to protect my sister Cindy from that criminal. Thanks to you I don't need to worry about her being hurt by that poltergeist any more. So now I have no more reason to stay here. I can finally cross over."

Alec's eyes were wide in shock. "Cross over? But - you can't! You're...my best friend Billy!"

Billy simply smiled back and shook his head as his body was becoming even more transparent. "I can't stay here anymore Alec, it's kinda against the rules..." Billy, still had Alec's hand grasped in his, "And you're my best friend too, Alec. We'll always be best friends. Thank you again for helping me protect my sister. Oh and Alec I have one more favor to ask of you, buddy." Billy suddenly removed his hand from Alec's and placed his sister's hand in Alec's instead. "Please look after Cindy for me?"

Alec and Cindy looked at each other both blushing. Alec was the first to turn away. "Um, yea, okay, sure." Alec agreed nervously.

Billy smiled warmly at the two of them. "Good, now I can finally rest in peace."

Alec seemed to come back to his senses and pulled his hand out of Cindy's. "Wait no! Don't go Billy!" He reached his hand out to his disappearing friend.

Cindy also seemed to realize just what was happening. "Brother!" She then shook her head realizing it was futile to get her brother to stay when he should cross over. "Brother, thank you for watching over me."

Billy nodded as he burst into dots of sparkling, blue light, which floated upwards towards the ceiling before they passed straight through and disappeared towards the heavens.

Cindy's eyes filled with tears and she hastily wiped them away before she stood up from the chair she had been sitting in to come over closer to Alec's bedside. "Alec, I want to thank you for saving my life and for saving my brother."

Alec scratched his cheek bashfully as he looked away, "Anytime..." He had always been a bit awkward around girls not really knowing how to act around them.

Cindy smiled brightly at that. "I have to get back to the orphanage, but I hope that one day soon we'll meet again Alec. You were so brave. I'll never forget you. Jinx I'll never forget you either." Cindy unexpectedly leaned forward and placed a kiss on Alec's cheek before she skipped away. "Bu-bye boys!"

Alec was left in a stunned state that he had just been kissed by a girl. He brought a hand to his cheek where Cindy had kissed him and had a dazed look on his face.

"Bye Cindy!" Jinx waved after her enthusiastically and smirked. "She's cute isn't she Alec? And she can see me which makes her special."

Alec seemed lost in thought however. "Is she?"

Jinx frowned and was about to try and say something to him when the door suddenly burst open and Mr. and Mrs. Suzuki strode through the door.

"Alec honey!" Laura rushed to the side of Alec's bed.

"Son!" Mori also rushed to Alec's side.

Alec, who had his head hanging down, his bangs covering his face, slowly looked back up at them. They seemed so far away from him in that moment though. How could they even begin to understand what he had just gone through? Or even what he was going through now having lost his best friend? Even when his parents were standing right there next to him for some reason he still felt so alone.

"Alec, are you alright?" Laura questioned seeing his strange look.

Alec nodded, "Sure, I'm fine, Mom."

Mori let out a breath of relief, "Thank goodness. We were so worried when we'd heard you'd been hospitalized again. We'd feared the worst-"

Laura cut him off. "This has *got* to stop. I can't take much more of this Alec. You're just being selfish in your actions by doing whatever you want. You need to think about your family more and how your actions are affecting us. I can't take much more of your...fiascos. You need to stop this...you need to try harder at being normal!"

Alec blinked back at her in shock. "Normal?"

Laura threw her hands up in exasperation. "You still don't understand. I've had enough...of the both of you. Of this family. I need...a break."

Mori looked over at his wife worriedly. "Laura, what are you saying?"

"I'm sorry Mori but this isn't what I wanted in life. I want a normal life and a normal family. This just isn't it. This family just can't make me happy. I shouldn't have to put up with all this. I deserve more. And that boy...is *not* my son!"

"Laura!" Mori's voice warned.

Laura looked somewhat abashed at her own words, but she still looked upon Alec with cold eyes. She gave Alec one last chilling look before she turned and left the room with Mori trailing helplessly behind her.

"Laura wait!"

Alec hung his head, defeated, his bangs shielding his dulled eyes. Everyone was leaving him...was he really so...unwanted?

Jinx sensed Alec's mood and instantly tried to cheer up his friend. "Hey cheer up Alec! You've still got me don't you? Who cares what she says anyways? Alec! Come on! Talk to me! Alec! Cheer up!" Jinx persisted and was tugging on Alec's clothing, hair and ear as Alec continued to ignore him until Alec finally snapped.

Alec just wanted to be left alone. His mind was in chaos at having just lost his best friend Billy and having his own mother say that he was not her son. He didn't have the patience to deal with a hyperactive fairy just then, and so Alec picked up one of the pillows from his bed and threw it hard at Jinx. It was a direct hit which sent the poor fairy sprawling onto the ground, his head spinning and looking a bit swirly-eyed.

"Where did all the little birdies come from?" Jinx was saying as he saw birds flying around his head.

"Be quiet Jinx! Just go away and leave me alone!" Alec yelled. "I never told you this before but when you're like this...you're just...annoying!"

Jinx pushed himself off the ground and stared back at Alec an indignant expression on his face. "Annoying? So that's how it is then? Well fine! Be that way! Alec Suzuki! If you want to be alone - then be alone! FOREVER!" Jinx yelled his last word as he flew out of the hospital window.

Alec sighed heavily and hung his head. Alone. Now he was truly alone. He had just lost his best friend...his mother was probably leaving him and his father...and now Jinx had left him too. Everyone was abandoning him. *All alone*, Alec put a hand in front of his mouth as he began to cry. *What have I done?*

Chapter 4:
YOKAI: DEMON

Billy had left him. Jinx had left him. His mother Laura had left him. Everyone had left him. And so now he was alone.

After Billy had crossed over and Alec had had the 'falling out' with Jinx, Alec had wanted to escape from the reality that had become his life. And he found a way - video games and MMORPGs (Massive Multiplayer Online Role Playing Games). Alec bought an XBOX live and many of the latest and most advanced games available to accompany it. He also bought the most high tech and innovative lab top he could find, so his computer system would be able to handle some of the intense graphics the games he was going to play had. In the online RPGs (Role Playing Games) Alec was able to become someone else. And Alec badly wanted to be anyone other than Alec Suzuki.

In the online virtual reality worlds Alec created a new identity. In the games he always chose to be a swordsman, or warrior class PC (Player Character). The persona he had come up with for himself was that of a powerful, loner type. His screen name was usually: Dranarch. In many of the games he played he had managed to reach the highest level, which in RPGs was usually level 100. He became unbeatable, powerful, invincible. In those worlds he was someone who wasn't useless. He was someone who wasn't unwanted. From his fellow players he had received praise for his accomplishments in level, skills and game play abilities. Slowly, however, Alec began to simply want to *become* his online persona Dranarch. But no matter how much he wanted to escape reality, the reality of who he really was still haunted him - he was Alec Suzuki the cursed boy, the Spirit Magnet, whom no one loved or wanted.

Alec was playing an advanced, live shooting game, when he heard his father knocking on his bedroom door.

"Alec...can I come in?" Mori's shaky voice came through the door.

Alec decided to ignore him and continued to concentrate on his game. He heard Mori opening the door and stepping into his room.

Mori flinched at the sounds of gunshots and cries coming from Alec's game and looked around at his son's room then shook his head despairingly. Video game cartons, game cd cases, game guidebooks, and gaming magazines littered the floor of his son's room. His son was continuing to play some violent game using his XBOX live and was completely ignoring him. This had become the usual. To Mori it seemed his son had shut himself off from the world and he knew this wasn't healthy for Alec. His son barely went outside any more. Just for school and as soon as he got home he would hole himself up in his room and play those video games of his.

Mori knew that he had to do something - something drastic to help his son. He was losing him to...virtual reality. He had to somehow make his son face reality and stop him from running away. Although, secretly Mori knew exactly what Alec was running away from and also knew of a way to help him.

"I don't blame you for the divorce son..." Perhaps Alec was punishing himself, Mori thought. "I still love you...but this place, this country, this house, it holds too many painful memories for me. That's why I've decided to take a job back in Tokyo.

Alec's fingers stilled on his game controller. Was his father about to abandon him too? Alec was panicking and could feel himself almost starting to hyperventilate. He couldn't take much more of this. He didn't want to be left alone. But Alec took a deep breath and managed to compose himself to at least hear his father out, his fists clenching around the game controller.

"So, you're just running away?" Alec said, his voice tinged with bitterness. His father had never been a fighter. He'd always been a pushover and had let Laura control him like a puppet. Now she had left and Mori was just going to sit back and watch it happen and do nothing about it. His father was a coward and Alec hated his father for that and for not protecting their family. For letting his mom leave. He wasn't the only one after all who wished he could have a normal family and a normal life.

"I'd like you to come to Japan with me - there's a boarding school there called the Izanagi Academy. It's a school where children who are...special go. Perhaps, they will be able to help you and understand you better than I can. I'm sorry Alec that I can't be the one to help you. I'm sorry for being so weak... and for breaking my promise to *her* but this is the only way I can think of to help you." Mori wrung his hands together, a guilty look on his face.

"A boarding school?" So he really was being abandoned after all. Alec hung his head, his white bangs shielding his stormy gray eyes.

. . . .

Mori Suzuki was driving his son to the Izanagi Academy, which was located in the outskirts of Tokyo. Alec was looking out his passenger's side window at Tokyo city as it passed them by. Mori's job had taken him to live in the very heart of Tokyo and so before they were leaving it Alec got to see just how filled with people and life the city was even when compared to a city as big as New York.

Alec was glad that his father had always spoken Japanese to him throughout his childhood and so at least the language barrier wouldn't pose a problem for him at his new school since he could both read and write fluently in Japanese. In the distance Alec noticed a tall, Eiffel Tower-like structure that had a lattice of orange-red and white steel bars that reached up into the sky. Mori informed Alec that this monument was Tokyo Tower.

As Alec continued to people watch from his passenger side window he came to one conclusion: *Tokyo is weird.* Everything there seemed strange and almost otherworldly. The city was so modern it felt as though he'd been transported to some kind of futuristic Blade Runner-like city. Alec's eyebrows rose when he saw people dressed in *cosplay. Cosplay,* a Japanese pop culture phenomena, short for 'costume play' was when young people dressed up as their favorite *anime* (Japanese animation) or *manga* (Japanese comic books) characters and tried to become them by roleplaying.

Being a huge fan of video games and comic books himself Alec did a double take upon seeing this. To see people dressed up as actual characters from things like comic books or even Japanese video games and to be walking along the street as though it were perfectly normal was an odd thing for Alec to accept. He rubbed his eyes several times before he decided he *was* actually seeing people dressed up in elaborate costumes like it was Halloween during the middle of the day.

What are all these people doing? Why are they all dressed up like that? When it's not even Halloween...?

Alec watched as one girl dressed in a pop culture, fashion trend called *Gothic Lolita* walked by and wondered why a girl would chose to dress up like a Victorian Doll with all the frills and lace like that anyways. But then he shrugged. Alec was beginning to enjoy himself now as he watched others who were cosplaying famous *anime* and *manga* characters. Alec saw a boy with dyed, spiky, blonde hair and a bright, orange *ninja* costume on. Then he noticed another boy in a long, red, trench coat with a pair of yellow spectacles perched on his nose.

Next, Alec saw a boy with a long, silvery-haired wig on, a red and white Japanese kimono, and a *katana* was strapped to his waist. *That can't possibly be legal?* Alec mused to himself at seeing someone carrying around a sword in broad daylight. Then he saw a girl skipping down the sidewalk with a set of mouse ears on her head, along with a matching orange, cat-shaped purse and a sailor, schoolgirl uniform on. Alec shook his head. *Tokyo is definitely weird but it's also...pretty cool too.*

Alec couldn't help the *deja-vu* feeling that tingled down his spine as he saw these people dressed up and 'role playing' since it was oddly similar to the feeling Alec got when he logged into a MMORPG and got to see all the customized PCs people had managed to come up with by changing their hair or eye colors, and creating unique outfits by combining items or changing colors. And then of course in the best RPGs 'role playing' was extremely important - to pretend to be someone else and to stay true to that character.

Alec couldn't help the hope from bubbling up in his chest as he saw this - maybe these people would be able to understand him and his need to escape from reality like they seemed to be doing and which apparently looked to be accepted.

It all seemed way too fast for Alec as his father practically dumped him on the steps of Izanagi Academy and sped away in his car. Alec watched him going, a sinking feeling in his stomach. He was all alone now.

An upperclassman student informed him that his luggage had already been sent up to his room and led him through the main school building and to his home room. Alec walked inside to see the 8th grade class of Izanagi Academy and that was now his class. He noticed the home room teacher turn his attention towards him and offer him a warm, lopsided smile. The teacher had a friendly but confident air about him with a scruffy chin and slightly messy, brown hair and kind, brown eyes.

"Ah, you must be the new transfer student - Alec Suzuki. Come and meet the class Alec." The teacher waved Alec to come over and stand besides him.

"I'm Takahashi-*sensei*." Takahashi-*sensei* bowed. "And this is my class, which you are now to become a part of. Class say hello to Alec."

"*Konichiwa* Alec. Hello Alec. " The class chimed obediently.

Alec noticed that the school uniform of Izanagi Academy was similar to that of many other Japanese schools and the boy's uniform was of a high-collared, black shirt and matching black slacks. The girls at the school had the popular, sailor outfit as their uniform, which consisted of a long-sleeved, white shirt that had a red bow that was tied about the collar. Then the outfit was paired off with a plaited, short, blue skirt.

The students in the class all stared at Alec curiously, many with friendly smiles on their faces. Alec sighed heavily. They may have looked friendly enough now but after the poltergeists started causing mischief around him and made him look like a fool any niceness that they might have shown him was going to go down the drain. He knew once he started acting like a weirdo by talking to himself and running away from invisible monsters that the students would once again label him the class clown.

Alec had already decided there was no point in trying to befriend anyone. Besides, even if he truly wanted to make some friends and somehow managed to despite his 'condition' it wouldn't be fair to them. He'd be putting his new friends in danger since Alec was a 'Spirit magnet'. And that was something Alec wasn't willing to risk. Alec had already decided before he got there that it would be best to distance himself from his fellow classmates and not to make any friends. It would be less painful to Alec anyways to have no friends from the beginning instead of making friends only to lose them once they found out the truth.

Alec merely nodded at the class. They all seemed a bit intimidated by his snow-white hair, icy, gray eyes, and stoic expression. *Good,* Alec thought. *If they're afraid of me, maybe they'll just leave me alone.*

"Class Alec's come all the way from New York City to study here with us. I know it must be a big change for him so try and be friendly with him." Takahashi-*sensei* continued to direct his class, several of them nodded. "Now let's see...how about you take that empty seat over there by Neji-*kun*." Takahashi-*sensei* pointed over to a seat by a window and which was next to a lanky boy, who had messy, black hair, and was wearing thick, square-framed glasses.

Alec nodded and obediently went over to take his seat.

The boy next to him immediately introduced himself to Alec, "Hey, my name's Neji. Nice to meet you." Neji stuck his hand out for Alec to shake.

Alec merely looked at Neji coldly before turning his back to him and facing the window. Neji's hand fell and Alec noticed his hurt expression before the boy seemed to wipe his expression clean with indifference and acceptance. Alec noticed that he seemed unfazed by Alec's cold response, almost as though he was used to that sort of treatment. That bothered Alec and almost made him turn around to take the boy's hand but he had to stop himself. He had to stick to his plan. And that was to avoid people and not make any friends and to keep people safely away from him - it was for their own good.

The students in the class were snickering at how Alec had refused to take Neji's hand and he could hear their muttering:

"Silly *otaku*, who'd want to be friends with him?"

What's an otaku? Alec wondered. There were still a few Japanese words he wasn't quite familiar with.

"Looks like even the new kid knows how to spot a loser."

Maybe this class already had their 'class clown' after all. *Man, I can relate to that. I know how he must be feeling but...I can't be friends with him.*

57

. . . .

Time flew by and before Alec realized it was already lunch time. Alec headed over towards the cafeteria following the other students and made his way into the lunch line. He picked up a tray and then paused at the selection of food he had to chose from. Alec raised an eyebrow at the strange looking food and didn't even know where to begin or what out of that strange assortment of food would even be edible. Most of the food were pieces of *sushi* and there were some cup *ramen* soups but...Alec was stumped.

Neji happened to be right behind Alec in line and began to recommend a few things to Alec. "You're never tried this kind of food before have you? Well, I'd stick to these and those at first. And the soup is always pretty good here." Neji pointed out a few types of sushi and to the soup.

"Thanks." Alec said gruffly as he quickly filled his tray with the recommended food items.

Neji had also filled his tray and was following close behind Alec. Alec managed to find an empty table and took a seat. Neji was looking around the cafeteria for a place to sit but all the other places seemed to be taken and the few places that had empty spaces were giving Neji odd looks which clearly said: 'Ew! Stay away geek!'

Neji bit his lip before coming over to Alec's table. "*Ano*, Um,...do you mind if I sit with you? Everywhere else seems to be full."

Alec shrugged. He wasn't heartless after all.

Neji let out a sigh of relief and quickly took his seat down across from Alec. He gave Alec a lopsided smile. "Thanks for that...though I can understand why you wouldn't want me sitting with you either."

Alec couldn't help but look up and frown at that. He knew he was going to regret this but the words were leaving his mouth before he could stop them. "Why wouldn't I?"

Neji blinked back at him in surprise, "Why? Because I'm an *otaku* of course."

"What's an *otaku*?" Alec questioned hearing that word again.

Neji's eyes widened, "You don't know? Well, I guess you can say I'm an obsessive fan of *anime* and *manga*." At Alec's questioning look he clarified. "Japanese cartoons and comics."

Alec used his chopsticks to plop a piece of *sushi* into his mouth. "What's so bad about that?" The *sushi* was pretty good but - *What I wouldn't give for a MickyD right about now.*

Neji just blinked at him, his mouth gawking open. "I suppose...it's just considered a geeky thing to be."

Alec shrugged at that. He never put much stock into what other people thought anyways. Alec knew he wasn't supposed to be getting friendly but couldn't help himself from continuing his conversation with the *otaku*. "So? I'm into video games. Everyone has something that they're into. I don't see anything wrong with that."

Neji suddenly looked at Alec as though he'd said the most wonderful thing in the world and Alec was beginning to get a bit uncomfortable as Neji was looking at him now a bit starry-eyed.

"Alec, you're a real cool guy, you know." Neji nodded adamantly, "I wish I could be more like you."

At this comment Alec began to choke on a piece of *sushi*. Someone actually wanted to be like him? What was the world coming to?

"I like your hair too by the way. I'm surprised the teacher's are letting you get away with it. Dyed hair isn't allowed, you know. It looks cool though I wonder if I could try getting away with it too..." Neji continued. "Though I doubt it'd look that great on me anyways." Neji laughed bitterly - at himself. And then let out a huge snort causing him to blush when he realized this.

Alec had managed to take a couple gulps of some green tea to clear his throat. "It's not dyed..."

Neji raised an eyebrow at Alec and then nodded knowingly and threw Alec a wink. "Yea, sure it's not."

Alec sighed. But he wasn't about to explain to Neji that his hair had turned white due to exorcizing a powerful poltergeist and overdoing it a bit.

Neji bit his lip nervously as he seemed about to say something to Alec. Then he burst out - "Alec, I'd like to be your friend."

Alec, who had finished his meal, stood up with his tray. "I'm sorry Neji. I don't *do* friends." He said coldly before walking away from the *otaku*.

"He's just too cool." Neji smiled as he watched Alec walk away.

Alec shook his head. He had almost slipped up. He couldn't start acting friendly now. He had decided he wouldn't make friends. Period. If he got close to someone...they would only end up leaving him in the end.

* * * * * * * * * * * * * * *

The end of the school day came quickly and Alec watched as students went off to do after-school club activities. *Maybe I should join a club?* Alec mused and then shook his head. No, it would be soccer all over again. He would end up putting his teammates in danger.

Alec began to head towards the dorm building but that's when he heard a familiar voice coming from over by the soccer field. It was Neji and he sounded like he was in trouble. Alec knew he shouldn't go or get involved but he couldn't stop himself. Alec ran in the direction of Neji's voice. He turned around the corner of one of the school buildings to see that three boys from their class had Neji surrounded and appeared to be bullying him.

"Where do you think you're going, geek?" The tallest boy of the group glared at Neji. He had silky, black hair, was wearing a blue headband to keep his bangs out of his face, and had dark narrowed eyes. He was already out of his school uniform and was wearing a pair of shorts and a t-shirt to practice soccer in.

Alec sighed, what was with schools always having a group of three bullies anyways?

Neji sighed in an exasperated manner, "I'm going to the computer club room where else would I be going? I'm the computer club's president and I have club duties to attend to so if you'll excuse me, Tatsuya." Neji tried to get past Tatsuya but Tatsuya simply sidestepped into Neji's path.

"I don't think so - Ken, Omi, let's do our thing." Tatsuya cracked his knuckles as he directed his two friends, which suddenly grabbed onto Neji and flipped him upside down and began to shake him.

Ken and Omi Alec noticed seemed to be dressed for soccer practice as well. One of the boys had short, curly hair and the other had a buzz cut.

"Hey! What do you think you guys are doing? Let go of me!" Neji struggled in their grasp, a deep frown on his face. "You bunch of bullies!" He shouted angrily at them.

The *jingling* of loose change could be heard in Neji's pockets and after a few more vicious shakes the money began to fall out of Neji's pockets and onto the grassy ground. Tatsuya went over to pick up the *yen* while his friends dropped Neji onto the ground with a *plop*.

Neji pushed himself up off the ground and dusted grass off his uniform while glaring at the three boys.

Tatsuya began to count the combination of coin money and paper money that had fallen out of Neji's pocket in the palm of his hand, "30,000 yen. Not a bad haul. From a spoiled, rich kid like you though I would have expected no less." Tatsuya shrugged. "Oh well, hopefully we'll have better luck, *next* time."

Tatsuya's friends snickered at the implication of his words. "Yea, we all know his pop is loaded and always seems to be sending him money for his stupid *anime* or *manga*. We'll put his money to better use." The curly-haired boy declared.

"Definitely, that's why you need to bring us some more money tomorrow." Tatsuya drawled, "You certainly don't need any more *anime* costumes. And this isn't nearly enough for the new video game I want to buy."

Neji frowned and just glared back at the boys. "No." But Alec could see the flash of fear behind his eyes.

Tatsuya's eyebrows rose, "No? Did you just say what I think you said? You're acting like you have a choice, Neji, which you don't. Perhaps, I need to make the situation a bit more clear to you. If we, the soccer team, say you're going to bring us more money tomorrow then you're going to bring us more money. Or else."

Neji's voice was shaky as he demanded. "Or else what?" But he still stood his ground.

Tatsuya went over to pick up a soccer ball and walked back towards Neji. "Or else this." He brought his arm back and then threw the soccer ball hard at Neji, aiming for his stomach. The air was knocked out of Neji with a gasp and he wrapped his arms around himself as he stumbled backwards and fell on his backside.

Tatsuya went over to pick up the soccer ball and looked down at the fallen Neji, "So now do you understand, *otaku?*" He raised the ball threateningly.

Neji just glared up defiantly at Tatsuya. "No, I won't give into bullies." But Alec noticed his body was trembling.

Tatsuya shrugged, his expression dark. "Have it your way then." Tatsuya brought his arm back preparing to throw the soccer ball again, this time aiming for Neji's head. Neji shut his eyes and raised his arms to block the blow he knew was coming. Tatsuya threw the ball so that it went flying towards Neji but then -

Neji opened his eyes when the ball never hit him to see Alec standing in front of him and that Alec had caught the speeding soccer ball with his bare hands. Alec had had just about enough of watching Neji getting bullied. He hadn't wanted to get involved but those guys had gone way too far. Neji could have really been hurt by that. Alec decided he had to teach these guys a lesson. Alec dropped the soccer ball and looked Tatsuya dead in the eyes. He then brought his leg back and then brought his foot forward to kick the ball at Tatsuya with his usual incredible force.

Tatsuya was knocked backwards and onto his backside. His friends, Ken and Omi, turned to gawk at Alec in surprise that someone had dared to mess with Tatsuya.

"Hey, it's the new kid." Ken started recognizing Alec by his signature snow-white hair. Ken was taller than Alec by a couple of inches at least and was the boy with the short, curly hair. "How dare he do that to Tatsuya!"

"Yea, you're right." Omi frowned and cracked his knuckles as he turned to face Alec, "I think the new kid needs a lesson on why you never pick fights with those on the soccer team. What do you say Ken?" Omi was the most muscular of the three boys and was the one who had the buzz cut, which Alec thought was sort of silly for a middle school boy to have. Alec knew he was trying to look tough but only managed to look like some kind of wannabe thug.

"Yea!" Ken smirked back. "He picked the wrong people to mess with. You're going to get it kid!" Ken ran over to the soccer ball that was next to Tatsuya and dribbled it towards Alec. He then kicked the soccer ball at Alec as hard and as fast as if he were trying to score a soccer goal.

Alec merely stood waiting for the soccer ball and appearing unconcerned. He waited until the very last moment before bringing up his leg and blocking the soccer ball with his ankle and then pivoting his leg at the same time so that he instantly sent the soccer ball flying back at Ken. It hit Ken right between the eyes and Ken was instantly knocked out. The force of the blow also sent the soccer ball flying back at Alec, who jumped up and let the soccer ball hit his chest to stop it. The soccer ball fell back to the ground and Alec made his way towards the last bully dribbling the soccer ball towards him.

Omi looked a little worried and was backing away from Alec, who had a fierce gleam in his silvery-gray eyes. "He looks like...a demon." Omi muttered to himself, and he almost thought he could see an aura enveloping Alec as he moved in to attack him. Alec kicked the ball forward and it hit Omi right between the legs. Opps. Alec hadn't really meant to do that. Honest. Omi brought his hands down between his legs as he crumpled over in pain, tears in his eyes.

Meanwhile, Junpei a boy with spiky, orange-brown hair and clear golden-brown eyes, and who happened to be captain of the 8th grade soccer team had been watching the entire scene before him with an amused expression on his face.

The sound of clapping was heard as Junpei made his way forward revealing himself. He threw at wink at a confused Alec before he turned his attention towards Tatsuya and his friends.

Tatsuya, Ken and Omi were just pushing themselves off the ground and about to jump Alec when they caught sight of Junpei, their eyes becoming as large and round as saucers.

"J-junpei-*san*!" Tatsuya stuttered, "What are you doing here?"

"Captain!" Ken and Omi declared nervously.

"I was doing some drills." Junpei said offhandedly, "Now as for what you guys were doing here. Tisk tisk tisk." Junpei wagged his finger at them. "Using a soccer ball to bully kids? I'm very disappointed in you Tatsuya. I expected better from you than such cowardly behavior. And to show such a lack of respect to the sport of soccer truly disappoints me." Junpei shook his head. "You're one of my best players Tatsuya but...maybe I should take you off the team, hmm?" Junpei tapped his chin thoughtfully.

Tatsuya looked horrified by this prospect. "*Iye*! No! Junpei-*san* please don't! Give me another chance. I promise I'll never bully someone with a soccer ball again!"

Junpei looked pleased and turned towards Ken and Omi. "What about you guys?"

"We promise too!" Ken and Omi immediately declared nodding their heads vigorously. "We'll never do it again."

Junpei nodded. "Good. Now go on and get out of here before I change my mind. Come on, shoo." Junpei waved his hands at them, dismissing them.

Tatsuya, Ken and Omi hesitated but then began to leave the field. As Tatsuya was passing Alec however he said in a low voice, "I won't forget this you punk kid. You'd better watch your back."

Punk? Alec raised an eyebrow at this. Maybe ignoring everyone, keeping quiet, and glaring at people was giving them the impression he was some kind of juvenile delinquent or something. Opps. Alec sighed. And they already thought his hair was dyed...

Ken and Omi both gave Alec death glares as they marched off the field following after Tatsuya. Alec shook his head, great his first day of school and he'd already made some enemies. At least these ones were alive.

Junpei was suddenly at Alec's side and slapping him happily on the back. "You did good kid. That was quite the show of soccer talent you put on back there. How about joining the team? We could use someone like you with those mad skills. What do you say?" Junpei gave Alec a hopeful look.

Alec blinked at Junpei in shock, not having expected such a request. He briefly entertained the idea of saying yes since his inner soccer-loving self was crying out for him to do so, but he quickly squashed the voice in order to refuse. He had already decided he wouldn't join the soccer team this time around no matter how much he wanted to. But before he could answer he was suddenly *glomped* by Neji, who tackled Alec in a crushing hug that sent them both crashing to the ground.

"Alec-*kun*!" Neji cried, "You saved me!"

"Neji...I can't...breath." Alec choked out, as he was beginning to turn blue from having Neji hugging him so tightly. Junpei chuckled at their antics.

"Oh, *wari wari*, my bad, sorry." Neji blushed in embarrassment as he got off of Alec and adjusted his glasses. He then looked over at Junpei and suddenly frowned at him - obvious dislike flashing in his eyes that surprised Alec. "*Junpei.* Alec's not going to join the soccer team because I'm going to get him to join the computer club."

Junpei raised an eyebrow at this. "Oh really? And why would Alec want to join a boring club like that one?"

Neji frowned and pursed his lips. "It's *not* boring. I just bought several new computers for the club actually and ordered some new software and game equipment for this popular MMORPG that's out. Of course Alec will want to join. There's no reason why he'd want to join some sports team where he'll have to run around and get all sweaty and covered in dirt and grime. I mean who would want to do that?"

Junpei looked insulted. "You're wrong! Soccer's the best! And what's wrong with getting a little sweaty from a bit of healthy exercise. You could use some exercise yourself there Neji you're looking a bit pasty and lanky if you don't mind me saying so. Holing yourself up in your computer room every spare moment you have instead of going outside once in a while is what's making you an easy target for bullies like Tatsuya." Junpei put out his hands in a helpless gesture. "Nerds - I'll just never understand them." He shook his head.

"Jocks - I'll never understand them." Neji shot back, glaring.

Alec frowned at the two of them speaking as if he weren't there. He hated things like that. Besides, who said he'd wanted to join either of their clubs in the first place? Although Alec had to admit that the MMORPG Neji had mentioned *had* peaked his interest and that deep down Alec would always love soccer and was secretly dying for the chance to join the team but... he had already decided he wouldn't join any clubs or teams. It was much too dangerous with his 'condition'. He'd only be putting his friends and teammates in danger if he joined either club or team. And he couldn't help but remember what had happened at the soccer game back in New York and how John had almost gotten flattened by that score board, a shiver went down his spine. Alec sighed, his heart heavy, as he turned to face them. He'd have to turn both of them down. It was for the best.

"Who says I'm joining either of your clubs?" Came Alec's cold voice. "I never mentioned I had an interest in computers or soccer. Besides...I have better things to do with my time." *Like...running away from poltergeist... fighting for my life...exorcizing ghosts and evil spirits. Yep, that about summed it up. Sigh.*

Junpei pouted at Alec, "Oh, come on Alec, you're so good. I can tell. I have an eye for talent. I just have to have you on my team."

"Don't listen to him Alec." Neji shoved Junpei out of the way, "If you're going to join something it has to be the computer club. Okay?"

Alec was beginning to get pissed by Junpei's carefree manner and Neji's pushy behavior. "I said NO." Alec suddenly yelled the last part at them.

Alec was about to storm off when Neji noticed a glowing, floating soccer ball was about to attack Alec from behind.

"Alec! Look out!" Neji called out a warning.

Junpei noticed this as well and pushed Alec out of the way just as the soccer ball crashed into the ground leaving a small crater from the force of the impact. Junpei raised an eyebrow at this strange occurrence. "Is it just me or did a soccer ball just try to kill Alec?"

"Yea, I think so..." Neji nodded vigorously, looking pale, "Do you think it was a g-ghost?" His voice trembled.

"I wonder if it was a *Yokai*..." Junpei frowned thoughtfully.

Alec was quite disturbed he hadn't sensed that attack. He must have been too distracted by his thoughts of soccer and computer games. It was definitely a *poltergeist* or evil spirit of some sort. He could sense it now. And it was definitely powerful. Darn. Something was after him again. He couldn't stay around Junpei and Neji any longer or they'd be in danger of getting hurt by this thing - he had to leave - now.

Without saying goodbye Alec took off in the direction of his dorm building leaving a confused Junpei and Neji in his wake. But he couldn't put his friends in danger. *Friends?* Alec shook his head.

"Hey wait!" Junpei called after Alec pouting. "He totally just ran away from us. He's hiding something..." Junpei bit his lip.

"Yea, he is." Neji pushed his glasses up his nose knowingly as he watched Alec stride away, a deep frown forming on his face.

* * * * * * * * * * * * * * * * *

Alec ran towards the dorm building and pulled out a slip of paper that he had written down his room number on. He entered the building and used the elevator to reach the appropriate floor before making his way down the hall in search of his room number which was #202. He finally found it and reached into his uniform pocket for his room key. He used the key to open the door and let himself inside, flipping on a light switch. It was a normal-sized room with two twin beds and a window that overlooked the soccer field. It would have been quite ordinary if not for the decorations that were on one side of the room.

Alec blinked

It had been completely decorated with *anime* and *manga* memorabilia. There were several *anime* magical girl posters taped to the wall on the other side of the left twin bed. Alec looked at the posters to see that most of the girls had on these strange costumes, which consisted of a sailor, school girl uniform. The magical girls all had strangely colored hair in colors like blue, pink or purple. Most had magic wands in their hands with either hearts or stars on the ends. Alec also noticed, gulping, that a lot of the costumes were very...*risque*. The skirts were extremely short and some of the necklines were very low cut. Alec blushed as he looked at one of the magical girls in particular and quickly turned away, averting his eyes.

Alec's attention was then drawn to a collection of figurines of *anime* magical girls that happened to be on the desk of whoever happened to be Alec's roommate. The figurines were all about 7-inches tall and were surprisingly detailed – some with little cat ears or sailor outfits or wings. But the fact still remained that they were *dolls* and Alec was beginning to wonder if he'd accidently entered a girl's dorm room somehow, but then remembered this was the boy's dorm building so that was impossible.

The figurines were so realistic Alec realized that if you peered under their skirts you could even see that they were wearing different colored underwear. Alec's eye twitched, was his roommate really a 13-year-old boy too? To have these kinds of things was beginning to make him wonder. Alec walked over curiously to take a peak and then he caught himself at what he was doing. *I am NOT a pervert! I'm only 13 for god's sake. Who is this crazy roommate of mine anyways? He's going to corrupt me!*

Alec shook his head. His roommate whoever he was - was definitely a total weirdo. *And I thought I was bad with my video game obsession, this is a LOT worse.* Alec nodded to himself vigorously and was forced to put the figurines of the girls in a drawer. They were bad for his health.

Alec noticed that whoever this boy was also had a shelf that was full of *anime* DVDs, SIM dating games, and *manga* graphic novels. But that's when Alec caught sight of the boy's video game collection. Alec couldn't help himself from coming over to the boy's book shelf and taking a look at some of the titles. He was surprised to find a few American titles there as well. And was fascinated and interested in all the Japanese MMORPGs that he had never even heard of or tried before. To think that so many virtual worlds he'd never even visited before existed. Each virtual reality world was different from each other - each with their own settings, classes, items, costumes, missions or quests. It was all just too exciting!

Alec began to take out several of the titles and was reading them when suddenly the sound of a key entering the lock on the door was heard and the door opened. Alec turned around to see who his weird roommate would turn out to be and saw that it was none other than Neji.

Neji walked into the room and shut the door behind him. He still hadn't noticed Alec on the floor surrounded by his video game titles. But when he finally did turn around and saw Alec his eyes widened in surprise. "Alec?" Neji's face turned bright red in embarrassment as he saw that Alec had already noticed all his *otaku* possessions. Neji was feeling a bit mortified because the person that he thought was cool and whom he wanted to befriend had just seen his entire *otaku* collection and probably thought he was a total weirdo now. "You're my roommate? Wow...I...no one has ever even come into my room before. I've never had a roommate since I'm on *otaku* and no one wants to room with me because of that. I usually don't show anyone all this...you must think I'm pretty strange huh?"

But Alec barely heard what he was saying since he was so engrossed in the Japanese MMORPGs. "Neji tell me about this game?" Alec held up a title. "I've never heard of it before...this one I've played." Alec motioned to another excitedly. "I got up to level 100 before the game began to become a bit boring. Leveling up is almost the best part of these games. And this one looks really interesting. I had no idea there were so many Japanese MMORPGs I've only really played the major American ones but I see you have those too."

Neji blinked back at Alec in shock and he felt tears prickling his eyes. He wiped them away with the back of his hand and before Alec could notice had put his glasses back on his face before hurrying over to Alec's side. "So you like playing MMORPGs too? I didn't know. That's something we have in common. Well...I'd really recommend this one here for starters..." Neji began to show Alec some of the latest games that had come out in Japan.

Alec nodded and was absorbing all of the information that Neji was telling him about the various games. Alec couldn't wait to get to try and play some of them.

Neji gave Alec a lopsided grin. "So you *are* into computers. Why did you pretend you weren't into them? You really should join the computer club after all."

Alec blinked back at Neji and looked down at the pile of game CDS that the two boys had piled around them during their conversation in surprise. Alec felt like hitting his head against the wall. He had messed up. He had let himself get carried way by his love for video games and MMORPGs and had been all friendly to Neji now for several hours. Dang. This was totally going against his plan on pushing people away. How to recover? Alec wondered.

Alec frowned and stood up going over to his side of the bedroom. "I'm not that into them. They're just something to pass the time with once in a while. That's all. I have a headache so I'm going to call it a night." Alec declared as he plopped himself down on his bed and pretended to fall asleep.

Neji wasn't bothered by this brush-off one bit and couldn't stop smiling. Alec had been the first boy to not make fun of all his *otaku* possessions. Neji got ready for bed and plopped himself down on his own bed while looking up at the ceiling. He found that he couldn't sleep though since he was so excited at having a roommate as cool as Alec. "I'm so glad you're my new roommate Alec...this is going to be so cool. Maybe we'll even get to be friends? I understand of course if you don't want to be friends with someone like me..."

Alec had to bite his bottom lip to keep himself quiet at that. He wanted to yell out - 'Of course I'll be friends with you!' But he knew he couldn't and so stubbornly kept quiet pretending he was asleep.

Neji however continued to be unfazed by Alec's cold and aloof behavior. After a long moment of silence Neji spoke up again into the darkness of their room. "Thanks again...for saving me back there. You were really awesome. I wish...I could be as cool as you or even that sports nut Junpei." Neji finished in a low voice.

Alec blushed at the unexpected praise. It made him feel embarrassed and slightly uncomfortable. No one had ever really praised him like that before. It was weird. *He's wrong about me...I'm not awesome. Or cool.* Alec turned over so that his back was facing Neji and pretended to snore. He heard Neji sigh and finally Neji went to sleep.

Alec shook his head and sighed. He let his head fall back onto his soft pillow. Why did Neji have to be his roommate of all people? He just wouldn't stop trying to befriend him or getting him to join the computer club. Why couldn't he just leave Alec alone since that's what Alec wanted. Right? *All alone.* Alec felt his throat tightening at the thought but shook his head trying to compose himself.

Alec lay awake and wondered about what he was going to do about the poltergeist that was after him. It had felt pretty powerful and Alec was worried but he had to get rid of it as soon as possible. The sooner the better before it began to cause damage to school property or put anyone in danger. He decided he'd get rid of it that very night. All he had to do was make sure Neji was completely asleep before he'd sneak out, track that poltergeist down, and exorcize it somehow.

Alec waited until the dead of night before he tried sneaking out of his room. He made sure Neji was sound asleep before going over and getting his soccer ball out of his duffle bag and then left the room.

Little did Alec know, however, that Neji was faking to be asleep when Alec snuck out of the room, leaving a very confused and worried Neji behind.

Alec snuck his way down the dorm hallway, keeping to the shadows, as he made his way towards the door that led to the staircase that went up to the roof. Opening the door Alec began to climb the stairs to the roof, and finally upon reaching the top he swung the door open. The roof of the dorm building was the perfect spot - at least for a battle. It was a large, flat, open area and there was plenty of room for Alec to make a good kick and to dribble. Alec dropped his soccer ball down in front of him, and looked up to see a full moon shining overhead – but it was no ordinary full moon this one was an ominous blood red color. Alec shivered and looked at the rest of the sky which resembled a piece of black velvet with silver and ruby sequins sewn into it. It was breathtaking. Alec was surprised he was able to see that many stars, being so close to the city. He had never seen many stars back in New York. Alec shook his head. He hadn't come out there to stargaze. What was important was that the moon and stars provided him with something very useful indeed - light.

Alec scanned the roof and began to reach out his senses to see if he'd pick up on anything. That's when he felt it - a malevolent and powerful presence. It had to be a poltergeist or evil spirit and since it felt familiar Alec assumed it had to be the poltergeist, which had been after him that afternoon.

"Show yourself. I know you're there." Alec called out.

Materializing there in front of Alec and hovering in midair was a strange, shadowy sort of creature that was demonic in appearance. It had pointed furry ears on either side of its head, large, black, bat-like wings, which were keeping it up in the air, and three glowing red eyes. The scrawny vampire-like creature was about four feet tall. When it opened its mouth to leer at Alec he could see rows of white, razor-sharp teeth and noticed its abnormally long incisors.

Alec gulped despite himself, this creature's presence was a bit different from the usual poltergeist or evil spirit he was used to dealing with and it had a slightly different sort of form that was less human and more demonic, devil-like, fanciful. Alec also noted that its presence was a lot more powerful than the mere 'poltergeist' Alec usually dealt with. Alec prepared himself for the battle to come, and which he knew was going to be one hell of a fight. He was beginning to wonder if maybe he had bitten off more than he could chew this time, but he also realized he didn't have a choice as he turned to face the creature, a steely look in his eyes.

* * * * * * * * * * * * * * * *

As soon as Alec left their room Neji bolted out and down the hall to Junpei's room. He didn't like the jock very much but he knew that Junpei was a tough guy and would probably be of more use in a crisis situation than he would. Neji wondered if Junpei would even talk to him though. They were kinda on opposite ends of the social spectrum – Neji being the most unpopular boy in their class and Junpei being the most popular boy in their class.

Neji didn't like Junpei for that exact reason, although now that he thought back even though Junpei's friends had always teased and picked on Neji Junpei himself had never really joined in the teasing, however there were times when Junpei hadn't stopped the teasing either. Neji frowned at that thought, but shook his head. Now was not the time to be holding grudges against Junpei but trying to get someone who could help Alec in a possibly dangerous situation. Neji had a really bad feeling about all this.

He pounded on Junpei's door and heard a muffled response from within.

"*Hai, hai,* yea, yea, coming..." Junpei opened the door, and Neji saw that his spiky, orange hair was even more messy than usual. His eyes widened in surprise when he caught sight of the *otaku* geek, Neji. "You? What's up?"

"It's Alec. I think he may be in some kind of trouble and I..." Neji glared at Junpei as if it were all his fault. "I'm not strong enough to save Alec on my own if the situation is dangerous. But I know you're tough Junpei. Will you... please help me?" Neji clenched his fists at his sides waiting to be refused.

Junpei shrugged and put out his hands in a helpless gesture, "Sure why not? How did you know I love being woken up in the middle of the night and dragged into potentially dangerous situations Neji? That was a joke." Junpei added at Neji's blank stare. "But anyhow let's go. If Alec's in some sort of supernatural trouble like I think he might be then we'll have to help him. I can't lose the star candidate for my soccer team after all. I have to protect my potential teammates."

Neji nodded, leave it to the popular kids to always have an ulterior motive. He rushed off with Junpei trailing close behind and Neji began to explain what he saw as they ran down the hallway.

Junpei yawned widely, "That's it? That's why you woke me up in the middle of the night Neji? Because you saw Alec leave his room with his soccer ball? I thought Alec was in some kind of mortal peril or something."

Neji blushed, looking abashed, and a little embarrassed. He pushed his glasses up his nose, "Yea, well, doesn't that seem suspicious to you? Where could he be going at this hour of the night?"

Junpei shrugged nonchalant. "Maybe he just wanted to go practice some soccer out in the field with no one watching, so he could practice alone. I've even done that before."

Neji frowned as they caught sight of Alec's departing form up ahead as he went through the door that led to the stairs that went up to the roof. "Then why is he heading for the roof?" Neji raised his eyebrows at Junpei expectantly.

Junpei blinked as the door closed in front of them. "The roof? That is odd. Come on let's go. I have a bad feeling about this all of a sudden."

Junpei and Neji quickly opened the door to the stairs and took them two at a time as they made their way to the roof. Junpei kicked the door open and they rushed out just in time to see Alec facing off with the shadowy, bat-like creature.

Junpei blinked at the creature in shock. "A *yokai*! Uh oh. What the hell are *yokai* doing up here? And where's the *Shinigami* Squad? Dang."

Neji gasped at the sight. "Epp! A-a-a demon? I'm against all forms of violence." Neji stuttered, taking a step back.

• • • • • • • • • • • • • • • • •

Alec's body was glowing with a blue-tinged aura as he gathered his spirit energy. When he had finished empowering his soccer ball, so that it too was bathed in a blue light, he was finally ready to attack the *yokai*. He wasted no time in kicking his soccer ball forward at the *yokai*, which was flying towards Alec, its claws outstretched ready to rip Alec apart. The soccer ball hit the *yokai* right in its stomach and burst through the creature to the other side, creating a hole in its body. The *yokai* instantly began to dissolve in the air as it was exorcized, crying out in pain, and then bursting into dots of light which disappeared.

Junpei and Neji's jaws were dropping at what they had just witnessed.

"He just exorcized a *yokai*...with a soccer ball. Crazy American *gaijin*." Junpei shook his head ruefully. "I wonder if he knows that's usually not how it's done at least not here anyways."

"Alec must be an exorcist." Neji pushed his glasses up his nose, a knowing look on his face. "He really is cool."

Alec still hadn't noticed Junpei or Neji yet since he was focused on the fact that he suddenly sensed more evil spirits in the area. *Uh oh!* Alec thought as more *yokai* suddenly began to materialize in the air hovering in front and around Alec. There were five in all, and they were surrounding him strategically. They all seemed to be the same type of monster or *yokai* Alec realized as he noticed that they had the same shadowy emaciated bodies, bat-like wings, three ruby colored eyes, and claws.

"Darn it." Alec rushed over towards his soccer ball and quickly dribbled it to attack one of the new *yokai*. He brought it up into the air with his foot and then kicked it at the *yokai* that was the closest to him and it was instantly exorcized by Alec's power - crying out as it was destroyed. Another *yokai* however took advantage of the fact that Alec's soccer ball was now nowhere near him and attacked. Alec dived out of the way and the *yokai's* sharp claws came down instead on the roof's floor. Pieces of cement flew up in the air as a small crater was created from the force of the impact of the *yokai's* demonic power. Alec gulped. These monsters were no pushovers. Alec ran towards his soccer ball dodging attacks from the *yokai* left and right. He finally managed to get his soccer ball back and had already kicked the soccer ball at another *yokai* and exorcizing it when he was suddenly attacked by a *yokai,* which had materialized directly in front of him, and had managed to catch Alec off-guard.

"Look out Alec!" Junpei called.

Weaponless, Alec was defenseless and he didn't have enough time to evade the attack as the *yokai* punched Alec hard in the stomach. Alec was sent flying backwards where he hit the door to the roof with a sickening thud. Alec slid down the door a bit swirly-eyed.

"Alec!" Neji yelled in a panic.

Alec coughed as he tried to push himself up and saw that the last remaining three *yokai* had all gathered in front of him, and one of them was holding his soccer ball in its clawed hand. The *yokai* smiled cruelly at Alec as it used its long claws to puncture a hole in the soccer ball causing it to deflate. The *yokai* then tossed the now useless soccer ball over the edge of the roof. Alec clenched his fists at his sides. *Darn it!* What the hell was he supposed to do now? Alec thought as he watched his only method of defense against these monsters get thrown away. *Is this the end?* The *yokai* began to move in for the kill, their clawed hands outstretched before them, their fangs dripping with drool, ready to rip Alec to shreds and devour him. When suddenly -

There was a bright flash of blue light that Alec thought resembled an arrow, and which headed towards one of the *yokai* that was instantly exorcized by whatever had hit it. Alec's eyes immediately shifted to the direction that the burst of light had come from and saw a beautiful, young girl wielding a bow. *So it was an arrow of some kind,* Alec thought in a dazed manner. The girl was dressed in the robes of a *miko* or shrine maiden with a white *haori,* or wrap shirt, and a pair of bright red *hakama* or split pants. Her brown hair was tied back into a high pony-tail by a pure, white ribbon.

Standing next to her was a young man dressed in the traditional garb of a monk with a white *haori* shirt and *hakama* pants in gray. From out of one of his sleeves the monk suddenly took out several strips of white paper, on which Alec noted were written *kanji* or Japanese letters. The monk suddenly flung these 'paper strips' which had begun to glow with a blue-tinged light at another of the *yokai,* that was instantly exorcized. Alec's eyes widened at this. Just what were those strips of paper really? And more importantly – *Just who are these guys?*

"*Aniki! Onee-san?* Brother! Sister?" Came Junpei's surprised voice.

Neji gave Junpei a curious sidelong glance, "They're your *siblings?*"

Junpei nodded, "Yea, Junko and Jin, they're students here in the 10th grade."

73

Alec watched as the *miko* seemed to gather her spiritual energy around her and in a manner similar to Alec was suddenly engulfed in a blue-tinged light. He watched as she pulled back on an invisible string which began to become more visible as her spirit energy was poured into her bow and then as she pulled back on the string a large Spirit Arrow was formed. She loosed the arrow against the remaining *yokai* and watched, a pleased expression on her face as it burst into dots of light and then disappeared.

Alec's head was spinning. He didn't get what the heck was going on. First off he had been about to get 'eaten' by some evil spirits or Japanese monsters when suddenly a girl started shooting 'magic arrows' and a boy flung 'magic strips of paper' at a demon and managed to defeat it! *This all has to be some kind of messed up dream or nightmare. Or maybe I fell into one of Neji's anime dvds, which happened to be cursed or something.*

Junko and Jin's eyes hardened as they turned their attention towards the startled Alec and stared at him with stern expressions on their faces.

Junpei and Neji rushed to Alec's side now that the *yokai* threat had passed. "Alec!" They both cried.

Alec's eyes widened in surprise at the sight of his friends, err, dorm mates running towards him. He tried to push himself up but his body felt drained of energy. "Yo. What are you guys doing here?"

Neji knelt down by Alec's side, "Are you alright Alec? You're looking a bit pale." He scrutinized Alec through his glasses as he adjusted them to peer at Alec more closely as if he could see right through him for internal injuries that Alec could be trying to hide.

Junpei, however, was less considerate. He slapped Alec enthusiastically on the back as soon as he got close to him. "Good job Alec! You managed to take out three bat *yokai* all on your own! And with a soccer ball no less! Crazy American punk!"

Alec coughed as Junpei continued to slap his back, but his brows furrowed at the unfamiliar word '*yokai*'. "Yokai? They weren't evil spirits or poltergeists?" Alec questioned. *I'm so confused...*

Junko suddenly strode forward and poked her finger into Alec's chest. "And just what kind of question is that? Of course those weren't poltergeists - those *yokai* are on a completely different level from ghosts or poltergeists. *Yokai* are a type of Japanese demon, monster or spiritual being. They sometimes manage to cross over from their own dimension or plane called the *Makai*. The type of *yokai* we just faced were bat *yokai*. These bat yokai have the tendency to eat the souls of people with high spiritual power in order to increase their own powers. What were you thinking taking on such monsters by yourself, kid? And without even a proper weapon - with a soccer ball no less!"

Junpei winced at his sister's special 'nagging voice'. He gave Alec a pitying look having been nagged by her several times himself and knowing it was not a pleasant experience.

"He obviously *wasn't* thinking." Jin came to stand next to his sister, and turned to glare at Alec, "What did you think you were doing coming out here alone at night and *way* past your curfew I might add, young man. Explain yourself and you might not get a detention."

Alec was beginning to get a bit frustrated by all this. Just who were these people? And why did they butt in to his business anyways? "Just who are you guys anyways? What's going on?"

"They're my older brother and sister, Jin and Junko." Junpei began to explain as he introduced them, "They go to the same school as us since you know Izanagi Academy goes all the way up to the 12th grade. They happen to be 10th graders here. They're also a monk and *miko* in training at the Izanagi Temple, which happens to be on the campus grounds, not too far from here through the forest."

"What about those paper strips, what were those?" Alec asked quickly. Things were finally beginning to make some sense. Those two, the monk and the *miko*, must be some kind of Japanese exorcists.

"Ah, those were *o-fuda* or 'prayer-strips'. They're long, strips of paper that have sacred spells or sutra written on them. They can be used to exorcize ghosts or evil spirits." Junpei helpfully explained. "Or in this case exorcize a *yokai*."

Jin's eye twitched as Alec continued to ignore him. "Hey, don't ignore me kid. You still haven't explained to me what you were doing out here fighting these *yokai* by yourself." He glared at Alec, who simply glared back, lightning seemed to flash between their eyes.

"What do you mean what was I doing? I was trying to exorcize the poltergeists, err, *yokai*, who were obviously after *me*. It's what I've always had to do. I've faced evil spirits and poltergeists on my own before this. Back in America I guess you could say I was a bit of a ghost hunter or exorcist. Don't you people realize it's dangerous for you to even be around me like this?"

The last thing Alec wanted was for people to get involved in this. He didn't want anyone to fight the monsters that *he* attracted or to have people try and fight to protect him. The last thing he wanted or needed was help. It was his fault the monsters were showing up in the first place, so it was his responsibility to get rid of them - it always had been.

Junko and Jin exchanged surprised looks.

Junko's expression softened. "You mean to tell us - you're really an exorcist?"

Alec nodded, "Well, um, yea, back in the states poltergeists and evil spirits were always trying to eat me but I managed to exorcize all of them just fine on my own."

Junko nodded knowingly. "A Spirit Magnet. You must have a very high spirit energy as well as..." She trailed off looking thoughtful, a frown coming to her pink lips.

Jin's eyes narrowed at him, "Just who are you kid? I haven't seen you on campus before."

"He's the new transfer student." Junpei explained helpfully. "He's in my class."

"The name's Alec Suzuki." Alec offered. "I'm 13 and am in the 8th grade here. I just arrived here today."

"And so the American boy exorcist makes his grand entrance to the spiritual world of Tokyo *ka*? Huh?" Jin shook his head ruefully. "You're right that the *yokai* were attracted to you and probably because of your high spiritual power, however, it is still completely unacceptable for you to be fighting *yokai* on your own like this. You need training and permission to face *yokai* at this school kid. You're not the only one with exorcist powers you know."

Permission? To defend himself? Alec was speechless at this nonsense.

"He's still just a kid," Junko started looking at Alec, "He shouldn't be out here fighting things like this when he's obviously had no true spiritual training. It's much too dangerous. You see, Alec, my brother and I have been charged with protecting this campus and keeping it safe from all *yokai* and evil spirits. It's our *job* to keep you safe."

"It's what we've been trained to do." Jin nodded, " It's not a job for a *child*. It's much too dangerous for a kid like you to even be trying to exorcise such powerful *yokai* in the first place. It's simply ludicrous - these *yokai* are way out of your league Alec. You're not in America anymore, things are different here, the spiritual world is more a part of the real world here in Japan. You must cease fighting the *yokai* and let us handle it, understand? It's for your own good." Jin crossed his arms over his chest and stared down at Alec.

Easier said than done. Alec blinked back at Jin in shock. *He just doesn't get it does he?* Suddenly indignant anger bubbled up inside of him. "I think it's you guys who don't understand. They're attracted to *me*. This is *my* problem and I plan to take care of it on my own - thanks. I have no intention of putting other people's lives at risk because of myself. No one has ever helped me or had to help me out before. And I don't expect anyone to either. Those *yokai* or whatever they are - are attracted to *me*, just like the evil spirits or ghosts that usually haunt me. So, you see, this has nothing to do with you guys. This is my fight - it always has been. I don't need anybody's help nor do I want any. So why don't you guys just butt out!" Alec yelled before opening the door to the stairs and slamming the door shut behind him.

"Alec!" Jin called after the white-haired boy, and shook his head. He then turned to Junpei as if noticing him for the first time, "Junpei what are you doing up here? It's dangerous - unlike your sister and I, you have no spiritual powers. Now run along off to bed."

Junpei gnashed his teeth together at this. "I was worried about my new friend, Alec. But it seems like he can take care of himself. Maybe he's right and you really should just butt out. He seemed to be doing pretty good by himself if you ask me." Junpei crossed his arms over his chest and raised his eyebrows at Jin in challenge.

"Well, no one asked you." Jin frowned and turned his attention to Junko, "We have to inform headmaster Yoru of this new development right away. It was no mere coincidence that brought Alec Suzuki to this school."

"Do you think he'll be trained as a *Shinigami* (exorcist)?" Junko asked curiously. "I wonder if that's wise. I sensed..."

Jin nodded, understanding his sister's unspoken words. "I know. He's so young to have so much spiritual power. He won't be able to control it properly. With that much power...I'd say he might be dangerous if his true powers are awakened. I'll say as much to the headmaster. Alec should not be allowed to train or unlock his true powers...at least for now."

"Until he is ready then?" Junko quirked her head at Jin,

"But isn't that up to Alec to decide?" Junpei frowned at his two siblings that seemed to be deciding Alec's fate. "You heard what he said - he doesn't want to put others in danger because of himself or have to depend on anyone. He wants to be able to protect himself. I think he should be trained as a *Shinigami* so that he'll gain the strength and control that he'll need."

"The sort of thinking the kid has is naive." Jin began, "This is for the kid's own good. His power should be sealed..." Jin stroked his chin thoughtfully.

"But the only *miko* who could do that is-" Junko was saying before Jin gave her a sharp look as if to say 'Shhhh!'.

Junpei and Neji exchanged curious looks wondering who Junko and Jin didn't want them to know about.

Chapter 5:
RedAki: The Red Demon

As Alec was approaching his home room class the hair on the back of his neck prickled in warning. He had a bad feeling about this for some reason. He reached his hand out for the door handle and hesitated - he could hear excited chatter coming from the inside of the classroom. Alec wondered what they could be so excited about this early in the morning then shrugged and opened the door. As soon as he entered all the eyes of his classmates were drawn to him and there was a sudden silence as if he had been the object of their current conversation. Alec gulped, *Uh oh.*

"There he is!" "It's Alec Suzuki!"

Suddenly, all of his fellow classmates came running up to him and formed a circle around Alec as they began to ask him random questions:

"Is it true that you're an exorcist?" "I heard that you defeated a bat *yokai* with a soccer ball!" "Did he really?" "How many *yokai* did you exorcize last night?"

They all looked at Alec expectantly waiting for his answer. Alec just stood there flabbergasted by this turn of events. "I...uh..." He was at a total loss at what to say. *How did everyone find out about what happened last night,* he wondered. Weirder still was that everyone seemed to believe it! And even stranger than that they seemed to accept what Alec was and even thought he was cool for it. Alec could only nod dumbly in response to their questions. This of course caused quite a stir.

"*Uso!* No way! That's *so* cool! Tell us more about it!" They began to pester Alec with even more questions. They were pressing in on him from all sides and Alec was beginning to feel a bit claustrophobic. He thought he might pass out when Neji suddenly came to his rescue.

"*Oi!* Hey! Make way, best friend coming through. Clear a path!" Neji began to push his way stubbornly through the crowd, which was hard for the lanky boy, who nearly got squashed between people. He came to stand next to Alec and began shooing people away with an imperious look on his face. "Alright everyone, show's over. Shoo. Give the guy some breathing room." Neji was waving his hands at the students, who glared at him.

"Who's this geek? Do you know him?" Someone asked.

"Who am I?" Neji pushed his glasses up his nose, "I'm Alec Suzuki's official manager." Neji whipped out a PDA (personal desktop assistant) and began typing away on it. "I'll see what I can do about penciling you guys in for an interview or autograph signing with Alec but for now he's really busy and needs to get ready for class. So if you'll excuse us."

Alec's classmates pouted and glared at Neji before returning to their respective seats.

Whew. Alec smiled and turned towards Neji with an amused expression on his face. He then raised an eyebrow at him, "Manager?"

Neji shrugged, "Whatever works to herd the sheep. Come on." Neji grabbed Alec's wrist and the two boys headed towards their seats, which were in the back of the classroom.

Junpei was already seated at his desk behind Neji's with his feet propped up on the desk in front of him. Alec was surprised to see him there since he hadn't been in the classroom the previous day but figured he must have been skipping.

"Hey guys," Junpei smirked at the two of them. Alec smiled back hesitantly and Neji just glared at the soccer captain. "So, it looks like since what happened last night was supposed to be kept a secret the whole school now knows that Alec is an exorcist."

Alec sighed heavily at this news and sunk down into his seat. "Just great..." Alec ran a hand through his snow-white hair. The last thing he wanted was all this attention.

Neji turned to look at Alec, "Alec, so is it really true then? Are you really an exorcist? Everything I saw last night wasn't just a dream? As your best bud I think I have the right to know." Neji's eyes were burning with curiosity.

Best bud? Alec blinked, but then he nodded, "Yea."

Neji's eyes sparkled, "Really? That is so neat!"

Alec stared at Neji in disbelief. He just couldn't see how his 'curse' could be considered neat and it irked Alec that Neji seemed to understand so little about the living hell that was his life. "No - no it's not. How would you like it if evil spirits...poltergeists...*yokai* were chasing after you and trying to eat you all the time! Hmm? It's not neat it's a curse! How could you possibly understand what it's like - or how I feel?" *I'm a walking bad luck magnet. Do you think someone like me can even have a best bud? No I can't. It's too dangerous for people to even be around me. I wish he'd understand. This is for his own good. He needs to stay away from me.* "And FYI we're *not* best buds. Just...stay away from me Neji. You're just annoying. You're nothing but a nuisance. So just leave me alone already." Alec turned to stare out the window, keeping his back to Neji.

Neji's eyes filled with unshed tears but he noticed that the entire class was staring at the two of them now and so he wouldn't let himself cry - not in front of *them*. So, instead he sat silently in his chair, his lower lip trembling.

Junpei turned to frown at Alec, a hard expression on his face. He knew just what Alec was doing and he didn't buy Alec's act for a second.

Alec felt Junpei's stare and turned to glare at him but saw that Junpei was giving him a look which clearly said: 'I don't buy your act for a second. And you're being a jerk..'

Alec swallowed and could feel the guilt swirling in his gut but he wouldn't allow himself to apologize to Neji.

Takahashi-*sensei* entered only moments later to find a strangely quiet class room. "*Ohayo minna.* Good morning everyone." He shrugged before taking roll call and beginning class.

Alec was glad for Takahashi-*sensei's* arrival since it gave him the excuse to ignore Junpei and Neji completely.

* * * * * * * * * * * * * * * *

Alec was seated alone at a table in the cafeteria during lunch. His fellow classmates kept their distance from him, slightly afraid of Alec after his sudden outburst. Neji was also eating alone and looking rather depressed. Neji sighed heavily as he merely poked at the food in front of him not having much of an appetite.

Junpei had just entered the cafeteria when he noticed Neji's forlorn expression. Shrugging he decided to go up to the geek and see what was wrong and why he wasn't sitting with Alec. Junpei plopped his tray down in front of Neji as he took the seat directly across from him, "Yo. What's got you looking so down in the dumps?"

Neji frowned at Junpei looking up from his lunch, "Why do you care? We're not even friends." He finished coldly. "And shouldn't you be sitting with your soccer buddies or something?"

It was Junpei's turn to frown at that. "I care. And sometimes I like a change of pace. Why aren't you sitting over with Alec? You guys are friends right?"

Neji began to laugh bitterly and his voice cracked as he spoke. "Friends?

Alec made it pretty clear I think that we aren't friends and that he wants me to stay away from him."

"I don't think that's true at all." Junpei's brown eyes sparkled knowingly. "I bet there's a good reason why he's acting this way. Don't you remember what he said last night? How he doesn't want to put people in danger because of him being a Spirit Magnet? He's probably just pushing you away because he doesn't want you to get hurt."

Neji sniffled and a long piece of snot that was hanging out of his nose went back up into his nose. "You really think so?" He gave Junpei a hopeful look.

Junpei nodded knowingly, "Yea, come on let's go sit with him. He looks rather lonely to me even though he's trying to hide it with his tough-guy, loner act."

"Hiding being lonely? That's so cool." Neji smiled lopsidedly at Junpei. "I wish I was better at hiding my emotions."

"It's not something to be proud of actually." Junpei shook his head. "It means that Alec has been used to being alone for a really long time. But he won't be able to get rid of us that easily now will he Neji?"

"Heck no." Neji pushed his glasses up his nose, a fierce expression now on his face. "It seems like we have a common goal for once Junpei. And that's getting to be friends with Alec."

Junpei nodded. "This way none of us will have to be lonely anymore."

Neji gave Junpei a strange look since he had just implied that *he* was in fact lonely but then Neji shrugged it off.

● ● ● ● ● ● ● ● ● ● ● ● ● ● ●

Alec let out a sigh of relief. He was enjoying the peace and tranquility of his lunch. Without Neji bugging him or trying to talk to him the entire time this was pure bliss. Alec looked across the table at the empty seat that Neji usually occupied. *Yep, pure bliss...*Alec sighed, a small frown on his lips. *Right?*

When all of a sudden Neji and Junpei took a seat at his table. Neji took his usual seat across from Alec and Junpei took the seat directly next to Alec on his left.

"Hey Alec," Junpei ruffled Alec's hair as he sat, "So when are you going to join my soccer team hmm?"

Alec stared at Junpei in shock, "Uh..."

Neji suddenly pouted, "Hey, Junpei, stop trying to hog Alec all to yourself. And Alec's not going to join your soccer team - he's going to join the computer club remember."

"Computer club?" Junpei waved his hand in a dismissive manner, "Why would Alec want to join that boring club again?"

"I told you - we just got some new computers recently. And I just bought all the equipment needed to play Yokai World. It's going to be great. And the more people I get to join the club and play the game - the more fun it will be. We could get people we know from the real world to form a team in the game. I know Alec likes MMORPGs too, so there." *Beat that!* Neji seemed to say as he stuck his tongue out and pulled down his left eyelid at Junpei.

Junpei ignored Neji's odd behavior. "Yokai World?" Junpei actually seemed interested. "I've actually heard of that game. It's a really popular virtual reality MMORPG that's supposed to be so real that it feels just like you're actually transported to another world when you play. A lot of people at this school are playing the game and I think the online world has over 8 million players already."

Alec was looking back and forth from Junpei to Neji while they were having this conversation, his head spinning. "Yokai World?" He asked suddenly, his interest piqued.

Neji pushed his glasses up his nose, his eyes twinkling. He knew he had Alec now as he immediately explained. "Yokai World is the most popular net game in Japan right now. It's a MMORPG with an advanced virtual reality interface. You have to wear a VR HMD (virtual reality head mount display) when you play the game. It's really cool and high tech."

"A virtual reality MMORPG?" Alec started, "I used to play regular MMORPGs back in the states..." He said wistfully.

Neji smirked. "Yokai World is totally different from those primitive MMORPGs. Yokai World uses the latest in advanced VR technology. The graphics are out of this world. You really feel like you've been transported to another world when you play."

Alec's lip twitched as he tried hard not to smile. An escape from reality... it was hard not to smile at the thought.

"How about after school you guys come to the computer club room and play Yokai World with me?" Neji questioned suddenly.

Junpei shrugged. "Sure. Sounds fun." They both turned to Alec expectantly.

Alec was a bit caught off-guard by this request. The last thing he needed was to start getting all buddy-buddy with these guys. "I dunno..." He hesitated though since the offer of getting to play an advanced VR RPG was extremely tempting.

"Great! It's settled then - after school the three of us will get together and play Yokai World." Neji declared.

Alec blinked at him in shock, he hadn't really said yes. These guys were such a hand full. Alec sighed, it was getting harder and harder to push these two away. But then did he really want to? A small smile formed on his lips, maybe it would be fun.

. . . .

The end of the school day came quickly and Alec was beginning to have second thoughts about playing Yokai World with Junpei and Neji and so was trying to sneak his way back to his dorm building before they could find him. However -

"Hey, there he is!" Junpei had spotted him.

"Alec!" Neji called out to him.

Junpei and Neji seemed to have been waiting for him in hiding and had suddenly popped out of nowhere to latch onto both of Alec's arms stopping him from escaping.

"Epp!" Alec squeaked as he was suddenly caught.

"Hey, where you going Alec?" Junpei gave him a knowing look, a twinkle in his eye, "We're going to play Yokai World remember? You're so forgetful." Junpei scolded him affably.

"Don't worry we forgive you." Neji nodded and the two boys began to drag Alec away back to the main school building where the computer club room was located.

"Hey! What do you guys think you're doing? Help someone! I'm being kidnapped!" Alec moaned as he was being dragged away. His cries however fell on deaf ears. "Why me...?" *I just want to be left alone...but I would also like to just escape from reality. It's a rush - a totally liberating feeling to get to become someone else. Oh well, I might as well try to have some fun.*

. . . .

Alec was pushed stumbling into the computer clubroom first by his would-be captors Junpei and Neji, who were probably worried he might try and escape again. The room was pretty spacious with six desks lined up in the center of the room for the six new computers Neji had told them about.

Alec noticed that at one of the computers towards the back of the room a girl of about the same age as them was seated at one of the desks and typing away at the computer before her at a very fast pace. Alec blinked at her odd appearance - she had short, black hair, which had been highlighted with neon-green highlights. She had a black, french-styled beret on the side of her head, and she wore a pair of lime-green, cat's eye shaped glasses on her face. She didn't look up as the boys entered and she seemed to be the only other member of the computer club.

83

Alec then noticed that Neji had also decorated this place with a bunch of *anime* and *manga* memorabilia and his eye began to twitch.

Junpei seemed to notice this as well as he whistled through his teeth. "Interesting decor. You really are an overzealous *otaku* just like they say." Junpei walked over to one of the walls that had several posters of *anime* 'magical girls' and his eyes rested on one poster in particular. Junpei's eyes seemed to turn into two large hearts and Alec noticed embarrassed that drool was dripping down his chin. "Although you do have pretty good taste." Junpei dragged Alec over to see the poster. "Don't you think so Alec? Isn't she a total cutie?"

Alec knew he shouldn't look up at the poster but did anyways. It turned out to be a poster of a character from a popular *anime* series about a magical girl, who was sometimes prone to bouts of clumsiness, and she was *cosplaying* in a low-cut, pink, frilly, waitressing outfit. Alec blushed at the sight and gulped, quickly turning his head away. "Uh, yea, sure, I guess so."

"Oh hey Rika!" Neji greeted the girl in glasses at the computer. "I got some guys to play Yokai World with me. Would you like to play with us?"

Rika looked up from her work to eye Alec and Junpei. She seemed to be sizing them up as she looked Alec over curiously and then turned her attention to Junpei, a small frown forming on her face. She adjusted her glasses on her nose before she then turned her attention back to her computer. "No thanks. I'm busy. Maybe later."

Junpei eyed Rika curiously. "That girl looks familiar, who is she?" Junpei questioned Neji.

"Oh that's Rika, she's in our grade and in our class, you know. You'd probably know that if you weren't always skipping classes Junpei. And Alec you haven't gotten to meet her yet since she was sick these past couple of days."

"Oh, that must be why." Junpei shrugged the matter off.

"Alright Alec, Junpei, chose a computer and I'll go get the needed equipment for playing Yokai World. The software has already been installed on the computers so we just need to set up the HMDs." Neji went over to a closet in the room and took out a large cardboard box.

Alec took a seat just as Neji was bringing him the game equipment. Neji handed him a game controller and something that looked like a combination between a helmet and a visor. Alec raised an eyebrow at this but didn't question it as he connected the game controller and then plugged in the VR HMD. He then put the HMD on his head and prepared to play the game.

Neji and Junpei connected their game equipment as well. "Now, you'll all have to create a new user account, a user ID name and chose a password before you can play the game. And then you just click on the icon on the desktop for Yokai World and log in." Neji explained to the boys.

Alec created his account and then moved his mouse to double click on the icon on his desktop which read - 'Yokai World'. Behind the red lettering was a blue icon of a ghostly fireball with slanted, red eyes. A window popped up and Alec began to type in the necessary information:

ID: Dranarch

Password: wings

logging in...

* * * * * * * * * * * * * * * * * *

As soon as Alec was logged in he was transported to the start town. Alec looked around at the virtual reality town in awe his mouth gaping open. It really did seem real. *So this is virtual reality?* Alec looked down at his hands and opened and closed them into fists. But no matter how real the place seemed to Alec he had to remind himself that it was just virtual reality, data.

The town had a medieval and gothic style to its buildings. And Alec felt the entire town had a sort of dark and spooky feel. Gray, swirling clouds hung high overhead in the artificial sky and black birds flew past. Most of the buildings were made of dark stone and Alec noticed a castle in the distance. There was a canal rushing past with a curving, stone bridge that ran over it and Alec noticed that the waters seemed like liquid silver. The detail of the place was incredible if Alec didn't know any better he'd say he really had been transported to another world. It was just like being in a dream but with more conscious thought and control over his body.

Alec began to 'people watch' as other PCs (Player Characters) passed him by. Alec watched as these PCs roamed the streets as they went about their business - some were trading items with other players, some had set up their own shops at a nearby market place to sell items they had gotten from killing game monsters, others were going into the shops along the cobbled street where Alec was currently standing to buy things from NPCs (Non player characters) - such as health potions, weapons, armor, or clothes.

Alec recognized many of the available 'classes' or 'game occupations' in the game. Alec spotted Monk PCs, who were dressed in *haori* and *hakama*, with bald heads and a red dot in the center of their foreheads, and most were seen carrying a staff or fan. There were *Miko* PCs wearing white *haori* and red *hakama*, and a few were seen carrying bows. He spotted several *Shinigami* (exorcists) and they seemed to be one of the most popular classes in the game. Their costume consisted of a black *haori*, black *hakama*, and many PCs had paired their outfits off with different colored *obi* belts but the most common color chosen for these seemed to be white. Most *Shinigami* were seen with a sword strapped to their waist.

He also noticed a PC walking by with a witch hat and a broom. He also caught sight of Ninja PCs lurking in the shadows - selling secrets and information to other players about rival Guilds. Alec saw Mage PCs with their longs staffs and capes. He then noticed a few PCs with *Noh* masks (Japanese drama masks) on their faces. And although PCs were able to carry their weapons in the start town, it was a 'safe zone' or 'PK free zone' so no one was able to attack each other there or try to steal other player's items.

Alec couldn't help but feel that the PCs resembled people dressed up for trick or treating. A chill went down Alec's spine in foreboding, *This place really is like a Halloween Town or something.* He even caught sight of a PC walking past with a pumpkin head. *Yep, there's definitely something up with the overall theme of this game...it couldn't be...? Naw.* Alec shook his head. *But...I'm beginning to get a bad feeling about this so maybe I should just log out...*

Just as Alec was debating logging out Neji caught sight of him.

"*Oi!* Alec is that you?" Alec recognized Neji's voice and turned around to see a tall, handsome Monk PC. Alec blinked, *That can't be Neji can it?* Alec knew that in Yokai World people's overall body type and facial features remained the same as they were in the Real World. The only things that players were able to change about their appearance were their hair and eye color, hair styles, and of course the different sets of outfits or armor that went with each class in the game.

There standing before Alec was an extremely well-built monk with slicked-back, black hair and who was wearing black, dark-blue, and silver monk robes. The PC before him also looked to be older than Alec, maybe a 10th grader. The monk was wielding a staff in his hands and had a lopsided grin on his face. He was also wearing a set of oval-shaped glasses on his face, which Alec had to admit were a lot cooler than the thick, square-rimmed glasses Neji wore in reality.

"Neji?" Alec's jaw dropped.

Neji strode forward confidently, in his element. "The one and only, although here I am known as the infamous Dr. M." Neji did a slight bow.

"*Oi!* Alec! Neji!" Junpei waved over to his friends as he caught sight of them and quickly ran up to them.

Junpei then skidded to a halt when he caught sight of Neji's PC body, which was somehow taller and more muscular than himself. Junpei simply gawked at Neji for a moment before he burst out laughing. "Oh my god! Neji? Is that really you...you look so...different!"

Neji's face flushed at Junpei's comment and he pushed his glasses up his nose to stare down at Junpei in a haughty manner. "Laugh now while you can, but here in this world I'm almost a god. You wouldn't want to make an enemy of me, Junpei."

Junpei continued to laugh, however, doubled over, his hands on his knees for support before he finally managed to pull himself together and wiped a tear from his eye. "I'm sorry." He apologized quickly. "I definitely wouldn't want to make enemies with someone who appears to be able to break the rules of the game like you can Dr. M."

Alec furrowed his brow in confusion. "What do you mean by that Junpei? That Neji can break the rules of the game?"

Junpei smirked and waved a hand at Neji's PC body, "He obviously did a bit of hacking into the actual game system to be able to change the data of his PC body to make it look like *that*. I have to say Neji I wouldn't have thought you had it in you. I'm impressed."

Neji despite himself, preened at Junpei's compliment. "Why thank you Junpei. At least you seem to know talent when you see it. I'll forgive your impertinence just this once."

"You're too kind, oh wise and powerful Dr. M. Oh how may I serve you?" Junpei did a bow with a flourish and Alec saw the smirk on his face. He was having a bit too much fun teasing Neji, who was taking all this quite seriously.

Neji was smirking and puffing up his chest while looking down at Junpei. "Don't worry I'll think of something, *minion*." Neji laughed maniacally and Alec shook his head at their antics.

Alec looked over the PC body that Junpei now possessed and saw that it didn't look much different from how Junpei appeared in reality except here he was wearing a martial arts, training *gi,* which consisted of a short-sleeved, orange shirt and a pair of slightly baggy, orange pants. It appeared that Junpei had chosen the Martial Artist class for his character. Alec noted with relief that Junpei's easy manner and warm smile hadn't changed a bit. He was a little envious of the boy's carefree nature and wished he could be more like him. But Alec had always been a bit of a worrywart.

Neji looked Alec up and down and saw that Alec had chosen the *Shinigami* class for his PC. Alec had decided to keep his shaggy, snow-white hair and silvery-gray eyes and was dressed in the same popular ensemble of a black *haori*, black *hakama*, and white *obi* belt tied around his waist that other *Shinigami* PCs had chosen. And he had a starter sword strapped to his waist.

Neji pushed his glasses up his nose knowingly, "You decided to be a *Shinigami*. A bit predictable don't you think Alec? Since you're already an exorcist in the real world. I would have thought you'd have liked to try something a bit different here in the game world." Neji shrugged. "To each their own. As long as you have fun then I guess it's okay. But I'm surprised you chose that class when you had seemed so adamant to be escaping reality."

Something about that unsettled Alec. "What do you mean?" His brow furrowed.

"Well..." Neji ran a hand through his slicked back hair. "I mean the main point of this game is fighting and capturing ghosts to then use to fight along side you here in Yokai World. So as a *Shinigami*, which is basically like a warrior-type class in this game, you're the best equipped class to fight ghosts on your own in single combat and capture them. It's a loner class really, which matches your personality to a T. The monk class is more of a support PC-" Neji was explaining when Alec cut him off.

"Whoa, wait a minute." Alec waved his hands frantically before him. "Are you telling me the entire theme of this game is...ghosts!"

"Yep. Isn't that cool?" Neji beamed at him, missing Alec's horror-stricken expression completely.

"Guess some people can't escape the reality of their lives no matter how much they try. Or maybe it's fate that you can't escape from? *Neh?*" Junpei chuckled at Alec's plight.

Alec just gaped back at Neji in pure shock. He had wanted to play a net game to escape reality not have reality haunt him into the game. If he had wanted to fight ghosts he might as well just log out and take a stroll in the forest or something...

"I'm logging out." Alec declared as he headed over towards the starter town's 'teleportation gate', which was this giant, floating, golden ring that was spinning around a glowing portal.

Junpei suddenly latched onto his arm. "Hey, where do you think you're going? We haven't even left town yet! We should go on an adventure or quest or something first."

Neji became equally enthusiastic. "Indeed, we should embark upon a quest immediately. It will be quite fun. And I know just the one we should go on." Neji had a mysterious glint in his eye.

Neji latched onto Alec's other arm and Alec was forcibly dragged towards the gate by both Junpei and Neji. *Why me?* Alec moaned in his head. *Why can't I ever make any 'normal' friends. Sigh.*

Neji raised his arm preparing to teleport the party of three to a new area. "Spirit Mountain!" Neji cried and the trio was instantly teleported.

* * * * * * * * * * * * * * * *

Alec, Junpei, and Neji found themselves scaling the rock face of a snowy mountain. Alec risked looking down at the drop and gulped. It was a very,

very long way down. If he were to fall he would definitely die. But it was just a game. Right? "Why me..." Alec sighed aloud. *It's just a game...it's just a game.* Alec repeated like a mantra in his head as he continued to climb up rocks with his bare hands. *An extremely realistic game...*

"We're almost there! Keep it up boys!" Neji yelled down at Junpei and Alec, who were scaling the mountain just under him. Neji had promised them earlier that there was just a little ways more to go and they would soon reach a mountain path that they could take the rest of the way up the mountain to their destination instead. Finally, they managed to reach the narrow path with clung to the side of the mountain.

They pulled themselves up onto the path and began their way along it. It was snowing, making it even more difficult for Alec and Junpei to keep up with the taller version of Neji in front of them. Alec was having to wade his way through the waist-deep snow and the rocks beneath his feet were quite slippery. Alec was edging himself slowly around a corner, hugging the side of the mountain with his hands, when he suddenly lost his footing and began to fall backwards. *Oh man!* Alec would have plummeted to his doom if it hadn't been for Junpei quickly reaching out and grabbing Alec's wrist just in time and pulling him back against the mountain face where he was able to grab at the rocks there. Whew. That had been a close one.

"Watch it Alec." Junpei smirked at him.

"T-thanks." Alec said a little shakily, as he ran a hand through his snow-white hair. The sensation of falling backwards had been quite real and had rattled Alec a bit.

They continued on their way until they reached the mouth of a cave that was cut into the mountain. There was a thick rope hanging from one end of the cave to the other and hanging on it were strips of *o-fuda.*

"O-fuda." Junpei noted, "That means a powerful demon or *oni* is sealed somewhere within the cave."

Alec gulped nervously, "A...demon?"

Junpei elbowed Alec in the side playfully. "Don't look so serious. This is a game remember?"

"Oh yea, right." Alec looked dubious.

"Come on, let's go inside shall we?" Neji smiled back at them. He was a little too happy in Alec's opinion and seemed completely in his element here in this virtual world, whereas Alec was beginning to feel powerless. Alec had always hated the feeling of not being in control in a situation where ghosts might be involved.

Neji waved his monk staff towards the sacred rope and it vanished. The party of three then began to make their way inside the cave. The cave was dark and Neji had to light the way using his staff, which glowed with a silvery light. And then, suddenly appearing out of the darkness was a giant floating head - it was hideous, with unhealthy, blue skin, sunken eyes, and half of its head was bald.

Alec pointed a trembling finger at the 'thing'. "Epp! W-what's that?" He backed up a step thinking it had to be another strange Japanese *yokai* monster.

"Calm down Alec, that's a game monster or mob." Neji raised an eyebrow at Alec's behavior. "Are you sure you've played MMORPGs before?" Neji narrowed his eyes at Alec in a scrutinizing manner.

Alec puffed his cheeks out indignantly. "Sure I have, just never one that was so real..." *And when in reality I see this kind of stuff everyday it makes it kinda hard to convince me that this isn't real. And without being able to use my real exorcist powers in this game I just feel so helpless all of a sudden...*

Junpei seemed to read his mind. "Do you feel a presence though?"

Alec blinked, and then reached out his senses and realized that Junpei was right. The mob in front of them had no presence. *It's not real - it's only data.* Alec let out a sigh of relief.

"If you're too scared let me handle it." Junpei smirked as he leapt forward into attack. Throwing a series of kicks and punches he made quick work of the low level mob and when the monster was finally destroyed Neji simply healed him back up to full health with a wave of his staff.

"Nice one, Junpei. Are you sure you haven't played these types of games before?" Neji questioned curiously.

Junpei shook his head, "No, but I'm a fast learner."

"I'm not scared." Alec pouted, already feeling better now that he knew he just had to use his 'sixth sense' to feel if the ghosts before him were real or not. Then he'd know if he really had to worry about them or not. "I'll take the next one!" Alec declared heading on ahead of Junpei and Neji into the cave. It wasn't long before the next mob appeared. This time it was a large floating skull, which was engulfed in blue flames, its teeth chattering. It looked real, and it looked pretty scary, but when Alec reached out his senses and sensed that there was nothing there - he smirked. It wasn't real. Alec unsheathed his starter sword and ran forward in attack, raising his sword. *I can do this. I won't let this game beat me. I'm the master of MMORPGs after all!* Alec brought his sword down upon the mob in a sideways slash.

The monster was quickly destroyed. He was only level 1, however, and had lost a lot of health and hit points during that short battle so Neji had to do a lot of healing afterwards. But Alec had to admit that it had been fun and couldn't wipe the smile from his face. *I did it.*

Junpei thumped him proudly on the back, "Good job, Alec. Looks like you're getting the hang of this."

"It is just a game. Nothing I can't handle." Alec smiled back.

The trio continued their way deeper and deeper into the cave fighting monsters that appeared before them, trying to get in their way. They were mostly low level mobs such as floating heads, floating skulls, and a few floating *Noh* masks. Finally they had defeated the last of these types of monsters and had made it to the central chamber of the cave. They stood in the entrance to the chamber looking in and could see that at the very end of the chamber there was a large prison cell, that took up most of the back wall. The cell had thick bars, and on them *o-fuda* had been wrapped. And then Alec saw a pair of glowing, yellow eyes from within the cell peering out at them. Alec gulped.

"What's that?" Alec questioned.

"That must be the demon. Let's go." Neji was the first to enter the chamber, and as he set his foot down a stone seemed to lower into the cave's floor. As the trio walked fully into the chamber they noticed that it had a high, curved, ceiling and that within the stone were large, gaping holes. Suddenly, the sound of bats was heard...

Alec looked around, wide-eyed at the cave walls, "What was that?"

"Bats?" Junpei suggested.

And then all of a sudden strange mobs began to fly out of the holes in the cave's ceiling and walls. They were skeletal, monkey-like creatures with no fur, and bat-like wings coming out of their bony bodies. When they grinned down at Alec and the others they revealed sharp fangs and Alec also noticed they had sharp-looking clawed hands.

Alec squeaked despite himself. "Epp!" But then he shook his head. *It's only a game!* Alec calmed himself and raised his sword before him in a two-handed grip. "I can do this!" Alec ran forward and began slashing his sword at the strange monkey mobs haphazardly.

Junpei joined in and using *taijutsu*, quick kicks and punches, began to take out several of the monkey mobs as well. However, they were still very low level (about level five at this point) and were losing their hit points fast as well as their health which was becoming dangerously low as they continued to fight the monsters. Junpei and Alec began to panic as more and more monkey mobs began to pour out of the holes in the cave.

"There's just too many of them!" Junpei exclaimed panting for breath, "Run for it!" Junpei decided as he took off running.

Alec sliced his sword through one more monkey mob before he looked up to see that there were still several creatures left. "Epp, wait for me Junpei!" Alec took off running with Junpei as the monsters began to fly after them, hot on their heels.

"Hey you guys!" Neji yelled after them, frowning, "Don't run away - fight them. I'll heal you!"

But the boys didn't seem to hear Neji as they continued to run for their lives.

Neji sighed and shook his head, "Guess I have no choice but to use *it*." He raised his hand, which was in a fist, and a ring on it began to glow. "I summon you - Tanuki!" From out of Neji's ring came a small ball of light, and it floated next to Neji where it then materialized into a *Tanuki* Ghost. The *Tanuki* Ghost looked like a combination between a man and a racoon. He was wearing a fighting *gi*, had boxing gloves on his paws and his face was that of a racoon. The ghost was semi-transparent and Alec noticed it even had a racoon's tail. It was most definitely the strangest ghost Alec had ever seen.

"*Ike*! Go get 'em Tanuki!" Neji directed his Battle Ghost forward.

The *Tanuki* Ghost seemed to respond to Neji's command and started forward towards all of the hovering, monkey mobs. It got into a fighting stance, boxing gloves raised before him, and then began using a fighting style that seemed oddly familiar to 'drunken boxing'. Neji's Battle Ghost began to make quick work of the mobs. Alec and Junpei watched a bit starry-eyed as Neji's Battle Ghost kicked some serious butt.

"Hey, what is that?" Alec asked curiously.

"He's my Battle Ghost, Tanuki. You see, in the game Yokai World there are mobs that you fight to gain experience points, skill points, gold, or items. Then there are level 100, A.I. (Artificial Intelligence), Battle Ghosts. Each area in Yokai World has a Battle Ghost that you reach at the end of clearing an area. You can fight them and if you manage to defeat them you can 'capture' them with this." Neji raised his hand to show them the golden ring around his finger, which had a round, red stone in the center of it.

"A control ring. It's a special game item. Once you've captured a Battle Ghost you can use them to help you fight mobs in the game. But mostly players use them to enter Ghostly Duels, which are PvP (Player versus Player) battles against other player characters. You fight each other, PC vs PC, Ghost vs Ghost, and if your Battle Ghost defeats their ghost, however, it can then help you to defeat your own opponent. The more duels you win the more points you earn and you get ranked in the game world. On the BBS (Bulletin Board System) on the Yokai World website the ranks of the top duelers or 'Ghost Masters' are listed. Of course everyone in the game is trying to get the number one rank and be the Ultimate Ghost Master."

"Ghost Master?" Alec said wistfully, looking intrigued.

Neji continued. "PCs in the game capture Battle Ghosts trying to get the most powerful or rare ones available and then they do battle against other players hoping to up their rank. Each duel you win helps you to get ranked higher. Everyone in Yokai World is trying to become the #1 Ghost Master. I'm currently ranked number 5. There's a reason why I brought you guys here. I heard that this area had a Battle Ghost that was very hard to get your hands on and so it sounded like the perfect opportunity to get one of you guys a really awesome Battle Ghost. If one of you manages to deliver the finishing blow to the ghost you'll be able to capture it and use it as your very own Battle Ghost. Here, take these." Neji reached into his robes and pulled out two more control rings. He then handed a ring each to Junpei and Alec. "I'm going to weaken the Battle Ghost and then on my signal attack. Got it?" Neji informed them.

"We gotcha." Junpei nodded.

Alec merely nodded.

"Now, let's free whatever *oni* has been sealed in here, shall we?" Neji smiled as he led the boys towards the back of the cave, which they were now able to get to since all of the monkey ghosts had been defeated. The prison cell was carved out of the back wall of the cave itself and Alec eyed the *o-fuda* that was wrapped around the bars. Inside the prison was a Battle Ghost, which resembled a man, who had monkey features. He had wild, messy hair, and excess facial hair was covering his face and chin. He had bright, golden eyes, and Alec noticed a ornate, golden headband around his head. He was wearing a red *haori* with matching red pants and there was a long, red *bo* staff strapped to his back. He was sitting in his cell and Alec noticed that the monkey man's expression was sad and wondered if he had been programmed to look that way since it was really quite realistic.

Neji waved his staff towards the bars of the cave, which suddenly disappeared. A twinkle seemed to form in the monkey man's eyes as he stood up and took his *bo* staff off his back, and held it out before him, prepared to do battle. He seemed pleased with the prospect of being free and getting to fight, a smirk forming on his lips. As soon as he stepped out of the cave the monkey man formed a strange, floating cloud underneath him and began to hover in midair. Alec's eyes widened at this unusual ghost that seemed oddly familiar somehow...

"Hey, is he supposed to be the Monkey King or something?" Junpei questioned Neji curiously.

Neji nodded, "Yep, he's Sun Wukong, the Monkey King, you have a good eye Junpei."

"Hey, what are you guys talking about?" Alec questioned, tilting his head at them.

"You don't know the story of the Monkey King?" Junpei questioned, "There's this Chinese folktale about a monk, who travels across India in order to get a hold of some sacred scriptures. To aid him on his quest the monk enlists the help of the Monkey King, Sun Wukong, a pig demon and a *kappa* demon. On their journey to the west they are met with several demons, who want to eat the monk's flesh and gain immortality. The monk's companions served as his bodyguards. The Monkey King was the most powerful of the monk's companions and protected the monk well. The Monkey King was said to be a demon that was born from a mountain rock, and who was raised by monkeys. He became a powerful warrior and then fought both heaven and hell to gain the immortality of the gods. It's a really cool story. I always wanted to be like the Monkey King myself. He never lets anything get in his way and always just keeps on fighting and moving forward."

"Time to get this battle started!" A bright light seemed to be forming around Neji and he then pointed his monk staff towards his Battle Ghost. "Go Tanuki! Shapeshift Data Copy Attack!"

Tanuki walked towards the Monkey King and its eyes seemed to glow - little flashes of green light seemed to be speeding past its solid, black eyes at an incredible rate. Alec thought Tanuki's eyes now resembled mini-computer screens. And then suddenly Tanuki seemed to change shape until standing in its place was no longer a *Tanuki* Battle Ghost but an exact copy of the Monkey King. However, there were slight differences that Alec noticed - such as the glowing red eyes and slightly darker and more sinister appearance of the copy. The copy formed a floating cloud underneath him as well, although it was a gray, storm cloud and not a white, fluffy cloud like the Monkey King had. He then hovered in mid air wielding his own black *bo* staff before him, prepared to do battle with his mirror image.

Alec, Neji, and Junpei watched as the two Battle Ghosts began to fight up in the air in the cave - their *bo* staffs clashing in quick movements. The copy swung his *bo* staff forward and caused it to elongate towards the Monkey King. The Monkey King jumped up and the *bo* staff simply passed underneath him. They charged each other in the air and their weapons continued to clash. But then the copy suddenly brought his *bo* staff forward and concentrated on having it wrap around the Monkey King like a snake. The Monkey King found that he couldn't move and the copy began to cause the *bo* staff to constrict...

The Monkey King was fading, his PC body flickering like data that was about to be erased, and was about to be defeated when Neji called back his Battle Ghost. "Come back, Tanuki! Alec! Junpei! One of you needs to deliver the finishing blow now - hurry!"

Alec looked up at the Monkey King and couldn't help but remember the sad expression he had seen on the Monkey King's face back when he had been inside of the cell - when he had been a 'captured' animal. Now the Monkey King was free and if Alec caught him then he'd lose that freedom right? But then again 'it' was just data? An A.I. program right? *Neh?* It's not like the

Monkey King's A.I. program had feelings...right? That would be impossible but...

Junpei, however, didn't hesitate as he leapt forward and delivered the finishing punch. The Monkey King was destroyed bursting into dots of light. Junpei raised his control ring and yelled, "Capture!" The small dots of light that were once the Monkey King flew through the air and were sucked into Junpei's control ring.

Neji seemed pleased. "Well done Junpei. The Monkey King now belongs to you. He'll have to rest up a bit before you can summon him again since he was just defeated. It should be a big help in leveling up. Now all we have to do is get a Battle Ghost for Alec."

Alec's brows shot up in surprise, before he frowned, "Who says I'm going to continue playing this game?"

Before either Neji or Junpei could answer, however, a large treasure chest suddenly materialized in the center of the cave's chamber. Neji's eyes seemed to sparkle. "Ooo. A treasure chest. I bet there's a great, rare item in there for having defeated the level 100, Monkey King, Battle Ghost and having cleared this area! Let's see shall we?" Neji waved his staff towards the treasure chest and it unlocked.

"Rare item?" Alec peered curiously into the chest.

"When you 'clear' a difficult 'area' in Yokai World you're rewarded with a treasure chest - they usually contain powerful, rare, or hard to get items like weapons and so forth. Some items are so rare you're able to sell the items online to other players for real money!"

"Real money? Dude that's crazy." Junpei shook his head, disbelieving.

Neji reached into the chest and pulled out what looked like a rolled up scripture. "Ooo. This is a Battle Scripture - you can use it to defeat high-level, ghost mobs. This is definitely a rare item." Neji nodded knowingly. "Here Junpei I think you should have it." Neji reached the scripture out towards Junpei.

"Thanks Neji," Junpei said as he reached out to take the scripture.

However, a voice suddenly rang through the cavern. "Hold it right there! You'll be handing that scripture over to me now. If you know what's good for you."

All eyes turned to see a *Shinigami* PC, who was wearing all red. His *haori* shirt and *hakama* pants except for his black *obi* belt were all a deep, blood-red color. He had spiked-up, black hair with red tips, a pale complexion and dark shadows seemed to surround the boy's eyes. His eyes were a fiery red that seemed to burn with anticipation. The *Shinigami* wore a cocky smirk and he was holding his sword by its hilt - he unsheathed his sword about halfway to reveal that the blade of the sword was pitch black. "Don't make me draw my sword." He drawled in a nonchalant manner.

Neji's eyes seemed to widen in recognition. "You must be the red demon, a.k.a RedAki, rank #3 Ghost Master in Yokai World. See that black-bladed sword of his? A black colored weapon means that he's a PKer."

"PKer?" Alec questioned quirking his head.

"Player Killer." Neji explained. "They're PCs in the game who kill other PCs to steal their items or money or just for the thrill of it. RedAki is an infamous PKer said to be very dangerous."

RedAki smirked at Neji's words, "A bunch of noobs (newbie players) know who I am. Don't I feel special? *Not*. Now, monk boy, hand over that scripture to me - now." RedAki was fingering the hilt of his sword, drumming his long, pale fingers along it.

Alec frowned thoughtfully, "So basically what you're telling me Neji is that guy over there is a game bully. I hate bullies." Alec's silver-gray eyes glared fiercely at RedAki and he unsheathed his starter sword to point it at RedAki in one fluid motion.

RedAki raised an eyebrow in surprise at this bold action, and decided to check Alec's screen name and PC data. "Dranarch huh? Level...5!" RedAki's eyes brows shot up to his hairline and he began to snicker. "You can't be serious. What kind of crazy noob are you? Thinking that you can take me on when I'm already level 87!"

"Try me." Alec unexpectedly charged forward and raised his sword in attack, bringing his sword upon RedAki is a high downwards slash.

With one fast motion RedAki unsheathed his sword and blocked Alec's attack. "Well, you've got guts, punk. I'll give you that. Or is it that you're just incredibly stupid. hmm?"

Neji raised his monk staff, "Don't worry Alec I'll back you up!" Neji immediately healed Alec as he took a blow from RedAki.

"Thanks." Alec said, now able to concentrate on his duel with RedAki without having to worry about taking any healing potions. Alec and RedAki's swords continued to clash, sparks flying up into the air but Alec's hit points were severely low, and his health was dropping fast. It wasn't long before he was already at his limit even with Neji's healing. Their differences in levels were just too great.

"Keh, I tire of this children's game. You can't fight a Ghost Master like myself without having your own Battle Ghost." RedAki suddenly raised his hand in a fist and a control ring with a large, red stone began to glow. "Come forth, Oni!"

A ball of red light shot out of RedAki's ring and materializing next to his master was an *Oni* Ghost. The Battle Ghost resembled a true *oni* or demon, and had red skin, black hair, and a scraggly, black beard. There were sharp fangs poking out of its mouth when it suddenly smiled. It had sharp, long, black nails, two horns were on either side of its head, and it was wearing a tiger-skin loin cloth. In its hands it wielded a giant, iron club.

"Rip them to pieces Oni!" RedAki's eyes blazed.

Alec squeaked and took a step back. He was no match for a level 100, *Oni* Battle Ghost!

"Don't worry Alec, I've got your back!" Neji came to stand next to Alec. "Go Tanuki! Shapeshift Data Copy Attack!" Neji yelled as the *Tanuki* Ghost came to stand in front of the *Oni* Ghost. Once again its eyes became small computer screens with glowing, green numbers flashing past until finally the *Tanuki* Ghost began to shapeshift until it became an exact mirror image of the *Oni* Ghost. Although once again Alec noticed that there were a few differences between the two Battle Ghosts. Neji's copy was looking more sinister than RedAki's Battle Ghost with eyes that glowed gold and the monster's hair and beard had turned snow-white.

RedAki's eyes widened in surprise, "But there's no such attack in this game." RedAki suddenly narrowed his eyes dangerously at Neji. "Just who are you...?" He began to check Neji's PC data. "Dr. M...huh? As in...Dr. Mimic! Dang! So you're that infamous, cyber-hacker, Dr. Mimic that I've been hearing about. You're ranked #5 Ghost Master in Yokai World aren't you?"

Neji smirked and pushed his gleaming glasses up his nose, "Indeed I am."

RedAki bit his lip. "Dang it." He turned his attention back to Alec. "Out of my way, I don't have time to play games with you, punk." RedAki suddenly attacked Alec very aggressively and with such speed that Alec was unable to block his attack. Alec looked down at his chest in shock and at the red slash that was there. He sunk down to his knees, badly wounded, his PC body glowing red in warning, and was about to die and be turned into a PC Ghost...

"Alec!" Neji yelled in concern and quickly healed his friend with a wave of his monk's staff.

"I'm coming Oni!" It was RedAki's voice.

As soon as Alec was healed he turned his attention back towards RedAki, who had gone to the aid of his Battle Ghost. The copy *oni* and RedAki's Oni were fighting each other with their giant, iron clubs. Their clubs swinging through the air and clashing with such force sparks were sent up into the air with each throbbing blow. But then the copy *oni* was suddenly moving faster than its opponent and moved past Oni's defenses and jabbed his club forward into Oni's gut.

RedAki was too late. "NO! ONI!" He cried as he watched the club pierce his *Oni* Ghost, and it was defeated. It turned into a ball of red light that went zooming back into RedAki's ring. "Dang it..." RedAki turned his sword to face Neji now. "You'll pay for that Four-eyes. You and your hacker tricks won't get the better of RedAki!" RedAki charged forward, sword raised, prepared to slice Neji in two when -

"Tanuki!" Neji called out to his Battle Ghost to aid him.

Tanuki came to stand right in front of its master and shielded Neji from RedAki's attack. RedAki's sword ended up clashing against one of Tanuki's boxing gloves. RedAki pushed his sword forward and Tanuki was beginning to get pushed back across the floor of the cave from the mere force of RedAki's power. Alec had to admit he was impressed that RedAki was able to push back a level 100, Battle Ghost like that all on his own. RedAki smirked confidently as Tanuki was moving back.

However - "You're not half bad, RedAki. To take on Tanuki by yourself like that but...tell me something can you defeat yourself? Tanuki! Shapeshift Data Copy Attack!"

Tanuki's eyes flashed with data as it sped across the two mini-screens.

RedAki blinked at the *Tanuki* Ghost in shock, "*Uso*! No way! It's copying my PC data! Dang it!" RedAki leapt backwards just as Tanuki finished copying RedAki's PC data and began to glow and then shapeshift until there standing in front of RedAki was now his own mirror image. Once again the copy's hair had changed to white and the eyes had changed to a golden color. The sword of the copy RedAki was also solid white. Copy RedAki got into a fighting stance and pointed his sword at the real RedAki.

RedAki bit his bottom lip nervously but got into a fighting stance as well as he prepared to fight - himself. RedAki was already pretty tired from having fought the *Tanuki* Ghost and Alec noticed that he was breathing irregularly and looked slightly pale as well. RedAki was also hesitating and seemed unnerved to be facing a look alike of himself. He frowned deeply as the copy RedAki suddenly smirked at him in a cocky manner. And that was the last straw.

"Wipe that smirk off your face, you danged copy! I won't lose to you! The original is always better than the copy! And I'm the real deal!" RedAki declared as he rushed forward in attack. He swung his sword in a hard, sideways slash and the copy RedAki raised his white-bladed sword to quickly block the attack. "Dang it...he can predict all my own moves. But I won't lose to him. I can't lose - I never lose." RedAki said like a mantra as he moved in for his next attack. RedAki feinted to the left but somehow the copy RedAki knew what he was going to do and managed to get past RedAki's defenses to suddenly stab RedAki straight through his chest.

RedAki looked down in a mixture of shock, horror, and awe at the sword that was sticking out of his chest. "I lost...impossible. I never lose...dang it. Screw you...you cheater!" RedAki was glaring at Neji as the copy RedAki removed the sword from RedAki's chest and he collapsed forward on the hard, stone floor. He was low on hit points and health, but had just enough so that he wasn't turning into a PC ghost right away.

"My guild mates will make you pay for this, you hacker!" RedAki spit towards Neji's feet.

Alec looked at RedAki concernedly and then turned to Neji, "Hey Neji, what's he talking about? Are you really this hacker Dr. Mimic? Are you really a cheat?"

Neji put an innocent expression on his face. "Alec, the point of this game is to win duels not to lose. In this world I'm not a loser.. I'm a winner. And I take pride in that fact. This is my world."

Alec frowned, "But you cheated. You shouldn't cheat. It's...wrong and it's also unfair."

Neji sighed and ran a hand over his slicked back hair, "Why do you care about that guy anyways? It's not like we even know him, or are even friends with him so what does it matter to play fair anyways? It sure doesn't look like he's the type to play fair to me. He's a PKer Alec. Those guys deserve to be PKed themselves any time you get the chance."

Neji tossed the scripture to Junpei, who caught it with a nod of thanks. Neji walked over and looked down at RedAki's fallen form seemingly enjoying the position he had put the infamous PKer. "Maybe we should finish him off... he could be carrying some rare items." Neji suggested thoughtfully, a gleam in his eyes.

Just as Neji was about to raise his staff upon RedAki, however, Alec stood in his way arms out to his sides. "Don't Neji, this is wrong and you know it. You didn't beat him fair and square in a one on one duel like you should have. Using not your hacking abilities but your game playing skills."

"Alec, he's a PKer." Neji began again. "He doesn't fight fair either. You're taking all this way too seriously Alec - it's just a game you know."

Just a game? Alec looked over at RedAki and his crestfallen expression. He looked so...defeated and broken in that moment. Vulnerable even. Alec could feel that his pain was actually real. Alec was sure he was not used to defeat and had taken the blow to his pride really hard. Alec was also sure that for RedAki, just like himself, even though game worlds weren't real they were real to them. Alec could just tell that RedAki felt the same way he did. It was a gut feeling that Alec couldn't shrug off - that they were kindred spirits in that belief.

"But even so," Alec began, a steely expression in his eyes, "Do you really want to sink down to his level then? I thought you were better than that Neji. Or is this really the kind of person you are? That once you have power you'll become just like the bullies that pick on you in the real world? I really hope you're just roleplaying Neji. Because if you're not maybe I was wrong about you being a cool guy."

Neji blushed and suddenly looked embarrassed. "You're right Alec...I'm sorry. It's just when I'm in this game and am roleplaying Dr. M sometimes his persona can just take me over you know. And he's nothing like my real self back in reality. Dr. M is cool and strong and nothing like me..." Neji lowered his staff. "I just don't want to be a loser."

Junpei patted Neji hard on the back. "You made the right decision. He isn't worth it."

"Right." Neji agreed. "Come on, you guys, it's getting late we should log out."

"Kay." Junpei agreed.

"Coming Alec?" Neji called after him as he and Junpei prepared to log out.

"Yea, I'll be right with you guys." Alec said offhandedly as he took one last look at RedAki. Their eyes met and RedAki had a surprised expression on his face that Alec had decided to save him.

Alec nodded and then logged out.

That night Alec couldn't sleep. He kept thinking about his fight against RedAki and how he had been defeated by the dark *Shinigami* so easily. Alec had this desire to become stronger, and to become a Ghost Master. Alec also really wanted to fight RedAki again. He knew that RedAki took MMORPGs just as seriously as himself, and was highly skilled in them. His skill and game play abilities maybe even rivaled Alec's own skill and knowledge of RPGs. *He's the perfect rival,* Alec thought. And Alec couldn't help but think to himself that when RedAki had been fighting the Tanuki Ghost on his own that he had looked pretty cool. Even if he was a bully and a PKer - Alec knew that he just had to fight RedAki again someday in a Ghostly Duel and defeat him with his own strength.

For us, it's not just a game. Not at all. It's real.

Chapter 6:
LADY VIRUS

Alec couldn't seem to get RedAki out of his head. He wanted to become a Ghost Master and to defeat RedAki in a one on one Ghostly Duel - fair and square as soon as possible. He was thinking such thoughts as he was making his way down the several flights of steep, stone stairs that were in front of the main school building and which led down to the areas where the track and soccer fields were. Alec wasn't really paying attention to where he was going until the hairs on the back of his neck prickled in warning. Alec turned his attention towards the top of the stairs and recognized Rika, who was about to go down the steps as well. Her arms were full of art supplies and the sailor outfit she was wearing was covered with splotches of paint.

Alec raised an eyebrow at her appearance - he hadn't known that Rika was into art. But that wasn't what had given him the bad feeling, he knew. He noticed a couple of snickering female students that were watching Rika with an expression of contempt and superiority. They were laughing at her, and making fun of her by whispering things behind their hands. Alec hated it when people did that - ganged up on other people. Bullied. It just rubbed Alec the wrong way.

It was at that moment that Alec noticed the group of female students seemed to be up to something - as Rika was nearing the top of the steps one female student casually put her foot out and Rika stumbled over it and towards the steps. Alec's eyes widened in shock and horror - she was going to fall down the steps!

"Rika!" Alec called as he watched her stumble forward onto the steps and begin to fall forward as she lost her balance. Alec knew he didn't have enough time to stop her fall and so did the only thing he could do - as she fell he caught her in his arms. The force of Rika knocking into him caused Alec to fall backwards but he knew this was going to happen and so simply wrapped his arms around Rika's body protectively making sure to shield her body with his own as they fell back and then down the steps.

He knew that Rika would be badly injured if she hit her head on any of the stone steps and so made sure to bring her head close to his chest. However, Alec had forgotten to think of his own well-being in the process as they tumbled painfully down the steps.

Though that hardly seemed to matter to Alec as they finally landed at the bottom of the steps. The back of Alec's head hit the final bottom step with a sickening *crack*. But even though he had been knocked unconscious he continued to keep his arms wrapped protectively around Rika.

Rika risked opening her eyes and was surprised to feel that her body felt no pain even though she and Alec had just fallen down several, steep, stone steps. She looked down to see who had caught her and protected her and her eyes widened in surprise when she saw that it was none other than Neji's friend, Alec Suzuki. He seemed to be unconscious, which made her furrow her brow in worry. She quickly realized the position she was in and pushed herself off of Alec's still form before kneeling down next to him and trying to stir him awake. "Alec?" Rika shook his shoulder and that's when she noticed the puddle of blood forming around the back of his head. She reached her hand behind his head and stared down at her fingers in disbelief when they came back red.

"Alec!!!"

* * * * * * * * * * * * * * * * *

Alec felt a cool hand pressing against his brow. It warmed his heart as it reminded him of those few rare moments where his mother Laura had checked his temperature during those times when he had been sick. But ever since Alec had started seeing 'ghosts' his mother had stopped these shows of affection. Tears prickled Alec's eyes at the thought but he willed them away. The hand left his brow and Alec wished that it could have stayed a little longer since it had seemed to make all the pain in Alec's body go away.

Alec heard a knock at the door and Alec guessed the person who had his or her hand to his forehead had gone to answer it. Alec opened his eyes and turned to watch as the school nurse opened the door to her office, which was also the school's infirmary where Alec currently was. As soon as she did so Junpei, followed close behind by Neji and a hesitant looking Rika entered the nurse's office.

Junpei immediately rushed over to Alec's bedside. "Alec!" He then noticed that Alec was awake. "Hey, guys it looks like Rika's knight in shining armor is awake." He threw Alec a wink.

Alec blushed as he began to remember what had happened. He remembered someone tripping Rika on the stone steps and then rushing to catch her. But then all he could remember was pain and then darkness. Alec reached up his hand and felt that there was a bandage wrapped around his head.

Alec gave Junpei a weak smile as Neji came to his bedside next, a worried expression on his face. "How are you feeling Alec?"

Alec tried to sit up, "Not so bad actually...just a bit sore." Though he knew he must be covered in ugly bruises from head to toe.

Junpei, Neji and Rika all looked relieved at Alec's words. Junpei, however, had a knowing look on his face. "That's all thanks to Haruna-*sensei*, the school nurse. She has the ability to heal people as well as some empathic abilities. She probably saved your life Alec."

Alec looked over curiously at the school nurse, Haruna-*sensei*, who was currently at her desk writing something down. She swivelled her chair towards them at the mention of her name however and gave Alec a warm smile. Alec blushed and smiled back since Haruna-*sensei* was unexpectedly very pretty. She had shoulder length, brown hair which had a flirtatious flip to it, and large, bright, brown eyes. She was wearing a pink blouse and black skirt underneath the white nurse's jacket that she was also wearing. She had very kind eyes, Alec decided. Alec also felt there was something oddly comforting about her presence that seemed to put him at ease.

"Thank you, Haruna-*sensei*." Alec began to thank her for saving him when Junpei's words seemed to sink in and his eyes widened. "An Empath... you mean, like a real one?" To Alec abilities such as having 'healing powers' or being an 'Empath' still seemed to be abilities that could only be possessed in a video game or MMORPG.

Junpei looked amused but nodded. Alec looked at Haruna-*sensei* a bit starry-eyed.

Haruna waved Alec's thanks away. "Just doing my job. It's my duty to protect you students. You were pretty banged up though when they brought you in here Alec. For a moment there I thought I might lose you. It was very heroic of you to save Rika like that but try and think of your own well-being a little more too. Sometimes it's not wise to be so selfless."

Junpei ruffled Alec's hair at the comment, "Good luck with convincing Alec about that Haruna-*sensei*. No matter how hard Alec tries to pretend he's a loner, tough-guy he's just a great big softy. It seems to be Alec's biggest character flaw - selflessness. He's always going around saving people, putting himself in mortal peril-"

"Junpei!" Alec looked embarrassed. "That's not true."

"He's just being modest." Neji chirped in. "He saved me from some bullies just the other day."

Haruna's eyes softened as she looked at Alec. "Your family must be so proud - you're really a good boy." Although Alec noted her voice sounded a bit sad and almost wistful as she said this.

Her words affected Alec to the core and he couldn't help the flash of hurt that crossed his eyes as he thought of how his parents had practically abandoned him at Izanagi Academy. But he quickly wiped his expression clean and put a tremulous smile on his face, but otherwise remained silent. Junpei looked at Alec curiously but didn't question Alec about his parents.

Alec noticed Rika hiding behind Neji and giving Alec a shy look. He gave her a hesitant smile before asking. "Are you alright Rika-san?"

Rika jumped but then nodded. "Yes, thanks to you, Alec-kun." She gave Alec a warm smile.

Junpei looked back and forth between the two and a wolfish grin formed on his face as he leaned over to whisper in Alec's ear and nudged Alec's side with his elbow, "You *dog*...girls just love the hero-type. You're going to be super popular once word of this gets around."

Junpei then turned to tease Rika, "Rika, have you fallen for the guy that saved your life? Perfectly understandable, happens all the time." Junpei nodded knowing, a perfectly serious expression on his face.

Rika blushed but couldn't help frowning at Junpei. "Junpei! Why don't you mind your own business! *Mou!* Geez!" She picked up a pillow and threw it at him. It hit Junpei smack on the face.

Junpei merely chuckled in response, Rika was so easy to tease.

Alec blushed at the comment. Then he remembered how those female students had tripped Rika on purpose - that had been really dangerous! "Hey! What about those girls that tripped you, Rika? Did you get to see who they were? We should tell the Headmaster about this."

Rika turned her head away, "Oh, that's really not necessary. I'm used to it..."

Alec narrowed his eyes at her and burst out. "No! It's *not* ok. If I see those girls again I'm going to give them a piece of my mind. That was totally dangerous! Someone could have been seriously hurt!"

"Well, someone *was* seriously hurt." Junpei reminded him giving Alec a pointed look.

Alec blushed and scratched his cheek thoughtfully, "Oh, yea, right."

Rika looked surprised by Alec's outburst but also a little pleased as well.

"Yea, you can beat them up with your soccer ball." Neji added helpfully.

"I can't do that Neji they're *girls*." Alec corrected him.

Junpei chuckled. "Lucky for them that they are. You can be kinda scary Alec when you're angry. Isn't that right Neji?"

Neji nodded and pushed his glasses up his nose, "Indeed."

Alec's jaw dropped, "I'm not scary! *Mou*! Geez! You guys!"

Rika giggled at the boys' teasing of Alec.

Haruna-*sensei* had a thoughtful expression on her face. "If you find out which girls they were Alec I will see that they are suitably punished for their actions."

"Really?" Alec's eyes lit up hopefully, "Thanks Haruna-*sensei*." He beamed at her.

There was a sudden knock at the door and Haruna-*sensei* went over to answer it. She opened to door to find a breathless student.

"Haruna-*sensei*! TenTen had a nasty fall on the track. I think she might have twisted her ankle but we're not sure." The track team member explained quickly.

"Oh dear," Haruna exclaimed and turned back to Alec and the others, "I'll be back in a bit. Try not to stay too long since Alec needs his rest." And with that Haruna-*sensei* took off with the track team member.

Neji was looking a bit starry-eyed as he looked at Alec. "You're so cool Alec. I wish I could be more like you and save people and be a hero in real life. That's actually why I chose to be a healing monk in Yokai World because I wanted to save people and have them all look up to me like I was a *somebody*."

Alec looked taken aback by the comment. No one had ever said he was 'cool' before. "I'm not..." Alec insisted. Alec wondered briefly why it did seem like he was always saving people lately. But that had to be because of all the bullies at the school and Alec hated bullies having suffered at the hands of bullies throughout most of his childhood. Alec knew what it felt like to be picked on and hurt by others and so didn't want others to go through all that, and so when he was able to stop it he just had to.

Junpei reached out and squeezed Alec's shoulder. "You are. Don't sell yourself so short Alec." He leaned in to whisper. "I know you've managed to get yourself at least one admirer, who seems to think you're pretty darned cool with all your heroics." Junpei winked at Alec and he knew Junpei was referring to Rika.

"Hey Alec, when do you think you'll be released?" Neji questioned thoughtfully.

Alec shrugged, "I dunno...why?" Alec quirked his head.

"Well, it's just that this weekend Yokai World is having a really cool 'in game event' based on the folktale of Kintaro." Neji explained. "If you clear the game event you will be rewarded with a special, one of a kind, rare item." Neji's eyes sparkled at the mention of the 'rare item'.

"Kintaro?" Alec questioned, although the name of the folktale sounded oddly familiar. His father had read him a few Japanese folktales when he was very little and had sometimes used them as bedtime stories.

"You don't know the story?" Junpei looked surprised, "It's one of the most popular Japanese children's folktales. It's about a boy, who was born with super-human strength. His mother was forced to abandon him in the forests of Mt. Kintoki where he was raised by a witch. Since he was all alone there in the forest he ended up making friends with all of the woodland creatures and it was said he befriended a giant bear that allowed Kintaro to ride on his back. Kintaro along with the bear and wielding an axe went off on many adventures killing *oni* and monsters. Even as a toddler Kintaro was supposedly so strong he could uproot trees with his bare hands and cut boulders in two with his axe. He was also known for winning sumo-wrestling matches against the bears in the forest, which is how he gained the respect of all the forest creatures."

"If you clear the game event you'll earn lots of experience points too. So it would be a perfect way to gain several levels quickly." Neji pushed his glasses up, a knowing look on his face.

Alec's interest had also been piqued by the mention of experience points and the rare item. He could really use the experience points to up his level in the game and maybe if he was lucky the rare item would be a new weapon since his starter sword was seriously lacking in power. And if his goal was to get to duel with RedAki he needed to become stronger.

"Sounds interesting, unfortunately I have a game on Saturday and so I won't be able to go." Junpei put out his hands helplessly.

Neji sighed wistfully, "Yea, there's this *anime* convention I really wanted to go to as well...so I probably won't be able to make it either."

"*Otakus.*" Junpei shook his head.

"What about you Rika?" Neji asked her.

Rika looked thoughtful before she frowned, "Unfortunately, I think I'm going to be busy then too. I'm working on some paintings that I'm going to be entering in a competition."

Alec pouted, "That's too bad. I thought it might be fun if we got to play the game together Rika."

Rika blushed at Alec's offhanded comment, "Oh? Well, maybe some other time."

Junpei got a knowing glint in his eye as he watched the interaction between Alec and Rika and decided to give the two of them some space. "Well, Neji I think it's time for us to go." He began to head towards the door.

"Huh why? I wanted to stay and talk with Alec a little longer." Neji frowned at the jock.

"Well, we have that *thing* that we need to do. Remember?" Junpei jerked his head at Alec and Rika, trying to get Neji to understand what he was planning.

Neji, however, was a bit dense. Neji blinked, "Huh? What are you talking about Junpei? What thing?"

Junpei smacked a hand to his forehead, "Oh forget it, come on you bonehead! Let's leave these two alone!" Junpei grabbed Neji by the back of his uniform and unceremoniously dragged him out of the nurse's office. "Good luck Alec!" Junpei called before shutting the door loudly behind them.

Suddenly, Rika and Alec were alone together.

Alec and Rika looked at each other in surprise at Junpei's comment and both blushed before looking away. Rika, however, gathered her courage and turned to face Alec once more coming to sit on the edge of his bed. She licked her lips nervously. "Alec-*kun*...I just wanted to thank you for saving my life."

Alec turned to look at her and simply smiled. "Anytime. What are-" Alec caught himself since he had been about to say 'What are friends for'. And Alec had to wonder what had happened to his no friends policy. Luckily, Rika didn't seem to notice.

Instead, she leaned closer to Alec with a worried expression on her face. "I'm surprised by how good Haruna-*sensei* was able to heal you...there was so much blood." Rika touched Alec's snow-white hair where before it had been streaked with red.

Alec gulped at her behavior. He had never been this close to a girl before... except for maybe Cindy.

"I just wish there was some way I could repay you." Rika tapped her chin thoughtfully.

Alec swallowed thickly. "You don't have to do anything Rika. I wanted to help you."

An idea seemed to come to Rika and she looked at Alec before looking away and biting her lower lip as if she was debating something. She then turned back to Alec a steely expression on her face. "I think I know how I can replay you, Alec-*kun*."

"Oh?" Alec asked nervously.

"With my first..." Rika leaned over Alec, and breathed the word right over his lips. "*Kiss*." She then softly pressed her lips against Alec's.

Alec's eyes widened in surprise before he closed his eyes. The kiss was probably only a few seconds long but to Alec it seemed an eternity before she finally pulled away.

Rika looked back at Alec and blushed apparently surprised by her own bold actions. "Oh my god...I can't believe I just did that!" She giggled to herself before quickly getting up off Alec's bed. "Well...I should...get going. Hope you feel better. See ya Alec-*kun*!" Rika declared as she rushed from the room.

Even if she had waited for Alec's response she wouldn't have gotten one since Alec was lying back on the bed in a stunned stupor, swirly-eyed and in shock at what had just happened. When he finally snapped out of his dazed state he raised a hand to his mouth and muttered to himself, "My first kiss..."

. . . .

Haruna-*sensei* had told Alec that he should stay in bed the entire weekend to rest up since he had lost a lot of blood, but the game event that Neji had mentioned had really piqued his interest. Alec needed those experience points and a new weapon for his goal of beating RedAki in a Ghostly Duel, and so Saturday morning Alec Suzuki was sneaking out of the nurse's office and making his way down the halls stealthily towards the computer club room. Alec looked around to see if any teachers were roaming the hall before quickly letting himself inside the club room.

He flipped on the light switch, and found the computer club room empty. Alec made his way over to a computer and began setting up. He put on his HMD, clicked on the Yokai World icon and began to log in:

ID: Dranarch

Password: wings

Logging in...

Alec materialized in the middle of the start town and saw a large, floating bulletin board that gave players all the information they needed to know about the currently ongoing game event. Apparently, the game event was being held in a newly created area called 'Kintoki Forest' and players had to go there first and find the NPC called Yama-ube before they could enter themselves into the game event. Alec went over to the teleportation gate, which was a spinning, golden ring around a glowing portal. Alec raised his fist and got ready to teleport himself to Kintoki Forest.

"Kintoki Forest!" Alec called out and was instantly teleported to the new location. Alec found himself at the entrance to a dark, spooky looking forest. It was definitely not an inviting looking place but Alec shrugged since what could he expect when the whole theme of the game was ghosts. Alec began to walk into the forest and looked over at the trees a shiver going down his spine.

The trees had dark, gaping holes in their trunks which to Alec seemed to look like mouths and eyes and the expressions on the trees looked like faces that were contorted or screaming in pain. The trees were also reaching their twisted, leaf-less branches upwards. Alec gulped. He wished he hadn't come on this game event alone. If only Neji and Junpei could have come with him. *Sigh.* Alec shook his head fiercely, he wasn't supposed to have friends anyways. *Neh?* Whatever happened to the lone, role playing gamer Dranarch? Huh?

Alec found a narrow forest path and began to walk along it until suddenly materializing in front of him was a rather small, old witch, who was currently sitting cross-legged on a soccer ball sized, glowing crystal ball that was hovering in midair.

At the suddenness of her appearance Alec squeaked and wind-milled his arms as he fell backwards onto his backside. "Oof!" Alec looked up at the little, old witch. She was probably only about a foot tall, had a very wrinkly face, and white hair which she had pulled back into a tight bun. She was dressed all in black with a witch hat upon her head and Alec noticed she had a small wand in her hand. She smiled an amused, toothless grin down at Alec as she peered at him from her perch on the crystal ball.

The old woman chuckled at Alec. "What are you doing down there *Shinigami* boy? This is a very dangerous place for one such as you." Alec had a feeling she was referring to his current pathetically low level.

Alec pushed himself up off the ground and stood, dusting himself off. He reached out his senses and realized in surprise the being before him was a NPC. "Who are you?"

"I am Yama-uba." The mountain witch informed him.

Wasn't that the name of Kintaro's mother? "I heard there was a quest here in this forest." Alec began.

Yama-uba narrowed her eyes at Alec. "This is the forest of Mt. Kintoki. It was once a beautiful and tranquil place. It wasn't always like you see it now. Well, of course it was my son Kintaro who kept the peace and harmony in this forest. It was he who befriended and tamed all the woodland creatures, as well as *oni*. With his uncanny strength they respected him and he led them. Kintaro's best friend was the bear that used to be king of this forest. Kintaro won a sumo wrestling match against this bear and earned the bear's loyalty and ever since then Kintaro and this bear were best friends and Kintaro used to ride the bear during his many adventures however...an evil came to this forest. And things changed. The rivers and streams dried up, the trees withered and died and turned charred black, and the creatures of the forest turned evil...bloodthirsty...and hungered for human flesh. My son Kintaro went off in search of the evil that has caused all this and has yet to return...I fear something has happened to him.

"Your quest should you chose to accept it is to find my son, and to help him rid this forest of the evil curse that plagues it. And in return, should you succeed, you shall be handsomely rewarded." Yama-uba reached her hand inside her crystal ball and Alec watched as her hand simply passed right through it and then she began to pull something out. Alec's eyes widened as he realized it was a large *Shinigami* sword or *katana*. "I shall give you this *Shinigami* sword. There is no other sword like this in all of Yokai World. So, *Shinigami* boy, do you accept this quest?"

Alec nodded, "Yes, I accept the quest."

Yama-uba nodded and her eyes seemed to turn into two small, computer screens as data flashed past. "Dranarch, you have been successfully entered into the Yokai World Kintoki Forest Game Event. Get past the evil creatures of the forest, find and rescue Kintaro, and rid the forest of the evil that is plaguing it in order to clear this event. Good luck." Yama-uba's voice had become synthesized and mechanical.

Alec nodded and then continued his way into the cursed forest. He soon came to a forest clearing and at the edges of the clearing Alec saw several pairs of shining red eyes. *Uh oh.* Alec gulped taking a step back. He looked up and noticed that there were several pairs of gleaming red eyes up in the trees as well. And then from out of the trees the forest creatures began to emerge - several were wolves, their coats a bright white, their eyes shining red. Alec also saw boars with black fur and red eyes that had long, sharp tusks. From the trees black crows began to swoop down cawing at Alec with their claws outstretched. Alec unsheathed his sword and held it in a two-handed grip before him as he faced the monsters.

The leader of the pack of wolves stalked towards Alec with purposeful steps and began to circle Alec menacingly. Alec kept his distance, waiting for the wolf to attack. As Alec watched the wolf he couldn't shake the feeling that the wolf and these creatures seemed almost real. There was just something about them...even when Alec knew it was just a virtual reality game. They seemed so real to Alec that it made him hesitate in attacking them - he really wasn't the type to find pleasure in killing furry, little, woodland creatures after all!

But that's when the white wolf attacked. The white wolf suddenly leapt up into the air at Alec and pounced on him, slamming him hard into the ground. Alec managed to block the attack with his sword. The wolf's claws were wrapped around Alec's sword as it pressed forward, snapping his jaws at Alec. Jaws which were dripping with drool as it tried to get closer to bite Alec's neck. A trickle of drool fell onto Alec's cheek and he squirmed beneath the wolf in disgust.

It's just a game...it's just a game. Alec muttered in his mind as he tried to push the wolf off of him. But as hard as Alec tried to push the wolf back it was impossible, the wolf was just too strong, but if Alec didn't do something soon he'd be dinner. Alec narrowed his eyes at the wolf as he psyched himself up to attack. He had no choice since he wasn't about to give up on the game event that easily. Alec pulled his sword back and suddenly rammed it forward impaling the wolf straight through its chest. *I'm sorry...*

Almost immediately however as Alec's sword pierced the chest of the wolf something seemed to fly up and out of the white wolf. It appeared to be a black ball of fire with shimmering red eyes. Alec blinked as the wolf that was on top of him suddenly changed into a brown haired wolf, with clear blue eyes and a friendly disposition. It gave Alec a long, wet lick on his cheek before jumping off of Alec. Alec looked shocked at the appearance of the now normal looking wolf and realized that it had been possessed. Alec turned his attention to the evil spirit that had been possessing the wolf and pointed his sword at it. Alec charged forward with a battle cry and with a quick slash of his sword through the air was able to defeat the strange monster as it was instantly destroyed.

Alec let out a breath of relief. It seemed as though a *Shinigami's* sword could only harm evil spirits, so Alec didn't have to worry about harming the woodland creatures. *Wow a sword that can only harm evil spirits, that's such a cool idea. I wish a sword like that existed in reality.* Alec turned to face the other forest creatures, who were closing in on him now, and a determined look formed on his face. *Don't worry, I'll free you all!* Alec charged forward and began to fight with the creatures. Each time his sword slashed through the air at one of the creatures it seemed to pass right through them and an evil spirit would then rise up out of them, which Alec would then have to destroy. The animals Alec had saved happily followed close behind him as he continued his way deeper into the forest.

Alec was forced to fight several wolves, boars, and crows before he finally managed to make it to the next area of the forest where more high level monsters began to attack him. The level of mobs Alec was having to face now were getting hard for him since he was still such a low level. It was then that Alec began to notice other players in the forest with him fighting off monsters in parties that they had formed. He was definitely not the only player, who had entered this game event with hopes of winning a new rare item.

In this area of the forest the creatures players were having to face were possessed tigers, *kirin*, and bears. Many players were falling to these higher level monsters and Alec knew he was barely hanging on by a thread - if it wasn't for all the health potions Neji had given him he would have been a goner. He watched as one player was killed by a tiger and then turned into a PC Ghost, which his party members then resurrected using a red potion.

The boy's PC body returned to normal and he was able to continue the game event.

Alec had no one in his party and so if he were killed that would be the end of the quest for him. That was when he noticed a small boy of around nine years of age running through the forest with a large, white and black striped tiger hot on his heals.

"AHHHH!" The boy screamed unabashedly as he sprinted through the forest.

Alec looked around to see if the boy was in a party and realized he was alone and so decided he would go to the boy's aid. Just as the tiger was about to pounce on the boy, who threw up his arms in desperation, Alec ran in front of the tiger and stood in its path. Alec rushed forward and ran his sword through the tiger's stomach. Almost immediately a large, black ball of flame with glowing red eyes rose up out of the tiger. The tiger, which was returning back to normal, changed colors so that its coat was now orange and black striped. Alec then raised his sword prepared to attack the evil spirit that had been possessing the tiger. He ran forward and used a high downwards slash of his sword to finish this evil spirit off, cutting through the flames. He then turned towards the boy to see if he was alright.

The sight that met him were two large stars, which Alec realized were the boy's eyes. "Wow! Thanks so much! *Nii-san!*"

Alec's eye twitched at the use of the nickname '*nii-san*' which meant brother. "Yea, no problem, kid." Alec looked the boy over and saw that he was a monk PC type. Alec also noted due to the type of staff he was carrying that he was a healing monk and not a battle monk. The boy was surprisingly young to be playing a MMORPG Alec thought, guessing the boy's age to be around 8 or 9 years old. Alec raised an eyebrow at him. "Aren't you a little young to be playing a game like this all by yourself? You should at least have a party."

The monk boy frowned. "I'm old enough to play. I'm nine and in December I'll be ten! Usually my friends are on to help me but they were all busy today..." The boy sniffled beginning to look sad as he thought of his friends.

Alec felt sympathetic towards the boy. "Actually, that's the same as me. My friends are also all too busy today to partner up with me in this game event. But I really wanted a new weapon and I need those experience points, so decided to enter the game event and try my luck anyways."

"Me too!" the boy nodded vigorously, "I want a new monk staff."

"Is that what class you are? A monk? What kind of monk are you?" Alec questioned curiously, an idea beginning to form in his mind.

"A healing monk." The boy confirmed for Alec. "I don't have much offensive power unfortunately." The boy chewed his lower lip fretfully.

"I'm surprised you managed to make it this far all on your own, not bad kid." Alec smirked, "Do you have your own Battle Ghost yet?"

The boy shook his head, "It's impossible for someone my level to get a Battle Ghost."

Alec nodded, "I have an idea. Why don't we party up? You back me up with your healing spells and I'll be able to make quick work of these mobs without having to use up all my health potions."

The boy's eyes widened in surprise, "Really? You want to partner up with me? Wow thanks *Nii-san!*"

"So what's your name kid? I'm Alec." Alec said being friendly.

"Keiichi." The boy grinned.

"Alright then Keiichi let's go kick some monster butt!" Alec raised his sword in the air.

"HECK YEA!" Keiichi punched his fists in the air.

It was just as Alec suspected, with Keiichi's help it was much easier to deal with the higher level mobs. And Alec was able to easily slay the evil spirits which were coming up out of the tigers and *kirin*. When Alec had first spotted the *kirin* he didn't want to hurt it since it was such a fascinating creature - otherwise known as the Chinese unicorn. It was solid black with a spiraled red and black horn in the center of its forehead, had red eyes and there were tufts of red hair on its hooves. But as soon as the possessed unicorn had targeted Keiichi, Alec had no choice but to attack it. He slashed his sword forward at the unicorn and an evil spirit come up out of the unicorn, which Alec then had to exorcize. When Alec turned back to look at the unicorn he saw that it had turned a beautiful sky-blue color, its mane had turned moon-white, its eyes had become golden, and its horn was now a spiral of gold and blue. It tossed its head happily, whinnying its thanks in Alec's direction, before prancing away off into the forest.

"Whoa." Was all Alec could find to say.

Keiichi seemed equally impressed. "Sometimes I forget this is a game...and even if it is only a game...that unicorn was pretty neat don't you think?"

Alec couldn't help but agree as he nodded vigorously. There was something almost magical about Yokai World. Perhaps, there was more to it than met the eye...

Alec and Keiichi then noticed a group of players walking by who were complaining about kill stealers:

"Those jerks totally stole our kill back there." "Yea, just who did they think they were?" "We should report them to System Admin." "Where did Grim go?" "Dunno..."

Alec and Keiichi watched as the group of three players walked swiftly through the forest, while looking back over their shoulders nervously and with worried expressions on their faces as if they were trying to get away from something or someone.

"What's kill stealing?" Keiichi asked Alec.

"It's when someone who's not in your party finishes off a mob you've been fighting and steals your experience points." Alec explained.

A sudden scream was heard ringing through the forest.

"What was that?" Keiichi squeaked as he turned around.

Alec furrowed his brow and gripped his sword a bit tighter. He had a bad feeling about this. Alec and Keiichi watched as three fast approaching figures ran towards the three boys, who Alec and Keiichi had been eavesdropping upon. With movements too quick to follow Alec and Keiichi watched as these shadowy figures cut down the players and PKed them. Their screams echoed through the trees eerily. The players fell to the ground as they were killed and Alec saw that they all turned into PC Ghosts. But since all their party members had died there was no one who could resurrect them and so the ghosts were forced to stay where they were. Alec knew if they chose to log out they would automatically be disqualified from the game event.

Keiichi's eyes widened in fear, "Player killers!" He was beginning to tremble. "Oh my god, see that mark with the crossed scythes and the two red Rs on their outfits? That's the Guild Mark of the Renegade Reapers Guild, the biggest PK guild in Yokai World! We're so screwed!"

Alec heard rustling and turned to face the line of trees and bushes, which were in front of him. From out of the dark trees RedAki strode forward! His black-bladed sword was resting casually across his shoulders, and he wore an almost bored expression on his face. That's when he caught sight of Alec and their eyes met. RedAki grinned in a very creepy manner which sent a chill down Alec's spine. That look...it was the look of a cat eyeing a mouse.

"It's...RedAki." Alec said aloud and Keiichi gasped probably having heard of him.

RedAki's attention turned for a second to Keiichi before he quickly dismissed him and turned to look at Alec again, an amused expression on his face. RedAki stalked forward with purposeful steps and brought down his sword so that it was poised and ready before him. Then RedAki suddenly burst forward and charged straight at Alec. Alec quickly brought up his sword expecting RedAki to try and PK him but at the last second the sword slipped past Alec's left side. Alec felt a rush of air passing his body and the sleeve of his *haori* shirt had been cut open. But Alec turned horrified to see that RedAki had stabbed Keiichi instead directly through the boy's heart.

"Keiichi!" Alec cried out.

Keiichi looked down at the sword in his heart in shock, blood dribbled down his chin and he took a step forward before falling flat on his face.

Keiichi's PC body began to glow before it transformed into a PC Ghost which hovered, trapped above the ground. Keiichi pouted in defeat looking down at his white and semi-transparent hands.

"Dang, I'm a ghost. This sucks." Keiichi complained.

Alec let out a sigh of relief. For a split second there he had forgotten all this was just a game...

RedAki casually walked over to where Keiichi's monk staff lay on the ground and picked it up to examine it before tossing it aside carelessly. "Garbage. That staff isn't even worth stealing anyway." RedAki then snapped his attention back towards Alec. "It's you...I remember you. You're the boy who was with Dr. Mimic." RedAki raised his sword and pointed it at Alec's chest. "Are you friends with Dr. Mimic?"

Alec frowned and decided to answer truthfully. "Not really..." *I'm not really friends with anyone.* He shrugged. "Aren't you going to PK me too?"

RedAki looked thoughtful. "Actually, I owe you one from the other day. Thanks. When Dr. Mimic almost PKed me I had been carrying a *lot* of rare items which I needed to sell online for real money...that was a close one, I must say. I would have been in a real pickle if I hadn't been able to get that money. So in return I'll offer you a deal...or rather an opportunity. How about you join the Renegade Reapers Guild and become one of us?" RedAki put out his hand for Alec to shake.

Keiichi gasped in shock. "Don't do it Alec!"

Alec looked surprised by the offer, but then frowned. "You want me to join your PK Guild?" Alec remembered how those kids had looked earlier when the RRs had PKed them. Their frightened screams. Keiichi's sad face. Alec shook his head. "I don't like bullies. I'm no coward to need a group of people behind me to feel safe, and not the type of person to use a group of people to gang up on someone else. I'm happy being a loner and guildless for now thanks. I don't need anyone, least of all you."

RedAki dropped his hand, a dark expression formed on his face. "Think you're too good for us do you? What are you some kind of saint? Not wanting to PK - when really it only makes the game more interesting. Especially getting to duel with other players. Don't you see? It's fun, it's a rush, having a *real* battle like that. When both parties have something *real* to lose. Since you can't lose your actual life in the game. And on the plus side you may get to steal a couple of rare items. Besides, I don't think you understand that the Renegade Reapers are one of the most powerful guilds in this game and if you're not with us - you're against us Alec. So, are you sure you don't want to join us? The other guilds out there are a bunch of weaklings compared to us anyways."

"I'll decide on my own which guild is right for me or worthy joining, thanks. Your guild just isn't right for me RedAki." Alec's gray eyes were icy as he looked back at RedAki.

RedAki seemed frustrated, and ran a hand through his spiky hair. "It's either join us or die, Alec-*kun*. What's it really going to be?" RedAki stomped his foot and appeared to be on the verge of a tantrum.

Alec raised an eyebrow at this. "A death threat? Is that really how you get people to join your guild? You guys must be pretty desperate for members. You're not used to not getting what you want are you RedAki? What a spoiled brat. You almost look like you're ready to throw a temper tantrum or something but sorry - this time you're not going to get what you want. You're not getting me. You're going to have to get used to it RedAki - not getting your way I mean. Now that Dranarch is playing this game."

RedAki shook his head disgusted. "A spoiled brat? You have some nerve calling me that. I guess I was wrong about you. Here I thought I saw someone with potential but now all I see is a total *baka*, fool. I'd stop playing this game if I were you Alec because you've just made the RRs your enemy. Well, have it your way then *baka*, prepare to die!"

Alec raised his starter sword and pointed it at RedAki. RedAki raised his own sword and charged forward. His speed was incredible. It was no use. RedAki passed Alec quickly and managed to disarm him in a flash, Alec's sword flying up into the air. RedAki turned back around to face Alec. Alec looked down at his chest and saw a large gash there where RedAki had wounded him. *Darn it.* Alec fell forward and knew he was dying. There was this odd tingling sensation as his PC body turned into a PC Ghost.

In his ghost form Alec watched as the other three RRs came up next to RedAki to see who he had PKed. One of them was a girl whose PC appeared to be of the Assassin Class. She had shoulder length, purple hair that was wild and flipped up at the ends. Her eyes were a bright magenta color that seemed to gleam playfully. She was wearing a high-collared, Asian-styled top and some black pants. On her hands were long, sharp, metal claws. On the front of her shirt was the Renegade Reapers guild mark with the two Rs on either side of the crossed scythes. However, unlike RedAki's guild mark which had the Rs in red the girl had her Rs in purple.

Standing next to her was a boy whose PC was of the Ninja Class. He was dressed from head to toe in black and had a face mask on that covered half of his face making him look even more mysterious. His messy gray-colored hair fell down and hid one side of his face. The one eye that was visible was almost solid black. He wore a utility belt around his waist and he was spinning *shuriken* on his fingers. On his chest was a larger version of their guild mark, the Rs were in red.

The last member of their party was another boy whose PC was that of a healing Monk. His monk robes were in black, red and gold. He also wore the Renegade Reapers guild mark on the front of his *haori* shirt with the letters in red. He had a short buzz cut and there was a red dot painted in the center of his forehead. He had narrow and fierce looking eyes with a tint of mischievousness.

"You two *bakas* can just stick around here and float while my guild members and I go and defeat the boss monster. Then we'll be the ones to win this game event. I *will* be taking back that rare item as a reward! Cya around losers! Catara, Smoker, Kiba - let's go." RedAki sneered as he began to walk off into the dark forest.

RedAki's guild members snickered at Alec and Keiichi's plight before following close behind RedAki.

Alec sighed heavily. They were stuck as ghosts now until the game event was over since if they logged out now they would automatically fail clearing the game event. *Dang!*

"Dang...this sucks. We were doing so good too." Alec began pouting.

Keiichi was near tears as he sniffled. "This is no fun...maybe I should just stop playing this game...what with all the player killers and all..."

Alec looked towards Keiichi surprised but understood how he felt. Powerless. It wasn't a fun feeling. "Keiichi..." Here was a kid who was just playing a game to have some fun and these stupid player killers had to go and ruin it for him. Alec clenched his fists angrily. He hated bullies...he hated player killers. If only he were stronger, he could have protected Keiichi. *Darn it!*

"Maybe someone will come by and resurrect us?" Alec suggested hopefully.

Keiichi frowned, "Like that would ever happen..."

The unexpected sound of a branch breaking was heard and the two boys looked up to see a player walking out of the cursed forest with a haughty expression on her face. Her PC was of the same class as Alec's, but was a female *Shinigami*. She looked to be a bit older than Alec, maybe a 10th grader, he decided. She was wearing a short, dark green *kimono* dress, which was quite low-cut and Alec noticed, blushing, that he could see quite a bit of her cleavage. There was a black *obi* sash tied about her waist and it had a giant bow in the back, the ends of which hung down all the way to the ground.

She had emerald green hair which was put up into a high ponytail and sparkling green eyes. In her hands she wielded a *naginata* (a long spear-like weapon with a curved blade on the end, which was known as being a popular weapon for female *samurai*). And for some reason Alec couldn't help but think she looked like some kind of Japanese Pop Idol.

119

"Well, what do we have here? You boys look like you could use a helping hand." A cat's paw smile formed on the girl's face.

Alec and Keiichi just gaped, open-mouthed at the beautiful girl in front of them in shock. And Alec couldn't stop blushing at how well-endowed she was. *Cough.*

Keiichi's eyes widened as he seemed to realize something. "You aren't by any chance...LadyV?"

Alec turned to look at Keiichi curiously, "LadyV?"

Keiichi turned towards Alec and nodded vigorously. "She's Yokai World's Game Idol, she's a very popular player and has tons of fans within the game. She even has her own fan club!"

Alec blinked, "Game Idol?"

LadyV's eyes sparkled with mischief. "You're a bright boy aren't you? Well, you're absolutely right. I'm the one and only LadyV come to your rescue and since you boys are just so cute I've decided to help you. Red Potion Activate! Resurrect!" LadyV yelled as she used two red potions to resurrect the two boys in front of her.

Alec and Keiichi patted their hands down their now solid bodies with relief once they were resurrected. Alec let out a sigh of relief. "Thank you so much." Alec bowed, glad that he wouldn't have to look down at himself and see his transparent hands since it had been a bit unnerving to him.

Keiichi rushed up to LadyV. "Thank you! Thank you! Thank you!" He was jumping up and down excitedly. "This is so cool! I can't believe we were just rescued by LadyV! So um..." Keiichi looked bashful for a moment before he pulled out a pen and a pad of paper from god knows where to hand over to LadyV. "Can I have your autograph? My friends are *never* going to believe this, if I don't come back with some proof!"

LadyV giggled, "Sure thing, kiddo." She took the pad of paper and pen and began to sign her autograph with a flourish.

Alec felt a trickle of sweat form on the side of his face in disbelief as he watched Keiichi get his autograph. *Can you really get autographs in a game world?*

LadyV then turned her attention towards Alec. "Dranarch huh? Add me to your party."

Alec blinked at her. "Huh? You want to party with *us*?"

"Sure." LadyV winked at Alec. "I have a feeling you'll be entertaining Dranarch."

Alec blushed lightly. "Call me Alec."

"Alright then Alec-kun. I *know* you want to get back at those player killers for what they did to you right? What better way than to win this game event?

Come on! Let's find those guys and show them a thing or two! What do you say boys?"

"*Yatta!* HECK YEA!" Alec and Keiichi cried out in unison. LadyV smiled devilishly.

Alec and his new party traveled through the forest until they arrived at the final area where the mobs they had to face were of the highest level and happened to be bears. Alec caught sight of more trees that looked as though they were crying out in pain and he couldn't help but feel sorry for them. *Don't worry, I'll set you free of the curse soon.* Alec and LadyV began to fight against the possessed bears with Keiichi backing them up with healing. They exorcized the bears quickly and easily and were able to destroy all of the evil spirits.

They finally arrived at a clearing where they spotted RedAki and his fellow guild members. RedAki had managed to awaken the boss monster of the final area of the forest, which happened to be a giant, black bear that was at least ten feet tall. It had fierce, golden eyes and Alec noticed there was a glowing, golden headband on its forehead with a sparkling, red ruby in the center.

RedAki and his guild members were currently fighting the giant bear. Alec watched as RedAki charged the beast with his black bladed sword but his attacks seemed to have no effect. That had to be a very high level boss monster indeed, Alec decided. He then watched as Catara, the assassin PC, rushed forward in attack with her claws but she too was pushed back easily by the bear. Kiba, the healing monk, was healing Catara and RedAki's injuries as quickly as possible with a wave of his staff. Then Alec watched as it was Smoker the Ninja's turn. He flung several sharp *shuriken* at the boss mob but it also seemed to have no effect as the *shuriken* merely bounced off of the bear.

"Doppelganger Attack!" Smoker cried as his PC body began to duplicate until there were now three mirror images of Smoker, which all moved in to attack the bear mob with a series of quick kicks and punches and *shuriken* throws.

"Hey, is that a real game power?" Alec questioned LadyV and Keiichi curiously.

LadyV nodded. "Yes, the Ninja Class has the unique ability to be able to form shadow copies of itself and they can also turn invisible so make very useful spies for the guilds in this game, which are always trying to find out each other's secrets."

Alec then noticed a small boy NPC in a square cage that was made out of twigs and branches that had been tied together. He realized the boy had to be Kintaro. "Hey, look there's Kintaro!" Alec declared pointing towards the cage.

Alec turned his attention back towards RedAki and his guild mates and saw that the rampaging bear had waved his giant paw towards them so that Catara and RedAki were both sent flying backwards. RedAki hit a tree with a hard *thwack* and Alec found he flinched in sympathy.

"Dang it!" RedAki swore as he pushed himself up off the ground. "We can't do this on our own. He's too powerful. Summon your Battle Ghosts now! Attack him from all sides! I summon you, Oni!" RedAki's Oni Ghost materialized next to RedAki before RedAki waved his hand forward. "Oni attack!" The *oni* demon charged forward, his large iron club raised and he swung hard at the bear mob. Still the bear mob seemed unaffected by the blows. Oni decided to try a fire attack next and opened his mouth to unleash his fiery breath upon the bear mob in an impressive display.

Catara was the next to quickly summon her own Battle Ghost. She raised her hand and a purple stone from her control ring glowed. "I summon thee! Nekomata!" A humanoid ghost with cat-like features materialized next to Catara. It had the face of a cat with lavender-colored fur and deep violet-colored eyes, but the body of a human woman. There were two long tails swishing back and forth behind the semi-transparent ghost. The ghost was dressed in a long, deep purple *kimono* dress. "Attack Nekomata!" Catara commanded and her Battle Ghost immediately went into attack. Nekomata formed a large black and purple ball of flame between her two hands before she then flung the fireball at the boss bear mob. The bear mob cried out in pain as the attack hit it dead on.

"Come forth, Enenra!" Smoker the Ninja summoned his Battle Ghost next in his gruff voice. He raised the hand on which he had his control ring and its gray stone glowed before his Battle Ghost materialized next to him. It started out as a small ball of smoke at first but then it grew larger and larger until it had become a wispy, ghostlike creature composed entirely of thick, gray smoke and was floating next to Smoker with glowing red eyes. "Attack Enenra!" The smokey Battle Ghost seemed to disappear and then he reappeared to be seen coiling his entire body around the neck of the boss mob. The bear growled and raised both of its claw to try and pry Enenra off.

The healing monk Kiba was the last to summon his Battle Ghost. "I summon thee, Ookami!" He raised his ring, which glowed a fiery red. His Battle Ghost materialized next to him and Alec couldn't help think he resembled a werewolf ghost. It had the face of a white wolf with red eyes, the body of a man, and a long, white, bushy tail that had a red-tipped end. The ghost was dressed in a red and white kimono shirt and hakama pants. "Attack Ookami!" Ookami used martial arts against the bear mob but when he threw a punch forward or a kick sideways flames shot forth from these attacks coming out of his hands or feet.

LadyV stepped forward and cleared her throat loudly. "I'm so sorry but that's *our* boss monster."

RedAki and his guild members turned around to face LadyV with expressions of disbelief on their faces. That is until RedAki spotted sight of Alec. "You again!" RedAki seemed to be gnashing his teeth. "You're becoming such a pain in the butt!"

Kiba leered in LadyV's direction, "Hey, check it out - it's LadyV."

"Lady who?" Catara sniffed, not liking the way Kiba was looking at this newcomer.

"LadyV, the Game Idol. She also happens to be a rank #4 Ghost Master. Didn't you know?" Kiba informed her.

RedAki looked more thoughtful now as he raked his eyes over LadyV. "I see, then she's not to be underestimated if she's really ranked number 4. And besides her name does seem oddly familiar...Smoker, Catara, Kiba, I want you guys to take care of them. I'll face the boss mob on my own with Oni. Don't you guys forget, I'm ranked #3 Ghost Master in this world. I can handle it. Now go!"

Catara, Kiba, and Smoker hesitated not wanting to leave RedAki but then nodded before turning around to face Alec and the others. They summoned their Battle Ghosts to their sides before they set their sights on Alec and the others, prepared to fight.

LadyV quickly turned to Alec and Keiichi. "Alec-*kun*, I'll handle these brats - you take care of RedAki and find a way to beat that mob!"

"Me?" Alec squeaked, "But I've only managed to get to level 30! What can I expect to do against that level 100 boss mob when I don't even have my own Battle Ghost yet?"

LadyV put a finger to Alec's lips to silence him and leaned forward close to his face. "Sometimes the answer lies not in physical strength but in here." She touched her forehead to Alec's forehead. He blushed at her closeness. "Sometimes you have to use your head, Alec." She explained before pulling back and then turning to Keiichi next. "Keiichi you heal Alec. Now go, the both of you!"

"*Hai* LadyV-*san*!" Keiichi nodded vigorously.

Alec nodded and ran off, followed close behind by Keiichi, towards RedAki and the bear mob. Catara, Kiba, and Smoker tried to head Alec off but LadyV stood in their way, a haughty expression on her face.

"Your opponent shall be me." LadyV smiled a cat's paw smile as she spun her *naginata* staff towards them.

Oni was attacking once more with his fiery breath and giving RedAki the perfect opportunity to move in undetected with his sword to deliver the boss mob a finishing blow, and was just raising his sword to deliver this harsh downwards slash when Alec suddenly stood in his way. RedAki's sword came down hard and Alec blocked the blow with his own sword catching the blade.

"You again." RedAki growled, "You're beginning to become a nuisance. Now get out of my way, punk!"

Alec had a steely look in his gray eyes. "No."

Suddenly, the bear mob slashed its large clawed paw through the air at both RedAki and Alec and they were both forced to break apart and jump backwards. The giant paw came crashing down and left a large crater in the ground where Alec and RedAki had been only seconds before, dirt and grass flying up into the air.

"Epp!" Alec squeaked, that had nearly done him in.

"Oni!" RedAki commanded his Oni Ghost who obeyed and moved into attack with his iron club once more. RedAki then ignored Alec and ran forward to attack the bear mob with his sword. Alec decided to do the same and also rushed forward, his starter sword raised. Alec saw a paw coming towards him again and raised his sword to block but the force from the bear's attack was too strong and Alec was flung backwards. He landed hard on his backside, his head was spinning, and he was a bit swirly-eyed. "Uhhh..." He looked up to see how RedAki was doing.

RedAki, who was level 87, was even struggling against the bear mob and having to dodge its swiping, claw attacks while trying to move in to slash at the mob with his sword. He managed to get a few hits in but the mob still had most of its health left. If RedAki was having that hard a time at level 87 what chance did Alec have, who was still only level 30, to defeat that powerful a monster?

That's when Alec noticed something interesting about the headband on the bear mob's head - it was glowing with a red light and every time the bear attacked its eyes seemed to glow red. And then for a moment the bear stopped attacking RedAki and tried to take the golden headband off of its head and during this time its eyes weren't red but a warm golden color. However, the bear had stopped trying to remove the headband when its eyes had returned to red. The bear seemed to be fighting against something, Alec realized. And he was sure it had something to do with that magical headband.

Alec smirked. Maybe, just maybe, Alec had found a weakness in the bear mob after all. He would have to thank LadyV for her advice later. Alec got into a fighting stance and prepared to move in to attack, his sword held out before him in a two-handed grip.

Meanwhile, LadyV was engaged in Ghostly Duels with the player killers: Catara, Smoker, and Kiba.

"I summon thee, Noppera-bo!" LadyV cried as she raised her hand and on it a green colored stone on her control ring glowed brightly. A flash of green light seemed to come out of her control ring and then a Battle Ghost materialized next to her. The Battle Ghost resembled a woman with extremely long hair that went down to her toes, but her face was completely blank, featureless, and its surface was as white and smooth as an egg. She was wearing a flowing, black kimono with sleeves that touched the ground. There was a white *obi* sash tied about her waist and the ends of the sash seemed to float behind her in the air eerily. "Attack their ghosts, Noppera-bo! Use Virus Delete Attack!"

Catara was moving in for the kill and LadyV had to block her sharp claws with the blade of her *naginata*. Catara jumped backwards to put some distance between LadyV again when Smoker moved in for his attack next and flung several deadly *shuriken* at LadyV. LadyV raised her *naginata* and spun it rapidly so that the *shuriken* were blocked and ricocheted off into the air. Kiba was merely standing near by and healing Smoker and Catara as they fought the Game Idol.

Catara's attention however was turned to her Nekomata Ghost. The Noppera-bo Ghost had shot her sleeve forward, and it seemed to lengthen and become longer almost as if the threads of the material were alive and then the sleeve attached and covered Nekomata's face. The Nekomata Ghost tried to take the sleeve off of her face but when she finally managed to do so Catara screamed - the face of Nekomata had been completely erased. "Ack! What's going on?" Catara cried in confusion, "That's *not* a normal game attack. What have you done to my precious Battle Ghost?"

The Noppera-bo Ghost had already set her sights on Kiba's Ookami Ghost next and stretched out her sleeves towards Ookami's face and latched onto it. Noppera-bo pulled her sleeves away to reveal that she had also erased the face of the Ookami Ghost.

"That Battle Ghost...isn't normal!" Kiba declared backing away from LadyV in fear.

"Darn it! Come back, Enenra!" Smoker commanded his Battle Ghost so that he returned safely to Smoker's control ring.

LadyV smiled a mischievous smile as she turned to face the frightened player killers. "And now it's your turn to get a little taste of your own medicine. Noppera-bo! Go get them!" LadyV's Battle Ghost floated towards the player killers now, ready to attack, and was raising her sleeves in a slow, creepy manner -

Noppera-bo's sleeves then shot forward, zooming through the air, and latched onto Catara and Smoker's faces before they could even blink. The players cried out as their faces were erased. Noppera-bo then dropped her sleeves to reveal that the PC bodies of Catara and Smoker were now faceless.

The frightened player killers reached up to touch their featureless faces and began to stumble around the forest panicking.

"No! Stay away!" Kiba yelled as he was targeted next. Noppera-bo shot out her sleeve though and it attached to Kiba's face and slowly began to erase his face as well.

The screams of his fellow guild members caught RedAki's attention and he turned towards them. He watched in shock as LadyV cried out 'Virus Delete Attack!' and he watched as the face of Kiba's PC body was completely erased. RedAki's eyes narrowed dangerously since that was *not* a normal game attack, which could only mean one thing - LadyV was a hacker.

RedAki clenched his hands around his sword so tightly that his knuckles turned white - he hated hackers. He knew that name had sounded familiar. How could he have forgotten? She was none other than the infamous, cyberhacker Lady Virus. "How could I be so stupid...dang it! She's Lady Virus! My guild mates don't stand a chance against her! What have I done?"

RedAki turned around to face LadyV, pointing his sword towards her, "How dare you do that to my guild mates! You're Lady Virus aren't you? The cyberhacker! Darn you! I hate cowardly hackers like you!" RedAki moved in to attack her.

Alec couldn't believe his luck. With RedAki distracted he could now execute the attack move he had planned for the bear mob. Alec charged the bear mob, his sword raised and had to dodge one of its swiping paw attacks. He then waited for the bear mob to lower its head as it snapped its jaws towards Alec. Alec gulped. *It's just a game. Now!* Alec leapt upwards into the air and brought his starter sword down hard onto the red jewel in the center of the golden headband that was on the bear mob's head. The bear cried out in pain and Alec's starter sword shattered. The bear mob swiped his paw at Alec in one final attack and Alec was thrown painfully backwards.

Alec fell hard but quickly pushed himself up off the ground and watched as the gem in the center of the headband cracked. And then suddenly an evil spirit floated out of the bear mob's body. This evil spirit was more human in appearance than the other evil spirits had been, however, its whole body was made of nothing but black shadow. Alec could see the ghost was wearing a kimono and was holding two war fans in each of its hands. It began to make it's way slowly towards Alec, its fans raised.

"I did it! Uh oh..."Alec began to back away as the ghostly figure approached him. "Epp!" He didn't even have a sword!

The bear mob, now that it was no longer possessed, began to return to normal. It's black coat turned to a warm, chocolate brown and its eyes returned to gold. As soon as this happened the bear went over to the cage that held Kintaro trapped and with a wave of its claws it freed Kintaro.

The ghost of what Alec decided looked like some kind of evil mage was almost upon the weaponless Alec when suddenly someone stood in its path. Alec looked up surprised to see Kintaro, who was wielding a giant axe before him. Kintaro looked back at Alec and grinned cheekily before rushing forward to attack the evil mage ghost.

Meanwhile, LadyV smiled unconcernedly as RedAki rushed towards her in attack, his Oni Ghost by his side. "Noppera-bo! Go get his ghost!" She commanded and watched as her Battle Ghost moved into attack. LadyV raised her *naginata* just in time to block a harsh downwards slash from RedAki.

"Hey, you're pretty cute." LadyV noticed as she looked RedAki over, "It's a shame bad boys aren't really my thing."

RedAki brought back his sword and tried to attack her again, but his attack was easily blocked. "Keh, flattery will get you nowhere, LadyV. I'll show you no mercy. Darn you hackers and your cheap tricks - for once I'd like you guys to fight fair!"

RedAki turned to see how his Oni Ghost was faring and his eyes widened in shock when he saw that Oni's face had been erased and he was now walking around blindly, waving his iron club haphazardly in the air before him. "Darn it!"

LadyV smiled mercilessly. "Now it's your turn I'm afraid. Noppera-bo get this little player killer. Now." Her Noppera-bo Ghost floated towards RedAki next and RedAki fearfully raised his sword to try and block her attack. Noppera-bo shot her sleeves towards RedAki and he slashed his sword at the sleeves but the sleeves wrapped themselves around RedAki's sword and yanked his sword away from him.

RedAki backed up as Noppera-bo was floating towards him. "Oh man, today is *so* not my day. I should have just stayed in bed." RedAki flinched as the Noppera-bo latched onto his face with her sleeve. In a matter of seconds she had erased the face from RedAki's PC body. The sleeves pulled back to reveal the smooth, egg-like surface that had become RedAki's face. RedAki unable to see, sunk to his knees in defeat and hung his head.

Meanwhile, Kintaro was still battling the evil mage ghost.

"Alec here!" Keiichi threw his monk staff at Alec.

"Thanks." Alec smiled as he ran off to help Kintaro. The evil mage ghost spun and attacked with his two fans in his hands in a deadly dance. Alec and Kintaro fought against the mage, their weapons clashing with the mage's fans, but together Alec and Kintaro managed to exorcize the mage ghost. The ghost cried out in pain before disappearing. As soon as the evil mage ghost was destroyed the entire forest began to change and the trees began to transform into beautiful, cherry blossom trees that were very much alive compared to their former dead state.

Slowly the branches regrew themselves and the trees began to fill with lush, green leaves, and then buds began to form on the branches. Alec watched in awe as suddenly all the buds opened up on the cherry blossom trees so that the entire forest was filled with the beautiful pink and white flowers. A harsh, magical wind blew through the forest as the curse was lifting and it began to carry cherry blossom petals through the air so that they swirled around Alec and the others, who gaped openmouthed at the beauty of it.

The curse of the forest had been lifted.

"We did it!" Keiichi cried out happily.

Yama-ube suddenly popped into existence in front of Alec and the others. "Well done, Dranarch, you saved my son, the forest creatures, and have removed the curse that has been plaguing this forest by defeating the mage, who had it under his evil enchantments. The same evil mage, which had possessed my son's friend, Mr. Bear. Mr. Bear was also a victim you see and as you can see they're very happy to be reunited." Alec looked over to where Kintaro was patting his bear's head affectionately. "I am pleased to inform you that you and your party have cleared the game event. You and your party shall be rewarded, Dranarch. Now, come and receive your rewards."

"Alright!" Alec smiled to himself as he walked up to Yama-ube and watched as she pulled out his new *Shinigami* sword from out of her crystal ball. She reached the sword out for Alec to take and he did so.

Keiichi walked up to her next and she pulled out a new monk staff from within her crystal ball and handed it to the healing monk. Lastly, LadyV was gifted with a new and improved *naginata* weapon.

Alec was all smiles until he noticed what had happened to the player killers and RedAki - the smile falling off his face.

Catara, Smoker and Kiba were still walking around disoriented and afraid. Catara and Kiba ran into each other stumbling backwards while Smoker ran straight into a tree. *Ow.* Meanwhile, RedAki was still kneeling on the ground with his head hanging down, a defeated aura around him. Alec noticed their erased faces, and remembered vaguely hearing something about a 'Virus Delete Attack' and RedAki accusing LadyV of being a hacker. Was what happened to them not normal? Was LadyV really this hacker named Lady Virus?

Alec frowned and decided to confront LadyV. "LadyV, thank you for helping us and everything but...um..are you by any chance a hacker? RedAki called you LadyVirus."

LadyV turned with a bright smile towards Alec. "Yes, that's right."

"So then...you cheated." Alec's frown deepened, "And what about what you did to them? Is it really alright to leave them like that...shouldn't you put them back to normal? It could be dangerous for them to remain that way if what you did isn't allowed within the normal game parameters."

LadyV's brows rose in surprise before a smile once again tugged at her lips and she approached Alec swaying her hips. She cupped his face with her hand and leaned down towards him. "You really are a kind boy, Alec-*kun*. That's exactly what I like about you."

All the anger seemed to drain out of Alec and he blushed as LadyV continued to bring her face closer to Alec's.

At that exact moment two players teleported to the forest. It was Junpei and Neji. Neji had used his hacker skills to directly teleport them to the end of the game event's final area. Junpei and Neji turned around and quickly caught sight of Alec.

"Hey Alec!" Neji called over to him.

"Hey, Alec who's-" Junpei was questioning when his eyes widened in shock.

The beautiful player and Game Idol LadyV had pressed her lips against Alec's in a kiss. Alec's eyes widened in shock before his eyes turned all swirly and he fell backwards in a faint once LadyV had released him.

Girl overload. Error...error...

LadyV licked her lips, cat-like. "What a cutie! And don't worry about those player killers Alec, System Admin will set them right when they come down here. You really are such a kind boy to worry about your enemies like that. Oh dear, just look at the time. I have to get going. But I'll be sure to catch you later, Alec-*kun*! Since you really are quite entertaining. *Ja-ne*! Bu-bye!" LadyV raised her hand and suddenly teleported away.

Junpei was slack jawed. "Just who was that total babe? And why did she kiss Alec!"

"That was LadyV," Neji informed him shortly, "She's a Game Idol."

"A Game Idol huh?" Junpei's eyes sparkled before turning into two large hearts, "Strike! I think I'm in love, Neji. Aw man, Alec's so lucky." Junpei pouted as he got a far off look in his eyes as he thought about LadyV.

"Yea..." Neji agreed somewhat sadly. "He is."

"Hey *Nii-san*...are you alright?" Keiichi was poking the still passed out and swirly-eyed Alec in the arm.

If Alec had known that things were only going to get even more crazy in Yokai World from here on, he may have stopped playing the game...

But this was only the beginning.

Chapter 7:
THE KNIGHT AND THE GHOST LADY

Alec *needed* a bath. He knew the middle school boys had their very own bath house and was currently looking for it. It was a Japanese thing - 'communal bathing'. Alec shrugged, he wasn't really comfortable with the idea having been raised in America and all, but decided to try and take a bath anyways deciding as long as he went extremely early in the morning he wasn't likely to run into anyone else. The only problem was the campus of Izanagi Academy was *huge*. Alec already had the tendency to get lost so the Academy seemed like a maze to him. Luckily, a fellow student caught sight of Alec as he was beginning to wonder where the heck he was.

"Yo. You're Alec Suzuki aren't you?" A boy wearing a baseball cap pulled down so that it shadowed half of his face and eyes approached him.

"Um, yea...do I know you?" Alec quirked his head at the boy. He seemed oddly familiar...

"No, but a lot of students know who you are - the American boy exorcist and 'Ghost Magnet'. Anyways, you look lost perhaps I could be of some assistance?" The boy offered.

Alec let out a sigh of relief. "Um, yea, that'd be great actually. I'm looking for the bath house."

"Ah, it's that building right over there." The boy smiled pointing off to the building just behind him.

"Oh great. Thanks." Alec bowed, and then took off towards the bath house. Alec looked back at the boy, who seemed to have an amused smirk on his face. Alec shook his head. *Naw...*He was probably just imagining things or being paranoid, Alec decided. Alec entered the bath house and his breath was taken away. The place was huge. There were several large swimming pools filled with hot, scented bath water. And Alec could see the steam coming off the water.

In a Japanese *onsen* or bath house it was customary to wash and scrub one's body and rinse it off with buckets of hot water *before* actually getting into the baths. So Alec went about soaping himself down and then pouring buckets of water over himself before stepping into the soothing, hot waters of the *onsen* - after of course wrapping a small towel around his waist. Alec wasn't quite Japanese enough to be comfortable with being naked in an open, public bath just yet.

Alec let himself sink down into the steaming, hot water with a blissful sigh. The water felt so nice and relaxing. His thoughts began wandering back to how that artsy-girl Rika had kissed him in thanks for saving her life back in the nurse's office. Of course, he didn't really remember what happened after that...and then he couldn't help but remember how the mysterious LadyV, Yokai World's #1 Game Idol, had stolen his second kiss while saying that Alec was a kind boy. Alec realized slightly unsettled that he couldn't really remember what had happened after that either...

Rika and LadyV were two girls that were very different. And yet...Alec couldn't help but think there was something oddly *similar* about the two of them. Although he couldn't quite put his finger on it. It was just a gut feeling. Alec was blushing as he raised his fingers to his lips pensively wondering what the connection between the two girls and the two very different kisses could be. One kiss had been slightly shy and hesitant while the other kiss had been wet and passionate. Was it just him or was the water getting hotter? Alec wondered, shifting uncomfortably in the water.

Then just as Alec was beginning to doze off he heard voices coming towards the baths - and they weren't boys' voices. Alec stiffened and paled. *Uh oh.* They were distinctively higher pitched and squeakier which could only mean they were - *gulp* - girls' voices! Alec's eyes widened in shock. *Girls!* A flash of memory crossed his mind as Alec remembered the amused smirk that boy, who had given him directions to the bath house, had. He had been tricked, Alec realized. *Epp!* The girls were *so* going to kill him thinking he was some kind of pervert or something - he was just sure of it! The hairs on the back of his neck prickled in warning.

There was only one thing he could think to do - hide. As soon as the girls walked into the bathing room Alec took a deep breath, held it, and went under water. He had to try and hold his breath for as long as possible. He had to buy some time while he thought of a plan on how to get himself out of this mess, to escape...

Vaguely Alec realized that he *had* noticed that the tiles and bathing accessories had been a bit *pink* in this bath house. *Oh man! I'm so screwed!*

While Alec was holding his breath underwater the girls were all helping to wash each other's backs, soaping themselves, and then rinsing themselves off before they got ready to enter the bath...the bath which Alec was currently in. Some of the girls wrapped towels around their torsos as they entered the warm, inviting waters.

Alec was beginning to turn blue. *I can't hold it much longer! Oh no!* Alec cried out in his mind as he was suddenly forced to come up out of the water, spluttering and gasping for breath.

All of the girls in the *onsen* turned to look at Alec's sudden appearance in wide-eyed surprise.

Alec flinched his eyes shut. *Here it comes. I'm done for...*He thought. He knew this was the point where all the girls would yell: 'AHHHHH! Pervert! There's a boy in the baths! Get him!' Yep, Alec had watched enough Japanese animation to know just what kind of a reaction to expect when a boy accidently or not so accidently ended up in a girl's *onsen*. Soon they'd be yelling and throwing the water buckets or soap bars in his direction as he ran for his life, while clutching his tiny towel around his waist. Yep, any second now, that was going to happen. Alec's life was flashing before his eyes when -

A squeal of delight suddenly rang up from the group of girls. *Huh? Squeal of delight?*

Alec risked opening one of his eyes to see what the heck was going on.

"Eeee! It's Alec Suzuki!" "Oh, is that really Alec?" "It is him look!" "Lucky!"

Alec opened his other eye and blinked at them in confusion. "Huh?" He couldn't help but quirk his head at them.

The scantily clad, middle school girls all began to crowd around Alec getting far too close to his 'personal bubble' Alec decided. Alec gulped as his face was mere inches away from one girl's cleavage. The girls were all wearing nothing but small, tightly wrapped, towels around their torsos, which revealed a lot of cleavage. Alec was surprised that for middle school girls a lot of them were pretty developed. Alec blushed, thinking of Neji's posters. This was all a bit too much for Alec to handle. And he was beginning to get a nose bleed...

"Alec, is it true that you risked your life to save Rika up on the front steps?" One girl ventured to ask.

All the girls looked at Alec expectantly and seemingly with baited breath.

Alec scratched the back of his neck nervously. Was that what this was all about? "Well, um...yea, I guess so."

"And is it true that you shielded her body with your own and got a nasty head injury, which Haruna-*sensei* had to heal for you? And that you nearly died?" Another girl wanted to confirm.

"Well, yea. It's really no big deal though-" Alec was saying.

But the girls cut Alec off before he could explain:

"Eeeee!!!" *Kawaii*! He's so cute!" "He's so brave!" "No, he's heroic!" "Our little hero!" "Hey Alec, let me help you wash your back? *Neh*?" "No way, I'm going to help Alec wash his back!" "No I am!" "No it's going to be me!"

Two girls each grabbed one of Alec's arms and began to play tug of war with him. Alec's eyes were beginning to get all swirly as the girls all began to treat him like a rag doll. "Can I please just wake up now...?" Alec muttered to himself as he was suddenly let go and flung into one of the girls so that his face was unexpectedly buried in her cleavage.

Alec's eyes bulged out of his head and he had 'girl overload' promptly passing out. After that the girls had fun washing Alec's back for him, shampooing his hair and tying it up in pink bows while he was unconscious before they got bored. Once they had finished their own baths they simply left the *onsen* and left Alec floating unconscious in the *onsen* forgotten. Opps. That's how Rika, who had come into the baths late, found poor Alec - floating face up in the water, swirly-eyed, and with his towel barely in place.

"Oh my god! Alec-*kun*!" Rika quickly dove into the *onsen* and rescued Alec out of it. She set him down on the pink tiled floor and leaned over him expectantly. "Alec...Alec! Oh no, he's not breathing...that means...CPR?" Rika's face turned bright red at the thought of what she was about to do. "Forgive me Alec-*kun*..." She whispered before lowering her head and pressing her lips up against his so she could blow air into his lungs.

Alec's eyes slowly came open and he looked up to see Rika's face mere inches from his own. *Girl overload...error...error...* And he promptly passed out. Again.

Rika looked relieved when she saw Alec awaken but then her expression turned to concern when he simply passed out again. "Alec? *Mou*! Geez!" Rika quirked her head down at him confused. "Boys..."

• • • • • • • • • • • • • •

Luckily, Alec managed to make it to home room on time and without further mishap. *Seriously*, he thought, *this school is going to be detrimental to my health.* He sighed and took his seat next to Neji and noticed for the first time that Rika was there too seated at a desk in the far back of the classroom. He gulped nervously and she looked up to meet his eyes. Then they both looked away from each other blushing. Junpei whose seat was behind Alec's watched this exchange with interest

A wolfish smirk forming on his face. "Hey Alec, is there something going on between you two? Hmm?" Junpei propped his chin in his hands and he leaned over to hear Alec's answer.

Alec waved his hands frantically before him. "N-no!"

"Really?" Junpei didn't look too convinced.

Neji frowned and was oddly silent about the whole thing.

"Well, I must say Alec you have odd taste. There are plenty of *normal* girls you could try going out with instead-" Junpei was saying before he was suddenly hit in the back of the head with a heavy text book. "OW!"

Alec looked behind him at Rika, who was wearing an innocent expression on her face. Although Alec noticed the slight smirk tugging on her lips. Alec shook his head. *Girls are scary...*

Junpei was rubbing the back of his head confusedly, where a *huge* bump had formed, and looking around wondering who threw the book at him.

Alec began to overhear some of his fellow classmates talking about Yokai World:

"The Kintoki Forest Game Event on Saturday was pretty cool..." "Yea, except for when the Renegade Reapers showed up. That totally sucked man - they ended up PKing everyone in my party before we could get a chance to fight the boss monster." "So did the RRs win then?" "Actually I heard some noob player named Dranarch won the event." "Really? Anyone know who Dranarch is?" The boy looked around the classroom curiously.

Neji and Junpei both looked at Alec, who looked back at them and put a finger to his lips and 'shhhed'. Alec shook his head frantically at Junpei especially when he noticed how Junpei's smile widened.

"It was Alec-*kun*." Junpei informed them nonchalant.

Alec frowned, "Junpei!" Alec *hated* being in the limelight.

The boys in the class were surprised: "*Uso*! No way!" "*Saiko*! That's so cool!" "Congratulations Alec!"

Alec blushed, feeling awkward and not used to praise. "It's nothing...I wouldn't have won if LadyV hadn't shown up and helped us."

The boys got even more starry-eyed at this news. "So it's true then? LadyV did show up during the game event! I'm like her biggest fan!" "Me too! Me too!" "Oh man, what I wouldn't give to get LadyV's autograph - you're so lucky Alec!" "Yea, LadyV is like so hot...she's definitely the hottest player in the game."

"What about Midoriko?" Another boy pipped up suddenly.

"Who?" Alec asked.

"You know, the mysterious ghost lady, who haunts the game." One boy informed him.

"That's just an urban legend though...a real ghost can't actually be haunting Yokai World. That would be impossible." Another boy said.

Alec's interest was piqued. "A real ghost?" He turned to Neji for confirmation.

Neji nodded and pushed his glasses up his nose. "Midoriko is an urban legend of the game Yokai World. She's supposedly this beautiful ghost lady, who haunts the game while in search of her long lost daughter, who apparently used to play the game too. They say her daughter died or something while playing the game and that her daughter's mind and spirit never left - trapped in the game."

"But I heard a rumor recently that she's not just looking for her daughter. A few days ago a player came into contact with her and they said she was asking them if they've seen or found someone called the *Guardian*." A boy pipped up.

"The Guardian?" Everyone seemed intrigued by this.

The boy nodded simply.

"But how do you know she's not just a NPC or a Battle Ghost?" Alec pressed.

"Well, for one thing she's a ghost that can *talk* and there are no ghosts in the game that have this ability. As advanced as the AI Battle Ghosts are in the game none of them can talk, none of them have emotions, or free will. They just follow their programs." Neji explained.

For some reason, Alec thought back to the Monkey King ghost and the sad expression it had on its face when it was trapped behind those bars...

Alec shook his head.

"They're just AI programs." Neji continued, a glint in his eye. "Midoriko is different in that she actually speaks to players individually and about different things. She's even been known to give people advice, foretell their future, or gift players with special items that don't normally exist in the game. Also, apparently she can bend the rules of the game. Just like how she can create game items that aren't supposed to exist."

"I wonder if she really exists..." Alec tapped his chin thoughtfully. "Trapped in the game then. If she does, maybe I can help her."

Junpei snorted. "Alec, she's just an urban legend. She's can possibly be real."

Alec pouted somewhat miffed but kept quiet. A ghost...trapped in the game due to her unfinished business no doubt. How sad. Alec thought, he was determined to help her if she turned out to be real...

"There's going to be another game event this weekend. I hear this time the prize is a really special AI Battle Ghost. One that can talk. Funny, how we were just talking about that." Neji informed everyone. "I think it's fascinating.

I'd love to be able to do a total data analysis on its program if I managed to win it."

"Is that really safe though? Creating an AI Battle Ghost that advanced? What if it develops a will of it's own or something and decides to like take over the game?" Alec questioned worriedly, a serious expression on his face.

Neji, Junpei, and the other boys burst out laughing causing Alec to blush in embarrassment. "Alec, buddy," Junpei wrapped an arm around his shoulders, "I think you've watched the *Matrix* one too many times."

An advanced, AI Battle Ghost...with enough intelligence to be able to talk. *It would be like getting to have your very own robot companion but since it's a part of a virtual world I guess it'd be more like getting to have your own personal hologram. Man, that is so cool.* Alec couldn't help but thinking. What young boy hadn't wished upon a star to get their very own robot buddy at one point in their life after all?

"A lot of people are going to enter to try and get their hands on that new ghost. You can bet our friend RedAki will be entering as well." Neji frowned pensively.

"Will you guys be able to play this weekend?" Alec looked at the two boys, a hopeful expression on his face.

Junpei and Neji both looked repentant. "Sorry Alec, I can't. There's another *anime* convention I plan on going to with some fellow *otaku*. You can come with us if you want." Neji explained looking guilty.

"And I have another soccer game - you're welcome to come root for me though." Junpei offered with a warm smile.

Alec's shoulders slumped, feeling defeated. He then turned to Rika at the back of the class. "What about you Rika?"

Rika shook her head so that her short bob moved back and forth, "Sorry Alec but I'm also going to be busy again this weekend. There's an art show competition at this gallery that I'm going to be entering some of my work in. I hope you understand."

Alec nodded understandingly. He didn't really know what he had been expecting - to feel so disappointed. His 'friends' (which he wasn't supposed to have in the first place) all had their own lives in reality whereas Alec did not. Yokai World was his life. His escape from the reality of his real life of being a boy exorcist that he didn't want to face or accept.

Junpei noticed Alec's crestfallen expression and put a hand on his shoulder. "Don't let us stop you from playing Alec. Maybe if you're lucky LadyV will show up and help you again." Junpei finished with a wink.

"Yea, maybe..." But Alec was doubtful the famous Game Idol would waste her time helping someone as low level as him again. There would be no reason to after all.

"Actually, I happen to know LadyV since we're both fellow hackers, and I know for a fact she won't be able to get online this weekend either." Neji informed them suddenly.

"Oh well...that's ok then." Alec tried to hide his disappointment. "I'll just play on my own and see what happens. It's no big deal." Alec waved their worries aside. Though his friends were still looking a bit worried and guilty despite Alec's continued reassurances.

Alec was still stubbornly refusing to join the soccer club or computer club (officially) since he didn't want to get closer to Junpei or Neji since they'd only be put in danger because of him if they became better friends. But at least he had Yokai World right? Alec sighed. He couldn't help but feel that his 'friends' were letting him down. But at the same time he couldn't help but feel excited by the chance of getting a powerful, one of a kind, advanced AI Battle Ghost that could talk.

So despite the fact that his 'friends' wouldn't be joining him Alec didn't let it get to him too much and counted down the days impatiently until the game event. He only logged on to Yokai World to do simple leveling up for his PC during the week but didn't go on any quests and didn't party up with anyone.

Finally, the weekend had arrived. Alec logged on to Yokai World and immediately materialized to the start town. In the center of town was a giant, floating, message board that contained the needed information about the current game event, which was called the 'Dragon Prince Game Event'. Not much information was revealed except the prize and the location where Alec needed to go to start the event - the newly created 'Palace of the Dragon or Ryugu-jo Area'. Where he would have to go and speak with a NPC named Taro and the Emperor of the Sea there to enter himself in the game event.

Alec recognized the name of the palace and realized the game event had to be loosely based on the Japanese legend of Urashima Taro. He remembered that his father had once told him the tale as a bedtime story...

FLASHBACK

Alec had been tucked into bed for the night but still wasn't sleepy. "Daddy, can't you please tell me a bedtime story? One of those weird Japanese ones? *Please*." Alec gave his father his best puppy-dog eyes.

Mori chuckled good-naturedly and relented. "Alright then. Just the one. Once upon a time, there was a kindhearted fisherman named Urashima Taro. One day Taro came across some children who were bullying a small turtle."

A six-year-old Alec pouted as he interrupted his father, "I hate bullies."

"That's good, son. Bullies forget that the people they bully have feelings too. And it's not right to hurt other people's feelings. Taro felt the same way, so feeling sorry for the turtle he decided to save it from the children and put it back in the sea. A few days later, a large sea turtle, which could speak, came to Taro and told him the small turtle he had saved had actually been the daughter of the Emperor of the Sea. And that the emperor wished to see Taro to thank him. The turtle magically gave Taro gills and riding on the back of the turtle Taro was taken to the underwater Palace of the Dragon. The palace was quite large and made entirely of bits of sparkling coral and shells of many different colors.

"Taro was then brought before the Emperor of the Sea and standing next to him was the turtle he had saved, which was now a beautiful princess. The emperor thanked Taro and the eyes of the princess and Taro met. It was love at first sight. Taro spent the next few days along side of the princess, spending each day quite happily, and he vowed he would marry her. However, he wished to go back to his village and ask for his ailing mother's blessing. The princess was sad to see him go and made him promise to return to her. Before Taro left the princess gave him a special box which she instructed him never to open.

"Taro was confused by this but didn't question the princess. Taro was taken back to the surface by the giant sea turtle. Taro went back to his village but everything seemed changed and his mother was no where to be found. He asked some local fisherman if they knew of Urashima Taro and they explained that he had been a fisherman, who supposedly disappeared some 300 years ago. Taro was in shock that only a few days seemed to have passed at the Palace of the Dragon when apparently back on the surface hundreds of years had passed. In his grief he absentmindedly opened the magic box. Suddenly, Taro's hair grew long and white, his skin wrinkled, and his back bent.

"The princess came out of the sea and told Taro sadly that inside the box had been his age. However, so that Taro could once again go to the palace with her she turned him into a crane and gave him a magic pill to swallow so that he could breath underwater while even in the form of a bird. In this way, trapped in another form, he was able to stay by his beloved princess' side." Mori finished with a smile.

Alec frowned, "He should have listened to the princess' warning. That was silly."

"You're right." Mori nodded. "A lot of people have a hard time listening to other people's advice and usually end up having to learn things the hard way. Sometimes you just have to believe in people, Alec. It can sometimes save you from a whole lot of trouble."

"Believe in people?" Alec said sleepily as he yawned, "Like I believe in you, Dad?"

Mori didn't respond but patted Alec's head affectionately before standing up to leave. "Good night son." He said somewhat sadly as he walked towards the door to Alec's room and left closing the door behind him.

"Night Dad." Alec whispered before falling asleep.

END OF FLASHBACK

Dad...He had believed in his father - a father who had abandoned him in this very strange school. Alec shook his head of such thoughts. He quickly walked over to the nearest teleportation gate and raised his fist preparing to teleport.

"Palace of the Dragon!" He cried.

Alec was immediately teleported to a sandy beach where there were several large sea turtles lined up all the way down the beach. Alec watched as other players were getting onto the turtle's backs and letting them head towards the sea - probably to take them to the underwater palace. Alec's eyes widened. It was quite an interesting sight. And there were a lot of players entering this game event apparently. As Alec approached one of the giant sea turtles he was briefly reminded of how he was forced to ride a sparrow to get to the Fairy Palace. There was a special type of harness on the turtle and Alec used this to pull himself up and onto the turtle's back.

Once he was securely on the turtle it turned towards the ocean and began to make its way into the water. Alec was going to hold his breath but once again belatedly remembered he was in a virtual reality world. The sea turtle took Alec down underneath the water and then swam deeper under the ocean's surface. The water was crystal clear and the sights Alec was seeing were breathtaking - there were brightly colored fish, sea horses, sunfish, starfish, shimmering coral reefs, friendly dolphins, and deep ravines that seemed endless as Alec looked down into them. The dolphins playfully swam circles around Alec as he and his sea turtle continued their way towards the palace.

And then Alec saw it up ahead - The Palace of the Dragon. It was just how Alec had imagined it when his father had told him that bedtime story - a palace under the sea made out of brightly colored pieces of coral and sparkling shells in pinks, blues, and yellows. The turtle swam up to the entrance and Alec saw that there were several other players dismounting from their own turtles and entering the palace through the giant entranceway.

Alec made his way inside through the main entranceway and walked down a long, high-ceilinged hallway. At the end of the hallway he was met with a set of two, large coral doors. Alec pushed on the doors and found himself inside the throne room. There seated in the high-backed throne towards the back of the room was the NPC of the Emperor of the Sea. He was an aged, old man with flowing robes of blue, white and silver, which seemed to move and float in the artificial water around them. He had bright, gray-blue eyes, a long, white beard, pointed ears, and a dotting of blue and green scales on his face. Next to him was another NPC that looked like an average human man wearing a simple kimono. Alec guessed him to be Taro.

"Dranarch," the emperor addressed Alec, his voice booming, "What has brought you here to my domain?"

Alec bowed, "I heard you were in the need of some assistance, Emperor."

The emperor stroked his beard, "Indeed I do, my daughter has been kidnaped by the evil Water Dragon Prince, Ryuu, and has been taken to his palace where he plans to marry her against her will."

Alec's eyes widened. "That's awful."

Taro stepped forward and began to speak. "I would gladly risk life and limb to rescue my beloved princess but unfortunately I cannot leave the palace - the enchantment here is the only thing keeping me young. If I step foot outside of this palace my true age will return and I shall die. So even though I want nothing more than to go to her side I cannot..." Taro looked imploringly at Alec. "Dranarch, I beg for your help. Please, won't you save her?"

"Dranarch, if you agree to save my daughter and succeed in this quest you shall of course be handsomely rewarded. So, do you accept this quest?" The emperor asked.

Alec nodded solemnly, "Yes, I do."

The emperor and Taro both smiled. "Good, Dranarch you have been successfully entered into the 'Dragon Prince Game Event'. The sea turtle you rode here shall take you to Ryuu's palace. Be careful for the way before you is perilous and fraught with dangers. Ryuu has summoned many *shikigami* (controlled spirits) of the sea to stop those trying to get to his palace. Good luck."

Alec bowed, "I shall do my best."

Alec left the Palace of the Dragon and mounted his sea turtle before they swam off now in the direction of Ryuu's palace. Slowly, the sea's appearance became less inviting as the sun seemed to be blocked out from shining down into the waters due to the narrow, rocky crevices Alec and his turtle were forced to swim through. Alec noticed below them that they seemed to be passing over what could only have been called a 'fish graveyard'. The sandy ocean bottom was littered with the bones of fish and some of the skeletons were so huge Alec knew they were of whales. Alec shivered, a chill going down his spine as he looked down at the bones.

And then the *shikigami* began to appear. The *shikigami* were ghostly sea monsters - jellyfish, eels, sharks, sting rays, and squids. They all had translucent, see-through, shimmering bodies, which like soapy bubbles had a rainbow prism of color to them. Some of the *shikigami* were just the bones of a fish that had been reanimated. The skeletal fish had long, razor sharp teeth and some had only one large glaring eye. Alec saw that all the creatures had glowing red eyes. Alec also noticed that most of the ghostly fish had *o-fuda* stuck somewhere on their bodies - either their chest or foreheads. *Strange.* Alec thought.

But Alec didn't have much time to muse on this oddity however as several giant jellyfish began to swarm around him. A jellyfish that was glowing with a yellowish light reached out its tentacles to suddenly wrap them around Alec's *Shinigami* sword. It began to tug at Alec's sword, trying to steal it away. Alec struggled with the jellyfish and as he was doing this another jellyfish was sneaking up on him from behind. Unexpectedly, this jellyfish wrapped its tentacles around Alec's torso and sent a nasty, electric shock through Alec's body. Alec cried out in pain and could see his *health* draining.

Alec activated his *Shinigami* sword and empowered it with energy before he sent an energy attack towards the jellyfish that still had a hold of his sword. He managed to slice through the jellyfish's tentacles and the jellyfish was forced to release him. Alec then waved his sword at the Jellyfish and unleashed an energy blast towards it so that the jellyfish was destroyed. Alec quickly used his free sword to slash and hack at the jellyfish that still had hold of his torso and finally managed to free himself. The jellyfish began to swim away from Alec but not fast enough as Alec lunged his sword forward and pierced the jellyfish's body and then unleashed another energy attack upon it so that it was blasted back and then blew up from the inside - pieces of gooey jellyfish flying everywhere. Alec was panting for breath after he had managed to defeat just two jellyfish. Alec quickly used a few potions to replenish his health. *That was a close one.* Alec frowned.

Alec had been leveling up during the week in his spare time but he was still no where near RedAki's level. Alec guided his sea turtle forward and they continued on their way. Up ahead, Alec suddenly caught sight of the Water Dragon Prince's undersea palace. It was made entirely out of pointy, spirals of black coral which shined with a silvery light as the sun's rays came through the water and hit its polished surface. However, in front of the palace was an army of ghostly *shikigami* and sea creatures lying in wait! Alec saw there were sharks, sting rays, eels, and squids.

All these creatures began to make a beeline towards Alec who squeaked at this with an - 'Epp!' And almost made his turtle turn around the other way to retreat. Alec shook his head and quickly pulled himself together, his eyes taking on a steely gleam. He then charged forward on his sea turtle prepared to exorcize the ghostly fish. The mobs were more powerful now and Alec was having a much harder time slaying them.

Then as they passed over a sunken ship several sharks that had been hiding inside suddenly swarmed out upon Alec. One shark swam straight for

Alec and he quickly raised his sword and managed to slice it in two. At the same time however an eel had decided to attack Alec and managed to wrap its tail around Alec's sword arm. Alec swore at himself that he had managed to get in that type of trouble again. At the same time another eel grabbed onto Alec's other arm. It seemed to Alec that the fish were planning something... and whatever it was couldn't be good.

Alec looked up and saw that a giant stingray was swimming towards him and suddenly had its barbed tail pointed in Alec's direction, aimed at his heart. The tip of the stingray's tail sparked with electricity. Alec gulped. *This doesn't look good.* And when Alec risked looking behind him he saw that a ghostly shark was ready to get him from behind. Outnumbered and cornered Alec knew he was done for.

Alec closed his eyes waiting for the sting of the stingray's tail or the cruel bite of the shark - both never came. Alec opened his eyes which widened as he saw a player riding on the back of a sea turtle by standing on it, with a gigantic sword in his hand and who was suddenly helping Alec out of his sticky situation by exorcizing the ghostly creatures that had Alec trapped.

Alec thought the player before him was one of the coolest PCs he had ever seen in the game before. He was of the *Shinigami* Class and dressed in the popular black *haori* and black *hakama*. There was a dark blue *obi* sash tied about his waist. He had this spiky, blue-black hair that went up in different directions but in a way that Alec decided looked 'cool' and not at all messy. Alec noticed he had deep, sapphire colored eyes, which were narrowed in a look of fierce concentration as he battled the mobs. In his hands he wielded the biggest *Shinigami* sword Alec had ever seen. It was at least four feet long (five including the hilt) and about a foot and a half wide. The entire blade was pitch black. *Can that really be a normal game weapon?* Alec wondered briefly. *I've never seen anything like it before.*

Alec watched with his mouth gaping open as the lone player easily slashed his sword through the stingray that had been about to get him and then turned to slice through the two eels, which had a hold of each of Alec's arms. He then sped past Alec, not missing a beat, and sliced through the shark that had been targeting Alec from behind - all of this happened in a matter of seconds.

All Alec could say was - "*Whoa.*"

The player guided his sea turtle to move him in front of Alec and in front of the huge army of ghostly creatures. He raised his control ring and summoned his Battle Ghost. "I summon you, Tengu!" From out of his ring came a small ball of light which quickly materialized into the player's Battle Ghost. It was a bird-like and half-human ghost with a man's body, a man's face except for his hawk-like beak, and intelligent golden eyes. It was also wearing a flowing, dark blue kimono. The Battle Ghost had a mop of messy black hair and ebony colored wings stretching out of its back and almost looking angelic Alec thought - however it also had the look of a fallen angel to it too.

"Tengu! Attack!" The player directed. "Use Lightning Attack!"

Tengu flew forward in the water and raised a long, golden staff with a golden ring on its end. A crackling aura of energy seemed to spiral up around the staff before Tengu waved his staff towards the army of ghostly sea creatures and unleashed a fierce lightning attack towards the creatures that were immediately caught in the electric attack and were shocked so fiercely they were immediately destroyed.

The player watched his Tengu begin to 'kick some serious butt' and smiled to himself before turning to Alec. "Hey kid, you okay?"

Alec looked back at the player a bit starry-eyed. *He totally just saved my life. He's so cool. He must be an upperclassman, at least 15.* "Yea, thanks a lot... um?"

"The name's Night. And you're...Dranarch?" Night checked Alec's PC data.

"Call me Alec." Alec smiled shyly back.

"Well then Alec, why don't you let me take care of these guys so you can go on ahead. The Dark Palace is just over there."

Alec furrowed his brow in concern. "And leave you here all by yourself?"

Night smirked and suddenly waved his gigantic *Shinigami* sword towards a group of at least a hundred ghostly sea monsters, which were suddenly obliterated by the huge energy blast that had shot out of his sword unexpectedly. "I think I can handle it."

"Wow." Alec's eyes were wide. "But why are you helping *me*?"

Night had a mysterious glint in his eye. "You better hurry Alec, you're no match for these monsters at your current level, now go!"

Alec hesitated before nodding, "Right."

Alec did as he was told and took off towards the palace slaying any ghostly monsters that came in his path. He looked behind his shoulder to see Night and his Battle Ghost making quick work of the ghostly sea creature army. Alec shook his head, that player was so powerful it was unbelievable. But then why was he helping Alec, a noob he didn't even know? It was strange to say the least and had Alec frowning deep in thought.

The sea turtle dropped Alec off in front of the palace and Alec quickly made his way inside. He ran down a hallway and opened the doors to the main throne room. As soon as he stepped inside Alec caught sight of RedAki, who was speaking with the NPC, the Water Dragon Prince, Ryuu. Ryuu had long, silky, black hair and piercing, emerald green eyes. As Alec looked at his face he noticed that he had pointed ears and a dotting of shimmering, silver scales on the sides of his face. Alec also noticed that he seemed to have a tail, which was swishing back and forth angrily behind him. In one hand he held a small turtle and in the other he held a small box.

"RedAki, you have two choices. You can fight me for the princess." Ryuu held out the turtle in his hand, "Or you can forget about the princess and I shall give you a rare treasure." Ryuu held out the small box in his hands. "If you chose the treasure you must take it and leave this place and forsake the princess and therefore fail in your quest. It is your choice, RedAki. Which do you chose?"

RedAki seemed a bit torn by this sudden offer. Alec eyed the box suspiciously since it reminded him of the old folktale and of what had happened to Taro, the hairs on the back of Alec's neck were also prickling in warning. "*Oi*! RedAki! Don't open that box!" Alec warned.

RedAki spun around to face Alec in surprise. "You again..." RedAki growled. "Why won't you just leave me alone! Or are you stalking me?" RedAki gave Alec a disgusted look.

Alec blushed. "I'm *not* stalking you, you weirdo! I'm on the quest to save the princess."

"I could care less about saving the princess, as long as I get some sort of treasure or rare item out of this thing." RedAki scoffed.

Alec had a worried expression on his face. "But what about Taro?"

RedAki laughed suddenly amused and ran a hand through his spiky red-tipped hair. "You're really getting into this roleplaying thing aren't you? You do realize this is a game right? Taro will be just fine without his princess."

Alec frowned, to him it wasn't just a game. And he was sure even if RedAki pretended he didn't care - that for RedAki this wasn't just a game either. "When I start something I intend to finish it. I gave Taro my word and even if this is a game I don't plan on breaking my promise - this place is real enough to me."

RedAki seemed stunned for a moment - a myriad of conflicting emotions crossing his face before it returned to a cool expression. "Is that so? Maybe we have more in common than I thought Dranarch but I still haven't forgiven you for making a fool out of me the last time! How can you hang around scum like those hackers anyways?"

Alec had the grace to look guilty as he looked over RedAki's face to make sure that all his features had returned to normal. "I'm glad the system administration was able to return your PC body back to normal. I was worried. Is your Battle Ghost okay too?"

RedAki sneered, "No thanks to you but yes my Battle Ghost Oni is back to normal as well. Anyways, as much as I'm enjoying this little chat of ours, I'm going to have to kill you now." RedAki shrugged at Alec's shocked expression. "Player Killer. It's what I do. You understand. And I'll be adding that nice, new sword of yours to my collection!" RedAki unsheathed his black *Shinigami* sword and got into a fighting stance.

Alec followed suit and unsheathed his own *Shinigami* sword and pointed it at RedAki. He eyed RedAki's black bladed sword and suddenly thought of something - *That guy Night had a black sword too...does that mean he's a player killer? No way! He seemed like such a nice guy...*

As Alec was distracted by such thoughts RedAki moved in for the kill. Alec barely managed to bring up his sword just in the nick of time when RedAki was already bringing his sword down upon him.

"Taking a nap?" RedAki sneered, "You should really try and pay more attention to someone who's trying to kill you!"

Alec was definitely paying attention now as RedAki swung his sword at him again. Alec just barely managing to block the fierce blow. Even with all his concentration Alec knew he was seconds away from losing. RedAki was just too good, too powerful, too much of a higher level. RedAki was pushing Alec back now as blow after blow rained down upon him and finally RedAki managed to disarm Alec, his sword flying out of his hands, and before Alec could even blink RedAki had rammed his sword through his torso. RedAki leaned in close to whisper in Alec's ear:

"I warned you to stop playing this game after you decided to make enemies of the RRs. But even then you continue to get in my way. As long as you continue to play this game I'm going to make your time here a living hell. It's the least I can do after you and your lot made fools out of us." RedAki smiled triumphantly and pulled his sword out of Alec's chest.

Alec fell forward and lay dying on the floor. He watched as RedAki walked over to pick up his fallen *Shinigami* sword. *Darn it!* He had worked hard to get that sword. Tears of frustration stung his eyes and he shut them tight as he felt he was close to dying. He knew that in a few seconds his PC body would be transformed into a PC Ghost body instead but...then there was this strange, tingling sensation in his body as his PC body was fading -

And then instead of being turned immediately into a PC Ghost body Alec found himself suddenly teleported somewhere. It was a strangely, dark place, literally pitch black. Alec couldn't see even an inch in front of him no matter how hard he squinted into the darkness. "Am I really dying?" Alec wondered in a sort of numb shock before he began to panic. "I don't want to die! Someone...please help me...!"

A tinkling voice rang through the air answering him. "Do not be afraid. Do not fear...you are not dying. You are safe. I brought you here simply because I wished to speak with you in private. I have been waiting for you... Guardian."

A ball of sparkling light suddenly appeared hovering before him and as the light intensified Alec was forced to shield his eyes that had just gotten used to the darkness. When he removed his hand and blinked a few times to adjust to the now semi-darkness he saw that a beautiful woman had materialized before him. But what freaked Alec out the most was that he could sense it - her presence. The spiritual being before him now was real. *She's a real ghost!*

The woman floating in the darkness before him was dressed in the robes of a *miko* - a white *haori* shirt and dark blue *hakama* pants. She had long, wavy, midnight black hair and deep blue colored eyes. There was a strange mark in the center of her forehead that looked like the tattoo of a third eye, and which had been inked in a dark purple.

"Who are you?" Alec's voice trembled, the hairs on the back of his neck were prickling.

"I am Midoriko." Alec recognized the name immediately as the ghost lady who was supposedly haunting the game world and looking for her daughter. Well, it looked like that urban legend was indeed true.

"You're...real." Alec breathed. "I've heard about you...you're searching for your missing daughter right? Is that your unfinished business? Because if it is maybe I can help you find her and then maybe you'll be able to crossover? I've helped other ghosts crossover before..." A sad expression crossed Alec's face as he remembered Billy.

"*Yasashi des neh?* You really are a kind boy Alec," Midoriko smiled warmly at him. "But for now I do not wish to crossover...and as for my daughter I actually already found her. But sadly she no longer remembers me anymore. She's lost her memory. Ever since then I've been searching for the only person who can help her - the Guardian. He is the one who is fated to protect my daughter and help her to fulfil her destiny. And you are the Guardian, Alec."

"*Me?* I'm the Guardian?" Alec squeaked.

Midoriko nodded. "Yes, I have foreseen it. You are the only one who can help my daughter stop a 'great evil' from being awakened and unleashed upon the world through means of this very game."

Alec's head was spinning. "A great evil? The game?...But it's not real right?"

Midoriko frowned. "Yokai World is no longer just a game. The players of Yokai World wished for this place to be real and so it has somehow become linked with the real land of *yokai* known as the *Makai*. There are now 'tears' all throughout Yokai World which lead to this true demon plane. Also, since the game world has become a bridge to the *Makai*, it has also become in a sense a bridge to reality. Now the demon and human worlds are dangerously coming closer together because of this. Yokai World has even become linked to *Yomi*, the land of the dead, also known as the underworld. The lines between the game, reality, and the spirit world...are blurring. Have you ever heard of a game called Angel?"

"Angel?" Alec blinked at the sudden change of topic.

"It's much like the Ouji board game you Americans play that summons ghosts to speak through a game board. Angel summons ghosts in much the same way. Well, think of Yokai World being a giant Ouji board. The players' wishes are summoning ghosts and *yokai* into the game...and soon into reality."

Alec paled. "That can't be good."

Midoriko shook her head. "It's not. But for now there's nothing we can do. Alec, take this." Midoriko grasped Alec's hand and on it suddenly appeared a control ring with a dark blue, sapphire-like stone. "Use it to protect my daughter, Yukino. So that the power to control her does not fall into the wrong hands. Oh and Alec, there is one more thing I'd like you to do for me if you can. Night...save him...save him from the dark path he has begun to tread upon."

Alec looked down at the new control ring on his finger and his head snapped up at the mention of the player Night. "Night? But he saved me earlier. He's incredibly powerful. How could he possibly need *me* to save him?"

"There are different types of strength, Alec. You possess a strength that sadly Night has forgotten about. It makes him vulnerable to his enemies..." Midoriko shook her head sadly. "You must protect him, promise me?"

Alec frowned and bit his lip. "I don't know if I can. I don't know if I'll be able to. I mean, what could I possibly do?"

Midoriko leaned forward and pressed her forehead against Alec's. "Believe in yourself, Alec, just as I believe in you. You're my only hope. The world's only hope. Only you can save them. I know this. Now I must go and you must return. You mustn't let RedAki win the game event. It must be you who wins the Dragon Prince, Battle Ghost. It shall help you follow your destiny. That Battle Ghost is very special and shouldn't fall into the wrong hands. Now... go..." Midoriko began to fade away.

Alec reached his hand out towards her suddenly, "Wait! Midoriko! How will I find your daughter? There's still so much I don't understand. That I need to ask you!"

Midoriko had already disappeared and only her voice remained, "Do not worry, the paths of your lives will cross soon..."

Alec suddenly opened his eyes to find he was now in a PC Ghost body as he should have been from the start. He looked over to see that RedAki was still walking towards Ryuu so only seconds seemed to have passed when to Alec it felt like at least minutes or even an hour had passed being trapped in the darkness. Alec saw that RedAki was still debating if he would try and save the princess or just take the treasure.

Night had just made his way into the palace and burst through the doors of the throne room suddenly. He quickly caught sight of Alec and rushed over to him. "Dang, what happened to you kid?" Night then looked over and noticed RedAki. "Oh. Don't worry kid I'll have you back to normal in a second. Red Potion Activate!" Night used a red potion to resurrect Alec, which caused his PC body to shift back into its normal form.

Alec patted his hands down his now solid body. "Whew, good to be back."

Night called out. "RedAki!"

RedAki spun around to face Night and his mouth opened in shock. "YOU! Night-*teme*, Night you jerk, what are you doing here?" RedAki's eyes flitted over to the now resurrected Alec, his eyes narrowing dangerously. "I swear, that guy has the devil's luck. He won't stay dead for longer than five seconds! Why are you helping him Night?" RedAki unsheathed his sword and pointed it in Night's direction while striding towards him with purposeful steps.

Night smirked. "I have my reasons." Night shrugged. "Maybe I plan to make him into a Guardian." Night turned to Alec and said in a hushed voice. "Alec, go and face the Water Dragon Prince, Ryuu. I'll handle RedAki. Go."

Alec hesitated since he was still confused about why Night was helping him...and why he had a black sword. *Just who is this guy, really?* But Alec nodded and rushed off to try and face Ryuu. *Sometimes you just have to believe in people...*Alec thought to himself.

RedAki scowled darkly. "Night...I don't get why you're helping him but it's sure as hell pissing me off. Reaper-*sama* a.k.a Master Reaper will be most pleased if I defeat you and take him back that mysterious sword of yours that's neither a hacker's creation nor a true game weapon...it's something... more. Something that blurs the lines between the game and reality. Or so Reaper-*sama* told me. And it sounds fascinating." RedAki licked his lips. "And if Reaper-*sama* doesn't want it for himself I think I'll keep it." RedAki drawled, his red eyes gleaming with mischief as he pointed his sword at Night. "Night...the #1 ranked Ghost Master in Yokai World...but not for long!" RedAki charged forward.

Night hefted his giant *Shinigami* sword into the air to block RedAki's attack. Sparks flew up into the air as their swords' blades grated against each other. RedAki leapt backwards and then brought his sword down upon Night in a downwards slash. Night, however, was ready for him and quickly blocked and then lunged his sword forward with an attack of his own. RedAki quickly parried this. The deadly dance had begun as the two *Shinigami* clashed against each other - *slash, block, slash, parry.*

Alec could hear the sounds of their battle raging on and he couldn't help himself from turning his head to look back at them. Alec's eyes widened as he watched their Ghostly Duel, his mouth gaping open in pure awe at their superhuman skill, speed, and power. It was a battle unlike any he had ever witnessed. Their movements were almost too fast for Alec's eyes to follow and as they began to get even more serious Alec thought he was merely watching flashes of energy colliding with each other in the air.

However, Alec's time to watch was cut short when suddenly a large, golden trident nearly sliced him in two. Alec had just barely managed to dodge out of the way. Alec looked up to see that Ryuu, the Water Dragon Prince, had moved in to attack him. Alec held his sword before him in a two-handed grip and prepared to face his enemy. Alec steeled himself and charged Ryuu recklessly. His sword clashed against Ryuu's trident but as Ryuu pushed back Alec was suddenly sent flying and then landed hard on his backside. *Ow.*

Alec pulled himself up off the ground and charged Ryuu once more. Again and again Alec's sword clashed with Ryuu's trident but the Dragon Prince was just too powerful and Alec kept getting flung backwards - the last time he landed smack on his face. *Man, that smarts.* Alec pushed himself off the ground once more and turned to face Ryuu. Alec's PC body was glowing red signifying the danger of his health being low. He was running low on hit points as well. The difference in their levels was just too great. How could he be expected to win against a ghost as powerful as this one?

"Is that all you've got *Shinigami* Boy? How pathetic." Ryuu gave Alec a condescending look.

For some reason LadyV's words rung through Alec's mind - *It's not always physical strength that wins a battle Alec...sometimes you have to use your head.*

"No - that's not all I've got, Ryuu." Alec pointed his sword at Ryuu again.

Ryuu smiled and was about to charge forward when suddenly he gripped his head and cried out in pain. He then stared at Alec with a completely different expression on his face from before - it was an almost pleading expression. "*Shinigami* Boy....only you can free me...Argh!" Ryuu gripped his head again and the same condescending expression as before returned upon the Dragon Prince's face. And then the Dragon Prince began to laugh maniacally at Alec and pointed his trident at him aiming for Alec's heart. "Now, you shall die, boy!"

Alec blinked, had he just imagined that? The Dragon Prince seemed to be struggling against an unseen force. LadyV's words and his last battle with the possessed bear came to his mind - there had to be something he was missing. Alec looked the Dragon Prince over and noticed how an *o-fuda* was stuck directly on his chest right where his heart would be. And the *o-fuda* talisman was even glowing. *That's it! The Dragon Prince Ryuu has been turned into a shikigami!*

Alec decided he would use all his remaining energy for his next attack. His sword and body began to glow with a blue-tinged light and then Alec charged forward his sword raised. Ryuu also charged forward, however, and his trident had a longer reach than Alec's sword and managed to pierce Alec through. Alec didn't let this stop him though and kept moving his body forward over the pole of the trident, so that he got closer and closer to Ryuu until he was able to slash at the *o-fuda* that was on Ryuu's chest even though Alec's reckless actions were killing him. The *o-fuda* disintegrated and a dark energy was released into the air. Ryuu cried out in pain as this cloud of black energy was being sucked out of his body.

Ryuu began to return to normal - now that he was no longer possessed and his hair which had once been midnight black suddenly turned into a pale, silvery blue color. His eyes remained emerald green and his robes turned from black and gold to a kimono of white, green, and blue. Ryuu immediately removed his trident from Alec, a sickened expression on his face.

The black cloud of energy began to take on the form of a woman, and then the form shifted into the image of a shadowy mermaid. Even though her body was an indistinct sort of shadow Alec could tell she was wearing a sort of crown on her head and that she had long, flowing, wild hair.

Alec put a hand to his wound to staunch the bleeding as he watched this happening.

"*Shinigami* boy, you have freed me from the evil Sea Witch's grasp!" Ryuu came to kneel before Alec. "I owe my allegiance to you now, Master." Ryuu held out his hand and handed something to Alec. Alec took the item and opened his hand to see that it was a control ring. This one had a bright, green stone in the center of it. Alec placed the ring on one of his fingers and it glowed - Ryuu was now his very own Battle Ghost.

Yatta! Alright! I have a Battle Ghost now. This is totally awesome! This thought filled Alec with excitement.

Ryuu stood and waved his trident at Alec and suddenly his wound was healed.

Alec looked down in awe. Apparently, his Battle Ghost even had slight healing abilities. "Wow...gee...thanks." Alec smiled a lopsided grin at his Battle Ghost.

Ryuu smiled back. "Not at all Master. Now in order for us to break the enchantment that has been placed upon the princess we need to defeat the evil Sea Witch Morgana, the Emperor of the Sea's second daughter."

Alec looked over at the evil Sea Witch Ghost in shock. "She's the emperor's daughter too?"

The ghostly mermaid suddenly floated forward. "Yes." She responded in a melodious voice.

"Then why?" Alec furrowed his brow in confusion, "Why would you kidnap your own sister and turn her into a turtle?" Alec questioned.

"Love." Morgana moaned. "When Taro came to the Palace of the Dragon he fell in love with my sister while I fell in love with him at first sight, from afar. It was an unrequited love. And so I grew hateful and jealous towards my sister and I ended up leaving the palace. I searched the seas for a way to make Taro fall in love with me but no such spell exists. You can't use magic to make someone fall in love with you. Even after I changed myself into a *Shikigami*, a controlled spirit, I still didn't possess enough power to make Taro fall in love with me and so I decided to kill the Dragon Prince Ryuu and turn him into a *Shikigami* as well in order to gain even more power. I then possessed him to kidnap my sister without my beloved Taro knowing it was me. If I can't have Taro...no one can!" Morgana declared and raised her hand towards the small turtle that was crawling around on the floor preparing to unleash some of her dark energy upon it.

"Dang it! The princess!" Alec realized and ran to stop her. Alec dove for the turtle and wrapped his arms around it, shielding the small turtle with his body. He felt a blast of dark energy hit his back and he cried out in pain.

"Master!" Ryuu yelled seeing his Master's plight.

Alec expected more pain to come when it suddenly stopped. Alec turned around to see that Ryuu was standing in front of Alec now, his golden trident raised before him. He was using his trident to slice through the dark energy and it was flying past Ryuu on either side of him.

Night and RedAki turned their attention towards Alec, who was now facing the evil Sea Witch Morgana all on his own. "Alec!" Night cried out in concern and rushed to his aid.

RedAki frowned after him. "Hey, wait you jerk! How dare you ignore me Night!" But then something caught RedAki's eye - it was the small treasure box that the Dragon Prince Ryuu had offered him earlier. A sly grin formed on RedAki's face - the treasure was all his now.

Alec blinked in surprise at his Battle Ghost, who was protecting him. He was able to stand with the turtle-princess in his arms. "Thanks, Ryuu."

"No problem, Master." Ryuu nodded.

Night reached Alec and put a hand on his shoulder. "You okay kid?"

Alec nodded. "Night? Yea...my Battle Ghost protected me."

Night looked over at Ryuu, who was currently battling Morgana, and an intrigued expression formed on his face. "Yea, I can see that. That's one hell of a Battle Ghost you managed to get your hands on, kid. Maybe I should help him. Alec what attacks can your Battle Ghost use?"

"Huh?" Alec knew he had just had an air head moment and wanted to hit his head on a wall in embarrassment.

Thankfully, Night was a very patient person. "It should be listed on your skill bar."

"Oh yea right...well let's see there's something called Water Attack...and then there's something called Water Binding Attack-"

Night cut Alec off. "Use Water Binding. That should work nicely. I have a plan." Night had a mysterious glint in his eye, Alec noted.

"Alright. Ryuu use Water Binding Attack! Now!" Alec called out to his Battle Ghost.

"Yes Master. Water Binding Attack!" Ryuu pointed his trident at the evil Sea Witch Ghost and out shot a stream of water, which began to coil through the air and then wrap its way around Morgana and then restrain her.

Night took this opportunity to charge forward and pierce Morgana through with his giant *Shinigami* sword, using a large energy blast attack at the same time. She began to be destroyed from the inside out. "Taro!" She cried out before she was exorcized and disintegrated by bursting into little dots of light.

Alec couldn't help but feel sorry for Morgana and her plight due to her unrequited love. She must have loved Taro a lot for her love to turn so deeply into hate. There was a fine line between love and hate, Alec knew. A tear slid down Alec's face out of pity.

Ryuu seemed to notice this. "Master? Why are you crying? Are you hurt? Shall I heal you?"

Alec wiped the tear away. "No, it's not a wound you can heal. It's a wound of the heart."

Ryuu quirked his head at Alec, "A wound of the heart?"

Alec nodded, "Yes, a wound of the heart can only be healed by love..."

"Love..." Ryuu shook his head. "Does not compute. Sorry Master, I do not understand."

"Uh..." Alec seemed to have realized he'd been talking to an AI Battle Ghost all that time and was suddenly embarrassed with himself. "Don't worry about it, you don't need to understand. I just felt sorry for her that's all. She loved Taro so much but her love for him became twisted into hate and turned her evil. It's sad to love someone who doesn't love you back. But really in the end true love is only true love if it's mutual I suppose. Well, it seems to me that true love always wins out in the end anyways."

Night ruffled Alec's hair. "That's pretty deep coming from a *gaki*, brat like you!"

Alec blushed a bit flustered.

"And where did you come across such words of wisdom if I may ask?" Night questioned curiously.

Alec shrugged, "Neji, my dorm mate, lent me some of his *manga*."

Night nearly fell over in shock. "You got all that from comic books...?"

Suddenly, the small turtle that had still been crawling on the ground began to glow with a blue light, and then it turned into a beautiful princess. She had long, sea-green hair that reached the floor and bright, sparkling, blue eyes. She was wearing a beautiful, silk kimono of blues and greens with long sleeves. And Alec also noticed that like the Emperor of the Sea she had pointed ears and a sprinkling of shinny, small, blue scales across her cheeks.

"Wow." Alec blinked as she smiled kindly in his direction.

Ryuu bowed at the princess' feet. "Princess, please forgive me for kidnaping you."

The princess placed a hand on Ryuu's head and smiled down at him. "You are indeed forgiven."

Just then, there was an ominous rumbling sound and the floors beneath them seemed to shake. It was the sort of tremor one felt when they were experiencing the start of an earthquake.

"Quickly! We must get out of here as soon as possible. The magic and enchantments that were keeping this palace together have gone now that the evil Sea Witch has been exorcized." The princess explained hurriedly. "One of you can ride me out." She declared and suddenly her body began to glow with a blue light before she morphed into a large, wingless, sea dragon with long whiskers and shimmering green and blue scales running all along her body and tail.

"Master, you may ride me out." Ryuu told Alec as he too began to glow with a blue light and then in seconds Ryuu had also turned himself into a sea dragon's form. Alec blinked at his Battle Ghost in shock. Unlike the princess' body which was solid looking since she was still alive the water dragon that Ryuu had turned into was slightly transparent and Alec could see the insides of his ghost's body including Ryuu's skeleton. Alec hesitated before getting up onto the back of his Battle Ghost. "Night, you ride the princess."

"Right." Night nodded as he got onto the princess' back. The princess immediately took off swimming gracefully through the water towards the entrance way.

"Let's go Ryuu." Alec commanded and Ryuu swam up and was also headed for the door. That's when however Alec caught sight of RedAki, who was currently struggling to open the lid of the small treasure box. *Uh oh.* "RedAki! Don't open that thing!"

"Keh! Like I'm going to listen to my enemy! You probably just want the treasure for yourself." RedAki declared.

"No you *baka*! Wait!" Alec insisted.

Too late.

RedAki finally managed to pry the lid off the box and suddenly a large cloud of smoke came out and engulfed RedAki's body. And then suddenly RedAki's PC body began to change - his back bent and his skin became wrinkled and his hair grew out long and white. In seconds his PC body had suddenly aged.

Alec shook his head and sighed. "Told ya so." *Why do people have to learn things the hard way?*

RedAki frowned, "What the hell...?" And then his eyes widened in shock and horror. "Level 1! Impossible! *Sona*...This can't be..." RedAki sunk to his knees in defeat.

"Ryuu we can't leave him there. Come on we have to go and get him." Alec directed his Dragon Ghost, who nodded and they swam towards RedAki. "RedAki!" Alec reached out his hand towards the player killer.

RedAki looked up bewildered at Alec's offer. He hesitated before taking Alec's hand and Alec pulled him up behind him on his Dragon Ghost's back.

"Let's go Ryuu!" Alec cried and the Water Dragon Ghost quickly swam out of the palace door just as the palace of black coral began to collapse. They just barely made it out alive.

"Woot!" Alec cheered as he looked back at the collapsing palace. "We just made it."

RedAki just frowned at Alec's enthusiasm. "Why did you save me?"

Alec shrugged, having forgotten RedAki was even there. "I couldn't just leave you there looking all pathetic." Alec smirked.

RedAki's expression darkened. "Keh, I never asked for your help. You know, I really don't like you, Alec. In fact I hate 'hero wannabes' like you."

"*Hai hai.* Yea, yea." Alec replied nonplused. He was having way too much fun getting to ride a water dragon to let anything RedAki said bother him. It

155

was an incredible feeling soaring through the ocean as though he were up in the sky. Alec gripped onto the scales on Ryuu's back as he looked down as they passed over the sea floor and areas where Alec could see the deep chasms that seemed to go down forever. It gave Alec the feeling of being up high. He knew the game was a virtual reality world and all - but to Alec it just felt so real.

Alec, RedAki, and Night soon arrived safely at the Palace of the Dragon. As soon as they reached the front entrance Ryuu and the princess turned back into their normal forms. The group then entered the palace and made their way towards the throne room where Alec would receive his reward. Alec turned around to see if RedAki was behind them and noticed that the *KuroShinigami* boy had disappeared. Alec shrugged, *Oh well, his loss. And here I was thinking of being generous and sharing some of my reward with him.*

The group entered the throne room where the emperor and Taro were waiting.

"Taro!" The princess cried as soon as she caught sight of him.

"Princess!" Taro called out to her.

She rushed up to him and leapt into his waiting arms. Taro then spun her around happily before bringing her in for a passionate kiss. Alec blushed and looked away trying to give them some privacy. Night laughed at Alec's shyness from watching two NPC and ruffled Alec's hair teasingly.

The emperor waved his hand at Alec beckoning him forward, "Thank you for saving my daughter, Dranarch. Come forward and receive your reward for a job well done indeed."

Alec stepped forward and knelt before the emperor. Alec was then given lots of experience points and gold. Alec stood up smiling broadly wanting to share some of the gold with Night only to see that Night too had mysteriously disappeared. Alec pouted, what was with those guys?

"What's wrong Master?" Ryuu noticed Alec's perplexed look.

Alec scratched the back of his head, "Oh nothing, just wondering where those guys ran off to."

"Night left a little while ago. RedAki left as soon as we reached the palace." Ryuu informed him.

"I see." Alec sighed. People always seemed to be leaving him - just like that. *I wonder who that guy really was ...Night...the kind Shinigami with the black sword...*

Chapter 8:
YUKI ONNA: THE BEAUTIFUL SNOW WITCH

Alec, Neji, Junpei, and Rika were all sitting outside under a cherry blossom tree by the main school building while having their lunches. Alec began to tell them all about his little in game adventure and how Night, the mysterious PC, had helped him to win the Dragon Prince Game Event.

Neji began to choke on his *ramen*. "Night! You don't mean the #1 Ghost Master in the game do you?"

Alec shrugged. "I dunno. but his PC name was Night."

"Did he have this big ass, black-bladed *Shinigami* sword?" Neji pressed and Alec nodded. Neji looked like he was going to be sick.

"Why are you so freaked? He seemed like a real nice guy...although I wonder why his sword is black. He didn't really seem the type to be a player killer."

Neji's expression was grim as he pushed his glasses up his nose. "That's because he's *not* a player killer, per say. He has a guild called the Guardian Knights - they call themselves an Anti-PK Guild. They go around and target player killers...basically they're PKKers (Player Killer Killers). It's a very small guild at this point. I think he only has like two other members left ever since the incident..."

"Incident?" Alec questioned curiously, leaning in.

Neji nodded. "They say Night's sister was playing the game, Yokai World, when something unusual happened to her. Night claims that his sister is now in a coma in real life and that her mind is trapped in the game somewhere as a PC who can't log out. The guild's purpose is to search for her and to also question members of the Renegade Reapers guild by force to get answers as well since Night claims their Guild Master, Reaper, had something to do with why his sister is now in a coma. This is also why the Guardian Knights have such a long standing rivalry with the RRs guild and also why they seem to hate each other. They're basically in the middle of a guild war. Anyways, you shouldn't get involved with an eccentric like him - you'll just be caught up in the middle of their war at any rate. There's no way his sister's mind is trapped in the game - it's completely illogical. And blaming Reaper for it - that's just crazy too. He just wants to justify his lust for killing other game players - it puts him on the same level as those guys I'd say." Neji took a sip of a cup of steaming green tea that he was holding thoughtfully.

"So...you really don't believe Night?" Alec ventured to ask.

Neji seemed thrown by this question. "Of course not - it's not at all logical. Yokai World is just a virtual reality game - no matter how real it may seem at times it's still just a game. Something like someone's mind or spirit getting trapped inside of it is utterly preposterous."

"Just a game *ka?* Huh?" Alec mused aloud and couldn't help but think back on Midoriko's words: *Yokai World is no longer just a game. The lines between the game, reality and the true spirit world have begun to blur...*

His father's words also seemed to ring through his head: *Sometimes you just have to believe in people Alec.*

Alec's thoughts couldn't help but stray back to Midoriko and how she had been looking for her daughter. He had sensed that she was in fact a real ghost so...could her dead daughter really be trapped in the game too, as a ghost? It didn't seem so farfetched or unlikely to Alec. And if that was possible then Night's sister could somehow have her mind truly trapped in the game somewhere.

Alec shrugged and didn't appear at all convinced by Neji's assurances that it was just a game though he didn't think Neji noticed. "I guess."

Junpei however had his eyes on Alec and seemed to realize what Alec was thinking. He smirked at Alec conspiratorially, who looked away awkwardly.

Alec looked up and he saw Rika, who had been staring at him. Alec blushed and Rika blushed a bright pink at having been caught staring at Alec. Alec quickly tried to appear nonchalant and tried to take another bite out of his sandwich and failed miserably as he missed his mouth by inches and ended up getting mayo all over his chin. *Smooth Alec, real smooth.* Alec then turned even redder in embarrassment.

Junpei nudged Alec with his elbow. "Food is supposed to be *eaten* not worn." He chuckled.

Alec was now choking on his sandwich at this point but he couldn't help himself. Anytime he looked at Rika he remembered that soft kiss she had placed on his lips for having saved her life and it just made it incredibly awkward for him to even be around her.

Rika suddenly took out a small *bento* lunch box and opened the lid to reveal that inside were several home cooked rice balls. She held out the box hesitantly towards Alec. "Alec-*kun* I made these plum flavored rice balls if you would like to try one?"

Alec blinked back at her in surprise and reached out his hand for one, "Oh, um, yea, sure."

Junpei, however, pushed Alec aside and took a look at the rice balls, "Ooo! Plum flavored rice balls! My favorite! Rika how did you know?" Junpei reached forward and grabbed one.

"I wouldn't eat that if I were you..." Neji warned ominously.

Junpei gave him a look before plopping the entire rice ball into his mouth.

"AH!" Rika exclaimed in indignation as she watched Junpei chewing one of her precious, homemade rice balls, which she had made specially for Alec. "My rice ball! That was for Alec, Junpei! Give that back right now!" Rika grabbed onto the front of Junpei's uniform and began to shake him roughly, so that his head snapped back and forth.

Junpei tried to speak with his mouth full but just ended up shrugging before he was forced to swallow the whole thing.

"Spit it out now!" Rika demanded but then pouted as she watched Junpei swallow it whole. She let go of him and sighed heavily.

Junpei smirked but then his face seemed to turn slightly green. He suddenly stood up and went over to Neji, yanking the boy's thermos from the geek's hand that was full of hot green tea and began to chug it down.

"*Oi*! Hey!" Neji said as Junpei stole his green tea.

Junpei wiped the back of his mouth with his hand once he had finished chugging the green tea and looked at Rika as though she were the devil. "You call *that* edible! What were you trying to do? Kill Alec or something? And here I thought you liked Alec..."

Rika flushed in embarrassment. "What are you talking about Junpei? My rice balls are delicious!"

Neji had an amused smirk on his face. "I tried to warn him..."

Alec was beginning to think Neji hadn't really wanted to warn the jock in the first place and was now enjoying himself immensely.

"Isn't that right Alec? You'll try one won't you?" Rika pressed as she held out the *bento* box towards him.

Alec was hesitating at this point with Junpei nearly throwing up and Neji's ominous warnings but as he looked back at Rika's hopeful expression he didn't have the heart to turn her down. He shrugged. "Sure, I'll try one, Rika."

"The brave soul..." Neji shook his head.

"Should we start planning for his funeral?" Junpei asked Neji conversationally. "I was thinking something plain and elegant...white flowers like lilies, narcissus, jasmine...you know."

Alec grabbed a rice ball and took a small bite from it. He nearly choked as he forced himself to swallow it down. How could someone have messed up so badly in cooking a simple rice ball! He could have sworn he had tasted peanut butter and anchovies in there!

"So...how is it Alec?" Rika pressed.

Alec's eyes were watering. "It's...good." He managed to choke out. "Hey Rika, what's that over there? I think I see a *yokai*!"

"Huh? What? Where?" Rika turned in the direction Alec had suddenly pointed.

Alec used that opportunity to throw the rice ball clear across the grass and into the soccer field. Neji raised his eyebrows at Alec's actions and Junpei chuckled amused.

"That was a pretty good throw. The baseball team would be lucky to have you. I didn't think you could do something so...tricky Alec. I'm impressed." Junpei smirked.

"Oh shut up." Alec frowned.

"That was just his survival instincts kicking in." Neji pushed his glasses up his nose knowingly.

Alec nodded vigorously in agreement.

Rika pouted at the boys suspiciously as she turned back around to face them and decided to settle glaring at Junpei instead. "You see, Junpei, Alec appreciates my cooking. Some people just have no taste."

Junpei just started laughing and soon Neji was laughing as well. Alec bit his tongue to keep himself from laughing but soon all three boys were laughing at Rika's horrible cooking skills.

That's when all three boys ended up with a rice ball *splat* on their faces. Apparently, Rika had gotten fed up with their laughing and had thrown her remaining rice balls at them.

The rice balls slid down the boys' amused faces.

"*Mou*! Geez! Boys!" Rika huffed as she got up and left them.

Alec shook his head as he wiped rice off his face. *That Rika sure has some violent tendencies...*

But when the three boys all turned to look at each other's rice covered faces they couldn't help but break out laughing again.

It was the end of the school day, and Alec was gathering his text books and preparing to go back to his dorm room when Takahashi-*sensei* pulled Alec aside.

"Alec-*kun* would you mind if I had a word with you?" Alec noticed Takahashi seemed worried about something.

Alec shrugged. "Sure." He looked up to see that Neji and Junpei were in the doorway waiting for him. "Go on ahead without me, guys. Takahashi-*sensei* needs me for something."

"Alright, see ya Alec!" Neji called as he left.

"*Ja-ne.*" Junpei gave Alec a salute.

Alec turned back to Takahashi-*sensei* hefting his book bag over one shoulder. "You wanted to talk to me about something, Sir?"

Takahashi-*sensei* seemed a bit nervous and ran a hand through his salt and pepper hair. "Alec-*kun*, I was wondering if you could do me a huge favor and deliver a tray of food to a certain student who...how shall I put this...due to his health never leaves his room. I usually have another student do it but since they're going to be too busy with club activities they asked me if I could find someone else to handle it."

And since I don't belong to any clubs that makes me the perfect candidate for this task huh? Well, I guess it does. Sigh. Alec shrugged. "Sure *sensei*, it's no problem."

Takahashi-*sensei* let out a breath of relief and looked relieved. It made Alec wonder just what he was getting himself into. "Great! Here's his name and room number. All you have to do is go to the cafeteria - the tray will be ready and waiting for you when you get here." Takahashi-*sensei* explained as he handed Alec a small slip of paper.

Alec shoved the info slip into his pocket as he made his way out of the classroom. Junpei suddenly popped up from next to the doorway.

"Yo." Junpei greeted nonchalant, but Alec who hadn't been expecting anyone to be there nearly jumped a foot in the air.

"AH! Junpei? Don't do that!" Alec put a hand to his racing heart. "You scared me half to death. What are you doing here anyways?"

Junpei chuckled. "You're a jumpy one aren't you? Curiosity got the better of me." Junpei smiled a cat's paw smile, hands behind his head in a casual manner. "So, what did Takahashi-*sensei* want?"

Alec shrugged. "Nothing much. He just wanted me to take a tray of food up to some student."

Junpei's eyes widened in a mixture of excitement and...fear? Alec hoped he read the last emotion wrong. "You mean to Akira's room?"

"Akira?" Alec took out the small slip of paper and read it: *Akira Asamoto Room 304.* "Yea, Akira Asamoto...why?"

Junpei put a hand on Alec's shoulder and looked at him with pity. "You, my friend, are about to be cursed."

"Huh? Wait what?" Alec spluttered, "But it's just some student who's too sick to leave his room right?"

"Ah, that's what they say but that's not the truth. He's not sick...well...not in the way you're thinking. He's a *hikikomori*." Junpei looked expectantly at Alec as if he had just revealed a juicy tidbit of gossip.

Alec just quirked his head at him. "He's a what?"

Junpei's face fell and he sighed, running a hand through his spiky hair messily. "You don't know what a *hikikomori* is do you? Well, I suppose that does make sense since you've been living in America these past 12 years." Junpei tapped his chin. "How shall I explain this. A *hikikomori* is a person who is perfectly healthy but of their own free will chooses to isolate themselves from society, even their friends and family by choosing to never leave their room. Some say becoming a *hikikomori* is sometimes caused by extreme social anxiety. Others say *hikikomori* are people who have suffered some kind of traumatic social or academic failure and feel as though they can't face the world anymore."

Alec furrowed his brow in confusion. "What do you mean they never leave their room? They'd have to sometime right? To buy groceries? To eat? Or go to work? School? Right?"

Junpei shook his head. "A *hikikomori* is someone who is simply trying to shut out the world and escape from reality. Sometimes they're pushed to this extreme due to too much social pressure on them at home from their family or by their school. Some families are able to simply support their *hikikomori* sons or daughters, so they don't really have to leave their rooms in order to make a living or to get food. Although some *hikikomori*, who don't have parents that are able to support them, have been known to make their own money to support their isolationist lifestyle by doing things like trading stocks online, and some have been known to play MMORPGs for hours so they can sell rare items for real money to other players."

Alec gulped. *Escape from reality?* He could totally relate to that. And that was sort of scary. That's why he had started playing video games and online RPGs in the first place after all. To escape the reality of his unloving parents, their constant fighting, and yelling...and his own problems due to the poltergeists and ghosts which were plaguing him. "So, they just chose to lock themselves away from the rest of the world. That's awful..." Alec shook himself. "What about the curse you mentioned?"

"Oh right, the curse." Junpei chuckled, "Well, it seems everyone at school has it in their head that whoever ends up bringing a tray of food to Akira ends up becoming a *hikikomori* themselves."

Alec paled. "Is the curse...real?" He squeaked.

Junpei nodded seriously. "Oh yes...the last boy that delivered Akira's tray has become a recluse as well." Alec was looking green at this point before Junpei burst out laughing and slapped Alec on the back. "You should see your face! Of course the curse isn't real Alec! I was just pulling your leg...that would be crazy."

Alec's jaw dropped before he glared at Junpei. "Junpei that wasn't funny."

"Oh yes it was," Junpei was still smirking, "Hey, mind if I come with you to deliver the tray? I want to see if I end up getting cursed. It sounds like fun." His amber colored eyes were twinkling with mischief.

Alec sighed. "You have an odd idea of fun, dude. But, sure, whatever, tag along if you really want to." Alec shrugged. *At least that way I won't have to go up there alone. Gulp.*

Alec, followed close behind by Junpei, made their way over to the cafeteria where the tray of food was waiting for them to take to Akira's room. The boys then made their way back to their dormitory building and then took the elevator to the third floor. They then began to make their way down the hall, Alec keeping an eye on the room numbers.

"Room 301...302...303...304. Here we are." Alec suddenly stopped in front of a door. The door looked normal except for an odd rectangular panel, a kind of mini-door, it had at the very bottom of the door and which was currently closed and locked. Alec shrugged and knocked on the door. "Um, hello, in there, Akira? I've brought you your food tray."

The sound of movement and scuffling came from within and then the sound of the bottom panel being unlocked was heard. The panel then opened backwards to reveal that it was a rectangular opening big enough for Alec to easily slide an entire tray of food under the door. Alec raised an eyebrow at this since he thought the boy was going to have to open the door to receive his food, but he put the tray down on the floor and slowly slid it underneath the door through the opening. Almost immediately the panel was shut with a *bang* and quickly locked once more.

Alec flinched at the sound and stood back from the door.

Silence~

"Um, your welcome." Alec called back. "Okay...now that was weird." Alec turned to Junpei with a forced smile. "So I guess that's it then?"

"Guess so." Junpei shrugged.

"I didn't say thank you." Came a sneer through the door causing Alec to jump.

"You really *are* jumpy, you know that." Junpei smirked.

"Oh shut up," Alec frowned and made his way closer to the door, "Oh... okay...um, if you don't mind me asking - why are you a *hikikomori*? Why won't you come out of your room?"

Silence~

Alec and Junpei waited for several minutes to hear a response.

"What are you stupid?" The voice suddenly perked up again. "You're not supposed to talk to me! *Baka*. Just who are you anyways? The usual boy who drops off my food never said a word to me and now they replace him with some annoying chatterbox!"

There was something oddly familiar about that voice and it unnerved Alec. "I'm Alec Suzuki."

"Alec?" The voice questioned curiously as if testing out the foreign name on his tongue. "Never heard of you...you must be a new student here."

Alec nodded and then realized Akira couldn't see this. "Um, I am. I'm a transfer student from America."

"Crazy *gaijin*. That explains it." The voice sneered, "So let me ask you something then Alec Suzuki. You want to know why I won't leave my room. But I think the real question should be why *would* I want to come out of my room? Give me one good reason why I should go back out there?"

Alec felt baffled. He thought he had just been asked something rather profound and was coming up rather short. A reason to live in reality? He of course could say something hypocritical like: 'What isn't out here that isn't worth living for?'. But recently Alec's life felt like some kind of horrible nightmare that he didn't want to be a part of, so he would be lying if he said reality was all peaches and cream.

"You know what Akira, I can't really give you a reason. It's something you kind of have to find out for yourself I think. Or maybe I'm just not the right person to ask that question. Sorry." *How can I blame him for wanting to stay in there. Reality is overrated.*

Silence~

And then - "Some help you are! Ha!" But the voice sounded bitterly amused.

"Wow that was depressing. I wonder if you just got cursed Alec!" Junpei was frowning at all this seriousness - he hated seriousness. That's why he clapped Alec on the shoulder and grinned at him. "You really *were* the wrong person to ask! But that's just because you haven't discovered a lot of life's wonders yet." Junpei turned towards the door. "I'll give you a good reason to come out of your room Akira - girls, you know babes, chicks, girlfriends." Junpei waggled his eyebrows and Alec thought it was too bad Akira didn't get to watch since it was pretty funny. "How are you ever gonna get a girlfriend if you hole yourself up in your room all day. Tsk tsk tsk. Or better yet, how are you going to have any friends? You must get lonely in there all by yourself." Junpei nodded knowingly. "Why else would you be talking to us Mr. I Don't Want To Leave My Room."

"A girlfriend? Keh. That's the last thing I need." The voice drawled. "Friends? Who the hell needs them! If that's all reality has to offer me then goodriddens! I don't need anyone! A girlfriend to use me? Friends to betray me and leave me? I think not. Now why don't you two losers just go away and leave me the hell alone!"

"Alright already, fine." Junpei pouted and put out his hands out in a helpless gesture. "I wonder if all *hikikomori* are as touchy or as sensitive as that one." Junpei chuckled and turned to Alec. "Right Alec?"

But Alec was far from being amused by this situation. Alec's gray eyes were stormy, Akira's words had seemed to affect him to the core of his being. He could relate to Akira a little too well for his liking and it was unsettling. He understood Akira and where he was coming from. Alec couldn't help but wonder if one day - what if he chose to just shut out the world as Akira had? It was something Alec wanted to do after all - deep down he knew this was true. He also knew that someone like Junpei who was always so outgoing, happy, and carefree couldn't even begin to understand how he felt.

"Junpei, don't tease him like that. It's not funny. Come on let's go." Alec said coldly as he began to walk off.

Junpei pouted before putting his hands in his pockets and following. "Kill joy."

- - - - - - - - - - - - - - - -

ID: Dranarch
Password: wings
Logging in...

Alec logged on to Yokai World and decided he would concentrate on doing some training and leveling up. He teleported to the Graveyard Area and unsheathing his *Shinigami* sword began to look around the place for mobs. The Graveyard Area was pretty bleak looking...with rows and rows of graves and curved headstones. On the headstones Alec could see the letters R.I.P had been chiseled into them. In the nearby leafless trees Alec saw several black crows perched and they flapped their wings restlessly and cawed down at Alec as they watched him with their beady red eyes.

Alec didn't have to wait very long since he was in a cemetery after all - before mobs began springing up out of the fresh dirt of the graves. Alec squeaked and took a step backwards as a skeleton clawed it's way out of a mound of dirt. Alec took a deep breath to calm his racing heart. *It's just a game. It just looks real.* Though Alec couldn't help but reach out his senses just to be sure. He let out a sigh of relief when he felt nothing, which meant the monster before him was simply data. Alec charged forward, his sword raised, and quickly slashed it through the skeleton mob. The mob was instantly exorcized. Alec smirked, this wouldn't be so hard after all.

Alec continued his way through the graveyard exorcizing more skeleton and zombie mobs that popped up out of the graves and faced him until he came to a more open part of the graveyard which had large, stone tombs that were spaced out. These tombs had stone statues nearby of angels, large stone crosses, and guardian beasts such as foxes or wolves. He knew that in this area the mobs would probably be more high level.

A chill wind suddenly blew through the graveyard, and Alec shivered. "*Brrrr...*" Alec blinked as he rubbed his arms. He had just *felt* cold air but... that was impossible since he was inside of a game. In the game world a player never really felt things like the pain from their battle injuries or the wetness of the water like when Alec had traveled to the Palace of the Dragon. So feeling a cold wind on his arms was very disconcerting indeed.

The lines between the game and reality...are blurring... Alec shook his head and tried not to think about that as he continued his way deeper into the cemetery. He noticed that in that area a light snow had begun to fall and a white blanket of snow was covering the tombs and stone statues making the place seem oddly peaceful. Alec reached out his hand and let a single snowflake fall onto his open palm. Alec's eyes widened when he felt the coldness of the snowflake as it melted. That was definitely *not* normal.

He crunched his way through the snow before he stopped suddenly when he caught sight of a lovely stone angel. She was carved out of white stone and was wearing a long flowing dress. Her wings were outstretched behind her and Alec saw that sadly one of her wings had broken off. She had her hands outstretched before her and her head slightly bent as if in prayer. She was covered with a light dusting of the sparkling snow making her look even more divine, ethereal. Alec stayed and looked upon the angel statue for a while before he could swear he heard the sounds of a battle. The hairs on the back of Alec's neck were prickling in warning and he had a bad feeling about all this so he quickly ran on ahead.

There in an open area of the graveyard Alec saw RedAki with his Battle Ghost Oni at this side. Alec also noticed RedAki's guild mates: Catara with her Battle Ghost, Nekomata, Kiba with his Battle Ghost, Ookami, and Smoker with his Battle Ghost, Enenra. They were all in a circle and seemed to be attacking someone with a series of deadly fire attacks from their 'fire type' ghosts.

Alec looked past them and gasped. There in the center of the group was a girl of about the same age as Alec. Alec instantly thought there was something oddly supernatural and otherworldly about her. She had long, black hair that reached her toes and bangs which almost shielded her eyes. But when she looked up at the RRs Alec was able to see her eyes and it caused him to gasp aloud. One eye was a beautiful, deep sapphire blue and the other was a rich, golden color. Her face was extremely pale almost to the point where she looked unhealthy. The long *kimono* she was wearing was midnight black and had a pattern of dark blue flowers on the material. She wore an *obi* belt about her waist in a navy blue color and a large bow was tied behind her back. Alec also noticed a gleaming silver necklace about her neck with a thick silver chain on which hung a pendant made up of a pentagram within a circle, and in the very center of the pentagram was a bright blue stone.

The girl's eyes narrowed at the Renegade Reapers and she reached into her *kimono* sleeve to pull out a giant fan, made entirely of feathers and in an Asian-style and then Alec watched awed as she began to dance, moving her fan elegantly through the air.

Alec blinked as he continued to watch her graceful movements as she spun and danced and waved her fan through the air. But Alec saw that her movements were no mere dance for as she waved her fan through the air she began to unleash powerful, ice attacks upon the Battle Ghosts that were attacking her, countering their attacks easily. Oni breathed his fiery breath in her direction and she quickly waved her fan in his direction sending a cold blast of wind and snow his way - this caused the fire to turn into mist and steam immediately as the two attacks collided in midair.

Nekomata threw a black fireball towards the ghost girl and she turned and with another wave of her fan managed to turn the entire fireball into a ball of solid ice with a powerful gust of icy wind - the fireball made of ice then fell down onto the snow covered ground. Enenra tried to attack her next and was stealthily materializing right next to the ghost girl, his smokey tendrils reaching out to grab her and hoping to catch her unaware. But the ghost girl noticed him and quickly spun so that a fierce wind seemed to pick up around her and protected and shielded her from Enenra's attacks. She then waved her fan in Enenra's direction and sent an extremely powerful blast of icy wind in his direction so that the smokey demon was dispersed and was having a hard time pulling himself back together again. Ookami rushed in to attack next and tried to throw a series of kicks and punches at the ghost girl but she gracefully dodged his attacks and then sent an icy attack of her own at him which encased the Battle Ghost entirely in ice, imprisoning him inside.

167

Kiba was forced to call his Battle Ghost back. "Ookami!" The ghost turned into a small ball of light and quickly reentered Kiba's control ring.

As Alec watched the ghost girl attack and dance at the same time he couldn't help but think to himself that she was very pretty. But more interestingly Alec saw that just like Midoriko her body was slightly see-through, transparent, ghost-like, which meant the girl before him had to be a real ghost. If she wasn't a Battle Ghost, which also had transparent bodies. But there was only one way to find out. So Alec reached out his senses towards her to feel if she was real and shockingly found that she was. She had a very powerful spiritual presence in fact, one which caused the hairs on the back of his neck to stand on end in warning. *She's a ghost...and a very powerful one...* Alec rubbed the back of his neck absentmindedly and suddenly had this bad feeling that something was going to happen.

"Darn it! RedAki, none of our attacks seem to be working." Catara huffed, "What's with that Battle Ghost anyways? She's much too powerful to be an ordinary Battle Ghost. And this snow *feels* real. What's really going on?"

"Reaper-*sama* warned me something like this might happen when we tried to capture her - that's why he gave me this." RedAki reached into his *haori* sleeve and pulled out what Alec saw was a large glass globe and that inside the globe were dancing red flames.

"What is it?" Kiba asked curiously, "Is that a normal game item?"

RedAki brought the globe up to his face and peered inside at the trapped, dancing flames that were licking the inside of the glass and Alec watched as RedAki's red eyes seemed to glow and flicker as the flames were reflected into his own fire-hungry eyes. The hunger Alec saw in RedAki's eyes unsettled Alec and that bad feeling still wouldn't go away...which meant something bad was about to happen.

And Alec had the feeling it had something to do with that globe of fire. Alec reached out his senses towards it and his eyes widened - that fire was real somehow but not only that, it was no normal fire. It felt as though it possessed some kind of spiritual or magical power and it felt...*evil*. It sent goose bumps running down his arms.

RedAki then turned with the globe in hand to face the ghost girl. Alec realized in horror what RedAki was about to do. RedAki was about to throw that globe at the ghost girl! And Alec could only imagine what would happen to her if that actually happened.

Oh shoot! Alec quickly ran forward, "No! RedAki don't do it!" And then he turned to look at the ghost girl, their eyes meeting fleetingly. "Look out!"

RedAki threw the globe at the unsuspecting ghost girl but Alec rushed forward. It all seemed to happen in slow motion to Alec as he flung himself in front of the ghost girl, arms spread wide to shield her. The globe hit the middle of Alec's back instead of the ghost girl's body. The globe then shattered and suddenly the magical flames engulfed Alec's entire body in seconds.

RedAki's eyes widened in shock when the globe that he had just thrown ended up hitting Alec instead of the ghost girl and watched as the flames engulfed Alec with an expression of mixed emotions on his face. Anger and surprise were quickly turning to worry...

As Alec was covered in the spiritual flames he was surprised and terrified to find that he could actually feel it - he could feel himself burning and he let lose a bloodcurdling scream of pain. Gods, he was in so much pain! It hurt so much! Through the haze of pain Alec wondered briefly if his body back in reality was still alright and doubted it because this intense pain felt so real.

RedAki's expression had settled on worry and slight regret. He hadn't meant for Dranarch to get hit with that attack. No 'real person' should have been hit with an attack like that. Reaper-*sama* had warned him that the fire inside was no ordinary fire and that it could be deadly to a normal player if they came into contact with it. And though he didn't really like Dranarch that didn't necessarily mean he wanted him dead. They were rivals after all. Reaper-*sama* had told him that if the player hit with the attack was weak-minded enough to *believe* they were actually being burned alive that in reality they would suffer mental damage and feel great physical pain by convincing their body that what they were feeling was indeed real.

The force from the globe exploding on impact had knocked Alec into the ghost girl and sent them falling to the snowy ground with Alec on top of her. Even through the pain Alec realized if he stayed on top of the ghost girl he would end up catching her on fire. He didn't have the strength to move but couldn't let that happen and so he gathered his remaining strength to call out in a feeble voice - "I summon you, Ryuu!"

Ryuu was immediately summoned out of Alec's control ring and materialized next to Alec and the ghost girl. The Battle Ghost immediately leapt into action.

"Master!" Ryuu's eyes widened in shock as he saw his master engulfed in flames. He quickly summoned his trident and pointed it at Alec and a burst of water came forth to douse the flames. The flames began to be put out and in seconds they had been completely squelched. The back of Alec's *haori* and *hakama* were smoking.

Alec was no longer on fire but he was still in a lot of physical and psychological pain. Alec was still on top of the ghost girl and his whole body was trembling violently from the aftereffects of the attack. Alec was also gasping for breath as he tried to calm himself down by telling himself he wasn't on fire anymore and that the fire hadn't even been real to begin with.

It's just a game...it's just a game. Alec knew it would be silly of him to start hyperventilating but he was very close to it.

The ghost girl looked back up at Alec a bit wide-eyed that this young, white-haired boy would risk so much to save her when he didn't even know her. Just who was he?

Alec's eyes were shut tight against the pain and tears were leaking through his eyelids and streaming down Alec's face. He had never been in so much pain. "God it hurts...please make it stop...oh god it hurts so much..." Alec whimpered.

Anger filled the ghost girl's eyes that this boy would let himself get so badly hurt while protecting her. And she became equally angry at the RRs who had done this to him.

Ryuu was also extremely angry by the state that his Master was currently in. He turned to face RedAki and the other player killers, his expression grim as he pointed his trident in their direction. "How dare you hurt my Master!"

Kiba blinked. "Dude, that Battle Ghost like totally spoke to us just now."

"Hey, you don't think that's the special A.I. Battle Ghost that was the prize for clearing the Dragon Prince Game Event do you?" Catara sneered, "How could a crybaby like that manage to get his hands on such a cool Battle Ghost? It's not fair." She pouted.

"Is it true RedAki?" Smoker questioned curiously, "Dranarch won that game event as well as managing to get his hands on the very first Battle Ghost that can talk? I thought you had entered that event."

RedAki looked over at the slightly traumatized Alec, who currently had his head in the ghost girl's lap, who was stroking his hair kindly as she tried to soothe him. She was leaning over Alec and whispering soothing things to him and slowly Alec's trembling and crying seemed to have stopped. RedAki shook his head and a stoic expression formed on his face. "Yea, it's true, he won."

"*Sona.* No way." Catara frowned, "I thought for sure you would have won, RedAki." She gave him a starry-eyed look, which RedAki completely ignored.

The ghost girl gently moved Alec so that he lay on the ground before she stood up to stand next to Ryuu. As soon as Alec was left by himself he curled up into a ball, bringing his legs close to his chest and wrapping his arms tightly around them. The ghost girl looked down at Alec with soft eyes. "You protected me...and now I will protect you, *Shinigami* boy." The ghost girl turned to glare at RedAki and the others. "You guys will pay for what you did. Involving this innocent boy in our Ghostly Duel is unforgivable. Why can't you jerks just leave me in peace! You're going to get it now!"

171

"And I shall assist you." Ryuu smiled at her side, his green eyes narrowing dangerously at RedAki and his guild mates.

RedAki was actually looking repentant before he caught himself, a cool, mask of indifference settling over his features. "We can't leave you alone even if we wanted to. We...I...have special orders from Reaper-*sama* to capture you. And so that's what I'm going to do."

"Reaper-*sama*?" The ghost girl shook her head, "I don't even know who that is."

RedAki shrugged. "Well, he sure seems to know you. He said he needs you for something, ghost girl."

This seemed to be news to the others. "Reaper-*sama* needs her for something? For what exactly RedAki? Are you keeping things from us?" Catara put a hand on RedAki's shoulder but he shrugged her off.

"Get off!" RedAki huffed exasperatedly, "That's all he told me okay, Catara? Come on, we must capture her no matter what."

Ryuu looked over at Alec, who was still curled up on the ground, and then back to RedAki. "I don't think so. Master obviously wishes to protect this girl even if it means his life. And so I shall protect her in my Master's place."

"Keh, what a joke." RedAki sneered, "Catara, Kiba, Smoker attack!" RedAki directed them.

"*Osu*! Right!" The Renegade Reapers all agreed and controlled their ghosts to move forward.

"Who says I need protecting," the ghost girl declared coldly.

Thick storm clouds began to gather overhead as the ghost girl was beginning to get serious. She waved her fan upwards and thunder boomed and then a heavy snow began to fall all around them. She seemed to be gathering more of her power because when Nekomata charged at her she waved her fan towards the Battle Ghost and completely encased her in ice. Enenra was next to try and attack the ghost girl and the Battle Ghost quickly met the same fate.

"Now Dragon Prince Ryuu! Finish them off before they melt the ice and escape!" The ghost girl directed Ryuu.

"Right." Ryuu nodded and charged forward with his trident and lunging his weapon forward pierced through the ice that had been encasing Nekomata so that it shattered. He then turned and shattered the ice that was encasing Enenra next so that the Battle Ghosts were exorcized and forced to return to their Master's control rings.

The ghost girl then turned her gaze towards Catara, Kiba and Smoker and slowly began to walk forward, her fan raised, a dangerous gleam in her two different colored eyes. The wind began to pick up around them and it was freezing cold.

Catara shivered and rubbed at her arms, looking at the ghost girl fearfully. "It's freezing out here! RedAki? What's up with that ghost? This wind...and snow...it feels real. But it can't be real can it?" She was trembling now. "If I die in the game...I won't die in reality right?"

Catara, Kiba and Smoker were all backing away from the ghost girl at this point...

RedAki had been positioned behind them and he seemed rather reluctant to move forward and attack the ghost girl as well. He still had his Battle Ghost Oni but their Battle Ghosts seemed to be useless against this one and the ghost girl seemed to have the help of Alec's special AI Battle Ghost, Dragon Prince Ryuu. It seemed that the tables had turned. RedAki frowned, today was just not his day.

The ghost girl raised her fan and smiled as she lowered it and pointed it directly at RedAki and his guild mates, "Now it's your turn. Prepare to die!"

Alec managed to struggle to his feet finally having sensed the very real danger RedAki and the others were suddenly in. The hairs on the back of Alec's neck were standing on end. "No! Don't!" Alec called out to the ghost girl. "Don't hurt them!"

"You can't tell me what to do!" The ghost girl snapped. "This has nothing to do with you. These Renegade Reapers have been trying to capture me for several days now. They just won't leave me alone! It's time I ended this game once and for all!"

Alec swallowed and began in a much firmer voice. "I said no, Yukino."

Yukino's head whipped around to face Alec, her eyes wide, "How do you know my name?"

Alec held up his hand revealing the control ring with the blue stone that was on his hand - *her* control ring. Alec had realized this when he felt a sudden connection between the ring and Yukino when he had suddenly had the urge to stop her from harming the RRs and realized that he could actually use the power of the ring to stop her and even control her if he wished. Alec shook his head at her - the message was clear. If he really wanted to he could just control her like a puppet but he wanted to give her the choice of stopping her actions of her own free will.

Yukino frowned darkly but lowered her fan.

Alec let out a breath of relief. *Phew.* Alec wiped the sweat from his brow. That had been a close one. He had totally just saved RedAki, Catara, Kiba and Smoker from some serious psychological trauma or physical pain that would feel so *real* it would have endangered their lives. Alec had just suffered the very real fire attack and was still slightly in pain from it, although he was now doing his best to ignore the pain, which he knew was all in his mind, but he wouldn't wish that experience on anyone not even his enemies.

Alec then turned to RedAki, "RedAki! I challenge you to a Ghostly Duel - the winner will get to have Yukino!"

Yukino's eyes narrowed dangerously at Alec, "I am not some prize to be won." She said in a very low voice though there was a tinge of worry to her voice that Alec picked up on.

Alec looked at her and their eyes met. "Don't worry just...trust me. I won't let him have you. I promise."

His silvery gaze was so determined and confident that Yukino couldn't help herself from nodding her head.

"What makes you think we'll agree to that!" Catara scoffed, flipping her hair in an irritated manner.

"Alright." RedAki smirked, suddenly agreeing in a nonchalant attitude.

Everyone turned to stare at RedAki in surprise.

"I accept your challenge Dranarch. Catara, Kiba, Smoker - don't be such a bunch of idiots. He just spared your lives or at least spared you guys from a lot of pain and psychological trauma. This is my fight now - so don't get involved. And no foul play either - and I actually mean that this time." RedAki added as he saw Catara get a mischievous look on her face.

"But RedAki what about Reaper-*sama*?" Catara whined.

"Screw Reaper-*sama*!" Catara sucked in her breath in shock. "This is between me and Dranarch." RedAki pointed his black-bladed sword at Alec. "This Ghostly Duel is inevitable between us."

"Yes," Alec agreed, "It is. I've been waiting for this." Alec unsheathed his *Shinigami* sword and got into a fighting stance.

"So have I." RedAki's red eyes glittered.

RedAki and Alec faced off, while their Battle Ghosts, Oni and Ryuu faced off as well circling each other. Catara, Kiba and Smoker were standing back to give the two *Shinigami* plenty of room for their Ghostly Duel.

RedAki suddenly charged forward and brought his sword down upon Alec in a high downwards slash. Alec brought his sword up and blocked it easily, ready for him.

RedAki looked surprised, "You've gotten better."

"Thanks." Alec smirked back and parried the blow and lunged forward with an attack of his own, which was skillfully blocked by RedAki. Their swords continued to clash and the duel had begun.

Meanwhile, Oni and Ryuu were also facing off. Oni started out with an attack of his fiery breath which shot out towards Ryuu as he opened his mouth. Ryuu countered this attack with a wave of his trident and a blast of water which shot out and the two attacks hit in midair and canceled each other out. Mist was filling the air around the duelers. Oni charged forward with pounding steps, hefting his large iron club - he swung it at Ryuu, who blocked the blow with his trident and their weapons clashed fiercely against each other.

Alec and RedAki were in a deadlock both pressing against each other's sword. Alec looked sideways to see how his Battle Ghost Ryuu was doing and saw that he seemed to be in a similar situation. "Ryuu - use Water Binding Attack!" Alec suggested.

"Yes Master." Ryuu nodded and leapt backwards to give himself some space between him and Oni. He then raised his trident and pointed it at Oni. "Water Binding Attack!"

RedAki was pushing against Alec's sword and trying to force Alec back, but upon hearing this attack command curiosity got the better of RedAki and he looked sideways to see what was going to happen to his Battle Ghost.

Ryuu pointed his trident at Oni and from out of his trident came coils of water which shot towards Oni and began to wrap around his arms and legs like ropes. Oni's club fell from his hands as Oni was completely restrained though Oni continued to struggle against his bonds.

RedAki raised an eyebrow at the attack. "I didn't know you were into bondage, Dranarch." RedAki mocked.

"Into what?" Alec quirked his head at RedAki.

RedAki looked back at Alec in disbelief and sighed. "Never mind, you brat. I suppose that joke is a few years ahead of your time."

Alec frowned thoughtfully wondering what the heck RedAki was talking about.

With Oni now restrained all Ryuu had to do was charge forward as he lunged his trident forward piercing Oni straight through the chest easily. Oni cried out and was exorcized. Oni turned into a small ball of light which returned to RedAki's control ring.

"Darn it!" RedAki swore. "Now it's two against one huh?"

"I don't need Ryuu's help to defeat you." Alec declared pointing his sword at RedAki once more. "Not this time."

"Big words, punk, let's see if you can back them up." RedAki charged forward and their swords clashed once more but then RedAki performed his signature finishing move and managed to disarm Alec with a twist of his sword - Alec's sword went flying up into the air and landed on the snowy ground a few feet away. It was always the same move that got him, Alec realized. He knew it was coming, in fact he could almost read RedAki's moves by now. Even though he still couldn't stop himself from getting disarmed at least this time he had a plan, so that he wouldn't get himself run through, not like the last time.

Alec suddenly sidestepped the attack he knew was coming - predicting RedAki's moves flawlessly.

"Ryuu! Throw me your trident!" Alec commanded quickly.

"Yes Master!" Ryuu quickly tossed Alec the trident and Alec managed to catch it easily.

RedAki was lunging his weapon forward just as Alec had expected him to do but now the trident was in Alec's hand and as RedAki continued to lunge his black-bladed sword forward towards Alec, Alec lunged his trident forward at RedAki at the same time - the trident's reach was longer and RedAki was suddenly pierced through his torso. RedAki looked down at this chest in shock, and Alec pulled out the trident.

RedAki put a hand to his wound in a stunned stupor. "You beat me... you actually beat me... today is *so* not my day." RedAki fell over and quickly turned in a PC ghost. RedAki pouted at Alec in his ghost form. "You cheated, you little punk. I thought you said you wouldn't use your Battle Ghost for help."

Alec shrugged. "Yea, my Battle Ghost, but not his weapon. Loop hole. Though I am sorry I had to win that way against you but I had a promise to keep."

"Touche." RedAki looked resigned.

"RedAki!" Catara, Kiba and Smoker ran up to him with worried expressions on their faces.

"Don't worry Aki-chan I'll resurrect you in a jiffy." Catara purred.

"Don't call me Aki-chan!" RedAki spat back, embarrassed as he saw Alec watching the exchange curiously.

"Man this sucks..." RedAki sighed and was then resurrected by Catara who used a red potion.

"So what do we do now RedAki? We can't just let them go..." Kiba was saying.

RedAki ran a hand through his spiky hair, "Oh yes we can Kiba. I lost. And I gave my word to Dranarch. I may have lost today but that doesn't mean there isn't a next time, Kiba.." RedAki turned to Alec. "You may have won our Ghostly Duel today but next time you won't be so lucky, Dranarch. You were only able to beat me today since our levels were almost the same due to that darned box from the other day that took my level back down to level 1. But it won't take me very long to surpass the level you're at. This is far from over. We will be back for Yukino and then I will defeat you and take her. Yukino will be mine. Count on it."

Alec clenched his fists at RedAki's words.

"But RedAki Reaper-*sama* will-" Catara suddenly looked fearful.

"Enough." RedAki cut her off. "I will take full responsibility for this.

Catara Kiba, Smoker, let's go. We need to report our failure to Reaper-*sama*." RedAki raised his arm and Catara, Smoker and Kiba all followed suit. "Renegade Reapers guildhall!"

"Renegade Reapers guildhall!" The other RRs cried in unison.

Alec let out a sigh of relief as they teleported away and he sank to his knees, no longer having the strength to keep standing. He was still in a lot of pain though it was slowly fading to a dull ache.

Ryuu looked over at Alec concerned. "Master! Do you need me to heal you?"

Alec shook his head. "No, I'm alright, I just need to rest a bit..."

Yukino walked over to Alec with delicate steps and peered down at him curiously. Alec looked back up at her and their eyes met.

Yukino's eyes narrowed. "Just who are you? Why did you save me?" She crossed her arms over her chest defensively.

"My name's Alec Suzuki. And I saved you because..." Alec blinked as he thought about this. Why did he save her? He had been about to say 'Because your mother asked me to' but Alec had tried to help Yukino even before he realized who she was. As soon as he saw her and realized she was a real ghost and was in trouble he had this immediate urge to help her. When he saw RedAki about to throw that dangerous globe of fire upon her - he just acted. It was a gut instinct that had made him protect Yukino. It was only when he sensed the connection between the control ring and Yukino when she had been about to harm the RRs that he realized that this ghost girl must be Yukino, Midoriko's daughter. But saying, 'It was a gut instinct' or something cheesy like 'my heart told me to' would sound stupid so...

"Your mother asked me to." Was what he ended up saying instead. Alec sighed. He had almost wanted to tell her that other reason.

Yukino's eyes filled with confusion, "My...mother? What are you talking about? I can't possibly have a-?"

"I met your mother Midoriko the other day. She said she had been searching for you in the game but that when she found you, you did not remember her - that you had lost your memory. She also told me you were in danger. I think now after seeing the RRs try and capture you I know why. And it was your mother who gave me this." He held up his hand to show her the control ring with the blue stone.

Yukino's eyes narrowed suspiciously at the control ring. "I sensed that earlier...I can feel it. So it must be my control ring. I guess that means I have a brat for a Master. This is just great..." Yukino sighed heavily, a frown forming on her pretty face.

Alec puffed out his cheeks indignantly. "Hey, don't call me a brat. I can't be much younger than you...?"

Yukino frowned, "I don't remember how old I am. And anyways how am I supposed to have such memories when I'm just an A.I. Battle Ghost?"

Alec was a bit startled by her words. "An A.I. Battle Ghost? Why would you think you're a Battle Ghost? You're a *real* ghost Yukino. I have the ability to *sense* ghosts so I can assure you that you're a real ghost. Unlike say this guy -" Alec jerked his thumb at Ryuu who nodded. "Ryuu here is an A.I. Battle Ghost, the first in the game with the ability to talk. When I reach my senses out towards him I feel nothing because he's just a program. But when I reach my senses out towards you I can feel your spiritual presence."

Yukino walked around Ryuu in a circle and inspected him curiously. "So what you're saying is I'm a real ghost? And that you talked to my mother in the game? But how is that possible...?"

"Your mother...is also a ghost who is haunting the game, Yukino. I'm sorry." Alec felt awkward about telling Yukino that her mother was dead too.

"I see." Yukino said sadly, "So...I'm alive...or rather...I'm dead and now I'm trapped inside of this game. I wonder what happened to me. I wish I could remember...something horrible must have happened to me to make me want to stay here. There must be something I need to do here - something that has to do with the game. But also if I'm a real ghost...then why do I have a control ring, Alec?" She looked back at Alec with a slightly frantic expression on her face.

Alec frowned. "I dunno..."

"All this time I thought I was a Battle Ghost that had somehow developed free will. But now you're telling me I'm a real ghost. That I have a mother...a past. But then there's the mystery of the control ring. Why were you given the ring and why does the ring have the power to control me. It's awful...I can feel our connection through the ring. I can feel how much power you have over me. You could make me do anything. I don't want to have a Master! I don't want to be controlled!" Yukino bit her lip and looked close to tears.

ACK! Alec began to panic when he noticed that Yukino was about to start crying - her eyes welling up with unshed tears. He had just made a girl cry! *Dang it! Good going Alec. Making a girl cry. Real smooth.* Alec began waving his hands frantically before him, "*Chottomatte*, wait a minute! Whoever said I was your Master or anything? I was just kidding before. If I'm anything to you it's...well your mother called me your Guardian. But I would be happy if we could be friends." Alec gave her a shy smile.

Yukino sniffled. "But the ring...?"

Alec shook his head, "Your mother only gave me the ring so that it wouldn't fall into the wrong hands. She probably didn't want the RRs to get a hold of it. That became obvious to me just now. Perhaps, they intend to control you via the ring although I'm not sure for what purpose. Your mother also told me..." Alec looked away slightly embarrassed, and scratched his cheek nervously with his index finger. "That I had to protect you."

Yukino gave Alec a tremulous smile. "So you won't try and control me then? We can be friends?"

Alec shook his head vigorously from side to side then up and down. "No! I would never force you to do something you didn't want to do. And I would be honored if we could be friends."

Yukino let out a breath of relief. "Really?"

Alec smiled warmly at her. "Really. So...friends?"

Yukino nodded. "Friends."

"Don't worry Yukino I'll help you find your lost memories and remember your unfinished business so that you can crossover." Alec assured her.

Yukino's brow furrowed in confusion. "Unfinished business?"

Alec nodded. "Yes, people usually only become ghosts if they have some sort of unfinished business they didn't get to accomplish while they were alive, and their souls can't move on until it's somehow accomplished. There must be some reason why you decided to haunt this game world just like you said before..." Alec tapped his chin thoughtfully. "That's what we need to find out."

Yukino eyed Alec thoughtfully for a moment. "Why are you going so out of your way to help me?"

"Why?" Alec quirked his head at her as if the question had stumped him. He couldn't think of a time he hadn't helped a ghost to figure out his or her unfinished business so that they could crossover. It had to be one of the main reasons why he had been cursed with the strange ability to see ghosts to begin with. He was destined to help them. It was his responsibility. "It's what I do." Alec gave her a lopsided smile. "My best friend was a ghost..." Alec's throat closed up as he thought of Billy but he forced himself to continue. "I've never told anyone this but...he was my best friend for years but then after he accomplished his unfinished business he had to leave me alone...I'm always alone now."

Yukino's eyes seemed to soften at his last words, which she seemed to be able to sympathize with. She reached out and took Alec's hand. "Me too. I'm also always alone. You know Alec I think we're kindred spirits you and I and that's why we found each other. We're both alone but together...we won't have to be alone anymore. Now, that we're friends and everything I mean. And even if I do find out why I'm haunting the game that doesn't necessarily mean I have to leave you Alec. I mean, what if you become my unfinished business. Then I can stay here haunting the game for you, so you won't be alone."

Alec looked up surprised at Yukino's offer. "You would do that, for me?"

179

Alec then looked down at their clasped hands a bit embarrassed, a slight flush coming to his cheeks. This was the first time he had ever held hands with a girl like this...

Yukino smirked suddenly, "Sure, why not. Besides, someone has to look out for you, so you don't do something stupid again like what you did back there with the fox fire. That was totally reckless, you brat." Yukino pulled her hand away and ruffled Alec's hair completely ruining the moment in Alec's opinion as she began to treat him like a little kid. "I'm sure Ryuu agrees with me. Don't you Ryuu?"

Ryuu nodded, his expression grim. "Yes, Master was being way too reckless. He should have summoned me and used me to protect you instead, Lady Yukino."

Alec looked back and forth between the two in shock at this odd exchange. "Lady Yukino...?" Alec shook his head.

"Are you sure you're feeling okay, you brat?" Yukino joked pressing a hand to his forehead.

Alec blushed and pushed her hand away. "I'm fine. And don't call me a brat. We're the same age! *Mou*! Geez!"

"Aw, but I've always wanted a little brother." Yukino declared suddenly looking at Alec a bit starry-eyed. "Won't you be my little brother? *Please*? Even if we are the same age Alec girls mature faster than boys so technically I'm older than you. So that makes me your older sister. And it's my duty to protect you, okay? This will be fun." Yukino had an amused expression on her face.

"Little brother?" Alec blinked and then pouted, "But I don't need a big sister to protect me...I'm supposed to be protecting you, Yukino."

"You're not the one who can control ice and snow." Yukino's eyes were teasing.

Alec faltered at that comment since she was right. She could control ice and snow and that was impressive. In fact, it was a rather odd ability for a ghost to possess. He had never heard of ghosts having those kinds of abilities. *She's right, she is powerful, perhaps even dangerous. She had been about to freeze RedAki and those other PKers after all and who knows what really would have happened to them in the game...or reality.* Alec shivered. Did that mean Yukino was evil? Alec paled. He was just beginning to remember a story his father had once told him about a ghost lady called Oyuki, who could kill people with her icy breath...

Yukino raised an eyebrow at Alec's odd expression. "*Nani?* What?"

Alec shook himself. "Nothing. It's just a bit odd that your powers seem to work in the game and that they actually feel pretty real too."

"When you put it that way - it is a bit strange." Yukino agreed.

"Your mother said something about how the lines between the game, reality and the real spirit world are blurring."

"My mother?" Yukino's face fell. "I wish I could remember her." Her eyes began to shimmer again with unshed tears.

Shoot! Alec realized he was about to make a girl cry again! *Someone call 911! Think Alec think!* He looked over at all the glittery, powdered snow and suddenly got an idea. He quickly made a snowball and threw it straight at Yukino. Although her body was see-through it was solid enough for the snowball to hit her with a *splat*.

Yukino turned to stare at Alec in disbelief. "You did *not* just do that! I can't believe you just did that. You are so dead!" Yukino quickly made a snowball of her own in order to retaliate and threw it straight at the giggling Alec. It hit him *smack* in the face.

A snowball fight quickly ensued. Alec quickly made another snowball to get her back and threw it at Yukino so that it hit her forehead, the snow falling down onto her black hair and around her shoulders. Alec took in a quick intake of breath as he saw how pretty she looked with all the sparkling snowflakes caught in her dark blue-black hair. *She looks...like a snow angel.*

They were going all out throwing snowballs at each other and were getting completely covered in snow and laughing up a storm all the while.

Ryuu was looking at them quizzically, his head quirked. "What are you two doing?"

Alec tried to calm down his laughter to explain, "We're having a snowball fight."

Ryuu raised an eyebrow, "A snowball...fight?"

Yukino nodded, giggling, "Yea, you make snowballs and throw them at each other. The one who scores the most hits wins."

"It's...fun." Alec put in, trying to explain.

"Fun?" Ryuu again looked perplexed.

"And the one with the biggest snowball wins!" Yukino declared throwing a snowball at Alec in the back when he wasn't looking and running off.

Alec shivered as some of the snow went down the back of his *haori* shirt, "*Brrrr.*" He then turned to face her. "Hey, that's not true! And get back here you! That was a cheap shot!"

Ryuu silently went over and began to make a snowball...

Yukino laughed as Alec chased after her but suddenly her eyes widened and she pointed behind Alec in surprise. "Alec look out!"

"Huh?" Alec turned around just in time to see Ryuu hefting up a gigantic snowball at least as big as Alec was, which he then launched towards the unsuspecting Alec.

"Uh oh." Alec squeaked as he was hit by the gigantic snowball and completely buried within the snow.

"Alec!" Yukino cried out, sounding half-amused and half-worried.

"Master!" Ryuu seemed to realize he had overdone it.

They both began to dig in the snow before managing to pull Alec out.

"You okay?" Yukino frowned down at him.

Alec was shivering from the cold but smiled back. "Yea, just tired." He plopped down on the soft powdery snow with a sigh. Then Alec suddenly had another idea as he remembered the stone angel statue, which had been covered in snow back in the cemetery. "Hey Yukino...have you ever made a snow angel?"

"Snow angel?" She tilted her head at him, "What's that?"

Alec seemed to realize that making 'Snow Angels' must be an American thing. "Here I'll show you." Alec began to flap his arms and legs in the snow and both Ryuu and Yukino were looking at him like he was crazy. He knew how stupid he must of looked but he didn't care since he knew what the finished product would look like. He carefully stood up and turned around to face his snow angel. He smiled since it looked pretty good.

Yukino and Ryuu both seemed surprised and slightly impressed by what they saw.

"Crazy American boy." Yukino sounded amused.

"Come on! Let's all make snow angels you guys!" Alec declared plopping back down into the snow.

"Aw what the hell." Yukino grudgingly agreed and plopped down in the snow on Alec's left side. Ryuu followed suit and plopped himself down on the ground on Alec's right. They began to flap and move their arms feeling like complete fools but having lots of a fun doing it. As Alec was moving his arms up and down his fingers brushed against Yukino's and he couldn't help but be surprised that for a ghost...her finger tips had seemed warm if only for an instant. He blushed as he realized how close they were and when he looked at her he couldn't help but feel that she seemed perfectly in her element like some kind of spirit of the snow or goddess or something. Though he knew how silly that sounded in his head and was glad no one could hear his thoughts.

The three of them all stood up carefully to see the imprints of their three snow angels. They were each lined up side by side and looked pretty good. Ryuu's snow angel was of course bigger than the other two and it almost looked like the angels were of a father, daughter and son or maybe...a big brother, older sister, and little brother.

Alec's teeth were chattering at this point, and he was almost blue from the cold. Yukino turned to look at him worriedly when she noticed him shivering.

"Maybe you should log out Alec, you're not looking so good." Yukino frowned. "You don't want to catch your death of cold and end up like me now do you?"

Ryuu was looking worried at that comment. "Master should log out."

"Yea, maybe you're right but...what are we going to do about you?" Alec bit his lower lip.

"Huh? What do you mean?" Yukino quirked her head.

"I can't just leave you here, you know, alone. Not when the RRs are after you...you can't enter a control ring like other Battle Ghosts right?" Alec gave her a curious look.

Yukino shrugged, "I dunno...why don't you go ahead and give it a try."

Alec nodded. "Right then. Control ring!" Alec raised Yukino's control ring to summon her inside and it glowed but then nothing happened. *Dang.* "Strange...it doesn't work. Maybe it's because you're a real ghost and all...if only there was a safe place in the game where I could take you." Alec tapped his chin.

"A guildhall would be a good place to take Lady Yukino." Ryuu suggested. "Since only members can enter. Do you belong to a guild yet, Master?"

Alec shook his head, "No, I haven't really had any invites and the only Guild Master I know is Night."

"Night?" Yukino frowned at the name, looking pensive.

Alec hesitated because of Neji's warning about how he shouldn't trust Night. Then his father's words about how sometimes one has to believe in people rang through Alec's mind once more. Alec decided to send Night a private message.

"I'm going to send him a PM (Private Message) now. But I don't know how long it will take for him to respond." Alec said as he typed the message to Night on his computer back in reality and then sent it:

Night
I need your help, it's urgent. Please contact me.
Dranarch

Bing. The sound of Alec receiving a PM was heard. Alec blinked as he received a PM from Night only seconds later. *Dang, that was fast.* Alec read the message:

Where are you?
Alec quickly PMed him back typing in:
Graveyard Area Coord x12 y34
Night messaged him back:
I'll be right there.

Night teleported himself to the Graveyard Area in the game and began to head towards Alec's coordinates. His feet began to crunch through the snow that had gathered and Night was surprised when he felt the chill wind. He raised his hand up and was even more surprised to *feel* the snowflakes, which were falling in the graveyard around him. *That's strange.* Night then spotted Alec and Ryuu up ahead.

"Alec, what's-" He had been about to ask 'what's the matter' when he looked over and saw Yukino standing there in the snow and his eyes widened in shock before he composed himself to look merely curious. "What...who...?"

Alec stepped forward in front of Yukino, a steely expression on his face, "She's a ghost. A real ghost, Night. Though I don't know if you're going to believe me..."

Night simply cut him off. "I believe you."

Alec was a bit startled by this, "Y-you do?"

Night nodded. "It would explain this unusual snowfall after all."

"Yea, right, well the thing is I just rescued her from the RRs." Alec was saying.

Night sucked in his breath. "RRs?" He looked worried.

"Yea, I don't know what they want with her but whatever it is it can't be good. So, she needs a safe place in Yokai World to stay, somewhere where the RRs can't get to her when I'm not here to protect her."

Night raised an eyebrow at this declaration, "Protect her?"

Alec waved that aside. "It's a long story. But I was thinking a guildhall could work because only members are allowed and since I don't know any other Guild Masters...I thought of you." Alec put his hands out in a helpless gestures.

Night smirked. "So, you want to join the Guardian Knights, kid? Along with...?" His eyes darted over to the ghost girl.

"Yukino," Alec supplied.

"Yukino...*ka*?" Night looked over at her and their eyes met. Alec thought he saw a flash of sadness cross Night's eyes before it disappeared, making Alec think he must have imagined it.

Yukino stared back at him curiously and she couldn't help but feel that there was something oddly familiar about Night. There was something *comforting* about his presence. Yukino blushed when she realized she was feeling strangely towards him. Why was she feeling this way? It unsettled her.

"Do I know-?" Yukino was saying as Alec cut her off.

"Well, I guess so." Alec shrugged. *Neji is so going to kill me.* "I'm sorry to be such a bother. So can we? I mean, can we join your guild?"

Night gave Alec and Yukino a warm smile. "Of course."

Alec still hesitated.

"Something wrong?" Night asked.

Alec looked over at Yukino and decided to grab Night's arm and pull him aside so he could talk to him alone. "Well, there's something else I wanted to talk to you about...it's about...your sister."

Night's eyes widened and he looked back over at Yukino before looking back at Alec. "Yes?"

"Is it true that you're looking for her? In the game I mean?" Alec asked.

"You could say that." Night began noncommital.

"And you think the RRs were behind your sister's disappearance and that's why your guilds are enemies and that's why you PKK for information on your sister's whereabouts?" Alec asked in a rush.

"Yes, does that bother you?"

Alec paused, thought about it and then shook his head. "No, after seeing what the RRs were trying to do to Yukino I believe you. And that's why I want to help you find your sister. But I don't think PKKing is the answer. I just don't feel it's right. It's sinking to their level."

"Sometimes one must become a devil to best a devil." Night responded coldly. And Alec remembered Midoriko's words about how he had to save Night....from himself.

Alec knew he couldn't force the matter though so left it at that. "I don't believe that but...I still want to help you, Night. And maybe I'll be able to find another way for you to best a devil."

Night seemed amused by this declaration. "Thank you Alec, for believing in me and for wanting to help me."

Alec smirked. "I could be saying the same exact thing."

Alec and Yukino quickly accepted the guild invite from the Guardian Knights guild that Night sent them. Now, that they were both members they could directly teleport to the guildhall.

Alec raised his arm, "Guardian Knights guildhall!"

Yukino, and Night followed suit and they were all instantly teleported to a large hall inside of an impressive, Asian-styled building with tiled and curved roofs. The guildhall was more of an entire building than just one room. The building had sliding *shoji* doors, *tatami* floor mats, and scrolls of Japanese brush paintings and wood block prints hanging on the walls.

Night led them from the main guildhall into a smaller room off to the side. Alec blinked when he entered and saw a series of strange floating keyboards and large computer screens that two Ninja Class players, with masks on their faces, seemed to be monitoring. Alec looked up at the images onscreen and realized they were screen caps and images of things happening within Yokai World. Most of the images onscreen were replays of the RRs as they PKed people and just general RR activities that currently were being monitored.

185

"Welcome, to the Guardian Knights." Night waved a hand around the control room.

"What's all this?" Alec asked walking forward to look at the screens.

"I've been monitoring the Renegade Reapers guild activity for some time...I'm just waiting for them to make their move." Night frowned as he looked up at the screens. "They're about to start something big...I can feel it...but that's why we, the Guardian Knights exist...to be there to stop them if we have to."

Alec nodded. "I understand. Don't worry Night, I've got your back."

Night smiled. "And I've got yours." He reached out his hand and Alec took it and they clasped hands in agreement. A silent pact being made.

Alec couldn't help but think - *So I'm a Guardian Knight now, Neji is so going to kill me.*

Chapter 9:
THE GRUDGE CURSE PART I:

The next morning, Alec woke up early so that he could head over to Izagani's extensive school library and search for information on the story of Oyuki that was buzzing in the back of Alec's mind and that needed confirmation. Alec was happy that no one was in the library at such an hour so that he was able to avoid awkward questions about why he was researching Japanese ghost stories.

It didn't take him very long to find a book which contained the tale of Yuki Onna or 'The Snow Woman'. Alec's eyes scanned over the story and he read the story that was about two wood cutters, a young boy of 18 named Minokichi and an old man named Mosaku.

One winter day, the two woodcutters were unable to return to their village due to a fierce snowstorm but luckily stumbled across an abandoned hut in the mountains and decided to take refuge there.

However, that very evening Minokichi was woken up from his fitful sleep to see a woman dressed all in white and with long black hair leaning over Mosaku and breathing her breath upon him which seemed like an icy mist. Minokichi was too scared to move when the mysterious woman in white moved towards him next.

She leaned over Minokichi, prepared to breath upon him and kill him as well but as her face drew closer and closer to Minokichi's she seemed to pause in her actions. Minokichi, who now had a chance to better look at this mysterious woman's face, saw that up close she was even more beautiful. Their eyes seemed to lock on to each other's and unexpectdly Yuki Onna pulled back and gave the boy a smile.

"I was going to kill you like the old man...but upon seeing how young and handsome you are I have changed my mind." Yuki Onna informed him. "However, if you ever dare to breath a word of this to anyone I shall kill you."

And with these words Yuki Onna left Minokichi. Minokichi immediately went to Mosaku's side and upon touching his body found it to be a frozen-stiff corpse. It took Minokichi a while to get over the shock and trauma of his encounter with the Yuki Onna and to get over Mosaku's death but he eventually did so and returned to gathering wood to sell with the help of his mother.

On one such day, as he was in the forest gathering wood he encountered a beautiful young woman named Oyuki, who he instantly fell in love with. He ended up marrying Oyuki and they lived happily together for many years and had 10 children. However, one day as Oyuki was sewing by lamplight Minokichi seemed to remember the strange encounter he had with the Yuki Onna and decided to tell his wife about it and how she resembled the Yuki Onna.

"When I gaze upon you now I'm reminded of this odd incident that happened in my youth and when I met a woman as strangely beautiful as you..."

After Minokichi finished his story Oyuki got up and enraged yelled at Minokichi.

"I am the very same Yuki Onna whom you met! I told you I would kill you if you ever told a soul about that encounter and so I should kill you but I will not because of our children. If you at all mistreat them I shall return and punish you! Farewell!"

And with that being said she melted before Minokichi's eyes and then turned into a mist that disappeared, never to be seen from again.

Alec set down the book thoughtfully, a frown on his face. A spirit of the snow, Yuki Onna, with the ability to breath an icy breath on people and kill them by turning them into frost-covered corpses. Alec shivered. And then there was Yukino...who was a ghost who could control ice and snow...

The similarities between the two were there and were quite unnerving. But Alec had felt Yukino was a real ghost...with a real past so she couldn't be some legendary spirit of the snow now could she? That wouldn't make any sense. But if she was somehow related to Yuki Onna did that mean she was an evil spirit that Alec should exorcize? Alec was so confused he didn't know what to do.

He wanted to say to himself that the girl Yukino hadn't seemed evil at all but when he remembered her cold gaze upon the Renegade Reapers when she had been about to freeze them to death - he wasn't so sure.

His new friend, Yukino, might be an evil spirit after all. Alec's heart clenched painfully at the thought and he decided to bury it deep inside of himself. Above all, Alec wanted to believe in her.

● ● ● ● ● ● ● ● ● ● ● ● ● ● ● ● ●

Alec was walking down the hall back from the library with his head full of thoughts of Yukino and the Yuki Onna. That's when Junpei suddenly caught sight of him.

"Yo Alec!" Junpei flung his arm around Alec's shoulders unexpectedly. "You look deep in thought, my friend. Thinking about a girl?"

"W-what? No! Of course not!" Alec sputtered while turning beet red.

"Hmm?" Junpei raised his eyebrows at Alec's frantic reaction. "That's so suspicious. Why are you blushing then aye Alec? You were thinking about a girl weren't you?"

"I wasn't...not really anyways." Alec ended up saying.

A wolfish grin formed on Junpei's face. "I knew it! Spill!"

"No!" Alec refused but then Junpei put him into a stranglehold.

"Come on Alec spill! Don't be stingy! Was it Rika you were thinking about?" Junpei questioned curiously.

"No, it wasn't Rika. It's someone I met in the game." Alec started and Junpei loosened his hold and Alec was glad he was able to breath again. "Whew, anyways, I met her in the game but she's...well, I don't know if you're going to believe me or not but she's a ghost."

Junpei's eyebrows shot up to his hairline. "A ghost? You met a ghost while inside of the game?"

Alec nodded. "Yes, her name is Yukino and...well, I just got back from the library. There was something about her that reminded me of the myth of Yuki Onna. Do you know that story?"

Junpei nodded, "Yep, that's a creepy one. The Snow Witch that lures people deep into the snow-covered mountains before she kills them with an icy kiss that ends up freezing them to death. Why? Does Yukino remind you of the Snow Witch?"

"Because she can control the elements of ice and snow." Alec admitted.

"You're pulling my leg." Junpei decided and gave Alec an amused look. "You're good Alec. You almost had me going there that you met Yuki Onna within the game. That would be a fun urban legend to start up for Yokai World though. But if you did meet Yuki Onna Alec you better be careful because..." Junpei went up to Alec and then began tickling him. "She's going to eat you all up!"

"Ah! Junpei stop!" Alec struggled to get out of Junpei's grasp and couldn't help but start laughing since he was especially ticklish. "Junpei!"

"She's going to kiss you with her icy blue lips Alec! *Ooo!~*" Junpei continued to tease Alec, "Say, can you introduce us? An icy kiss wouldn't be such a bad way to go." Junpei waggled his eyebrows.

I don't think he took me seriously. Alec just sighed and shook his head. *Jocks...*

* * * * * * * * * * * * * * * *

Junpei then proceeded to drag Alec to the soccer field since it was still pretty early and they had a lot of time to kill before home room and Junpei wanted to play a little one on one soccer with Alec - best three out of five.

They began challenging each other for the soccer ball and Alec used some fancy footwork to get the ball away from Junpei and quickly headed off running with the soccer ball as he dribbled it towards Junpei's goal, which Junpei was supposed to protect.

"Oh man!" Junpei whined as he ran down the field and tried to get in front of the soccer goal in time to try and block Alec's shot.

Alec saw that Junpei was trying to get in front of the goal but it was already too late. Alec smirked as he used his spirit energy and knew he'd manage to get this particular soccer ball past Junpei's defenses. "Try this!" Alec used his toe to bring the soccer ball into the air a bit before bringing his leg back and then forward so that his ankle collided with the soccer ball and sent it flying forward towards Junpei at a rapid speed. The soccer ball was glowing with a blue-tinged light.

Junpei raised up his arms and prepared to try and block Alec's soccer ball. That was until he saw how fast it was going and that it was glowing like a comet.

"Oh shoot!" Junpei swore as he dived out of the way of the soccer ball which went flying past him and hit the net of the goal, spinning. But the net wasn't able to hold the soccer ball for very long as the soccer ball ended up eating a hole in the net in seconds and kept going.

Junpei whistled through his teeth as he stood up and looked back at the hole in the net. He was lucky he had chosen life over pride on that one. "Whoa, dang boy, you sure you don't want to join the soccer team? We'd be happy to have you."

"I'm sure." Alec said noncommital as he ran over to get the soccer ball so they could start again. "Come on!" Alec urged Junpei as he dropped the ball in the center of the field and they began to try and steal the soccer ball away from each other again. It was Junpei this time that managed to get the soccer ball away from Alec.

"Yes!" Junpei smiled to himself as he ran down the field towards Alec's goal.

Alec swore and quickly ran after Junpei but his vision was suddenly getting blurry and Alec blinked rapidly trying to clear it. Then a wave of dizziness seemed to pass over Alec and he could feel himself falling forward -

Junpei was just about to make it to the goal when he turned around to find out why Alec wasn't chasing him. He was startled to see that Alec had fainted.

"Alec!"

* * * * * * * * * * * * * * * * *

Alec was in and out of consciousness as Junpei carried him to the nurse's office. He heard Junpei enter the nurse's office and how Haruna gasped in surprise at the sight of the semi-unconscious Alec.

"Junpei? What happened?" Haruna-*sensei* got up from her desk and rushed over to the boys.

"He just...collapsed." Junpei shrugged with Alec still on his back.

"Put him over there on the bed." Haruna-*sensei* directed Junpei, who did as he was told and gently set Alec down on one of the beds. Haruna-*sensei* then came over and put a hand to Alec's forehead. "He's burning up! He has a very high fever. I'll see if I can lower it..." Haruna put her hand on Alec's forehead and kept it there as she concentrated on her empathic healing abilities - her hand beginning to glow with a blue-tinged light. After a while she took her hand away, frowning. "I did what I can but...there's something almost unnatural about his fever...I don't think..." Haruna trailed off and bit her lip, before shaking her head. "Let's let him rest for now."

Alec was dimly aware of them speaking and glad that they weren't going to try and rouse him to ask him any questions just then. For some reason he was feeling completely wiped out.

He awoke about a half an hour later, and looked up at the now familiar ceiling of Haruna-*sensei*'s office. He could feel that a cool, wet towel was on his burning forehead. Alec tried to sit up and immediately regretted it as his head spun. "Ugh, my head." Alec put a hand to his forehead.

Haruna-*sensei* and Junpei immediately came to his bedside as he woke up.

Junpei looked at Alec worriedly, "Alec buddy? You okay?"

Alec nodded, "Yea, what's wrong with me? What happened?"

"You fainted." Junpei informed him.

Alec's eyes widened.

"Junpei-*kun* brought you here after you collapsed. You are running an awful fever and I recommend that you stay in bed for the rest of the day or at least until your fever goes down, Alec-*kun*." Haruna-*sensei* instructed him.

"A fever..." Alec had a feeling of dread well up inside of him for some reason.

Haruna-*sensei* nodded. "It doesn't *feel* like a normal fever to me either. I can't really explain it. Do you have any idea what might have caused it so that I can decide on a better treatment?"

Alec wondered what Haruna-*sensei* could possibly mean but then found himself thinking back to when he had saved Yukino from that globe of fox fire and how he had *felt* like he was being burned alive. His mind had been on fire and he remembered how he had briefly wondered if his real body would be affected since the pain had felt so real but...how could he tell Haruna-*sensei* that he thought he developed a fever from something that happened to him in an online game. She'd never believe him or think he was crazy.

So instead of telling the truth Alec shook his head. "I dunno..."

Haruna-*sensei* frowned knowingly, sensing that Alec was keeping something from her (she was an Empath after all) but decided not to press him about it. She nodded. "Alright then Alec, just lay back and get some more rest then. You should feel better. But if you remember anything, anything at all tell me okay? It could be very important." She frowned at him.

Alec nodded and he watched as Haruna-*sensei* went to get him a fresh towel. She came back and placed it on Alec's forehead and absentmindedly brushed a stray white hair from Alec's face. She was looking down at Alec but Alec realized she wasn't really looking down at him, but rather at something from her past. She had a very sad look on her face and Alec suddenly wished he could make her feel better. She continued to stroke his head and Alec blushed as her kind touch reminded him once again of his own mother...and of how nice it felt to be taken care of. Alec looked away embarrassed as he realized what he was thinking.

Haruna-*sensei* seemed to realize what she was doing and pulled her hand back suddenly. She moved away from Alec's bed with a sigh. "Junpei, don't stay for too much longer, alright? You have to get to class soon and Alec-*kun* needs his rest."

Junpei nodded.

"I have to finish some paper work. I'll just be right over there if you boys need me." Haruna-*sensei* declared as she made her way towards her desk.

Junpei turned to Alec, a curious glint in his eye. "So...you like Haruna-*sensei* don't you?"

Alec's eyes widened and he spluttered, "What? I never said anything like that! I mean, I like her but...I don't like her, like her, you know."

Junpei didn't look convinced. "Sure, then why were you looking at her all doe-eyed for then?" Junpei raised an eyebrow at Alec, waiting for his response.

Alec looked away with a sigh, "I was...thinking of how much she reminded me of my mother." A sad look crossed Alec's face.

Junpei seemed caught off-guard by this. "Your mother? Is she...?" Junpei trailed off suddenly looking out of his element.

Alec shook his head. "No, she's not dead. But...I might as well be dead to her."

Junpei furrowed his brows in confusion at that statement. "What do you mean?" He gave Alec a curious look.

Alec frowned, "Just forget it okay. I don't want to talk about her."

Junpei pouted but knew that Alec had closed himself off. Junpei shrugged and put his hands out in a helpless gesture. "Alright fine. I won't ask. But if you ever want to talk about it I'm here Alec." Junpei headed towards the door. "I gotta get to class anyways so I'll see you later."

"Yea...see ya..." Alec said halfheartedly as he turned his back to the door.

* * * * * * * * * * * * * * * *

Alec woke up several hours later and looked over at the clock next to the bed and saw that it read: 7:30 pm. Alec plopped his head back down on his pillow and chewed his lower lip thoughtfully as he wondered why he had this nagging feeling that he had forgotten something important. His eyes widened when he suddenly realized he had never gone to leave Akira his tray of food that day! Alec quickly sat up in bed, the wet towel falling off his forehead, and looked around the darkened nurse's office. Haruna-*sensei* was nowhere in sight.

Alec decided he'd sneak out and make his way down to the cafeteria hoping that the covered tray of food would still be there. Alec pushed himself out of bed, wobbling slightly, his legs feeling like jelly, and then he steadied himself as he made his way to the door. His forehead was still burning and he was still feeling a bit dizzy but he managed to make it down to the cafeteria alright and as luck would have it the tray had been kept out. Alec grabbed the covered tray of food and began to make his way back to the dorm building, crossing the school grounds. He made his way inside and took the elevator to the appropriate floor before making his way slowly towards Akira's room.

Alec blinked his eyes as his eyesight was getting blurry again and wondered if he was going to make it. He wished he could steady himself on the walls but his hands were full with the tray. Finally, he made it to Akira's room. Alec carefully set down the tray of food and was about to knock when he heard some sort of muffled noise coming from within. Curious Alec put his ear up to the door and his eyes widened when he realized the sound he was hearing was of someone crying. Akira was crying.

Alec was suddenly filled with guilt. Akira was probably crying all because of him and how he had forgotten to bring him his food. Akira was probably feeling hungry, alone, and forgotten...not good things to feel. Alec knew this from personal experience - how many times had his mother forgotten to pick him up at school? And had just left Alec there to fend for himself and figure out a way to get home all on his own? And sometimes he'd been forced to walk home in the rain or snow. How many times had his mother been too busy or concerned with other things to prepare Alec his lunch?

Alec took a deep breath and knocked on the door.

Alec heard a shuffling sound from within as Akira was pulling himself together. "Wh-who's there?" The voice cracked but it was still cold and standoffish.

"It's me Alec, I brought your tray of food."

A pause. Then - "You're late! *Baka!*" *Grrrr.* He could hear Akira growling from the other side of the door.

"I know, *wari, wari.* It's my bad, sorry." Alec swiftly apologized, his hand behind his head as he bowed at the door repeatedly.

Alec heard the sound of the bottom door panel being unlocked and then it was swung open. Alec bent down and slid the tray under the door. And then the mini-door was swiftly closed and locked again.

Alec stood and leaned his back against the door for support since he was feeling a bit dizzy again. "You know, I'm really sorry I'm late. I didn't forget about you and...I'm sorry I made you cry." Alec said awkwardly.

There was the sound of someone choking on food coming from the other side of the door.

"*Nani?* What!" The voice choked out. "I wasn't..." The voice trailed off and then. "I wasn't crying because of that."

Alec raised an eyebrow. "Why were you crying then?"

A pause. Then - "None of your business! *Baka* brat! Why the hell would I tell you anyways?"

Alec shrugged. "Yea, I guess you're right."

There was a long silence before Akira spoke again. "You know the other day...why did you say you were the wrong person to give me a reason to leave my room?"

Alec sighed. "Because I understand only too well how you feel. Sometimes I too just want to run away from reality and shut it all out. Just shut everyone out and escape from the reality of my life."

"You do?" Akira almost squeaked in surprise.

"Yea, sometimes...I wish I could just stay locked up in my room and never come out...just like you."

"Why?"

"You probably wouldn't believe me if I told you..." Alec thought about how the poltergeist and ghosts were always chasing him, and how now in this strange school the ones taking care of the poltergeists were a monk and *miko* while he wasn't even allowed to exorcize ghosts anymore. What a load of boloney. What did they expect Alec to do when they came after him?

"So you want to be a *hikikomori*...just like me?"

"Yea, um, I guess so." Alec shrugged.

There was another long pause and then Akira broke out into a strained sort of laugh, but it was laughter nevertheless and Alec had never heard Akira laugh before. "You really are a *baka* brat!"

Alec couldn't help himself - he started to laugh too. "Yea, maybe I am." He agreed.

After they had both had a good laugh Alec pushed himself away from the door prepared to go back to the nurse's office. "I need to go - to get back to -" Alec was feeling dizzy again and he put a hand on the door to keep himself standing. He was feeling a bit nauseous all of a sudden as well and put a hand to the front of his mouth wondering if he was going to be sick. He blinked when he realized his vision was fading. *Aw man, I'm going to pass out. Great, just great.*

THUD

• • • • • • • • • • • • • • • •

"Alec?" Came Akira's worried voice, "Alec you okay? What happened? Alec!"

From inside the *hikikomori*'s room, a 12-year-old boy with spiky black hair and dark shadows around his eyes from lack of sleep, hesitated at the door to his room. He reached his trembling hand out and finally reached for the doorknob. Slowly, he turned the knob and opened the door. There lying on the floor in front of his now open door was a boy of about the same age as him with snow-white hair and very pale skin. Akira noted that he appeared to be unconscious.

Akira rushed to Alec's side and turned him over onto his back to try and wake him up. "Alec?" Akira lightly shook Alec's shoulder, but Alec didn't wake up. Akira noticed Alec's flushed appearance and how Alec was breathing in and out irregularly. Akira put a hand to Alec's forehead and quickly brought it back. He was burning! "*Shimatta.* Darn it. He's burning up..." Akira looked around frantically wondering what he should do...he couldn't very well take

Alec to the nurse's office could he? He was a *hikikomori* after all. He wasn't supposed to be able to leave his room. Akira looked around the deserted hallway and noticed how quiet it was. It was almost like the inside of his room - dark and quiet. Maybe no one would be around if he brought Alec to the nurse's office now in the middle of the night, and just dropped him off there.

Akira took a deep breath. *Yea, I can do that.* Akira reached out and hoisted Alec up onto his back so that he was carrying Alec piggy-back style to the nurse's office. *I can't believe I'm doing this. This Alec baka brat owes me one for sure. I'm going to suffer psychological trauma because of him for being out of my room. I better not run into anyone....it could scar me for life.*

Akira made his way out of the dorm building and took his first steps outside. He nearly fell forward in shock. It was so *open* out there underneath the night sky. It was just so...overwhelming. The sky was so high and the stars were shining so brightly and they seemed to be...laughing at him. He was sure of it! He could see their eyes and mouths open in laughter and they were pointing and laughing at what a fool he was being for helping some kid he didn't even know.

*Baka...Baka...Baka...Baka...*The stars seemed to jeer down at him.

Akira was beginning to hyperventilate. *Calm down Akira...one step at a time.* Akira focused on looking forward, ignoring the laughing stars, and took a deep breath before he put one foot forward and then slowly another. He painstakingly made his way in this manner towards the main school building where the nurse's office was.

Akira made his way into the building and finally he had made it to the nurse's office. Once again he hesitated, should he knock? That would mean he'd have to talk to another human being face to face but...he couldn't just leave Alec there without making sure he'd be okay right? Again, Akira was torn with what he should do before he decided on actually knocking. Akira chewed on his lower lip nervously as he waited for the door to be answered.

In seconds, Haruna-*sensei* was at the door. She opened it up and her eyes widened as she took in the sight of Akira and Alec. "Alec! What happened to him? Did he faint again? And um...who are you?"

Akira blushed at the nurse's forward manner but quickly composed himself. "He was delivering my food tray. What is he sick or something? You should get someone else to deliver my food until he's feeling better. The idiot... pushes himself too hard." Akira crossed his arms over his chest.

Haruna seemed to realize who Akira was. "Ah, you must be Akira. Alec has had a very unnatural fever all day today, hopefully I'll get someone else to have a look at him by tomorrow and he'll be set right. And I'll make sure to have someone else deliver your food to you tomorrow. Thank you for bringing him here Akira. That must have been very hard on you. You must be good friends with Alec-*kun* to go through so much for him."

She seemed to be able to see right through him and this unnerved Akira a *lot*. "It was nothing...and we're not friends!" Akira sneered before turning on his heel and bolting from the room. He couldn't stand being so out in the open any longer. He was sure that pretty nurse was laughing at him too behind her pretty, smiling face, behind that mask of hers!

Haruna's sad eyes watched him leave. "What a poor, lonely boy but..." She looked down at Alec, who was resting in the bed again, "Maybe someone has been sent to save you too."

•••••••••••••••••

Alec heard a knock at the door to the nurse's office and pretended to still be asleep as Haruna-*sensei* let them inside.

"I'm so glad two people from the *Shinigami* Squad could come so quickly." Alec heard Haruna-*sensei* say as she ushered them inside.

"We're here on Yoru's orders. It seems he's taken an interest in the welfare of this boy." Alec recognized that voice - it was Jin, Junpei's annoying older brother.

"You don't mean-?" Haruna was about to ask when Jin raised his hand to silence her.

"He's awake." Jin declared and Alec flushed with embarrassment wondering how Jin had known. Alec also wanted to know what the *Shinigami* Squad was exactly. And who was this Yoru guy? Alec opened his eyes and sat up in bed hoping for some answers.

Alec scratched his cheek with his index finger feeling a little awkward for eavesdropping. "Yo guys."

"Hey Alec." Junko greeted in a surprisingly friendly manner. Jin merely nodded in his direction

Haruna turned back to Jin and Junko. "So can you guys tell what's wrong with him?"

Jin nodded and looked over at Alec his brow furrowed, seemingly seeing something that no one else could see - and that happened to be an aura of black, negative energy that seemed to be surrounding Alec. "Yes, he's been cursed."

Alec squeaked. "I've been what?"

Jin smirked at Alec's discomfort. "Well, not quite *cursed* per say but you've come into contact with a large amount of negative, spiritual energy and it's affecting your body and causing that nasty fever. Don't worry, I'll have you cured in a jiffy." Jin reached into the sleeve of his *haori* shirt and pulled out a long, blank *o-fuda* and a paint brush. With a flourish he wrote down a quick spell with black ink in *kanji* letters and then before Alec could even blink Jin had slapped the *o-fuda* directly onto Alec's forehead and began muttering a sutra to himself.

Alec felt a strange tugging sensation in his gut and then Alec could suddenly see all of the black, negative energy being forced out of his body and his eyes widened. If he could see his own forehead he would have seen that the written *kanji* on the *o-fuda* were glowing with a blue, purifying light. Once all of the negative energy had been purged from Alec's body he felt completely exhausted and sank back down onto the bed panting for breath.

Haruna placed a hand to Alec's forehead and breathed a sigh of relief.

Jin however still looked troubled. "That was a very dangerous amount of negative spirit energy to be inside of someone. It's only because you're an exorcist, Alec, that you were probably able to even maintain consciousness at all. If it had been anyone else, say a normal human without any high spiritual abilities, it could have been much more serious."

Alec's eyes widened at this statement.

"Now the important question is how did this happen?" Jin narrowed his eyes at him. "Who did this to you Alec?"

Alec looked away not really wanting to tell them the truth since he was pretty sure they wouldn't believe him, but he also knew he didn't have a choice. Alec sighed. "I was in the game...RedAki...used a globe of fire on me..." Alec muttered keeping his voice low.

Jin's expression darkened. "What was that? Speak louder, kid. You were in the game? Do you mean Yokai World?"

Alec nodded. Jin and Junko exchanged a worried look.

"Could *they* be making their move?" Junko questioned her brother.

Alec looked up curious. "They?"

Jin noticed Alec's curious look and gave Junko a stern glare which clearly meant: 'Shhh!' She nodded in response.

Jin looked down at Alec, an imperious expression on his face. "Nothing you need to worry about Alec. We'll handle it from here."

Alec puffed out his cheeks in irritation. Jin was always trying to leave him out of things and it really got on his nerves. He was definitely being treated like a little kid. *Once again left out of the loop*, Alec couldn't help but think, *This school is weird. There are so many secrets. There's definitely more than meets the eye to this place...and I intend to find out what it is.*

Alec watched as Jin and Junko continued to talk to each other in low, urgent voices and then to Haruna-*sensei* before they sped out of the nurse's office. Alec felt completely drained and fell back onto the bed and quickly went to sleep...

* * * * * * * * * * * * * *

Guildhall of the Renegade Reapers, Yokai World...

RedAki felt very nervous and more than a bit worried to have been summoned by Reaper-*sama* to see him in his main audience chamber. He entered the hall where Reaper-*sama* was seated towards the back of the room in a red, outrageously high-backed, throne chair. Reaper-*sama* always had this intimidating, calm, deadly presence about him RedAki noted as he observed him. Their eyes met – red clashing with golden yellow. Eyes that would have been beautiful if not for the flames RedAki thought he could see leaping inside of them. Flames that hungered for a cleansing destruction. Reaper had long, silky, blood-red hair which he had pulled back into a pony-tail. He was dressed in an all-black Shinigami outfit with a red *obi* tied about his waist, and was wearing a flashy cloak that had a deep red lining. He was drumming his long, pale fingers on the arm of the throne chair impatiently as he waited for RedAki to approach him and RedAki noticed how his nails had been painted black. He also noticed that Reaper-*sama* had a control ring on each of his fingers making RedAki wonder just what ghosts or *yokai* his Master had up his sleeve...

RedAki's attention turned to the young lady that was standing next to Reaper, that he knew as Shino. In the game she possessed a Witch Class PC. She had long black hair, half of which was done up in a top knot and from which long, deadly looking, golden hair pins were sticking out. Her lips were painted in red and her upper eyelids had also been lined in red. She was wearing a black, sleeve-less, silk *kimono* that had a *freaky* pattern of red eyes on it, and around her waist she was wearing a matching red *obi* sash belt. Hanging from her neck was a necklace on which hung a pendant of a triangle with an eye in the center – the all seeing eye.

RedAki had heard rumors about Shino and about how she had visions of the future. RedAki shivered as her own dark eyes met his and he felt as though she could see straight through him. She gave him a once over and immediately seemed to sum him up as - rival. Rival for Reaper's affections that is and she leaned in closer so that she could rest her hand on Reaper's shoulder, giving RedAki a smirk as if to say, 'Ha, beat that!' RedAki couldn't help but feel jealous that Shino had managed to get so close to the man he looked up to and clenched his fists at his sides. She really annoyed him. RedAki couldn't help but stare at the strange tattoo she had in the center of her forehead, which was of a third eye and that had been inked in red. *Freaky...*

To Reaper's right, stood a Ninja Class PC, named Sumi. RedAki had always thought this guy was really creepy. *The Freak and the Creep. Ha! Who needs them when Reaper-sama has me?* He was dressed all in black and wore a half-mask on his face. He had silky, bright pink hair and light brown eyes. And what was with that spiked collar around his neck? *What a weirdo.* RedAki shook his head. Sumi never said much to the point that he irritated RedAki just for that, but the *ninja* always stuck by Reaper's side like glue - almost like a second shadow. And that also irritated RedAki since any time he wanted to spend time with his Master that creepy guy Sumi would be there and just silently stare at RedAki from afar as if *he* would do something to his Reaper-sama! Ha!

RedAki walked down the aisle and kneeled on one knee before Reaper. Out of the corner of his eye he could see a guilty looking Catara, Kiba and Smoker. *Those guys...did they rat me out about the duel?*

"You wished to see me, Reaper-*sama*?" RedAki bowed his head.

Reaper drummed his long nails on the arm of his chair. "I'm extremely disappointed in you RedAki-*kun*."

RedAki gulped, "I'm sorry Reaper-*sama*."

"You let Yukino slip through your fingers even after I gave you the *hoshi no tama (fox fire star-ball)*. Do you have any idea what this means? What you've put at risk?"

RedAki nodded. "Yes, Reaper-*sama*..."

Reaper shook his head. "I don't think you do. I heard you even let them go." Reaper said in an off-hand way but his voice was dangerous.

RedAki gasped, so his 'friends' did rat him out. *Great, just great.* "Dranarch and I had a Ghostly Duel - he won. We had a deal-" RedAki was trying to explain when Reaper waved his hand and cut him off.

"You disobeyed my orders, RedAki. This makes me very sad..." Reaper shook his head.

"I'm sorry, my Lord." RedAki bit his lower lip.

Reaper stood up and strode forward with swift, purposeful steps. "Not sorry enough I'm afraid." He reached out his hand and grasped RedAki's chin, forcing RedAki to look up at him. "How could you betray me so RedAki-kun? I believed in you, trusted you and now you've broken that trust. I'm hurt. You'll have to be punished - you do know that right? It's the only way a good school boy learns his lessons."

RedAki swallowed nervously. "Y-yes, my Lord."

Reaper summoned his power and a red-tinged aura seemed to flare to life around him. He stroked RedAki's cheek almost fondly before he then placed his fingers lightly onto the side of RedAki's face and kept his hand there as he concentrated his power. "This is me at my most masochistic self." Reaper said as he let his touch burn RedAki's face. RedAki cried out in pain and tried to pull back but Reaper wouldn't let him. RedAki felt like his mind was one fire from whatever Reaper was doing to him and wondered how something in a game could feel so real and so horrible. *Was this how Dranarch felt when the hoshi no tama broke on him?*

Reaper stood back and examined his handy work. "Now will you obey my orders without fail. If you do not you know now what shall happen."

RedAki nodded vigorously, and his head spun dizzily. "Yes."

Reaper smiled and clapped his hands together. "Good, then I shall grant you a new power." Reaper began to take one of the control rings off of his own finger and then handed it to RedAki. "With this Battle Ghost you should be able to get Yukino for me. Shino has foreseen your victory. Do not fail me."

RedAki took the ring from Reaper's hand and quickly slipped it on his ring finger. "Yes, my Lord." He looked down at the ring and could almost feel the power coming from it. "A new power..." His red eyes seemed to brighten with new life and hope. Perhaps, with this power he could beat Dranarch.

"Let that mark be a reminder of your failure to me RedAki. If you please me I will consider removing the mark. Understand?" Reaper drawled as he walked back to his throne and took a seat gracefully.

RedAki stood up and composed himself. "I understand, my Lord." He bowed, a secret smile on his face. *This is going to be fun. Here I come Dranarch!*

⁂

Alec had been resting up for several days, and unbeknownst to him during this time RedAki and his new Battle Ghost had been reeking havoc and spreading chaos throughout Yokai World...

When Alec was finally allowed to leave the nurse's office he went straight away with Junpei to the computer club room where they had arranged to meet up with Neji and Rika and all play Yokai World together.

"They'll be happy to see you Alec - this will be the first time in a while all of us have managed to get together to play Yokai World." Junpei was saying.

Alec smiled back happily, "Yea."

Alec opened the door and went inside, closely followed behind by Junpei. It was oddly quiet and Alec stopped in his tracks - Junpei running into him from behind - as he caught sight of Rika and Neji, who seemed to have either fallen asleep or fallen unconscious while playing Yokai World since they were both collapsed onto their keyboards in front of their computers and still had on their HMDs. But the way they were positioned was very awkward and almost looked like -

Alec gasped. *No! They can't be...?*

"Hey, Alec what's wrong?" Junpei questioned peaking around Alec and taking in the sight of the collapsed forms of Neji and Rika.

"Neji? Rika!" Alec rushed over to Neji first while Junpei rushed over to Rika's side. They both quickly checked their friends for a sign of a pulse and both breathed out sighs of relief when they found one. They then took off their HMDs and set them aside.

"They're both alright but...why won't they wake up?" Alec bit his lip worriedly. "Their sleep is unnatural almost like they're in a coma or something."

Junpei was looking at Rika's face without her glasses - noting that there was something oddly familiar about it. "Hey Alec, have you ever noticed that without her glasses Rika is kinda cute? Although she's still average when compared to say LadyV. As you know I'm LadyV's biggest fan. I think I could even be in love with her, Alec." Junpei sighed wistfully.

Alec frowned and shook his head, "Junpei! This is no time for jokes - go get some help! This is serious!"

Junpei seemed to snap out of it, "Right, sorry, I'll go get the nurse!" Junpei hurried off to fetch help.

Junpei returned moments later with help in tow and Rika and Neji were both diagnosed as being in comatose states and were quickly rushed to the hospital. It all happened in a bit of a blur to the stunned Alec, who just couldn't believe that this was all real - that this was actually happening. In a daze, he walked back to the computer club room which was now empty. Suddenly, he felt someone tap his shoulder from behind and he nearly jumped out of his skin. He spun around to see that Junpei had followed him back to the computer club room.

"Junpei! Man, you really have to stop doing that," Alec let out a breath of relief.

Junpei chuckled, "Right, sorry about that Alec." Junpei's expression turned serious as he looked around the computer room. "What do you think happened to them to make them fall into a coma like that?"

Alec looked thoughtful, "I dunno but...I have a feeling it has something to do with Yokai World."

The lines between the game, reality and the spirit world have blurred...

Alec took a seat at his usual computer and double clicked on the Yokai World icon. As soon as he had logged on he noticed that he had an email waiting for him and clicked it open. Alec's eyes widened when he saw who it was from - it was from Neji. "Hey, Junpei get a load of this - it's an email from Neji and it was sent...just a few minutes ago."

Junpei came over to Alec's side and peered over his shoulder, shaking his head, "But that's impossible, Alec..." Junpei frowned.

Alec shrugged and began to read the email aloud:

Alec

This is Neji...I don't know if you've heard about everything that's been going on in Yokai World during your bed arrest or if they're still trying to keep all this from you. But...RedAki seems to have gotten his hands on a new Battle Ghost that for some reason no one has been able to even lay a scratch on let alone destroy. Even my hacker skills couldn't touch that Battle Ghost. RedAki has been going on a PKing rampage trying to lure you out...along with some Battle Ghost he claims you have called Yukino. Do you have any idea what he's talking about?

Anyways, the people who've been PKed by his Battle Ghost are falling into comas. When I recently fought against RedAki I also ended up being PKed by his Battle Ghost. It was strange. I didn't die properly and come back as a PC ghost as I was supposed to. It was weird but my mind was on fire and then when I woke up next I was still in the game but no longer able to log out...I'm currently in the game world now...along with LadyV - it appears she's also unable to log out. I'm writing you to tell you all this and to warn you that Yokai World isn't safe right now and not to log on. It's much too dangerous. I hope you get this email and keep yourselves safe by not playing the game.

Neji

Alec and Junpei exchanged startled looks. "Neji and LadyV are both stuck in the game world?"

Junpei shook his head. "But that's...impossible. It's just a game."

Alec turned around to look at Junpei, biting his lip. "It's not just a game - not anymore Junpei. I can't explain this to you now but...trust me on this. I have to log on and speak with Neji and LadyV. I have to find out what's going on so I can help them somehow. And I have to confront RedAki - I can't let him continue to hurt people like this. I don't understand why he's doing this anyways...he almost seemed like he wasn't such a bad guy the last time we faced each other and had a Ghostly Duel. He had seemed almost...honorable. Something must have happened. And I intend to find out. If you're scared you can just stay here and keep on eye on my body for me."

Junpei raised an eyebrow, "Scared? No way, dude, I'm coming with you. You're going to need my help with this - I know it. And besides what are friends for - I've got your back Alec."

Alec smirked. "Okay then. Let's go!"

The two boys logged on to Yokai World and immediately teleported to Kintoki Forest where Neji had revealed he and LadyV currently were. Alec recognized the forest from the Kintoki Forest Game Event. The entire expanse of this forest was now covered with large, ancient-looking, cherry blossom trees, which were all beautifully in full bloom. It was quite breathtaking - for a game. Alec had to keep reminding himself.

Alec and Junpei searched around until they came to a clearing where they spotted Neji and LadyV, who was besides him.

"Neji! LadyV!" Alec ran up to them.

"Alec." Neji frowned. "I thought I warned you not to play the game right now. It's too dangerous. What if you end up like us?"

Alec pouted, "I couldn't just leave you guys here. I want to help you."

"Hey, there Alec-*kun*," LadyV threw Alec a playful wink that caused him to immediately blush.

"Hey guys," Junpei casually greeted them, hands behind his head.

"Neji, we read your email. Is it true that RedAki did this to you? You really can't log out?" Alec pressed.

Neji nodded grimly. "Rika and I were playing when-"

Alec suddenly looked around the clearing as if expecting to see Rika there. "Hey, wait a minute, where is Rika anyways? I saw her in a coma back in reality so she has to be here with you..."

Junpei was studying LadyV's face when his eyes suddenly widened. "AH!" He pointed a finger at her in shock. "LadyV...you're Rika aren't you?"

Alec looked over at Rika and his jaw dropped, "Rika? *Uso!* No way!"

LadyV put out her hands in a helpless gesture, "Guess the cat's out of the bag now." LadyV sauntered over to Alec and used her index finger to bring up his jaw and close his gaping mouth. "Alec you can close your mouth now. Is it really that hard to believe? It's called - role*playing*." She purred the last part of the word.

Roleplaying...? Alec gulped back in shock. So Rika was just acting the whole time? Pretending to be...what? Flirty, sexy and confident in the game while back in reality she was sorta awkward but really smart and maybe a little weird. But then if she was just play acting then did that mean those times she had kissed Alec were nothing but an act as well? Alec's heart clenched painfully in his chest. His first kiss...was an act? *Aw man. This sucks...*Alec hung his head.

Junpei was looking amused now as he looked LadyV over. "I can see the resemblance Rika but..." He began to stare at her chest area. "I see you used your hacker skills to make a few improvements to your-"

BONK

LadyV quickly bonked Junpei over the head with the staff of her *naginata* while blushing furiously. "Junpei! *Mou!* Geez!"

"*Itee!* Owie!" Junpei moaned as he rubbed the giant bump that was now on his head. "Rika do you always have to be so mean to me?" Junpei pouted at her. "Take into consideration that you've shattered a young boy's dream!

I'm seriously vulnerable right now. I've just lost the love of my life." Junpei put a hand to his heart and mimicked heartbreak. Alec felt that Junpei was probably being half-serious and half-joking about the whole thing.

"So?" A cat's paw smile formed on Rika's face, "The only one I want to *play* with is Alec-*kun*." Rika came up behind Alec and started drawing circles on his chest with her index finger. "*Neh* Alec? Won't you play with me?"

Alec turned bright red and struggled to get out of Rika's grasp. "Rika!" He finally managed to free himself and stumbled backwards.

Junpei and Neji both chuckled at Alec's plight. Alec just frowned at them until a dark thought came to him. Now was not the time for fun and games. "Hey guys, I just thought of something. What happens if you get PKed now...since you can't log out? What would actually happen to you?" Alec questioned.

Neji seemed to sober up as well. "It's hard to say but...the body can't live without the mind. We could end up dying for real."

Alec sucked in a breath and looked around. "Where's RedAki?"

Neji opened his mouth and was about to respond when -

"Right here." Came a drawling voice.

The hairs on the back of Alec's neck stood on end. Alec slowly turned around and came face to face with RedAki. And standing next to him was a sultry, fox-lady Battle Ghost.

"May I present to all of you my new Battle Ghost, Tamamo-no-mae." RedAki smirked as he gestured towards the ghost lady with a wave of his hand.

The female ghost had the appearance of a human woman except for the set of fox ears that were coming out of her head and the set of swishing fox tails that Alec saw were behind her and which were covered in orange fur. She had bright, orange-copper colored hair, bronze colored skin and fiery, ruby colored eyes. She was wearing a red silk kimono with a golden *obi* sash belt. Her lips were painted red and as she looked at Alec and the others Alec watched as her lips curved into a mischievous smirk.

"I knew you'd come for your little friends." RedAki sneered. "Even though you said Dr. M and LadyV weren't your friends to begin with - you're a bad liar. They're obviously your friends since you logged on as soon as you found out they were in trouble and rushed over here to see if they were alright."

But Alec's eyes were still transfixed on Tamamo-no-mae, his eyes wide. The spiritual power that he was sensing from her was incredible, and it was also overwhelmingly *evil*. He also sensed that this spiritual being before him was indeed a *real* ghost. But she was too powerful to be just a mere ghost so Alec figured she must be a *yokai*. He remembered his father had mentioned something about *kitsune* or fox-spirits once and how they were mischievous and powerful spirits that could shapeshift and use fire.

Alec was feeling a little overwhelmed by the intense power he was sensing from Tamamo-no-mae and his body began to tremble.

Junpei put a hand on Alec's shoulder and looked at him worriedly. "Alec, what's wrong buddy?"

Alec tried to pull himself together. "That ghost...it's real. It's...also too powerful to be just a mere ghost she must be a *yokai* or maybe she's even a *kami* (god)."

Junpei looked at Tamamo-no-mae curiously. "A real *yokai*? Inside of the game? How is that even possible?"

Alec shook his head. "She's a real *yokai*. You have to believe me Junpei and she's extremely dangerous. I have to...I have to stop him." Alec unsheathed his *Shinigami* sword and pointed it at RedAki. "Ryuu!" Alec summoned his Battle Ghost and Ryuu materialized besides him, trident in hand.

"RedAki! Why are you doing this? Why have you brought *that* into this world?" Alec demanded, his sword unsteady due to Alec's still trembling body.

RedAki's eyes were hard. "Why? You know why - Yukino. Hand Yukino over to me now and I'll spare the lives of your little friends. If not you better get used to the idea of making some new ones."

Neji looked over at Alec curiously. "Yukino?"

Alec was feeling a bit guilty he hadn't told Neji about Yukino but...she was a *real* ghost and he wasn't sure if Neji would have believed him that he had seen a ghost *inside* the game but not only that - Yukino was in danger and he had been forced to ask Night for help. Something he was sure that Neji wouldn't have approved of after Neji had warned Alec about him. He had only ended up telling Junpei about her since he had managed to catch Alec off-guard. And Junpei hadn't really seemed to take him seriously about the whole thing anyways.

"Darn it RedAki! I won't hand Yukino over to you. And I'm not going to let you get away with hurting my friends and all of this. This ends here!" Alec charged forward and raised his sword.

RedAki looked bored as he blocked Alec's attack. Alec noted he had been leveling up.

"Ryuu! Attack that Tamamo-no-mae! But be careful!" Alec commanded.

"Yes Master!" Ryuu declared and instantly moved into attack Tamamo-no-mae, waving his trident forward and unleashing a water attack upon her.

Tamamo-no-mae dodged the attack smiling and appearing amused. Ryuu tried again and this time Tamamo-no-mae formed a fireball in her hand which she flung in the direction of the spray of water to counteract it and caused it to turn into mist. Tamamo-no-mae then formed two small fireballs, one in each hand, and danced spinning and released the fireballs upon Ryuu at top speed, one after the other in a consecutive attack. Ryuu spun his trident quickly before him forming a shield which blocked the two fireballs. Whew. But Ryuu wasn't out of the woods just yet as Tamamo-no-mae seemed to be gathering her power, a golden aura flaring to life around her.

She brought her two hands together and seemed to be forming a large fireball there which became bigger and bigger until she unleashed the fireball at Ryuu while keeping her energy flowing forward so that her attack almost resembled a comet with its tail of fiery energy. Ryuu brought his trident forward and sent a blast of water Tamamo-no-mae's way. The two attacks hit - each trying to overpower the other - water versus fire. But then Ryuu was being pushed back and the fire attack overpowered his water attack so that the flames hit Ryuu. Ryuu cried out in pain as the flames consumed him.

Alec turned his attention away from RedAki and to Ryuu. "Ryuu!"

Singed and smoking Ryuu sunk to his knees and looked over at Alec worriedly, "I'm sorry Master, I have failed you." Ryuu collapsed and then turned into a small ball of light which shot through the air and reentered Alec's control ring.

RedAki suddenly leapt backwards distancing himself from Alec and directed Tamamo-no-mae waving his sword forward, "Tamamo-no-mae! Finish him off!"

Alec looked back at RedAki in disbelief that RedAki would really order Tamamo-no-mae to kill him. Alec frowned and gritted his teeth. This wasn't just a game anymore...this was real. Tamamo-no-mae was forming a fireball in her hands to unleash upon Alec as he took a step back in fear. He knew that the awful pain he had felt the last time would soon be felt again. And he knew it was futile to try and do anything to stop it - he didn't stand a chance against that *yokai*. She was just too powerful. He was done for. Alec's body was trembling as he remembered that awful pain from before...

Tamamo-no-mae danced while laughing maniacally and released her fireball upon Alec.

"Alec!" Junpei cried as he rushed forward suddenly and shielded Alec from the attack with his own body. Alec's eyes were wide in a mixture of surprise, shock, and horror as he saw Junpei suddenly become engulfed in red and gold flames and then cry out in pain from the attack as his body and Alec knew - his mind - was burning. Junpei fell to the ground with a thud and then he 'died' his PC body disappearing for a moment before then suddenly reappearing but not as a PC ghost as it should have but as a PC body once again though his body thankfully didn't have any of the horrible burns on it as it did only seconds before. It was odd however that Junpei's PC body hadn't turned into a ghost and Alec was worried that Junpei was now lying on the ground unconscious.

"Junpei!" Alec rushed to his side and reached his hand out to take his pulse. Thankfully, Junpei was alive but unconscious. Alec stood up and turned to face RedAki, his eyes narrowed in fury. "RedAki! How could you do this! How dare you hurt my friend!"

"And here I thought you once told me you didn't have any friends." RedAki said sullenly.

Alec was a bit startled as he realized that this was indeed true but he quickly composed himself and pointed his sword at RedAki and Tamamo-no-mae prepared to fight a losing battle.

However -

Night suddenly materialized before Alec. And to Alec it was like seeing the arrival of his guardian angel. Night looked so powerful, confident and unbeatable with his gigantic *Shinigami* sword raised before him and his blue-black hair seemingly shining.

Alec blinked in surprise but couldn't help the rush of relief that flooded him. "Night!"

"Night!" RedAki growled, "What in blazes are you doing here? Don't get involved!"

Night ignored RedAki and turned to Alec, "Alec, take the others using group teleport to the safety of the guildhall immediately. I'll handle RedAki."

Alec smiled back, trusting in Night's judgement. "Alright, be careful." Alec quickly typed in the names of his friends and prepared to do a forced group teleport. He hoisted Junpei up, and slung his arm around his shoulders and walked towards Neji and LadyV. "Now - Group teleport!" Alec declared and as his friends accepted the party invite they were all instantly teleported to the Guardian Knights guildhall. The ground beneath the players glowed as a magic circle of golden light and filled with strange symbols formed and then they disappeared as they were teleported.

RedAki tried to stop them but he was too late. "No wait! Dang it! *Shimmata!*" RedAki spun around to face Night and growled. "You! Jerk! You keep getting in my way Night! But not for long..."

Night got into a fighting stance and held his giant *Shinigami* sword out before him and pointed it towards RedAki. "I can't allow you to continue to hurt the people in this game world. This has to stop, RedAki."

RedAki spoke in a nonchalant drawl, "You're beginning to sound a lot alike, you and that punk brat. If you want it all to stop Night then perhaps we can make a deal. You know what I want. And I know you're protecting her now Night, so why don't you hand Yukino over and all the PKing will stop."

Night had a steely look in his eyes as he looked back at RedAki, "Never, I'll never hand Yukino over to the likes of you! Or over to Reaper! You'd have to kill me first."

RedAki shrugged and pointed his sword at Night. "Have it your way then."

Night summoned his Battle Ghost. "Tengu!" He cried and Tengu materialized next to him, ready to face Tamamo-no-mae.

RedAki raised an eyebrow and smirked amused. "You actually think your Tengu ghost has a chance against Tamamo-no-mae?"

Night appeared surprised. "Tamamo-no-mae? The real...?"

RedAki nodded, "Yes, now prepare to have your butt whooped Night. This is going to be so much fun." Flames of excitement seemed to leap in RedAki's red eyes.

Night ran towards RedAki. "I promised her! I promised her I'd protect her. I gave her my word." Night charged forward and raised his sword as he moved to attack RedAki. RedAki raised his sword and their swords clashed as he blocked the first blow.

"Why do you care so much about that ghost girl?" RedAki sneered, "Or is it just that you're worried you won't be able to use her for whatever crazy scheme it is that you're planning?"

Night blinked. "What are you talking about?"

"Don't play dumb," RedAki snarled, "Reaper has told me about what you're up to."

Night frowned thoughtfully. "I think you've got this all backwards - you're the ones that are planning something."

RedAki scoffed, "Liar! He said you'd say that. You're not to be trusted Night and I believe Reaper because Reaper to me is...." RedAki trailed off as he dodged an attack from Night and delivered one of his own. "The person I admire."

Meanwhile, Night's Battle Ghost was facing Tamamo-no-mae, he waved his golden staff forward and unleashed a sparkling, lightning attack towards Tamamo-no-mae at top speed, so fast that she wasn't able to dodge the attack in time. The attack hit her and wounded her as she was engulfed in the powerful electric shock, but her wounds seemed to disappear in a matter of seconds whereas had she been a normal Battle Ghost she would have been completely and utterly destroyed. Tamamo-no-mae formed two fireballs, one in each hand, and spun dancing before releasing the fireballs upon Tengu.

Tengu leapt out of the way and used his extreme speed to continue dodging Tamamo-no-mae's attacks. Tengu was known for being one of the most destructively powerful Battle Ghosts in the game due to his elemental control of lightning. Tengu began to fly circles around Tamamo-no-mae as she tried to hit him with her fire attacks. The blasts that were missing Tengu began to set the forest of cherry blossom trees on fire. The beautiful cherry blossom petals going up in flames, and it had begun to rain fire as the flaming petals fell to the ground sadly.

However, Tamamo-no-mae closed her eyes and concentrated on finding the exact location of Tengu as he continued to fly circles around her and suddenly she leapt forward and reached out with her hand. And then suddenly Tengu was in her one-handed grip, her fingers closing around his neck and then she used her elemental power to set him on fire. Tengu struggled in her grasp as the flames consumed him but it was a futile struggle and he was easily defeated by her. Tamamo-no-mae tossed Tengu aside and he turned back into a ball of light that flew back into Night's control ring.

Night looked down at his control ring. "You did well Tengu. I was able to obtain valuable information because of you and I was able to observe all of her attacks. Don't worry I will avenge you. Now that I am armed with the knowledge I need to defeat her." Night turned and pointed his sword towards Tamamo-no-mae.

RedAki raised an eyebrow. "You intend to fight Tamamo-no-mae on your own? What are you crazy?"

However, there was a small smile on Night's face as he faced Tamamo-no-mae and as he held his sword it began to glow blue with his spirit energy. Even while in the game it appeared as though Night was able to use his spiritual powers.

RedAki was beginning to get worried as he watched Night. "Hey, what are you doing? *Masaka*...No way...Reaper did warn me your sword was not of this world...oh no! Tamamo-no-mae! Look out! Use Shapeshift Attack!"

Night was rushing forward, his sword raised, ready to slice Tamamo-no-mae in half when - Tamamo-no-mae began to glow with a golden light and suddenly shapeshifted until she had turned into a girl that resembled Yukino except for the fact that both of her eyes were sapphire blue. Night swung his sword at Tamamo-no-mae only to end up stopping his sword mid-swing. "Yukino...?"

RedAki watched interested, "So Tamamo-no-mae turned into that ghost girl...which means that she's your greatest weakness or that she's the person you care about the most, but then why Night? If the ghost girl is just a tool like Reaper said she is why do you feel so emotional about her? It doesn't make any sense."

Yukino smiled sweetly at Night and reached her hand out towards him. "*Onii-san...!*"

RedAki's eyes widened. *No way - brother? Just what the hell does that mean? Is the ghost girl...Night's dead sister?*

Night looked conflicted as the ghost girl reached out to him but he kept his sword poised and ready to strike.

"*Onii-san*...you're awful! Do you really intend to kill me?" Yukino looked at Night imploringly and her eyes began to fill with tears. "Why brother? Why do you hate me so?"

Night's hand was trembling and his sword suddenly fell from limp fingers. "Yukino...I don't...I wouldn't..."

"Shhh." Yukino said as she moved forward and embraced her brother. Night stepped into her embrace and sighed in contentment. "*Onii-san*...I knew you loved me." An evil smile formed on Yukino's beautiful face. "Now we're going to die together *Onii-san* just like mother and father did..." She suddenly set Night on fire and he was engulfed in flames.

"Remember, that player is special too. Just like those hackers." RedAki reminded her mercilessly as he watched Night being set on fire and tortured with an almost bored expression on his face. RedAki picked something out of his ear and then flicked it away carelessly as he continued to watch. "So make sure you make it a grudge curse Tamamo-no-mae."

"*Hai, hai, Master.*" Tamamo-no-mae said and her voice sounded somewhat sarcastic as she used RedAki's title.

Night cried out in pain and struggled against Yukino's grasp but the pain was already too much for him - his mind was on fire and his struggling soon ceased.

"Foolish brother..." Yukino purred. "So foolish..."

She let go of Night when he had no more fight left in him and he fell to the ground unconscious. His PC body died and then instead of turning into a PC ghost ended up disappearing for a moment only to then reappear a few seconds later so that Night's unconscious form was now laying on the ground. Night began to murmur something in his unconscious state, as if he were trapped in a nightmare...

"Mother...father...sister...no..." Night moaned in his sleep.

"Good work, Tamamo-no-mae." RedAki praised as he walked up to Night and looked down at him with eyes full of hate, "That was a close one. He almost exorcized you back there. We have to be more careful." RedAki kicked Night's sword away from his limp fingers so that the sword skidded across the ground. "Now, I'll finish you off Night and this time it will be for good." RedAki raised his sword and prepared to bring it down upon Night. "I've been waiting a long time for this. I'll never have to see your cocky, perfect face again. Goodbye Night."

RedAki's sword flashed as it came down through the air-

Chapter 10:
THE GRUDGE CURSE PART II:

Alec, Junpei, LadyV, and Dr. M all teleported to the Guardian Knights guildhall where Yukino was waiting.

"Alec!" Yukino said enthusiastically when she saw him.

"Yukino!" Alec greeted and ran up to her. She in turn ran up to him and they were about to hug - probably due to a lapse of sanity on Yukino's part before she pulled herself together and took a step back instead and coughed awkwardly.

"Are you alright?" She questioned him.

Alec nodded, "I could be asking you the same thing."

"I'm alright, or as good as I can be considering I'm not even allowed to leave this place - it's like I'm a prisoner here." Yukino complained morosely, a frown forming on her pretty face.

LadyV watched the exchange between the two of them with interest.

"Hey, who's that Alec?" Neji questioned coming up next to him and eyeing Yukino curiously since she seemed to be a Battle Ghost but one that could talk.

"Oh, guys, this is Yukino. She's...a real ghost." Alec explained, a hand behind his head in nervousness. His friends were so going to kill him for not having said anything...

Neji's eyes widened, "Yukino? You mean she's the ghost that the RRs seem to be after? *Uso!* No way! Why didn't you tell me? And why are they after her anyways?"

LadyV looked Yukino up and down before dismissing her. "Hmph, I don't see what's so special about her."

Alec shrugged, "I dunno...but Night and his guild are helping me to protect her."

Neji frowned. "I thought I told you not to trust these guys, Alec. Thanks for listening to me." His voice was edged with sarcasm. "How come you didn't come to me for help instead?"

"Neji...it's not like I had much of a choice. It was a bit of an emergency and I needed help fast. Night was there to help. You were off at another one of your conventions. Anyways, maybe you're wrong about him. He seems like a pretty okay guy to me." Alec put in hopefully.

Neji opened his mouth to retort when Junpei began to stir awake, groaning.

"Ugh, my head." Junpei stood up and looked around, "Um, where are we?"

"The Guardian Knights guildhall. I might as well tell you guys that I'm a member of the Guardian Knights now." Alec informed them.

Neji and Junpei's jaws dropped, "You're what!"

Alec looked away and scratched his cheek nervously, "Well, yea..."

"Alec, where's Night?" Yukino asked as she looked around, "Didn't he leave to go and get you guys?" She began to look worried.

"He's facing RedAki." Alec explained.

Worry turned to anger. "Alone? Why didn't you stay behind to help him, Alec!" Yukino narrowed her eyes at him.

A guilty look flashed across Alec's face. "Well, um, you see...I'm sorry. I wanted to stay behind but Night wouldn't let me."

"I should be by his side, helping him." Yukino scowled. "But he wouldn't let me leave the guildhall. Dang it...I hate this. I hate being protected by everyone." Yukino sighed heavily. "This is so not my style."

Alec reached out his hand towards her about to put it on her shoulder but then he hesitated and let it drop down to his side instead. He had wanted to say - 'I understand how you feel.'

Junpei watched the interaction between Alec and Yukino curiously and a sly grin formed on his face as he sidled up to Alec and elbowed Alec playfully in the side. "So, is *this* why you didn't want to tell the others about her? Because she's kinda cute." Junpei waggled his eyebrows at Alec.

"Junpei!" Alec spluttered and flushed as he looked over to Yukino hoping she hadn't heard him. He let out a breath of relief when he saw that she hadn't. In a low voice Alec spoke to Junpei. "Besides, she's a ghost."

Junpei leaned in and whispered back. "Love knows no bounds."

Alec seemed a bit startled by this response and blushed slightly as he watched Yukino out of the corner of his eye. Alec shook his head trying to clear it of such unsettling thoughts, his bangs falling over his eyes.

Both boys seemed to fail to notice how LadyV a.k.a Rika was eyeing them with eyes sparkling green with envy.

Just then the two Ninja PCs, who were Night's loyal followers, walked into the main hall. "It looks like they've arrived safely." A male ninja dressed all in black and with a face mask on that only revealed his brown eyes observed.

The other ninja was a female PC, who was also wearing a face mask though her hair was done up in a high ponytail. She seemed to be startled when she caught sight of Junpei. "Junpei? What are you doing here!" And then she quickly put a hand over her mouth as if she had said something she shouldn't have.

Junpei raised an eyebrow at the female ninja before him. "Um, do I know you?" Though Junpei had to admit to himself there *was* something oddly familiar about her.

"No.2..." The male ninja began in a warning tone.

Alec sighed, he was getting a little sick of secrets so decided to ignore the mysterious ninja and spies of Night for the time being. "Junpei, how are you feeling, bud?"

Junpei cracked his neck from side to side, "Perfectomundo. I'm fine...I... oh god...I can't log out!" Junpei's eyes widened in horror as he suddenly realized this.

No.1 shook his head condescendingly. "You two shouldn't have entered Yokai World at all - it's extremely dangerous. And until we can think of a way to stop RedAki and his new Battle Ghost no one should be playing the game. You kids aren't the only ones who have encountered RedAki's new Battle Ghost and become comatose. Follow me." No.1 directed them to follow him and he led them to a large chamber where inside were rows upon rows of beds with unconscious or sleeping players lying on top of them. "These kids are all in comas, their minds trapped in the game for some reason we can't figure out."

Alec clenched his fists are his sides until his knuckles turned white.

"Why don't you just hand Yukino over to the RRs? Then they'd stop all this." LadyV said offhandedly.

Alec's jaw dropped and he looked at LadyV in disbelief.

No.1 however shook his head, "Yukino falling into the wrong hands has greater consequences for the game world than what you see here."

"Then you know why the RRs are after her?" Alec pressed.

No.1 fell silent.

No.2 put a hand on No.1's shoulder, "Maybe we should tell them..." Her soft feminine voice persisted.

"That's not for us to decide. He told us not to tell them just yet. It's up to him." No.1 shrugged her hand off his shoulder coldly.

"I'm getting sick of this - of being left in the dark! What the hell is going on? Why won't anyone ever give me a straight answer around here?" Alec snapped at No.1.

"Whoa...Alec lost his temper...now that's scary." Junpei whistled through his teeth.

No.1 didn't seem too fazed however. "Instead of having a tantrum like a child, if you want answers why don't you ask Night yourself."

Alec crossed his arms over his chest. "Fine! Maybe I will. *Hmph*!"

Alec glared at No.1 and he glared back, his eyes shadowed and slightly menacing looking because of the face mask.

Night suddenly teleported and materialized into the room along with them. He looked a bit tired and worn but otherwise seemed alright, though Alec noticed his sword was missing.

"Night!" Yukino called and to Alec's utter surprise she rushed up to him and hugged him warmly and in what Alec felt was a very familiar manner.

What was this odd, twisting feeling in Alec's stomach as he watched this exchange?

Yukino looked up at Night a bit starry-eyed, "Are you alright? We were so worried. Did you defeat RedAki?"

Night put his arms around her and returned the hug before moving away from her and patting her on the head affectionately. Then he smiled down at her - actually smiled! Alec had never seen Night smile like that before, at least not like *that* with true happiness. But then as Night looked down at her his expression darkened. He frowned and shook his head. "I'm sorry Yukino, I failed to keep my promise. RedAki he...defeated me."

Alec gasped. "Does that mean you...?"

Night nodded, "I can no longer log out."

No.2 rushed to Night's side at this statement and took his arm, "Night! What about your body back in reality...?"

"No.1, No.2 I want you to see to it that my body makes it safely to a hospital in reality. More importantly, I want you to check on *her* and make sure that she is still safe. The enemy could be trying to take advantage of the situation to get to my sister. You must protect her at all costs." Night then turned to Alec. "Alec, you must log out and get Junpei safely to the hospital as well."

Alec nodded but then hesitated. "But what about all of you? I can't just leave you here like this. I...I want to help." Alec looked at Night imploringly.

Night put a hand on Alec's shoulder and shook his head. "It's much too dangerous. RedAki is in the possession of a real *yokai*. You don't stand a chance against them at least not as you are now. You don't even have your own Battle Ghost and you lack the ability to use your exorcist powers within the game."

Alec nodded but took a step back. "I agree I don't have a chance alone but..." Alec turned to Yukino and met her eyes. "*We* do."

Night followed their exchange. "No. *No.*" He said the word a bit fiercer the second time. "We cannot put Yukino in danger."

"But Night, he's right I'm the only *real* ghost in the game world that could probably take on this so-called real *yokai* that RedAki has gotten his hands on." Yukino tried to convince him.

Alec smiled and nodded knowing they had won.

Night however didn't appear convinced. "No, you don't understand. You're more than a mere ghost Yukino I....there's a whole lot more to all this than you think."

"Then make us understand. Tell us what's going on!" Alec stamped his foot.

Night shook his head and bit his lip. "I can't tell you...it's too dangerous. Don't you see? I'm just trying to protect you - both of you. Now, Alec, you must take Junpei to the hospital or do you not care about your friend's welfare?"

Alec sighed heavily and gave Junpei an apologetic look. "Sorry Junpei, I'll go and help you right away."

Junpei gave Alec a lopsided grin, "Don't worry about it buddy - I know you just want to help."

Alec, No.1 and No.2 all logged out - the familiar golden circle filled with symbols materializing underneath them before their bodies glowed with a golden light and then they disappeared.

⚫ ⚫ ⚫ ⚫ ⚫ ⚫ ⚫ ⚫ ⚫ ⚫ ⚫ ⚫ ⚫ ⚫

Alec logged out of Yokai World and took off his HMD and turned to see how Junpei was faring - Junpei was slumped over his computer completely unconscious and comatose. Alec quickly ran out of the computer room to get Haruna-*sensei* and then an ambulance was called for Junpei. This time Alec went with the ambulance to the hospital since he also wanted to see how his friends Neji and Rika were doing in reality.

Hospitals were one of Alec's least favorite places - with his ability to see ghosts he often times couldn't tell who was still alive and who was already dead. It sent chills down his spine. So keeping his eyes on the floor in front of him he made his way to the room where his three friends were being kept. Alec opened the door and quickly let himself inside. Alec walked over to check on Neji, and then Rika, and lastly Junpei - all three of them seemed to be sleeping peacefully in their beds. Alec let out a sigh of relief and pulled up a chair - he didn't want to leave them just yet. He was feeling a little bit lost, and a little bit powerless on how to help his friends...

His eyes were beginning to burn with unshed tears but then he heard voices approaching and quickly used the back of his hand to wipe his eyes while he tried to pick up what the voices were saying -

Jin the serious monk along with Junko his kind but feisty, archer sister made their way into the room unexpectedly.

"What are we going to do about Yoru? It seems like we'll be able to awaken the others but as for Yoru...his curse seems a bit different from the others - more powerful. We couldn't even come close to cleansing it." Junko was going on worriedly, chewing on her bottom lip.

"Maybe it's for the best. When he wakes up he's going to have our heads when he finds out *she* was taken and that we let it happen right under our noses even after he warned us to look after her." Jin frowned.

"What do you think they're going to do to the poor girl? Hasn't she suffered enough?" Junko said sadly.

"Look on the bright side, due to recent events we now have a clue about why she fell into a coma in the first place - she was cursed. And in a very similar way to the way Yoru was cursed and they both won't wake up. Which means, if we manage to figure out how to wake up Yoru then we'll be able to wake her as well." Jin smirked confidently.

"You're right but now that she's been taken from us-"

"We'll get her back." Jin finished firmly.

They looked up from their intense conversation and were a bit startled to see Alec in the room seated calmly in his chair and twiddling his thumbs innocently. Alec tried to appear nonchalant and as though he hadn't been eavesdropping on them *again*.

Jin's eyes narrowed at him, "You again, what are *you* doing here?"

Alec was filled with indignation. "These are my friends!" He waved a hand at the three beds. And as soon as the words left Alec's mouth he was surprised to find that they were true - that somewhere along the way he, Rika, Neji and Junpei had in fact become friends.

Junko noticed Junpei on the bed for the first time and rushed over to her little brother. "Junpei!" Jin calmly followed his sister.

Jin turned around to glare at Alec again icily, "If you two hadn't logged on to Yokai World this wouldn't have happened. You would think that knowing the cause of your fever you would have been smart enough to avoid logging on to Yokai World but no, you're just a *baka* brat."

Alec frowned. "I logged on to Yokai World to try and find some answers to help my other friends." Alec waved a hand at Neji and Rika.

"Well, did you find any?" Jin asked with a touch of superiority.

Alec crossed his arms over his chest. "Yea, as a matter of fact I did."

"Well?" Jin raised an eyebrow expectantly.

Alec stuck his tongue out at Jin and pulled down his lower right eyelid. "Like I'll tell you, *baka!*"

Jin took a step back in shock at Alec's immaturity, "Why you little *baka* brat!"

Lightning was flashing between the two boys' eyes and Junko tried to placate them by raising her arms between them. "Now boys, play nice. We have more important things to attend to right now than fighting - like saving these kids."

Alec pouted but regained his composure and Jin did the same turning serious once more. He turned his attention to Junpei his eyes narrowing as if he were seeing something that Alec couldn't see. "Junko, it doesn't appear as though he was given a special curse like Yoru. I should be able to exorcize the negative spiritual energy from inside of him."

Junko let out a breath of relief. "I'm so glad."

Jin reached into his *haori* sleeve and pulled out a blank *o-fuda* and a paint brush. He quickly wrote a spell on the *o-fuda* and then slapped it onto Junpei's forehead. Jin pulled back and made some sort of hand sign and began to chant. Alec watched as the dark, negative energy which had now become visible was seen being purged from Junpei's body.

Alec, Jin, and Junko all watched and waited with baited breath as the color seemed to return to Junpei's cheeks and he slowly opened his eyes. Junpei took the oxygen mask off his face and sat up in bed peering at his older brother, older sister, and Alec. "Hey guys." He said somewhat weakly, but smiled warmly at them.

Junko was a bit teary eyed. "Junpei!" She flung her arms around Junpei and hugged him close, "We were worried you might never wake up..."

"Sis...you're choking me..." Junpei gasped and then tried to laugh at his sister's behavior.

Alec looked away feeling as though he were intruding upon a personal moment. Alec returned his attention to Neji and Rika who were still soundly asleep in their beds. If Jin had been able to cure Junpei so easily then maybe he could cure Neji and Rika too. Alec bit his bottom lip as he turned to face Jin. "Jin-*san*...could you...please try and exorcize my other friends too?"

Jin waved his hand dismissively at Alec's concern. "I was already about to try." Jin wrote up another *o-fuda* and slapped it to Neji's forehead next. The negative spirit energy could be seen coming out from his body and Alec and the others waited expectantly to see if he would wake up as well - but after several minutes Neji remained comatose.

Alec chewed on his lower lip fretfully while Jin narrowed his eyes at Neji, a knowing expression forming on his face. "It's just as I suspected."

"What is?" Alec was getting impatient.

"I sensed the curse was different on Neji. The curse and the energy trapped within him is more powerful and so more difficult to purge. This curse won't be broken so easily. Allow me to try the girl next." Jin made another *o-fuda* and walked over to Rika's bedside and then slapped the *o-fuda* to her forehead. He made his usual hand sign and began to chant some sacred sutra before the negative spiritual energy was beginning to be purged from her body. But Alec noticed this time that even after Jin had finished there was still an aura of black energy swirling around Rika. He could see it now for some reason. The group waited to see if Rika would wake up but she remained sleeping even after several minutes.

"I'm afraid this girl's curse is different as well...more powerful." Jin tapped his chin in thought. "One could say it almost feels like a grudge curse."

"A grudge?" Alec quirked his head.

Jin nodded, "But for it to be a grudge curse the person who cast or ordered the curse must have had a grudge or personal vendetta or deep hatred towards the victim - does that make sense?"

Alec thought about how much RedAki hated Rika and Neji because they were hackers and bent the rules of the game Yokai World. He also realized that RedAki had seemed to hate Night the most and hoped that wherever he was that Night was alright.

"Yea, that makes sense alright." Alec ran a hand through his shaggy hair nervously.

"Alec-*kun*, what were you able to find out in the game? Any information you discovered could help us figure out how to cure the ones that cannot be awakened through normal techniques." Junko asked in a kind voice.

Alec hesitated but then nodded. "I don't know if you're going to believe me but here goes. In the game there's a player named RedAki - he's gotten his hands on a real *yokai* named Tamamo-no-mae."

At the mention of the name Tamamo-no-mae Junko and Jin both sucked in their breath.

Alec continued on not having noticed. "It was this Battle Ghost who attacked Rika, Neji, Junpei and another player named Night...he's probably in a coma somewhere as well."

"Are you sure about that name? Tamamo-no-mae?" Junko pressed.

"Yea, why?" Alec responded.

Junko and Jin exchanged a look but then they seemed to come to an agreement and nodded at each other.

"Tamamo-no-mae is a very well known *yokai* of Japanese folklore. You've really never heard of the tale of Tamamo-no-mae before, Alec?" Jin asked Alec, a bit surprised.

Alec shook his head.

Jin nodded and a steely look formed in his eyes. "Guess I have no choice. I shall tell you the tale. The story of Tamamo-no-mae is really the story of the beautiful courtesan of a Japanese emperor, who was named Konoe. Tamamo-no-mae was supposedly the most beautiful and intelligent woman in all of Japan at the time of the emperor's reign. She was only 20 years old but was able to answer questions about just about anything, on a variety of subjects such as music, religion, or even astronomy. Because of her unique combination of beauty and intelligence Konoe fell deeply in love with her and the Imperial Court also regarded her highly.

"Konoe's life seemed to be perfect in every way with Tamamo-no-mae at his side, that is until one day he mysteriously fell ill. Konoe immediately hired the best and most well-known priests and fortune-tellers to try and figure out what was wrong with him but none of them could figure it out. That was until he hired an astrologer named Abe-no-Yasuchita. It was Abe-no-Yasuchita who managed to discover the truth behind Konoe's illness. Apparently, the astrologer was able to see past Tamamo-no-mae's mask of illusory beauty and was able to see her for what she truly was: a two-tailed, demon fox-spirit with great spiritual power.

"It was Tamamo-no-mae who had been causing the emperor's illness in an evil plot to steal the throne. Once her identity was discovered however Tamamo-no-mae fled the palace. Konoe was heartbroken at Tamamo-no-mae's betrayal but also extremely angry and so he hired the two most powerful samurai of the age to go after Tamamo-no-mae to kill her. Tamamo-no-mae had a premonition of her own death however at the hands of Miura-no-suke, one of the two samurai. She decided to appear to Miura-no-suke in a vision in order to beg for her life. However, he refused to spare her life and the next day when Mirua-no-suke discovered Tamamo-no-mae on the Plain of Nasu they had a fierce duel ending with Miura managing to defeat Tamamo-no-mae by shooting a sacred arrow at her heart. Tamamo-no-mae's spirit became a vengeful ghost. But so powerful was she in life that she became even more powerful in death...or so they say."

Alec shivered. "A two-tailed fox-spirit..." Alec remembered the orange, fur-covered ears and the two tails that he had seen coming out from the back of Tamamo-no-mae's *kimono*. It all made sense. But how had RedAki managed to get his hands on such a ghost or *yokai* in the first place? Alec wondered.

"If RedAki really has managed to get his hands on a *yokai* as powerful as Tamamo-no-mae Yokai World is in great danger." Junko started fretfully.

"Indeed." Jin agreed, his expression grim. "System Admin should perhaps be informed but...that could put those currently trapped in the game in danger..."

"If only the grudge curse could be broken. But how?" Junko wondered aloud.

Jin stroked his chin thoughtfully. "Perhaps, if Tamamo-no-mae were defeated then the curse would be lifted."

"Defeated? You mean exorcized?" Alec questioned curiously.

"Exorcized. Purified. Destroyed. It's all the same really but...in order to defeat Tamamo-no-mae in the game world a real exorcist would have to face and destroy her there and have the ability to summon their exorcist powers within the game..."

"A real exorcist - you mean like me?" Alec questioned curiously.

Jin realized he had been speaking aloud and turned to glare at Alec. "No of course not! You wouldn't have enough power to take on Tamamo-no-mae on your own - it would be pure suicide!"

Alec however was looking thoughtful. *So, the only way to get Rika, Neji, and Night to wake up is to defeat Tamamo-no-mae.* Junko and Jin exchanged worried looks upon seeing Alec's expression.

Junko put a hand on Alec's shoulder, "Alec-*kun*, I know you want to help your friends but it's too dangerous, you mustn't try to face Tamamo-no-mae on your own."

Alec gave her a reassuring smile. "Don't worry I'd have to be a total *baka* to want to face a *yokai* that powerful all on my own."

Junko let out a sigh of relief.

While Alec thought to himself - *Which is why I don't plan on facing her alone...*

• • • • • • • • • • • • • •

As soon as Alec left the hospital he made his way back to Izanagi Academy and then straight to the main school building where the computer club room was. He knew what he had to do and he wasn't going to let anyone stand in his way. Alec logged on to Yokai World and immediately teleported himself straight to the Guardian Knights guildhall. He *popped* up in the center of the hall where he saw LadyV, Dr. M and Yukino all speaking with each other. Luckily, there was no sign of Night or his ninja. As soon as Alec popped up in the center of the hall Dr. M and LadyV had called out to him but Alec simply ignored them and quickly strode over towards Yukino.

"Alec?" Yukino furrowed her brows at Alec's odd behavior. Alec then grabbed her by the arm and quickly pulled her aside so that he could talk with her in private. Dr. M and LadyV looked equally surprised by Alec's odd behavior. "Alec ow! What are you doing?" Yukino hissed.

Alec let go of her arm and turned around to face her, a serious expression on his face. "Yukino, I don't have much time before Night or his lackeys probably come in here and try to stop me. I found out how Neji and Night and the others can be awakened from their comas - Tamamo-no-mae must be defeated for the curses to be lifted."

"Tamamo-no-mae?" Yukino frowned thoughtfully.

Alec nodded, "She's a very powerful *yokai*...I don't think I can defeat her on my own. I hate to ask this of you but I'd like your help. Though I understand if you'd rather stay here where it's safe - either way I'm going to try and face her. I'm the only one who can exorcize her since I'm the only real exorcist in the game besides Night, who I think is an exorcist as well. I'm the only one that stands a chance."

"So, you'd like my help? And you're willing to face her on your own if I refuse?" Yukino looked thoughtful. "You wouldn't stand a chance against a ghost so powerful that it defeated Night so easily. It would be quite pathetic to watch really as you were completely and utterly defeated by her. So that's why I'll help you." Yukino smirked.

Alec felt relieved. "You will?"

Yukino tossed her long, straight hair over her shoulder, "Of course, you would die a horribly slow, bloody, and painful death without my help. It would be absolutely *dreadful*."

The odd way Yukino said 'dreadful' made Alec think she meant to say 'wonderful'. And the way Yukino's eyes were sparkling made Alec wonder if she really would like to see something gruesome like that. Alec gulped nervously as he thought back to what he had read about Yuki Onna and his worries that Yukino may be evil...

"You'd be just like a poor little lamb tied up and left for the slaughter... or rather left in a cave of ravenous wolfs or maybe lions. Or maybe-" Yukino was going on thoughtfully.

Alec cut her off - "Yukino, I get the idea."

"Oh right, sorry." Yukino looked a bit abashed. "Although I must say it's pretty stupid to be doing this since the odds are against us and I really should be trying to stop you since that would be the logical thing to do but...I think we're screwed either way so we might as well give it a shot." Yukino shrugged.

"Your upbeat confidence fills my heart with hope." Alec muttered sarcastically. "I know the chances of us actually winning aren't too high but... in times like this you just have to have guts." Alec put out his hand for Yukino to take. "The guts to take a chance for Night and the others."

"Guts huh?" Yukino took Alec's hand and they shook on it. "Recklessness for the sake of others, you really are a *baka* brat, Alec." Yukino smiled fondly at him. "But that's what I like about you."

Alec blushed, though he knew she had said the comment offhandedly and that it didn't really mean anything special.

Just then Night entered the guildhall, followed close behind by his lackeys No.1 and No.2. They caught sight of Alec and Yukino speaking to each other in hushed voices and immediately became suspicious.

"Alec wait!" Night called out to him.

"Oh shoot! We have to teleport now!" Alec grasped Yukino's hand and raised his arm. "Teleport Kintoki Mountain!" A golden, glowing circle filled with a pentagram and symbols appeared beneath Alec and Yukino's feet on the floor and they were instantly teleported.

"No Alec!" Night yelled.

But it was too late. Yukino and Alec had teleported back to the forest where they began their search for RedAki. They went straight away to the area where Night and RedAki had had their previous battle and saw the scorched cherry blossom trees that were still smoking. Alec looked at the blackened and charred cherry blossom trees sadly since they were his favorite kind of tree.

The sound of a branch breaking was heard and Alec and Yukino spun around to see RedAki and Tamamo-no-mae.

RedAki appeared amused at the sight of them and began in his drawling voice, "I didn't think you'd actually be stupid enough to come looking for me all on your own Dranarch - especially not after what happened the last time and certainly not after what happened to Night." RedAki took off a large sword that had been strapped to his back and revealed it to be none other than Night's own *Shinigami* sword which RedAki had stolen.

Alec spoke to Yukino in a low voice, "Face Tamamo-no-mae but if she's too much for you I want you to teleport straight away back to the guildhall. Mostly, I only want you to weaken Tamamo-no-mae enough for me so that I can finish her off by using my exorcist powers. Understand?"

Yukino nodded and responded in an equally low voice, "I understand though I don't plan on running away."

Alec faced RedAki and unsheathed his own *Shinigami katana* and pointed it at RedAki. "Things will go a bit differently this time around, RedAki."

"We'll see about that, Dranarch." RedAki smirked right back at him.

Alec looked over at Tamamo-no-mae curiously for a moment and their eyes met. Her clear, ruby-red eyes seemed to see straight through him, down to his very soul. He realized in that moment that Tamamo-no-mae was indeed a real spiritual being with her own thoughts and feelings. He couldn't help but wonder how she felt about being RedAki's ghostly pawn. His eyes went to her neck where he noticed she wore a golden control collar, which was connected to the control ring that was on one of RedAki's fingers. Alec's eyes were then drawn to the red-stoned ring on RedAki's hand. *If Tamamo-no-mae is simply being controlled...what is her true will? What does she really want? What would she do if she were free? Would she have harmed all these people anyways? She's supposed to be evil...*Alec mused.

Tamamo-no-mae's fiery red hair seemed to be alive and ablaze as she looked over at Yukino who was at least a foot shorter than herself. "A little girl is to be my opponent this time? I do believe I'm being sorely underestimated. Though I sense she is *real*..."

Yukino calmly took out her magic fan, "I'm not just a little girl." She raised her feathered fan upwards towards the sky and thick storm clouds instantly began to gather there and a heavy snow began to fall along with a fierce, chilling wind beginning to blow through the skeletal trees.

Tamamo-no-mae's brows rose in surprise. "There's only one *yokai* I know that is able to control the snow..." She narrowed her sparkling red eyes at Yukino. "I see now..." She cackled, amused. "Well, then, this should be fun. Try not to bore me little girl!" Tamamo-no-mae formed two small fireballs, one in each of her hands and danced and spun before she released the fireballs upon Yukino.

Yukino calmly waved her fan and a fierce blast of cold wind was issued forth from her fan and completely destroyed the fireballs. Tamamo-no-mae bit her bottom lip in frustration and flung more fireballs Yukino's way in retaliation. Yukino gracefully dodged the attacks so that the fireballs went flying past her and began to set the cherry blossom trees on fire once more. Tamamo-no-mae used her two hands to form a more powerful fire attack - the same attack that had finished Night off. When she was ready she then unleashed it upon Yukino. Yukino waved her fan forward and unleashed a blast of cold air mixed with snow. The two attacks collided and canceled each other out in midair. It seemed they were evenly matched.

As RedAki and Alec's swords clashed, RedAki was keeping tabs on the battle between the two ghost girls and frowned when he saw that they appeared to be on equal footing. He decided Tamamo-no-mae needed to kick things up a notch. "Tamamo-no-mae! Don't underestimate her! Use Shapeshift Attack!"

Tamamo-no-mae raised an eyebrow at this order but did as she was commanded having no other choice. Tamamo-no-mae used her spiritual power to read her opponent Yukino's mind to discover the person Yukino seemed to care about the most. Then Tamamo-no-mae's body began to glow with a golden light and then she shapeshifted into none other than - Night. She was an exact copy of Night in his *Shinigami* clothes and even with his original *Shinigami* sword, that RedAki now had, in her hands.

"Tamamo-no-mae has the ability to read minds." RedAki began to tell Alec conversationally, "She'll pick the person that her opponent cares about the most and turn into them. It seems that little ghost girl must have a crush on Night." RedAki snickered, amused.

Alec's eyes widened in surprise at this and his stomach did a little flipflop - though he didn't know the reason why.

Yukino stared back at Night in shock. "Night?"

Night smiled at Yukino innocently even as his sword was beginning to glow with a golden light. Night was then suddenly charging forward, sword raised, and in seconds he was in front of Yukino and swinging his sword at her. Yukino didn't react fast enough and a powerful blast of energy hit her and she was sent flying backwards with a cry. Yukino struggled to push herself up off the snowy ground but sat on her knees as she watched Night approach her stunned.

"Use fire! Tamamo-no-mae! I want to see her burn. I want to see this stupid forest *burn*!" RedAki declared suddenly and Alec could see flames flickering in his own red eyes that seemed to be filled with a lust for destruction. "Burn everything!"

"Yes, Master." Night said as he swung his sword at the surrounding cherry blossom trees which instantly began to ignite as his attack was unleashed upon them. The skeletal trees becoming engulfed in the swirls of red, orange and yellow flames, the petals bursting into fire, and then as they began to fall to the ground it appeared as though it were snowing fire. The heat was so sweltering that the snow fall that Yukino had summoned melted before it reached the ground.

A ring of fire was surrounding Yukino now as she knelt in the snow, a bewildered expression on her face. Fire..it was everywhere.

RedAki seemed to be losing control of himself. "Yes that's it! Burn! Let it all burn!" RedAki began to laugh maniacally. "Let everything just burn away!" RedAki ran a finger down the side of his cheek and Alec noticed for the first time a strange burn mark that was there. He was about to open his mouth and ask RedAki about the scar when suddenly Yukino screamed -

Fire...it was everywhere. Flames...they surrounded her. The temple was on fire. How had the fire started? Eleven-year-old Yukino did not know, all she knew was that she couldn't find her mother or her father...and she had been calling out to them for several mintues now. Her lungs were filling with smoke and they burned painfully so that she started coughing.

"Tosan! Father! Kasan! Mother! Yoru!" She remembered then calling for her brother knowing that if anyone would save her it would be him. In moments, she didn't have the strength to walk anymore, the smoke and fire and heat were just too much for her and she sunk to her knees, her body being wracked with coughs, tears streaming down her face. "Yoru..."

Suddenly, the door to the main temple chamber was kicked open by her older brother, Yoru, who went straight to his little sister. "Yukino!"

Yukino looked up through the smoke to see the worried face of her brother and smiled despite everything. "Yoru!" She reached her hands out to him and he immediately scooped her up into his arms and began to shield her from the flames and the heat with his own body.

Yoru began to head for the door and part of the ceiling gave way, crashing down in front of Yoru and Yukino. Yukino screamed and clutched at Yoru's robes frightened. "Yoru! I'm scared."

Yoru stroked his sister's hair soothingly. "Shh...it will be alright Yukino. I'll get you out of here safely, trust me."

Yukino nodded into her brother's chest and clung closer to him. Yoru dodged falling debree and finally managed to get to the front door which he kicked open. They managed to get outside safely and turned to face the temple which was completely on fire now. Only its curving, tiled roof remained intact. Dirty, with ashcovered faces, singed clothing, and tears streaking down Yukino's face - brother and sister watched as the temple suddenly collapsed as it burned to the ground.

"Mother...Father...?" Yukino questioned in a low, tremulous voice.

Yoru shook his head, and Yukino buried her face in Yoru's chest as she began to cry. Yoru stroked her hair and back to comfort her as sobs wracked her small body. There was a steely look in his eyes as he looked up at the burning temple. "Don't worry Yukino, I'm here for you. I'll never leave you and I'll always protect you. And I'll avenge our parents' deaths...when I find out who did this...I will show them no mercy."

Yukino was still on the ground clutching at the sides of her head as the lost memory fragment assaulted her fragile mind and she cried out - "Iyeee! Nooo! Mother! Father! Yoru!"

Night walked towards her, surrounded by flames, his giant sword raised and pointed it towards her, "But Yukino I'm right here..."

Yukino looked up, eyes wide, tears streaming down her face, and with a sinking feeling in his stomach Alec noticed that the strong ghost girl he had come to know was trembling. "Yoru?"

"Finish her!" RedAki directed Tamamo-no-mae, "But remember we need her mostly alive to bring before Reaper-*sama*."

"Yes, *Master*." Tamamo-no-mae said the last word full of bitterness and sarcasm as she approached Yukino and raised her sword - still in Night's form.

Alec seemed to snap out of his stupor. "Yukino no!" Alec quickly rushed forward and just as Night's sword would have sliced Yukino in two he brought up his sword and managed to block the attack deflecting the blow.

Night brought his sword back and slashed it at Alec who brought his sword up to block again but was forced backwards, skidding across the ground, from the force of the blow. He looked back at Yukino concernedly, who was still trembling on the ground. "Yukino! Snap out of it! I need you!"

As Alec's sword clashed now with Night's he decided it was now or never. Alec tried to remember how it felt to empower his soccer ball with his spirit energy back in reality. He began to try and summon his spirit energy and have it form around the blade of his sword but for some reason the game sword wasn't responding to what he was doing. *Dang it!*

"Fade away...I just want to fade away..." Yukino was muttering to herself and a strange, icy blue aura was forming around her...

RedAki then noticed that a strange energy aura was flaring up around Alec and was begining to get worried. He decided this duel had dragged on long enough. RedAki charged forward and planned on attacking Alec from behind while he was busy concentrating on Night. "Die!" RedAki cried as he lunged his sword forward towards the unsuspecting Alec -

The hairs on the back of Alec's neck prickled in warning but it was too late. Alec knew he was going to be run through from behind. However -

"Ice Daggers Attack!" Came an ethereal, tinkling voice that sounded like wind blowing through a wind chime made of glass.

Alec spun around to see a female ghost waving her feathered fan at RedAki. From out of her fan came several sharp daggers made entirely of ice, which shot in RedAki's direction and forced him to leap backwards out of the way.

"Dang." RedAki swore.

Alec blinked and looked around for any signs of Yukino but she had disappeared and now there in her place stood another female ghost who had long, flowing, ice-blue hair, and shining golden eyes. She was wearing a stunning, all-white kimono with a baby-blue *obi* sash tied about her waist, the ends of which flaoted behind her eerily. Her face was pale and her ears were pointed and elvish. She had this mysterious, elegant, serene, goddess-like air about her, Alec decided. But there was also something else about her... something slightly sinister and deadly.

"Yukino?" Alec squeaked.

"Alec, concentrate on RedAki while I handle Tamamo-no-mae. Wait for my signal." Oyuki directed him in her soft, lilting voice.

Alec could only nod dumbly, "Um, yea, sure..." Alec turned back towards RedAki.

Oyuki waved her fan at 'Night' and yelled - "Reveal!"

Night's image shimmered and then it was replaced with the image of Tamamo-no-mae. The illusion had been broken. Tamamo-no-mae was left looking amused. "Oyuki, I was wondering when you'd come out and face me. I was begining to get bored with that little girl, so fragile, so emotional - poor little thing. I was about to put her out of her misery. After all, it's not really her that they need is it? Or am I wrong about that?"

Oyuki nodded at Tamamo-no-mae, "Tamamo-no-mae, it's been a while. As for my Lady Yukino...the less you know about her the better. Though I think that in killing her you would have been making a grave mistake. I would think your new...Master would have commanded you more wisely. To think the great Tamamo-no-mae is now the pawn of some pyro-boy."

Tamamo-no-mae frowned, "It's not by choice that I am his ghost! Kaguto captured me." She put a hand to her throat where the control collar was. "And then he gave me to this boy. Anyways, I could be saying the same thing about you. You seem to be nothing more than a pawn as well now..." Tamamo-no-mae eyed the similar control collar around Oyuki's neck but that was in the guise of a sapphire necklace. "Ah, how the mighty have fallen, *yokai* being forced to serve mere *humans*." She spat the word, disgusted.

"Indeed." Oyuki agreed with a curt nod, "However, I choose to serve Yukino mostly of my own free will and the boy wisely doesn't seek to control me."

"Making friends with humans again Oyuki? That is so like you. Wasn't it a mortal man that you fell in love with all those hundreds of years ago? Where is he now? Oh, that's right - he's dead." Tamamo-no-mae's red lips formed into a grin, "Humans and their pathetically short lifespans. It's a wonder you were stupid enough to fall in love with one of them to begin with. I heard he ulitmately betrayed you anyways. Humans are not to be trusted, Oyuki... look after all at what they did to *me*. And it's not just me...Kaguto is enslaving many *yokai* from the Makai. He's...up to something."

Oyuki frowned. "I'm surprised your new Masters haven't informed you of their aims. Although I suppose they just see you as a tool...or someone that cannot be trusted with their secrets. But enough chit chat Tamamo-no-mae. You are right that most humans cannot be trusted but I believe some can be. And the girl who is now a part of me and the boy who is her Guardian - I believe these two are on our side or at least the side of *yokai*. And so I will fight for their sakes. Prepare yourself, Tamamo-no-mae!"

"And I too shall fight, because I have no choice. But also because I've always wanted to fight you!" Tamamo-no-mae began to summon her power, "Here I come Oyuki!"

Meanwhile, RedAki and Alec were still locked in their Ghostly Duel. RedAki looked sideways at Oyuki curiously. "What ghost is that? Oh, I get it now. I knew there was more than meets the eye to that ghost girl - she always gave me a creepy feeling. To think the *Yuki Onna* lay dormant inside of her! That must be the real reason why Night is so preoccupied about the ghost girl - it's really Oyuki he's after!"

Alec furrowed his brows, "What are you talking about?"

RedAki raised an eyebrow at him, "Don't you know? The real reason why Night is protecting Oyuki? He plans to use her to-" Alec continued to look clueless and RedAki's smile broadened. "You really have no idea what's going on do you? And even so you're caught completely in the middle of all this."

Alec frowned. "No, I don't." He said through gritted teeth. "Why don't you enlighten me?"

RedAki snickered. "I could but...it's more fun to leave you in the dark. So, I don't think I will. You'll find out soon enough that all this time you've been on the wrong side when Night shows his true colors."

Alec's expression turned to worry. It had been something he had been wondering about in the back of his mind for a while now. What was Night really up to? What was really going on? What part did Yukino have to play in all this? Why couldn't they tell Alec? And Night...could he truly be trusted? Neji had tried to warn him about Night but he hadn't listened.

*Save him...save Night from the dark path he has chosen...*Midoriko's words echoed through his mind.

Alec shook his head. "No! I trust Night. It's you who are on the wrong side RedAki." Alec took a deep breath and began a little more confidently. "I mean look at what Reaper has made you do - PK innocent people and put them into comas, all to get his hands on Yukino. He's probably going to use her for something really evil too. And you think I'm on the wrong side? Ha!"

RedAki shrugged, "The ends justify the means - it's all for the greater good Alec. You'll see. Night is the evil one."

"What happened to your cheek RedAki?" Alec suddenly asked.

RedAki gasped and put a hand to cover his scarred cheek self-consciously, "Nothing..."

"Did your beloved Reaper-*sama* do that to you? Did he punish you?" Alec persisted.

"I deserved it!" RedAki suddenly cried out, "I disobeyed him!"

231

Alec took a step back in shock at RedAki's admittance. "So it's true then. That jerk...he shouldn't have hurt you. It was my fault. I'm the one who stole Yukino away."

"Why the hell do you care?" RedAki snapped.

Alec sighed, "Why...?" He looked up at RedAki and their eyes met. "Because we're *rivals*. And that means something - at least, it means something to me."

RedAki was a little thrown off by Alec's words but before he could form a response his attention was then drawn away by Tamamo-no-mae and Oyuki's fierce battle that was beginning to become even more intense.

Tamamo-no-mae was throwing fireballs and Oyuki was countering with ice daggers that came flying out of her fan like magic. And then Tamamo-no-mae materialized a scepter and held it before her as she gathered a lot of her elemental power around her and suddenly she sent a large fiery blast towards Oyuki. Oyuki waved her fan forward and sent a pretty powerful icy blast of her own, filled with swirling snow that made it hard to see. She then tucked her fan away into her sleeve and cupped both of her hands together before her and formed a giant icicle. She held the icicle like a sword in her hand as she suddenly charged forward using her own snow attack as cover as she approached the unsuspecting Tamamo-no-mae.

"Wait no!" RedAki tried to warn Tamamo-no-mae.

But it was too late. Oyuki was suddenly upon her and she rammed the icicle forward so that it pierced Tamamo-no-mae's chest. Tamamo-no-mae looked down in shock.

"*Bakana*...Impossible..." RedAki looked at Tamamo-no-mae in disbelief.

Alec frowned and though he didn't like it he used RedAki's moment of distraction to disarm him and then in RedAki's stunned state Alec managed to get past RedAki's defenses and stab RedAki through the stomach, effectively PKing him.

"You punk...you actually PKed me! Oh shoot." RedAki moaned as his PC body died and then he came back as a PC ghost. RedAki watched in horror as he began to lose his items that were dropping to the ground from having been PKed.

"Alec!" Oyuki called to Alec, signaling him that now that she had managed to weaken Tamamo-no-mae that it was his turn now.

Tamamo-no-mae sunk to her knees with the icicle still imbedded in her chest.

RedAki's control ring and Night's *Shinigami* sword fell to the ground where Alec was able to pick them up - much to RedAki's chagrin. He quickly put on Tamamo-no-mae's control ring and sheathing his own sword wielded

Night's sword instead. Alec strode forward to stand in front of the defeated Tamamo-no-mae and gathered his exorcist powers, and his spirit energy. His sword and body began to glow with a blue-tinged light. He then poised his sword ready to finish Tamamo-no-mae off.

"Now, I shall excorsize you, pitiful *yokai* and the curse upon my friends shall be broken." Alec looked down at her with stormy gray eyes.

Tamamo-no-mae looked up in horror, she could feel Alec's spirit energy actually radiating off of the sword now. "An excorist...impossible...and that sword...it's not of this world is it? No! Wait! Please don't kill me! I'll do anything! Please! Spare me! I...I didn't mean to do any of it. I was only being controlled afterall - it's not fair." Tamamo-no-mae pouted as she hung her head in defeat.

Alec's eyes were as cold as ice. "Life isn't fair, *sayonara*." Alec raised Night's glowing sword and brought it down upon her.

Tamamo-no-mae closed her eyes awaiting the blow - which never came. She openned one eye cautiously and then the other to see that Alec was instead strapping Night's sword to his back.

Alec smiled down at her. "Tamamo-no-mae, you are dead. As you know, I could have excorsized you but I've decided not to. This is because you were being controlled and so it didn't feel right to punish you for crimes you didn't commit of your own free will."

Tamamo-no-mae blinked at Alec in surprise. "But why...? I'm your enemy, I hurt your friends."

Alec nodded, "Yea, you did. That's why I'm going to let you go on one condition - I need you to tell me how I can release my friends from the grudge curse. Is there any other way to do so without having to kill you?"

Tamamo-no-mae nodded, "Yes, I could remove the grudge curse myself although I don't really feel like traveling to the human plane anytime soon. But there is one other way - I simply will have to give you the power to break the curse on your friends. Meaning, I will pass my curse breaking power onto you."

Alec smiled a lopsided grin, "Wow, you'll really do that?"

Tamamo-no-mae smirked, "*Surre...*" She purred. "After all, you're such a nice little *morsel*, I mean boy." Tamamo-no-mae corrected herself.

BONK

Oyuki suddenly hit Alec over the back of his head with her fan. "Don't be so trusting boy. Tamamo-no-mae is your enemy."

"Ow!" Alec pouted, rubbing the back of his head. That really hurt. There were even tears in his eyes.

Tamamo-no-mae frowned and then pouted, "Correction - I *was* his enemy. Have you forgotten I was being controlled to fight him and his little friends. And besides he has my control ring now, so really I think it's safe to say I can't do anything to harm him right now. And this kind, delicious-looking boy has decided to spare my life. So I owe him a life debt. I don't know how special that is in the human world but you know how important that is in *our* world. But I think that passing my curse breaking power to him should make us even. Wouldn't you agree Alec-*kun*?"

Alec blinked, "Um, yea, sure."

Oyuki sighed at the exchange. She turned to glare at Tamamo-no-mae one last time. "If you harm the boy you will have to answer to me."

"*Hai, hai.*" Tamamo-no-mae agreed in a sing-song voice, not sounding at all concerned. "Now Alec...close your eyes..."

"Huh? What?" Alec was saying as Tamamo-no-mae stood up and approached him. She was then standing only a foot away from him when she suddenly cupped his cheek in her warm hand. "Wait! What are you...?"

"Hey what are you doing!" Oyuki demanded to know as well.

"I'm passing my curse breaking ability to the boy. What do you think I'm doing...? You really need to get your mind out of the gutter Oyuki." Tamamo-no-mae teased without taking her eyes off of Alec. Their lips getting closer and closer.

"Hey, wait just a minute! There must be a more civilized way to-!" Oyuki was saying.

Too late.

Oyuki gasped and raised a hand in front of her mouth as she did so.

Tamamo-no-mae pressed her lips passionately against Alec's and began to kiss him deeply as she passed on her curse breaking powers to him. Alec had at first blushed at the sudden kiss, had then turned red as it continued, and was now getting a nose bleed as the kiss was deepened. By the time Tamamo-no-mae finally pulled away from him and was licking her lips Alec was already in complete 'girl overload mode'. Alec stumbled backwards in shock before completely falling backwards, his eyes all swirly.

"You made him pass out." Oyuki complained. "And was a kiss *that* long really necessary?"

Tamamo-no-mae smiled a foxy grin. "Would you kill me if I said no?"

"I might." Oyuki narrowed her eyes at her rival.

"I better stay quiet then." Tamamo-no-mae laughed gleefully.

"*You*-! You are impossible!" Oyuki threw her arms up into the air.

"Well, at least I didn't kill him. I've kept my promise. I only hope he will keep his." Tamamo-no-mae looked over at the still swirly-eyed Alec.

Oyuki looked over at Alec too, a fond expression on her face. "Alec is an honorable boy."

A mischievous glint formed in Tamamo-no-mae's eye. "Oh? I think you like him."

Oyuki blushed. "I most certainly do not! He's just a little boy."

"So, wasn't the man you eventually made your husband a boy you saved from a snowstorm up in the mountains?" Tamamo-no-mae prodded.

"I don't have to answer that, *hmph*!" Oyuki huffed uncomfortably. "But I don't like him, that I can assure you."

"I don't believe you even for a second. I think the little boy with the kind and noble heart has managed to melt your heart of ice, Oyuki. Let's put it to the test then shall we?" Tamamo-no-mae giggled as she suddenly shoved Oyuki hard from behind so that she stumbled forward.

"What are you doing?" Oyuki cried as she suddenly fell forward, windmilling her arms as she tried to stay upright, but failing and falling right on top of Alec.

"You should go ahead and kiss him if you like him. You may never get another chance." Tamamo-no-mae teased.

Alec was just beginning to stir awake.

Oyuki was looking down at Alec curiously and was suddenly startled by the resemblence that Alec had to that same little, lost boy she had saved during a snowstorm all those years ago and whom she had later encountered in a hut in the mountains when he had been trapped there by a snow storm. Alec did indeed remind her of her long, lost love. A kiss? Or a kiss of death? Then Alec could stay with her forever...as a ghost by her side back in her world. Oyuki began to summon her power while lowering her face towards the unsuspecting Alec.

"Alec!" Yukino had woken up inside of Oyuki at this point and sensed that Alec was in grave danger. "Alec wake up! Oyuki no!" Yukino screamed from within Oyuki's mind. She then gathered her strength to regain control of her body and of Oyuki.

Oyuki's body began to glow with a bright silvery-blue light and suddenly she changed back into Yukino's body.

Alec blinked his eyes open and saw that Yukino was unexpectedly on top of him with their lips a mere inch apart. "Yukino?" He tried to sit up and instantly regretted it as their lips brushed up against each other.

Yukino's eyes widened before she quickly scrambled off of Alec and stood. "Yuck!" Yukino wiped her lips with the back of her hand. "A kiss from a little *baka* brat!"

Alec pushed himself up off the ground, a bit disoriented, and a little flushed. "What happened?" Alec was trying not to feel too hurt by Yukino's reaction to their accidental kiss.

"You total *baka*!" Yukino complained. "Oyuki was about to give you the kiss of death, you moron! And you would have just let her!" Alec failed to notice how worried she looked.

Alec gulped, kiss of death? That didn't sound so good. He knew he had sensed something *dark* from Oyuki.

"Kiss of death?" Alec quirked his head at Yukino.

"Haven't you heard of how the *Yuki Onna* freezes men to death with her icy kiss?" Tamamo-no-mae questioned Alec referring to the tale.

Alec's eyes widened and he swallowed nervously. He had almost been killed - by a kiss. "Epp." Alec squeaked. Junpei would have gotten a kick out of that one. 'Not a bad way to go' He could just picture Junpei saying that as he waggled his brows at Alec. But as for Alec himself - he wasn't a pervert! There was no way he could have enjoyed a kiss of death from Yukino...right?

"Now he gets it." Yukino shook her head. "You're so slow, it's a good thing I'm here to watch out for you." Yukino nodded vigorously.

Alec was acting sheepish with a hand behind his head as he agreed, "Yea..."

An amused laughter drew both of their attention back towards Tamamo-no-mae. Alec had nearly forgotten about her. He looked down at his new control ring and concentrated on its power and on his will to free Tamamo-no-mae. The control collar around her neck glowed before snapping open and dropping to the ground. Tamamo-no-mae was now free.

Yukino's eyes widened in shock. "Oh my god, what did you just do Alec? Don't tell me you just freed Tamamo-no-mae? What are you crazy? She'll kill us!"

Alec however was looking back at Tamamo-no-mae and she was looking at him her expression serious now. She nodded her head regally at Alec, pleased he had kept his promise. "Oyuki was right, for a human you are honorable, Alec. Thank you, and until we meet again! *Chu~*" Tamamo-no-mae blew Alec a goodbye kiss before turning to go.

"Hey, wait! How exactly do I use your curse breaking power?" Alec called after her.

A cat's paw smile formed on Tamamo-no-mae's face. "You kiss the cursed person and the curse will be lifted of course."

Alec's eyes widened in shock. "*Ch-chu?* K-kiss! " Alec stuttered. "B-but... some of my friends are...guys!"

Tamamo-no-mae laughed. "I *so* wish I could be there to watch Alec kiss his little friends! But alas I really must get back to the Makai. Responsibilities of being a demon lord and all. *Ja-ne!*" Tamamo-no-mae called before she was suddenly gone, disappearing in a blast of fire.

Alec was looking a bit green.

Yukino frowned. "Well, at least she didn't kill us. That was lucky." Yukino spun around to face Alec. "No thanks to you." She scowled at him.

Alec looked a bit bashful at her words. He knew the crazy risk he had just taken in trusting an evil *yokai* like Tamamo-no-mae. Although, he could feel the new power coursing through him. And all that from a kiss...Alec put his finger to his lips remembering the passionate, fiery kiss. He almost blew a fuse...

Yukino looked over at him and thought he was remembering their kiss and blushed slightly. "*Baka*...you're making such a big deal. It was just an accident. I hope that wasn't your first kiss?" She asked curiously, and somewhat hesitantly.

Alec lowered his hand. "No, it wasn't."

Yukino looked both surprised and a little disappointed, "Really? Oh...I see."

"Jealous?" Alec suddenly pipped up with a small, timid smirk.

"Hmph! Of a *baka* brat? No way. I was just wondering who would want to kiss a little kid like you?" Yukino shot back.

Alec puffed out his cheeks, "Plenty of girls, actually." He crossed his arms over his chest and gave her a haughty look.

Yukino flushed at his comment, "Liar!"

"Am not."

"Are to!"

"Am not!"

They both looked at each other panting for breath, both red in the face - and then they burst out laughing at the silliness of it all. Still smiling at each other they teleported back to the Guardian Knights guildhall to tell their friends the good news.

Chapter 11:
NEKOMATA: THE TWO-TAILED CAT DEMON

Alec threw the door to the hospital room open where Jin, Junko and Junpei where still waiting with the sleeping Neji and Rika. They were startled at his abrupt entry as Alec strode inside with purposeful steps making his way over to Neji's bedside first.

"Alec?" Jin called after him, "What are you doing here? Hey, I'm talking to you, kid!"

"Alec?" Junko questioned concerned.

But Alec just ignored them going straight to Neji's beside. Alec was looking a little pale as he began to lean over his unconscious friend. *Gulp.* It was now or never.

"Hey, what are you-?" Jin was asking when Alec suddenly leaned over and pressed his lips to Neji's.

Jin's mouth fell open in complete shock and Junko gasped in surprise while covering her mouth with her hand. Junpei was looking as though he might pass out when he began to notice the golden light that was glowing around Alec and that was being passed into Neji's body. The curse mark on Neji's chest that was over his heart and which read in *kanji* letters - *sleeping death* began to fade. Neji then began to stir as the mark finally disappeared altogether.

Neji opened his eyes and was a bit bewildered to find Alec still kissing him.

Alec realized Neji was awake and quickly pulled back, his eyes meeting Neji's. And then both boys blinked before exclaiming simultaneously:

"YUCK!"

Alec quickly ran over to the sink in the hospital room's bathroom and began to rinse out his mouth while Neji was vigorously wiping his lips with the back of his hand. Once Alec had finished gargling he came back inside the room.

Neji was looking at Alec with a confused expression on his face and a slight flush to his cheeks. "Alec, you know I like you as a friend and everything and I do think you're a real cool person and all, but I'm sorry I can't return your feelings." Alec's face began to turn beet red at Neji's words. He was completely mortified at the misunderstanding.

"Neji, it's not what you think-!" Alec waved his hands frantically before him, "I was...it's a new spiritual ability I've gained. It's a curse breaking power."

Junpei was looking amused. "A curse breaking power? Where you have to *kiss* the person for it to work? Dude, I could put that ability to some good use." Junpei began to chuckle and Alec sent him a death glare. Junpei noticed and tried to calm himself down before wiping a tear from his eye with his index finger, he had been laughing so hard. "Sorry, buddy, but you have to admit it was hilarious. You having to kiss Neji and wake him up like sleeping beauty or something!"

"Junpei! This is serious!" Alec puffed out his cheeks angrily. "Besides, it's what Tamamo-no-mae told me to do." Alec sighed heavily at Junpei's antics. He really deserved to become a saint after all this, Alec thought.

"Tamamo-no-mae?" Jin broke in quickly, "She gave you this power?"

Alec nodded.

Neji pushed his glasses up his nose, finally beginning to understand what was going on. "Oh, I see. Then, thanks man. I owe you one." Neji gave Alec a timid smile.

Alec smiled back. "No prob. Anytime."

Junpei was pouting since he didn't get to have his fun. "Hey, you're taking this rather calmly aren't you Neji? I mean you were just kissing another boy!"

Neji blinked and ran a hand through his greasy hair, "He only did it to save my life. I can't be ungrateful now can I?"

Junko went over to inspect Neji's chest and let out a sigh of relief that the mark was completely gone. "Well, whatever it is it seems to have worked. The curse mark is no longer there."

Junpei got a mischievous gleam in his eye. "Ah, that's right Alec you still have to wake the *real* sleeping beauty from her slumber a.k.a. Rika otherwise known as Game Idol, Lady V. Who would have thought?" Junpei rubbed his hands together in anticipation.

Alec looked over to Rika's sleeping form. She was the girl, who had given him his first kiss and whom Alec thought he might have a small crush on. But ever since he found out she was also LadyV he had mixed feelings about her. Was she just toying with him all along? How did he really feel about Rika? He knew he cared for her as a friend but as more than friends? He wasn't so sure.

Alec approached Rika's bed feeling nervous and somewhat guilty. He couldn't help the flush that came to his cheeks as he leaned down and looked upon Rika's sleeping face. He had to admit, Junpei was right, she was pretty cute without her glasses.

Neji was scowling deeply as he watched Alec leaning over Rika and almost looked like he was about to stop him or say something but remained silent. Junpei was simply once again amused. "Come on Romeo, sweep her off her feet already." Junpei waggled his brows playfully.

Alec gulped as he leaned over to press his lips against Rika's. He could feel the warm tingling feeling of the curse breaking power flowing through him and then passing into Rika's body. The golden light was warm, inviting, and pure and Alec knew it wasn't anything harmful. A few moments later Rika began to wake.

Alec was pulling back when Rika suddenly wrapped her arms around Alec's neck trapping him and pulled him back in for another kiss. This time she deepened the kiss while Alec struggled to pull away, his face as red as a tomato at this point. Finally, Rika let him go and Alec stumbled backwards gasping for breath and looking like he might pass out at any second.

Rika sat up in bed, an amused expression on her face, as she licked her lips cat-like. "*Mmm* I was having the most delicious dream about you Alec."

Alec was a bit startled by her forward attitude. *She's acting like LadyV now...where did my slightly shy and awkward Rika go? Pout.*

Alec was a bit speechless. "I was just..."

"Saving your life Rika." Neji offered a serious note to his voice, "He has a new curse breaking ability. He has to kiss the cursed person to pass on purifying spiritual energy. *That's* why he kissed you."

"Oh." But Rika was still all smiles. "Thank you Alec for saving my life." She threw a wink at him. "Again."

Alec grinned back goofily despite himself, "Anytime."

Jin and Junko looked at each other and exchanged a knowing look before nodding.

"Alec, there's one more person we need you to wake up for us please." Junko told him.

Alec blinked. "Um, yea, sure." Alec began to follow Jin and Junko and called over his shoulder to his friends. "I'll catch you guys later."

Jin and Junko led Alec down the hall to another hospital room where when he entered Alec saw a 15-year-old boy with short, spiky, blue-black hair lying back comatose on a bed. There was something oddly familiar about this boy and Alec's eyes widened as he realized. *It must be Night!*

Alec slowly walked to Night's beside, "Night?...Is that really you?" Alec quickly leaned over and pressed his lips to his hero's in order to awaken him. Alec's body glowed with a golden light and he could feel the warmth spreading through his limbs. He felt Night beginning to stir and quickly pulled away from him.

Night began to sit up, a slightly confused expression on his face. "Alec? What are you doing here? Did you and Yukino defeat Tamamo-no-mae? Is Yukino safe?"

"Well, um, you see, about that..." Alec looked away and scratched his cheek nervously, "I kinda...lethergo." Alec said the last part in a rush but Night caught every word.

His sapphire colored eyes widened. "You what!"

Alec waved his hands frantically before him as he began to explain. "Wait, let me explain. Tamamo-no-mae was just being controlled...I had to free her. And in exchange for sparing her life Tamamo-no-mae gave me her curse breaking power."

Night's eyebrows rose. "Ah, so that's why you kissed me. I thought you might have a secret crush on me, which would be understandable since I'm your mentor and everything but-"

Alec was all flushed. "No! You got it all wrong. I was just breaking the curse! *Mou!* Geez! Each and every one of you are a bunch of perverts! You all need to get your minds out of the gutter - this is a PG rated story you know!"

Night suddenly turned serious. "Alec, listen to me - this is very important. You spared Tamamo-no-mae's life and in return were gifted her curse breaking power. You're both even now. Everything's balanced. Which means if you ever encounter Tamamo-no-mae again you have to be careful. She won't owe you anything. She could...eat you."

Alec gulped, "But I don't think she'd do that...she's...not so bad."

"She's a *yokai* Alec and a very powerful one. She's not to be trusted. Remember that." Night narrowed his eyes at him.

Alec pouted but said nothing, acting stubborn. Call it a hunch but he had sensed good in Tamamo-no-mae, and were all demons and *yokai* truly 100% evil? Alec didn't think so. Nothing in the world was black and white, to Alec things were just shades of gray.

Night looked over at Jin and Junko noticing them hovering in the doorway for the first time. "Ah, Jin, Junko, tell me, how is my little sister?"

Jin and Junko exchanged a nervous glance.

"We tried to stop him..." Jin began.

"We're so sorry." Junko hung her head. "We failed you."

"Yoru, he's...taken her." Jin explained.

Yoru blinked at them in shock before bursting out. "WHAT! You let them take my sister?"

He was beginning to get angry and the lights overhead in the hospital room were flickering ominously. Alec also watched mystified as items on the bedside tables began to rattle as if there were an earthquake or something. The hairs on the back of Alec's neck were prickling in warning as well.

Junko quickly grabbed Alec's arm and began to drag him forcibly from the room, "Alec-*kun*, it's too dangerous for you to be in here right now with Night like this. You have to get out of here. Let Jin handle this."

"But-" Alec was saying as he was pushed out of the room. Alec turned around, prepared to go back inside and just as Junko closed the door in Alec's face he watched in surprise as a vase of flowers lifted up off the table next to Night's bed and then was slammed into the far wall, shattering to pieces.

"How could you let this happen? My sister!" Night yelled and Alec could hear more stuff smashing into the walls and breaking. "If Kaguto lays one finger on my sister - I'll kill him!"

"Yoru! Calm down...we'll find her. Don't worry. And when we do Alec will be able to wake her up! There's hope now Yoru!" Alec recognized Jin's voice, though he had never heard the boy's voice sound so strained.

"Sister! Nooo!" Night yelled and the sound of a few more things smashing into the walls was heard.

Then there was silence and Alec was surprised when he could hear the muffled sound of someone sobbing pitifully. Alec's eyes widened in shock as he heard Jin's soothing voice, "*Shhh* it's alright, Yoru. I promise we'll find her."

"*Sister...*" Yoru moaned pathetically, "I failed her...I've broken my promise..."

Alec had a sinking feeling in his stomach upon learning that Night's sister was in danger. Alec clenched his fists at his sides feeling utterly powerless to do anything.

After Night had calmed down Junko left the room to check on Alec and closed the door softly behind her.

"Junko, isn't there anything I can do to help?" Alec asked her pleadingly.

Junko shook her head sadly, and patted Alec's head. "You've done more than enough already. You really are a good boy. No...for now there's nothing you can do. But when we get Yoru's sister back you're the only one who can awaken her. Now go back to Izanagi Academy. Everything will be fine now - thanks to you."

Alec nodded but still had a twisting feeling in his stomach that wouldn't go away.

●　●　●　●　●　●　●　●　●　●　●　●　●　●　●　◦

By the time Alec returned to Izanagi Academy he realized it was time to bring Akira his dinner. He hurried to the cafeteria and quickly grabbed the tray that was waiting for him and hurried off to Akira's room. He had his soccer ball with him since he had decided on doing a little 'secret soccer training' afterwards. But when he was about to knock on the door he heard a sudden crash from within that was quickly followed by another.

"Damn you! Dranarch!" He heard Akira yell and then the sound of something else breaking was heard.

Alec worriedly knocked on the door. "Akira? Akira open up! What's wrong?"

"Darn it all to hell!" Akira was yelling from inside and Alec could hear him overturning what was most likely a chair.

"Akira? I'm coming in!" Alec decided to empower his soccer ball for this task and then kicked the soccer ball directly at the door so that it was forced open.

Alec saw that the entire room was in complete disarray - with chairs overturned, books and papers were scattered everywhere, and there were several broken items on the floor that had been flung at the wall. The severely pissed off *hikikomori* boy was about to throw a lamp at the wall next when Alec rushed up to stop him.

"Hey! Stop!" Alec grabbed the boy's arm and spun him around to face him.

Alec had actually never seen Akira, the *hikikomori*, face-to-face before and his eyes widened slightly as he took in his overall goth-boy appearance. The boy was very pale, and there were dark shadows under his eyes that were either naturally caused by insomnia or perhaps makeup, Alec decided as he took in the rest of the boy's outfit. He was dressed all in black, his short black hair was spiked up, and he was wearing a silver chain necklace on which hung a silver skull charm. But what unsettled Alec the most was the burn scar he saw on Akira's left cheek...

Akira's eyes widened as he looked back at Alec but for different reasons. "You! It's you again! Get the hell out of my room!" Akira began to shove Alec towards the doorway.

"It's you...you're RedAki aren't you?" Alec said as he was being shoved out.

Akira stopped dead in his tracks, a startled expression on his face. He then narrowed his eyes suspiciously at Alec, "Just who are you?"

"It's me...I'm Dranarch." Alec admitted.

Akira's eyes widened and then narrowed in anger. "YOU! It's you! I hate you!" Akira strode forward and grabbed Alec by the front of his school uniform before lifting him up in the air and slamming him hard into the back wall. "Do you have any idea what I've been through because of you! Kaguto he-" But Akira stopped himself, biting his lip.

But Alec had already figured it all out. He raised a hand tentatively towards the ugly scar on Akira's face. "He...punished you didn't he? You should really go and see Haruna-*sensei* for that."

Akira glared, "That's none of your business! Besides why do you even care? Why are you even here?"

But he set Alec down nevertheless. Alec brushed himself off. "I'm here... to help you. Come on let's go to the nurse's office."

Akira stepped back. "Keh, you don't get it do you? This is a spiritual wound, it will never go away - never. I'll be a hideous scar face for the rest of my life. Yet another reason why I shouldn't leave my room." Akira let out a defeated sigh. "I hate my life."

"I hate your life too," Alec agreed nodding, "Why don't you just...leave the Renegade Reapers and Kaguto? I mean he's such a jerk to you. Why are you so loyal to him anyways? And I...I could help you get out of here. I could help you stop being a *hikikomori*."

"You don't understand." Akira ran a hand through his spiky hair, "Kaguto he...he was the only person to ever acknowledge me. He made me feel as though I actually had worth or value. Also you...you know too little about what's actually going on to understand. You don't even know what either side is after or what they believe in. Say I should pick your side for example. You're Yoru's little pawn but he doesn't even let me train my spiritual abilities because according to him they're not...right. That's why I don't want to be on your side. I like my side because they at least accept me the way I am. I'm wanted by them. And I don't intend to ever leave this room."

"I don't think I need to understand much. Look at what that jerk did to you! How can you follow someone who would do that to you after one little failure? He's a sick, twisted lunatic!"

Akira was turning red with anger, "Don't call him a lunatic. How dare you insult Master Kaguto! Kaguto was the only person to ever show me kindness!" Akira grabbed Alec's shoulder in a painful grip.

Alec stubbornly glared back, unfazed, "He kidnaped *her* you know."

Akira blinked. "Huh?"

"*He* kidnaped Night's sister - she was in a coma in the real world. Are you really going to follow a guy like that? A guy who kidnaps little girls?" Alec raised his eyebrows at Akira.

"I don't know what you're talking about." Akira scowled darkly, "You're obviously lying."

Alec clenched his fists in frustration. "And you are an idiot! To follow a guy like that - he's a freakin madman!"

"I told you not to badmouth him!" Akira said as he shoved Alec back and then suddenly punched Alec hard across the face.

Alec's eyes widened in shock and he put a hand to his throbbing cheek. Akira had just hit him. No one had ever hit him like that before. And before he knew what was happening Alec had clenched his own fist and flung it at Akira in return. He watched satisfied as Akira stumbled backwards, blood running down from a split lip. Akira wiped the blood away with the back of his hand and sneered. Akira then rushed at Alec and flung another punch. Soon the boys were going all out, throwing punches at each other left and right and Alec found that he actually enjoyed it.

The two boys stood minutes later glaring at each other, both covered in bruises, sporting black eyes, split lips, and both of them were panting for breath. "Get out. Just get the hell out." Akira groused through gritted teeth.

"Akira...wait. I'm sorry. I don't know what came over me." Alec started as the effects from the adrenaline rush from the fight were beginning to wear off. "I can help you."

"GET OUT! YOU LIAR! AND LEAVE ME THE HECK ALONE!" Akira yelled at the top of his lungs as he shoved Alec hard so that he stumbled back out into the hallway. Alec blinked as Akira slammed the door closed in his face with a loud bang.

Alec flinched at the harsh sound. A sinking feeling in his stomach developed as he looked at the closed door. *What have I done?*

Alec left dragging his feet sadly down the hall, regretting how he had handled that entire situation. But when he had heard Night crying back at the hospital it was like something had snapped inside of him. It was the first time he'd ever been in a fist fight like that. Usually, when bullies picked on Alec he just let them beat him up, without returning a single blow but today... he had fought back. And it felt good.

Alec returned to his dorm room and Neji was there waiting for him. Neji's brow furrowed in worry as he took in the sight of Alec's battered form.

"Alec! What happened?" Neji rushed up to Alec, a PDA (personal desktop assistant) in his hand that he had been tinkering with and was currently upgrading.

Alec merely went over to sit on his bed and hung his head down with a heavy sigh, his white bangs covering his stormy gray eyes as he stared down curiously at his hands. The skin was scraped off of his knuckles in places and he was bleeding. Alec was trembling slightly and he fought to calm himself before he spoke."I was...in a fight."

"A fight? With whom?" Neji's eyes widened.

"Akira...I mean, RedAki." Alec amended. "They're the same person."

Neji gasped. "RedAki...you mean to tell me that RedAki is the *hikikomori* you've been taking care of all this time!"

Alec nodded and was filled with bitter regret. He looked down at this hands...those hands of his that he had used to hurt someone. He clenched his hands into fists, angry with himself.

He's not my son! He's a monster! - Laura's voice rang through his mind.

Maybe he really was a monster, to just snap like that. Alec had been frustrated that Akira had been right when he said that Alec didn't really know anything. Also the anger had been building inside of him that he was powerless to do anything to help Night out about his sister and so Akira's harsh words had been the straw that broke the camel's back, so to speak. Alec hadn't even known the true depths of his own pent up anger and frustration until he had suddenly snapped and taken it out on Akira.

Alec's voice wavered. "I shouldn't have done that. I shouldn't have hit him....I hurt him. And it's not even him I'm really mad at." *The one I'm mad at is me.*

Neji pushed his glasses up his nose thoughtfully, "But who started the fight?"

Alec shrugged, "We both did but I instigated it, I guess. I insulted Kaguto a.k.a. Reaper, and got Akira pissed. And then I got pissed that he could care about a guy like that." Alec couldn't hold it in any longer and hot tears of frustration began to fall down his face. "I hurt him when really all I wanted to do was help him. I'm so stupid. I totally screwed things up. Now Akira hates me and now...he'll never leave his room And it's all my fault."

Neji sat down next to Alec and put a casual arm around his shoulders and Alec turned to cry into Neji's chest. "There, there Alec." Neji tried to comfort him somewhat awkwardly. "Don't beat yourself up about it. It was just a fist fight. We're boys, it's normal for boys our age to get in fights. It's no big deal really."

"It is a big deal - to me." Alec sniffled. "I just...snapped. It's like there's this other side of me that I don't even know about. This evil side. What if my mother was right and I'm...a monster?"

Neji frowned, "You're no monster Alec you're...our guardian angel. You saved everyone today. We'd all still be in comas if it wasn't for you. We owe our lives to you. You're no monster - you're a hero."

Alec just continued to cry. "I'm no hero. I'm not even close." *I failed to save Akira after all...and he truly needed to be saved from himself. And I'm failing Midoriko...how can I save Yukino or protect her? And how can I save Night?*

Alec ended up crying himself to sleep that night.

· · · · · · · · · · · · · · · · ·

The next day, before classes started Alec decided to go to Haruna-*sensei's* office to get his wounds from the fist fight healed. As soon as he entered the door Haruna began to fuss over him like a mother hen.

"Oh dear! Alec-*kun* what happened to you!" Haruna-*sensei* quickly ushered him over to a chair where she began to inspect the cuts and bruises on his face and hands.

"I...got into a fight." Alec admitted, feeling worse about it than before. Haruna-*sensei* was such a nice person but she probably thought Alec was some kind of juvenile delinquent or something now.

"I see." Haruna-*sensei* looked grave but didn't say anything as she began to lay her hands on his skin and heal him with her empathic power, a tingling sensation coming over his cuts and bruises.

Alec hung his head ashamed. "I'm...sorry."

Haruna-*sensei* raised an eyebrow at him and ruffled his hair. "You really are a good boy." She smiled at him in a warm manner.

Alec looked up at her in shock, eyes wide. "How can you say that! I got into a fist fight...and I beat up another student! Who didn't even deserve it!"

Haruna-*sensei* frowned, "But you really are a good boy because you regret a thing like getting into a fist fight. You are a thirteen-year-old boy Alec, fights happen. Stop putting so much pressure on yourself. You're still a boy."

Alec shook his head. "No, you don't understand. I..." Alec felt sick as he considered telling Haruna-*sensei* that he had actually enjoyed the fist fight against Akira. But he just couldn't bring himself to tell Haruna-*sensei* since she was just so nice and to have her think badly of him would hurt more than anything.

Haruna-*sensei* frowned and she pushed the corner of Alec's mouth up with her index finger. "Smile, smile. You need to turn that frown upside down mister. What will all the girls think if they see you looking like that today. Today is a special day after all."

Alec blinked. "Huh? Girls?"

"I have to get you all healed up so you'll look your best today. You do know what day it is *neh?*" Haruna-*sensei* pressed, a playful twinkle in her eyes.

Alec gave her a blank look.

"It's Valentine's Day, silly." Haruna smiled lopsidedly at Alec's clueless nature.

Alec's brows rose, "Oh. Dang, I forgot to get something for Rika. She's the only female friend I have."

"Bzzz." Haruna made the sound of a buzzer beeping 'incorrect' like on a game show. "No, no, Alec, it's only in America that boys buy girls things on Valentine's Day. In Japan it's a little different, you see, girls buy the boy they like chocolate or some times they make their own homemade chocolates to reveal their true feelings. If the boy accepts the chocolate it's the same thing as accepting the girl's feelings and saying you like her back. So you have to be very careful not to just take chocolate without meaning it Alec. Or else you'll hurt some girl's feelings. Then it's not until White Day that boys buy the girls they like or the girls who gave them chocolates on V-day something. Usually you give something 'white' in return like white chocolate or marsh mellows. So, this girl, Rika, do you think she'll give you chocolate?"

Alec shrugged, "Probably..."

Haruna-*sensei* frowned, "You don't look too happy about it though."

Alec sighed, "It's just I don't really know how I really feel about her. I mean, I thought that I liked her but then I found out something about her and now I'm not so sure. But I do care for Rika as a good friend. I dunno...I'm confused I guess." *I still don't know if Rika really likes me or if she's just roleplaying. I felt something for her but now...I don't know how I feel.*

Haruna-*sensei* took a seat at her swivel chair. "Well, if you don't think Rika's the one you like, do you have anyone else that you would have given a present to? Think Alec, who would make you feel all giddy inside to make smile with something you gave her? Or who would give you butterflies in your stomach if they suddenly showed up offering you chocolates today? Do you have someone like that?"

For some reason Alec suddenly pictured Yukino all dressed in pink and giving Alec chocolates and completely acting out of character for her as she confessed her feelings of love for him. He was surprised that this visual image did give him butterflies in his stomach. But just because the idea of Yukino giving him chocolates made him smile it didn't mean that he 'liked her liked her' right? Naw.

Alec almost laughed aloud since it was the most ridiculous thing he could have imagined. Yukino wearing pink and acting all girlie! *And* giving him chocolates! Like that would ever happen. Hell would freeze over first. Yukino wasn't into those girlie sorts of things and didn't see Alec as more than a little brother. She also clearly seemed to have a thing for Night. He wasn't even sure how he felt about her. And besides she was...

A ghost.

And Alec was surprised that this thought made him feel a great sense of sadness. Like someone had taken his heart and clenched their hand around it painfully. But it was only natural to feel sad about thinking of Yukino being a ghost because she was his good friend. That feeling wasn't anything special, Alec decided.

Alec shook his head. "No, I mean, yes, but...she'd never give me chocolate. She's not the type of girl to be into all this 'girl stuff'." *And even if she did want to give me chocolates how could she - trapped inside a game world?*

Haruna smiled knowingly, "Sometimes the girls who seem all tough on the outside are actually quite soft on the inside. She may pretend she doesn't like girlie things but deep down she may actually like them quite a bit. She may be a bit more girlie than you think. I think Alec, she may end up surprising you."

Alec got up from his seat and shrugged, "Yea, maybe. I better go." Alec dragged his feet to the door and Haruna-*sensei* watched him go, a slightly fretful look on her face.

Alec was walking down the hallway when a couple of girls suddenly called out to him.

"Oh, hey there he is! Wait up!" The girl called out and Alec turned around to face the two girls and eyed the wrapped Valentine's Day chocolate in their hands. He raised an eyebrow at the girls and looked behind him to see who they were calling out to. But there was no one behind him. Alec turned back around to face them and pointed at himself with a look that asked - 'you mean me?'

The girl nodded and smiled shyly as she walked towards him. Once she was standing in front of him she reached her hands out with the chocolate and offered them to Alec. "Alec, will you accept my chocolate?"

"Uh...?" Alec was completely caught by surprise that this pig-tailed girl was suddenly giving him Valentine's Day chocolates. And then he remembered what Haruna-*sensei* had warned him about:

If the boy accepts the chocolate it's the same thing as accepting the girl's feelings and saying you like her back. So you have to be very careful not to just take chocolate without meaning it Alec. Or else you'll hurt some girl's feelings.

The girl's friend elbowed her to the side, "Reina," She whined, "Stop hogging Alec all to yourself. He has to accept my chocolates as well." The girl reached out her chocolates towards Alec next.

"Uh..." Alec looked at the two girls awkwardly wondering what he should do but desperately not wanting to hurt their feelings.

Reina frowned, "Yukari! I got to him first."

"Did not, we both saw him at the same time." Yukari shot back.

"Uh...*Moshi Moshi*? Hello hello?" Alec tried to get their attention as they began to fight over who was going to give Alec their chocolates first.

Alec was beginning to slowly back away from the girls since they had become conveniently distracted. However -

A large group of girls had just turned the corner at the end of the hall and had spotted Alec and the two girls.

"Look there he is!" "It's Alec Suzuki!" "Alec? Where?" "Eeeee!"

Uh oh.

Alec took another step back as he saw the manic gleam in the girls' eyes and noticed they all had chocolates in their hands. The hairs on the back of his neck were prickling in warning. This was worse than being hunted by *yokai* or poltergeist Alec decided, nodding vigorously to himself. Alec decided there was only one logical course of action in a situation like this one - run.

And run he did.

"After him!" "Don't let him get away!" "Let's get him!" The group of fan girls began to give chase.

As Alec ran down the hall he looked behind his shoulder in disbelief - *They're actually chasing me! This is ridiculous!* "Ack! Why are you all chasing me?"

"Because you're running away *baka*!" "That's right, you have to accept our chocolates!" "We spent hours making them!" They demanded.

"I'd rather not, thanks!" Alec shot back as he continued to run.

Just then Neji and Junpei ducked out of an empty classroom and grabbed onto Alec so fast he didn't know which way was up and then he found himself suddenly brought inside the safety of the science room where Junpei quickly shut the door.

Junpei put a finger to his lips for silence and Alec nodded as they heard the gaggle of girls running past the science room like some kind of stampede. Alec let out a breath of relief. *Gulp, girls are scary. Even more so on Valentine's Day.*

Junpei smirked, "You dog, it seems they're still your fans for having saved Rika."

"Aw man..." Alec pouted, "You have to do something to help me Junpei, girls are scary..." Alec shivered, a chill going down his spine at the thought of being cornered by all those girls.

Junpei and Neji laughed at Alec's plight. "Wish I had his problem." Neji said as he plopped a bonbon into his mouth from a red heart-shaped box.

"And where did you get those?" Junpei asked raising an eyebrow curiously.

"Oh these." Neji held up the box of bonbons, "A girl gave them to me and told me to give them to Alec. You don't mind right?" Neji asked Alec as an afterthought. "Chocolate stimulates my brain waves."

"Not at all." Alec smiled, amused.

Just then the door suddenly opened and all three boys jumped at least a foot in the air. But it was only Rika. She quickly slipped her way inside and closed the door behind her. "Hey guys, so this is where you've all been hiding huh? Though I don't know why you're hiding here *Junpei*. Who would want to give chocolates to a cocky, egotistic jock like you. Hmph!" Rika glared at him.

"You just haven't learned to appreciate my finer qualities yet, cutie, give it some time." Junpei winked at her. "No girl can resist my charisma forever." Junpei waggled his fingers at her as if his 'charisma' would float in the air towards her.

Rika waved her hands in front of her trying to dispel Junpei's 'charisma', "Charisma? *Pu-lease*. I think you mean cooties! Keep those things away from me! Ew!" She then turned her attention to Alec noticing him for the first time. "Oh! Alec when did you get here? I have something for you." Rika reached into her sailor uniform and pulled out a small box wrapped in silver paper with a blue ribbon wrapped around it. "Chocolate...I made it myself."

"Oh, uh, you really shouldn't have..." Alec had a hand behind his head bashfully as Rika approached him. Rika was about to hand Alec her chocolates when they heard a sudden pounding on the door.

"Alec! We know you're in there! Come on out!" The fan girls cried.

"Aw man, what are we going to do?" Alec moaned. "Maybe I can jump out the window..." Alec looked over to the windows of the science room.

"It's a two story drop..." Neji warned.

"Don't worry, you all just leave it to my genius." Junpei declared and took out a duffle bag. "I figured something like this might happen today so I came up with a battle plan." He took out what appeared to be a white haired wig. "Neji and I will dress up like Alec and then we'll all make a break for it. The girls won't know which one of us is the real Alec so they'll have to give up. Simple really. Oh and we'll all have these matching sunglasses as well to help with the disguise and they just make me look cool."

Alec raised an eyebrow, "I dunno Junpei, do you really think that's gonna work...?"

Junpei gave him a thumbs up, "Trust me."

The two boys quickly put on their 'Alec disguises' which consisted of a white wig and black sunglasses. Alec only had to put on the matching sunglasses. All three boys already had matching clothing because of their black, high-collared school uniforms.

Rika looked the boys over and looked at the slightly taller, more muscular, and tanner version of Alec who was Junpei and then the slightly more scrawny and wimpy Alec who was Neji before she burst out laughing. All three boys frowned in response.

"Sorry," Rika apologized when she got herself under control, "But I really doubt you're going to fool anyone with those costumes of yours. It's like so obvious."

"Well, all we have left to do is put it to the test." Junpei declared and suddenly opened the door to the science room.

"Junpei!" Alec squeaked as he peaked his head out and was immediately spotted. "Ack!" Alec took off running. Neji followed suit and quickly ran off in the opposite direction.

Junpei smirked pleased at how well his plan was working out as he watched the two boys run off and the fan girls' reaction to this development:

"Oh no! There are two of them!" "Which one is the real Alec?" "Half of you go that way!" "The other half will go this way!" "Let's go!" The fan girls directed each other.

Junpei shook his head ruefully as he watched the crowd of girls disperse, "They're a pretty well organized group - those fan girls of Alec."

"Yea," Rika pouted, "But even I didn't get a chance to give Alec my chocolates."

"You could always give them to me instead," Junpei waggled his eyebrows at her playfully.

"I think not." Rika said snottily and put her chocolates back inside her school uniform.

"Can't blame a guy for trying," Junpei put out his hands in a helpless gesture, "Well, I better go help with the diversion!" Junpei rushed out of the classroom and struck a pose while trying to appear 'dashing'. "Ladies? Were you all looking for me?"

"Look there he is!" "Get him!" "I have some rope!" "He won't get away this time!"

Rope? Gulp. Junpei had been thinking he might stick around but...after that last comment Junpei took off running as well. "Mommy!" Alec was right girls really could be scary, Junpei decided as the girls followed hot on his heels.

• • • • • • • • • • • • • • •

Meanwhile, Alec had managed to make it outside the main school building and was running alongside the soccer field when another group of girls spotted him. Alec looked from side to side for a place to hide and then spotted the storage closet. He quickly made his way inside and shut the door behind him. He turned around to see that the storage closet was quite large and filled with soccer balls, gym mats, basket balls, bats, baseballs, and all kinds of other sporting equipment for all the sports clubs.

Unexpectedly, Alec sensed a ghost-like presence, the hairs on the back of his neck prickling, and he rubbed the back of his neck absentmindedly in response. He looked around suddenly having the eerie sensation that he was being watched. That's when he noticed a pair of yellow eyes peering out at him from underneath a pile of gym mats. Alec slowly walked towards the eyes and leaned down to have a closer look. There in the shadows he could see the shadowy form of a cat. Alec let out a breath of relief - "It's just a cat...here kitty kitty..." Alec crooked his finger at the cat. "Don't worry I won't hurt you."

The black cat slowly made its way out from underneath the mats and Alec gasped when he saw that it had not one but two long silky tails. "A *nekomata*...a cat demon..."

The *nekomata* calmly padded forward and peered up into Alec's startled gray eyes. Alec found himself staring back but then realized that he couldn't seem to look away. He was completely captivated, trapped by the *nekomata*'s golden gaze. Alec felt as though he were losing himself, falling, into their luminous depth. Those strange golden eyes seemed to be able to see right through Alec all the way to his spirit. And then an odd sensation overtook him. His stomach flip flopped and goose bumps broke out all over his arms. And then all of a sudden the world seemed to grow *HUGE* all around him. And then when he blinked next he found himself looking at - himself.

It was a freaky feeling for Alec, like looking at a mirror's reflection but not quite the same. Alec watched himself smile this evil twisted grin and didn't even know his face could make that sort of expression. It was most definitely creepy.

"Foolish *gaijin* boy, everyone Japanese knows never to look a *nekomata* in the eyes lest their soul be eaten. You're lucky I merely decided to do a soul-swapping with you since this body of yours was just too perfect to pass up. With this body my powers will be magnified at least ten fold! Now, I think I'll go have some fun with this body, *Ja-ne. Baka.*" The *nekomata*, who was now in Alec's body, declared before he strutted to the metal door of the storage closet and swung it open to let himself outside. He quickly left and Alec could hear him closing and locking the door from the other side.

The sound of the locking door seemed to snap Alec out of his stunned stupor. He couldn't quite believe this was actually happening. A real *nekomata* had just done a soul-swapping with him and stolen his body!

"Hey, wait!" Alec cried out and found that instead of his normal human voice all that came out of his mouth was - "*Meow! Meow!*" Alec put a paw to his mouth in shock and then looked down at his hands to see that instead of human boy hands he now had paws with razor sharp claws.

Alec heard the sound of the *nekomata* walking away from the now locked storage closet. He was trapped. "Aw man..." Alec moaned. "This can't be happening. Why me?"

Alec stood on his hind legs, a very un-catlike thing to do and looked at the locked door in despair. *A nekomata just switched bodies with me, great just great. As if this day couldn't get any weirder...*

Alec looked around the storage closet until he noticed a small window. Alec climbed onto some of the boxes that were under the window and then jumped the rest of the way so that he managed to grab a hold of the window ledge with his small paws, his claws digging into the ledge to keep him there as he hung on for dear life. He then managed to scramble himself up and pushed at the window at the same time so that it opened and then Alec managed to squeeze himself through. It was a long drop. Alec squeaked until he felt his body naturally twisting itself so that he was able to land on all fours. *Whew. Thank god for cat-like reflexes.* Alec quickly looked around and caught sight of his body a.k.a. the *nekomata* walking back towards the main school building.

"Oh, no you don't!" Alec declared as he ran off towards the *nekomata* running on all fours now since it was faster. "*Oi!* Hey you! Wait up!" Alec shook his head in frustration when all that came out of his mouth were a bunch of 'meows' again.

Alec had almost managed to reach the *nekomata* when suddenly all the hairs on his back stood on end in warning and Alec spun to look sideways where Alec noticed a dog had spotted him. *Uh oh.* The golden haired dog didn't look too friendly either and was eyeing Alec as though he would make a nice snack. The dog's lips were drawn back into a ferocious growl and Alec could see the drool dripping down the dog's canines. *Ew. Gross.* Alec shivered. He guessed the dog was a kind of golden retriever and was surprised at his behavior since he had always heard that kind of dog was friendly, well, maybe to humans.

Alec took a step back and the dog growled as it approached Alec. Alec hissed back at the dog despite himself and shook his head. The hairs on his back still wouldn't go down either and it was an uncomfortable feeling. *Well, big dog, big teeth. Seems like there's only one thing for me to do. Run!*

"Epp!" Alec squeaked as he decided to take off running, the angry dog right on his heels. *Today is so not my day!* Alec moaned in his mind as the dog chased him into the forest that was close to the main school building and on the school grounds. Alec saw trees flash past in his vision as he continued to run and he had never realized how big this forest on campus actually was before. The chase continued until Alec suddenly came out into a clearing where there was a temple of some sort. It was a traditional, Japanese temple with curving, tiled roofs, a large golden prayer bell was seen hanging off to one side, and a *kami* (god) shrine was also nearby.

There in the courtyard before the main temple building was a sight that made Alec skid to a halt and caused his eyes to widen to the size of saucers. He saw Junko and several other girls dressed in *miko* robes, a white *haori* shirt and red *hakama* pants. The *miko* all had bows in their hands while Junko was instructing them in archery. However, this was no normal archery. Alec watched as Junko was explaining to the girls how to summon their spirit energy before releasing an arrow so that it was enveloped with a blue-tinged light and so would effectively exorcize any ghost or *yokai*. Alec's little cat mouth dropped open as he watched more than one of her students sending off glowing spirit arrows towards their targets.

Alec's attention was then drawn towards some young monks-in-training, who were sparing with each other in the center of the main courtyard. Though once again these were no ordinary sparing matches. Jin seemed to be teaching a fellow student a few unusual tricks. Jin's body was enveloped with a blue-tinged light and his blows seemed to be faster and more powerful than was probably humanly possible as he spared with his opponent. Jin's pupil was following suit and also enveloping his body and fists with his spirit energy to add both power, speed, and strength. Then Jin was getting into a weird fighting stance with both of his hands cradling thin air which he brought back and then suddenly forward so that a blue energy blast was unleashed towards his sparing partner - much to Alec's complete amazement. The energy blast hit the monk in training who was flung backwards onto his backside. Ouch. The monks clapped and jeered, impressed by Jin's obvious skill.

Alec realized as he watched them that Junko and Jin were not only teachers but that the people they were teaching were also fellow students. Alec was able to recognize a few people he had seen around campus before. Alec was a bit shocked to be watching his fellow students training in their spiritual powers. Learning things like how to make spirit arrows and form energy blasts. It was totally unreal. They were controlling that same blue light, or what Alec realized was his spirit energy that Alec used to empower his soccer ball.

Alec couldn't believe that there were this many people at Izanagi Academy with spiritual powers just like him. What was with Izanagi Academy anyways? And why was the school training its students like this? For what purpose? And if these students were allowed to train in their spiritual powers and abilities then why wasn't Alec allowed to train too? It couldn't have been his age since Alec noticed a few boys his own age training with Jin.

It's just not fair. Alec frowned, pouting. *Why am I always left in the dark about everything? There are so many secrets in this school like this training for kids with spiritual powers and I knew nothing about it. What are they all training for anyways? For what purpose? It's like the school is forming an army...but against what? This sucks, I want to learn how to better control and strengthen my own powers too. Why doesn't anyone seem to understand that? What is it that they think they're protecting me from?*

However, Alec didn't have much more time to muse on these plaguing questions since the dog was suddenly behind him now, and barking loudly managed to chase Alec towards Junko and her archery students. Alec ended up having to run under Junko's legs just to avoid getting eaten alive by the dog and caused Junko to squeak out in surprise and miss her mark on the bull's eye as she loosed her arrow in a rather crooked manner. The dog was still right behind Alec and he had no choice but to then run straight through the middle of Jin and another monk, who were in the middle of sparing.

All eyes were now on the scruffy dog that was chasing a black two-tailed cat.

"A *nekomata*?" Jin frowned worriedly as he caught sight of the two tails. He then called out to his sister, "Junko! It's a *nekomata*! Quick!"

Junko was already in motion raising her bow, knocking an arrow and aiming it at Alec.

Ack! No way! Junko's going to exorcize me! Epp! Alec squeaked frantically in his mind as he somehow managed to dodge her first arrow attack. *Whew! That was close. Now I've got a bunch of monks and miko trying to exorcize me, great, just great.*

Alec decided to take his chances back in the forest instead of with the exorcist and demon hunters in training and took off running back in the direction of the forest. *What the hell is up with this school?*

"Junko, don't lose sight of him. I have to go and get my *o-fuda*!" Jin cried as he ran off into the main temple building.

"Right. I'm on it bro!" Junko called as she began to chase after Alec. Jin caught up to her moments later. "He went this way." Junko directed him as they both took off into the woods in pursuit of the *nekomata*. As Junko was running after him she managed to knock another arrow and send it flying Alec's way. Alec jumped into the air as the arrow flew right under him. How he had managed to dodge that attack he couldn't even fathom. *Well, at least I've managed to lose the dog. Though I've picked up a monk and miko.* They were hot on his tail, err, tails.

"How do you think a *nekomata* got onto the school grounds?" Junko questioned worriedly, as they continued to run.

"The tear most likely." Jin frowned, "We can't let it get to the school.

Nekomata are extremely dangerous. There's no telling what it will do if it comes in contract with a fellow student!"

Too late! Alec thought as he continued to run. *I wish they could just figure out it's me already.* "Junko! Jin! It's me Alec!" But all that continued to come out of his mouth were a series of panicked 'meows'.

Alec managed to dodge another arrow but this one nicked his ear painfully. *Ow! Why do things like this always happen to me! I wonder what the nekomata is doing in my body anyways. I hope to god it doesn't hurt anyone.*

Alec had a really, really bad feeling about all this.

A shiver went down his spine.

• • • • • • • • • • • • • • • •

Meanwhile, the *nekomata,* in Alec's body, was approaching the school building when he was suddenly approached by all these middle school girls who were holding chocolates in their hands.

"Alec!" "Alec-*kun!*" "Please accept my chocolates." "Here Alec I made these especially for you."

The girls all rushed up to him and reached out their chocolates.

The *nekomata* raised an eyebrow in surprise at them but then a cat's paw smile formed on his face. This was going to be good. This kid's body was going to be even more useful than he might have originally thought. *Merry Christmas to me.* A mischievous glint formed in his eye.

A few moments later, found the *nekomata* in Alec's home room seated in a chair with his feet propped comfortably up on the desk before him. His desk was piled high with Valentine's Day chocolate while a group of giggling girls surrounded him and fed him bonbons one by one as if they were grapes. Yep, life didn't get any better than this. Why hadn't he decided to leave the *Makai* for the human world sooner?

Takahashi-*sensei* was watching the 'girl shy' Alec in disbelief as he let the middle school girls fawn all over him and lavish him with attention. He was so stunned he had just frozen up in shock and hadn't even started class yet. All the middle school boys were hovering just outside of the classroom doorway with evil glints in their eyes as they watched Alec and the girls. They were incredibly pissed that Alec had somehow managed to get all the attention, affections, and chocolates of all the middle school girls for himself on Valentine's Day. The boys were filled with anger and jealousy and were secretly plotting Alec's downfall.

It didn't help matters much that Alec was openly gloating from all the attention he was managing to receive from the middle school girls.

Junpei and Neji were approaching home room when they spotted the group of boys waiting outside the door curiously. They pushed their way past the group confused about what they were doing exactly, before walking in and seeing Alec surrounded by swooning girls and piles of chocolate. Both their jaws dropped.

Junpei was the first to recover. He shook his head and used his finger to shut Neji's mouth shut next.

"Is that really Alec?" Neji gaped.

Junpei frowned thoughtfully as he looked at Alec's haughty expression, an expression he'd never seen on his friend before. "We're about to find out. Come on."

Junpei, followed close behind by Neji, strode up to Alec. "Hey there Alec." Junpei greeted, arms crossed over his chest.

Alec looked up, a bored expression on his face. "Hey guys." He said nonchalant.

"So, what's all this?" Junpei waved a hand at the fan girls. "I thought you said you didn't like Valentine's Day or chocolate?"

"Who me? I love Valentine's Day." The *nekomata* smirked, "Chocolate... girls...what more could a boy ask for?"

The girls giggled in response as Alec threw his arms around two of them, a sly grin on his face.

"Okay, Mr. Alien Body Snatcher, where is Alec and what planet have you taken him to!" Neji was starting forward, rolling up his sleeves, when Junpei pulled him back grasping the back of his uniform's collar, Neji struggled futilely against the jock's strong grip.

"Stay back Neji, this isn't some sci-fi movie. You could get hurt." Junpei warned him before starting forward.

"So, what do you guys want?" The *nekomata* raised an eyebrow at their antics, "Want some chocolate or something?" He held out a box of bonbons in their direction.

Neji was instantly won over by the Alien Body Snatcher. "Sure!" Neji grabbed the box, took off the lid and began to dig in.

Junpei sighed and shook his head. "None for me thanks. What I'd like to know is where is Alec and what have you done with him?" Junpei narrowed his eyes at *nekomata* noticing the creature's golden eyes. Those eyes were definitely not Alec's.

A twisted smile formed on the *nekomata*'s face before he clapped his hands. "Well done boy, you found me out. Looks like the cat is out of the bag, so to speak. Though more accurately speaking, the cat's out of his body." The *nekomata* stood up abruptly and grabbed a handful of the handmade chocolate before suddenly tossing them at Junpei. "Catch!" The *nekomata* said before he ran for the door. "I'm outta here."

Junpei threw up his arms to block the chocolate and quickly had to grab Neji who wanted to stay and pick up all the fallen chocolate. "Neji! Come on! He's getting away! Come back here you imposter!" Junpei yelled as he took off after the *nekomata*. Neji was right behind him though lagging a bit since his arms were laden with goodies and what Neji liked to think of as 'girl's affections'.

The *nekomata* was laughing gleefully as Junpei chased after him and was skipping more than actually running away when suddenly the *nekomata* went to an open window and jumped out.

"Alec!" Junpei cried in fright, wondering what would happen to the boy's body. But as Junpei and Neji reached the window and looked down they saw that the *nekomata* had landed safely and was off and running.

"Dang it! He's getting away! Come on." Junpei said as the boys took off towards the stairs.

· ◇ ● ● ● ● ● ● ● ● ● ● ● ◈ ● ◇ ·

Meanwhile, Alec was still trying to get away from Jin and Junko as he made his way around another corner and down a long stretch between two buildings only to realize a bit too late that it was a dead end. *Oh shoot!* Alec squeaked in his mind as he spun around and stood on his hind legs, his little paws on the wall behind him as Junko and Jin rushed forward. Junko was already raising her bow and knocking an arrow, which she aimed right at Alec's heart, prepared to finish him off.

Alec gulped, *Oh no, I'm done for.*

But then he heard Junpei's voice - "I think he went this way! Quick!"

And then suddenly Neji and Junpei were there with them. Junpei looked confused to see his brother and sister there until he spotted the trapped *nekomata*.

Neji's eyes widened as he saw the two-tailed cat, "Holy guacamole, a real *nekomata*..."

Junpei looked over at the *nekomata* and his golden-brown eyes met with the silvery gray eyes of the *nekomata*.

"Junpei! It's me! Alec!" Alec tried to call out. *"Meow! Meow! Meow!"*

Alec hung his head in defeat. He was sure there was no way Junpei could have possibly understood any of that. But Junpei's eyes widened startled and he then quickly spun to face his sister. "Oh shoot! Junko! Don't!"

But Junko had already released the arrow upon Alec. Alec shut his eyes and waited for the inevitable but luckily the inevitable didn't come to pass. Alec opened his eyes to see Junpei run towards the zooming arrow with superhuman speed and use a karate chop to break the arrow in half before it

259

could reach Alec. He was safe. *Phew. Close one. Again.* Alec let out a heavy sigh and feeling exhausted slumped down against the wall.

Junpei was standing protectively in front of Alec now, his arms out at his sides. "You idiots! You almost killed my best friend!"

Junko blinked worriedly. "You don't mean..." She looked at the *nekomata* and gasped upon noticing the silvery gray eyes. "Alec-*kun*?"

Jin's eyes narrowed suspiciously at Junpei, who was not supposed to have any spiritual abilities whatsoever and who was now claiming a *nekomata* was in fact Alec Suzuki. "Explain yourself, Junpei." Jin demanded.

Junpei stepped aside and pointed at Alec, "Didn't you guys hear what he said just now? And besides...his eyes...his presence it's Alec. Can't you see?"

Jin looked surprised. "You could hear his mind-voice? And you can sense Alec's spiritual presence?"

Junpei shrugged, "Well, yea, but it's probably because Alec and I are such close friends - it doesn't mean anything. I know what you're thinking Jin, you want to know if my spiritual powers have awakened but they haven't." Junpei pouted and turned around to pick up Alec and hold him in his arms protectively.

"Thanks for saving me Junpei." Alec looked up at him, with what he hoped was a grateful expression.

Junpei smiled down at the cat. "I owed you one anyways. Now we have to find that body snatching *nekomata* before something...*weird* happens."

"Weird?" Alec quirked his head at Junpei.

Junpei nodded grimly. "The *nekomata* who stole your body is apparently a chocolate loving, playboy."

Alec's eyes widened in horror. "*Sona*, oh no..."

● ● ● ● ● ● ● ● ● ● ● ● ● ● ● ● ●

Meanwhile, the *nekomata* was peering around corners to see if Junpei or Neji were still after him. Someone suddenly tapped him on the shoulder and the *nekomata* jumped about a foot in the air.

He turned around to see a girl with a bob of black hair that had bright green highlights. There was a french beret on her head and she was wearing black knee socks. She had a pair of green-framed glasses on her nose and the *nekomata* noticed the box of chocolates in her hands.

"Did I scare you Alec?" Rika sounded amused.

"Not really," the *nekomata* shrugged and grinned back at her.

"I wanted to talk to you alone, if that's okay?" Rika questioned quickly looking around to see if they'd be interrupted by any other fan girls.

The *nekomata*'s grin widened, "That's more than okay." He put an arm around her shoulders. "Where do you have in mind?"

"How about the roof?" Rika said, surprised at Alec's sudden boldness.

"Puurfect." The *nekomata* agreed.

Rika and the *nekomata* made their way up to the roof of the main school building and faced each other. Rika began to speak. "Alec I...wanted to know if you'd go out with me?" Rika held out her chocolates to Alec and held her breath.

The *nekomata* took a step forward and took the chocolates from Rika's hands, "Sure." He agreed nonchalant.

Rika looked up surprised and with a pleased expression on her face. "Really? So then does that mean that you like me too?"

The *nekomata* smiled slyly and took a step forward to remove the glasses from Rika's face. "Of course, how could I not like a cute girl like you?"

"Oh Alec!" Rika exclaimed excitedly as she threw her arms around Alec's neck, "You know, I was saving you a very special present. But I think I'll give it to you now. You see, I bought this cherry chocolate flavored lip gloss...just for you." Rika declared as she began to move in to kiss Alec.

The *nekomata* was leaning in as well, a triumphant smirk on his face.

However, at that exact moment Junpei, along with the real Alec in his arms, Neji, Jin, and Junko opened the door to the roof and all rushed out.

"No Rika! Don't kiss him! That's not Alec it's a *nekomata*!" Junpei called out a warning as he ran towards the pair.

Rika opened her eyes in shock and noticed the glowing golden eyes for the first time and the strange twisted smirk on Alec's lips that she had never seen on his face before and took a startled step back.

"*Nekomata*! Get away from her!" Junpei yelled angrily.

Junko quickly knocked an arrow and loosed it towards the *nekomata* who was forced to dive out of the way.

"Hey! That's my body! Be careful!" Alec tried to say when once again all that came out of his mouth were 'meows'.

Jin quickly took out an *o-fuda* from his sleeve. "If I can get close enough I can exorcize the *nekomata* from your body Alec."

The *nekomata* however turned to face the group with a confident expression on his face. "You pathetic humans are no match for me. Not now that I possess this body which has amplified my powers!" A black and purplish-tinted aura began to form around the *nekomata*, flaring to life all around him, the malevolent energy crackling. The *nekomata* raised a hand in the air. "*Shikigami*! Evil spirits! I summon you!" Suddenly, from out of thin air appeared many strange ghost-like creatures. They had heads that were skulls and were surrounded by black flames and had long tails also composed of flame. Their teeth began to chatter as they floated in the air eerily.

And then the flaming, skull-headed spirits flew forward in attack. Junko quickly began shooting at them with her bow and arrows exorcizing the creatures left and right with her spirit arrows as they hit their marks flawlessly. Jin was throwing *o-fuda* at them and also managing to exorcize the evil spirits with ease.

The *nekomata* pointed his finger directly at Alec, "Kill the cat! I've decided to stay in this body - forever!" He began to laugh maniacally.

The flaming skull spirits all flew towards Alec who was still in Junpei's arms. *Epp!* Junpei looked fearful but then a steely glint formed in his eye. His friend was in danger and he couldn't just stand back and do nothing. So forming his free hand into a fist Junpei flung it forward at the first skull spirit that was upon him.

Alec noticed that Junpei's fist was glowing with a blue-tinged light and watched awed as Junpei's fist connected with the skull spirit, and the skull cracked as it was exorcized. Junpei blinked down at his fist in shock.

The sound of Neji's panicked yell was heard as the geek was suddenly surrounded by several skull spirits with nowhere to go. "Ack! Help!"

Junpei quickly set Alec down on the ground. "Alec, stay out of sight. I have to help Neji!" Junpei rushed over to Neji's side and used a flying side kick to exorcize one of the flaming skull spirits. Then with a flurry of quick kicks and punches he managed to take out the rest, his fists and feet surrounded by the glowing blue light.

The *nekomata* was rushing toward Jin now ready to attack. Jin quickly got into a fighting stance ready to met him. The two began to fight, throwing deadly punches and kicks at each other with extreme speed and strength. Jin's body and hands were glowing with the blue-tinged light of his spirit energy while the *nekomata*'s hands and feet were also glowing but with a black and purple colored energy which was his evil spirit power.

Jin then got into a fighting stance and cupped his hands together as he began to form a ball of energy between his hands. Alec recognized what he was doing - he was going to create a spirit energy blast. Although he noticed that the *nekomata* was copying Jin's stance and that he also seemed to be forming an energy blast. Then they both suddenly released their attacks upon each other, the two blasts of energy colliding in the air. But then the *nekomata*'s dark energy blast seemed to be pushing Jin's attack back until it had overpowered it completely so that the blast hit Jin in the chest and he was flung backwards.

"*Aniki!* Bro!" Junpei cried out.

"Jerk!" Junko aimed her bow and fired. The *nekomata* turned his attention to her next and he caught the arrow that had been speeding towards him and simply snapped it in half using his one hand. The *nekomata* then rushed towards her as she fired arrow after arrow upon him but with his extreme speed and catlike reflexes he was able to gracefully dodge all of her deadly spirit arrows. Then as he was almost upon her the *nekomata* quickly formed an energy blast in his two hands and brought his hands forward to unleash the blast upon her. Junko was surprised when the blast hit her chest and she too was knocked painfully backwards, where she lay unconscious on the ground.

"*Onee-san*! Sis!" Junpei cried out.

The *nekomata* looked down at the fallen forms of Jin and Junko and shook his head at them. "I would have thought two members of the *Shinigami* Squad would have put up more of a fight. I guess the rumors of their power are a bit over exaggerated back in the *Makai*."

"*Shinigami* Squad?" Alec caught the reference and shook his head. *More mysteries...*

"You big jerk! How dare you hurt my brother and sister!" Junpei declared as he got into a fighting stance. "You'll be fighting me next. And this time you won't be so lucky."

"Gladly." The *nekomata* replied with a cocky smirk and cracked his neck from side to side before moving into attack.

Alec watched in awe, as Junpei and the *nekomata* began to exchange blows. He hadn't known Junpei was so skilled in the martial arts. The exchange of quick kicks and punches, blocks and blows, was faster than the eye could easily follow. Alec noticed how Junpei's body but mostly his fists and feet had begun to glow with a blue-tinged light, which meant that Junpei was somehow controlling his spirit energy now. And then the *nekomata* was forming an energy blast to send Junpei's way but Junpei mirrored his movements and began to do the same.

The aura around Junpei flared larger than before as Junpei gathered all his spiritual power to form the blast and then both released their energy blasts at each other. The attacks hit in midair, the crackling ball of blue light combating with the sparking ball of dark purple and black energy until Junpei's attack managed to overpower the *nekomata*'s! The *nekomata*'s eyes widened in shock as he was hit in the stomach by Junpei's blast and sent stumbling backwards.

The *nekomata* looked up next to see Jin, who was gripping his wounded side and peering down at the *nekomata* with a merciless expression on his face. Jin grinned, "Time to leave that body, *nekomata-san*." He slapped a glowing *o-fuda* down on the *nekomata*'s forehead before the cat demon could even blink.

Alec felt the same strange tingling sensation again, and his stomach was flip flopping before he blinked - and looked down at his hands. His human hands. Alec broke out into a large grin and looked up at his friends, a thankful look on his face. "I'm back."

The *nekomata* spirit was back in his body now and was trying to sneak away. However, Junko had gotten up as well and prepared an arrow. "Not so fast kitty cat, where do you think you're going hmm?"

The *nekomata* hissed before he bolted for the roof door but Junko was faster and unleashed her spirit arrow upon him, a flash of blue light streaking through the air as it hit its mark and exorcized the *nekomata* into nothingness. "#$@% you *Shinigami* Squad!" It cried out as it was destroyed.

Junpei helped Alec to his feet and Jin and Junko rushed over to them, followed close behind by Neji.

"You alright there Alec?" Junpei asked.

Alec nodded, "Perfectomundo."

Junpei ruffled Alec's hair as Neji came up to them. Rika was feeling a bit awkward and was merely watching everyone from a distance.

Jin looked over at Junpei a serious expression on his face before he broke out into an actual smile, "You did good back there little bro." He ruffled Junpei's hair much like Junpei had done to Alec. "Oh what the heck, come here and give your brother a hug!" Jin grabbed Junpei and pulled him into a hug before he began to strangle the life out of him.

Junpei was pleasantly surprised and blushing. "*Aniki*! Stop you're embarrassing me! Not in front of my friends! *Mou*! Geez!"

Jin pulled back and put his hands on Junpei's shoulders before looking at him eye to eye, his expression serious once more. "Why not? It's a time for celebration. Junpei, now that your powers have finally awakened you must begin your spiritual training immediately so that you can become a part of the *Shinigami* Squad just like your sister and I. You'll make mother and father so proud."

"You will join us won't you?" Junko asked, all smiles.

Alec bit his lower lip feeling left out again. *Shinigami* Squad? What was that exactly? Something like the Ghost Busters or something? And now Junpei was going to get to join but...as for Alec...he was still being left out of the loop apparently. Darn it.

Junpei shrugged, "I dunno...I guess so."

Junpei noticed Rika's forlorn expression, "Hey guys, I think we should leave these two love birds alone. They have a lot to talk about."

Jin and Junko nodded and followed Junpei off the roof. Neji hesitated before following them as well.

Alec turned to Rika and bowed, "I'm so sorry Rika..."

Rika walked forward. "Don't be, it's not your fault the *nekomata* possessed your body. You heard everything then?" Alec nodded. "Then...what do you say Alec will you go out with me? You already know I like you."

Alec bit his bottom lip, "Rika...I'm sorry but I don't think I can return your feelings. I'm not really sure if I like you as more than a friend or not. I mean, if you were to ask me if I liked you or didn't like you I'd say I like you Rika but this is all just so new to me. I've never gone out with a girl before. I'm not sure how I feel. But I think if we could get to know each other better and maybe start out as friends then...I guess we'll see what happens. So what do you say, Rika? Friends?" Alec put out his hand for her to shake.

Rika raised her eyebrow at his handshaking idea, "You are such a boy, but you're also a real nice boy Alec." She took Alec's hand and smiled. "I won't give up on you so easily you know. You're still my hero after all."

Alec blushed, "Yea, um, well..."

Rika took her hand back and put her arms behind her back as she playfully skipped backwards a few steps, "Don't worry Alec I won't try and kiss you. For now, we'll just be friends. Thank you for being honest with me Alec. I...I have to go."

Rika rushed away and Alec thought he saw tears in her eyes. Alec frowned, he really hadn't wanted to hurt her feelings but it was true that he didn't know how he really felt about her yet. He had always been bad around girls - except for maybe one a.k.a. Yukino, who had become one of his best friends recently. Things just seemed so natural around her for some reason.

She may just surprise you... Haruna's words echoed in his mind for some reason.

Naw. Alec shook his head, smiling. The last thing Yukino would do was give him a Valentine's Day present. She wasn't like that at all. Alec decided to take the chocolate that Rika had given him and leave it in front of Akira's door. However, as soon as he stepped out into the hallways of the main school building his fellow male classmates caught sight of him. Alec took a step back nervously - he could feel their malevolent intent. *Uh oh...*The hairs on the back of Alec's neck were prickling in warning.

"Look! There he is!" "Get 'em!" The boys declared as they all ran towards Alec, their eyes glowing like demons.

"Epp!" Alec squeaked as he took off running in the opposite direction. He was doing a whole lot of that lately he realized. He looked over his shoulder and saw that the boys were still in pursuit so it wasn't like he could stop running anytime soon.

Alec didn't see the banana peel on the floor until it was too late -

Covered in toilet paper after having been caught and teepeed by the boys, Alec finally managed to lose the boys and make his way to Akira's room where he stood outside the door. Poor Alec was looking a bit like a mummy, still partially covered in toilet paper, and he was still a bit swirly-eyed and dizzy from having been thrown in a trash can and rolled down the hallway a few times. But Alec decided it could have been worse - at least the trash can had been empty this time. He looked around to make sure no one was watching him before setting the small box of chocolates on the floor in front of Akira's door. Alec then took a step back and knocked on the door before he took off running, a smirk on his face.

· · · · · · · · · · · · · · · ·

Akira waited a beat before poking his head outside. He then looked down and saw the wrapped box and raised an eyebrow at it. He quickly took the box inside and closed the door behind him with a kick. He smiled to himself, *A secret admirer ka?*

He looked around his room nervously as if someone were spying on him before he cautiously opened the gift. He undid the blue bow and slowly lifted off the lid of the box. He peered inside and saw that there was a chocolate heart inside with the words - '*I love Alec*' written across it in blue icing. Akira's eyebrow twitched. He then tossed the box along with the chocolate heart at his bedroom wall so that the chocolate heart was broken in two.

"Alec *no baka*! Alec you idiot! I hate you!" Akira seethed. "I don't need your pity..."

· · · · · · · · · · · · · · · ·

"Achoo!" Alec sneezed and rubbed his nose with his index finger as he was sitting down at his computer in the computer club room, ready to log on to Yokai World. He put on his HMD and logged on as fast as he could. He had been happy to get chocolates from Rika but for some unfathomable reason he really wanted to see Yukino.

Alec had gone straight to the Guardian Knight's guildhall where Night told Alec that Yukino was at a different area and mysteriously enough she was waiting for him. He teleported there and found himself in front of a towering, Gothic-styled cathedral. It was made of large, gray stones and Alec could see a stained glass, wheel-window above the main entrance, and then looked up to see sinister looking, winged gargoyles perched on the ledges of pointed spires leering down at him. Alec made his way inside and saw Yukino at the end of the church standing in front of a large stone statue of a winged angel. Although this angel was a bit different from the angels Alec was used to seeing in churches since this one was wearing a *kimono* but she still had large feathery wings on her back.

Alec slowly approached not wanting to disturb Yukino's private moment and as he neared the angel and peered up into her stone face, he gasped. That face - he knew that face. It looked just like Midoriko - Yukino's mother. He was sure of it. Alec came to stand next to Yukino and she knew he was there without having to turn to look at him.

"Yo." She greeted him.

"Hi." Alec started shyly.

"She's beautiful isn't she?" Yukino questioned, her eyes still on the stone angel's face.

Alec nodded.

"They say she's the guardian of Yokai World. Her name is Midoriko." Yukino explained to him.

Alec's brows rose, so it really *was* a statue of Midoriko. "She's...your mother." Alec informed her.

"I had that feeling..." Yukino turned to face Alec now, "That there was some connection between us. Her face seemed so familiar and now I know why. Thank you."

"No problem." Alec smiled, and thought back to something he just remembered. "Say, Yukino, the other day when we fought against Tamamo-no-mae, you remembered something didn't you?"

Yukino nodded as she too thought back to that day, "I did. I remembered..." She was beginning to tremble and Alec wanted to hit himself on the head for making Yukino try to remember memories that were obviously painful ones. He put a hand on Yukino's shoulder and shook his head.

"It's alright, you don't have to tell me. I'm just glad that you're starting to remember. I really want to help you with your unfinished business." Alec reminded her.

"Yes, I know." Yukino let out a breath of relief as she let the memories slip away again. She then gave Alec a curious look. "Shouldn't you be on a date or something? It's Valentine's Day you know. Night told me."

Alec blushed and looked down at his feet. "Yea, I know but I'm exactly where I want to be right now."

It was Yukino's turn to blush slightly in surprise. "Oh." Was all she said and there was a long awkward silence between them before Yukino cleared her throat. "That reminds me. I got you something. Wait here." Yukino said before running off to one of the pews where she had apparently hidden something.

Alec waited for her to return and when she did she had something hidden behind her back. She smiled at him mischievously before revealing what it was. She took the item out from behind her back and Alec saw that it was an extremely long *katana*. And it was no ordinary *katana* either, it was stunning and took Alec's breath away. It was almost as tall as Yukino herself and the hilt was wrapped in crisscrossed white and silver ribbons. The sheathe was a solid gleaming silver color.

It wasn't quite what Alec had been expecting for his Valentine Day's gift, but then again coming from Yukino he should have known better. He smirked somewhat amused at this turn of events. "A *katana*?" He raised one eye brow at her. *How romantic.*

She smiled back and handed the *katana* to him. "Yep, and this is no ordinary *katana* either - this one can break the rules of the game and bend the rules of reality just like Night's sword can. A famous computer programer and spiritualist made the sword using a combination of technology and magic. That means you'll be able to use your spiritual powers in the game if you have to."

"Whoa." Alec looked down at the sword in awe. It was quite heavy and he couldn't get over how long it seemed. He held the sword at his waist and prepared to unsheathe it. He pulled the sword out in one quick, fluid motion but unfortunately was only able to get the sword out about half way. Alec blushed red with embarrassment having done something so stupid in front of Yukino like that. *Dang, this sword is way too long. How do I properly unsheathe it all the way? I must look like an idiot.*

Yukino nodded, "You have to learn the right way to draw it. There's a special trick to drawing such a long sword. Allow me to show you." Yukino reached out her hands and Alec willingly handed the *katana* to her. Yukino then held the *katana* at her side and then in one swift elegant motion she unsheathed the *katana*. The blade was long and bright polished silver with a glowing, blue burn mark that mimicked ocean waves running along the entire length of the sword blade. Yukino looked so deadly, powerful yet at the same time beautiful in that exact moment, with the massive sword in her hands that Alec blinked at her a bit in shock as though he were seeing her for the first time and felt somewhat in awe of her.

He enthusiastically clapped his hands together at her show of skill.

With another fluid motion she was able to re-sheath the *katana*. She then handed the *katana* back to Alec. "Now, you try."

Alec tried to follow the elegant motion that Yukino had performed but didn't quite get it right. Alec sighed in defeat but then he felt Yukino suddenly standing behind him and she put her hands on Alec's arms. He gulped - he could feel Yukino pressing up against his back. "No, here, let me show you, like this - you have to become one with the sword, the sword is an extension of yourself. And your movements must flow like water."

Alec nodded, blushing more fiercely than before at Yukino's closeness. Yukino was completely oblivious to the effect she was having on Alec.

They both worked through the movements until finally Alec got it right.

Yukino stepped back and smiled pleased. "Good. Now..." Yukino put her hand out before her and Alec watched wide-eyed as it began to glow with a blue-tinged light and then suddenly a sword made entirely of ice was formed in her right hand. She then held the ice sword out before her in a two-handed grip. "We can spar."

Alec hesitated. "But you're a-"

Yukino wagged a finger at him, "Ah, ah, ah, don't tell me you were about to say something silly like 'but you're a girl'." Yukino suddenly charged forward and brought her sword down upon Alec in a downwards slash, and her blade immediately clashed with Alec's silvery blade that had been brought up just in the nick of time to block her swift and deadly attack.*Whew*! "Don't hold back Alec - because I sure as hell won't! I'm a battle ghost remember? I live for battle!"

Alec smiled back as he realized her immense skill. "Alright then, have it your way." He said as he began to get serious as well.

Their swords clashed in a deadly dance as the two sparred together - the *Shinigami* boy and the battle ghost.

"Hey, Yukino, how did you learn to fight so well with a sword?" Alec asked as they sparred.

Yukino looked thoughtful for a moment before answering, - "My brother taught me."

Chapter 12:
Nopperabo: The Faceless Ghost

Rika was in her dorm room with her roommate Sakura. Sakura was one of the more popular girls in their grade and was very pretty. She had long, light brown hair and honey-colored eyes. Rika seemed to feel that even though they were in different social circles Sakura liked her and thought of her as a friend. Although Sakura was the head of the unofficial Alec Suzuki fan club... and that *was* rather weird. Rika had a few hours before home room started and she had wanted to redo her bright, neon green highlights and decided to ask Sakura for her help.

"Sakura? Could you help me redo my highlights?" She questioned politely.

Sakura looked surprised before she smiled, "Sure roomie, although I don't know how good I'll be at doing highlights - it's a little bit complicated isn't it?"

Rika shook her head. "It's easy, you just paint straight lines. I know you can do it Sakura."

"Alright then, if you insist." Sakura shrugged.

And that was how poor Rika had ended up with a botched dye job that day. Sakura had apologized profusely explaining that it was a *lot* harder than it seemed to paint straight lines of hair dye and bleach on someone else's head. Rika had forgiven her but...that hadn't solved the problem. So that was how Rika had ended up entering home room that morning with a GIANT beret on her head with all of her hair concealed under it. Trying to act as natural as possible she went over to Alec, Neji and Junpei.

"Hey guys." Rika greeted.

"Hey Rika." Alec gave her a shy smile remembering how she had revealed

271

she liked him and declared she wouldn't give up on him either, just the other day.

"Yo Rika." Neji nodded to her.

Junpei eyed Rika's hat curiously. "What's with the giant beret? You usually wear that other one..."

"Oh, this?" Rika tipped her beret forward trying to appear nonchalant. "This is just a new fashion statement of mine. You'll see, everyone will be wearing them soon. It's super cute *neh*?" But Junpei saw right through her nervous fidgetiness.

Junpei narrowed his eyes in suspicion at her. "*Sou*? Oh really?" Junpei turned away from her as if he had bought her 'little act' before spinning back around and making a grab for her beret when she was least expecting it. "Aha!" Junpei managed to pull it off and low and behold - Rika's botched dye job.

All eyes in home room turned to Rika.

No longer did Rika have her perfectly done green highlights - but now had rainbow colored hair, in a myriad of colors - pink, blue, yellow, purple, and green.

Sakura and her two friends, Tami and Rena, were giggling uncontrollably off to one side of the class room. Junpei and Neji burst out laughing as well and soon everyone in the class followed suit and began to laugh - all expect for Alec.

"Your hair!" Junpei gasped between breaths, "What happened? It's looks just like tie dye! It's crazy!"

Poor Rika was absolutely mortified, her face bright red and her eyes were filling with unshed tears, until however -

Alec quirked his head at her, observing her new hairdo thoughtfully. "Actually, it's not so bad. In fact, I think it looks really cool. You think you could do some tips or something to my hair Rika? I was kinda getting bored with my snow-white hair."

Rika's eyes widened in surprise, and the fan girls - Sakura, Tami, and Rena all gasped in shock. The rest of the students in home room looked a bit stunned as well since they usually followed Alec's lead and he had just said that he thought Rika's latest hair blunder, err, style was 'cool'. And if Alec Suzuki said it was cool - well then it was.

Rika sniffled and wiped away her unshed tears and smiled broadly at Alec, "Sure thing! I think blue tips would look hot on you Alec."

"You can just dye my hair later then okay?" Alec said offhandedly.

"Sure." Rika lowered her voice, "Thanks."

Alec lowered his voice to whisper back, "No problem, what are friends for *neh*?"

She blushed in response.

"Hey, you have to do my hair too then Rika!" "Mine too!" "I want tips like Alec's going to get!" "*Oi!* Don't leave me out. I want a cool new hair color too!" "I think I'll get red tips..." "I was thinking of going blonde, what do you think?" Came the voices of Rika's fellow classmates as they were suddenly all asking her to dye their hair and give them a new look later. And it was all thanks to Alec, leading the charge of going against school rules and being a rebel.

Sakura, Tami, and Rena were pissed that Rika had somehow managed to turn the tables and was now being praised for her unique hair style and color sense. Sakura chewed on her thumb nail angrily as she watched Rika getting showered with attention from not only *her* Alec but the entire class as well. *Ch!*

• • • • • • • • • • • • • • • • •

Rika was entering the girl's bathroom when she began to overhear a conversation between her roommate Sakura and her two best friends Tami and Rena.

"Grrr...I can't believe that weirdo Rika. How does she do it? Every time we try and make her look bad she somehow manages to turn things around and actually look good! I hate it! I hate her. I can't stand her anymore." Sakura was venting in frustration.

Tami twirled a lock of her short, curly brown hair around her finger thoughtfully. "She does seem to have the devil's luck. Even with that time you tripped her down the front steps and Alec Suzuki ended up catching her!"

Sakura was chewing on her thumb nail again, "As head of the Alec Suzuki fan club I cannot allow this sort of thing to happen again. We cannot continue to let that girl do whatever she wants with Alec. We have to protect him for her evil clutches. Alec is supposed to be mine! As the most beautiful and popular girl of our grade it is only natural that Alec Suzuki be my boyfriend but that weird girl is in my way! We have to do something." She declared with a toss of her long, light brown hair.

"I don't know what Alec sees in her anyways or understand why he's even friends with Rika in the first place. Everyone else knows she's an oddball." Rena shook her head, and tucked a stray, dark strand of hair behind her ear.

"Alec's just too nice for his own good. He's just being friends with her out of pity, most likely." Sakura said knowingly and Tami and Rena quickly agreed, nodding their heads.

"No one is allowed to be that close to my Alec - I'll show her." Sakura declared, clenching her fists.

Rika kept a hand over her mouth to keep from gasping aloud, having overheard everything. She quickly stepped backwards and made her way out of the bathroom unseen and unnoticed. Rika was stunned, she had thought Sakura was her friend and liked her and that the hair dye incident was an accident but now she found out it had been on purpose! Sadness was quickly turning to anger. Anger at those girls for thinking they were better than everyone else - that they could just do whatever they wanted. Anger at being called 'weirdo' and 'oddball' for years, before Alec came to the school, was welling up inside of her. Though she knew she purposefully went against the norm it still hurt. And if it wasn't for Alec transferring in this year she would have had to put up with what she had been putting up with all through middle school so far. The teasing, the insults, the pranks. But when Alec came and befriended her and Neji, their fellow students had started to treat both of the geeks a little bit better.

Alec was the mysterious, new transfer student who everyone thought was oh so cool and followed his every lead. It hadn't taken him long to get his own fan club at all. And now with Alec as her friend, her weirdness was beginning to be seen as 'coolness'. Rika sighed. Alec-*kun*...what would she have done without her knight in shining armor?

· · · · · · · · · · · · · · · · · ·

Rika was still fuming as she had headed to her art class. She managed to make it to class on time thankfully but then began to fall behind on their assignment to do a self portrait. She stood with a blank canvas before her, for once uninspired about what to paint. She was in conflict. How should she portray herself? She began to paint her portrait but with how her hair used to look with its perfect green highlights, she then painted in her signature beret, her sailor school uniform, and her black knee socks. But when she was about to paint in her facial features she held her brush back. She decided to leave her face blank, which made her look just like a *nopperabo* - a faceless ghost.

Faceless...identity-less...emotionless. Who was Rika really? She knew she wasn't really LadyV, that was just a role she had managed to create but sometimes she wished she really were LadyV and not 'Rika'. LadyV was beautiful, powerful and confident. Things that Rika felt she was not. She wished her face and body were also like LadyV's, then maybe Alec wouldn't have turned her down. So with feelings of confusion and anger towards the people who made her feel this way, and who had ever made fun of her, Rika completed her self portrait leaving the face blank.

When class was over the other students left the art classroom first with Rika being the last to leave.

No one was there in the empty art room to see what happened as Rika's painting began to glow with a blue-tinged light and then the image of herself, the faceless student, began to emerge out of the painting slowly. The faceless girl began to crawl her way out onto the floor before pulling herself up off the ground, while letting her bangs shield her featureless face as she made her way towards the door.

If the *nopperabo* Rika had lips they would have been formed into a smile.

⬤ ⬤ ⬤ ⬤ ⬤ ⬤ ⬤ ⬤ ⬤ ⬤ ⬤ ⬤ ⬤ ⬤ ⬤

It was late after school, after club activities even, when Sakura was walking along the middle of a hallway alone and on her way to the bathroom. She wanted to go there quickly and then make the walk back to her dorm building before it got too late. Her music club activities had kept her at school really late that day. She couldn't help looking over her shoulder every five seconds since she felt the school was really creepy late at night. A chill went down her spine and she shook her head thinking she had to be imagining things. She entered the girl's bathroom and was surprised to see Tami crying over by one of the sinks, her face in her hands.

Sakura's expression turned to worry as she approached Tami. "Tami, what's wrong?"

But Tami ignored her and simply continued to cry and moan pitifully.

Sakura hesitated before reaching a hand out to touch Tami's shoulder, "Tami!"

Tami suddenly turned around and lowered her hands to reveal she had no face - the entire surface of her face was as smooth and as featureless as an egg!

Sakura screamed and quickly ran out of the bathroom. She rushed down the darkened hallway until - she spotted Rena up ahead.

Sakura let out a breath of relief as she approached her other best friend, "Rena, oh thank god."

Rena turned around and eyed Sakura curiously, quirking her head at her, "What's wrong, Sakura? You look like you've seen a ghost." Sakura missed the note of amusement in Rena's voice.

"I just saw Tami crying in the bathroom when something horrible happened!" Sakura was saying in a rush.

"Oh? Something horrible happened, you mean like this?" Rena put her hand over her face and brought her hand down wiping her facial features right off her face.

Sakura let out a piercing scream as she bolted away from the faceless ghost.

• • • • • • • • • • • • • • • •

It was the dawn of a new day at Izanagi Academy and everyone was waiting for the arrival of Takahashi-*sensei* in the their home room.

"Hey, where's Sakura?" Someone was asking Tami.

"She's in the nurse's office." Tami informed the female student.

Rika, who was hanging out with Alec, Neji, and Junpei, looked over at the two girls curiously.

Rena began to explain, "Oh, it's awful! Last night Sakura saw a *nopperabo*!"

"A real *nopperabo*! *Uso*! No way!" The female student gasped.

Rika's eyebrows raised in surprise.

"*Nopperabo*?" Alec questioned his friends. The name sounding somewhat familiar.

"A faceless ghost - like the Battle Ghost LadyV has back in Yokai World." Junpei began to explain.

Alec nodded. That's why the name had sounded so familiar.

Junpei was chewing his bottom lip worriedly. "If what they're saying is true this is *so* not good. Jin and Junko aren't on campus since they're away on *Shinigami* Squad business. If a real *nopperabo* has managed to come here through the tear we're in trouble. They're extremely dangerous and have immense spiritual power. They're shape-shifters and steal people's faces. It's not until a *nopperabo* is defeated that the people's faces will return to them. And a person who has had his or her face stolen cannot live without their face for very long - usually only a few hours."

Alec shivered. *Nopperabo* sounded like a very dangerous ghost indeed and if there really was a *nopperabo* out on the loose in the school it could mean trouble. If Jin or Junko really weren't around that only left Alec or Junpei with the ability to exorcize such a ghost. Alec decided he'd start to patrol the school after dark and see if he could lure out and exorcize the *nopperabo* on his own. He decided it shouldn't be too hard, not when he was a Spirit-Magnet after all.

Rena and Tami were looking at each other fearfully at the thought of coming into contact with the *nopperabo*. Rika was smiling a secret smile to herself happy that Sakura had finally gotten what she deserved.

• • • • • • • • • • • • • • • •

Alec had patrolled the halls of Izanagi Academy's main school building the night before but with no luck. Then he ended up finding out the next day that there had been another attack - this time Tami and Rena had apparently both seen the *nopperabo* in the girl's bathroom and had been frightened so badly that they were in the nurse's office recovering from the traumatic experience. Alec kicked a wall in frustration. He should have...what? Checked the girl's bathroom last night? But that was sort of 'forbidden territory' since after all he *was* a boy. But he had to protect the girls somehow. What if Rika was attacked next? He'd never forgive himself.

Already a school urban legend was forming about the *nopperabo*. But Alec knew that this *nopperabo* was no mere legend. It was real. Also, the fact that members of Alec's 'fan club' were being targeted made Alec feel oddly responsible for what was happening for some reason.

Alec was torn about what he was going to do. But decided that that night he couldn't allow another attack to happen right under his nose like that. And so after school when he began his 'secret patrol rounds' he decided to check the girl's bathroom for the *nopperabo* first before moving on to patrol the rest of the hallways with his trusty soccer ball in hand.

Alec was about to sneak into the girl's bathroom, while feeling a bit guilty about the whole thing, when he suddenly felt someone tap him on the shoulder. Alec jumped and spun around to see a smirking Junpei standing there, hands on his hips.

Junpei then raised an eyebrow at Alec as if to say 'Were you really going in there?'. Alec's hand was still on the doorknob to the girl's bathroom. "Whatcha doing Alec? Spying on girls? Didn't think you had it in you, buddy."

Alec turned bright red from Junpei's teasing and he waved his hands frantically before him in a negative gesture. "*Gigao no!* No! That's not it! I was, you know-" Alec stuttered.

"You were going to search for the *nopperbo* weren't you?" Junpei had already figured it out, but enjoyed giving Alec a hard time. He was just too fun to tease. He then noticed Alec's soccer ball, and his expression turned serious. "Alone? But you're forgetting you're not alone Alec." Junpei stepped forward and ruffled Alec's shaggy hair affectionately.

"Junpei!" Alec hated being treated like a little kid just because he happened to be a bit shorter than the other boys in his grade.

Junpei pushed the door to the girl's bathroom open without hesitation, "Let's go."

"Um, right!" Alec quickly followed behind him.

The two boys entered the girl's bathroom and checked all the stalls but the *nopperabo* was nowhere to be found. Junpei shrugged, "It doesn't look like the *nopperabo* is here tonight."

"Let's go check the halls." Alec suggested as he made his way back outside.

The boys then began patrolling the hallways next and were turning a corner when they spotted something down the end of the hallway - It was

Rika and she was kneeling down in the middle of the hallway on her knees, with her face in her hands and she appeared to be crying for some reason. Perhaps, she had come across the *nopperabo*? Alec thought. Alec and Junpei quickly rushed to her side.

"Rika? What's wrong?" Alec was reaching his hand out to her.

Junpei had stopped a few feet away from her and was giving Rika a curious look since he noticed that her highlights seemed to be back to normal.

Rika slowly raised her head and then lowered her hands from her face. Alec squeaked - *Epp!* And took a step back when he saw Rika's now featureless face. He took another step back as Rika stood and began to approach him.

"A real *nopperabo*..." Alec mouthed, a chilling feeling coming over him and the fear unexpectedly froze him in place.

Rika was almost upon him, reaching her hand out to caress Alec's face when -

"Alec, look out!" Junpei quickly pushed Alec out of the way, landing on top of him. Junpei got off of Alec and held his hand out to Alec to help him back up.

Alec took his hand shakily. "Thanks, I don't know what came over me." Alec ran a hand through his messed up hair uncomfortably.

"Don't sweat it." Junpei turned to face the *nopperabo* and began to concentrate his spirit energy so that his hands and feet began to become enveloped with a blue-tinged light. "I can handle it. Just leave it to me this time!" Junpei rushed forward and began to dish out a couple of quick kicks and punches towards the *nopperabo*. Alec was surprised when he saw her easily dodging Junpei's intense attacks. She was fast, which meant the best way to get rid of her was to have one of them distract her just as Junpei was doing now while the other could prepare to attack her from behind undetected. Alec just had to wait for the right moment -

Alec reached out his senses and ignored his fear. His sensed that she was definitely a spiritual being of some kind with a dark aura but she wasn't actually all that powerful compared to some of the ghosts Alec had encountered in the past. This filled him with the confidence he needed to put his plan into action. Alec summoned his spirit energy and empowered his soccer ball in his hands before dropping his soccer ball on the floor before him.

"Junpei! Get out of the way!" Alec called, and Junpei quickly obeyed diving out of the way. Alec sweat-dropped, it almost looked like Junpei was afraid Alec would blow him up along with the *nopperabo*. Alec shrugged. Whatever. As soon as Junpei was out of the way Alec kicked his glowing soccer ball with all his strength at the unsuspecting *nopperabo*. It hit the *nopperbo* in her stomach and then she exploded -

Junpei and Alec as well as the floor and walls were all suddenly splattered with -

Oil paint.

Splotches of different colored paint were now all over the place. And Alec and Junpei were covered from head to toe in a rainbow of colors. They were both in wide-eyed shock. That had been no 'normal' *nopperabo*. They then both turned to look at each other and both boys burst out laughing - they both looked as though they'd been tie dyed.

"What a mess." Junpei shook his head looking at the paint splattered hallway. He rubbed a hand through his hair to remove some green paint from his orange-brown locks. "Yuck."

"Aw man, we're going to have to clean it up too, you know." Alec pouted. "This is going to take all night..." Junpei was already trying to sneak away when Alec caught sight of him. "Junpei! You can't just leave me here with this mess!"

"Oh yes I can!" Junpei said as he tried to take off running when Alec clamped a hand onto his shoulder to stop him. "No one will know it was us if we just leave now. There's no real reason why we have to clean up this mess, Alec. If your conscience says you have to clean it up then by all means go ahead but leave me out of it." Junpei turned around to give Alec his best glare.

Alec glared back before he changed tactics and let his eyes turn puppy-dog like, his lower lip trembling, "But Junpei...aren't we friends?"

"Oh no, not the puppy-dog eyes! You brat!" Junpei tried not to look at Alec and back away from him but it was already too late. "*Mou!* Geez!" Junpei ran a hand through his spiky hair and sighed. "Alright already you win! I'll help you clean up and yes we're friends. Though sometimes I wish you were a little more like me."

Alec smirked, "Thanks Junpei." He beamed at the jock.

"Yea, yea." Junpei waved his hand through the air in a dismissive gesture but couldn't help but smile back.

The two boys went over to a broom closet and took out the needed cleaning supplies before they began to mop down the hallway.

"So this is what we get for being heroes? Some reward huh?" Junpei shook his head ruefully as he continued to swirl water, paint, and soap on the floor.

"You can say that again, but no one ever said being a hero was easy." Alec shrugged and pushed his sleeves back before grasping his own mop.

The next day, Rika was on her way to her art class when Sakura suddenly tripped her. Rika went flying onto her art supply bag and the paint tubes inside burst open so that she ended up getting paint all over the front of her school uniform. Since Rika was an orphan there was no way she would be able to afford a new school uniform, and so if she wasn't able to get the paint out she'd end up having to look like a messed up piece of art work for the rest of the school year...

Sigh.

Sakura immediately feigned regret, and Rika was surprised she never noticed how fake it sounded before, "Oh! Rika, I'm so sorry! I didn't see you there. You will forgive me right? You always do. Because you're the very best roommate." Sakura smiled sweetly before she, Rena, and Tami walked off leaving Rika still lying there in a puddle of paint.

Rika stayed like that for a while, emotions of sadness and anger warring within her. It was hard to find the motivation to stand up. She just wanted to melt into that puddle of paint somehow and just fade away. She hadn't played Yokai World in a while now and found she missed that other world almost painfully, where she could completely escape reality and become someone else.

Rika finally pushed herself up off the ground and made her way to her art class.

· · · · · · · · · · · · · · · · ·

Alec, Junpei and Neji were all eating lunch outside in their usual spot underneath this nice cherry blossom tree they had discovered. Alec and Junpei both had shadows under their eyes from having to stay up all night and clean the entire hallway of the paint from the strange 'paint ghost' as Alec liked to think of it. They had already started eating when Rika arrived. She sat down with a huff and began to unwrap her *bento* boxed lunch.

All three boys looked over at Rika curiously when they saw that she was covered in paint. Alec's eyes widened in concern. "Rika what happened?" He was already fearing the worst and wondering if another paint ghost had attacked.

"Nothing." Rika frowned as she stuffed a piece of omelet into her mouth using her chopsticks.

"Get a little carried away in art class did ya? What with that crazy artistic spirit of yours it's understandable." Junpei teased lightly.

Rika however was *not* in the mood for Junpei's teasing or jokes right about then. So she simply stuck out her tongue and pulled down her lower left eyelid at him - definitely not a very cute or attractive thing to do, in Junpei's opinion.

Junpei shook his head. "That was *so* not cute. I still can't believe *you're* LadyV." Junpei sighed wistfully, "How it pains my boyish heart to have my balloons of hope and delusions of grandeur popped right before my eyes." Rika just sent him a death glare in response and Junpei coughed uncomfortably as he continued. "Don't worry Rika, Alec and I feel your pain."

"That's for sure..." Alec muttered as he began to take a sip from his bowl of *ramen* noodle soup.

Rika eyed the two boys suspiciously, "What are you guys talking about?"

"Last night Alec and I went after the *nopperabo* on our own and found it stalking the hallways...actually oddly enough it had taken on your appearance, Rika." Junpei began to recount the adventure.

"Mine?" Rika seemed startled.

Junpei nodded, "And then Alec and I attacked it. Alec finished it off with his killer soccer ball move, but then it burst into-" Junpei leaned forward as Neji and Rika were both doing the same, curious expressions on their faces. "Paint." Junpei finished with an amused smirk.

Both Neji and Rika face-faulted, Neji nearly choking on a *naruto*, or tiny fish cake, from his ramen soup.

"Paint?" Rika spluttered in disbelief.

Alec nodded vigorously, "We spent all last night cleaning up that mess. It was awful."

Rika looked thoughtful - A *nopperabo* resembling her and made of paint was haunting the school? *Oh my god, could it be my nopperabo self portrait came to life!* Was something like that even possible? Rika wondered as she stood up suddenly, having the insight to go and check on her painting. "I...have to go do something. See ya guys." Rika said hurriedly as she rushed off.

Alec watched Rika go, a worried expression on his face, while Junpei just shrugged off her strange behavior. "Girls."

• • • • • • • • • • • • • • • • • •

That night Alec and Neji were fast asleep in their dorm room when the hairs on the back of Alec's neck suddenly prickled so fiercely that he sat up in bed. He peered through the darkness of his room and then he heard the sound of a far away scream.

"Alec...?" It was Neji's trembling voice in the darkness.

"Yea?" Alec asked back.

"Did you hear that?"

"Yea, I did, let's go." Alec hopped out of his bed and headed towards the door, but not before picking up his trusty soccer ball along the way, Neji following close behind him. As soon as they opened the door they saw that Junpei was outside in the hallway waiting for them.

"Junpei." Alec greeted.

"Alec. Neji." Junpei nodded to them both.

"What's going on?" There was a fierce gleam in Alec's silver eyes.

Junpei shrugged, "I dunno but I think the scream came from the girls' dorm building."

Alec nodded, "We had better go check it out then. It could be another one of those strange *nopperabo* or paint ghosts or something. And someone might get hurt."

Junpei agreed, "Yea, let's go."

So Alec, Neji, and Junpei all rushed over to the girls' dorm building and found that several girls were currently running out of the building and screaming -

Alec and co. then noticed that something was chasing them - *Yokai!* Alec's eyes widened as he watched the different and strange looking *yokai* floating and chasing after the middle school girls. Alec recognized among them *nekomata*, *nopperabo*, *kitsune*, and *tengu* all dressed in *kimono* and also saw floating *Noh* masks. It was almost like watching Yokai World game mobs coming to life in the real world or like watching some kind of strange demonic parade. Alec also saw strange animated items that seemed to be possessed such as paper lanterns, umbrellas, and pots that all had gleaming eyes or one or two feet coming out of them strangely.

Junpei raised an eyebrow at the sight, "Whoa, it looks just like the *Hyakki Yako*."

Alec turned towards him, not recognizing the term. *"Hyakki Yako?"*

Junpei nodded, "The 'night parade of one hundred demons'...it's said that once a year the *yokai* of the Makai World come to the human world and walk the streets one summer night in some kind of parade and that any unlucky human to come across their parade will be eaten..."

Alec gulped at the suggestion and quickly shook his head. Now was not the time to worry about becoming a *yokai* snack - he had to help those girls! Alec and Junpei immediately sprang into action.

Alec empowered and kicked his soccer ball at a *nekomata* and it burst into paint which ended up covering two squealing middle school girls, whom it had been about to attack. "Sorry!" Alec called as he dribbled his soccer ball in the direction of another monster.

Junpei formed a spirit energy blast in his two hands before aiming it at a *nopperabo*, which was also turned into a puddle of paint as it was destroyed.

"It's more of these weird paint spirits!" Alec called over his shoulder to Junpei as he took out another strange floating *Noh* mask spirit.

"There must be someone or something causing all this." Junpei declared as he flung another energy blast at a *tengu*.

"But who would be targeting my fan girls anyways?" Alec questioned suddenly, as a connection seemed to be forming in his mind.

"Someone who was jealous maybe?" Junpei joked back but that's when it hit him. Someone who had to like Alec a lot in order to be jealous enough to have these girls attacked - someone who had a connection to *paint*. It was suddenly so obvious. "Oh my god, Alec are you thinking what I'm thinking?" Junpei turned to stare at him.

Alec furrowed his brows before blurting out - "You don't think?" Junpei nodded grimly. "*Rika...*" Alec sounded disappointed.

"She's obviously doing something to create all these fake *yokai* - she must be in the art room or something. I'll stay here and you go and stop her. It has to be you Alec." Junpei directed him.

Alec nodded, "Right, thanks Junpei."

Alec rushed off towards the main school building and quickly made his way to the art room where he knew he'd find Rika. He quickly entered the art room and found Rika sitting in front of a giant canvas. Alec eyed the canvas and saw that it was a painting of some sort of demon parade in a night setting. Rika was currently adding more and more *yokai* to the parade with every elegant stroke of her brush.

"Rika!" Alec called out to her and when she didn't respond - so deep in concentration in her painting it seemed - he rushed up to her and grabbed her shoulder to turn her around to face him. When she spun around to face him Alec noticed the odd expression on her face - her eyes seemed to be glazed over as if she were in some kind of trance. Alec watched in awe as more *yokai* began coming to life from her painting of the Demon's Night Parade that Rika was working on and were all flying out the window in a train and Alec saw that they were all mysteriously headed towards the girls' dorm building.

Alec gripped Rika's shoulders with both hands, "Rika! Snap out of it!" Alec gave her a little shake but nothing seemed to work. Alec paused, he had just gotten an idea - a crazy idea - but an idea none the less of how to snap Rika out of her trance. Alec gulped nervously and looked down at Rika's lips. Well, it was worth a shot. Alec decided. Alec slowly leaned over and pressed his lips to hers before quickly pulling back. "Come back to me, Rika." He whispered in a low voice.

Rika's eyes became less hazy and she then blinked back at Alec, a confused expression on her face. "Alec? What...?"

Then Rika's eyes flicked over to see the *yokai* which were coming to life and eerily emerging from her painting. Her eyes widened as she watched them flying towards the open window in the art room to where they were then flying outside and lighting the night sky with the paper lanterns Rika had painted to have each of the *yokai* holding. Rika gasped, "Ah! What in the world is going on?"

"You're doing this Rika. It must be your spiritual power to be able to paint things that come to life. You must be unconsciously empowering your drawings with your spirit energy in order to fulfill a certain purpose. Do you know what purpose that might be exactly?" Alec asked lightly, having the sinking feeling he already knew what her answer would be.

Rika's eyes widened knowingly. "Oh my god...but I didn't...I didn't really mean for it to happen. I don't really want to hurt anyone it's just - I was so tired of them teasing and making fun of me. I just felt so angry at them and wanted justice - for them to just get what they deserved."

Alec nodded understandingly. "You have to stop them Rika before someone does get hurt."

"But how?" Rika bit her bottom lip.

"Paint something for the sole purpose of getting rid of everything you've painted. You have to concentrate as you paint it, think of its true purpose and give it some of your spirit energy." Alec informed her, somehow knowing that this was true.

"I don't know if I can..." Rika hesitated, still unsure of herself.

Alec put a hand on her shoulder, "I know you can. I believe in you Rika."

Rika blushed and nodded, "Alright, if you say so, Alec-*kun*."

Rika pushed her sleeves back, a determined look on her face and raised her brush high in the air before bringing it down upon another clean canvas, which she had set up. "*Yosha!* Alright! Here goes nothing!"

* * * * * * * * * * * * * * *

Junpei's breath was coming in and out in short gasps, he was running low on spirit energy, but the *yokai* just kept coming and coming. He didn't know how much longer he could last before he would let one of those *yokai* slip by him and then one of the girls behind him would be hurt. "Dang it!" He punched through the air and destroyed another floating *Noh* mask which burst into paint. He looked across the school grounds - it looked as though there had been a paint ball tournament or something, splotches of different colored paint were everywhere.

A floating and bobbing *nekomata* was about to get Junpei from behind when Alec and Rika ran up to him. "Junpei behind you!" Alec called out a warning.

Junpei spun around and punched the creature just in time. He saw Alec and Rika and breathed a sigh of relief. That's when he noticed the small (about the size of a teddy bear), strange but cute creature in Rika's arms. It resembled a *kappa* Junpei realized as he looked it over and took in its green frog-like body, webbed feet, round yellow eyes, duck bill-like mouth, and the tortoise shell on its back.

Junpei raised an eyebrow, "A *kappa*?"

Alec smirked coming to stand at Junpei's side, "No ordinary *kappa*."

Rika strode forward and raised her *kappa* into the air. "K-chan! Do your thing!" The *kappa* then opened its duck bill-like mouth and then a strong wind seemed to pick up and swirl around the group. Then Alec felt this suction force that seemed to be pulling everything in the direction of the *kappa*'s open mouth, so that Alec and his friends watched as suddenly all the paint spirits were getting sucked into the *kappa*'s mouth until in mere seconds there were no *yokai* left haunting the students. Phew!

The *kappa* closed its mouth when he was done and then he burped. "Erp! *Gouchisousama*! Thanks for the meal."

Junpei sweat-dropped at that. And Alec's eyebrow twitched. "That's one way of doing it, I guess - kinda makes a guy feel a bit inadequate though, Rika ." Junpei joked.

Rika grinned back, and soon Alec and Neji broke out laughing at Junpei's comment.

And so the day was saved.

By a *kappa*.

. . . .

However...It was another unusual day at Izanagi Academy, students had gathered in home room ready to start the day. Alec's fellow classmates were now sporting their new dye jobs courtesy of Rika and so the students were all looking very colorful with their rainbow colored hair styles - some with just the tips of their hair colored differently while others had bleached their hair entirely and went blonde or even pink for a more dramatic effect. Sakura, Rena, and Tami were all scowling since this strange fashion trend had come about without them having had a say in the matter.

The students in the classroom were currently all talking about how cool Alec, Junpei, and Rika had been when they had protected the girls' dorm from the mysterious paint spirits:

"Alec, Junpei, and Rika were just so cool the other night. Protecting all of us like that." "Yea! Alec and his soccer ball kicked butt!" "Junpei's energy blasts were frickin awesome dude!" "And Rika's weird pet was pretty amazing too!" "Yea it was."

Sakura was chewing on her thumb nail again in complete disbelief that this was happening. "How did this happen? She's done it again! Grrr...will I ever win against her? Rika...one day I will get you back!" Sakura vowed to herself.

"Although I heard the *nopperabo* is back and haunting the school again." The students began to change topic. "Yea, I heard about that too..." Another student agreed and the rumors caught Alec and co's interest. "On the forest path close to the boys' dorm building a *nopperabo* was spotted there. It had on a long sleeved, black and red *kimono*." "Epp! Scary! I'm definitely not going anywhere near that place!" "Yea, I guess I'll have to find another way back to the dorms..."

Alec and Junpei exchanged a look and both nodded, a silent communication having passed between them. They would be checking out the forest path tonight.

· · · · · · · · · · · · · · · · · ·

That night, Alec and Junpei set out for the forest path to see if they'd encounter the *nopperabo*. But with Alec, the Spirit Magnet, along it wasn't long before the *nopperabo* made her appearance.

Alec and Junpei had been walking down the middle of the forest path, dark tree branches hovering over them on either side, when suddenly the shadowy figure of a woman stepped out from the trees and onto the path directly in front of them. She had extremely long, midnight colored hair, and was wearing a black and red *kimono* (just as the students had described) with a red chrysanthemum pattern on the material, and wore a red *obi* sash tied about her slim waist. She had her long *kimono* sleeve raised to cover her face as she walked out before them but then she slowly lowered the sleeve to reveal her face - and Alec and Junpei gapped as they saw she had no face. The surface of her face was pale white, blank, and smooth. She was the *nopperabo*. *Gulp.* Alec swallowed.

"My face...my face....where is my beautiful face?" The faceless ghost moaned as she strode forward.

The hairs on the back of Alec's neck were standing on end. He reached out his senses and felt that the ghost before him was extremely powerful. He was afraid but quickly bottled his fear and acted quickly - he wouldn't let himself freeze up again, not like the last time, he decided. He empowered his soccer ball and dropped it before then kicking it straight at the *nopperabo*. Alec's soccer ball flew through the air but then seemed to hit an invisible shield that surrounded the *nopperabo,* but which was merely the pure aura of spirit energy radiating off the *nopperabo,* which managed to deflect Alec's soccer ball and with such force that the ball bounced off and hit a nearby tree which broke in half from the force of the impact, splinters of wood flying up into the air.

"Whoa." Alec breathed as he watched the large tree topple over. *This is so not good.*

The *nopperabo* continued to approach Alec, and she seemed to glide across the ground in a spooky manner, "My face...my face...do you have my face, you *delicious* boy?"

Uh oh...Junpei had a bad feeling about all this. "Alec! Stay away from my best friend, you monster!" Junpei attacked the *nopperabo* creating an energy blast in his two hands and sending it off towards the *nopperabo* Kamehameha-style but the energy blast just hit the invisible shield and was deflected.

"Don't get in my way, boy." The *nopperabo* turned her attention to Junpei and she raised her sleeve and caused it to shoot out towards Junpei, the length of her sleeve in a very abnormal fashion, becoming impossibly longer, before it grasped Junpei, the ends of the sleeve like ribbons wrapping tightly around Junpei's body, and then the *nopperabo* lifted Junpei off the ground and flung him into a nearby tree. He hit the tree with a painful sounding *thwack* and slid down the tree trunk where he sat in a slightly dazed state and could only watch in horror as the *nopperabo* approached Alec next, a sinking feeling in his stomach.

Alec was too afraid to move when the *nopperabo* had her sleeve shoot forward and latch itself onto Alec's face. Alec screamed in pain and horror as he felt his face being 'peeled' off like a mask. Alec had never felt something so painful before in his entire life. The *nopperabo* pulled back her sleeve and there in her hand she now held a face mask, which had the features of Alec's face.

Junpei watched in horror as Alec's now faceless body fell backwards and landed to the ground with a soundless thud where it lay unmoving. Alec had probably passed out from the shock and pain of having his face removed, Junpei realized. "Alec!"

The *nopperabo* put the face mask of Alec's features over her blank face and her face seemed to merge with the mask until it became one and her face became Alec's. "Face...face...a beautiful face at last! Buwhahaha!" She let out an evil cackle. The *nopperabo* then slunk back into the shadows of the forest leaving Junpei and the unconscious Alec behind.

• ● ● ● ● ● ● ● ● ● ● ● ● ● ● ●

Junpei had gathered his remaining strength to take Alec's unconscious form to nurse Haruna's office right away. Haruna-*sensei* was distraught to find Alec the way he was, and Neji and Rika were quickly informed of what had happened. They had rushed over to the nurse's office as soon as they'd heard to see their friend.

Junpei looked down at Alec's still form angrily, and clenched his fists. "Dang it. The *nopperabo* is real and she's just too powerful...I wish *Aniki* or *Onee-san* were here...I'm just not strong enough...darn it..." Junpei's knuckles were turning white.

"There must be something we can do." Rika looked desperate. To see her knight in shining armor in this state, unnerved her.

Junpei seemed to think of something. "That's it, Rika! *You* can save Alec! All you have to do is paint some really cool monster that can defeat the *nopperabo*!"

Rika looked back at Junpei bewildered, "You want me to what? Junpei...I dunno if that will even work. This is totally different than before. Before it was the paint spirits *I* created so it was easy to overpower them with my will but this is a real *nopperabo*...I don't think anything I could create would be a match for her." Rika hung her head and began to ring her hands together.

"Rika, you have to help me save Alec." Junpei placed a hand on her shoulder and forced her to look up at him. "I can't do this alone. I need your help. The only way Alec will get his face back is if the *nopperabo* is defeated. And he won't stay alive long in his current condition...this is a matter or life or death." Junpei urged her.

"I dunno..." Rika still hesitated, her insecurities getting the best of her, "I'm not like LadyV, Junpei. I'm not cool or confident or powerful. In reality, I'm just me. I don't think I can do it."

Junpei huffed, "Then you're just going to give up? Give up on Alec? Just stand back and do nothing while Alec dies? I thought you were his friend Rika...maybe even something more than just a friend." Junpei shook his head at her, a disappointed look on his face.

Rika looked hurt. "I am but...I just don't think I can do anything to help him...I'm being realistic, Junpei."

Junpei threw his arms up into the air in frustration, "Fine! Be that way! I don't need your help. I'll defeat that *nopperabo* all on my own. Hmph!" Junpei stormed out of the nurse's office and slammed the door behind him with a loud bang.

"Junpei wait!" Rika called after him. She bit her lower lip thoughtfully as she looked back at Alec's faceless form.

"Rika, he's right you know." Neji cleared his throat and pipped up, "At least, you have the power to do something. If I had spiritual abilities like you guys I would do everything in my power to help save Alec. And do you know why Rika? Because he's my friend. And I sure as hell don't have many of those. I'm just the class nerd after all. But you know what, he never really seemed to care. That meant a lot to me. Rika, you know if you were in his place he'd be doing everything to save you right? That's just the kind of person Alec Suzuki really is."

Rika frowned and lowered her head, her bangs covering her eyes, which were swirling with confused emotions. "I know that..." She sighed heavily. "You're right Neji." She looked up, a steely look now in her brown eyes. "I have to at least try and do what I can. And hope that will be enough."

"It will be." Neji gave her a thumbs up. Neji watched her leave the nurse's office, a fond expression on his face. "I know you can do it Rika. You're an incredible person Rika even if you don't seem to be able to see that yourself. And...I believe in you, Rika-*chan*. I always have. Dang...if only I could have said all that to her face." Neji ran a hand back through his oily hair and chuckled at himself. "I'm so pathetic, like that would ever happen."

⸰ ⸰ ⸰ ⸰ ● ● ● ● ● ● ● ● ● ● ● ● ⸰ ⸰

Junpei returned to the forest path on his own, he was determined on facing the *nopperabo* and getting Alec's face back no matter what. He was not the type of person to forsake a friend in need, after all.

"Nopperabo! Show yourself! I know you're here!" Junpei called out loudly in the direction of the trees.

From out of the trees came the *nopperabo*, eerily she lowered her sleeve that had been covering her face to reveal that she still had Alec's face. It unnerved Junpei to see Alec's familiar silver-gray eyes peering back at him in a face that was now oddly sinister looking, and he shivered as she smiled at him, a chill going down his spine. Alec wasn't meant to smile like *that*.

"Give it back." Junpei growled. "Give my friend's face back! Give Alec's face back! You monster!" Junpei rushed forward in attack. His fists were glowing with a blue-tinged light as he brought his hand forward hoping to grasp Alec's face and peel it off the *nopperabo*.

But the *nopperabo* moved faster. "Meddlesome boy, I believe I have no choice but to kill you." The *nopperabo*'s sleeve flew out at Junpei, extending like a web, strips of material wrapping around Junpei suddenly, only this time they seemed to coil more and more tightly around him. Then Junpei could feel the strips of cloth wrapping around his throat and begin to constrict, choking him. He found himself suffocating, gasping for breath until -

"Unhand that boy at once!" It was an oddly familiar voice Junpei thought to himself in a daze.

Junpei painfully turned his head to see that it was none other than LadyV, the Game Idol, his goddess of good fortune - as he had sometimes liked to think of her. His eyes were already beginning to appear star-like as he gazed upon her. There she was LadyV, in all her usual glory with her emerald green hair in that high ponytail of hers, wearing her black and green, short kimono dress, her *naginata* in her hands, and even her Battle Ghost, Nopperabo, was at her side.

"LadyV...but that's impossible..." Junpei gasped out. "I must be seeing things. Wonder if that means I'm dying. But if LadyV is my angel in heaven then maybe dying isn't so bad." A pained half-smirk formed on Junpei's slightly blue face.

LadyV charged forward lunging her *naginata* toward the *nopperabo* so that she was forced to let go of Junpei and leap backwards away from the deadly curved blade. Junpei fell to the ground gasping for breath, and his hands went up to his sore throat that was throbbing in pain. LadyV was continuing her attack and the *nopperabo* decided to try and retaliate by sending her long sleeves flying at LadyV. But LadyV quickly sliced her *naginata* through the air and cut through the attacking sleeves easily. The *nopperabo* pulled her sleeves back frowning and as LadyV moved into an offensive attack again the faceless ghost was forced to gracefully dodge LadyV's attacks. The *nopperabo* was able to do so easily with her quick *yokai* reflexes and speed.

LadyV saw that this wasn't going to go anywhere and so called out to her Battle Ghost to help her. "No-chan!"

No-chan waited for the right moment and then popped up behind the *nopperabo* and wrapped its own spider web-like sleeves around the *nopperabo* so that she was suddenly trapped.

The *nopperabo* was unable to move and LadyV took this opportunity to spring forward and with her *naginata* raised pierced the *nopperabo* through. The *nopperabo* cried out as she was exorcized and her body disintegrated as she disappeared. The face mask, which held Alec's features, fell to the ground and LadyV went over to pick it up. LadyV then walked over and handed the face mask to someone and Junpei's eyes widened when he caught sight of who it was.

It was Rika.

"Here you go, Master." LadyV said, with a bow in Rika's direction.

Junpei's expression was one of total surprise, "Rika? You came..." His voice was hoarse from nearly being strangled to death. He was looking at her now with misty eyes. "Rika...I knew you'd come."

"Of course I did, *baka*." Rika smiled back. "My alter ego LadyV was the only person I could think of who could defeat a *nopperabo* in reality, so I decided to paint her and her Battle Ghost, No-chan. In my mind LadyV is just so powerful and invincible that I knew she'd win and I guess since I was able to create her that way it must have worked."

Junpei smiled lopsidedly at her. "Man, that was awesome, Rika! *You're*... frickin awesome!"

Rika blushed at the unexpected compliment. "Junpei..."

It was then Junpei's turn to blush. "Sorry, what I meant to say is that LadyV was awesome, as usual."

Rika appeared amused by that. "I am LadyV remember? *Baka*." But she didn't look nearly as mad at Junpei as she normally would have.

"Oh right, I knew that." Junpei laughed nervously, a hand behind his head, "What I meant to say is that your painting of her was neat, duh."

"Riiight." Rika didn't sound too convinced.

The sudden sound of clapping was heard and this caused Junpei and Rika to spin around towards the sound. They saw that Jin and Junko had just returned to the school.

"Very impressive skills you have there Miss Rika. To have defeated a true *nopperabo* on your own is quite impressive." Jin praised her.

"It seems your spiritual powers have awakened. Yoru anticipated as much... soon you'll begin your training with Headmaster Yoru so you can one day be on the *Shinigami* Squad." Junko informed her pleasantly.

"Me?" Rika squeaked. "Be on the *Shinigami* Squad? Train with Yoru? I dunno..." It was all rather overwhelming.

Jin put a hand on her shoulder, "We need those like you Rika, nay, Japan needs people like you to protect her from outside spiritual threats. Won't you help us?"

Rika was a bit caught off guard by all this but looked over at Junpei, who gave her a small reassuring nod. Rika then looked back at Jin and Junko, still hesitating but then she nodded. "I suppose...I'll try my best."

Jin and Junko smiled, "Welcome Rika to the *Shinigami* Squad. We're glad to have you aboard."

Jin put his hand out for Rika to take and Rika once again hesitated before she took it. Junpei placed his hand overtop of Rika's and his brother's and gave Rika a sly grin. Junko followed suit and placed her hand on top of everyone else's.

A new addition to the *Shinigami* Squad had been made.

* * * * * * * * * * * * * * * *

Junpei and Rika quickly headed over to Haruna's office to bring Alec back his face. Junpei immediately went over to Alec's beside and then placed the face mask on Alec's blank face - it glowed with a blue light before re-bonding with Alec's head. Alec's eyelids fluttered and then he opened his eyes. Shocked, he brought his hands up to his face and felt for his eyes and nose and mouth. Tears of relief shone in his gray eyes. "My face! It's back Junpei you-!"

But Junpei raised his hand to cut him off, "Uh, uh, uh, Rika's the one you really ought to be thanking this time around."

Alec looked over to Rika and smiled warmly at her, "Thanks Rika."

Rika blushed back at him. "Your welcome, Alec-*kun*, I know you'd have done the same for me."

They looked into each other's eyes dreamily (or at least Junpei thought it looked a bit dreamy) until -

Junpei frowned and decided to interrupt them. "Guess what Alec? Rika's going to join the *Shinigami* Squad! Isn't that cool?"

Alec was a bit shocked by the unexpected news and wondered why a flash of hurt seemed to pass through him before he felt happy for Rika. "Um, yea, that's great Junpei. You know I've been meaning to ask you this but what exactly is the *Shinigami* Squad?"

Junpei easily began to explain and Alec almost felt silly he hadn't just asked Junpei sooner. "A group of spiritualists, exorcists, mages, and mediums with the power to protect Japan from spiritual threats. You see, Japan is a land with very close ties to the spirit world or Makai...It's not uncommon for ghosts or *yokai* to travel to this plane occasionally and start mischief. That's what the *Shinigami* Squad is for - to protect normal humans from *yokai* and ghosts."

"I see." Alec frowned, "Why do you think it is that Jin doesn't want me to join up with you guys? Or to begin my training?" Alec questioned.

Junpei shrugged, "Sorry bud, I really have no idea. I'll talk to him though if you want me too. Though I'm sure he must have a good reason."

"Hmph! Well, then I want to hear it." Rika crossed her arms over her chest. "It makes no sense why he hasn't been asked to join the *Shinigami* Squad - he's an exorcist and a very powerful one too!"

Alec sighed heavily, "It's alright guys, it...it doesn't really matter anyways."

"Alec..." Junpei looked at Alec worriedly.

Alec tried to mask his emotions better when he sensed Junpei's concern. "You're right, Jin probably has a good reason. I...I need to be alone for a while. Cya." Alec left his speechless friends and a worried Haruna-*sensei* behind as he ran from the nurse's office. He decided to go to the soccer field and do some of his secret soccer training. As he trained and dribbled his soccer ball down the field Alec wondered why Izanagi Academy still possessed so many secrets and why Alec was always kept in the dark about everything...

But there was one thing Alec knew for sure - he intended to find out.

Chapter 13:
NUE: The Japanese Chimera

Alec's class had a planned field trip to Kyoto the very next day. Alec was extremely excited since he'd never been to Kyoto before. Once the class arrived there - Alec, along with his friends - Rika, Junpei and Neji ended up sightseeing and hanging out together. First, they ended up tagging along with Rika, who wanted to buy a new *kimono* while they were there. Most of the girls in their class had also insisted on going '*kimono* shopping' since Kyoto was famous for its *kimono* stores. Alec, Junpei, and Neji had been somewhat reluctant to follow Rika into 'girl territory' as they liked to think of it. But after Rika had stepped out of the dressing room wearing a beautiful, pale green kimono with a pattern of golden vines embroidered on the silk along with a dark green *obi* sash tied about her thin waist - they soon changed their tune. Alec thought she definitely looked cute with her fixed green highlights and she wasn't wearing her usual beret either.

Junpei let out a whistle of approval as Rika spun around to show off her new *kimono* to the boys. Rika blushed in surprise at Junpei's reaction since she was almost sure that he would have teased her. Alec noticed that Neji was literally drooling as he admired Rika in her new *kimono* and a sudden thought crossed Alec's mind. Did Junpei and Neji like Rika too? Or was it merely in his overactive imagination?

Well, he didn't know much about girls...or attraction or dating...so he didn't really know what Junpei or Neji thought of Rika. He had always thought he was the only one who had harbored a bit of a secret crush on Rika, but lately he was having suspicions that Neji and Junpei harbored secret feelings for her as well. Maybe Alec should have said 'yes' to going out with her after all but...Alec really wasn't ready for a relationship yet. He was still very shy, awkward, and bad around girls - or at least he felt so.

After Rika paid for her *kimono* the group headed over to Kiyomizu-dera, which was a temple considered to be a national treasure of Japan, and which had an incredible view of the Kyoto landscape from it's large balcony stage.

Alec, Rika, Junpei and Neji all looked out at the beautiful panorama view of Kyoto city before them. "*Steki*! Beautiful!" Rika declared and then suddenly pulled an easel out from nowhere along with her brush set and paints. She also pulled out her signature beret from her *kimono* sleeve and set it on the side of her head before setting to work at painting the beautiful landscape before her.

Alec felt a trickle of sweat form on his brow from this. Where Rika had hidden that easel or brushes or those paints Alec couldn't quite fathom. All three boys looked at Rika at that exact moment as she commented on the landscape, and all three of them responded simultaneously with a wistful note in their voices: "Yea..."

Alec blinked and looked over at Neji and Junpei in surprise. They looked equally surprised at having been caught complimenting Rika albeit in an indirect way of course. Alec frowned - how had this happened? Did all three boys harbor secret crushes on Rika now? And shouldn't that bother Alec more than it seemed to? He found himself merely feeling oddly amused by the whole situation.

Junpei came over to nudge Alec in the side. "So, you going to take the plunge?" He looked over at Rika pointedly.

Alec flushed at the question.

Junpei merely laughed at Alec's discomfort. "I'm only kidding, Alec, it's an expression here. Did you know? 'Jumping off the Kiyomizu-dera stage' has the same meaning as the saying 'taking the plunge' as in getting married. There's also this Edo tradition from hundreds of years ago where people, who were said to have survived jumping off the stage, had their biggest wish granted. Do you have a wish Alec?" Junpei teased thinking it would have something to do with Rika.

Alec looked down over the stage's edge and gulped. It was quite a long drop down to a steep hill lined with trees. "A wish *ka*?" Alec thought of his wish to be left alone by ghosts and now *yokai*. How free his life would be if he could live like a 'normal' teenage boy. Alec was absentmindedly walking towards the end of the stage distracted, his thoughts full of his wish, when Neji and Junpei were forced to grab his arms and pull him back.

"Alec dude!" Junpei warned, "I was just kidding."

"Alec." Neji said with concern in his voice and a scowl on his face. "You don't believe in that old Edo tale do you? It's just a story. I really doubt your wish would actually come true if you jumped off and risked your life. It's completely illogical." Neji nodded to himself before pushing his glasses up his nose knowingly.

Alec shook his head while coming out of his slight daze. "Sorry about that guys. I just zoned out there for a minute."

Rika gave Alec a worried look and was opening her mouth to ask Alec something when the group suddenly heard a commotion coming from inside of the temple. A commotion which seemed to consist of a bunch of overly excited and giggling girls.

Alec raised an eyebrow, "What do you think is going on?"

Junpei stroked his chin thoughtfully before a knowing look came into his eyes, "Ah, the girls must be over by the love stones."

"Love stones?" Alec questioned, quirking his head at Junpei.

"Yea, they're - it's better for you to see them than for me to try and explain it. Come on." Junpei began to drag Alec off by the arm. Rika and Neji were following close behind them.

They entered an area in the temple where a large number of the middle school girls from their class had gathered, including most of the girls that were in Alec's fan club as well as the 'fan club president' Sakura, and her two friends Tami and Rena. Alec saw that there was a large stretch of open space where there was a large stone sitting at one end and another large stone similarly seated at the opposite end of the space. He watched as girls closed their eyes or were blindfolded before they stood from the first stone and tried to cross the space and make it to the other stone. The girls were stumbling in the general direction of the other stone and some had completely gone off course. It strangely reminded Alec of 'pin the tail on the donkey'.

Alec's eye twitched as he watched one girl land flat on her face, "Um, Junpei, just what are those girls doing?"

Junpei grinned, "It's said here at the temple that if you manage to get from one stone to the other with your eyes closed that your true love will love you back, silly huh?"

Neji smirked and shook his head, "Girls...that's completely illogical." He adjusted his glasses, "*Neh* Rika?" Neji turned to see that Rika had run off along with the rest of the girls to the starting rock. "Rika?" Neji sweat-dropped, a trickle of sweat forming on his brow in disbelief.

Junpei was sweat-dropping as well at Rika's girlie behavior but then shrugged.

Alec smirked, "Sometimes I forget Rika is a girl." Neji and Junpei gave Alec a weird look and Alec waved his hands before him nervously as he tried to explain. "I mean, we're just such good friends and all. And I'm bad around girls but around Rika I feel okay."

Junpei looked off wistfully towards the first love stone, "You don't think it works?" He asked in a low voice to Neji.

"Only one way to find out." Neji declared and Alec watched amused as his two friends ran off towards the starting love stone.

"I will win Alec's love!" Sakura declared as she made her way towards the second stone. Alec sweat-dropped at this. He still didn't get why all the girls in his grade gave him all this attention that he felt he didn't deserve and it still made him extremely uncomfortable.

Rika licked her lips, "Alec..." She closed her eyes and began to walk forward, her hands outstretched before her. Junpei and Neji started walking along besides her and they all began to walk towards the other stone at the same time. Junpei was farther ahead of Rika when he suddenly turned right and started walking in that direction, so that Rika ended up knocking into him accidently. "Ack!" Rika squeaked as she unexpectedly fell on top of Junpei in a tangle of limbs.

Junpei opened his eyes and blinked up to see that Rika had fallen on him, "It worked." He breathed, a somewhat mystified expression on his face.

Neji had successfully made it to the second rock and opened his eyes. He turned around and was smiling triumphantly, that is until he caught sight of Rika and Junpei and his smile quickly slid right off his face.

Most of what was going on seemed to go right over Alec's innocent head.

Rika ended up blushing down at Junpei when she realized what his words had implied but then she also realized their current position. "*Hentai*! Pervert!" She quickly got off of Junpei and gave him a hard slap as he was trying to sit up, which sent him flying into the nearby temple wall.

BAM

Junpei slid down the wall and groaned, a large bump forming on the back of his head. "I think she likes me..."

Clueless, Alec went over to Rika to offer her a hand up, and Rika blushed as she took it. All of his fan club girls were turning green with envy from the extra attention that Rika had just received, but Alec was still completely oblivious to it all as the girls tugged at their hair in frustration, or bit their nails in response to Alec paying more attention to the 'weird artsy-girl' as they had dubbed Rika, than to them.

Alec looked over at the love rocks and wondered to himself briefly whose heart he would like to win. Rika's? Or...perhaps, Yukino's? Alec blinked surprised that Yukino's ethereal image had entered his mind. He couldn't possibly like the goth, Battle Ghost girl could he? Instead of the cute Rika? Naw. Alec shook his head and decided to stay away from those love stones since they were putting odd ideas in his head.

That's when Alec suddenly had the strange feeling that he was being watched. He reached out his senses and felt that there was indeed a spiritual presence. The hairs on the back of his neck were prickling and he went back outside to the balcony stage following the presence and where it seemed to be the strongest. It appeared to be strongest over by the stage's edge and Alec peered down. Rika had followed Alec with a concerned and somewhat curious expression on her face.

Alec was worriedly looking down upon the steep hill of trees and forest, while rubbing the back of his neck when Rika came to stand besides him.

"What's wrong Alec?" She asked.

Alec was about to respond when he suddenly felt a huge surge in spirit energy coming from somewhere. Before he realized what was happening it appeared as though a large spirit energy blast had hit the balcony stage more or less in front of Alec, but instead of breaking at Alec's feet the stage instead broke away under Rika's feet. She stumbled forward as the stage broke away from underneath her and she suddenly felt herself falling. Rika spun around panicked and reached out her hand as she fell backwards. "Alec!"

"Rika!" Alec was quick to react and dove for her hand as she fell. He almost thought he wasn't going to make it for one terrifying split second but then his hand closed around Rika's. Whew. Safe. He was lying on his stomach now, Rika's hand still in his as she was dangling down over the broken edge of the stage. Alec watched as one of her *zori* sandals fell off Rika's foot and fell down to the steep hill below. Rika looked down at the sheer drop as she too watched her shoe disappear and squeaked in fright. It was a long way down.

Rika looked back up at Alec, a pleading expression on her face. "Please, don't let go."

There was a steely look in Alec's clear gray eyes. "I won't."

Alec wouldn't let her fall - no matter what. He summoned his spirit energy and it began to pulse around him. He then used this added strength that began to fill him to swiftly pull Rika up and back onto the stage, so that she was now standing in front of him.

Rika had watched in awe as Alec's body had been enveloped in a blue light and then how the muscles in his small, lithe body had seemed to bulge as he concentrated on using his spirit power to pull her up and onto the stage in front of him.

Rika was a bit stunned to be on solid footing once more, but soon overcame her shock before flinging herself at Alec and wrapping her arms tightly around him in a fierce hug. She buried her face in his chest and murmured, "I was so scared..." And indeed Alec could feel her body still trembling.

Alec frowned and absentmindedly stroked her hair in a comforting gesture. He was too worried to be embarrassed about how Rika was suddenly so close and in his arms. *This was no accident. I sensed something. Whatever it was must be behind this. Dang it.* Alec had sensed a spiritual presence after all, which meant that attack had probably been meant for him and *not* for Rika if it turned out to be a ghost or *yokai*. That also meant Alec had just put Rika's life in danger.

Junpei and Neji had rushed up to them. "Alec!" Junpei called.

"Rika, you guys okay?" Neji asked.

Rika pulled back from Alec and nodded, "*Hai*, thanks to Alec-*kun*." Rika looked back up at Alec. "Alec, you saved me again."

Alec nodded distractedly. *Darn it...my friends almost got hurt because of me. This is what I was worried would happen all along...* He frowned grimly as guilt seemed to swirl in his stomach.

Junpei was distracted with fussing over Rika but Neji's keen eyes noticed Alec's unease. "Alec, what's wrong?"

Alec was rubbing the back of his neck since the hairs there were still standing on end, "I just thought I sensed...no never mind. It's...nothing. " He didn't want to worry his friends - he had already decided he would be taking care of this on his own later.

Little did Alec Suzuki know that three mysterious figures were watching him from the shadows with amused expressions on their faces...

"Hmm how heroic." A girl's voice edged with sarcasm spoke. "I didn't think he'd risk his life to save her. How boring." The girl appeared to be pouting.

"I still don't see what the big deal about this guy is. But it seems he's a bit more skilled than we originally thought." A male voice drawled in a dull tone.

"I think we'll have to kick things up a notch if we're going to have any fun. Let's put Alec Suzuki to the test and see if he has what it really takes to be an exorcist. We'll see how those sissies in the *Shinigami* Squad handle things shall we? This is going to be fun." The third mysterious figure sounded amused and was rubbing his hands together at the prospect of putting Alec's exorcist abilities to the test.

The three figures began to laugh maniacally as they envisioned unpleasant things happening to Alec and his friends.

* * * * * * * * * * * * * * * * *

Right before sunset Alec and his fellow classmates followed Takahashi-*sensei* to a traditional, Japanese-styled hotel that Takahashi-*sensei* had generously booked for them. The hotel was luxurious enough to even have its own hot springs, bathing pools in the back of the establishment for them all to use. As soon as they got back, Junpei and Neji 'convinced' Alec to go to the hot springs bath with them. Alec was still a bit uncomfortable with the whole concept of 'communal bathing' and would have preferred to stay in his room. But with both Neji and Junpei forcibly dragging him outside it was impossible to escape them. Junpei slid the *shoji* doors to the back open and stepped outside, followed by Neji and Alec, who was clutching a small towel around his waist self-consciously.

Alec looked outside and gasped as he saw how nice the hot springs bathing pools actually were. They were surrounded by an Asian-styled garden and steam was rising off the waters invitingly. Alec looked up to see a clear, starry, night sky overhead. The entire ambiance was rustic and tranquil. Alec could even hear the sounds of crickets and cicadas coming from the nearby bushes and trees. Junpei was the first to enter the bathing pool and he let out a contented sound as he did so. Neji was next to enter the waters and was followed after by the still somewhat reluctant Alec, who sat in the bathing pool quite a ways away from Neji and Junpei.

Junpei chuckled at Alec's modesty, "Let's compare sizes." He suggested jokingly.

Alec turned red and Neji looked disgusted, "Let's not." Both boys ended up saying at the same time.

Junpei chuckled at their irk. "Worried you'll come in second place, guys?"

Before either boy could respond they heard the sound of giggling girls from the other side of the fence, which separated the men's bathing pools from the women's bathing pools.

A cat's paw smile formed on Junpei's face as he realized this and he swam towards the fence to eavesdrop better while putting his ear to the fence. Despite himself, Neji soon followed after Junpei. Alec shook his head at the two of them but ended up following after them anyways when his curiosity got the better of him.

On the other side of the fence, in the girls' hot springs pool Rika, Sakura, Tami, and Rena were all bathing. They had all wrapped towels around their torsos for modesty's sake and just in case any of their fellow male classmates stupidly decided to try and spy on them. This of course had been Rika's idea since she knew what Junpei was like.

Sakura was looking over at Rika in a scrutinizing manner. "Hmph, why does Alec keep choosing you when he could have a real woman like me? I'm much more developed." Sakura put her hands to her chest to make her point.

Rika blushed and crossed her arms protectively over her own chest at the comment. True she was slightly smaller than Sakura but for a thirteen-year-old she was rather over-developed in her opinion. "He hasn't chosen me or anything. We're just friends." Rika decided to tell the truth, even if it stung a bit.

"*Sure...*" Sakura didn't sound very convinced. "Then why is he always saving you?"

Rika blushed and didn't respond. She didn't really know the answer to that either.

Meanwhile, Alec was blushing bright red as he overheard the conversation about him. Junpei was looking amused and Neji was looking scandalized. "Hey Alec, give me a leg up would ya?"

Alec gawked at Junpei indignantly. He definitely didn't like the idea of Junpei spying on *his* Rika! "I most certainly will not! You're such a pervert Junpei! You shouldn't even be thinking of doing such things since we're still in middle school."

Junpei pouted, "Kill joy...it's just a harmless peek. Aren't you at all curious by what she meant by 'developed'?"

Alec blushed and shook his head vigorously, "No! I definitely am not!"

Meanwhile, the conversation was continuing on the other side of the fence and so the boys leaned in to begin listening once more.

"I wonder who's *bigger* Junpei or Alec?" Rena was thinking aloud.

"I would have to say it's my Alec-*kun*." Sakura nodded knowingly.

"I'd have to put my money on Junpei myself." Tami declared.

From the other side of the fence, a cocky smirk had formed on Junpei's face and he was looking a bit smug.

Rika was blushing during the strange conversation and decided to wisely stay out of it. "I say we find out..." Sakura trailed off and had a mischievous look in her eyes as she eyed Rika like a mouse about to get pounced on by a hawk. Sakura then continued in a low voice that the boys on the other side of the fence weren't able to overhear - "You're going to find out for us, Rika. We'll even give you a leg up."

Rika paled, knowing if she refused her dorm mates would probably pour shaving cream all over her while she was sleeping that night or come up with some equally evil prank to pull on her otherwise.

Meanwhile, Junpei had somehow managed to convince Neji that Alec should be the one hoisted up to take a peek over the fence in order to find out which girl had the 'best assets'. Something which Alec didn't even know what Junpei was talking about. And so Junpei and Neji were hoisting Alec up while the terrible trio were hoisting Rika up at the exact same moment, so that oddly enough they both ended up peering over the fence at the exact same time.

Their eyes unexpectedly met. Rika immediately blushed in surprise as she looked down to see Alec's half naked body. Alec couldn't seem to help himself either from looking down from Rika's face curiously, and was suddenly met with the sight of Rika's cleavage, which could be seen just above her towel. Alec's face flushed, turning bright red before he got a massive nose bleed, which promptly caused him to pass out.

Girl overload...error...error...

As Alec was no longer able to support himself, Junpei and Neji were suddenly finding it very hard to keep Alec standing straight at the fence and were forced to let him go. Uh oh...

Rika was so embarrassed by this turn of events that she quickly wrapped her arms around her chest, but this sudden movement caused Sakura and Rena to lose their hold on Rika's legs so that they were also forced to let go of her. Rika suddenly found herself flying forward towards the passed out Alec. She wind-milled her arms in the air trying to grasp the fence for support, but ended up grabbing onto Alec instead. At this point Neji and Junpei's hold had slipped from Alec, so that both Alec and Rika ended up flying backwards and into the hot springs with a tremendous *splash*.

When Alec began to regain consciousness he could confusedly feel Rika's small chest pressing up against his bare chest. Once he figured out what was actually going on and that Rika had somehow fallen on top of him *and* that they were both half naked he promptly passed out again from 'girl overload'. Alec lay back in the water passed out and swirly-eyed.

Rika looked down at the dizzy-eyed Alec in concern. "Alec!"

Junpei and Neji were both drooling at the sight of Rika in nothing but a towel, and she seemed to notice this as she got off of Alec and wrapped her arms and towel more tightly around herself. "*Hentai!* Perverts!" She stuck her tongue out at them both.

Neji frowned and pushed his glasses up his nose, "Rika, I do believe you made a mistake just now by saying 'perverts'. When I'm sure what you meant to say was 'pervert'. Since it's just Junpei whose the pervert here really."

"Oh really? I didn't make a mistake Neji." Rika huffed at him, hands on her hips. "Your nose is bleeding by the way."

Neji's eyes widened in surprise and he quickly covered up his nose, thoroughly embarrassed by the evidence of his attraction to Rika.

However, a scream was suddenly heard from the terrible trio on the other side of the fence. Alec was instantly awake, the hairs on the back of his neck were prickling, and he was completely alert while in 'hero mode'.

He looked back at the others, a serious expression on his face, "Wait here."

Alec then summoned his spirit energy and used the extra strength and power to leap over the dividing fence easily to the other side and to the girls' bathing pools in one quick movement.

Junpei looked back at Neji and Rika, "Neji look after Rika - it might be too dangerous for you guys."

Junpei then followed suit and also jumped over the fence joining Alec on the other side. Neji frowned deeply, watching them go with mixed emotions playing on his face. Sure, he was a normal human but that didn't mean he had to like being left behind or not being able to help his friends. Neji clenched his fists in frustration at feeling utterly useless.

Alec and Junpei landed on the ground next to the main bathing pool to see that a bunch of monkeys with white furry bodies, red-skinned faces, open mouths revealing sharp fangs, and unexpectedly glowing, golden eyes were approaching Alec's fan girls.

"Monkeys?" Junpei raised an eyebrow at them before his expression darkened, "How dare they attack innocent, bathing maidens!" Junpei cracked his knuckles menacingly. "I'm so going to kick their butts." Junpei's fists were beginning to glow.

Alec reached out his senses and sensed that there was a powerful, evil presence close by and he also sensed that there was some sort of evil energy trapped within the monkeys. He put a hand on Junpei's shoulder stopping him. "Wait Junpei, don't hurt them. Those monkeys aren't themselves - leave this to me."

With the extreme speed that Alec now possessed when his spirit powers were activated he surged forward and began to merely touch the monkeys lightly on their foreheads with his index finger and managed to expel all the negative, dark spiritual energy that for some reason had been possessing the monkeys with his purifying touch. Exorcizing the monkeys wasn't easy however. They tried to attack Alec at the same time as he tried to help them, and Alec was forced to dodge and leap out of the way from their attacks before he managed to touch them on their foreheads. He also had to touch them long enough to completely expel all the dark spirit energy trapped inside of their bodies.

Junpei and Alec's fan girls watched in awe as the dark energy left the monkey's bodies by Alec's glowing touch. Once the dark energy was expelled, the monkeys seemed to instantly return to normal. Their eyes no longer glowing eerily with a golden light and they were no longer wearing feral expressions of hunger on their faces. Instead, they became cute and harmless, albeit mischievous, monkeys.

Junpei's eyes widened as he realized just what was going on, "They're

303

possessed. I'll help ya Alec!" Junpei began forming small energy blasts (about the size of a golf ball) that he sent the monkeys' way, and which when they hit the monkeys didn't harm them but instead managed to expel the dark spirit energy from their bodies.

The possessed monkeys tried to stop Alec and Junpei as they began to exorcize the others one by one, but between Alec with his purifying touch and Junpei with his energy blasts they were making quick work at returning the possessed monkeys back to normal.

One monkey unexpectedly leapt at Sakura, but Alec noticed this out of the corner of his eye and lunged at it quickly grasping it around the neck while concentrating his cleansing spirit power at the same time, so that the monkey was returned back to normal by the time they both hit the water with a splash. That had been a close one though, and Alec realized that Sakura had almost been bitten by a possessed monkey - because of him. Again, Alec felt guilt swirling in his stomach giving him an uneasy feeling.

Alec's fan girls watched in a combination of shock and admiration as Alec and Junpei finished exorcizing the monkeys. Alec let out a breath of relief. Phew. His fan girls were safe. He felt oddly responsible for their safety after all.

Sakura rushed over to Alec, swimming through the hot springs pool, in order to thank him, "Oh Alec! You saved us! Thank you."

"No prob." Alec scratched his cheek nervously, suddenly feeling a bit bashful as the scantily clad fan girls began to surround him and thank him exaggeratedly. He averted his eyes as best he could and tried hard not to stare at the half-naked girls knowing he'd just pass out from girl overload if he did.

Tami had shyly gone up to Junpei, "Thank you for your help."

It was Junpei's turn to act bashful now. "Anytime, babe." Junpei sent her a wink when he had recovered from his initial surprise. She blushed deeply at this.

Neji and a worried Rika had managed to climb the fence somehow and fell with a loud *splash* on the other side at that moment.

"Is everyone okay?" Neji asked, coming up out of the water.

Rika quickly scanned the hot springs pools for any sign of Alec and noticed that he was off by himself and petting the heads of some of the monkeys. She raised an eyebrow at this, what were those monkeys doing there in the hot spring pools anyways? And then she noticed that Junpei was crowded around by Alec's fan girls, who seemed to be thanking him profusely for having saved their lives or something. She frowned at this and flipped her hair in an irritated gesture before making her way over to Alec's side. "Alec-*kun*!"

Alec turned and flashed her a bright smile, which almost took her breath away. "Rika!" He was starting forward but as he wadded through the water one of the monkeys had decided to grab onto the towel that was wrapped around his waist. Before Alec realized what was happening the monkey had pulled the towel completely off - leaving Alec naked!

Rika's face turned beet red and she gasped when she couldn't help herself from looking down. Sakura, Rena, and Tami turned around to see what all the fuss was about before they all blushed too at the sight of a naked Alec and began to giggle madly in response. Junpei was looking impressed while Neji wore a sympathetic expression for the shy Alec on his face. Alec was completely mortified and quickly covered himself with his hands as he made a mad dash for the inside of the hotel. *Why me?* Alec moaned in his mind.

* * * * * * * * * * * * * * * * *

Later that night, Alec found that he couldn't sleep a wink. He was still worried about the dark spiritual presence that he had sensed earlier and that had to have been behind the possessed monkey attack. He knew *something* was after him. And his friends continued to get into dangerous situations because of him. Rika had almost fallen off the balcony stage to her death and Sakura had almost been bitten by a possessed monkey. He decided he had to do something about this before it was too late.

Alec was currently lying on a futon in a room that he was sharing with Junpei and Neji, who were also both lying on futons on the floor not too far away from Alec. Alec gave up on sleeping and got off the futon determined to face whatever it was that was after him alone, along with his trusty soccer ball of course. Neji woke up at the sound of Alec pulling his soccer ball out of his duffel bag and watched as Alec snuck out of their room. Worried about his friend, Neji decided to secretly follow Alec since he didn't want to be told to stay behind again.

Alec went outside of the hotel where all his fellow classmates and Takahashi-*sensei* were staying to try and guard it. As soon as he was outside he sensed a powerful spiritual presence and a *yokai* materialized before him. It was a *yokai* unlike any Alec had ever seen before. This *yokai* was so strange that the more Alec looked at it the less he could figure out what it was exactly. It's overall shape and appearance seemed to be a patchwork of different creatures molded together such as a *tanuki*, a monkey, a tiger and a snake.

The creature before him had the white, fur-covered and red-skinned face of a monkey with fierce, glowing yellow eyes. It's body was that of a large, orange and black stripped tiger, and Alec couldn't help but notice that it's claws looked razor sharp. Behind the strange creature Alec saw two emerald green colored snakes that were the creature's tails. The *yokai* glared back at Alec before letting out a loud, horrible screech.

Despite it's odd and frightening appearance Alec managed to keep his cool. "There you are." Alec didn't allow his concern to show as he gathered his spirit power to then empower his soccer ball. As soon as he was ready he wasted no time in kicking the soccer ball directly at the unsuspecting *yokai*, who didn't quite understand what Alec was trying to do. "Eat this!" Alec cried before he sent off his attack. His soccer ball hit the chest of the *yokai* dead on and the *yokai* cried out in pain as it was exorcized. "I knew there was something after me. Dang, that was almost too easy...." Alec let out a sigh of relief.

Alec was too preoccupied with his own thoughts to notice that another Chimera-like *yokai* was materializing behind him. One clawed hand was reaching out from a dark, circular vortex of subspace that the *yokai* had managed to open in midair and was about to rip a hole into Alec's chest -!

Neji, however, who was close by noticed this. "Alec! Look out!" Neji leapt forward just as the clawed paw would have pierced Alec through and the *yokai* ended up wounding Neji instead.

Alec turned around in complete surprise to see Neji with a clawed, tiger's paw poking out of the center of his chest, blood gushing out and around the wound. The clawed paw removed itself and Neji fell forward, a pool of his own blood surrounding him where he lay unmoving.

Alec's eyes widened in complete horror - "Neji!" Alec then turned towards the *yokai,* which was stepping out of the hole from subspace with glowing eyes filled with hunger and bloodlust. "You jerk! How dare you hurt Neji!" The *yokai* merely opened its mouth and let out another unsettling screech at Alec as it stepped all the way out of the hole and stood on all fours in front of Alec licking its bloodied, clawed paw as its snake tails swished back and forth behind the creature.

This *yokai* was the same strange Chimera-like type as the other *yokai* Alec had just faced and Alec saw in an unnerving manner that the more he tried to see what the Chimera *yokai* looked like it seemed to shift shape. Alec started when he thought she saw a completely different looking creature than the one standing before him, but then his vision returned to normal and the *yokai* was the same as it had appeared before. Alec rushed over to his soccer ball, empowered it, and then kicked it swiftly at the *yokai* with all his strength and power. The soccer ball glowed like a comet with a tail of energy as it hit the *yokai* and exorcized it into nothingness.

307

Alec quickly rushed over to Neji's side and kneeled down besides him. He reached out a trembling hand to check for Neji's pulse, but before he could even do so he suddenly sensed more spiritual presences materializing all around him. Alec looked up to see several *yokai* beginning to materialize in a circle around where he and Neji were. They all appeared to be of the same type of *yokai* as the other two with sinister monkey faces, tiger-like bodies, and snake tails. Several of them had hungry looks in their eyes as they eyed Alec's tasty looking body and sensed his delicious soul.

Alec stood and put his foot on top of his soccer ball as he faced the *yokai* prepared to face them all on his own. Alec was super pissed since he thought Neji could very well be dying and his spirit energy aura flared up wildly around him, waves of blue light surrounding his body, and blinding the group of *yokai* momentarily from the sheer amount of power. He then wasted no time in moving to attack *yokai* after *yokai* with his soccer ball. Running and dribbling. *Dribble. Dribble. Dribble.* Dribbling the ball to the next *yokai* to then take his shot while having to dodge deadly attacks from the *yokai* as they slashed their claws at Alec or tried to take a vicious bite out of him. Then the *yokai* were suddenly opening their mouths and breathing fire unexpectedly at Alec.

Things were beginning to heat up. These blasts of fire missed Alec as he easily dodged and avoided them. However, the blasts ended up hitting the hotel that was behind Alec instead. Alec watched as the hotel began to catch on fire and then the flames began to lick their way up the sides of the building quickly since it was no ordinary fire but demon fire. To Alec's horror, in minutes the entire hotel seemed to be engulfed in flames and he could hear panicked screams coming from within.

"Neji! Rika! Junpei! *Minna!* Everyone!" Alec cried out.

Alec was panting for breath since he had been fighting for several minutes by now and was cut, bruised, and bleeding from head to toe. His spirit energy was also running dangerously low. Things were beginning to look a bit hairy to Alec and he wondered how he would get out of this one unscathed.

The combination of the sight of the fire and the screams caused an unexpected fragment of buried memory within Alec to surface at that exact moment -

A beautiful and kind faced woman, with a pair of round glasses on her face, was cradling Alec protectively in her arms, but as he looked up at her he saw that she was faceless. Or rather he couldn't remember the woman's face, but as he breathed in he realized he could remember her smell - jasmine. They were suddenly surrounded by fire and he felt the beautiful woman bringing him closer to her body, shielding him from the heat and the flames. Somehow he knew she was crying because of him...

"Don't cry, momma." A small, chubby hand went up to his mother's face.

"No! Not again!" Alec cried out in fear and then he shook his head to clear it of these strange images. Images of something that had happened to him long ago but something that he had forgotten about. Were those really his memories? Just what could it mean? Who was that woman? She couldn't possibly be his mother...His mother was Laura Suzuki after all. Right?

Rika and Junpei were among the first to rush out of the burning hotel building.

"Guys!" Alec called out to them as his vision cleared and he caught sight of them.

Junpei rushed over to Alec and unexpectedly bonked him hard over the head.

"Ow! What was that for?" Alec demanded, tears in his eyes as he rubbed the large bump on his head. "That hurt Junpei."

"That's what you get for not waking us up to help you!" Junpei declared, frowning at him.

"Oh right, the fire! What about the others?" Alec looked over towards the burning hotel worriedly.

All of a sudden, Rika pulled her easel from out of thin air again and set it down before her with her paint brush in hand. She rolled up her *kimono* sleeves and placed her black beret over her head and to the side. "You guys just leave that to me!" She declared licking the tip of her paint brush before putting it to the canvas on the easel before her.

Rika began to paint with a flourish of her paint brush and both Alec and Junpei watched in awe as in a matter of seconds she had managed to paint an exquisite drawing of a beautiful and mysterious looking woman with long black hair, blood-red lips and an all white *kimono*. The painting began to glow and then the woman began to emerge from the painting in a rather ghost-like manner. She then floated out of the painting and faced the burning hotel building.

Storm clouds that were gray and swirling began to gather high overhead and a chill air began to blow around the group before snow began to fall all around them. The mysterious woman began to blow an icy breath upon the flames before her and began to put them out. She reminded Alec of Yukino so much he couldn't help himself from asking Rika who this woman was supposed to be.

"Who's that?" Alec demanded.

"The legendary *Yuki Onna* of course. Though she's not the real one if that's what you mean. This is the *Yuki Onna* which exists only in my imagination.

Anyways, you boys just leave the fire to me and concentrate on those strange *yokai*! Just what are they anyways, they kinda look like *tanuki*."

Junpei looked over at the remaining *yokai* and his eyebrows raised as he saw what Rika had meant. "They must be *Nue*."

"*Nue?*" Alec questioned tilting his head.

Junpei nodded, "A sort of Japanese Chimera. They're said to be made up of a monkey, a *tanuki,* a tiger and a snake. Although that's not their real appearance at all. It's said their real appearance is something humans can't even begin to comprehend, so that when a human looks upon a *Nue* their mind comes up with an image it can understand. They're extremely powerful and can breath fire. The *Nue* must have been controlling those monkeys from before."

Alec frowned and along with Junpei they turned to face the *Nue* once more. Though Alec's strength was beginning to leave him...

Takahashi-*sensei* was currently leading students out of the hotel including: Sakura, Tami, and Rena, as well as some of the other girls, who happened to be fan girls of Alec's. Sakura's beautiful hair appeared to be a bit singed on the edges and her pajamas had burnt holes in places. The class managed to get out of the building safely but were now gaping open-mouthed at Alec and Junpei as they battled the *Nue* and as they watched *Yuki Onna* use her icy breath and control of the snow to put the flames out on the hotel.

Rika noticed that Alec and Junpei were beginning to tire and decided to paint some ice and water type *yokai* to help fight the fire type *Nue* that the boys were currently facing. The *ink-yokai* began to leap out of the canvas and began to engage the *Nue* in battle. It was a funny sight since the only water type *yokai* Rika could seem to think of had been *kappa* and now several small *kappa* were hopping out of Rika's canvas and shooting blasts of water out of their duck bill-like mouths at the *Nue*.

However, most of the *Nue* were ignoring Junpei and Rika's ink-*yokai* and had their attention solely focused on Alec.

One *Nue* motioned with his clawed paw for Alec to come closer, "Come closer you delicious boy...let me smell you...let me taste you...let me eat you..."

Other *Nue* were stalking around Alec, forming a circle around him, and echoing the other's words, "Yes...let us taste you...let us eat you!"

The other *Nue* continued, "You must know boy, that if a *yokai* consumes your soul their power will be magnified a hundred fold. Oh yes, we know all about you Alec Suzuki back in our world of the Makai. You're a bit of a celebrity."

Sakura tossed her singed hair over her shoulder in disgust, "The *yokai* want to eat Alec's soul? So, *he's* what these *yokai* are really after? So then it's his

310

fault all these horrible creatures are here in the first place! And it must be all his fault that all these awful things keep happening at Izanagi Academy!"

A hush seemed to fall over all of Alec's fellow classmates at these words.

Seems like the jig is up, Alec thought, *now they know I'm a Spirit Magnet.*

"Alec...son of the dragon demon, Lord Ryuuzaki...we've been hunting you for a long time and now we've finally found you! Thanks to some help from Izanagi's rival clan. It seems the protections of Izanagi Academy are able to usually shield your presence from our sight, but now that you're not at the school your spirit signature is as clear as day." The *Nue* continued licking his lips as he eyed Alec hungrily.

Alec stepped back in shock at these words. Son of the dragon demon, Lord Ryuuzaki? What was he talking about? "Huh? Dragon demon, Lord Ryuuzaki? Who's that? What are you talking about - I'm just Alec Suzuki. Laura and Mori Suzuki's son."

"Lies! We *yokai* know the truth! The truth of your blood Alec Suzuki! It calls to us. Half-demon that you are! You have the blood of the most powerful Demon Lord of the Makai flowing through your veins, which makes you more powerful than any of us, however if we manage to eat your soul and your body we will gain immense spiritual power. Power that will even rival that of your father's! And so it is worth the great risk to face you like this."

Alec was completely bewildered by this turn of events. He was half demon...? But that was impossible. He was human. Right?

"Why do you think ghosts and *yokai* are always hunting you? It's for your delicious soul and body! Because you are the son of the dragon demon, Lord Ryuuzaki and his *miko* lover!"

Alec's head was spinning in disbelief. *No, it can't be true. I don't believe it. I'm half yokai? Impossible...no way! This can't be happening...!*

Alec was too distraught to fight the *Nue* as they closed in on him. Junpei and Rika noticed this but were too busy with their own *Nue* to help him right away. But if they didn't help him soon he'd be done for! Alec was gripping his head with his hands over his ears while trying to block out the words of the *Nue*, trying to block out the world. *Just fade away...I just want to fade away.* The *Nue* were almost upon him -

"Alec!" Junpei and Rika's worried voices filled the air around him.

The *Nue* raised his paw filled with razor sharp claws high into the air before bringing it down upon Alec, however -

Yoru suddenly appeared in front of Alec. Alec blinked and saw that Yoru was wielding a strange sword with a blade that seemed to be made entirely out of pulsing blue light. Yoru quickly used his Spirit Sword to make quick work of the *Nue* that immediately threatened Alec's life. Yoru's sword sliced through the chatterbox *Nue*'s monkey head with ease and it was immediately exorcized. The *Nue* cried out in pain as it disintegrated into the air.

Next, glowing *o-fuda* and sacred arrows were seen flying through the air and hitting *Nue* left and right so that they were exorcized.

Junpei turned to see none other than his brother and sister, Jin and Junko, "*Aniki! Onee-san!*"

Rika smiled brightly, "The *Shinigami* Squad!"

Rika, Junpei, Yoru, Jin and Junko began to work together to exorcize the rest of the *Nue*, while Alec was still frozen in shock and unable to move. When the last of the *Nue* had finally been destroyed Rika looked around as if she were searching for someone.

"Hey, where's Neji?" Rika asked worriedly, and this was when Alec came out of his stunned stupor, his stomach plummeting as he turned to look towards Neji's fallen form.

Rika immediately followed his gaze and gasped, covering her mouth with her hand as she noticed Neji's unmoving form, and the pool of blood that surrounded him. "Neji...No!" Rika cried. "*Iyeeee!*" Rika sunk to her knees and began to cry into her hands.

"Rika." Junpei knelt at her side and tried to sooth her, placing a tentative hand on her back. Rika turned to face him and flung herself into Junpei's chest and began to cry into his shirt. Junpei hesitated before wrapping his arms around her to comfort her, a confused expression on his face.

Yoru quickly rushed over to Neji and knelt down to take his pulse. His expression grim. "He's still alive. Jin call an ambulance - hurry!"

"*Hai*, Yoru-*san!*" Jin quickly ran into the hotel's front lobby where there miraculously was still a phone available. Jin easily made his way inside since the flames had been thoroughly put out by then and began to dial up the ambulance.

In what felt like hours but were just a few minutes an ambulance arrived at the scene and Alec, a somber expression on his face, watched as Neji was lifted onto a stretcher and an oxygen mask was set over his face. Once Neji was loaded into the ambulance car and the ambulance began to drive away Alec turned towards Yoru.

Yoru turned towards Alec sensing his eyes on him, and their eyes met. "Yoru."

"Alec."

Alec clenched his fists at his sides, his knuckles turning white. "Is it true then? What those *Nue* said about me? Is my real father a *yokai*? I'm...half *yokai*?"

Yoru nodded, "It's true."

Alec was shaking with anger now, for being kept in the dark about so many things for far too long. "Just who are you, really Yoru? Or should I say Night?"

"I am the Headmaster of Izanagi Academy and am also the leader of the Izanagi Clan, an ancient demon hunting clan, which founded the school with the purpose of finding and training those with spiritual powers and with the potential to become a part of the clan or the *Shinigami* Squad, which as you already know is in charge of protecting Japan from spiritual threats. I recently inherited the position of Headmaster and Head of the Clan from my late father..." Yoru explained calmly.

"Is my bloodline the reason why I was forbidden to train my spiritual powers?" Alec pressed.

Yoru hesitated before saying. "Yes, but-"

At the word 'but' Alec didn't want to hear anymore. He had heard quite enough. He felt betrayed. People close to him had known the truth of his existence all along but had kept it from him. He desperately wanted to escape from reality, a reality that currently seemed to be crushing in on him from all sides, suffocating him painfully. "I hate you. I hate all of you!" Alec cried as he ran off.

"Alec-*kun*!" Rika cried after him concerned.

"Alec!" Junpei called after his friend as well.

But it was no use, Alec was already gone.

• • • • • • • • • • • • • • • •

Alec managed to hitchhike his way back to Izanagi Academy. As soon as he was back he decided to head up to the computer club room and log on to Yokai World.

ID: Dranarch

PASSWORD: wings

Alec logged on to Yokai World and materialized in the center of the starter town with its tall, gray stone buildings, Romanian feel, gothic architecture, and canals with racing dark water. He noticed the floating bulletin board in the middle of the town square and walked up to it and read that there was currently a game event underway, one that had the theme of the folktale 'Peach Taro' apparently. Alec shrugged thinking it sounded rather interesting and decided that it would help to get his mind off things. Alec raised his arm and said: "Onigashima Island!" So that he was immediately teleported to the island, and therefore entered himself into the game event.

Alec vaguely remembered his father, err, Mori-*san*, (since if what that *Nue* had said was true then his real father was some dragon demon Lord named Ryuuzaki), telling him the folktale once as a bedtime story. The story went

313

that there had been an elderly couple, who had both longed for a son and one day when the old woman went down to a stream nearby her home to wash clothes she found a mysterious peach that had been floating downstream. She brought the peach home for her husband to see and as they both cut it open to eat it they discovered that a small boy was inside the peach instead of the peach's pit. The boy declared he had been sent from heaven to be their son.

The boy was named *Momo* for the word 'peach' and *Taro* for 'eldest son' a.k.a. Momotaro. When he grew older Momotaro ended up going on an adventure to slay a powerful demon lord, who had taken over an island with his *oni*, or fellow demons. On the way to the island Momotaro befriended a talking dog, monkey and a pheasant to help him on his quest. With their help Momotaro was able to defeat all the *oni* in the demon lord's army and penetrate the demon lord's fort where in a one on one battle Momotaro won against him. Momotaro then returned home to live out the rest of his days in peace and tranquility.

As soon as Alec materialized on the island's beach *oni* mobs began to appear. The *oni* resembled RedAki's Battle Ghost Oni since they were large, muscular creatures with red skin, scraggly black hair and beards. Alec also noticed they had glowing, golden eyes and horns coming out of either side of their head. In their hands they were wielding either large swords, clubs, or battle axes. The creatures were also wearing nothing but tiger-skinned loin cloths.

Alec smirked as he drew his new *Shinigami katana* and pointed it at them. These low level mobs didn't even stand a chance. Alec charged forward and slicing his *katana* through the air made quick work of the *oni*. Alec then continued his way deeper into the forest. He encountered more *oni* as he continued his way, some which had become more powerful but they were still no match for Alec's unique sword. However, Alec found it a bit strange that even though this was a game event he didn't encounter any other players.

Alec could only think of one explanation for this - the RRs, or Renegade Reapers, must be PKing on the island so that no one would clear this game event except for them. Alec knew he would have to be careful not to be caught off guard by the crafty RRs. So, Alec continued his way until he came to the demon lord's fort. It had a high wooden fence surrounding it but as Alec defeated several *oni* on guard he saw that there were no longer any *oni* guarding the main entrance, which meant someone had already managed to break inside. Alec went through the entrance to the fort to see the bodies of several fallen *oni* littering the bloodstained ground. And then, up ahead Alec saw something -

RedAki a.k.a. Akira was currently in a one on one battle with the great demon lord himself, Ura. Ura was a huge and intimidating *oni* with wild red hair, a tangled red beard, gleaming yellow eyes, curved black horns on his head, huge steel-like muscles, and was wielding a gigantic, double-edged battle axe. RedAki must have PKed all the competition to come this far and have Ura all to himself, Alec realized. But strangely enough RedAki didn't seem to be in his best form, Alec noted, as he continued to watch him fight. RedAki's blows weren't having much of an affect on Ura either and then Alec could have sworn he saw RedAki look a bit dizzy before he regained his composure and kept on fighting.

But when Alec saw that RedAki was swaying on his feet he knew something was definitely wrong. RedAki continued to clash with Ura relentlessly but he appeared completely worn out. RedAki raised his black *katana* to block a blow, but then Alec saw that the next blow from Ura caused RedAki to sink to one knee. RedAki was panting for breath and he couldn't seem to find the strength to lift his sword as Ura swung his battle axe through the air at him again. RedAki was about to be cut in two -

When Alec rushed forward and stood between Ura and RedAki just in the nick of time, blocking Ura's blow with his own *katana* and protecting RedAki from the deadly axe swing.

RedAki's eyes were wide. "Dranarch?"

Alec looked back at RedAki and smirked, "The one and only. What's up RedAki? This isn't like you..." Alec turned his attention back to Ura and raised his hand, so that the blue stoned, control ring there glowed. "Ryuu! I summon you!" Alec summoned his Battle Ghost Ryuu who materialized into existence by his side. "Ryuu, go get 'em!" Alec said with a grin as Ryuu summoned his trident and surged forward to attack Ura, who leapt backwards. Alec watched pleased as Ryuu's trident clashed with Ura's battle axe sending sparks into the air. Alec was then able to turn around completely to face RedAki.

Alec reached his hand out to RedAki to help him up. RedAki blinked in surprise but took Alec's hand anyways.

"You okay?" Alec gave him a questioning look.

RedAki nodded looking a bit frazzled, "Yea...I think so."

Alec nodded back, "Good, then let's get this guy! Together!"

"I don't need your help." RedAki sneered but got into a fighting stance anyways facing Ura as Alec did the same. Alec and RedAki moved simultaneously to attack Ura and Ryuu stood back to give the two *Shinigami* some room. Alec and RedAki were able to read each others movements and knew exactly how to attack to catch Ura off guard. Ura looked to one side and then to the other as the two *Shinigami* approached him from both sides simultaneously and Ura didn't know which way he should attack first until it was too late.

Alec and RedAki's swords flashed as they slashed them through the air as the two boys crossed paths past Ura while delivering their finishing blows, and Ura was defeated with a cry as he disintegrated into little dots of light and data. A large, heavy looking treasure chest dropped out of the sky suddenly, and rocked back and forth heavily before it settled in front of Alec and the surprised RedAki.

RedAki appeared sullen as he looked at the treasure chest that he knew Alec had earned. But Alec simply smiled back at RedAki knowingly, "Well, go ahead and open it RedAki. You need the treasure more than I do, *neh*? You sell rare game items for real money online and that's how you've been paying your tuition at Izanagi Academy right?"

RedAki's eyes widened in surprise that Alec had figured this out, but he nodded curtly. RedAki then approached and opened the chest with a wave of his hand. Inside the chest was a GIANT peach. RedAki blinked as he reached in and hefted it up into his arms as he pulled it out. Dang, it was heavy.

"A peach..." Alec blinked, "I wonder what you do with it."

RedAki shrugged, "Dunno, but as long as I manage to sell it for lots of money I don't really care. I better put this thing into my inventory for now." The peach suddenly disappeared. RedAki turned to stare at Alec curiously for a moment before he let out a reluctant - "Thanks."

"No problem." Alec was all smiles, thoroughly pleased with himself for having helped RedAki out since he knew he owed the boy one.

RedAki walked towards Alec but suddenly appeared faint as he stumbled. Alec reached out and caught RedAki's shoulder to support him and to keep him standing, "Hey, you alright? Do you need a health potion or something?"

RedAki shook his head and regretted doing so since the second he did it just made his head spin worse than it already was. "No, I don't, moron. My health is currently at 100%."

"But then why?" Alec was asking when-

RedAki suddenly collapsed into a faint. "RedAki!" Alec hadn't been expecting this and so RedAki dropped to the ground with a loud thud. Alec was more than a bit freaked out about this since a player didn't normally just collapse in the game like this - a player would either need to be wounded heavily for this to happen and even then could be healed with a health potion or spell. Or a player could fall and die, but even then would come back as a PC ghost right away. But a player didn't normally just collapse into unconsciousness like RedAki did unless...Uh oh...

Alec knelt down by RedAki's side and shook his shoulder, "RedAki? What's wrong? Wake up! Akira!" Alec frowned, what if RedAki a.k.a. Akira was in a coma for some reason? *Epp!* Perhaps, he had even been cursed. And if that were the case there was only one person who could help him.

"Akira! Hang on, okay? I'll be right there." Alec told RedAki before reluctantly logging out and leaving RedAki's collapsed body alone and still in the game.

Once Alec had logged out, he quickly removed his VR HMD and rushed out of the computer club room and back to the dorm building and then all the way to Akira's room. "Akira? It's me Dranarch, I mean Alec, open up!" Alec pounded on the door as soon as he reached the boy's room.

There was no response. Alec gathered his spirit energy and used it to give him the strength needed in order to kick the door in. What he found when he ran inside was that Akira was collapsed at his computer and unconscious. Alec rushed over to him and shook him roughly by the shoulders.

"Akira! Wake up! You need to log out of the game! Please be alright. I really don't want to have to kiss you..." Alec trailed off as he looked down at Akira's unconscious face and gulped as he thought about how he might have to kiss Akira in order to break whatever curse might be upon him.

Akira luckily seemed to stir in Alec's arms however, "Alec...?" He said weakly and Alec was glad when Akira turned to his computer and logged himself out of the game world. Alec let out a breath of relief. Phew. Akira then tried to take off his HMD but seemed too weak to accomplish this for some reason, so Alec helped him to remove it. *Is he sick?* Alec wondered.

"What's wrong with you?" Alec's eyes narrowed at him. Akira looked awful, there were heavy, dark circles around his eyes, which meant that Akira hadn't slept in days. He was also looking even paler than the goth boy usually did. Akira opened his mouth to speak when his stomach suddenly rumbled and he blushed in embarrassment.

Alec raised an eyebrow, "You're hungry? When was the last time you ate?"

Akira looked away at that. Alec frowned when a sudden thought occurred to him - after he had the fight with Akira he hadn't told anyone that the *hikikomori* would need someone else to bring him his food. He had meant to but with everything else going on he had completely forgot. Which could only mean that no one had brought Akira food for the past several days *and* it was all his fault! Opps. *More than just opps! I can't believe I did that!* Alec was totally disgusted with himself. He had almost let a fellow student starve to death!

"Akira...oh my god...I'm so sorry. I forgot to tell someone to bring you your meals." Alec hung his head in shame, his white bangs covering his shadowed gray eyes.

"Sure you didn't just forget on purpose?" Akira turned his dark eyes to glare at Alec now, and Alec saw that his eyes held a mixture of hurt, betrayal and anger in them.

"On purpose?" Alec snapped, "Of course I wouldn't forget something so important on purpose! You nearly starved to death in here because of me! You have the right to be angry with me just - Wait here. I'll go and get you some food right away! Don't go anywhere!" Alec yelled behind him as he rushed out the door.

"Where could I go?" Akira muttered to himself hopelessly, "Doesn't he remember I'm a *hikikomori*...?"

Alec rushed to the cafeteria and quickly had some soup made for Akira. He didn't think the boy's stomach could handle much else not having had anything inside of it for *days*. Alec was feeling completely ashamed for what he had done. He didn't know if he could forgive himself but he vowed to himself at that moment that he would never forget Akira's meals again, no matter what. Akira needed him. He made his way back to Akira's room as fast as possible and helped the weak Akira to a small table where he could sit and eat his soup.

Alec watched him worriedly as Akira ate and took a seat at the table across from him. Alec was still feeling a lot of self-hate. "I'm sorry." He whispered again. He couldn't help it, one time saying sorry just didn't feel like enough.

"Say that again and I'll shove one of my dirty socks in your mouth. I'm not deaf - I heard you the first time, *baka* brat." Akira groused.

Alec nodded, "Right sor-" Alec managed to catch himself just in time at Akira's death glare. Alec gulped. After a moment of watching Akira eat he looked thoughtful. Alec ran a hand through his snow-white hair in an agitated gesture. "Man, today is so not my day. I wish I had just stayed in bed and never woken up...maybe even just dreamed all day. Dreams can be so much better than reality, you know? Maybe I'll just lock myself in my dorm room and never leave and just keep sleeping and sleeping and dreaming and dreaming. Forever." Alec's voice held a wistful note to it that made Akira raise an eyebrow in question.

Akira looked up from his soup and his eyes met with Alec's, "Why? What happened?"

Alec let out a heavy sigh. "To make a long story short, during our class field trip to Kyoto, our class was attacked by *Nue*, they're a type of *yokai*. Though you probably already know that. My friend Neji was critically wounded because of me...students were put in danger because of me..."

Akira furrowed his brows in confusion, "What do you mean by 'because of me'?"

"I...I'm a Spirit Magnet. Ghosts...*Yokai*...you name it, they want to eat my soul in order to gain power. That's why those *yokai* attacked us. It's all my fault I-"

Akira shook his head and interrupted Alec. "No it's not. That's not exactly the real reason why those *yokai* attacked you or were even there. The *yokai* were summoned by someone to attack you and your fellow classmates. More specifically anyone with high spirit power or anyone that might be on the *Shinigami* Squad were their real targets."

"What are you talking about?" Alec narrowed his eyes suspiciously at Akira.

"Izanami Academy. Have you heard of it? It's a school a hell of a lot like this one but located in Kyoto. Three students from Izanami Academy summoned those *yokai* to attack you and your classmates. They were curious about you, *Shinigami*-in-training, and wanted to test your strength, you know have a little fun." Akira shrugged. "They were particularly interested in you, however, since there are all these rumors flying around about you, and how you're Yoru's new pet project."

"How do you know all this?" Alec demanded.

"Why do you think I was at that game event alone today, *baka*? Catara, Kiba, and Smoker...as you know them in the game world...happen to be students from Izanami Academy in reality. They told me online about their plan to have some fun with the *Shinigami* in training from their rival school while they were in Kyoto, their territory might I remind you, though I didn't think they'd go as far as to try and kill one of you..." Akira chewed on his lower lip seemingly agitated.

"But why would kids from Izanami Academy do that? What do they have against our school?" Alec had a confused expression on his face.

"*Baka*, haven't you been listening to a word I've been saying?" Akira slapped a hand to his forehead and shook his head back and forth in an exasperated manner. "Both schools are preparing kids with spiritual powers to combat the supernatural or evil spiritual forces that threaten Japan. Izanagi Academy and Izanami Academy are for lack of a better way to put it - rivals. Izanagi Academy is home to the *Shinigami* Squad and Izanami Academy is home to the *Kuro-Shinigami* League as they like to call themselves. The two schools used to be one but split due to differences of opinion on the proper ways to combat and defeat ghosts and *yokai*.

"The *Kuro-Shinigami* believe the ends justify the means - they'll use any means necessary to defeat *yokai*. For example they believe it's okay to control *yokai* using Magic Control-Tech in order to use them to fight against other *yokai* in battle. They also believe in the genetic experimentation of *yokai* in order to research their powers and find ways to pass these powers on to the *Kuro-Shinigami,* so that they can stand up easily in battle against *yokai* if need be."

Alec looked horrified. "Control technology...and genetic experiments on *yokai*? That's awful!" Alec was thinking of Tamamo-no-mae specifically as he said these words.

Akira was looking amused, "Somehow I knew you'd say something like that. You're such a softy. Well, don't worry, Izanagi Academy and the *Shinigami* Squad don't believe in control tech or experimentation on *yokai*."

"You sure seem to know a whole lot about all this. And about Izanami Academy." Alec narrowed his eyes at Akira suspiciously once more, "Why is that exactly?"

"Ever since Yoru refused to train me in my powers I've held it against him. That's why I decided to join up with the Renegade Reapers whom I knew were a part of the Izanami Academy. I consider myself a part of Izanami Academy actually even if I live here at Izanagi Academy. You see, my spiritual ability is that I'm able to control *yokai* through the means of 'spirit strings'. I've been given the nickname the Puppet Master by some. But since Yoru doesn't believe in controlling *yokai* he won't let me advance my powers."

Alec was impressed, "You can really control *yokai*?"

Akira nodded, a pleased expression on his face, "Yep, but tell me Alec what is it you're able to do? If the *yokai* attacked you and you actually managed to survive then you must have some sort of spiritual ability."

"My abilities lie in exorcism and curse-breaking mostly. I can empower a soccer ball with my spirit energy and I use it as a weapon to exorcize ghosts or *yokai*." Alec explained, a serious expression on his face.

Akira paused before he then broke out laughing, "A soccer ball? Man, that's hilarious." Akira continued to laugh and began to beat the table top before him with his hand as he only seemed to laugh harder. Alec's eye twitched in annoyance, obviously the soup had done a good job in reviving him.

Alec then frowned at Akira before he looked thoughtful. "Akira." Alec licked his lips and wondered if Akira would answer him. "Could you tell me what the real life connection between Kaguto or Reaper-*sama* is?"

"Reaper-*sama*? He's the Headmaster of Izanami Academy, duh. Don't you know anything? His real name is Kaguto and he's part of the Izanami Clan, you probably know Night or Yoru is part of the Izanagi Clan right? Those two clans have had a long standing rivalry that goes back for hundreds of years. The clans were the founders of the two schools. You really are clueless. And yet you're a *Shinigami*-in-training." Akira shook his head at Alec. "Unbelievable."

"No, I'm not." Alec revealed a tinge of bitterness in his voice. "Yoru won't let me train either, though his reasons are different from yours. I-" Alec hesitated about telling Akira he was a half-demon and decided to just go ahead and say it. "Apparently, I'm half *yokai* or something. So I feel your pain, Akira. I know what it feels like not to belong."

Akira's eyes widened. "You're a half-breed? A *hanyou*? I see...you know, at Izanami Academy they wouldn't care anything about that. And besides, Kaguto says Yoru is going to put Japan in a whole lot of danger. Do you really want to be on the wrong side?"

Alec sighed, now that Akira had brought up 'this' again. "I believe in Yoru...even if he doesn't believe in me. He's probably just trying to protect me from myself or something noble like that."

"He should believe in you." Akira scoffed, "Yoru is just being stupid. You're such a goody two shoes it makes me sick. I don't know what Yoru could possibly be worried about. You're a good person Alec Suzuki. I know...you did just save my life after all."

Alec blushed and looked away, "Yea, well, um...I still wish I could just crawl under a rock and disappear, just escape reality. My life has become so crazy all of a sudden. I just don't know what to believe. My real father might be a *yokai*...I know nothing about my supposed *miko* mother either, if she even really existed. I guess that means I was adopted and I never knew. It's like my whole life has just been turned upside down and nothing makes sense anymore. I'm so confused. I don't know what I should do."

It was Akira's turn to look thoughtful. "Yea, but you can't keep running away."

"Running away?" Alec's head snapped up.

"You're already a part of reality Alec, whether you like to admit it to yourself or not. You're tied to it since you have friends and people who care for you in reality. You don't belong to just yourself anymore. I on the other hand have no ties to reality, with no friendships and no parents, so can escape reality and exist in the game world for example, and be perfectly content alone. Are you really going to turn your back on them? And abandon your friends?" Akira gave Alec a pointed look.

Alec opened his mouth to say that he didn't have any friends either, after all he wasn't supposed to have any friends - but then he promptly shut it. Akira was right, even though he had tried not to make friends since he was afraid of them getting hurt because of him somehow Neji, Rika, and Junpei had all managed to worm their way into his life and his heart and had become his friends. Alec's eyes widened as he realized this. He had friends - people he needed to protect. People whom he cared about and who cared about him in return. Akira was right, he had been running away.

"Are you really such a coward, Alec? I didn't think you were." Akira continued relentlessly.

I'm no coward. Alec shook his head. *He's right, I can't keep running away from the reality of my life anymore. I've already become connected because of my friends and I need to become stronger if I'm going to be able to protect them. I need to confront Yoru about my training and if he won't help me perhaps Kaguto will!* "You're right Akira. I won't keep running away."

Akira nodded sagely, "I knew you wouldn't run away forever. Now go - you need to talk to him don't you? To Yoru?"

Alec nodded, "Yes, yes I do."

Akira watched Alec go, a sad look on his face. If it worked out between Yoru and Alec that would mean they'd go back to being enemies when for a split second Akira thought - *Oh this is what's it's like to have a friend.*

⋅ ⋅ ⋅ ● ⋅ ● ● ● ● ● ● ● ● ● ⋅ ⋅ ⋅

The next day, Alec went to the Headmaster's Office. He had actually never been there before and hesitated before knocking on the door.

"Come in." Came a voice Alec instantly recognized.

Alec entered and saw the back of a chair behind a large, mahogany desk. The chair swivelled around to reveal Yoru sitting there. Alec blinked at Yoru's appearance in reality which to his surprise wasn't much different from his overall appearance within the game world. Yoru had spiky, blue black hair, the same sharp sapphire colored eyes he had come to know in the game, and was tall and slightly muscular - though Alec thought his game body might have been just a tad more muscular. Although Alec had to admit to himself it was a bit strange to see Yoru in such normal clothing - he was currently wearing an all black suit with a dark blue tie. Apparently, Yoru really was the Headmaster of Izanagi Academy after all. Yoru looked mildly surprised to see Alec.

Alec stalked up to the desk and slammed his hands down on the desk top loudly despite Yoru's slightly intimidating, confident, and composed manner,"Yoru, I want to begin training my spiritual powers."

Yoru's eyes narrowed at Alec. "Why?" Yoru questioned as he steepled is fingers together thoughtfully.

Alec clenched his fists, "I need to become strong enough to protect my friends."

Yoru and Alec stared at each other for a moment before Yoru broke out into a wide grin. "Good answer. Welcome to the *Shinigami* Squad Alec."

Alec blinked, that had almost been too easy. Maybe he should have just asked Yoru for this a long time ago. Oh well.

Chapter 14:
The Tale of Okiku: The Plate Ghost

Yoru had told Alec to meet him the very next day at the Izanagi Temple, which was on the school grounds, so that he could begin his training.

"First things first, you need a proper weapon with which to face the *yokai* with instead of that silly soccer ball of yours. Observe - the Spirit Sword." Yoru was explaining when he held out the hilt of a *katana* that had no blade out before him in a two-handed grip. Goose bumps went down Alec's arms and legs as Yoru began to summon his immense spirit energy and his body began to glow, surrounded by a blue-tinged light. And then Yoru summoned a blade of pure spirit energy, willing it into existence. "Spirit Sword!" Yoru cried as a sword blade composed entirely of blue light a.k.a. spirit energy burst forth from the hilt of the sword and flared into life.

Alec recognized this sword as the same type Yoru had used to save him from the *Nue* back in Kyoto.

"To properly create a Spirit Sword one needs an iron will, a strong determination, and great spirit power. I believe you have the potential to possess all these things Alec." Yoru gave Alec a small smirk.

Yoru then caused his spirit blade to dissipate and strode inside the temple to get Alec his very own Spirit Sword to practice with. When he came back outside with it Alec saw that it was similar to Yoru's in that it was merely a *katana's* hilt with no blade. "These Spirit Swords were created using a complex combination of magic and technology." Yoru informed Alec as he handed Alec one of these hilts. "Now, Alec I want you to try and form a Spirit Sword."

Alec nodded and held out the sword hilt in a two-handed grip before him. He concentrated hard and summoned his spirit energy, so that his spirit aura surrounded him like flames and then Alec cried out, "Spirit Sword!" A blade slowly flickered to life but its appearance was unstable and not as solid as Yoru's had been. But Yoru seemed pleased anyways that Alec had managed to form a blade on his first try.

Yoru nodded, "Good. Now we can spar." Yoru used his one hand to grip his Spirit Sword and formed his spirit blade in an instant to then point his sword at Alec with a merciless look in his eyes while he got into a fighting stance.

Epp! "Already?" Alec squeaked, taking a step back.

Yoru's deep sapphire eyes were as cold as steel. "Yes, we need to test that blade of yours, which in turn will be testing your will, determination and your power all at the same time. Now, prepare yourself!" Yoru moved forward to attack.

Alec brought up his flickering sword just in the nick of time to block a vicious swipe from Yoru's sword. Yoru pushed his sword forward, and was easily pushing Alec back. Then as blow after blow rained down upon Alec he found he could only block the attacks. And then Alec's blade shattered. *Epp!* Yoru put his Spirit Sword to Alec's throat and Alec gulped. Yoru pulled his Spirit Sword back while looking grim.

"Again." Yoru got into a fighting stance again and waited for Alec to reform his spirit blade. "You must learn to create a blade that will never break. A blade that is an extension of yourself."

Alec concentrated on reforming his Spirit Sword again but it was still unstable and flickering. Alec sighed heavily at himself.

"Now, attack me." Yoru urged Alec on. "And don't hold back."

Alec hesitated at Yoru's words since he of course didn't want to hurt Yoru. But Alec charged forward anyways with his sword moving haphazardly through the air while Yoru elegantly blocked Alec's attacks with minimal effort.

"Your will is weak. Your determination is weak. Your strength is weak. I thought you told me you wanted to become stronger to protect your friends, Alec? Now come at me seriously. As if you mean to kill me." Yoru commanded.

Alec frowned at Yoru's words. *Kill?* Alec didn't want to kill or hurt anyone. He just wanted to protect his friends. He charged forward but his doubt made his sword weak and Yoru managed to shatter it easily.

Alec was panting for breath and he was feeling frustrated with himself since he didn't really understand why his will seemed so weak.

Yoru raised his sword before him once more. "Again." Yoru's own Spirit

Sword was perfect Alec noticed a bit chagrined. It was glowing blue, pulsing with energy, solid.

Meanwhile, close by Rika was training with Junko, who was supervising her as she painted ink-*yokai* and practiced on empowering her drawings with her spirit energy so that they came to life. Junko had asked Rika to paint a *nekomata* for starters and the black two-tailed cat had easily leapt off the canvas. Next Junko asked Rika to paint a *kitsune* or fox spirit, but Rika was getting distracted by the sounds of Yoru and Alec sparring. She noticed out of the corner of her eye as Alec's Spirit Sword shattered once more and her heart clenched painfully in her chest.

"Rika concentrate." Junko chided her.

"*H-hai!* Sorry *sensei!*" Rika blushed and returned her attention to willing the fox spirit to come to life. But she couldn't help herself from looking over at Alec worriedly again out of the corner of her eye.

Also, training at the temple was Junpei, who was currently sparring against his brother Jin, their feet and fists were glowing as they fought each other using martial arts and dealt a series of complicated kicks and punches, blocks and blows. They had moved on to using energy blasts against each other at one point and Jin felt he was pleased by his brother's progress. However, Junpei became distracted as he heard Alec's cry of surprise as Yoru shattered his sword once more and Alec was flung backwards onto the ground while looking a bit swirly-eyed.

"*Alec...*" Junpei's voice was tinged with worry.

Jin frowned at his brother and used his brother's distraction to put Junpei into a painful stranglehold.

"Pay attention to the opponent who's in front of you Junpei - it could mean your life." Jin scolded his brother while tightening his hold.

"OW! *Hai! Aniki!* Alright already! I get it, I get it! You're hurting me! *Itai!*" Junpei whined while struggling to get out of his brother's hold.

Yoru was showing Alec no mercy as he attacked him again, and Alec was forced to dodge and block the vicious attacks as best he could. But Alec wasn't giving up and charged Yoru again. Alec's blade was becoming more solid as he thought to himself - *I must protect them, my friends, humanity. I must become stronger...*

Yoru raised an eyebrow upon seeing that Alec's sword had become stronger all of a sudden, but frowned seeing that it still wasn't good enough. Which meant Alec was still filled with doubts. And until he confronted these doubts and overcame them Alec's sword would be completely useless in real combat. For now, Yoru decided, his sword still wasn't ready. Yoru could guess the doubts that Alec had - Alec was probably being silly and doubting whether or not he was okay with killing *yokai*. But Yoru knew that Alec would have to overcome this if he intended to become a true *Shinigami*. Hesitation in the heat of battle after all was a very good way to get oneself killed.

Alec was feeling more confident as he confronted Yoru this time with his almost completely solid Spirit Sword, and this confidence showed on his face.

Yoru raised his sword and voiced Alec's inner doubts, "Don't get so cocky, brat. Do you really think your sword is strong enough to slay *yokai*?"

Alec's feelings of confidence vanished and he faltered at Yoru's words. Before he could compose himself Yoru surged forward swinging his sword at Alec, and as soon as it clashed with Alec's Yoru was able to easily slice through Alec's sword causing it to shatter into brilliant dots of light. Alec was flung backwards with a cry of pain. Alec sat back on the ground gasping for breath, and his body was trembling from the low spirit energy he now had.

Yoru frowned down at him, a disappointed look on his face, "Pathetic. You cannot hesitate to slay your enemies in battle Alec. You must not hesitate to slay *yokai* when the time will call for it. You must not show mercy to your enemies. This is your greatest weakness. This doubt is holding you back. You must overcome all of your doubts and strengthen your will and determination in becoming a true *Shinigami* if you are to create a proper Spirit Sword. I don't believe your heart is in this one hundred percent, and until it is this is a complete waste of my time. You have to be serious about this training Alec or it will be pointless. I believe that is enough for today. Classes will begin shortly." Yoru turned on his heel and left Alec still sitting on the ground.

Alec hung his head in defeat, his white bangs shielding stormy gray eyes, and he clenched his fists hard enough that he could feel his nails digging into the soft skin of his palms. *Doubt...ka? Huh?*

* * *

After their training, Alec, Rika and Junpei all headed over to the main school building and then to their home room. As soon as Alec entered the room there seemed to be this odd hush that fell over everyone. *Gulp. Now that's a bit odd,* Alec thought. He looked around the classroom curiously wondering what was going on. He noticed Sakura, Rena, and Tami and waved over to them, but strangely they turned their faces away from him. Alec shrugged feeling confused and made his way over to his desk, which was towards the back of the classroom. As he passed a group of boys he heard one of them mutter -

"*Yokai scum*...Demon scum..."

Before the boys started snickering at Alec behind their hands.

Alec's eyebrows rose. *Ah, so that's what's going on.* There was a sinking feeling in Alec's stomach all of a sudden and he could feel bile rise up in his throat. Now that his class knew he was a Spirit Magnet *and* half *yokai* they were going to shun him apparently. Alec sighed heavily. This was exactly what he had expected all along, and knew deep down was what would happen when his fellow classmates found out the truth about him. He had prepared himself for this but...as he tried to convince himself that it didn't matter he was finding it a bit harder than he thought it would be as he continued his way to his desk. His fellow classmates had accepted him, befriended him, more than that they had made him out to be something he wasn't - cool. And now that they had turned on him Alec couldn't help but feel hurt and was surprised by how much this betrayal actually stung. Somewhere along the way he realized he had made the mistake of letting himself care too much.

He was so distracted by his own thoughts he didn't notice when Tatsuya put his foot out so that Alec tripped and fell flat on his face with a loud smack. *Ow. Man that hurts.* Alec could feel tears stinging in the corner of his eyes.

Junpei glared at Tatsuya and cracking his knuckles ominously, "Hey, Tatsuya, you bonehead, what the hell did you do that for? Huh?"

Tatsuya paled as he looked up at Junpei since everyone was well aware Junpei was extremely skilled in *taijutsu*, or martial arts. "Uh, n-nuthin Junpei..." Tatsuya stuttered nervously, putting his hands up before him in a surrendering gesture.

"Didn't look like nothing to me," Junpei growled as he started forward, but Alec put a hand on Junpei's shoulder to stop him. Junpei turned to look back at Alec, who shook his head at him.

"It's not worth it Junpei." Alec said in a low voice, "And it doesn't bother me. I don't care what they think."

"Well, I do." Junpei frowned but reluctantly followed Alec to the back of the classroom. "That really pisses me off. They have no right to treat you like that just because..." Junpei trailed off and bit his lower lip.

"I'm half *yokai*?" Alec mercilessly supplied for him. "But it's true isn't it? I'm-"

"No! You're not!" Junpei put a hand on Alec's shoulder and looked him in the eyes, "You're not a demon. You're my best friend and I could care less that you were half *yokai*. Isn't that right Rika?"

However, Rika hesitated looking startled before simply nodding, "Um, right." She gave Alec a somewhat strained smile. Sadly, Alec could see the fear that lurked in her eyes. And that hurt. Really hurt. If he had wanted at least one person to believe in him, it would have been Rika...

Alec hung his head, his white bangs shadowing his sad gray eyes.

Takahashi-*sensei* arrived at their home room and sensed that there was an odd tension in the air as he stepped inside. Takahashi-*sensei* shrugged and began his English lesson. Takahashi-*sensei* was not only their home room teacher but also their English teacher. "Let's begin class shall we? Open your English books to pg 356. Now, how about we have Alec read the following passage to show you all the correct pronunciation." Takahashi-*sensei* turned to Alec, "And then translate the following passage into Japanese, Alec."

"Yes, sir." Alec stood and read the passage and then flawlessly translated the passage into Japanese. He then sat back down when he was finished.

Takahashi-*sensei* nodded, a pleased expression on his face. "Well done Alec. Class you should all make a note of Alec's pronunciation. I'm sure that if any of you have any questions on how to pronounce an English word properly Alec would be happy to help you, isn't that right Alec?"

"*Hai, sensei.*" Alec said in a monotone voice.

Takahashi-*sensei* raised an eyebrow at the odd, heavy silence in the classroom. Usually, by now the students would all be enthusiastically praising Alec for his English skills. But today it almost seemed as though they were all ignoring Alec on purpose. Sometime was definitely wrong. Takahashi-*sensei* coughed nervously and continued his lesson. "Well, anyways, let us continue to page..."

Alec, Junpei, and Rika were all about to head to lunch when Takahashi-*sensei* stopped Alec. "Alec, may I have a word?"

"Of course, Sir." Alec told his *sensei*, and turned to his friends, "I'll catch up with you guys." Alec's friends nodded and continued their way out of the classroom.

Alec noticed Takahashi-*sensei* seemed worried about something since his brow was furrowed slightly as it oftentimes was. Alec decided Takahashi-*sensei* really could be a worry wort and thought he'd tell his teacher not to worry so much otherwise he'd give himself wrinkles. But before Alec could say so his *sensei* spoke. "Alec, I couldn't help but notice how the class attitude towards you has changed. Is there something wrong? Perhaps, there's something I could help you with? I can speak with them if you'd like."

Alec shook his head, somewhat surprised by his teacher's worry for *him* of all things. He had almost been sure Takahashi must have been worrying about something having to do with Haruna-*sensei*. "Thanks for your concern *sensei*, but it's nothing I can't handle."

Takahashi frowned, "Well, if you say so, but I'm here to help Alec if you ever need advice or anything. Don't forget that." He ruffled Alec's shaggy hair affectionately. "You're a good boy, Alec."

Alec's eyes prickled with tears since that touch had reminded him of Mori's infrequent, fatherly touch. "Yes, Sir." Alec rushed off to the cafeteria without a backwards glance since Alec felt if he looked back at Takahashi's accepting gaze he'd break down for sure. It was moments like this when Alec felt he was truly alone.

• • • • • • • • • • • • • • • • •

Alec was late arriving to the cafeteria and Rika and Junpei had already taken their seats at a table. The group couldn't eat outside that day at their usual spot under the cherry tree since it was raining heavily. Alec hurried through the lunch line and got himself a tray of food before he spotted Rika and Junpei.

Tatsuya, who had been watching Alec and waiting for the right moment, managed to put his foot out to trip Alec up again as he was quickly heading over to his friends' table, but this time when Alec fell forward he ended up landing face first onto his tray of food with a messy *splat*. Alec blushed thoroughly embarrassed as he pushed himself up off the tray and began trying to clean himself off using a whole lot a paper napkins from a nearby table. A few students were snickering at his expense and then Alec sensed someone was hovering over him. He looked up, not really at all surprised, to see that it was Tatsuya, who wore an evil smirk on his face, though Alec could also see the shadows of hate and fear behind his eyes.

"Oh, here let me help you," Tatsuya sneered as he dumped his entire tray of food over Alec's head. "*Demon*." He snarled.

A gasp went through the cafeteria at the boy's words. Alec just sighed and wiped some of the *ramen* noddles from his hair. *Aw man*. He was a complete mess. He turned around planning to ignore Tatsuya and head off to the bathroom, but Tatsuya wouldn't give up since he wanted to get a rise out of Alec.

"Aren't you going to say something to defend yourself, *demon*? Aren't you going to fight back, coward? Or you won't because it's true then? I guess being a half-breed doesn't make you any stronger than us after all. Say something-" Tatsuya grabbed Alec's arm in frustration from the lack of response and spun him around.

Alec dully wondered if he was about to get punched when suddenly Junpei stood up in his chair and flung a bowl of pudding at Tatsuya, so that it hit him smack on the face. A few students now laughed at the Tatsuya's expense. Tatsuya was red faced and furious and quickly reached over to someone's tray to grab a handful of fried rice before flinging this at Junpei across the room. "Demon lover!" He accused as Junpei ducked and the handful of fried rice ended up hitting a student sitting at the table directly behind Junpei and Rika.

"FOOD FIGHT!" Someone yelled.

Chaos ensued as food went flying through the air over the cafeteria tables. It was a little bit of deja vu for Alec as he ducked under a table with Junpei and Rika ending up joining him soon after with mischievous looks on their faces. "You alright there, Alec?" Junpei asked with an amused smirk.

Alec smiled gratefully back, "Yea, thanks."

Rika smiled at Alec too, but then looked away, a conflicted expression on her face.

* * * * * * * * * * * * * * * *

After school Alec had agreed to meet with Junpei and Rika in the computer club room so that they could all play Yokai World together and get their mind off things. Mainly, how Neji was still in a coma in the hospital...

Alec was walking down the hallway, which led to the computer room when three boys suddenly grabbed onto him. Alec struggled halfheartedly wondering what they were up to this time. He immediately realized that it was Tatsuya and his friends Ken and Omi *again. Sigh. These boys really need to get a life...don't they have anything better to do than to pick on me?*

"You sure had everyone fooled didn't you, *demon*? But I always knew there was something *off* about you. I won't forgive you for lying to us. You're not welcome in this school anymore, demon. We want you to leave and if you don't we'll make your life a living hell. Here's a taste of what you'll get if you continue to stay here." Tatsuya grinned, an evil glint in his eye.

Ken and Omi shoved Alec into a half full trash can, put the lid on it tightly, and began to roll Alec down the hallway. They gave the trash can one last push before running off - not wanting to get caught. Alec rolled down the hallway and hit the far wall with a crash. He popped out of the trash can due to the impact and was all dizzy, swirly-eyed, and covered in foul smelling garbage. *Today is just not my day.*

Alec stumbled to the computer club room where Junpei and Rika were already waiting. When he entered the room Junpei looked up from his computer and gave Alec a strange look.

"Dude, what happened to you? You look like something the cat dragged in...or threw up for that matter." Junpei's lip twitched despite himself.

"Nuthing." Alec shrugged not wanting to worry Junpei.

"You have a banana peel on your head, you know." Rika informed him smartly.

"Thanks." Alec peeled it off and threw it aside.

All three friends then logged on to Yokai World and immediately teleported to the Guardian Knight guildhall. Night, No.1, and No.2 along with Yukino were there.

Yukino smiled serenely when she saw Alec, "Alec-*bozu*." She teased walking over to him and she seemed to *glide* across the floor, Alec thought. "Hey guys." Yukino also greeted Junpei and Rika.

"Hey Yukino." Alec smiled warmly back.

"Heya," Junpei winked at her.

LadyV merely nodded and was eyeing Yukino curiously as if she were an oddity.

"What's new?" Alec questioned the goth girl.

Yukino's deep blue eyes actually sparkled, "Oh it's dreadful!" Yukino began excitedly, much to Alec's chagrin. "Players are going crazy with posts on the BBS, (bulletin board system). Apparently, players are claiming that they've encountered real ghosts within the game - but not real Battle Ghosts like what happened with Tamamo-no-mae. They're claiming to encounter their dead parents, or dead brothers or sisters. Or even their long lost loves."

LadyV was suddenly looking very pale.

Alec blinked at Yukino's reaction to this strange news since she seemed a little too happy that all this weird, 'morose' stuff was going on in Yokai World. Well, that was probably normal for her, he realized. "*Real* ghosts?" Alec turned to Night, "Is that even possible?"

Night frowned darkly, "Perhaps, but that's what I want you to find out for me Alec. I have a new mission for the Guardian Knights - to investigate this new game phenomena and find out if players truly are encountering real ghosts within the game. And to discover why this is and how we can prevent this from occurring in the future. The game area that's had the most real ghost sightings is the Haunted Mansion Area. I want you all to go there and investigate right away. Maybe the tear is somewhere around there. Once we've located the tear we have to make sure it's monitored so that no more ghosts are allowed to come into the game world."

"Tear?" Alec quirked his head, looking like a curious puppy dog as he did so.

"A dimensional portal, which leads from the game world to the *real* underworld a.k.a. *Yomi*, apparently." Night explained.

Alec frowned, "A dimensional portal? Do things like that really exist?"

Night's expression was grim. "Yes, but they're not supposed to just pop up randomly. It's not a normal occurrence. That's why we call it a tear and not a portal. A tear is an imbalance in reality - an anomaly."

Alec shrugged, he wasn't too surprised real ghosts were crossing into Yokai World since it only made sense when he got to meet Tamamo-no-mae, a real *yokai* from the Makai, (a spiritual world that was inhabited by an entirely different race of supernatural beings called *yokai*), in the same manner.

Alec turned to Yukino, "Yukino, you'll come with me won't you?"

Yukino nodded somberly, "Of course, someone has to watch out for you, Alec-*bozu*."

Alec turned to his other friends next, "Junpei? LadyV?"

Junpei smirked, "Just lead the way, bud."

LadyV hesitated before nodding. Yukino narrowed her eyes at LadyV, thinking that the hacker was acting quite strangely from her normal self, which was usually all over Alec by now...

Alec raised his arm as he prepared for a group party teleport. "Haunted Mansion Area!" A large, glowing, golden pentagram formed underneath the group as they were instantly teleported to the Haunted Mansion Area.

Alec, Junpei, LadyV, and Yukino all stood looking at this spooky mansion house that was towering before them, and which was surrounded by dark, leaf-less, skeletal trees in which ravens with glowing red eyes were sitting and eyeing the group. The mansion's outer walls were all a stark, white-gray color and there were several tall, staring windows, which revealed the mansion had two floors. A pale, cloudless, gray sky was seen overhead. Everything about the immense mansion house was cold, unfriendly, and intimidating.

Alec gulped.

"That house gives me the creeps." LadyV shivered.

"Just remember it's only a game," Junpei reminded her and tried to snake his arm around LadyV's shoulders - to comfort her of course. "But I've got goose bumps too."

LadyV didn't even bat an eye as she shrugged Junpei's arm off of her. Junpei pouted in response but was pleased LadyV looked a little less worried.

"There's something about it though..." Alec reached his senses out and thought for a moment he could sense the presence of a real ghost. *Uh oh.*

"I like it." Yukino looked upon the house with a pleased expression on her tranquil face. "My kind of place. Looks homey to me."

Alec couldn't help but smile at Yukino's odd comment. *Well, even if she is a Battle Ghost it seems she's a goth girl deep inside as well.* Alec thought to himself slightly amused.

LadyV flipped her hair irritatingly over her shoulder, "Well, of course *you* would - you're a ghost. Hmph!"

Yukino just kept smiling serenely to herself, and she seemed to be immensely enjoying herself. Her amusement was beginning to rub off on Alec, who oddly enough felt like laughing as he watched her.

"Let's go inside." Alec directed them and Yukino quickly followed him up the pebbly pathway that led to the house and that was composed of tiny, white stones. He noticed that LadyV and Junpei were lagging behind and shook his head at them bemused before continuing to the entrance. He stood at the front door and noticed there was a large, golden knocker of a menacing looking *oni* head with horns in the middle of the door, but Alec decided to simply ignore it as he turned the knob to the front door and began opening the door instead.

"I wouldn't go in there if I were you." The *oni* head suddenly spoke up in a gruff voice.

Alec blinked back at the doorknocker in shock. "Oh? And why's that?"

The *oni* head raised an eyebrow at their group, "Strange things have been happening in there...and the place is haunted. You should level up a bit more boy before trying your luck in this place."

"I think we can handle it." Alec replied before swinging the door open all the way.

"Well, if you must go....beware of plates." The *oni* head warned Alec ominously.

"Plates? Thanks for the advice." Alec nodded a bit confused.

The group ignored the *oni* head's continued protests as they entered the mansion to find themselves in a large, spacious entrance hall that had a gigantic stairwell before them that led to the second floor and that was covered in a red carpet. A giant, dusty, crystal chandelier hung in the center of the entrance hall shedding a warm glow upon the floor. As soon as the door shut eerily behind them ghost mobs began to appear. Alec reached out his senses and found that they were indeed just normal game monsters. They looked like dark, shadowy shades with glowing red eyes.

"They're not real. They're just normal ghost mobs." Alec reassured his friends before he unsheathed his new *katana* and pointed it at the mobs.

Junpei got into a fighting stance following Alec's lead. LadyV summoned her *naginata* and spun her weapon in a complex pattern impressively before aiming it before her. Yukino pulled out her magical fan from within her *kimono* sleeve and raised it high above her.

"These guys are small fries." Junpei grinned.

"All too easy." LadyV agreed.

"They certainly don't stand a chance against us do they? I almost feel sorry for the cute little ghosts." Yukino pouted.

"Did you just call those ghosts...cute?" LadyV raised an eyebrow at her and shook her head as Junpei and Alec chuckled.

The group then moved in to attack the ghost mobs while coordinating their moves. Alec with his new sword slashed it through the air and easily sliced through them. Junpei with his quick kicks and punches managed to exorcize several in the blink of an eye. LadyV used her *naginata* and attacked a ghost mob piercing it through with a quick jab. Yukino waved her fan and finished off several ghost mobs with her Ice Daggers Attack, shards of ice

flying through the air to impale the ghosts and destroy them. All in all, they managed to defeat the ghosts quite easily.

They then decided to go up the main center staircase until they were on the second floor. They made their way down a narrow hallway, where there was a dusty red carpet under their feet and creepy hanging portraits were on the walls that Alec had the sneaking suspicion were watching them. The group was keeping an eye out for more mobs when LadyV suddenly felt something on her shoulder.

LadyV let out a piercing scream and the group turned around to see that a rusty suit of armor had come to life. LadyV ended up throwing her arms around Junpei in fright while Alec raised his sword and attacked the suit of armor. Alec noticed a pair of yellow eyes glowing at him from inside the helmet. Alec stabbed the front chest of the armor, so that a ghost rose out of the armor escaping in fear - the armor had been possessed. Alec slashed his sword through the air and made quick work of the evil spirit. He turned around and blinked in surprise as he saw LadyV hugging Junpei tightly. Yukino also seemed surprised by this as her mouth dropped open slightly. Alec coughed politely to get their attention.

LadyV jumped away from Junpei as soon as she realized what she was doing while Junpei had a smug expression on his face. Alec decided to simply ignore all this and continued on his way down the hall with Yukino at his side. Alec opened the door at the end of the hall and they entered into a large dinning room. There was a long table in the center of the room covered with an assortment of food. The table itself was covered with a white tablecloth and plates were piled high with meats, fruits, and delicious looking desserts. Alec even caught sight of a roasted pig with an apple in its mouth. Alec drooled and wished he could eat data. There was a crystal chandelier hanging in the center of the room just above the dinning table and which was sending a warm glow upon the room.

"That food looks so good..." Alec pouted and his stomach suddenly growled loudly. He blushed in embarrassment.

"I feel your pain, man." Junpei's stomach was also rumbling to join in with Alec's.

"Boys." LadyV shook her head, "Is all you think about, food?"

"Well, I think about food, soccer, and girls." Junpei shrugged. "And that's about it."

LadyV sighed and put her face in her hand.

Alec suddenly sniffed the air and realized he could actually *smell* the food. Now, that was weird. Alec blinked. "Hey, Junpei I can smell the food. Does that mean it's real somehow?"

"Only one way to find out." Junpei tucked a napkin into the neckline of his *haori* before picking up a fork and knife. The two boys were about to dig in when -

"I wonder if it's poisoned." Yukino wondered thoughtfully, "Alec why don't you try and eat something and see what happens."

Alec gulped, his hunger quickly receding. "Pass. I don't feel like getting a virus or something anytime soon."

"How boring." Yukino pouted.

LadyV eyed the food curiously, "That's obviously some kind of spiritual trap. You *bakas*." She scolded them and Alec and Junpei had the decency to look sheepish.

The door closed and locked behind them suddenly and they had no choice but to cross the floor and try and make their way to the other side of the dinning room where another door was waiting for them. However, as they started forward the plates, glasses, silverware, and chairs all started to rattle. Some of the plates were rattling so badly that they ended up falling off the table and shattering as they hit the floor. The chandelier overhead began to flicker and swing slightly throwing odd shadows onto the dinning room table ominously and Alec noted it was just like a poltergeist's influence. But when Alec reached out his senses he didn't sense anything real, so realized this was all still just part of the game.

"A poltergeist?" Junpei questioned Alec, who shook his head.

"Not a real one anyways." Alec informed him.

"Thank god," LadyV let out a breath, "That would *so* not be fun. Game mobs I can handle but real ghosts..." LadyV shivered thinking of the *noppera-bo*.

"Oh, I have to disagree. I think it would be fun to meet a real poltergeist since I never have before. I wonder what they're like." Yukino's eyes twinkled.

"Just take a look in a mirror, *ghost* girl." LadyV scowled at her.

"Ghosts don't have reflections, you know." Yukino informed her plainly.

LadyV's eyebrow twitched, "It was an *expression*. Oh never mind." She sighed in an exasperated manner.

Just then the plates began to hover off the table and went speeding towards Alec and the others.

"Ack!" LadyV dived out of the way.

Yukino calmly waved her fan at a couple of the plates and her ice daggers shattered through them. "Now, *this* is fun."

Alec dove under the dining table to hide and found that Junpei was already there as well. They looked at each other and blinked. "Hey, I thought *you* were protecting the ladies." Junpei frowned thoughtfully.

335

"Well, I thought *you* were going to do that, Romeo. I've had enough plates thrown at me for one day." Alec sighed heavily, thinking back to the cafeteria food fight.

"We better get back up there," Junpei realized.

"Yea...suppose so..." Alec agreed reluctantly, thinking of the possessed door knocker's warning.

Alec and Junpei crawled out from under the table to see LadyV getting chased by flying plates and Yukino breaking plates left and right as she did her fan dance. Alec raised an eyebrow at LadyV. "Just use your *naginata* against them V!"

"Easy for you to say. They're *creepy!*" LadyV looked behind her, hesitating on whether or not to face the possessed plates and then decided to keep on running away instead. "Those plates have beady little eyes! And they remind me of that ghost story..."

"Oh, I know the one." Junpei was saying as he punched through a plate, *"Bancho Sarayashiki*, The Dish Mansion at Bansho, it's about this beautiful servant girl named Okiku, who worked for a *samurai* named Aoyama Tessen and how he wanted to marry her. When she refused him, however, out of anger he decided to blackmail her, and so broke one of the family's precious delft plates of which there were ten. He told Okiku he would lie for her to keep her out of trouble as long as she would only agree to marry him since everyone thought *she* broke the plate. However, she once again refused his proposal and driven mad with grief and anger he ended up throwing her down a well. Her spirit could not rest because of the wrong done to her and she ended up haunting the well. Nightly, she would call out numbers counting from one to nine. But when she would reach the number ten she would let loose a bloodcurdling scream, which represented the plate that she had not broken but was killed for."

LadyV shivered, "That's the one!"

Alec gulped. "Plates..."

At that moment, the center of the tablecloth began to rise up from the dinning table until it formed the shape of a woman with long hair. The she-ghost began to moan in a pitiful way and approached Alec and the others as she floated off the table and still hovering above the floor came towards them. *"One..two...three..."*

"Epp! It's Okiku!" LadyV declared scrambling backwards away from the ghost.

"You're right," Junpei paled at the sight.

"She's just a game mob!" Alec insisted as he reached out his senses and felt nothing. "Ryuu!" Alec decided to summon Ryuu to help him defeat this ghost mob since LadyV and Junpei seemed to have scared themselves stiff with

336

the telling of the ghost story. Ryuu materialized next to Alec and immediately attacked the ghost lady with his trident. Alec followed suit and charged the ghost lady slashing his *katana* through the air.

Yukino looked at the ghost of Okiku curiously, "But that's not the real Okiku, you know I've met *her*."

Alec blinked back at her in shock, "You mean to tell me you've met the *real* Okiku, Yukino?"

"Oh yes, we had a very pleasant chat just the other day. She didn't seem too happy though. And she was going on and on about how *samurai* are the worst. And something about plates but I didn't really get what she was talking about." Yukino was babbling on unconcernedly. "She told me how RedAki had tried to capture her since he needs a new Battle Ghost for the upcoming tournament."

"RedAki?" Alec started as he slashed his sword at the ghost of Okiku only to have her block his attack with a fork. She was more powerful than she appeared apparently. Alec dodged another plate that had been flung at him while Okiku had yelled - 'Nine!' "What tournament?" Alec asked.

"Oh, didn't you know? There's going to be a tournament in the game in a few days to determine who the Ultimate Ghost Master of Yokai World is. We'll be entering of course, won't we Alec?" Yukino smiled back at him.

Alec smiled a lopsided grin back at her, "Um, yea, sure, I guess so." He returned his attention back to the ghost of Okiku.

"You know in the story all you have to do to get rid of her is say 'ten'." Yukino informed Alec thoughtfully.

"I really don't think that saying ten is going to do anything." Alec shot back when suddenly Okiku let out a bloodcurdling scream and disappeared with a *pop*. Alec lowered his sword, "Well, that was a bit anticlimactic."

A treasure chest suddenly appeared before the group and Alec opened it with a wave of his hand to find that inside was a giant plate. "The tenth plate...I bet RedAki could get a lot of money for this rare item." Alec put the plate into his inventory for safe keeping and looked around to see where Junpei and LadyV had gone. He bent down and peered under the table to see that the two of them were hiding under there together. Alec cleared his throat. "BOO!"

"AHHH!" Both LadyV and Junpei hugged each other in fright and Alec laughed at their behavior.

"You'd make a fine ghost, Alec." Yukino winked at him and he blushed.

After LadyV and Junpei had gotten out from under the table the group headed over to the door at the end of the dinning room. Alec flung the door open -

And Rika gasped.

Alec looked inside and saw a stunning ballroom with a black and white checkered, marble floor. But that wasn't all. Ghostly couples of NPCs were doing the waltz around the room as a band of skeletons in top hats and bow ties played music for them on a stage towards the back of the room. The ghostly couples were human in appearance but were slightly transparent. Some of the women were dressed in either sparkling ball gowns or ornate *kimono*, but most of the men were in slick suits. They were all wearing ornate feathered, beaded, or sequined masks on their faces. It was a phantasmagoric masquerade.

Alec raised an eyebrow at the sight of a bunch of ghosts dancing a waltz and looked over to see what Yukino thought about all this and saw that her eyes were sparkling with delight. This made Alec's eyebrow raise a little higher - he wouldn't have thought Yukino was the type to like girlie things like dances.

Alec smirked as a sudden idea popped into his head. "You want to dance don't you, Yukino?" Alec's voice held a tinge of amusement.

Yukino blushed and Alec thought she looked a lot cuter that way, "Dance? Me? Whatever gave you that idea? I don't want to dance. Hmph! Dances are totally girlie and stupid and..." Yukino trailed off wistfully as she watched the ghosts dancing elegantly in circles across the dance floor and sighed. "Oh what the hell. Come on, let's go!" Yukino grabbed Alec's wrist and ended up dragging him to the dance floor.

Alec blushed at the sudden feeling of Yukino's hand on his wrist and then gulped nervously as he was forced to put his hands in the right positions so that they could waltz together - one hand around her waist and the other holding her hand.

LadyV was gawking in disbelief at the two of them as they began to dance together to the haunting melody that was playing. Junpei sauntered up and stood casually next to LadyV in a nonchalant manner. "They make a nice couple, don't they?" He turned to LadyV and bowed before offering his hand out to her with a flourish, waggling his eyebrows at her. "Would Milady care for a dance?"

LadyV tossed her hair at him, "Hmph, dance? With you? I think not..." She returned her attention back to Alec and Yukino's dancing.

Junpei pouted, "Oh come on Rika, pu-lease? When you look like LadyV I can't help myself from being a bit enamored with you." He admitted in a low voice, almost hesitantly.

LadyV blushed unexpectedly in response, "Well..." She saw Alec blushing in Yukino's arms and frowned suddenly. "Oh, alright, but just one dance." LadyV conceded.

"*Yatta!* Yes!" Junpei punched the air and dragged LadyV off to the dance floor.

As Alec danced with Yukino he couldn't help but think she was pretty and elegant...for a goth girl, Battle Ghost. Alec noticed Rika and Junpei dancing together with an odd pang in his chest.

Yukino noticed this as well, "What's up with LadyV today? Usually she's all over you by now. I'm surprised she didn't drag you to the dance floor while peppering you with kisses. If I didn't know better I'd say she was avoiding you." She quirked her head curiously at Alec wondering if he was hiding something from her.

Alec nodded. "She has been distant...ever since she found out back in reality..." Alec gulped wondering how Yukino would react to the news. *Aw, what the hell.* Alec decided. He was used to be friendless anyways. "That I'm half *yokai.*"

Yukino raised an eyebrow. "You're a *hanyou?*" She looked at Alec thoughtfully. "But that's no real reason for her to start acting differently. You're still you after all." Yukino smiled openly at him. The first real truly open smile she'd ever given Alec before.

Alec's eyes widened startled at her comment, which sounded so matter-of-fact. And at her smile his heart seemed to suddenly kathump in his chest. Alec couldn't meet her gaze as he asked the following question. "But aren't you...afraid of me? What if I turn into an evil demon and try and eat you or something?" Alec said in a rush.

To Alec's surprise Yukino chuckled lightly. "Eat me? Alec...you're my friend. I trust and I believe in you. You accepted me for what I am - a ghost. You didn't run away or scream in fear or turn away in disgust when you saw me, but accepted me and became my friend. So, it's only natural that I do the same for you. And true friends stick by each other no matter what *neh?* If LadyV is really your friend she won't care either."

Alec let out a breath of relief, pleased that at least Yukino had accepted him for what he was even if she did still treat him like her little brother or something most of the time. He smiled fondly as he thought this last part. Maybe it wasn't so bad having an older sister.

Just then, Alec suddenly sensed a ghostly presence. He turned his head, eyes searching to figure out which ghostly couple was real and then spotted them. With his *Shinigami* eyes he could see the glowing, blue aura that they possessed whereas the fake NPCs just felt empty and had no spirit aura. The woman, who was dancing, was beautiful with long black hair and she was wearing a dark green *kimono* with a golden *obi* tied about her waist. The man dancing with her was also handsome but Alec couldn't fail to notice the giant, bloody, claw marks that were on the front of his suit. Now, that he observed them a little closer, he saw that both of them were covered in blood stains, but with their bodies transparent it made it hard for Alec to see the blood on them at first. Alec frowned since they had obviously met a violent end.

"Hey, guys a real ghost couple! Over there! Look!" Alec pointed at the couple.

Yukino, and Junpei turned to see which couple Alec was pointing to. LadyV then turned and her eyes widened as she caught sight of the couple, and she gasped in response raising a hand to her mouth. "Mother...Father...?"

Junpei gave LadyV a sharp look, "Your parents? Are they...?" *Dead.* Junpei couldn't bring himself to say the last word.

LadyV nodded numbly and let go of Junpei to rush across the dance floor towards her parents. "*Oka-san! To-sama!* Mother! Father! "

The ghostly couple stopped dancing and turned to face LadyV curiously.

"It's me Rika!" LadyV explained since she was currently inside of her LadyV, PC body.

Rika's mother and father peered at her curiously for a moment before they seemed to recognize her or perhaps they sensed her own spiritual presence. Her mother's eyes were the first to widen. "Rika? Is that really you? *Anata,* dear, it's Rika!"

Her father stared at her a moment longer before nodding gruffly, "My little girl, Rika." He acknowledged her but then he looked over her skimpy, low-cut *kimono* outfit and coughed, "Muffin-head? Must you wear such revealing clothing?"

But LadyV just smiled teary-eyed at them and flung her arms around them both. "Mother! Father! What are you both doing here?"

Rika's mother stroked her head, "We thought we might get to meet you here Rika. The other ghosts were saying such things back in Yomi."

LadyV pulled back to look at her parents curiously, "But why?"

"Rika dear, you need to stop blaming yourself for our deaths. It's time that you learned the truth of what happened that night. That rainy night when me and your father were on our way back from that party, and we had called home to let you know we were on our way. That night you had told us to hurry home-"

LadyV paled at her mother's words remembering how she had sent her parents to their deaths. If only she hadn't said anything. If only she hadn't made them speed through rush hour traffic in the rain then maybe her parents would still be alive and with her now.

"We didn't get into a car accident because of you Rika." Her mother finished, shaking her head.

LadyV furrowed her brow in confusion at her mother's words. "What do you mean?"

"Rika, our deaths were no accident. We were attacked that night by *yokai*." Her father revealed.

LadyV looked startled. "*Yokai*? But why?"

"They sensed my spiritual power and wanted to eat my spirit." Rika's mother began to explain. "Your father tried to protect me...and died that night because of it. He ended up swerving off a bridge when the *yokai* attacked us but luckily we crossed over before they could eat our souls. I sense you've inherited my spiritual power Rika." Rika's mother looked worried. "You must be very careful around *yokai*, Rika. They're not to be trusted."

LadyV nodded, "I understand." She sniffled as tears threatened to spill down her cheeks.

Rika's parents exchanged a look. "We have to return to Yomi now. We don't have much power to remain in this plane. We merely wanted you to know the truth Rika. We're so happy we got to tell you everything." Her mother informed her, ending with a warm smile.

"We're very proud of you Rika. We heard you're a *Shinigami*-in-training now." Her father told her, a pleased glint in his eye.

Rika nodded, too moved and choked up with emotions to say anything.

"*Anata*...we must hurry." Her mother told her father, placing a hand on his arm. He turned and nodded at her.

"Bye Muffin-head." Her father told Rika.

"Bye sweetie." The couple turned to go and floated away across the dance floor. "Oh and Rika." Rika's mother turned back around to face her. "Rika honey, you're not alone. You have wonderful friends. Remember that." She looked at Junpei, Yukino, and Alec especially, her gaze lingering on him for a moment longer than the others before she smiled warmly at them all.

They then continued to float away and LadyV's legs seemed to give out beneath her and she sunk to her knees in shock. Junpei rushed to her side and comforted her while she began to cry into her hands. Alec and Yukino rushed up to them.

"Junpei, look after LadyV will ya? Yukino, let's go follow Rika's parents. They'll lead us to where the tear is!" Alec declared.

Yukino nodded, "Right. Good idea Alec."

Alec and Yukino rushed after Mr. and Mrs. Nakamura as they floated away leaving their daughter behind. The ghost couple floated to an outdoor balcony and Alec and Yukino followed them outside onto it. Alec watched as they floated down from the balcony and entered a garden that was behind the mansion. It was dark out and so Alec couldn't see the garden very well but saw several bushes of twisted and thorned vines. Upon closer inspection Alec saw that they were rose bushes but that someone had cut off all the heads of the roses for some reason.

Alec and Yukino hopped down from the balcony, holding hands, and continued to give chase through the one-time rose garden. They followed the ghosts deeper and deeper into the garden until they came to a clearing where there was a rather large, stone well. The well had a strange marking on the ground around it that was glowing with a fierce red light and that looked like a jagged claw mark that had slashed the earth there.

Alec and Yukino watched as Rika's parents floated down into the well and disappeared. Alec skidded to a halt in front of the well and gulped. He risked peering over the edge of the well and saw nothing but darkness below. He quickly stepped back shaking his head frantically. "Uh uh, no way - there's absolutely *no way* I'm going down there! I've read about how these types of horror stories end!"

Yukino grabbed Alec's wrist and pulled him towards the well excitedly, "Come on Alec! What are you waiting for? This should be fun."

"Your idea of fun gives me the heebie jeebies." Alec insisted as Yukino continued to drag him forward, his feet making ridges in the dirt as he tried to stay put.

Yukino turned to smile at him, "Don't worry. I'm with you. I won't let anything happen to my cute, little brother." She ruffled his shaggy hair playfully and Alec blushed and swatted her hand away.

"*Mou!* I'm not your little brother." He insisted with a puppy-dog pout.

"But if something does happen to you we'll haunt the world together forever *neh*? So look at the *bright* side of things. Now let's go!" Yukino pulled Alec up with her onto the ledge of the well as she jumped up. And then before Alec could stop her they jumped down into the well together.

"But I don't want to be a ghost!" Alec cried as they fell down the well. A bright light seemed to surround them as they fell and then all of a sudden they hit the bottom with a thud. Alec groaned and rubbed his backside as he stood up. Yukino had landed perfectly on her feet, and Alec puffed his cheeks out indignantly at that. Alec moved forward but nearly tripped over something. He looked down and paled - human bones and skulls littered the bottom of the well. *Gulp.*

"Um, Yukino..." Alec began nervously.

Yukino however seemed completely calm and right at home at the bottom of the spooky well surrounded by skulls. "Hmm." She looked thoughtful as she inspected the interior of the well and seemed to remember something. "Oh yes, now I remember why this place seems so familiar. This is where I met Okiku." She picked up a skull and quirked her head at it in an interested manner.

Alec turned white as a sheet. "You don't mean the real Okiku do you?"

Yukino nodded airily as she tossed the skull carelessly aside, "What else would I mean, silly."

Alec began to laugh nervously at that as he peered around through the semi-darkness. Suddenly, there was a bright flash of light and a ghostly being began to materialize in front of Alec and Yukino. Alec gulped as he took in the appearance of the ghost before him. She appeared to have the head and torso of a woman but the lower half of her body was that of a snake. *Epp!* Alec hated snakes. She had long, scraggily, wild black hair and from her dark eyes she seemed to be crying tears of blood. Her long snake tail was made up of shiny, green and black scales.

Alec reached out his senses and immediately wished he hadn't since the being before him was in fact a *real* vengeful ghost! *This is so not good.*

Okiku looked over at Yukino unconcerned, but when she turned her attention towards Alec her eyes seemed to narrow at him dangerously as she took in his *Shinigami* outfit along with his *katana*. Both his clothes and his sword resembled what a *samurai* of Japan's Feudal Era would normally wear. A flash of anger crossed her face. "Samuuuraiii!" She wailed.

She sent her tail forward so that it wrapped itself around Alec before he could so much as raise a finger against her. Her tail then began to coil tightly around him. "Samuraiiiii....*Shineee*....Diieeeee...!" She hissed.

Alec was looking a bit blue in the face as Okiku continued to let her tail constrict around poor Alec's torso. "Yukino...little help here..." Alec gasped painfully.

Yukino frowned at Okiku but didn't appear too concerned.

She's definitely not worried enough! Thought Alec frantically. *Doesn't she get it that I'm about to suffocate to death here!*

"Okiku, you're being very rude. Alec's my friend." Yukino tried to calmly explain.

But Okiku ignored Yukino and turned her hateful eyes towards Alec, which seemed to burn a hole straight through him. "One...? Two...? Three....?" Her voice began, each number like a question, demanding the truth from Alec. "*Ichi?...Ni?...San?*"

Alec was choking as Okiku tightened her hold on him even more. "Yukino! Do something! *Please!*"

Yukino pouted, "Oh very well, you leave me with no choice Okiku." She summoned her fan and waved it at Okiku so that a barrage of icy daggers flew at her.

But the ice daggers hit an invisible force field that surrounded Okiku and appeared to melt on contact.

Yukino furrowed her brow in confusion and then she seemed to remember something. "Uh oh, I forgot how powerful she is. No wonder RedAki wanted to capture her..."

"Six...Seven...Eight...Nine...?" Okiku continued and with each number her hold on Alec became tighter and tighter. He knew that when she reached ten he would suffocate and that all the bones in his body would be broken if he didn't do something to stop her. "*Roku...Hana...Hachi...Kyuu...*"

Yukino had finally become worried. "Alec! Okiku let him go!"

Alec thought that Yukino must have heard the sound of one of his ribs cracking. Alec grasped the part of Okiku's tail, which was around his neck and tried to pull it away from his throat so he could speak. "TEN!" Alec managed to choke out suddenly, "I know...you didn't steal the last plate Okiku!" Alec gasped.

Okiku, who had been about to let out a bloodcurdling shriek, closed her mouth with a snap and peered down at Alec curiously before suddenly releasing him so that he fell down to the bottom of the well and out of her grasp.

Alec pushed himself up off the well's floor and having a sudden idea decided to summon the tenth plate from his inventory to hold out to Okiku. He was still gasping for breath as he did so. "Here...it's the tenth plate. Everyone knows you didn't break it Okiku. There are even folktales about you now, you know. You should...rest in peace."

Okiku gasped in surprise at this gesture and took the plate slowly from Alec with trembling fingers. Suddenly, her body seemed to shift and change until standing in front of Alec was no longer the half-snake half-human woman, who had been transformed into a *yokai* by her hatred and regret. Now standing in front of Alec was a beautiful ghost woman with long, wavy hair, who was wearing a pale pink and white *kimono* with a dark pink *obi* tied around her waist. Her porcelain-like face and clear brown eyes were suddenly warm and kind, and her lips rose pink. But Alec noticed she was still crying tears of blood...

Alec stepped forward and hesitantly reached out his hand to brush away one of the blood tears with his thumb. "No need to cry...I believe you." Alec kindly told her with deep sincerity in his voice.

Okiku's expression softened and she actually smiled back at Alec warmly. She started in a low musical voice, "Thank you, you kind *samurai* boy."

Okiku then burst into a ball of light that flew up into the air and zoomed out of the well to disappear deep into Yomi World as she crossed over.

Yukino gave Alec a surprised look, "That was a nice thing you did for her, Alec."

Alec smiled back goofily, "I hope to be able to do the same thing for you someday remember?"

Yukino blinked back at him in surprise and a slight blush rose to her cheeks, "I had forgotten. Anyways, put your arms around my neck. We're getting out of here."

"*Hai?*" Alec hesitated before going over to Yukino and doing as he was told while feeling oddly embarrassed at the close contact he was suddenly having with the goth ghost. What was wrong with him lately? It was just Yukino after all. Yukino summoned an icy wind with her fan and it lifted them up, spinning, and out of the well to then plop down on the forest floor outside.

Alec immediately let go of Yukino and took a step back before he then looked around the dark forest where they had ended up. It looked like any other normal forest except perhaps a tad more...lifeless. "So this is Yomi? The underworld?" Alec shivered at the thought.

"Well, only one way to find out. Let's go explore." Yukino's eyes sparkled at the thought of having an adventure in the land of the dead.

Alec shook his head at her and followed close behind as she started off without him.

Alec and Yukino continued their way through the dense forest. Alec heard a rustling in the trees around them and looked up to see shadowy figures concealed in the branches but that appeared to be bird-like. Alec squinted through the dark foliage but could only make out that the creatures were large, almost the size of a small human and had wings. The hairs on the back of Alec's neck were prickling in warning and he rubbed the back of his neck agitated. Alec reached out his senses and felt that the creatures hiding within the trees were real. A chill went down Alec's spine. *Gulp.*

After that Alec walked a bit closer to Yukino.

Yukino raised an eyebrow at his odd behavior. "Want me to hold your hand, Alec-*bozu?*"

Alec just frowned at her and silently shook his head.

On a few lower branches Alec and Yukino spotted some crows that seemed to be watching them curiously with their beady, red eyes. Upon closer inspection Alec saw that the crows weren't like normal crows at all but had three eyes and once again he was sensing a very real presence from them. "Oh they're so cute." Yukino cooed when she caught sight of them.

Alec nearly fell over in shock. "One of these days you're going to be the end of me, Yukino." He shook his head in disbelief.

There was more rustling in the trees and this time when Alec looked up he saw a pair of golden eyes peering at him and then the creatures that had been hiding emerged from the surrounding trees and flew down at them. *Epp!* They were definitely some kind of *yokai* Alec realized. They were about the size of a small human - 4 to 5 feet tall. They were human-like but also bird-like. The *yokai* were wearing the robes of a Buddhist monk and the female ones appeared to be wearing *kimono*. They had pale, almost bluish skin, pointed elvish ears, most of them had dark blue hair, golden eyes, and when Alec looked down at their hands he noticed they had extremely sharp, raptor-like claws. Alec could see that they all had two black feathery wings coming out of their backs. But Alec knew these beings were far from being angels. He could sense their malevolence.

"*Karasu-tengu.*" Yukino breathed besides him as she recognized the *yokai*.

"*Karasu-tengu?*" Alec questioned.

Yukino nodded, "They're a type of crow demon."

Alec quickly unsheathed his *katana* and Yukino took out her fan. Alec didn't have a choice but to defend himself and he slashed his sword through the air as one *karasu-tengu* was almost upon him. However, he watched in surprise as his sword simply passed straight through her. Alec was forced to leap back out of the way as the *karasu-tengu's* clawed hand came down hard upon the ground instead, dirt and rock flying up into the air where Alec had been only seconds before. *Gulp.*

"What a beautiful boy. How delicious you look...do let us eat you..." The *karasu-tengu* crooned as she walked towards him.

"I'm skin and bones really. I doubt I'd taste all that good." Alec waved his hands frantically before him and backed up several steps.

"Ah, but what we want most is you tasty spirit. Come to us, boyo, and let us eat you!" The *karasu-tengu* crooned beckoning him with their clawed hands.

"I think I'm going to have to pass on that one." Alec raised his hand so that his control ring glowed, "Ryuu! Come forth!"

Ryuu, however, would not materialize. Alec blinked down at his control ring in confusion. "Ryuu! Ryuu!" He tried again and again to summon his Battle Ghost but to no avail. He looked back at the approaching *karasu-tengu* and did the only thing he could think of doing at a time like that -

RUN!

Meanwhile, Yukino danced and waved her fan elegantly through the air so that her ice daggers shot out at the *karasu-tengu* that were fighting her and as soon as the daggers hit them they were exorcized and defeated. She then turned to see Alec being chased by a group of blue-haired female *karasu-tengu*. She shook her head at him, he was such a playboy.

"AHHHH! Yukino help meeee!" Alec yelled.

Yukino raised an eyebrow at this but quickly came to Alec's aid, "Hey birdbrains! Over here! Stay away from Alec-*bozu*!" She waved her fan and several *karasu-tengu* were hit with Yukino's ice daggers which were glowing with a blue light.

"Yukino, my sword's not working." Alec pouted. "And Ryuu won't come out."

Yukino sighed in an exasperated manner, "Your sword doesn't exist in this plane of reality - you have to use your spirit energy and empower your sword for it to be able to do any damage here. Also, this isn't the game world anymore so data like Ryuu simply can't exist here. Our bodies aren't really here either, right now just our minds and souls exist in this place. However, we can still suffer spiritual damage just not physical damage understand?"

Alec blinked. "Oh, yea, right, I knew that." Alec summoned his spirit energy and his *katana* glowed with a blue light as he then turned to attack the *karasu-tengu* again and this time as his sword slashed through the air it actually wounded the *karasu-tengu* so that they cried out in pain as they were purified and destroyed.

Between the two of them Alec and Yukino managed to defeat the rest of the *karasu-tengu* with no further problems though Alec had to admit they were some of the most powerful *yokai* he had ever had to face. He knew he would have been hard pressed to face those creatures without Yukino by his side. Alec and Yukino continued their way through the forest when they suddenly came out onto a barren clearing of dry, cracked earth and where up ahead Alec saw a giant cave close to the bottom of a mountain. From one side of the cave's mouth to the other a thick rope had been hung and Alec could see there were *o-fuda* hanging down from the rope as well, which meant something must be sealed within the cave.

Alec took a step forward towards the cave and was immediately overwhelmed by the sheer amount of dark spirit energy he felt. The energy seemed to be all around him and it caused Alec, who felt as though he were being crushed by the energy itself, to sink to his knees. Yukino turned to look at Alec worriedly.

"Alec? What's wrong?" She frowned down at him.

"That cave..." Alec gasped, "I sense that a malevolent presence is within there. I've never felt an evil presence so powerful before in all my life."

Yukino turned to look towards the cave curiously, and noted that it seemed oddly familiar to her. She took a step forward and then unexpectedly a flood of memories seemed to assault her all of a sudden. Yukino cried out in pain and gripped her head as the onslaught of memories came upon her.

"Yukino!" Alec stumbled to her side in concern and put a hand on her shoulder just as Yukino was remembering...and then Alec realized that his head was being flooded by the images and memories too...

Alec ended up seeing memories of Night and Yukino playing Yokai World together. They both looked a little different from how they now looked however. Yukino had the same colored eyes for one thing and her PC type seemed to be that of a Mage and not a Battle Ghost nor was it transparent. Together, brother and sister, battled against different mobs in the game while smiling at each other and appeared to be having a lot of fun. The memories then began to slow down to show one memory in particular...

Alec recognized the setting as the guildhall of the Guardian Knights. He saw Night speaking with Yukino in harsh tones...

FLASHBACK

"Yukino, where are you going?" Night demanded placing a hand on Yukino's shoulder which she shrugged off coldly.

"That's none of your business, *Onii-san*." Yukino scowled.

"You're going to see *him* again aren't you." Night sounded both disgusted and disappointed.

"So what if I am." Yukino tossed her long, raven-black hair over her shoulder, and turned to glare at her brother challengingly.

"Yukino, I forbid you to see Kaguto again." Night glared back at her. "He's dangerous. He's only trying to take advantage of you...trying to trick you. He doesn't really care about you - you must realize that. I mean, you're only 12 years old. Kaguto on the other hand is already a teenager. He doesn't have time to play children's games with you. He's up to something. I know he is, and I intend to find out what that is. Why else would he be hanging around you?"

Yukino turned red with anger and clenched her fists at her side. "You don't know anything about us. Kaguto is my friend. He understands me. He likes me. Not even you, brother, can truly understand the darkness that lies in my heart. Not like Kaguto does. No one understands me. No one but him!" Yukino rushed away from Night and raised her hand into the air. "Teleport!"

"Wait! Yukino!" Night rushed to where she had teleported but it was too late as his hands grasped air. "*Yukino...*"

· ● ● ● ● ● ● ● ● ● ● ● ● ● ● ●

Alec saw that Yukino had teleported to the Haunted Mansion Area. She took off towards the garden that was behind the mansion and strolled through it. It was dark in the garden since the clouds were thick in the artificial night sky that hung overhead blocking out the moon, and so the colors of the flowers and plants could not easily be seen. Yukino continued on until she reached a slight clearing in the garden where in the center stood a sparkling fountain that was spraying curves of water. And there standing next to the fountain was a cloaked and hooded figure.

Yukino ran towards this person without fear. "Kaguto!"

Kaguto slowly spun around, his cloak swirling in the air and revealing a deep red lining. He then lowered his hood to reveal a handsome face with golden eyes, and long, blood-red hair, which was tied back into a pony-tail so that loose strands framed his face on either side. His face was ghostly pale, his eyes were heavily lined in black, and he also wore black lipstick. His outfit was that of a *Shinigami* - a black *haori* shirt along with black *hakama* pants. Yukino noticed that Kaguto was wearing a necklace she had never seen him have on before. It had a thick silver chain from which hung a silver pentagram, which had a sparkling blue sapphire imbedded in the center of the star.

Kaguto grinned as she approached, "Yukino-*chan*, here for you." He strode forward and tucked a rose behind her ear. Yukino blushed at the gesture. "A unique bloom for a unique girl such as yourself. It suits you perfectly, Yukino."

"Kaguto...what is this place?" Yukino began to inspect the garden, "I've never gone this deeply into the garden before."

Kaguto smiled as he waved a hand at their surroundings, "A rose garden. I know how much you love flowers and so when I found this place I just knew I had to show it to you."

The clouds overhead suddenly crossed over the moon so the moon's rays were able to shed light upon the darkened garden. Yukino gasped as the color of the roses surrounding her were revealed. They were all a stunning, midnight blue and their leaves and thorns were pitch black.

"It's beautiful." Yukino gasped.

Kaguto looked down at her with a fond expression on his face. "Indeed." He walked forward and cupped Yukino's cheek. "You are like a little rose bud - one day, when you grow up, you will blossom into a beautiful rose, Yukino."

"Oh Kaguto, do you really think so?" Her blue eyes shimmered with emotion.

Kaguto nodded seriously, "I know so. You will grow up to be even more powerful and beautiful than you are now. And then when you're old enough we could get married." Kaguto suggested casually.

"Really Kaguto?" Yukino's eyes widened. "I can't wait to grow up." She breathed, a wistful expression on her face.

"Really." He murmured and ruffled her hair so that the pentagram dangled down before her eyes and captured her attention.

"What a lovely necklace." Yukino's eyes seemed to be glued to the necklace.

Kaguto spoke in a nonchalant manner. "You like it? Then it's yours." Kaguto moved to take it off of himself.

"Oh no!" Yukino waved her hands before her, "I couldn't. Not when it looks so good on you."

Kaguto smirked to himself as he took off the necklace and then he moved slyly behind Yukino to put the necklace on her, clasping it from behind.

"It's nothing special, just a rare game trinket, after all." A control ring with a deep blue stone on Kaguto's hand glowed with a faint light as he moved away from Yukino. "Consider it an early birthday present." He tucked a stray strand of red hair behind his ear and gave her a rather dashing smile that managed to take her breath away.

Yukino looked down at the pentagram pendant and fingered it thoughtfully. "Thank you." She whispered, too stunned to say more.

"You look cute." Kaguto ruffled her hair affectionately.

"Kaguto! *Mou!* Geez!" Yukino batted his hand away, "Stop treating me like a child."

"But you are a child." Kaguto chuckled and shook his head ruefully. He then reached his hand out for her to take. "Come, there is another place I wanted to show you. I think you'll like it."

Yukino hesitated before placing her hand in Kaguto's. He then led her through the rose garden until they reached the stone well. Kaguto helped her to climb onto the ledge with him and then together they jumped down into the well. Once they had traveled through the tear and were then in Yomi but still at the bottom of the well Kaguto helped Yukino to climb out of it. Then Kaguto led her through the forest of Yomi by the hand until they came to the clearing where the entrance to the cave was visible.

"We're here..." Kaguto announced, a mysterious glint in his eye.

Yukino looked towards the cave and gasped. "But that's...the spiritual power coming from that place is *real*, Kaguto. Just where are we, anyways? We're not inside the game anymore are we? How did we get here? Just what is this place?" There was a note of panic in Yukino's voice.

"We're inside of Yomi..." Kaguto began conversationally, "And that cave before us is the home of my mother...Izanami."

"Izanami?" Yukino's brows rose at the mention of the Japanese creator-goddess turned goddess of the dead, "Your mother? What are you talking about? That's...impossible. You're being ridiculous. This is all a joke right Kaguto? Ha ha. Very funny. Let's go back now alright?"

"I am the reincarnation of her son Kagu-Tsuchi. When I stumbled across this place in the game she reminded me of who I truly am. She also asked me for my help. You see, I have no way to set her free. But you do, Yukino-*chan*. You possess the ability to break the seal on this cave, which is trapping my mother inside. You who are a medium and seal-breaker of the Izanagi Clan. Oh Yukino, won't you please help me free my mother?" He reached out his arms beseechingly to her.

Yukino took a step back. "Night was right about you...all this time...you were just trying to trick me. I can't believe this - I thought we were friends but you want to use me to break the seal on the cave and unleash Izanami! Do you even have any idea what that would mean? Yomi must have become linked to the game somehow, and if she's able to use the game to enter reality... she'd destroy everything! She's the goddess of the underworld for *kami-sama*'s sake! She'd turn the world into hell. Burn everything to ashes! It would be the destruction of our world."

Kaguto broke out into a psychotic grin, "I know." He said in such a casual manner that Yukino gasped. "That's exactly what I wish for. Revenge. Revenge on this world that rejected me because I'm different. Justice, upon a world that gave me a mother that even tried to kill me! This world Yukino is flawed. It needs to be destroyed and then redone! And it would be I who set things right."

"Your mother really...?" Yukino trailed off in shock.

Kaguto nodded grimly, "She always suspected there was something wrong with me. Strange things always seemed to occur around me, you see. Things like accidents, or things would randomly blow up or set on fire when I was around. This led her to believe that I was possessed and she took me to several shrines to get 'exorcized'. Let's just say some shrine priestesses were nicer than others." Kaguto shivered at the memory. "What my mother didn't know was that I was causing the accidents. Whenever I became anxious, afraid, or angry my power would become uncontrollable and would unleash itself. Once my mother figured out the connection she decided I was a demon and tried to strangle me to death...Luckily she failed."

"Kaguto...I'm so sorry." Yukino met his sad golden eyes with her own sapphire colored eyes that were filled with pity.

Instead of looking soothed by Yukino's pity Kaguto instead looked disgusted. "I don't need your pity, Yukino. My eyes were opened that day. That day...I killed my parents. I was just so angry when I awoke from being unconscious after my mother had tried to kill me and left me for dead. I remember...how my power just went out of control and soon everything around me was on fire. Of course, the fire didn't hurt me...but it destroyed the house along with my parents. And then I was free.

"However, people never accepted me and I was shunned and feared once my abilities were discovered. I ended up having to live in hiding as a *hikikomori*. My only escape became the game Yokai World. Although, it's strange that my curse became my blessing. It was through the game that I stumbled upon this tear which leads to Yomi. And it's here in Yomi that I was able to meet my *real* mother. Yes, Yukino, my real mother.

"She revealed to me that I was the reincarnation of her long lost son and how she needed my help. She awakened my powers fully. I now have full control over the element of fire. And I can also create it at whim. She gave me a new purpose. I knew I would find a way to free her someday and together we would take over the world, mother and son! Together we would destroy everything, make it all beautiful and pure and white. All will be consumed in my purifying flames! And then we would create something new, a beautiful land just for the two of us. However, I've become rather fond of you Yukino, perhaps you could be a part of my ideal world as well."

Yukino backed away in horror, "Become a part of your new world? You're crazy!"

Kaguto scowled deeply. "Yukino, I'm truly disappointed. I thought if anyone would understand me, and the darkness in my heart that it would be you - a kindred spirit. You, who also hate this world though for different reasons. Sadly, if you won't help me then I'll be forced to kill you, Yukino-*chan*." Kaguto began to summon his power into his hand, which was enveloped in a glowing red light, so that a giant scythe materialized there. It was a large, intimidating weapon and it was enveloped in red flames that coiled around the long pole and the curved and deadly blade.

Yukino's expression darkened. "I'd like to see you try." She brought her hands together and formed a sort of hand seal, the tips of her index fingers touching in a steeple shape. "I summon the ghost known as *Oyuki* to me now!" A ball of light suddenly appeared in the sky and then shot down into Yukino's body and seemed to be absorbed into her, possessing her, and one of Yukino's blue eyes changed to gold. "I call upon the power of *Oyuki* to aid me in the task before me now!" A magic fan suddenly materialized in Yukino's hand and she waved her fan in Kaguto's direction. "Ice Dagger Att-" But then suddenly and unexpectedly, Yukino found that she couldn't move. It was as though she was suddenly frozen in place by some unseen force.

Kaguto laughed gleefully and held up his hand to reveal a glowing, blue-stoned ring. Yukino narrowed her eyes at the ring.

"You fell right into my trap, Yuki-*chan*." Kaguto stroked the ring on his finger lovingly, "Now that you've merged with the ghost Oyuki I can use this ghost control ring to control you as well!"

Yukino blinked in surprise, "But that's- Impossible! That's just a game item so how can it control real ghosts?"

"Ah, but this particular ring is *not* a mere game item nor is that necklace

I gave you. I created this control ring using a combination of advanced magic and technology. Mother helped of course. We also made the matching control collar, or should I say necklace, which you now wear upon your neck. And which looks lovely by the way. And now you'll be forced to obey my will as I control the ghost you've temporarily become one with. Now come. Resistence is futile."

Kaguto walked forward and Yukino felt her body moving of its own accord and found herself walking to stand next to Kaguto and in front of the cave's entrance. Yukino felt herself summoning her spiritual power and then she watched as below her feet a giant glowing pentagram made up of her own blue-tinged spirit energy formed beneath her and began to glow and pulse with energy. Then her hands were forced together and began to form hand seals as she was made to chant the spell that would release the seal upon the cave and upon Izanami.

Yukino's eyes widened in horror as she tried to fight Kaguto's control, but it was impossible. Her body was no longer her own. "No! Someone help me!...Mother! What do I do?" Yukino called out when she managed to regain control for just a moment.

Suddenly, a bright ball of light appeared in the red sky of Yomi and Midoriko materialized before them in her *Shinto* priestess robes, a bow in her hands as she floated in midair. She began to form a spirit arrow with her bow and aimed at Kaguto. "Stay away from my daughter, Kaguto!" She loosed the arrow upon him and it flew through the air where it hit his hand - the hand that possessed the control ring. His hand and part of his arm were instantly purified, turning into ashes. The ring fell through the air and landed on the ground. Midoriko swooped down, flying through the air, and snatched up the control ring before Kaguto could grasp it with his other hand.

"NO!" Kaguto cried angrily as the ring was stolen from him.

Midoriko turned to Yukino, "Yukino I don't have enough strength to remain here much longer. You must leave this place immediately - hurry!"

Midoriko suddenly disappeared.

Kaguto was howling in pain from the wound Midoriko had given him. Though his hand and arm in reality remained intact he had still suffered great spiritual damage from Midoriko's attack. And he found back in reality that strangely his right hand and arm wouldn't move.

Enraged Kaguto spun towards Yukino, and with his good hand he pointed his giant scythe at her, "Do it! Unseal her! Free my mother! NOW!" He bellowed, spit flying from his mouth, a crazed expression on his face.

Yukino glared back defiantly at Kaguto, "No."

Kaguto's expression turned murderous. "Then you shall be cursed!" He began to gather an immense amount of power as a red aura of energy formed around him, and red flames seemed to lick his body. He then lunged his scythe forward and pierced Yukino through her heart in one swift, deadly motion. Yukino's body was immediately engulfed in flames and she screamed out in pain as her mind and spirit were assaulted by the attack.

Kaguto removed the scythe from her body and she fell slowly backwards. Yukino's body disappeared as her PC body was destroyed and then her PC body reappeared a few moments later in midair only to then fall backwards onto the ground where Yukino lay unmoving. Her PC body did not turn into a PC ghost as it was supposed to, but had become oddly transparent.

Kaguto walked over towards her fallen form, a dark look on his face, "You made me do this Yukino-*chan*. I thought you were my friend, that you understood me, but you wouldn't help me. Why? Why must I always be betrayed by humanity?" Kaguto spat the last word.

Night suddenly rushed out from the forest's edge and caught sight of Kaguto hovering over his sister's unconscious body. "Yukino! Kaguto you bastard! Stay away from her!" He rushed towards them, his massive *Shinigami* sword raised.

Kaguto leapt backwards, "Keh, no need for me to stay. Teleport!" Kaguto raised his arm in the air and instantly teleported. After all, Night was a dangerous person, and a wise man did not needlessly put himself into harm's way, Kaguto thought.

Night rushed to Yukino's side and cradled her limp body in his arms. Yukino's eyes fluttered open. "Where am I? Who...am I?"

Night peered down at her, his brows furrowed in concern. "Yukino?"

Yukino blinked back up at Night, "*Dare*? Who...are you?" Night's heart broke into a million pieces at these words. "What is this strange place? Why am I here?" Yukino's voice was veering towards panic now.

"Yukino, it's me, it's-" Night was trying to explain when Yukino violently shoved Night away from her and got out of Night's embrace.

She stumbled away from Night and grasped her head in pain as she tried to remember. "No! Stay away!" Yukino suddenly panicked as Night took a frantic step towards her and raised her arm. "Teleport!"

"Yukino! No! Wait!" Night called after her but Yukino had already disappeared. Night fell to his knees in despair and defeat, hanging his head. He began to punch the parched earth in frustration with his fists. "Oh little sister...I failed to protect you...Yukino...Yukino...Yukino..." Night punched the sandy ground with each time he said his sister's name - until blood and dirt mixed together.

END OF FLASHBACK

Alec blinked, he was back in Yomi with Yukino at his side. He turned to face her and saw that she too seemed to have returned from her memories. He licked his lips which had felt dry all of a sudden. "Yukino...do you remember?" He asked tentatively.

Yukino nodded slowly, "I do." She managed to croak out before falling forward in a faint. Alec managed to catch her in his arms easily since he was kneeling by her side.

"Yukino!" Alec called out in concern and decided he should take her back to the Guardian Knights guildhall right away. He hoisted her up into his arms and carrying her bridal style began to head for the forest when -

A honey-coated voice called out to Alec:

"Alec Suzuki...don't go...kind boy...beautiful boy...free me...if you let Yukino free me in return I shall grant you a wish. Perhaps you would wish for spirits and yokai to finally leave you alone? Or I can bring your mother back to life perhaps. Does this interest you?"

Alec turned around at the sound of the voice in surprise and realized it had to be the voice of Izanami, the goddess of the underworld there in Japan, known as Yomi.

"My real mother?" Alec had to admit he was a bit curious about her. Had she loved him? Would she have been kind to him whereas Laura had never shown him much kindness? What was she like? Was she beautiful...homely? Would she be proud of him or scorn him? These questions couldn't help themselves from buzzing around in Alec's head.

"How would you like to see her now?" The voice that was dripping with sweetness offered and without waiting for an answer a bright ball of light suddenly formed in the red sky overhead and shot down to hover in front of Alec.

A ghostly woman instantly materialized to stand directly in front of him. She had long brown hair that was tied back into a pony tail, large round glasses were on her face giving her an intellectual look, and she was wearing a plain white button-down blouse and brown slacks. Alec couldn't help but think she looked extremely 'normal'. But there was something oddly familiar about her Alec also realized in surprise. Deep in his subconscious he realized that he knew this woman.

"Mother?" Alec quirked his head at her.

Sarah (for that was his mother's name) looked at the white-haired boy with gray eyes in front of her and gasped, a hand coming to her mouth, "Alec?" She rushed up to him and caught Alec by surprise by throwing her arms around him. She stroked his hair fondly and Alec thought he remembered the gesture. Alec hesitated before he slowly wrapped his arms around Sarah and hugged her back.

Sarah pulled away from Alec after several moments and looked into Alec's face searchingly, "Alec, what are you doing here? Are you dead?"

Alec shook his head, "No mother, I-"

But Sarah cut him off, "Then you can't stay here! You must go back to wherever you came from. It's much too dangerous for you to remain here in the land of the dead."

"But mother...Izanami mentioned she could bring you back to life." Alec couldn't believe the words were leaving his mouth. He hadn't known he'd been tempted by Izanami's offer until he voiced his feelings aloud.

Sarah looked frightened rather than pleased by the prospect, but then her face softened and her expression turned sad, "Oh Alec, that's so sweet of you to want me back and believe me I would want nothing more in this world than to be able to return to you, my son but...my time has passed. Alec, are you alright? Is Mori-*san* taking good care of you? You're not alone right? Mori was a colleague of mine when I had traveled to Japan studying as a linguist here, you see. He...had been in love with me. I asked him to look after you for me when...I could no longer do so myself." Sarah explained in a rush.

Alec wanted to tell his mother about how Mori had abandoned him, and left him at Izanagi Academy to fend for himself. He wanted to tell her how he had screwed things up by causing his adoptive parents to get a divorce. That he *deserved* to be alone now. He had been the cause of his adoptive parent's unhappiness after all. But what ended up coming out of his mouth instead was - "Yea, don't worry mother. Everything's fine. Of course, I'm not alone." Alec swallowed thickly before voicing the question that was on the tip of his tongue. "Mother...am I really half *yokai*?"

Sarah nodded, her expression suddenly turning wistful.

"Then...who's my father? Is he dead? Is he alive?" Alec asked curiously.

Sarah bit her lip and looked thoughtful before continuing. "Alec...the tale of how I met and fell in love with your father is best left for another time. You must leave this place quickly and get that young lady to safety as soon as possible. She is not safe here as you very well know. I really shouldn't be asking you this Alec, but if you think you can, come and visit me again. It was nice seeing your face. I had forgotten...you've grown up to be so handsome." Sarah patted Alec's head affectionately.

Alec blushed at his mother's kind words. "Thanks mom." He looked down at the unconscious Yukino in his arms and knew he had to bring her to Night as soon as possible. "You're right mother, Yukino comes first. I'll...come again if I can." Alec promised before he raised his arm. "Teleport!"

Alec and Yukino teleported to the Guardian Knight's guildhall where Night and his *ninja* were waiting.

Night's eyes widened in worry when he saw Alec carrying Yukino's unconscious form, "Yukino? What happened?"

Alec frowned at Night since now he knew that all along Night had known about the existence of Yomi within the game, or rather that there was a way to get to Yomi from the game. And that even knowing that Night had still sent them to investigate the appearances of ghosts in the game *and* so had put Yukino's life in danger. But most of his anger drained away when he remembered how Night had tried to protect his sister and how devastated he had looked afterwards when he had failed. Alec couldn't get the visual image of Night's blood-covered fists out of his mind.

Alec shook his head. "Yukino and I discovered the tear that leads to Yomi. It's the one that leads down through the well. But you already know all about that don't you Night?" Alec prodded.

Night blanched at Alec's admission. "You took Yukino to Yomi! Why did you do that?" He stalked angrily towards Alec.

Alec glared back and lightning seemed to flash between both their eyes. "You told us to investigate where the real ghosts were coming from."

"Yes, investigate but *not* to actually go anywhere. I had simply wanted to know if the tear had opened again." Night ran a hand back through his spiky hair in an exasperated fashion.

"Well, you could have told us instead of keeping us in the dark about every little thing." Alec groused. "You knew Yukino was your sister all along didn't you? She's the girl who's in the coma, isn't she?" Alec demanded.

Night was shocked Alec had managed to figure all this out. "How do you know this?"

Alec waved his hand through the air, "Yukino got her memories back and I got to see them too."

Night looked at the still unconscious form of Yukino in Alec's arms. "She...remembers?" Night gulped and suddenly looked nervous.

Alec nodded and Yukino began to stir awake. "Ugh, my head..." She opened her eyes and turned to see Night and her eyes widened with recognition. "*Onii-san*...Brother." A small smile formed on her lips.

Night blinked back at her in surprise, "Yukino..."

A grin broke out across Yukino's face as she leapt out of Alec's arms and sprinted towards her brother, "*Onii-san!*" Yukino flung herself at the unsuspecting Night, who managed to catch her in his arms.

"Yukino, you remember me?" Night was startled, his head spinning.

Yukino wrapped her arms fiercely around her brother and looked up at him nodding vigorously, "Brother...I'm so sorry..." She apologized for having forgotten him.

Night patted her head, "There's nothing to be sorry for..." Alec felt the unspoken words of 'It is I that should be sorry' were there.

Alec chewed on his bottom lip as he watched the touching moment before him and was beginning to feel uncomfortable since now wasn't the time to argue with Night. Although he wouldn't let Night off the hook that easily. He decided he'd scold Night about Yukino later. Alec knew it must have been painful for Night to have been searching for Yukino for so long within the game only to find that his sister had forgotten him. And now she finally remembered him again. They could finally have the reunion they should have had a long time ago. Alec felt so awkward upon intruding on this brother and sister reunion he decided to log out.

Alec raised his arm - "Log out!"

Alec logged out of Yokai World and removed the VR HMD from his head. He looked around the computer room and saw that Rika and Junpei were no longer there. He sighed remembering Rika's face that night when she had found out about her parent's death and how she had looked at him afterwards. *Sigh.* He looked down at his watch and realized it was pretty late and he still hadn't delivered the tray of food to Akira. Alec quickly headed over to the cafeteria and fetched Akira's tray before heading to the boy's room. Alec brought his soccer ball along with him since he felt like playing a little soccer on the field alone that night since it helped him to get his mind off things. An idea was forming in Alec's mind as he walked down the hall. Maybe, just maybe, he would somehow convince the *hikikomori* to come out and play a little one on one soccer with him that night. *Well, it's worth a try at any rate.* Alec shrugged.

Alec arrived at the dorm building and then up to Akira's room. He knocked on the door to Akira's room and Akira opened the bottom panel so that Alec could slide the food tray under the door. Alec did so and flinched as Akira slammed the mini-door shut afterwards and began locking it again.

"*Ano*...Um...can I come in?" Alec questioned tentatively.

There was a long pause before Alec heard the sound of several locks being unlocked, and then Akira opened the door to lean on the doorframe in a nonchalant manner as he eyed Alec and his soccer ball curiously - "Well, what do you want?" Akira drawled in a bored tone.

"I just wanted to tell you that I took your advice. I confronted Yoru and he's letting me start my spirit training. He's training me himself actually." Alec informed him.

Akira's eyes widened in surprise before his expression darkened, "Well, good for you." He tried to close the door on Alec but Alec swiftly put his foot in the door.

"As it turns out though I can't even form a proper Spirit Sword. Pretty pathetic huh?" Alec continued speaking as if Akira wasn't currently slamming the door into his foot again and again in a frustrated manner.

Akira sighed heavily and stopped trying to close the door. "Yea, so?" He glared at Alec angrily

Alec swallowed and decided to just go for it. "I'm going to go out and play some nighttime soccer, wanna come?"

Akira blinked at Alec in surprise before he spat out, "I'm a *hikikomori* remember? I can't leave my room!"

Alec quickly reached out and grabbed Akira's wrist. "You don't know until you try. Come on, it will be fun." Alec began to pull Akira out of his room.

Akira instantly began to panic, "No! Let go of me! I can't go out there! They'll...They'll...." Akira stammered nervously.

Alec's eyes narrowed at Akira and realized that Akira's *hikikomori* problem probably had a lot to do with social anxiety. "*They*? No one will be out there Akira. It's the middle of the night. Or are you afraid you'll totally get your butt whooped by me, hmm?" Alec challenged.

Akira looked torn between fear and anger before he said in a low voice, "Are you sure no one will be out there?"

Alec smirked, "Positive."

Akira forced himself to smile back, his lips twisting into a sort of twisted sneer. Alec realized he probably didn't smile much. It was pretty painful to watch. "You're on then, Alec-*bozu*."

So Alec, with Akira in tow and practically clinging to him, managed to make it out to the soccer field where the two boys began to play a little one on one soccer. Alec had to admit that Akira was pretty good except that he seemed to get tired easily - probably due to the lack of exercise from being locked in his room all the time. But Akira was also able to summon his spirit energy and use it to increase his speed and strength, which made up for his lack of true strength so that he was playing on equal footing with Alec in no time.

After they had played for a while, best 3 out of 5, they collapsed on a grassy area besides the soccer field, panting for breath. The two boys looked up at the starry night sky, and noticed the full moon that was shining over head.

"You see, it's not so bad out here now is it?" Alec said while admiring the stars. You could never see stars so well back in New York, after all.

"Maybe not..." Akira admitted as he turned to look at Alec out of the corner of his eye, "Because of you..." He said in a low voice so that Alec couldn't hear.

There was a small smile tugging on Alec's lips as he suddenly thought of something - Yukino was alive.

Chapter 15:
THE TALE OF LORD RYUUZAKI

Alec, Junpei, Rika, and Neji were surrounded by yokai. They were everywhere. Alec held his Spirit Sword in a two-handed grip before him and faced off with the yokai as he summoned a glowing blue blade of light and energy to flare into existence. Junpei's fists and feet were glowing with his spirit energy as he got into a fighting stance prepared to fight the yokai. Rika was painting some ink-yokai of her own to fight with while Neji was standing back cheering his friends on and trying to stay out of the way.

"Don't worry Alec we won't let those yokai eat you." Rika assured Alec.

"Yea, buddy, we'll protect you." Junpei seconded.

"I won't let anything happen to my best friend." Neji agreed.

"Minna..guys..." Alec's voice was thick with emotion.

Alec slashed his sword through the air and was happy to see Junpei making quick work of some yokai with his energy blast attacks. However, that's when they heard a piercing cry - it was Rika's voice.

Alec and Junpei turned to see Rika getting cut down by a yokai that had slashed its sharp claws at Rika's back while she had been busy painting more ink-yokai.

"Rika!" Alec cried out worriedly. He rushed towards the yokai, his sword out before him, but he was flung back with a simple wave of the yokai's clawed hand as a powerful energy blast hit Alec in the chest and sent him flying backwards.

"Jerk!" Junpei charged forward and aimed a series of quick kicks and punches at the yokai, however, the yokai was much faster and got past Junpei's defenses easily and stabbed Junpei in the chest with its clawed hand.

Alec pushed himself up off the ground just in time to see Junpei fall. "Junpei!"

Alec hadn't noticed a yokai sneaking up on him from behind until he turned around at a sudden sound - his eyes widened in horror when he saw that Neji had stepped in front of the yokai's path to protect Alec. Neji was cut down by the yokai and lay on the ground unmoving. Neji had sacrificed himself to save Alec once again....

His friends had all died protecting him...

"Neji!" Alec yelled to the sky in despair.

Alec awoke with a strangled cry, which had been much louder in his head than it was in reality. He was panting for breath and a thin sheen of sweat had formed on his brow. He could still remember his friends being killed all around him because of his weakness and inability to protect them. Alec clenched his fists around his bed sheet. Instead they had protected him. And then...

"Ouch!" Alec flinched in pain - something had just bit him! Alec flung the tangled sheet off his bed to find that his entire mattress was covered in fire ants. ACK! Alec scrambled out of bed trying to brush the fire ants off his skin but they obstinately clung on, fiercely biting him, so that Alec was forced to run into the shower fully clothed in his pajamas and turn the shower head on so that it blasted cold water down upon him. Finally, as the ants were hit with the cold spray of water they were washed off of him.

As Alec shivered in the shower he realized this had to be a prank. He could suddenly hear the sound of muffled laughter coming from outside of his doorway and frowned to himself. *Very mature guys...it must be Tatsuya and his lackeys again.* But sadly Alec understood why they had done it. It was because Alec was a *hanyou*, or half-breed. And in their eyes that pretty much meant that Alec was the same as the enemy. And Alec really couldn't find too many flaws in their logic.

Alec hung his head letting the cold water beat down upon him for a good thirty minutes, so lost in his own tumultuous thoughts he hadn't noticed the time slipping by, before when his body had begun to shiver violently he finally turned the shower off.

· · · · · · · · · · · · · · · ·

Before Alec had to head over to Izanagi temple to begin his morning training session with Yoru he quickly stopped by Haruna-*sensei*'s office to get something for the painful bites that covered his entire body and even part of his face. Haruna-*sensei* took one look at the poor figure Alec made all red and swollen before having to hide a giggle behind her hand, unable to help herself at the utterly pathetic sight that Alec made.

Alec frowned and turned around to leave the nurse's office.

"I'm so sorry Alec-*kun*!" Haruna-*sensei* quickly apologized as she led Alec over to the bed and sat him down so she could apply *Caladryl* lotion to the bites on his face and chest. "You really just look so pathetic."

Alec pouted, "Is that your *professional* opinion then?"

Haruna patted Alec on the head, "Well, you look just like a flea bitten puppy that's all. You just bring out my maternal instincts looking all droopy-eyed and pathetic." Haruna explained as she continued to apply the lotion to his bare chest.

Alec blushed at that and remained quiet as Haruna tended to all his bites. Her soft touch...it was like a mother's. *Mother*...Alec decided he would go back to Yomi later that day to see his mother again if he could manage it.

When Haruna-*sensei* was done Alec headed out of the nurse's office and out of the main school building towards the forest he'd have to go through to get to Izanagi temple. However, before he managed to reach the forest's edge he was unexpectedly jumped by some boys in his grade.

"Look there he is! The demon! Get 'em!" Came an oddly familiar voice.

Alec looked up startled to see who had a hold of him this time and sighed heavily. It was Tatsuya and his cronies, Ken and Omi again.

"Oh it's just you guys. Isn't it a little early in the morning for bullying?" Alec began in a monotone voice.

"It's never too early to make your life miserable." Tatsuya sneered and tucked a stray hair behind his ear to fix his perfect mushroom cut hair do. "Let's get 'em up there." Tatsuya directed his friends.

The boys began to haul Alec over towards the school's flag pole. "Hey, wait a minute. What are you going to do? Let me go!" Alec struggled against their grasp half-heartedly since after the whole fire ant prank that morning he was having trouble drudging up enough real motivation to fight back. He just felt so tired, of everything. And besides, he didn't even have his soccer ball with him so how could he really be expected to fight back. Tatsuya and his friends were taller, stronger, and bigger than Alec was.

Tatsuya and Ken lowered the flag while Omi held onto Alec. Then Tatsuya removed the flag from the hook before he directed Ken and Omi to hold onto Alec while he walked behind the unsuspecting boy. Then before Alec realized what was going to happen Tatsuya had reached forward and grabbed a hold of the back of Alec's boxers and attached them to the flag hook. *Uh oh*. Alec's eyes widened when he realized what was about to happen.

Tatsuya smirked before quickly directing Ken and Omi to raise the 'flag'. Alec struggled futilely as he was being raised up off the ground by the back of his boxers and then his expression scrunched up in pain as he suffered from an awful wedgie.

"Enjoy the wedgie from hell!" Tatsuya cackled gleefully at Alec's plight as Ken and Omi continued to raise Alec higher into the air.

Alec bit his lip to keep from crying out in pain since the 'wedgie from hell' was extremely uncomfortable and even more so the higher Alec was suspended off the ground. Alec's face had turned bright pink and he began to struggle in earnest to get off the flag hook somehow as tears of pain formed in his eyes. *What a great way to start the day huh? Sigh.* Alec hung his head, finally giving up and realizing that no one would be coming to his aid any time soon.

Tatsuya, Ken, and Omi were laughing so hard at Alec's plight they were laughing on the ground now and had drawn the attention of several other students so that a small crowd began to form around the suspended Alec. Most of the other students joined in the laugher thinking Tatsuya's prank was extremely funny. Others looked a bit conflicted about what was going on but didn't move to do anything about it. Luckily, Junpei and Rika were passing by on their way to Izanagi temple and spotted what was happening to Alec. Rika gasped and raised a hand in front of her mouth when she caught sight of Alec dangling pathetically from the flag hook by just his boxers.

"What the hell is this!" Junpei growled as he stalked forward, "What's going on here? Who's responsible for this?" Junpei glared at the crowd accusingly. They all managed to look somewhat guilty, but a few managed to point over in Tatsuya's direction discreetly.

The three boys were still laughing on the ground but sobered quickly when they heard Junpei's harsh voice. They pulled themselves off the ground and turned to face Junpei. "We're just teaching that demon a lesson." Tatsuya began conversationally.

Junpei cracked his knuckles, "Big mistake Tatsuya. When you pick on Alec Suzuki you pick on me too." Junpei charged forward and flung a punch at Tatsuya before he could even blink. Tatsuya fell backwards onto the ground and Ken and Omi quickly came to his aid. Ken threw a punch at Junpei, which Junpei easily dodged moving to the side, and then he tripped Ken up as he charged forward. Ken fell forward and got a face full of dirt. Then as Omi was trying to attack Junpei next from behind Junpei spun around and delivered a hard uppercut to the large boy's jaw that sent him up into the air before falling backwards with a hard thud.

Junpei wiped his hands off, and a cocky grin formed on his face. Beating the crap out of bullies was a great way to start the day, Junpei decided.

Rika covered her face as Junpei gave the three boys a couple extra painful kicks while they were on the ground, but she was soon peering through her fingers curiously with a slight smile on her face. Junpei just wanted to make sure they learned *their* lesson well and what better way to teach someone than through reinforcement, he decided.

By the time Junpei was done with Tatsuya, Ken, and Omi the boys were quite a sight. The three boys were all covered in large, well-deserved bumps and bruises. Tatsuya was sporting a black eye, Omi was missing a front tooth, and Ken had a strange mark on his face from hitting the ground face first. As they struggled to stand they had to lean on each other for support. If the vain Tatsuya could have seen the ugly bruise around his eye in a mirror he would have died of mortification.

"We won't forget this Junpei! You...demon lover! Any friend of that demon will suffer our wrath you got that? Let's go boys!" Tatsuya shot back but his voice was trembling and he was merely trying to keep up appearances since Junpei knew Tatsuya was wisely afraid of really pissing Junpei off. The three boys ran or rather limped off away from Junpei as fast as they could.

Junpei chuckled heartily as he watched them go and then turned towards the gawking crowd next and raised an eyebrow at them as he cracked his knuckles, "What are you all still doing here? Show's over. Scram. Unless you have something you want to say?" Junpei gave them his 'ultimate death glare' and they all ran away screaming. Junpei smirked in response. Sometimes it was fun to be bad. "Rika help me get Alec down from there."

"Oh, right." Rika quickly obliged and the two of them began to lower Alec down from the flag pole.

As soon as Alec was on the ground he sunk to his knees clutching his groin in pain. "Ow..." Alec looked up at Junpei with unshed tears in the corners of his eyes. "You don't know how much that hurt."

Rika gave Alec a pitying look and bit her lip as if she wanted to say something.

Junpei nodded his head in sympathy, "I feel your pain little buddy. Can you stand?" Alec struggled to stand and Junpei helped him up and ruffled his hair. "You okay now?"

"Yea, thanks Junpei." Alec managed a small tremulous smile since most of the pain was fading. "You saved me..." *Ah, the theme of the day. I really am pathetic.*

"Dude, what happened to your face?" Junpei gawked when he had finally noticed the red bites that were all over Alec's face, and that were covered in pink *Caladryl* lotion.

"Oh, some of the boys thought it'd be funny to put fire ants in my bed this morning. That's all. I really gotta remember to lock to my door tonight. I'm bitten *all* over."

"That's horrible!" Rika blurted out and looked surprised at herself that she had said this.

Junpei began to tease Alec, "Oh ho! Did Nurse Haruna put that lotion on *all* your bites Alec? *Everywhere* on your body?" Junpei suggestively waggled his eyebrows.

"Junpei!" Alec turned bright pink. "Haruna-*sensei* gave me the bottle of *Caladryl* lotion so I could treat the places I couldn't let her, um, see."

Junpei chuckled and ruffled Alec's hair, "Come on, we gotta get to Izanagi temple. Yoru and the others are waiting for us."

"Yea...right." Alec muttered unenthusiastically.

The trio headed over to the temple to begin their spirit training lessons. Alec had dragged his feet the entire way there. He really wasn't feeling up to training with Yoru that day after everything he had been through just that morning, and not counting the haunting nightmare that was in the back of his mind and that wouldn't seem to leave him alone.

Junpei was going to be training with his brother again and Rika was going to be training with Junko. When they arrived the trio went their separate ways and Alec went off to find Yoru.

Yoru tossed Alec his Spirit Sword and Alec concentrated on forming his spirit blade. The sword glowed and the blue blade flared into existence. Alec held it out before him in a two-handed grip, pointing it at Yoru, who also summoned and formed his Spirit Sword. The nightmare was still fresh in Alec's mind and it urged him to try harder that day to form a better Spirit Sword. Alec felt a lot of pressure on his shoulders to become stronger. However, as much as Alec tried to push himself harder that morning he still couldn't seem to manage to form a better Spirit Sword than before and Yoru also seemed to be disappointed.

Yoru shook his head and charged Alec, his spirit sword raised, and Alec was forced to form his own Spirit Sword in retaliation. Their blades clashed and Alec's shattered. Alec leapt sideways out of the way as Yoru's sword came down upon the ground and left a small crater there. Alec quickly formed his sword again and tried charging Yoru this time but his sword's blade was still flickering.

Yoru scoffed at his attempt at an offensive attack, "Your sword is still too weak. What did I tell you the last time? You need a strong will and determination to form a proper Spirit Sword. But just as your sword wavers I can sense that your heart is wavering with doubt and hesitation *still*." Alec could hear the anger in Yoru's voice.

Alec frowned, "I just don't understand why must I slay the *yokai*? What if I can save them? I understand that sometimes I will have no choice but to slay them, but when I can I think I should try and help them, Yoru. I just want to protect my friends. I'm not training like this so I can learn to kill or become some kind of human weapon. I'm just doing this for my friends."

"A Spirit Sword is a tool to slay *yokai* with yet you insist that you don't want to hurt *yokai* if you don't have to. Even if they are evil, or even if they are endangering the lives of your friends?" Yoru shook his head at Alec. "You need to harden your heart Alec to become a proper *Shinigami*. The sword must become an extension of yourself, of your will to protect your friends and slay the *yokai* that oppose us. Such a weak sword will not be able to protect anyone nor slay *yokai* successfully."

"There must be some other way." Alec insisted. "What I want is...what I truly want is to be able to save my friends and the *yokai*." Alec admitted.

Yoru looked surprised by this admission, "There is no other way. You must chose Alec. Who will it be? Humans...or *yokai*? Who's side are you really on? You can't save them both. It's this kind of naive thinking that makes your sword weak. *Yokai* are the enemy, Alec."

Alec was shocked by how hateful Yoru's words had sounded and his blade shattered as Yoru pressed forward in attack. Alec fell backwards from Yoru's powerful blow and was panting for breath as he pushed himself back up off the ground to face Yoru once more. Alec frowned thoughtfully, "Then aren't I your enemy as well?"

"That's different. You're one of us now." Yoru said simply.

Is it really that simple? Alec wondered. Had he really already chosen a side? And what side was that exactly? Did he really intend to slay *yokai*? Alec simply didn't want to hurt anyone, not if he didn't have to. He just wanted to protect his friends and prevent them from coming to harm but...Yoru continued to insist that until he let go of his doubts his sword would continue to be weak. That he had to harden his heart to gain strength. Was that really true? Was becoming a demon-slayer the only way to gain the strength to protect his friends? Deep down, Alec really didn't want to believe that.

*Save him Alec...*Midoriko's melodious voice rang in Alec's head all of a sudden. He shook his head and tried to concentrate on Yoru instead, who was still before him.

"Yes, I am one of you." Alec nodded as he charged Yoru.

"Good." Yoru smiled as he raised his sword as Alec's clashed with it. "You're getting close to awakening your true power. You're still too kind-hearted though Alec. You cannot show mercy to your enemies since they will only end up betraying you in the end. Such as how you let Tamamo-no-mae live. That was a mistake. It was foolish. Don't you agree Alec?"

Alec faltered and his sword shattered as he staggered backwards, "But she...I sensed...Tamamo-no-mae isn't *all* evil Yoru! I didn't have to slay her. Tamamo-no-mae didn't *need* to die. Besides she was being controlled by Akira. She's not on Kaguto's side and shouldn't have to pay for his crimes. I know you want to get your sister back, but taking it out on innocent people is wrong."

"Innocent?" Yoru's voice turned angry, "She's a *yokai* Alec, a creature of pure evil. Don't tell me you're on her side?"

Alec shook his head frantically, "N-no I'm not." He stuttered.

"What happens if Tamamo-no-mae ends up killing one of your friends because you left her alive Alec?" Yoru asked coldly.

"She...wouldn't do that." Alec insisted, his voice wavering.

"Then who's side are you on?" Yoru demanded.

"Yours...no hers...I don't know..." Alec bit his lip so hard that it bled.

"Again you hesitate. Show me your will to protect your friends! You must chose Alec! Who will you chose to protect - us or them? Chose!" Yoru charged forward and their swords clashed.

"I...I don't know!" Alec pushed his sword back but then it shattered. He was flung backwards with a cry.

Yoru shook his head at him with a disappointed look in his eyes. "Until you face me with a firm heart that holds no more doubt or hesitation then this is pointless." Yoru turned around to leave Alec on the ground.

Alec stubbornly pushed himself up off the ground, "Wait, Yoru, don't go. Even if I don't really know my choice yet. I do know I will protect my friends, whatever the cost." Alec formed his Spirit Sword and charged Yoru from behind.

Yoru turned around and one-handed managed to block Alec's blow with his own Spirit Sword, "That's still *not* good enough." Yoru brought his sword back and then forward with such force that Alec's sword was once again shattered in seconds.

Alec stumbled backwards and sunk to his knees, panting for breath.

Yoru lowered his sword and scowled. "That's enough for today."

Alec, however, struggled to stand, his legs feeling like jelly, and formed his Spirit Sword once more. It was now flickering even worse than before. "No. I can keep going Yoru. You don't understand. I have to become stronger as soon as possible. I have to be able to protect them now. I'll do whatever it takes, Yoru. I'll train harder...there has to be something I can do..." Alec staggered forward.

"It's impossible for you as you are now Alec." Yoru shook his head at Alec. "You need to first confront the doubts and fear in your own heart and overcome this before you can become a true *Shinigami*. You must find your own path as an exorcist. Only you can decide the path you are going to take. Even I can't force you."

Alec held his flickering sword out in a two-handed grip before him and stumbled forward painstakingly towards Yoru, "I know that but...I don't care about all that. All I know is...all I understand is that I must protect my friends." Alec insisted stubbornly and took another unsteady step forward but began to lose his footing. Alec forced himself to take another step forward but then felt himself falling forward as his vision darkened. *Aw man, I think I'm going to pass out. This sucks.* Alec thought before he indeed fell to the ground unconscious.

Yoru looked down at Alec's fallen form with a thoughtful expression on his face. Junpei and Rika saw that Alec had passed out and rushed over to his fallen form. Both of them ignored Junko and Jin's calls for them to 'get back here!'.

"Alec!" Junpei called.

"Alec-*kun*!" Rika cried out in concern.

"He's alright, he just expended a great deal of spirit energy. He just needs a little rest and he'll be as good as new." Yoru informed them in a nonchalant manner.

Rika and Junpei however glared at Yoru accusingly since he seemed to have been going quite hard on Alec during their training.

Yoru shrugged having read their expressions easily as if to say 'So?'.

"We're running out of time. Kaguto is on the move...fires have been breaking out all across Tokyo and I know he's behind them. It won't be long now before we'll have to fight them - the Izanami Clan and their *Kuro-Shinigami*. Alec must be ready...Midoriko told me in a dream that he could be our only hope."

"Midoriko?" Rika questioned.

Junpei leaned in to whisper in Rika's ear, "Yoru's deceased mother...she was a powerful *miko* known to have been a Dream-Walker, one that could cross into people's dreams, but could also see the future in her own dreams through prophecy."

Rika and Junpei looked down at Alec's battered and bruised form. And Rika's expression softened. "Why does he push himself so hard?"

Junpei frowned down at Alec, "He wants to protect us. Especially you Rika. I hope you realize that."

Rika blushed, "Oh Alec..."

. . . .

Alec was taken by his friends to nurse Haruna's office so that he could rest and recover. However, his sleep was plagued with nightmares...

Alec and his friends were facing yokai once more when Tamamo-no-mae suddenly appeared before them, a teasing smile on her face.

"Look! It's the fox witch! Let's get her!" Junpei declared charging forward.

"No wait!" Alec stepped in front of Junpei's path with his arms spread out, and his back to Tamamo-no-mae, "Don't hurt her!"

369

Tamamo-no-mae grinned and flung a fireball at Alec's back.

Rika however managed to push Alec out of the way, "Alec!" She cried and was hit by the fireball instead, her body bursting into flames as she collapsed.

Alec's eyes widened in horror at the sight, "Rika!"

Junpei pushed past Alec angrily. "Rika! You she-demon!" He turned to Tamamo-no-mae, "You'll pay for that!" He attacked Tamamo-no-mae by throwing an energy blast her way. She threw a fireball in retaliation and her attack easily overpowered his. Junpei was hit in the chest and sent flying backwards with a cry where he lay unmoving on the ground.

"Junpei!" Alec cried.

Neji turned to face Alec a stricken expression on his face, "Alec! Why? Why aren't you doing anything? Why didn't you kill her Alec? Why didn't you fight her? Why did you let Tamamo-no-mae kill Rika and Junpei? I thought we were your friends Alec! Or are you just a monster...a devil...a demon...a yokai...! You're one of them aren't you?" Neji pointed a trembling finger Alec's way.

Alec backed away in horror, "No! No...I'm not!" Alec shook his head frantically.

Tamamo-no-mae threw a fireball at Neji next and he was consumed in flames, his body falling to the ground to join the others.

"Neji!" Hot tears were streaming down Alec's face. But then unexpectedly the bodies of his friends began to stir and they rose up, pushing themselves up off the ground, the flames still surrounding their bodies eerily.

"Alec...why? Why did you forsake us? Aren't we friends?" Junpei questioned coming towards Alec, stumbling forward.

"Alec...why did you betray us?" Neji demanded also walking towards Alec.

"Deep down I knew...I knew all along that you would chose them." Rika spat.

"Is this the side you've chosen Alec?" Junpei asked. "Have you really chosen them?"

"No!" Alec shook his head frantically.

"Choose Alec..." "Choose..." "Choose..." Junpei, Rika, and Neji's voices echoed around Alec as they grasped his arms and demanded that he answer them. Alec could feel the flames enveloping his own body now as they transferred from his friends and onto him. The heat and flames and smoke that was all around him now was beginning to become unbearable as it consumed him.

"NO!" Alec screamed as his entire body burst into flames and he disintegrated into ashes.

Alec awoke with a start quickly sitting up in bed. He was gasping for breath and he felt that he was covered in sweat. His eyes also stung from unshed tears. Alec wrapped his arms around his trembling body and hung his head as he tried to compose himself. *It was just a dream...just a dream...* Alec said like a mantra in his mind.

Haruna-*sensei* was at his side in an instant with a concerned expression on her face, "Alec?" She put a hand to his forehead. "Are you alright?" She stroked his head while trying to take some of his pain away with her empathic ability. "Did you have a nightmare?"

Alec put his face in his hands as he remembered how he had let Tamamo-no-mae kill his friends. It was just like Yoru said...he'd have to chose...What the hell was wrong with him? Why was he hesitating?

Alec shook his head and let out a shaky breath, "No, I'm fine. Really. I...I have to go!" Alec struggled to get out of bed and tossed the sheets aside. As soon as his feet were on the floor he quickly rushed from the room.

"Alec-*kun*!" Haruna's voice carried after him but he ignored her.

Alec rushed down the hallway to the computer club room and entered quickly. He wanted to log on to Yokai World and go to Yomi so that he could talk to his mother. He desperately needed to know more about his father. Somehow Alec knew that knowing the whole story about where he came from would help him make the choice he knew he had to make. He needed to know more about himself, especially that part of himself before he could decide what side he should really be on.

Alec logged on to Yokai World and teleported to the Haunted Mansion Area. Once there he then went through the rose gardens and to the well. Taking a deep breath he jumped onto the ledge and then jumped down into the well, which was a tear that lead to the true Land of Yomi. He made it through the *tengu* forest without incident and then went straight to the cave. Alec's mother instantly appeared out of thin air as if she'd been expecting him.

"Alec...you came back?" Sarah breathed happily.

Alec nodded, "Mother..." He took a hesitant step forward and then walked up to her, "Mother I need to know...I need you to tell me more about who I really am. Where I come from. I need you to tell me about how you met my father and more about him." Alec requested in a rush.

Sarah nodded understandingly, "I promised you didn't I? That I would tell you the story of how I met and fell in love with your father. And so I shall." A small wistful smile played on her lips before she began. "I used to live in New York. I worked as a linguist there. I traveled to Tokyo when I was given an interesting opportunity to research a recently discovered language found in several ancient Japanese texts.

"When I arrived there I met up with another linguist named Mori Suzuki and we quickly became friends. On one of the days I was investigating an ancient text about *yokai* and which had several parts written in a language no one had ever read before, something unexpected happened. I didn't know it at the time but that book about *yokai* was actually a tear which led to their world - the Makai World.

"When I opened and read a few lines from the book I was suddenly transported to the Makai World and once there I found myself in the midst of a horrible battlefield..."

FLASHBACK

"*Itteeee!* Owwie!" Sarah rubbed her backside from the hard fall she had just experienced and on unsteady legs pushed herself up off the ground. Her eyes widened at the sight before her and she rubbed her eyes not believing what she was seeing. What had happened to the library? Her eyes widened even more when she realized that what she was now seeing before her was real. She had somehow been transported into the middle of a bloody battlefield...

On one side of the field were groups of riders on black horses, who wore dark clothing and armor in deep violet, blacks and golds. Sarah saw that they had pointed elvish ears, and strangely colored eyes and hair. Their hands seemed to be clawed and when they fought they seemed to possess a supernatural power that normal people just didn't have - power which was able to fling their opponent backwards with such force the opposing rider *and* horse were flung away from them by this power once it was unleashed.

Sarah saw that the opposing force were mostly mounted on white horses and wore light colored armor in whites, golds, and emerald green. Sarah saw that these beings who were fighting also had pointed ears and strangely colored eyes. *They almost look like elves.* Sarah thought to herself, but quickly tossed the idea aside when she noticed their unusually long nails or claws and the fangs that seemed to poke out of their mouths when they smiled.

Sarah watched in awe as the combatants seemed to be attacking each other using elemental attacks as well. The dark army seemed to be skilled in fire attacks and Sarah watched as the opposing force countered these fire attacks with water and ice attacks.

Sarah didn't know this at the time, but she had unluckily landed on the side of the battlefield where the *Nekomata* army was, lead by the leader of the *Nekomata* Clan, known as Lord Kyohei. Three riders in dark clothes and armor became curious as soon as they spotted Sarah on the battlefield and wondered what a mere human woman was doing in the middle of a battlefield and so rode up to her.

"Look a human!" A *nekomata* rider declared.

"A human woman? What's she doing here on the battlefield?" Another rider quirked his head at her.

"Do you think she's a priestess?" One rider hissed nervously, and Sarah watched fascinated as she saw two tails coming out from the back of the rider's pants swishing behind him in an agitated manner.

"We had better find out. Look how strangely she's dressed though...I don't think she's from our world." One *nekomata* suggested thoughtfully.

"We had better bring her back to Lord Kyohei." The *nekomata* nodded.

"Although perhaps we could have a little fun with her first." One of the *nekomata* riders licked his lips, revealing two small fangs, "What do you say guys?" Sarah couldn't help but feel the *nekomata* was eyeing her in much the same way a cat would eye a canary.

Epp! Do they want to eat me or something? Sarah wondered fearfully.

The other two *nekomata* snickered in response and Sarah saw one of the *nekomata* licking his claws in anticipation. They rode up to Sarah and then dismounted from their horses to approach her since she was no threat to them. "Come here human wench. We won't hurt you - much." The *nekomata* reached out and grabbed Sarah's shoulder suddenly.

Sarah instantly freaked out and batted his hand away with a cry. "*Iye!* No! Don't touch me! I'll be ruined for marriage!" However, unexpectedly her mere touch appeared to possess enough power to blast the *nekomata* backwards. The *nekomata* flew back and landed on the ground with a hard thud where he lay unmoving.

Sarah blinked down at her hand as if seeing it for the first time ever. *Uh oh...*She thought when she noticed the angry expressions the *nekomata* now wore on their faces. *This is so not good. Where's a knight in shining armor when you need one? Why couldn't I have fallen into a fairy tale instead of a demon folktale!* Sarah took a step back away from the approaching *nekomata*.

The other two *nekomata* were not happy campers and had drawn their *katana* and strode forward with purposeful steps towards the retreating Sarah. "Don't give us any more trouble wench...we're going to take you to our Lord." Sarah wondered if she imagined it but they almost sounded worried.

Sarah shook her head knowing that couldn't be true. There was no way these strange beings could be afraid of her. Not when she was totally freaked out by them. And now that the *nekomata* warriors were approaching her with their swords drawn she was more frightened than ever. "*Iyyyee!* Nooo!" She screamed and covered her face in her hands. A fierce wind seemed to pick up and swirl around her, but what it really was, was her spirit energy and then there was a flash of blue light as she suddenly forced this energy outwards, purely by instinct, so that it blasted the two *nekomata* back and with such power that they were instantly exorcized and turned into dust.

As Sarah watched the *nekomata* be destroyed she became even more frightened by this confusing turn of events and her power seemed to go out of her control. She let out a scream as her spirit energy shot out of her body uncontrollably and engulfed about half of the battlefield in a blue-tinged light. The *nekomata* that were unlucky enough to be near her were all immediately exorcized by the purity of her spirit energy and were turning into piles of dust.

Meanwhile, elsewhere on the other side of the battlefield, Lord Ryuuzaki of the Northern Lands, dragon *yokai* in charge of the dragon *yokai* army, noticed that Lord Kyohei's forces were suddenly converging towards one spot on the battlefield and wanted to know why. What was so important over there that the *nekomata* had seen fit to diverge their forces to that area and completely ignore his troops? Ryuuzaki's pride was somewhat stung and he decided he had to find out.

Ryuuzaki turned his steed and rode hard towards the area just in time to see a huge burst of purifying light destroy about fifty or more *nekomata* warriors. And Ryuuzaki was sure that there had definitely been a woman's scream coming from the center of this sudden carnage. Eyes wide but without fear Ryuuzaki rode forward past the piles of dust that were once *nekomata* warriors.

What he saw was something completely unexpected - a rather plain looking woman was kneeling on the ground in the center of all the piles of dust - all that remained of the purified *nekomata*. She appeared to be crying but upon hearing his approach on horseback she turned her tear-streaked face to look up at him. He saw that she was wearing round glasses and had chocolate-brown hair, which was tied back into a simple ponytail. He also noticed her odd clothing, which consisted of a normal white, button-down blouse and a pair of brown slacks along with some sneakers. The clothing was strange to Ryuuzaki since it was unlike most normal clothing found in the Makai.

Then their eyes met. Her warm brown eyes seemed to widen as she took in his overall appearance and she murmured to herself in a low voice, "So beautiful..." Before she suddenly fainted.

Ryuuzaki raised an eyebrow at this strange human woman. She didn't seem to look like a priestess, or act like one for that matter, but the power she had exhibited earlier had definitely been that of a priestess, Ryuuzaki decided. *Perhaps, she could come in handy...*

A dragon soldier came riding up to Ryuuzaki and peered down at the fallen woman curiously wondering what his Lord intended to do with her. "Lord Ryuuzaki, the *nekomata* are retreating for today. What shall we do? Should we pursue them?"

Ryuuzaki dismounted and picked up Sarah's limp body into his arms. "Today's battle is over thanks to this woman. We take the priestess with us. She could be quite useful to have against our enemies if we can convince her to help us." He walked back to his horse and placed Sarah on his saddle first before swinging himself up on the saddle behind her.

"Yes, my Lord." The dragon soldier bowed his head.

With Sarah in his arms Ryuuzaki and his dragon *yokai* army rode back to the palace of the Northern Lands.

⬝ ⬝ ⬝ ⬝ ⬝ ⬝ ⬝ ⬝ ⬝ ⬝ ⬝ ⬝ ⬝ ⬝ ⬝ ⬝ ⬝

Sarah awoke to find herself in a richly, decorated room, fit for a princess really, and with an oriental style. She saw that her glasses had been put on a night table besides her bed and she reached out for them blindly before putting the large, round frames on her face. She sat up in bed and peered around the room. It was dark but the light from a full moon outside was shedding ample light into the room from a set of large, glass paned doors, which led to an outdoor balcony, and so she was able to see most of the room easily.

That's when she suddenly heard the sound of a flute. It was a beautiful and haunting melody, and curiosity getting the better of her Sarah got herself out of bed to see if she could hear it better from the balcony. She made her way outside onto the balcony and peered over the edge to see that her balcony overlooked the royal gardens. They were impressive and even with just the moonlight to see by Sarah saw the ponds and little bridges that were found throughout the gardens.

And there in the center of the garden and playing upon a flute was none other than Lord Ryuuzaki. Sarah gasped as she laid eyes upon the handsome demon man. He had long, flowing, silvery-white hair and bright blue eyes flecked with silver. He was wearing an ornate white and golden *kimono* with an emerald green and gold *obi* sash belt tied about his waist and that had a pattern of yellow crescent moons on it. Standing there beneath the moonlight Sarah couldn't help but think he was stunning - the way the moonlight made his silvery hair glow took her breath away. To Sarah it made him look just like some sort of angel. Though with the sharp claws and fangs she amended in her thoughts that he was more of a fallen angel.

She was leaning over the edge of the balcony to get a closer look at him when she accidently lost her balance. She began to fall over the railing and wind-milled her arms helplessly as she tried to regain her balance, "Oh no! Epp!" Sarah suddenly tipped over the railing and found herself falling down through the air when -

She suddenly wasn't falling anymore. She blinked and realized she had been caught and was in someone's arms. She looked up to see that Ryuuzaki's face was now mere inches from her own and blushed scarlet. The demon lord had saved her. She looked past him and realized he had summoned a pair of wings in order to catch her mid fall. The wings were fascinating Sarah thought as she pushed her glasses up her nose to observe them better and saw that they were silvery gray in color, leathery in texture, and bat-like in shape.

"You saved me. Thank you." Sarah began hesitantly finally finding her voice, being so close to such a god-like man was incredibly unnerving for her. She'd never even been on a date before let alone be this close with a man. She had always stuck to her books for companionship. Being this close to him she saw that his eyes weren't merely blue but had flecks of silver and green in their depths as well.

Ryuuzaki nodded, "Your welcome." He flew down gracefully into the center of the garden before gently setting her down on her feet.

Sarah looked around and wondered what had become of the bloody battlefield and then she remembered how Ryuuzaki's face was the last thing she had seen before she passed out which must have meant - "You saved me back there as well didn't you?"

Ryuuzaki nodded again.

"Why?" Sarah shyly ventured to ask.

"Because Priestess I need your help." Ryuuzaki admitted, a serious expression on his face.

"Priestess? I'm not a priestess I'm just a linguist." Sarah tried to explain.

Ryuuzaki quirked his head at her, "A linguist?" He looked her clothes over once more, "Are you from the Makai?"

Sarah shook her head. "Is that what this place is called? No, I'm from the...well, real world...you know America? New York? I was in Tokyo though when I somehow ended up here. I was reading this strange book..." Sarah trailed off.

Ryuuzaki's multi-colored eyes seemed to gleam knowingly. "A book? Ah, yes a tear...I see now. You're from the human plane aren't you? But you still possess powerful exorcist abilities, did you not know?"

"Exorcist abilities?" Sarah furrowed her brow in confusion, and couldn't help but think back to when this strange power had erupted from out of her body and destroyed the *nekomata*...She shivered uncomfortably at the memory.

Ryuuzaki nodded. "Right now this world is at war. Well, the four Demon Lords are always fighting each other for territory. But right now I, Ryuuzaki, Lord of the Northern Lands, am waging a war against Lord Kyohei, Lord of the Southern Lands and his *nekomata* army. In the last battle I sustained tremendous losses. Lord Kyohei is extremely powerful - he and his army have the ability to raise the dead making his army almost unstoppable."

Sarah gulped, "Raise the dead?"

"Your world is also in danger. If Lord Kyohei succeeds in his endeavor and conquers all four lands - meaning he defeats the other two Demon Lords, the Lord of the East and the Lord of the West respectively, as well as myself, he plans to take over the human world next. So, won't you please help us, Priestess? Grant me your power...the power to save both our worlds and join me. Together, with our powers combined I know we can beat Lord Kyohei." He reached his hand out to her in a beseeching manner.

Sarah bit her lip as she looked at Ryuuzaki's outstretched hand. This was all like some kind of crazy dream - a handsome demon lord was at war and needed *her* help to save the world? Naw. It was crazy! But as she looked up and met those silvery blue eyes of his her reservations faded away and she found her body moving forward on its own, and her hand moved to place itself in his. And she realized in that moment that she wouldn't refuse this demon man anything.

He closed his powerful, calloused hand gently around her delicate fingers and smiled at her warmly and she smiled back hesitantly beginning to blush. *He really is so handsome...*

* * * * * * * * * * * * * * * *

Time passed, until it was the day of the final battle. Lord Kyohei's *nekomata* army with their undead fallen comrades were facing off against the dragon demon army, and both groups were still in their humanoid forms. Although, at any moment they would decide to kick things up a notch and take on their true forms. Sarah found out that full *yokai* have the ability to take on a humanoid form and also a beast form. While in their beast form they are sometimes granted powers they do not normally possess while being in their humanoid forms and at times became even more powerful. A *nekomata yokai* would turn into a large, two-tailed cat about the size of a tiger, or in most cases about twice or three times that size. While the dragon *yokai* would actually turn into full sized dragons when in their beast form.

The battle was coming to its climax when the *nekomata* and *yokai* were beginning to show their true forms. Lord Kyohei, when he transformed into his 'beast shape', turned into a giant, black two-tailed cat with bright, violet colored eyes. He was about the same size as the silvery, green and blue scaled dragon that Ryuuzaki had become when he had transformed into his beast form. The multi-colored scales on Ryuuzaki's body glittered in the sunlight blinding Sarah's eyes. Sarah rode on Ryuuzaki's back, clutching her arms around Ryuuzaki's neck tightly, as they flew through the air towards Lord Kyohei at top speed.

Lord Kyohei and Lord Ryuuzaki attacked each other in midair. Lord Kyohei opened his mouth to unleash a large, black fireball towards Lord Ryuuzaki, who did the same opening his mouth and unleashing a powerful lightning attack at Kyohei. Their attacks collided in midair, neither overpowering the other until both attacks were dissipated.

"*Sarah, lend me your power - now.*" Ryuuzaki spoke to her telepathically.

"Alright." Sarah nodded and concentrated on summoning her spirit energy so that when Ryuuzaki was forming his next attack and unleashed it upon Lord Kyohei she let her energy burst forth as well to intertwine with Ryuu's own demonic energy so that they became one - the holy spirit energy of a priestess mixing with the dark energies of a *yokai* lord. Swirling together the energies went flying towards Kyohei, who opened his mouth to unleash another fireball attack upon them, but Sarah and Ryuuzaki's attack cut through his attack easily, and hit the *nekomata* square in the chest. Kyohei was pushed back as the holy and dark energies enveloped him, overpowering him, until he was purified and exorcized into nothingness.

With their lord defeated the *nekomata* army began to retreat. A victory cry went up through the ranks of the dragon *yokai* army in response - they had won.

Ryuuzaki flew down to land among the cheering dragon army. He transformed back into his humanoid form and held Sarah in his arms to steady her since she had used a great deal of her spirit energy for that final attack. He then turned her around to face him and removed her glasses before kissing her deeply and passionately.

An approving cry went up through the dragon *yokai* army in response to their lord kissing the human woman, who had helped them defeat the *nekomata* army. "*Whooo!*" They beat their swords or spears on their shields loudly creating quite the ruckus. Sarah was blushing beet red by the time Ryuuzaki saw fit to let her go.

That day, they all celebrated the victory brought about by their Lord Ryuuzaki and the mysterious 'Priestess' as they liked to call Sarah.

That night, as they celebrated their victory over the *nekomata*, Sarah and Lord Ryuuzaki lay down together under a willow tree in the royal gardens, and under the light of a full moon they kissed again. Sarah was swept away by his love that night...

INTERMISSION

"Then what happened?" Alec interrupted his mother's story. He licked his lips and was leaning forward when she had suddenly paused in her tale.

"Now that..." Sarah waved her finger back and forth at Alec, "Is a secret. For now at least. I'll have to wait till you're a bit older to tell you what happened between Ryuuzaki and I that night. You're only 13-years-old after all and this story is rated PG. But suffice it to say I had a wonderful night with your father. A night which gifted me with you...

"The next day I told Ryuuzaki I had to return back to the human world, my world, home. He located a tear back in the Makai and I was able to get back to Tokyo safely where Mori was waiting for me. I gave birth to you in Japan but when you were only a few months old *yokai* suddenly attacked us and burned down the apartment complex where we were living. I was able to exorcize most of them with my powers, but I worried for your safety and decided I should move back to America, thinking we'd be safer there. Mori offered to come with me.

"And we were safe for five years. During those five years Mori stayed by my side. He had always loved me and he never asked who your father was. But then on your 5th birthday...Lord Kyohei's son came to our door. I was shocked to see a *nekomata* there in the middle of New York City and so I didn't react fast enough...."

FLASHBACK RESUMED

Knock. Knock. Came an insistent knock at the front door.

"Coming!" Sarah called as she went to answer the door. She opened it and saw a boy with glossy black hair, bright violet colored eyes, pointed ears, and noticed two little fangs that were peaking out of his mouth as he grinned at her. She looked down at his hands to see that he had long, black claws. She gasped in sudden realization. "A *nekomata*."

"Why hello there, Ryuuzaki's Priestess." Kyohei's son suddenly materialized a giant sword in his hand and brought it forward to run Sarah through the heart with it. Before she could even blink, in one fluid motion he had done so, and then had removed his sword. "And goodbye. With this my revenge is complete, father." The *nekomata* turned to walk away, but then stopped for a moment as if he had sensed...something. Kyohei's son shrugged before continuing on his way without looking back.

Sarah sunk to her knees and placed a hand over her bleeding heart. She was dying...

"Sarah!" Mori quickly came to the front door and found Sarah there in the doorway bleeding. "What happened? Who did this?"

"Mama?" Sarah weakly turned her head to see that her five-year-old son had come to the door and was looking at her with a worried expression on his face.

"Alec..." She choked out, as blood dribbled down her chin, and then she reached out a hand to stroke his cheek fondly, "Be a good boy for mama... Mori...please take care of my son...I beg of you..."

"Sarah!" Mori gripped her hands, "Just hang on. I'll call an ambulance they'll-"

Sarah shook her head, "It's too late for me Mori...thank you for being such a good friend to me all these years...thank you for loving me." She stroked his cheek fondly before she fell forward.

"Sarah!"

END OF FLASHBACK

Alec had had his face in his hands but then he looked up with a startled look on his face. "I...remember. I don't know how I'd forgotten...Mother...I remember you."

"Oh Alec!" Sarah flung her arms around him and he hugged her back fiercely.

"But what happened to Lord Ryuuzaki?" Alec questioned.

Sarah shook her head sadly, "Time passes more slowly for demons than it does for us short-lived humans. Ryuuzaki probably didn't realize how much time had passed when it was already too late. I never got to see him again. So, I don't know. He's not here in Yomi, so he must still be alive out there somewhere in the Makai World..."

Alec frowned as he looked down at his watch and saw that it was time to go and give Akira his food tray. The time had flown by. "Mother, I have to get going. Perhaps, I'll come again and see you." Alec shyly offered.

Sarah shook her head. "It would be better if you didn't Alec..."

Alec took her hands anyways, "I'll come again. I promise. Log out!" Alec raised his arm and logged out of Yokai World.

⸱ ⸱ ⸱ ⸱ ⸱ ⸱ ⸱ ⸱ ⸱ ⸱ ⸱ ⸱ ⸱ ⸱ ⸱ ⸱

Alec left Akira his tray of food without saying anything and headed back to his lonely dorm room to sleep. Neji was still in the hospital in a coma and so Alec still had their dorm room all to himself. That night at least he remembered to lock his door. But that still didn't stop him from having another nightmare...

Alec was in a dark forest surrounded by yokai, who wanted to eat him, and he was all alone. He was swinging his Spirit Sword helplessly through the air at them left and right, but his sword was already beginning to flicker due to his low spirit energy. His sword's blade suddenly shattered and he was left defenseless. There were just too many of them!

One yokai swiped a long, clawed hand towards Alec and his sword was knocked to the ground. The trees around Alec seemed to be growing larger until the light in the forest grew dimmer and dimmer until only pitch black, darkness surrounded Alec on all sides, but luckily he could still sense the presence of the demons and yokai. Alec knew he was surrounded and that he was doomed, but as the cold fear spilled through his veins, another emotion seemed to possess him...

Anger. He was filled with a dark anger and hatred towards the yokai, who were attacking him, and some strange power seemed to be awakening inside of himself. Then Alec could feel himself transforming...his ears were becoming pointed...his nails were growing out into claws...his incisors had lengthened into fangs...two short horns had sprouted on either side of his head...a pair of silvery bat-like wings sprouted from his back and he grew a tail. In this new form Alec could feel an immense power thrumming through his veins.

Power - it consumed him. He sensed his invisible enemies and attacked them in the darkness slashing his clawed hands through the air at them. He killed and killed and killed all of the yokai around him easily without having to see them. Their bodies falling to the ground all around him but then suddenly light returned to the forest and Alec was able to look down at the bodies of the yokai he had slain -

Alec's eyes widened in horror as he saw instead the dead bodies of his friends - Rika, Junpei, Neji, Takahashi-sensei, Haruna-sensei, Yoru, Junko, Jin...he had killed all of them without even realizing it! He had let his bloodlust and inner demon overtake him and he had killed them without knowing who they were! His friends...

"NO!" Alec cried.

Then the bodies of his friends began to rise up off the ground and Alec could see that they were dead but that they were moving or at least their bodies were moving. He could also see the horrible wounds he had inflicted upon them - horrible claw marks and slash wounds and bite marks. They began to sway on their feet as they approached Alec, and their mouths and eyes stretched open in an eerie, zombie-like manner...

"Alec...why...? Why did you kill us Alec?" Haruna-sensei questioned, a hurt look on her face.

Alec looked down at his clawed hands in despair and saw that they were covered in blood. Human blood. "No...I didn't mean to...I didn't know..." Alec began to futilely explain. "It's not my fault!"

"You let yourself become a demon Alec..." Takahashi-sensei shook his head at Alec while appearing sad and disappointed.

"Demon..." "Monster..." "Devil-child..." Their voices filled the air around Alec until lastly Alec heard Laura's accusing voice. "That child is not mine..."

Alec put his face in his hands and could horribly feel his horns. He raised his head and cried out to the night sky. "NOO!"

Alec woke up choking for breath, a scream dying on his lips. He looked at his hands and saw that they were normal and not covered in blood. He raised his hands to touch his head and felt that there were no horns and let out a sigh of relief. No - he wasn't a demon *yet*. But what if that did happen? What if he did end up turning into a demon and hurting his friends? What if he did let the demon blood within consume him? Then his friends would be in danger. He couldn't let that happen...

So, Alec decided to do the only thing that seemed logical to him at the time. He would just have to push them away.

Alec was so distracted by the nightmares that he'd been having that he did poorly during his next training session with Yoru. Once again he failed to produce a solid Spirit Sword and Yoru seemed more than disappointed. The boys at school were continuing to play pranks on him but Alec could hardly care less since he had more important things on his mind. Alec had decided to distance himself from his friends, which as it turned out wasn't too difficult since it seemed his friends had distanced themselves from him. Rika and Junpei had been spending a lot of time with each other all of a sudden and seemed to be leaving Alec out of the loop. Not that he minded...

Neji was still in the hospital and Alec couldn't help but feel utterly alone. Perhaps, it was for the best that his friends were ignoring him. He had wanted to push them away in the first place right? But then why did it hurt so much? Alec decided to set up a computer in his dorm room so that he could log on to Yokai World without having to use the computers in the computer club room and risk crossing paths with Rika or Junpei there. Once he had everything set up he ended up logging on to Yokai World and ended up going to Yomi to see his mother...

Alec's mother appeared before Alec with a surprised look on her face, not having expected to see her son back so soon, "Alec? Honey what's wrong? I told you not to come back here - it's much too dangerous."

"Mom..." Alec's voice was all choked up, "I just had to see you...I just feel so...alone." Alec rushed up to her and buried his face in her chest.

"Oh Alec," Sarah whispered sadly and wrapped her arms around him, not able to push her own beloved son away. With tormented eyes Sarah stroked Alec's snow-white hair trying to comfort him as he cried.

However, since Sarah was a ghost she had no sense of time and days passed with Alec simply letting himself cry into his mother's embrace...

• • • • • • • • • • • • • • •

Meanwhile, back in reality Alec's friends were beginning to get worried about Alec since they hadn't seen or heard from him in several days. Junpei was sure that Alec was hiding or locking himself up in his room, but when he had gone to Alec's room earlier that day there had been no answer when he knocked on the door. Junpei came to the conclusion that Alec had probably set up a computer in his room to be able to escape reality and play Yokai World without having to use the computer room. Junpei convinced Rika to log on to the game with him so that together they could try and find Alec. Then they could talk to him and convince him to come back to the real world - back to them.

Rika and Junpei materialized in the Guardian Knights guildhall and Yukino instantly greeted them.

"Hey guys," She looked behind them, "Where's Alec? Isn't he with you?"

Junpei shook his head, "Actually, that's why we're here Yukino. You haven't seen Alec at all have you? We have reason to believe he's somewhere in the game..."

"No, I haven't." Yukino frowned. "Why did something happen?" Yukino narrowed her eyes at them and was surprised with she saw LadyV flinch.

Junpei shrugged, "Well, we can't find him back in reality and we think he's holed himself up in his dorm room, but he won't answer the door, so I think he's probably logged on to Yokai World and can't hear us banging on his door in the real world, you know."

"It's all my fault." LadyV started biting her lip, "I need to apologize to him, say I'm sorry. I need to explain...I've just had a lot on my mind after finding out the truth about how my parents died and Junpei has been there for me, but we only recently realized that we've been unintentionally ignoring Alec. We didn't mean to do it but I know Alec must think we've been doing it on purpose."

"It's easy to see why Alec ran away." Yukino added cryptically and LadyV looked pale. "You guys are *supposed* to be his best friends and yet you were completely ignoring him..." Yukino sighed. "Knowing him, he's probably off sulking somewhere by himself and thinking about something stupid."

"We *are* his friends." LadyV insisted.

"Well, sometimes you guys sure don't act like it." Yukino frowned at them, hands on her hips.

"We know and we're really sorry. So do you have any idea where Alec might have gone in the game Yukino?" Junpei questioned her with a hopeful look in his eyes, "We tried all the major areas but there's no sign of him, but I can tell from my friends list that he is currently logged into the game."

"No..." Yukino looked thoughtful, tapping her chin. "Sorry."

"We have to find him. Despite what you might think of us Yukino we're really worried about him. We have to apologize. And there's someone else who's really worried about him too." Junpei explained.

"Who?" Yukino quirked her head at him.

Junpei stepped to the side to reveal -

"Dr. M!" Yukino blinked. Alec had mentioned to her how Dr. M had been in the hospital due to a *yokai* attack and had been in a coma.

　　　　　　· ● · ● · ● · ● · ● · ● · ● · ● · ●

Yukino had a pretty good idea of where Alec had run off to if he was currently logged into the game, but in an area that his friends couldn't find him. That narrowed it down quite a bit actually. Which was why Yukino headed over to the Haunted Mansion Area the minute LadyV and Junpei had left the guildhall, and used the well to get to Yomi. Before she told LadyV and Junpei where Alec was she wanted to speak to him first and get his side of the story. She made her way through the *tengu* forest and it was just as she suspected - there was Alec a little ways in front of the cave and he was crying into some woman's arms.

Yukino approached with delicate steps on her *zori* sandals. "Alec?"

Alec wiped his tears with the back of his hand roughly before he pushed himself away from his mother and turned to see Yukino. He looked a bit surprised to see her there but quickly stood to face her.

"Yukino?" He gave her an uneasy smile. But Yukino noticed he appeared to be swaying on his feet and realized that it had to be from staying logged into the game for several days without food.

"*Baka*...Alec where have you been? Your friends are very worried about you." Yukino frowned at him, hands on her hips. She had to resist the urge to whack him over the head for being so stupid and careless about his own well being.

Alec blinked. "My friends? I don't have any friends. I'm all *alone*..." Alec's voice cracked on the last word.

Yukino took another step forward and shook her head, "You're wrong Alec. I'm your friend aren't I? And the others told me how worried they've been about you. They also told me how they wanted to apologize. They didn't realize they had been ignoring you until it was already too late. They didn't mean to hurt your feelings, Alec. So come back to us." Yukino reached her hand out to Alec.

Alec shook his head. "No Yukino...you don't understand. It's better off this way. I can't have any friends..." He took a step away from her.

"What are you talking about?" Yukino furrowed her brow in a confused manner.

"It's too dangerous for my friends to be around me. I'm a Spirit Magnet and ghosts and *yokai* are always going to be attracted to me because they want to eat my soul. If my friends stay near me their lives will be put in danger because of me. Also...what if I end up turning into some kind of demon and end up hurting them? I have *yokai* blood flowing through my veins Yukino. I don't know what I'm capable of..." Alec was beginning to sound hysterical.

"Alec no *baka*! You are an idiot!" Yukino exclaimed suddenly making Alec flinch, "You say you don't want to hurt your friends but you already have! They're worried sick about you and are blaming themselves for your running away. LadyV was near tears when I last spoke with her. You don't belong to just yourself anymore Alec, you belong to your friends too. And by pushing them away you're hurting them Alec - something you claim you don't want to do. Also, if you're not close to your friends to protect them when something does happen you'll be the last to know your friends were in danger and that they needed you. You have to stay close to your friends Alec to protect them. Running away will just ensure that your friends come to harm."

"But Yukino...I'm afraid of...myself...of my inner demon." Alec admitted in a low voice.

"That's just stupid! I know you Alec and I know you're a good person. You wouldn't hurt a fly if you didn't have to. I can sense the pureness of your heart, or did you forget back in reality I'm a *miko*. I also pride myself on being a good judge of character. I trust you Alec...even knowing you're half *yokai* I know you would never do anything on purpose to hurt me or your friends. I believe in you so you should also believe in yourself Alec. Have faith in yourself like I do. I know you won't let your inner demon overpower you - ever. You're too strong and kind and nice for that to happen." Yukino put a hand to Alec's heart. "You're a good person Alec. I know."

Alec was blushing now. "Yukino...I...thank you."

Yukino was standing in front of Alec now but she gave him a harsh look and suddenly slapped him hard across the face.

Alec put a hand to his cheek in shock, "Ow! **Yukino**? What was that for?" Alec pouted.

"That's for being a *baka* and a coward. I thought you were braver than this Alec. You've been afraid of nothing but your own shadow. You only have one choice you need to make. Are you going to be someone who needs protecting or are you going to be a protector? You need to decide that. Or are you going to keep running away forever?"

"You're right Yukino. I won't keep running away anymore and I think I know what my choice is." Alec shook his head ruefully. "I still can't believe you really slapped me. For a second there I thought you were going to..." Alec trailed off, an amused expression on his face.

"What?" Yukino raised an eyebrow, "Kiss you? Yea, right, like I'd ever do something like that. And if I were going to kiss you Alec it would be when you've stopped being a *baka* brat, and someone I can't help but see as my pathetic little brother, and when you've become a true protector. Someone strong, brave, powerful - a real hero. Yea, but right now, I'd never kiss a boy like you. I mean, yuck!" Yukino stuck her tongue out at him playfully.

"Right. Guess not." Alec sniffled and wiped a tear away smiling tremulously at her. But thanks to Yukino knocking some sense into him - literally - he was feeling quite better.

Yukino leaned forward and wiped one of his tears away, "Boys don't cry Alec." She shook her head at him. "But..." She placed her hand on Alec's head and brought his head forward to her chest, "If you ever need a shoulder to cry on Alec, I'm here for you. You're *not* alone."

Alec was startled by Yukino's unexpected embrace, and he didn't dare move. "Thanks..."

"There, there." Yukino patted his back mechanically.

"You're really good at this comfort thing aren't you?" Alec joked, his voice tinged with sarcasm.

"Don't make me hurt you." Yukino replied back in her monotone voice.

Alec gulped.

Sarah laughed at the two of them and they turned their attention towards her. "You two are just so cute together."

This caused both of them to blush. "Mom! We're not like that!" Alec insisted.

Yukino quickly pulled back from the impromptu embrace she had given Alec but he had just looked so pathetic she couldn't help her inner girl from reacting. Yep, that was it. Completely justifiable - anyone would want to hug a cute, wounded puppy dog right?

"Yea, we're just friends. Distant acquaintances really." Yukino put in, "He's like a little brother to me."

Alec sighed at that reminder.

"So, Alec have you decided what you're going to be?" Yukino questioned curiously.

"Yep." Alec gave her a thumbs up, "I'm going to be a protector!"

"Good boy." Yukino ruffled Alec's hair as though he were a puppy. "Train hard and maybe when you grow up you can be."

"*Mou*...Geez...Yukino..." Alec whined as he batted her hands away. He hated it when she treated him like a little kid when they were basically the same age. Curse his genes for being an inch or two shorter than she was!

"We should get going to the guildhall. There's a surprise waiting there for you." Yukino revealed with a wink.

"Alright." Alec turned towards his mother, but his mother smiled at him and shook her head. "Goodbye for now, mother. Teleport!"

"Teleport!" Yukino echoed and the two of them were instantly teleported to the guildhall.

• • • • • • • • • • • • • • •

Alec and Yukino materialized in the Guardian Knights guildhall and saw Junpei and LadyV had returned and were waiting for him and then Alec caught sight of someone else and his eyes widened.

"Dr. Mimic...Neji..." Alec's voice was thick with emotion, his eyes filling up with tears. "Neji!" Alec rushed up to his friend.

"Heya Alec." Dr. M gave Alec a lopsided grin. "What's with that face? I'm completely hunky dory now. I'm more worried about you. LadyV and Junpei have been telling me about how the school's been treating you lately. It sounds awful."

Alec shook his head. "It's nothing - not anymore. It's good to have you back Dr. M."

"Good to be back." Dr. M pushed his glasses up his nose as he looked Alec up and down, "You're looking scrawny. How many days has it been since you've eaten? Geez, I'm out of it for a little while and everyone decides to go on a starvation diet!"

Alec blushed, "A few days I guess...I'll eat something as soon as I log out." A sudden thought came to Alec and he paled. "Uh oh!"

"What is it Alec?" Dr. M questioned.

"Akira...I completely forgot that since I was starving myself in my room Akira wasn't getting his meals either. Opps." Alec rubbed the back of his neck bashfully.

Dr. M chuckled, "Man, he is going to be so pissed..."

"Epp." Alec squeaked thinking of how Akira was probably going to blow up at him.

Meanwhile, back in Akira's room the *hikikomori* boy was lying back on his bed while his stomach was grumbling loudly. Akira was trying very hard not to think about food...

"Alec Suzuki...you're a DEAD MAN!"

Chapter 16:
WHITE DAY

Alec had woken up extra early to avoid any crowds or people as he headed over towards Izanagi temple to begin his daily Spirit Sword training. As he was walking through the woods, however, he suddenly heard a faint cry -

"*Help!*"

For some reason this cry also seemed oddly familiar. Alec rushed through the woods in the direction that the cry had come from and he soon passed through the woods into a clearing where Alec saw a sparkling water fall and a stream in front of him. And there by the stream were three *Shinigami*-in-training: two monks and one *miko*. He recognized them from his daily *Shinigami* training at the temple as being - Toji, Rito, and Rei.

The scene that was happening before him both shocked and surprised him. Toji and Rito were both holding onto the arms of a small winged creature and seemed to be dunking it under the water of the stream. And Rei seemed to be holding something in her hand that oddly resembled a wand...

When Rito and Toji pulled up the creature, which was spluttering for breath, they began to question it harshly as if they were having some kind of interrogation - "We demand you tell us what you are? You filthy little *yokai*!"

Alec's eyes widened to the size of saucers when he realized just who and what the creature was - "Jinx!" Alec's expression was a mixture of shock, worry, surprise and happiness.

"I can't understand what you're saying!" Jinx choked out in English to the two monk boys. Without his wand, Alec realized, he was unable to cast a spell on himself to speak or understand Japanese.

Jinx turned at the sound of his name to see Alec. "Alec!" Jinx gave him a pleading look with his bright blue eyes.

Alec's eyes narrowed dangerously at the three *Shinigami*. "What the heck do you guys think you're doing?"

Rito looked indignant, "That's really none of your business, Alec. We discovered this suspicious looking *yokai* and we're simply interrogating it. We want to find out what kind of *yokai* it is and what kind of a threat it posses before we decide if we should exorcize it."

Alec clenched his fists at his sides angrily. "Jinx is not an it. Nor is he a *yokai*. He's a fairy. And he's *not* suspicious he's my friend. Now, you guys are going to let him go. Or else." Alec growled the last part, and his voice turned as cold as ice.

"Or else what?" Rito scoffed, "Your behavior makes this 'thing' even more suspicious, Alec. It makes sense that a *yokai* like yourself would protect another *yokai*. Sticking up for one of your own, aye Alec? This *yokai* must be dangerous, so I say we exorcize it right away. Rei!" Rito said her name like a command.

"*Hai*, Rito." Rei took an arrow from her bag and knocked it to her bow before aiming it straight at Jinx, who Rito and Toji had a hold of between the two of them, each monk holding onto one of Jinx's tiny little arms.

"No!" Alec yelled and began to think frantically about what he could do. He didn't have his soccer ball with him, so wondered what else could he possibly use to fight back with. His hand went to his waist absentmindedly and he felt the hilt of his Spirit Sword. He had forgotten he had the Spirit Sword with him that day. He grabbed the hilt and concentrated on summoning his spirit energy to form the Spirit Sword's blade. He held the sword out before him in a two handed grip and then suddenly the Spirit Sword flared to life - a glowing, blue blade made of spirit energy formed, and this time it was both powerful and solid looking.

Rei released her arrow upon Jinx, who shut his eyes as the arrow was flying towards him. But the arrow didn't appear to hit him right away so he hesitantly opened his eyes again to see Alec rushing forward with a glowing, blue sword of light. Jinx raised an eyebrow at this. Alec quickly stood between Jinx and the oncoming spirit arrow and slashed his Spirit Sword through the air cutting the arrow in half.

Alec then turned to face Rito and Toji. "Let him go." He repeated in a low voice as he pointed his Spirit Sword at them.

They instantly released Jinx, but then both monks turned to face Alec with confident expressions on their faces, after all they had witnessed Alec's recent training sessions with Yoru and had seen firsthand how bad Alec was at keeping his Spirit Sword solid. They had admittedly been intimidated by

Alec at first, not used to seeing him so angry, but had quickly managed to pull themselves together. It was easy not to find Alec very intimidating when one got to watch Yoru kick Alec's butt on a daily basis by shattering Alec's weak and flickering Spirit Sword multiple times and making it look easy. They had nothing to fear from Alec. The Alec they knew - the Alec of yesterday.

Rito and Toji let their fists and feet glow with their spirit energy and moved into their fighting stances prepared to face Alec. But Alec was no longer the same boy as the boy from yesterday - he no longer held doubt or hesitation in his heart. And even as Alec himself realized this he couldn't help but wonder why. *Why is my sword so different today? Why am I not hesitating? Is it because I've figured out that my sword is not a tool to slay yokai with...but to protect them with? And that I also intend to protect human beings? Is that the decision I've come to? Yes, that's it! I've finally figured out the path I need to take - I will protect both humans AND yokai.*

Alec charged forward and with his superhuman speed gained by using his spirit energy to empower his muscles he passed Rito so quickly it didn't look like Alec had done anything to him until Rito's monk's robes began to fall around him in tatters and strips of cloth. In the blink of an eye, Alec had managed to slice all of Rito's clothes off effortlessly. Alec's gray eyes were twinkling with amusement.

"Ack!" Rito exclaimed and quickly covered himself. Rei blushed and covered her eyes, but was seen peaking through her fingers anyways.

Toji frowned and looked pretty pissed at Alec as he decided to form an energy blast attack with both of his hands and which he then flung at Alec. Alec raised his sword and holding it like a baseball bat moved it through the air with a confident smirk on his face. "Batters up!" Alec hit the energy blast and sent it flying back at Toji. It hit Toji in the gut and sent him flying backwards into the stream. "Going, going, gone." Alec said as he watched Toji getting washed away down the stream. "I believe that's a homerun." Alec chuckled mercilessly.

Alec turned to face Rei next, "Now, if you'd please hand over Jinx's wand-" Alec held out his hand expectantly.

Rei frowned and shook her head stubbornly at Alec, "Why are you so good all of a sudden? You shouldn't be able to handle a Spirit Sword like that - just yesterday you were worse than an amateur. I mean, you totally sucked."

Alec blushed at that but shook his head and explained. "I was a different me yesterday than the me of today." *And it took Jinx being here for me to realize that. Yukino made me realize I wanted to be a protector and Jinx made me realize what I want and need to protect. I owe those two a lot.*

"No, I refuse to believe that someone can change so quickly. I think it was just luck that let you cut my arrow before. And I'll prove it to you!" Rei knocked another arrow to her bow and quickly fired it at Alec. Her arrow was engulfed in the blue light of her spirit energy. *Shinigami*-in-training such as herself would use real arrows before they became powerful enough to form arrows out of thin air like Junko could and which were completely made up of spirit energy. Alec moved his sword through the air and surprised her by easily blocking her arrow and cutting it in half.

"Impossible." Rei breathed. She raised her bow and shot at Alec again and again. She sent arrows at him in quick succession but he was able to move his sword swiftly through the air and cut through all her arrows easily. Rei sunk to her knees in stunned defeat. "You're just not...human."

Alec stalked towards her and reached his hand out. "Jinx's wand, please."

Rei blinked up at Alec with a slightly fearful expression on her face before she reached into her *haori* sleeve and pulled out Jinx's wand and handed it to Alec with trembling fingers.

Alec tossed Jinx his wand and Jinx caught it. Jinx put his wand to his throat and quickly chanted a spell so that he could start speaking and understanding Japanese.

Jinx watched as Alec dissipated his sword and he looked at his savior with wide, teary, doe-eyes before Jinx flew straight at Alec and hugged him, burying his face in Alec's chest. "Alec! I was so scared! What's with this school? Why can so many people see me here? It's weird! I think they were going to kill me!"

Alec put a hand on Jinx's head and patted it in a comforting gesture. Alec scowled, thinking back to those other *Shinigami*-in-training, and found he was totally pissed at them. In fact, they were lucky Alec let them get off the hook so easily. Alec had been enjoying giving those three a taste of their own medicine - perhaps a little too much. Alec shivered. "Shhh, it's alright Jinx. I won't let anyone hurt you."

Jinx sniffled and looked up at Alec. He had a long drip of snot hanging from his nose, which he sniffed back up into his nostril. "Really? You aren't still mad at me?"

Alec shook his head. "Aren't you the one who should be mad at me? I'm the one who pushed you away Jinx. I didn't want to lose anymore of my friends. I also didn't want you to get hurt because of me. But Yukino's right. I was just being stupid. It's just like she said - pushing my friends away will only hurt them and then when they're in trouble I won't know about it. Just like what happened just now. If I hadn't gotten here in time Jinx..." Alec shook his head. "I need to start keeping my friends close. I never stopped being your friend Jinx."

Jinx's expression brightened considerably, "When I talked to Cindy about what you did she told me the same thing. That you pushed me away not because you didn't like me but because you *did* like me."

Alec scratched the back of his neck bashfully, "Yea, I know it's stupid but it's true. I've been a total *baka*. But my friend Yukino helped me get a clue."

Jinx tilted his head, curious, "Yukino?"

Alec nodded, "She also helped me realize how stupid all my fears and doubts have been recently. She told me that the only choice I had to make was whether I was going to be the type of person that needed to be protected or would be doing the protecting. And now thanks to you Jinx the last piece of the puzzle has fallen into place for me and I now realize what I must do - what path I am to take. Yoru was wrong. He said I had to chose - would I protect humans and my friends or would I protect *yokai*. But he didn't realize there's another option - I intend to protect both humans and *yokai*. My sword is not a tool to slay *yokai* with - it's simply a tool to protect those I care for with.

"You see, Jinx, I found out while I was here at this school that I'm actually a *hanyou*, I'm half-*yokai*. My father apparently was a powerful *yokai* warlord. Half of the blood that flows through my veins is *yokai* blood and the other half is human. That's why one part of me is meant to protect humans and the other part is meant to protect *yokai*. If I can I will try and stop both sides from fighting each other altogether. If I can somehow help the spirit world find peace and live in harmony with the real world then we could have true peace and no one else would have to die...That's what I truly wish for anyways." Alec shrugged slightly embarrassed with his admission.

Jinx just smiled. "That's just like you Alec - you're completely naive and idealistic, but at the same time really cool. I'm proud to have you as a friend Alec. I always knew you were a special sort of human. I bet you have a greater purpose in all this somehow. So...is this Yukino your girlfriend?"

Alec turned bright red. "What? No! She's just a friend - that's all." Alec waved his hands frantically before him.

Jinx pouted, a disappointed look on his face, "That's too bad. She sounded really wise if you ask me. And it seems like you owe her one if she helped you to overcome your stubborn streak at pushing your friends away, and in finally believing in yourself."

Alec looked thoughtful, "Yea, I owe her a lot actually..." Alec shook his head in disbelief at Jinx actually being there, all the way in Tokyo. "I still can't believe you came all the way to Tokyo to see me Jinx. Not that I'm not happy to have you here. It's good to have you back."

Jinx blushed at the unexpected praise. "Yea, well, the Elders weren't too happy with me after that whole fiasco of showing magic in front of humans and I had this nagging feeling you might need my help. Although it looks

393

like you have things under control." Jinx eyed Alec's deactivated Spirit Sword. "Where's your trusty soccer ball?"

Alec held up his Spirit Sword in one hand and let it flare to life, the blade now solid blue and glowing. "I've upgraded my weapon of choice." Alec grinned.

"I can see that." Jinx raised an eyebrow at the peculiar weapon. "Any particular reason?" Jinx was a bit surprised the see the pacifist Alec he had known with such a deadly weapon as a sword in his hands. It was a bit unnerving.

Alec frowned, "Japan is a hell of a lot more dangerous than America was where spiritual threats are concerned. The magic and spiritual world here is still strong and alive and it hasn't weakened as much as it has in America. And I sense...something *big* is going to happen soon. It's just a gut feeling though." Alec shrugged. "But I want to be ready for it. I need to be ready to take on anything. Whatever it is."

Jinx nodded in understanding, "Actually it was the Elders who mysteriously suggested you may be needing my help in the near future. They also hinted that 'something big' was going to happen here."

Alec looked a bit surprised by this news but then waved it off. "Well, whatever it is I'll be ready."

"*We'll* be ready." Jinx corrected him, "You're not alone Alec."

Alec couldn't help but grin at that. "Yea, I know. I also have a bunch of annoying new friends here, who constantly remind me of that fact, but even though they sometimes get on my nerves I wouldn't give them up for anything in the world. Come on, let's go show Yoru my new Spirit Sword. I think he'll be surprised."

• • • • • • • • • • • • • • • • •

Alec and Jinx, the bad luck fairy, headed over to Izanagi temple where Rika and Junpei were already currently training with Jin and Junko. All eyes were immediately drawn towards Alec and the mysterious, tiny creature that was casually perched on Alec's shoulder and swinging his feet back and forth.

Yoru approached Alec and eyed Jinx curiously, "And who's this?"

"This is my friend Jinx. He's a fairy. And no he's not a *yokai* or some kind of malevolent spiritual being." Alec decided to clarify once and for all. "He's a magical creature from America."

Yoru narrowed his eyes at Jinx, "*Yokai* is a broad term which can refer to any sort of spiritual being such as your friend Jinx whom only people gifted with spiritual powers can see. So your friend, in a sense, is a *yokai*." Yoru was frowning thoughtfully.

Alec just shrugged in an obstinate manner. "Whatever."

Yoru decided to change the subject. "Have you made your choice Alec?"

Alec smirked, "Yea, I have. Want me to show you my new sword?"

Yoru smiled back challengingly. "Please do." Yoru formed his Spirit Sword with one hand and pointed it at Alec.

"Jinx go over there so you'll be safe, and try and stay out of trouble. Yoru and I are just going to have a friendly little sparring match." Alec motioned towards the edge of the courtyard. Jinx looked from Yoru to Alec with a skeptical expression on his face, before nodding and flew off to watch the two *Shinigami* from a safe distance.

Alec formed his Spirit Sword in a two-handed grip before him and the blade pulsed with energy and power. This time his blade was solid, strong, and did not waver.

Yoru arched an eyebrow in surprise, "Impressive - now let's put it to the test shall we?"

"That's what I'm here for." Alec nodded and Yoru charged forward and their swords clashed. Yoru was surprised to note that Alec was not pushed back. Then Alec moved his sword through the air quickly and Yoru was forced to block the cunning attack. Then they began to spar on par with each other in a deadly and impressive dance. *Slash. Block. Slice. Dodge. Slash. Parry.*

Everyone at the temple, all the *Shinigami*-in-training, had stopped their spirit training as they turned to watch in awe as Alec was fighting equally with Yoru.

"What is your decision?" Yoru questioned him curiously, no longer sensing hesitation or doubts in Alec.

"You said I had a choice to make, Yoru. That I had to choose between protecting my friends and protecting or siding with *yokai*. Well, you're wrong." Alec's silver eyes flashed.

Yoru faltered in his step at Alec's words and Alec almost managed to land a blow, but instead cut his sword through the sleeve of Yoru's *haori* shirt. The onlookers gasped simultaneously in surprise at they watched this.

"There's a third choice available." Alec began to explain as their swords continued to clash as Yoru regained his footing. "And that is the path I have chosen - to use my sword to protect not only my friends and humanity but also *yokai*. My sword is not a tool of destruction but a tool of protection!"

Yoru blinked back in shock at Alec's answer before shaking his head pityingly at Alec. "I didn't think you were so naive. If you plan to protect your friends from attacking *yokai* for instance you will be forced to kill those *yokai*. That's the only way."

Alec frowned, "No, you're wrong Yoru. You've blinded yourself to only one path when there are many. There's always another way. Sometimes I will be forced to kill them but other times my voice will reach the *yokai* and I'll be able to save them too. Don't you see Yoru? Don't you understand? I want to save them both!" Alec swung his sword hard at Yoru, who was forced back.

Yoru looked stunned and then angry as he blocked Alec's attack. "You really are just a *baka* brat. Stop being so foolish and naive. You can't stop *yokai* and humans from fighting and hating each other so easily Alec. This is a conflict that's been going on for thousands of years."

"I know but that doesn't mean I can't try." Alec pouted with a stubborn expression on his face.

"You're only going to end up getting yourself killed by having such overly kindhearted sentiments. I already told you a *Shinigami* cannot have a heart - it will only make you weak. Emotions like mercy...or even love are weak emotions Alec that will make you hesitate in the heat of battle!" Yoru swung his sword at Alec hard.

Alec bit his lip, "You're wrong, you just don't understand how powerful someone can become when they have someone to protect or when they have love in their heart. But I'll show you Yoru. I'll save you from yourself! Just like Midoriko asked me to do!" Alec pushed Yoru's sword back, and then charged forward with a sudden burst of power that shattered Yoru's sword.

Everyone gasped and then fell silent, stunned.

"*Midoriko?*" Yoru whispered his mother's name startled as his blade shattered in his hand.

Alec nodded. "She warned me you were going down the wrong path - one filled with hatred, anger, and revenge. Those emotions won't make you stronger Yoru - they'll make you weaker. You won't really be winning if you win your battles like that. You may think you got what you wanted but in the end you'll realize it was a hollow victory. Do you really want to become what you most dislike about your enemies just to defeat them? Become a devil to best a devil? Why not stay an angel and try to save the devil instead? A truly strong person can stay an angel and defeat devils. Only a weak person needs to become a devil to best devils. Think about it Yoru. It's what Midoriko would have wanted."

Yoru blinked back at Alec in shock stunned by his words.

Alec dissipated his sword and turned to walk away from Yoru after having said those final words. "Let's go Jinx." Alec called and didn't look back as he left the temple grounds. Yoru's eyes followed Alec as he left and seemed at a loss for words. Jinx obediently flew after Alec's retreating form.

* * * * * * * * * * * * * * *

Alec and Jinx made their way back to Izanagi Academy and several students were giving Jinx odd looks since not many Japanese students knew what a fairy was. Although Alec found it equally strange that so many students were able to see Jinx at all. Yep, Izanagi Academy was definitely not a normal school.

The usual three troublemakers - Tatsuya, Ken and Omi, tried to pull a prank on Alec as he passed by under one of the school building's windows and threw down some rotten eggs at Alec from their strategic position at the window. Yep, Tatsuya needed a life and had been planning this all morning. Jinx, however, noticed this 'sneak attack' and quickly waved his golden, star-tipped wand at the rotten eggs.

"Transfiguration! Flowers!" Jinx's wand glowed with a golden light.

The golden light hit the eggs and with a *poof* of purple smoke they were transformed into - water balloons.

The water balloons crashed down upon Alec completely soaking him and making him look like some kind of half-drowned, puppy dog. His shaggy, white hair became plastered to his face and covered his eyes.

Jinx looked at Alec aghast, "Alec! I'm so sorry!"

Alec brushed his wet bangs away from his eyes and looked back at Jinx before he burst out laughing - much to Jinx's total surprise. "Ah, well, water balloons are so much better than rotten eggs any day, thanks Jinx." Alec wiped a tear from his eye since he was laughing so hard.

Jinx brightened at this. "No prob."

"Hey, Jinx, how about you try sending a swarm of butterflies at them." Alec suggested mischievously.

"Butterflies?" Jinx quirked his head at Alec. "You know I'm bad at summoning things Alec."

Alec winked. "Just do it."

Jinx shrugged, "Well, ok, you're the boss." Jinx waved his wand through the air. "Summoning Charm! Butterflies!" From out of Jinx's wand instantly came a swarm of - killer bees. The bees were at least three times larger than normal bees with hard, sharp looking stingers and red eyes. They zoomed up towards the three boys hovering in the window and began to chase the boys down the hallway as they tried to run away.

Alec had to hold his stomach he was laughing so hard it hurt. "Nice one, Jinx."

Jinx puffed out his chest proudly but then his expression turned to worry, "But Alec why were those boys going to throw rotten eggs at you anyways?"

Alec sighed heavily, his mirth quickly fading, "It's because the whole school knows I'm half *yokai* now. They think I'm the enemy..."

Jinx frowned, an angry expression forming on his face. "*Hmph!* That's ridiculous! Didn't you tell them you want to protect them? Ungrateful jerks!" He puffed his cheeks out.

Alec just shrugged, "They won't listen to me. Don't worry about it anyways Jinx. I'm getting kinda used to it."

Jinx crossed his arms over his chest, "Well, I'm not okay with it. I want to teach those bad humans a lesson."

Alec shook his head suddenly looking worried. "Jinx don't. It's really not necessary. Please. You'll just make things more difficult."

Jinx frowned stubbornly but nodded letting out a huff of breath. "Alright."

· · · · · · · · · · · · · · · · · · ·

The day seemed to fly by for Alec and he learned to just ignore the odd looks the students were giving him for having a fairy sitting on his shoulder. Before he knew it, it was already lunch time and Alec and Jinx decided to head outside and sit under the cherry blossom tree, which was Alec's favorite spot to eat lunch. They were eating alone when Junpei suddenly appeared and casually sat down with them.

"Yo Alec!" He plopped himself down across from Alec and noticed Jinx on Alec's shoulder. Jinx looked back at Junpei curiously and quirked his head at him. Junpei's eyes widened at the fairy's movement. "Whoa, so the rumors are true then and you've made yourself a new little friend. He's a fairy isn't he? Care to introduce us?"

"Junpei this is Jinx. Jinx, Junpei. Jinx is an old friend of mine from America. And yea he's a fairy." Alec grinned.

Junpei shook his head in disbelief, highly amused, "Only you would be friends with a *real* fairy Alec. You never stop surprising me. Crazy Americans. But you know, everyone's been talking about how you've gotten yourself 'yokai reinforcements' - they're all afraid of the little guy. And I heard something about killer bees..."

Alec and Jinx blinked at each other. "Afraid of Jinx?" Alec burst out laughing.

Jinx turned a bit red. "Hey! I could be dangerous if I wanted to!"

"Oh, it's not that you're not dangerous - you're a walking, taking, natural disaster. The bad luck fairy Jinx. I just mean they think you're *deadly*. Now that's just crazy. I don't think they know anything about fairies here do they Junpei?" Alec wiped a tear of mirth from his eye with his index finger.

Junpei shook his head, "I don't even know much about fairies myself but..." He shrugged. "I don't really need to know anything. If you trust Jinx and say he's your friend then I want to be Jinx's friend too. As long as he won't steal my teeth. I heard something about that...and I'm pretty attached to mine."

Alec burst out laughing again and it was a few moments before he was able to calm himself down.

"What?" Junpei asked, a clueless look on his face.

Alec smiled a lopsided grin at him, "That's the Tooth Fairy, Junpei. And the Tooth Fairy doesn't steal teeth. When children loose their baby teeth they place the tooth underneath their pillow and while they're asleep that night the Tooth Fairy comes and replaces the tooth with money."

Junpei raised an eyebrow at the tale. "Money huh?" Junpei turned to Jinx, "So you're *not* the Tooth Fairy?"

Jinx tried to keep a straight face and failed. "Nope, sorry."

"Too bad..." Junpei said wistfully. "I'm low on cash right now."

"I can see why you like this guy, Alec. He's amusing." Jinx grinned. "Any friend of Alec's is a friend of mine. Put 'er there, friend." Jinx stuck out his small hand towards Junpei, who took it in between his thumb and index finger smiling.

"Where are Rika and Neji?" Alec's brow furrowed as he searched the grounds with his eyes.

"Ah, Neji mentioned something about an invention he's working on and I guess he wanted cyber hacker Rika's help." Junpei then decided to change the subject, a glint in his eye. "So Alec, do you realize what day it is?"

Alec shrugged.

Junpei clicked his tongue disapprovingly at Alec. "It's White Day, Alec. So what are you going to give Rika?"

Alec was totally caught off guard by this new development. "Uhhhh... Errrrr..."

Junpei narrowed his eyes at Alec. "Don't tell me you haven't even gotten Rika a present yet?"

"Uh..." Alec scratched the back of his neck nervously.

Junpei shook his head in an exasperated fashion. "That is so like you Alec. You don't understand the feelings of a young girl's heart at all do you?"

Alec shrugged, "Well, I am a boy..."

"Is Rika Alec's girlfriend?" Jinx quirked his head at Alec. "What about Yukino?"

Junpei shot Alec a curious look. "Yukino?"

"No, she's *not* my girlfriend. Neither of them are! *Mou!* Geez!" Alec waved his arms frantically before him.

"Well, as far as I know Jinx, Rika is Alec's main squeeze and Yukino is just Alec's friend. Besides, Yukino is...well, a ghost. Can't have much of a lasting relationship with someone who's already dead now can you?"

"He's made friends with another ghost has he?" Jinx nodded knowingly. "Alec just loves setting himself up for heartbreak."

"He's done this before?" Junpei blinked.

Alec had a guilty expression on his face. "Junpei about that - Yukino is actually alive."

"Huh?" Junpei's jaw dropped comically.

"I recently found out Yukino is alive, but she's in a coma in real life while her mind is trapped in Yokai World - it's a VR game Jinx." Alec explained for Jinx's benefit before he continued. "Anyways, I think she was cursed just like you guys were Junpei."

Junpei nodded, "Whoa...but then where is she? Why haven't you broken the curse on her yet?"

Alec sighed heavily feeling the weight of Yukino's present state on his shoulders. "She was recently kidnaped by a man named Kaguto in reality - he's known as Reaper in Yokai World."

"Reaper? Dang." Junpei ran a hand through his spiky hair. "Man oh man, so are you, I mean we, going to try and find her?"

Alec nodded adamantly. "Yes, but I don't even know where to start. But I do know someone in reality now, who may be able to locate her for me. Whatever the case I'll find her eventually - and when I do I'm going to save her."

"So you going to get Yukino a White Day present too?" Junpei questioned Alec, an odd sort of curious expression on his face.

Alec blinked. "I hadn't really thought about it..."

"Alec, you're so clueless when it comes to girls." Junpei sighed and put out his hands in a helpless gesture. "Well, don't you worry, you have Junpei here to help you out. I have some great ideas about what you can get those lovely ladies. You had better take notes Alec."

Alec literally took out a pad of paper and a pen to take notes, waiting in rapt attention for Junpei to begin.

Junpei coughed. "Alright, well, girls like things like flowers, chocolates, poetry, expensive jewelry, and expensive clothes. And I have reason to believe they like pink things though since this is White Day it's traditional to find the girl you like a white colored gift."

Alec quickly scribbled everything Junpei was saying down.

Jinx raised an eyebrow at Alec's strange behavior and then turned to Junpei, "Have you ever even had a girlfriend before?"

"Well, no..." Junpei admitted looking a little flushed. "But...I do have my own fan club and that's got to count for something. Also the girls in our grade always go to my soccer games and cheer for me so they must like something about me. And that's got to be because of what I know about making girls happy. Anyways, Alec, lucky for you I have the perfect idea for a gift you could give Rika. Something special and that no one else will be able to give her."

Alec looked hopeful, "Really? What is it?"

Junpei leaned forward to whisper in Alec's ear, "A kiss."

Alec pulled back, blushing furiously, "Junpei!"

Junpei and Jinx both laughed at Alec's discomfort. "He's so clueless." They both agreed.

⸰ ⸰ ⸰ ⸰ ⸰ ⸰ ⸰ ⸰ ⸰ ⸰ ⸰ ⸰ ⸰ ⸰ ⸰ ⸰

Alec was pondering what to get Rika while walking down the school's hallways, but still couldn't make up his mind while Jinx tagged along with him. *Flowers...? Yukino likes flowers but how would I manage to find flowers in a game world? Chocolate...maybe I could try and make some but I don't know how to cook. Poetry? That's Yukino's thing but I wouldn't even know what author to chose. Expensive clothes and jewelry? I don't have any money and I wouldn't even know what to pick out...*

Alec sighed heavily. He felt he still needed a bit more advice on the whole White Day thing and so his feet seemed to be taking him to Takahashi-*sensei*'s classroom.

"I still need a bit more advice on what to get Rika for White Day, Jinx." Alec was tugging at his shaggy hair in frustration. "I'm going to go ask a teacher of mine for some help. Let's go Jinx." Alec continued his way down the hall with purposeful steps now.

Alec knocked on the door to Takahashi-*sensei*'s classroom and heard the teacher say 'come in'.

He entered and saw Takahashi-*sensei*, who was seated at his desk and looking a bit depressed as he looked down at a small box that was sitting in front of him. Alec looked at the box curiously, which was wrapped in white paper and tied with a red ribbon.

"Takahashi-*sensei*?" Alec took a hesitant step into the classroom, a worried expression on his face.

Takahashi-*sensei* was startled out of his reverie and immediately tried to hide the box in the drawer of his desk, shoving it inside and out of sight. He looked up then to see that it was Alec and let out a sigh of relief. "Oh, Alec, it's only you. How can I help you?" Takahashi-*sensei* steepled his fingers before him.

Only? Alec's eye twitched. "Well, *sensei*, you know how you told me I could come to you if I ever needed advice on something?" Alec was feeling a bit awkward and uncomfortable about the subject he was about to bring up as he shifted nervously from foot to foot.

Takahashi-*sensei* raised an eyebrow at his uneasy behavior, "Oh, why yes, of course. What is it?"

Alec gnawed on his lower lip. "Well, I want to give a friend of mine a gift for White Day but I don't really know what I should get her. My friend Junpei suggested flowers, chocolate, poetry, jewelry or clothes - but what would a girl my age really want?"

Takahashi-*sensei* blinked at Alec in surprise, "Oh! And who's the lucky girl?" Takahashi-*sensei* leaned forward suddenly interested.

Alec blushed, "Rika."

"Ah, well, since Rika is rather...artistic I think she'd appreciate a gift that was *made* more than a gift that was *bought*. So why don't you make her something...unique."

Alec smiled at the idea. "Yea, you're right. That does sound like her. Thanks a lot *sensei*!" Alec beamed, suddenly feeling a weight off his shoulders.

"Not at all." But Takahashi-*sensei* sighed, "Ah, if only things could be as easy at my age..."

"*Sensei*? Is something wrong?" Alec had a gut feeling his teacher's unease had something to do with that white box he had seen. "Do you need any advice?"

"It's not advice that I need. It's more like...confidence." Takahashi-*sensei* set his forehead down on the desktop before him. "Ah, there's just no way! I just can't do it!" Takahashi-*sensei* began to hit his head on the desk in front of him repeatedly.

Alec was beginning to get worried. "Do what?" Alec looked at his teacher alarmed.

"Give my White Day present to Haruna-*chan*." Takahashi-*sensei* moaned and suddenly covered his mouth with his hands when he realized he had actually admitted to this out loud with a look of horror crossing his face.

Alec's eyes grew wide in surprise. Haruna-*sensei*? Before things suddenly became clear to Alec and he smiled slightly. "Haruna-*sensei* is really nice. You shouldn't worry so much about it *sensei*. Just go for it."

"Easy for you to say." Takahashi-*sensei* sighed, "I've been trying all day to give her my present but she's been really busy and I can't seem to find the right moment. Tons of male students are giving her presents too, you see... and some of the other male teachers as well. The *younger* male teachers...I don't have a chance..."

"So what you're saying is you just need the right opportunity to give her your gift *neh*?" Alec tapped his chin in thought and then his eyes brightened as he came up with something. "I have an idea. Just leave everything to me *sensei*!" A mischievous gleam had oddly formed in Alec's eyes.

Takahashi-*sensei* looked at Alec's expression worriedly, "Uh Alec? You're scaring me..."

● ● ● ● ● ● ● ● ● ● ● ● ● ● ● ●

Takahashi walked down the hallway with an unconscious Alec in his arms feeling like an idiot. "This is never going to work..." When he finally reached the nurse's office he took a deep breath before calling out to Haruna. "Haruna-*san*!"

"Coming!" Came Haruna's voice as she opened the door to see the unconscious Alec in Takahashi's arms. "Oh dear! What happened to him this time?"

"I don't know. I just found him unconscious in the middle of the hallway. I think he's been neglecting to eat properly again. You know, vegans." Takahashi shook his head at the word 'vegan' as he made his way into the nurse's office.

"Oh dear, set him over there on the bed for me will you." Haruna directed.

"*Hai.*" Takahashi set Alec down on the bed and then moved out of the way as Haruna began to check Alec's temperature and pulse with a small frown on her face.

Takahashi looked around the nurse's office surprised that he and Haruna-*sensei* were finally alone and that there were no other students or teachers around. It was a golden opportunity if Takahashi had ever seen one. *Chance!* Takahashi knew it was now or never. He swallowed audibly before gathering his nerve to speak. "*Ano*...Um...Haruna-*san*?"

Haruna turned her head to look at him, "Yes, *sensei*?"

Takahashi reached into his pocket and pulled out the small white box. "Here - for White Day." He fumbled as he handed her the box and closed his eyes, not wanting to have them open to see her reaction.

Haruna blinked in surprise. "For me?" She took the box. "Thank you. What is it?"

Takahashi opened his eyes in surprise and let out a breath of relief that she hadn't rejected the idea of receiving a gift from him right away. "Open it and see." He declared with a lopsided smile.

Haruna unwrapped the small box to reveal that inside was an angel-shaped silver pendant. "An angel?" She breathed.

Takahashi blushed at his silly idea for a present. "I chose it because you're the guardian angel of this school and of it's students. I know that sounds cheesy but to me it's true. You don't have to wear it if you don't like it..."

Haruna shook her head. "No! I love it!" Haruna clutched the pendant to her chest happily.

Takahashi looked surprised but pleased, "*Honto?* Really?"

Haruna nodded vigorously. "Oh yes." She leaned forward to kiss Takahashi on the cheek unexpectedly. "Will you put it on me?"

"Sure thing." Takahashi was looking a bit smug as he moved closer to help Haruna with the necklace. That's when the teachers both noticed the empty bed.

"He wasn't really sick was he?" Haruna asked in a low voice.

Takahashi smiled, "Nope."

Haruna smiled back. "He really is..."

"A good boy." Takahashi finished for her and they both ended laughing at having said nearly the same thing at the same time.

• • • • • • • • • • • • • • • • •

Alec asked some passing students if they knew where Neji was since Alec decided he wanted to ask the inventor for his help in making a handmade present for Rika.. The students informed Alec that Neji was currently in the 'lab room' as they called it. Alec shrugged at the name and had the students give him directions. Then Alec and Jinx headed over to the lab. Alec had been a bit surprised when they had said 'Oh, he's at the lab' - *This really is a weird school.*

Alec and Jinx found the lab rather easily and Alec knocked on the door, which had a simple sign on it that read: LABORATORY.

"Coming!" Came Neji's voice before he opened the door. When Neji stood in the open doorway, Alec saw that he was wearing a white lab coat with a pair of black rubber gloves, and that he had a protective visor on, which he raised to look at Alec and Jinx. Alec also couldn't help but notice the blow torch in Neji's hand that was thankfully turned off.

Alec raised an eyebrow at his geeky friend, "Um, hey Neji?"

"Oh, hey Alec. Come on in." Neji greeted as he walked back into the lab with Alec and Jinx following close behind. Neji shut the door behind them and Alec was able to take a look at the lab before them. It was a rather large room with several super computers, but the most intriguing thing about the place were all the long tables in the lab on which were several random objects Alec had never seen the likes of before, and assumed they had to be some of Neji's crazy inventions that he had heard about.

"What is this place exactly Neji?" Alec murmured as he looked around the lab - some of the equipment there was extremely high tech and he wondered how a school could afford to have a place like this.

"Ah, this is the inventors clubroom. Pretty neat huh? I come here to work on my latest inventions." Neji waved a hand at a nearby table.

"Inventions?" Alec's eyes darted towards the table to see what was on it and noticed a bunch of weapons. A trickle of sweat formed on Alec's brow as he saw the size of some of the guns, which looked like some sort of lazer gun. The kind of gun one would find in a science fiction movie or maybe a RPG game. "Uh Neji...why are you inventing weapons of mass destruction?" Alec shivered. Some of those weapons were HUGE. *Is that a rocket launcher? And that's a bazooka?* Alec knew Neji was a little unhappy with the world and all but still - this was a bit extreme.

Neji just grinned, "Not just ordinary weapons Alec. They're anti-ghost and anti-*yokai* weapons. So that even a normal person like myself can kick some ghostly butt like you can!" Neji finished explaining enthusiastically.

Alec blinked. "Neat. How do they work exactly?" Alec was eyeing the weapons suspiciously.

Neji pushed his glasses up his nose as he began to explain. "Oh, they use an artificial spirit energy, which I've developed and-"

"Hey, what's that?" Jinx cut Neji off when he suddenly pointed over to one lab table in particular.

Alec turned to look over at the table as well and blinked. He then walked over to take a closer look. From the looks of it there was some kind of manikin or mechanical doll on the table. Its limbs were all made of metal, and its shape was that of a humanoid female. It looked to be some pretty high tech stuff, Alec thought.

Alec's eyes widened when he realized what he must be looking at. "Is that what I think it is?" Alec breathed in awe.

Neji smirked proudly, a somewhat haughty expression on his face as he adjusted his glasses on his face, "Yes, that's right. She's my latest creation - the first of her kind. Battle RoboGirl 2.0!" Neji declared with a flourish, waving his hand in her direction.

"*Oi!* Hey, wait a minute, 2.0?" Jinx frowned. "Wouldn't that mean there was a 1.0?"

Neji ignored him.

Alec's gray eyes, however, were sparkling. "Wow, a real robot! Is that even possible? It's like I've fallen into a sci-fi novel."

"Better that than the horror novel our lives usually seem to be." Neji joked and then puffed himself up. "Nothing is impossible for my brain. Sometimes it pays off to be a geek. She'll be able to kick some serious ghostly butt once I'm done programming her and completing her AI personality chip. So Alec what brings you here?"

"Oh yea, I was wondering if you could help me make Rika a present. You know, for White Day and everything. Maybe like a piece of jewelry or a hair barrette or something." Alec shrugged at a complete loss.

Alec missed the flash of hurt that crossed Neji's face before Neji slipped on an expressionless mask. "For Rika? Yea, sure, why not? I can help you with that. It'd be easy - a piece of cake, for someone like me." Neji began to laugh somewhat bitterly making Alec narrow his eyes at Neji in confusion and wonder why his friend was acting so strangely all of a sudden.

However, while the boys had been talking Jinx had gotten bored due to his short attention span, and while looking down at the dormant robot suddenly had an idea. Jinx grinned as he decided he'd help Neji finish his robot a bit faster and waved his wand through the air and yelled: "Animate!" Before he pointed his wand at the robot, and a bolt of golden light hit it dead on.

The fembot sat up and its eyes glowed red as it came to life. "Power on... Battle RoboGirl 2.0 activated." Came a female sounding, synthesized voice.

Alec and Neji turned in surprise to see the fembot that was currently trying to get up off the table. "Oh no...Jinx what did you do?" Alec immediately turned towards the fairy.

"I...uh...I just wanted to help so I animated the robot..." Jinx hid his wand behind his back with a guilty expression on his face.

Alec's eyes narrowed angrily. "Jinx, what did I tell you about using your magic around my friends."

Neji frowned thoughtfully as he watched the fembot, "She shouldn't be able to even move since I haven't installed her power source yet. And she definitely shouldn't be able to talk yet since her AI personality chip is no where near being finished. This is bad...I've only completed some of her programming..."

The fembot was now walking awkwardly towards them. "Target... identified. Attack mode...activated." She seemed to lock her sights on Alec and Neji. "Mission...terminate." The fembot's monotone voice continued.

*Uh oh...*Alec took a step back. "What exactly did you finish programming?" Alec questioned worriedly.

"I've only managed to install her combat data, battle simulations data, martial arts data, and weapons training data so far." Neji was also backing up away from the fembot. Not a good sign, in Alec's opinion.

"Oh, is that all." Alec said calmly before he gave Neji a look and burst out. "Neji! What were you thinking! Tell me there's nothing else?"

Alec was not comforted by the guilty expression that formed on Neji's face at that moment.

Just then, however, before Neji could answer the fembot suddenly leapt towards Alec in attack. Alec jumped backwards and the fembot's hand came down hard on one of the invention tables that Alec had tried to hide behind. The powerful karate chop that the fembot gave the table caused it to break neatly in two - the inventions spilling all over the floor.

"Ahh!" Alec tried to get out of her way as the fembot began to give chase. The two boys were forced to scramble out of the way as the fembot continued after them and she reached one of her hands out towards them before she suddenly started spinning, leaping, and twirling around the lab as she chased the boys. Alec looked back at her baffled before realizing she really was *dancing*. As she began to spin and dance like a top while executing dangerous jumps she ended up knocking things over about the lab causing things to break, and small explosions were beginning to rock the lab and set things on fire.

"Ah, that's her dance program." Neji informed them all nonchalantly.

Alec appeared incredulous that a mere dance program was doing this much damage. "Dance program? You've got to be kidding me. I thought she was supposed to be a battle robot."

Neji blushed guiltily, "A *cute* battle robot." Neji corrected Alec helpfully. "You know, like from the *manga - Battle Angel Alita*." Neji tried to explain before shrugging. "What? It seemed like a good idea at the time." Neji said in his defense when Alec merely gawked at him.

Alec shook himself and got back to business. "How do we shut it off?" Alec questioned as he dived out of the way as the fembot executed a flying side kick towards him, but since she missed him ended up jumping over him instead.

"We can't." Neji shook his head. "It doesn't even have a power source installed yet. The fairy magic must be animating it." Neji's eyes widened in realization.

"Jinx! Do something!" Alec yelled as he was forced to dodge a deadly plié.

"But you told me not to use magic!" Jinx whined, a confused expression on his face.

"Just use it! Things can't get any worse than this! Just try and stop her!" Alec cried as he ran from the fembot and suddenly tripped. Alec landed face first on the floor and groaned in pain. *Uh oh!* Alec looked behind him to see that the fembot was almost upon him.

"*Yosha!* Alright then! Deactivate!" Jinx waved his wand at the dance-crazed robot and a blast of blue magic light shot towards it and enveloped the robot that was instantly incased in solid ice.

"Phew." Alec wiped the sweat from his brow as he stood back up, "That could have been a *lot* worse. That was great Jinx, you didn't even blow anything up. You'll just have to thaw her out later or something, eh Neji?" Alec turned to look at Neji.

Neji, however, was looking around at the chaos that had become his lab. It was a complete mess - small fires had broken out all over the place, several of his inventions lay smashed and broken on the floor, and wires were beginning to fizzle and snap ominously. Alec also turned to see the destruction. "Uh... opps." Alec began to laugh nervously with a hand behind his head. "Neji I'm really sor-" Alec was trying to say when Neji cut him off.

"Out." Neji said in a low voice before he turned to face Alec with a fierce look in his eyes. "GET OUT!" Neji's oily hair was sticking up all over the place, and he was smoking slightly as he pushed Alec and Jinx forcibly out the door of the lab and slammed the door in their faces.

"That went well." Alec sighed, *So much for getting help from Neji. Now what do I do? Aw man...* Alec scratched his head thoughtfully. "I suppose I could try and bake Rika something. Let's go, Jinx." Alec took off, leading the way to the home economics room. As soon as they got there Alec took out a cookbook and realized he didn't have any ingredients - double opps. "Uh..." He stared down blankly at the list of ingredients for making marshmallow-covered brownies feeling a little like a moron.

"Just leave it to me, Alec!" Jinx declared reading Alec's mind. With a wave of his wand several ingredients appeared out of thin air as well as bowls, spoons, measuring cups, a mixer, and cooking tray.

Alec poked a bag of flour suspiciously with his index finger wondering if it was going to explode or something. It was definitely too good to be true that one of Jinx's summoning spells hadn't backfired.

Jinx frowned at Alec's actions and pouted. "Hey."

"Sorry." Alec began to get the ingredients ready, "Your magic picks the weirdest times to work, you know."

"Well, definitely when it's important." Jinx declared and with another wave of his wand Alec was suddenly wearing an apron and a chef's hat.

"Now, Jinx, as much as I appreciate your help, I have to make these marshmallow-covered brownies without any more magical assistance or else it won't count. Okay?" Alec gave Jinx a stern look.

Jinx nodded vigorously, "I understand, Alec!"

"Good." Alec nodded and set to work. It didn't take Alec long before he had the brownie mixture ready and spread in a pan. He then covered the batter with large white marshmallows until the entire mixture was covered. Alec smirked down at his hard work and wiped a hand across his brow managing to put a mark of flour on his forehead. He preheated the oven and then opened the oven when it was ready to slide his tray of brownies inside. He set it to the appropriate temperature and stood back to wait. "Now we just have to let them bake. They'll be ready in about 45 minutes. I'll go and clean up in the meantime. Don't touch anything, Jinx." Alec called over his shoulder as he headed for the sink.

"*Hai, hai!*" Jinx raised his hand in assurance.

Alec was washing the dishes and after about 20 minutes Jinx was beginning to get extremely bored as he watched the brownies *slowlyyy* baking and decided to speed things up a bit with the help of some fairy magic of course. After all, fairies were renown for their baking skills, so Jinx was sure he would be able to get the spell right. He waved his wand at the oven door.

However...

"Alec!" Jinx called a few seconds later.

Alec quickly rushed over, "What's wrong?"

"Alec, I'm so sorry. I just wanted to help you bake the brownies faster..." Jinx began to apologize.

"Oh no..." Alec rushed over to the oven and peered inside, "What did you do exactly?"

"I..dunno..." Jinx shrugged. "It was supposed to finish the brownies but I don't think that's what happened because they still look the same."

Alec shot Jinx an exasperated look before he watched as the brownie mixture suddenly seemed to be expanding until it was overflowing from the pan at an alarming rate.

"Oh shoot! I better take them out." Alec declared reaching for the oven door.

"Wait Alec, no!" Jinx tried to stop him.

Too late. Alec opened the door to the oven and loads and loads of batter and marshmallow began to pour out until the entire room was beginning to be filled with the sticky mixture.

"Ahhh!" Alec yelled frantically as he was buried beneath brownie batter and marshmallow. "Jinx!"

"Alec!"

A few sticky minutes later...

A slightly singed, dust covered, bruised, cut, and now marshmallow-covered Alec stood outside of the door to the home economics room. Alec sighed heavily, thinking about how he had at least enough luck to survive that entire fiasco but just not enough luck to have actually *prevented* it. Sigh.

"Alec I'm so-!" Jinx began but Alec coldly cut him off.

"Don't bother. Come on, let's go." Alec started off down the hall. Jinx trailed behind him, hanging his head dejectedly as he flew through the air. Alec looked back at Jinx out of the corner of his eye and sighed. "I'm not mad at you Jinx. I just don't know what I'm going to make Rika now..."

At that moment, they happened to be passing a classroom where the sewing club was currently meeting. Alec looked in to see some girls from the club currently making dolls. He suddenly got an idea and decided to walk in. "Hey, girls mind if I-"

The girls all looked up to see Alec covered in marshmallow goo and brownie batter. Then they seemed to recognize him, which only made things worse. "AHHH! It's the demon boy! Run!" The girls all got up from their desks and fled the room like a stampede. "That must be his true form! How hideous!"

"*Ano*...Um..." Alec called helplessly after them, a trickle of sweat forming on his brow, "I'm just going to borrow a few things alright?" Alec said to the now empty room. Did a tumbleweed just roll by?

Jinx snickered at the girls' odd behavior. "The girls at this school are weird, Alec."

Alec sat down at one of the desks with a sigh, "Sometimes I wonder who the real weird one is." He began to sort through different materials, ribbons, thread and needles that the girls had left behind and began formulating an idea in his head for what to make Rika. "*Yosha!*" Alec rolled up his sleeves and set to work.

∙ ∘ ∙ ∙ ∙ ∙ ∙ ∙ ∙ ∙ ∙ ∙ ∙ ∙ ∙ ∘ ∙

With his completed gift now in hand Alec walked down the hallway towards the art room. He had somehow managed to make a stuffed, white bear with a tiny, black beret on its head. It was a little misshapen but Alec thought a girl would deem it cute enough. Alec was still a mess and now his hands were all covered in band-aids to boot, but he thought that probably didn't matter much. He was feeling much too excited and impatient to give Rika his White Day present so he didn't want to waste the time to take a shower and clean himself up a bit first before he saw her.

Jinx frowned at Alec's band-aid covered hands that he had pricked one too many times with the needle. "Alec, you should have let me help you."

Alec shook his head. "No, that's alright, besides using magic is like cheating. I wanted to make Rika something...from, you know, um, the heart." Alec blushed a bit when he said this. "Besides, I'm pleased with the finished product. I just hope Rika will be too."

Alec walked into the art room, followed close behind by Jinx, but then stopped suddenly when he saw just what was happening inside. Jinx bumped into Alec's back due to his sudden stop.

Jinx rubbed his now red nose, "Ow, Alec what's wrong?" Jinx peered around Alec's shoulder and gasped.

Three art students seemed to have Rika pinned down, or rather half of her body was pinned down over a desk and one of them had a pair of scissors in her hands, and this girl was hovering over by Rika in a threatening manner.

"People like you shouldn't be coming to this school, Rika. We don't need people like you here. You're just a total waste of space." The girl with the scissors was saying.

"Demon-lover..." One of the other art students muttered under her breath.

"How about we show you what happens to demon-lovers like you at this school, Rika." One of the other girls suggested.

"We'll teach you a lesson about being friends with the enemy or any demon - hold her down girls." The girl with the scissors directed her friends.

"Say goodbye to your hideous hair, Rika." The girls laughed cruelly.

Rika struggled in their grasp. "No! Let me go!"

Alec took one look at the glinting, sharp, steel blade of the scissors being raised above his friend before he instantly saw red. He tossed Jinx the bear absentmindedly as he strode forward, "LET HER GO!" His voice boomed throughout the art room.

The three girls all turned around towards the doorway to see a severely pissed off Alec. Rika looked up too from the awkward position of half her body on the desk and saw that Alec's eyes were glowing eerily with a blue-tinged light. Rika's own eyes widened at the sight.

Alec's aura had also begun to pick up around him.

"His eyes...they're the eyes of a demon." The girl with the scissors gasped as the scissors fell from her limp hands.

"Ah! It's the demon boy himself!" The other girl student realized backing away for the door.

The series of overhead track lighting in the art room began to flicker ominously and then the bulbs began to break one by one showering glass down upon the girls, who immediately freaked out and let go of Rika to then turn and run out of the room as fast as they could while screaming in fright and yelling something about demons.

Jinx watched as they ran out the door and spun towards them. "Uh, uh, uh, you won't get off the hook that easily! Transfiguration! Super size!" Jinx tossed Alec's bear up into the air and it became super sized, about 7 feet tall. It also began to walk on its own. "Alright then, Mr. Bear go give those girls a great big bear hug!" Jinx directed the bear.

The large stuffed bear nodded and began to walk out the door of the art room and then down the hallway after the fleeing girls. Jinx flew after the girls to make sure the bear scared the beejeezes out of them, and began to laugh somewhat maniacally as he got to watch the bear *glomping* them.

Jinx thought it was less than they deserved for saying all those hurtful things towards his friend Alec.

Rika was no longer being pressed against the desk and so backed away from it, only to sink to her knees in shock however. A concerned Alec quickly went to her side to help her up and reached his hand out to her. *"Daijobou ka?* Are you alright, Rika?"

Unexpectedly, Rika violently smacked his hand away. *"Iye!* No! Stay away! Don't touch me - you *demon!"* She raised her head to glare up at him fearfully.

Alec's worried expression turned to hurt.

Rika gasped as she realized what she had just done and covered her mouth. She shook her head in horror. "Alec...I'm sorry...I didn't mean to..."

But her words and voice were weak and Alec could hear the doubt in them, so he turned to walk away from her instead. He didn't miss the sound of Rika's breath of relief being let out as he did so either - it was like a knife being twisted in his heart.

Junpei had suddenly appeared in the doorway to the art room, and took a look at the chaos that the art room had become before whistling through his teeth, "Whoo wee! What happened here? Alec?" Junpei went up to him first but Alec wouldn't meet his eyes and he kept walking out of the room and past Junpei. Junpei shrugged at his friend's strange behavior, but that's when he noticed Rika, who was still on the floor on her knees so he rushed up to her. "Rika, are you okay?" He knelt down next to her, a confused expression on his face. "What happened here?"

Rika sniffled as she looked up and saw Junpei. She then launched herself at Junpei, *glomping* him and crying into his chest. "Oh Junpei! I was so scared!"

Junpei patted her back, and stroked her hair. "Uh, there, there. I'm here now." He began to help her up awkwardly. "You alright now then?"

Rika smiled back tentatively, "I am now."

Alec hovered just outside of the doorway, not really wanting to, but unable to stop himself from eavesdropping on his two friends that seemed to have forgotten all about him.

"Oh yea, I almost forgot. I have something for you, Rika. Catch." Junpei tossed her something.

Rika caught the nondescript brown paper bag and looked at it curiously.

"A White Day present." Junpei explained acting nonchalant as he placed his hands behind his head.

Rika opened the brown paper bag and reached inside it to pull out a white and black polka dot beret. Rika's eyes widened in surprise and then they sparkled with delight. "Oh Junpei! I love it! Thank you so much!" She spontaneously gave Junpei another hug thoroughly surprising the jock.

Rika looked up while in Junpei's embrace, and Junpei looked down at her, their eyes meeting. They both seemed to realize just how close they were to each other in that exact moment and blushed. They both quickly jumped away from each other in an embarrassed manner. Then they looked at each other with guilty smiles on their faces before they burst out laughing at the strangeness of the entire situation.

Jinx had come back to the art room at that point, with Alec's stuffed bear, which Jinx had returned to its original size, and found Alec standing just outside of the art room conspicuously.

"Hey Alec, I'm sorry I borrowed your present." Jinx reached the bear out to Alec. "Here."

"Why don't you keep it..." Alec murmured as he turned to walk off.

"But Alec-" Jinx insisted and suddenly Alec broke off into a run "Wait!" Jinx called after him hopelessly. When Alec had already turned a corner at the end of the hall Jinx quirked his head in confusion completely dumbfounded at Alec's actions. "What happened?" Jinx turned to look inside the art room...

· · · · · · · · · · · · · · · · ·

Alec wanted to escape reality really badly all of a sudden, and so decided to log on to Yokai World. He teleported to the Cathedral Area and entered it to see the statue of Midoriko at the far end, which seemed to be glowing from light being reflected from the stained glass windows and onto the statue. Alec walked down the center aisle towards Midoriko and that's when he noticed the strange mark on the ground around the statue and which was similar to the glowing, slash mark that had surrounded the well back in the Haunted Mansion Area.

This mark was also glowing with a red-tinged light as Alec approached. "What's that? It looks like the same mark that surrounded the well that led to Yomi. Could it be another tear? And if so does it also lead to Yomi?" Alec wondered aloud.

Alec moved his hand forward to touch the statue of Midoriko but instead of feeling a solid surface beneath his fingers he felt nothing but thin air. He hadn't been expecting this and so ended up stumbling and then falling forward into nothingness. An invisible force had seemed to seize him and drag him into the tear. He could feel himself being teleported somewhere and then all of a sudden the world stopped spinning by him and he was there. Wherever 'there' was.

Alec blinked and looked around finding himself to be in an elaborate garden. Flowers were everywhere, surrounding him on all sides. The flowers were like nothing Alec had ever seen before. They were the strangest flowers Alec had ever laid eyes upon - they oddly looked tropical since they came in a variety of bright colors like magenta and sky-blue and neon green. The flowers were also surreal and animalistic at the same time due to their unusual size and strange markings like spots or stripes. Alec knew because of this that he had to still be in the game since flowers like those couldn't possibly exist in reality.

Alec caught sight of an orange and tiger-stripped flower and reached his hand out towards it knowing that since he was in the game he wouldn't really be able to feel anything but being drawn to the unique flower for some reason anyways. But he was in for a surprise when he did feel something as his fingers touched the petals, and not only that, he sensed some kind of spiritual presence from the flowers, which meant they were in fact alive. *Uh oh.*

Alec gasped in surprise and took a step back. "It's real."

"Of course I'm real! Foolish boy!" An angry feminine voice growled.

Alec backpedaled, "Ack! It spoke!" Alec lost his balance and landed on his backside inelegantly. "You totally just spoke to me didn't you?"

"Maybe I did." The flower purred.

Alec shook his head in disbelief. No maybes about it.

That's when all the flowers started moving strangely before him as they began to chatter earnestly with each other, their flowery heads bobbing up and down excitedly. "What's a human boy doing here? Do you think our Mistress knows?" Alec saw a strange yellow lillie with cheetah spots talking.

A giant, green and pink, fly trap began to speak. "How did he get here? Foolish human boy. Mistress will be angry..."

"He's such a pretty boy...Mistress will surely eat him..." A giant blue and yellow daffodil turned towards Alec.

"He does smell delicious..." The flytrap was taking a sniff.

After that comment all the flowers began to sniff the air curiously in Alec's direction. Alec was thoroughly unnerved that he could actually *hear* them smelling him.

"He does! He does smell delicious!" The tiger lily agreed.

The strange flowers all began to stretch eerily towards Alec to sniff the air. Alec began to frantically scoot across the ground away from the flowers, completely freaked out by their odd behavior. He quickly got to his feet and ran down a garden path, which was surrounded on both sides by flowers that all seemed to lean towards him as he ran past them. Alec also caught quick snippets of what the flowers were saying as he passed them by:

"Oh how delicious he smells!" "Wait boy let us smell you!" "Wait! Come back! What's your hurry boy?"

Alec, however, had no intention of stopping anytime soon, and so ran and ran until he entered an enclosed garden area where the flowers there were oddly silent since they had yet to bloom. Alec let out a breath of relief as he entered this area and noticed that there was an impressive stone fountain in the center of it of a majestic nine-tailed fox, which was spouting sparkling water from its mouth. The fox appeared to be sitting and looking up at the moon. *A kitsune?* Alec mused as he eyed the statue curiously.

A flash of movement caught Alec's eye and he turned to get a better look. Alec gasped when he saw that there in the center of the secluded garden was none other than - Yukino! She was suddenly there standing by the fountain of the nine-tailed fox and Alec saw that she was surrounded by glowing, golden fireflies that seemed to swirl around her making her appear as though she had a golden aura. Alec was even more surprised to see that Yukino was dancing in a traditional Japanese manner with two fans in either hand and then Yukino began to sing softly - this sweet, haunting melody...

Her singing made Alec's breath catch in his throat and his heart skipped a beat. The sight before him had him mesmerized and he found that he couldn't move or breath. He suddenly didn't want Yukino to realize he was there and therefore stop her singing and dancing. Alec's heart was thudding so loudly in his chest, however, he was almost sure Yukino had to have been able to hear it. Alec quickly ducked behind a bush to hide and scolded himself for his actions. *Why the hell am I hiding?* But Alec continued to watch her dance and sing in secret while the glittering fireflies circled around Yukino in a dream-like manner.

She's so beautiful...but wait a second. I don't like Yukino do I? I can't possibly 'like her like her' neh? Right? Naw...

Alec had never really thought of Yukino like that or as more than a friend, but seeing her dance and sing and be beautiful and girlie and graceful - for once it was stirring something unexpected inside of Alec. Something that he had never felt before. Something that had probably been there all along. Was it *like*? Alec blushed as he continued to watch her.

"I think...I might actually like Yukino." Alec gasped to himself. *Epp!* He quickly covered his mouth realizing he had said his last musing aloud.

Yukino suddenly stopped singing to look over to where Alec was still hiding behind the bushes. "Alec, you can stop hiding. I know you're there." Came Yukino's amused voice.

"Epp!" Alec squeaked before he bashfully stood up from behind the bushes, scratching the back of his neck nervously. "Ehehehehh..." He began to laugh nervously. "You got me."

Yukino just grinned playfully at him and oddly enough she *giggled*.

Alec raised an eyebrow at this since Yukino never *giggled*, before he

415

shrugged it off and looked around the enclosed garden of white flower buds curiously, "So how did you find out about this place Yukino?"

"The same way you did." Yukino carelessly explained, "So, why were you watching me?"

Alec turned bright red. "Uh..." He scratched his cheek with his index finger. "No reason..."

Yukino quirked her head cutely at him, "What? Do you like me or something?"

"No!" Alec burst out, before amending, "I mean...I dunno...maybe..." He stammered, blushing, bashful. He swallowed his nervousness, and decided it was now or never. "Yes, I think I do like you, Yukino." *I can't believe I just said that!*

Yukino was slinking towards him with an unreadable expression on her face. *Epp!*

*Please don't kill me...please don't hate me...please don't hate me...*Alec was saying like a mantra in his mind sure that Yukino had taken his confession in the wrong way and probably hated him now.

Yukino was less than a foot away from him when she spoke. "I see." She reached out her hand to cup Alec's cheek. "Do you want to kiss me?"

Alec's eyes widened in shock. *This has to be a dream. Maybe I hit my head really hard when I fell through that tear or something. There's no way this can be real. Maybe I should just go with the flow then?* Alec licked his lips and gulped as he looked down at Yukino's rosy colored lips. "Uh...no? Yes...I dunno...is this a trick question? Yukino I-" But before Alec could finish with - 'Don't think I'm really ready for this yet' -

Yukino had stood on tiptoe to suddenly press her lips against Alec's. And just like that she was suddenly kissing him right on the lips. Alec stood stiffly still in shock, his eyes wide before he realized he was keeping them open and closed them, giving into the kiss.

However, just as he was beginning to enjoy the kiss -

"Alec *no baka!*" Came a harsh, and slightly angry sounding voice.

Alec frowned, *Wait a minute, isn't that Yukino's voice?* He quickly pushed Yukino away from him and turned to look in the direction of the voice and saw - Yukino? *Huh? What's going on?* He turned back to the Yukino, who was in front of him and who had just kissed him, and not to mention whom he had just confessed to only seconds before. Alec's head was spinning.

The Yukino before him licked her lips, an amused expression on her face. "That was a delicious kiss, boya."

*Uh oh...*Alec recognized that deep, throaty voice. The 'Yukino' in front of him suddenly shape-shifted and then standing before him was none other than Tamamo-no-mae, the fox witch.

Alec's jaw dropped, "Tamamo-no-mae!" He blushed in embarrassment. He had totally been tricked by her! "But then wait...where are we if you're here?"

"You've stumbled upon the Makai world, the true world where *yokai* and other spiritual beings reside. This is my home and this happens to be my garden. Did you know that you're trespassing here? You've been a naughty, naughty boy Alec. And naughty boys need to be punished." Tamamo-no-mae reached out and stroked Alec's cheek.

"Get away from him!" Yukino declared as she suddenly formed her ice sword and lunged forward in attack towards Tamamo-no-mae, who was forced to leap backwards away from Alec and out of the way of Yukino's deadly ice sword as it came crashing down upon the ground.

Tamamo-no-mae raised the sleeve of her *kimono* and revealed the deep slash that Yukino had managed to make in it with her ice sword. "*Yare yare*, my oh my, I do believe you're jealous."

Yukino instantly spluttered, "J-jealous! Of a kiss with a little boy? Ha! I only like older men, thank you very much. And I'm most definitely *not* jealous!"

Though she was blushing Alec wasn't able to see her face, so her words were like an arrow to his boyish heart. *Ouch.*

"I just...care for him like a brother and I intend to protect him from your evil clutches!" Yukino declared as she pointed her ice sword at Tamamo-no-mae.

"Evil clutches? How amusing. I'd like to see you try. The boy is *mine*. Come and try to take him from me if you can." Tamamo-no-mae shape-shifted into Night's form and was wielding Night's gigantic, signature *Shinigami* sword before him. "I don't appreciate how you interrupted my play with the boy. And just when it was getting good too."

Yukino glared back at 'Night', "Careful, I think you're forgetting this is a PG rated story. Besides, playtime's over. I won't let you lay one more finger on Alec. How dare you try and corrupt him! And how *dare* you use *my* face to trick Alec into trusting you! Oh, you'll pay for that one, *dearly*!" Yukino charged forward and her ice sword clashed with Night's *Shinigami katana*.

"I wouldn't have pegged you as the possessive type, Yukino dear." Night mocked.

"That *baka* brat needs me to look after him. I will protect Alec-*kun*!" Yukino shot back as their swords continued to clash.

"Impressive, your brother's face doesn't seem to effect you as it once did." Tamamo-no-mae observed thoughtfully.

Yukino smirked. "I'm a different person today than the me from yesterday.

I'm the me of today! And this me knows her real brother. You can't trick me anymore Tamamo-no-mae!"

Alec seemed to snap out of his stunned stupor to realize for a moment that it appeared that these two girls were fighting over him. Naw. But Yukino did seem to be trying to protect him and that was unacceptable, Alec decided. He had decided just yesterday that he would become a person that protected - not one that needed to be protected. Alec unsheathed his white *katana* and pointed it towards Tamamo-no-mae, a steely look in his gray eyes.

"Tamamo-no-mae! Get away from Yukino!" Came his calm and deadly voice.

Yukino looked behind her and was surprised by the fierce expression on Alec's face. "Alec-*kun?*"

Tamamo-no-mae shrugged carelessly and lowered her sword before returning to her true fox lady form. "I was just having a little bit of fun, Alec-*kun*." She pouted by way of apology.

Tamamo-no-mae then teleported so that she was instantly standing right next to Alec, and then she leaned down to whisper in his ear, "I'd keep her in the garden a little while longer if I were you. The moon flowers are about to bloom and they only bloom once every 400 years so I assure you it's worth the wait. I'm sure she'll like it. Good luck." Tamamo-no-mae threw Alec a wink.

"Tamamo-no-mae what are you doing? Get away from him!" Yukino growled as she rushed forward.

Tamamo-no-mae just turned around and skipped backwards playfully before disappearing suddenly into thin air. Her mischievous grin lingering in the air for a moment before disappearing with a *pop,* making Alec think of the Cheshire cat. "Goodbye you two. Don't stay up past your bedtimes!"

Yukino started off in the direction that Tamamo-no-mae had disappeared, but Alec grabbed her wrist to stop her. Yukino spun around in surprise. "Alec?"

"Wait Yukino, there's something I'd like you to see." He shyly let go of her wrist.

Yukino nodded, "Okay, what is it?"

"It's a surprise..." Alec gave her a shaky smile, "Hey Yukino, how did you get here anyway?" Alec decided to ask her something normal since he was beginning to act weird around her. He shook his head like a dog trying to rid his mind of strange thoughts.

"I went to the cathedral to speak with mother and noticed the tear. I only touched the statue before I ended up here. You know how I love flowers so I just couldn't help exploring the place. Did you see those cute talking flowers? They were my favorite."

Alec shivered, "Cute? I thought they were really creepy."

Yukino laughed, "You would. So what's this surprise?" She pressed.

"Well…" Alec scratched his cheek nervously, wondering how much longer he would need to stall her when suddenly all of the surrounding flower buds began to open revealing long, silvery-white petals that seemed to shimmer in the moonlight.

Yukino gasped in delight as she looked around the flower garden as the flowers were opening up all around them. "It's so beautiful."

"Happy White Day, Yukino."

Yukino turned to face Alec in surprise, "You planned to bring me here for…all this didn't you?"

Alec nodded sheepishly, hoping that he didn't look too guilty since this whole thing had in fact been Tamamo-no-mae's idea.

Yukino stepped forward and placed a quick kiss to Alec's cheek. Before she then skipped backwards and smiled in amusement at Alec's stunned expression. "Thank you."

Alec raised a hand to his cheek in shock, blushing.

But then Yukino leaned in and ruffled his hair, messing it up thoroughly, "*Baka* brat, that was very sweet of you."

Alec pouted, she still saw him like a kid brother it seemed. "*Mou!* Geez! Yukino!" But he smiled back anyway and she grinned at him in return.

They both admired the blooming moon flowers together in silence with the moonlight shining down upon them, and the fireflies playfully flitting through the air. Alec had to admit it was an unexpected romantic atmosphere. He looked at Yukino out of the corner of his eye. He wanted to confess to her but found that he couldn't. He knew that he'd get rejected by her after all and he decided that it would just be too painful. It was better to have hope than despair.

"I wish there was music…" Alec murmured to himself, *Then I could ask Yukino to dance.*

"Why?" Yukino asked curiously. Alec turned towards her in surprise since he hadn't thought she'd be able to hear that.

"Oh, um, because…I'dliketodancewithyou." Alec said in a rush and then immediately turned red from embarrassment.

Yukino raised an eyebrow at him. "Oh." She paused thoughtfully for a moment. "Too bad there isn't any."

But then an eerie song began to play filling the air around them with music. Alec and Yukino looked around them in shock wondering where the music was coming from. Alec then noticed that the moon flowers were swaying and moving oddly as though from vibrations.

"Oh my god, it's coming from the flowers." Alec gaped at the moon flowers in shock.

"That's so neat." Yukino smiled looking pleased.

Alec shivered, "I think you mean creepy."

Yukino reached out her hand to Alec, "Well, did you want to dance with me or not?"

Alec felt himself blushing for like the 100th time that night but nodded. "Um, oh, yea, sure..." *Smooth, Alec, real smooth.* Alec shook his head at himself. He then took Yukino's hand and they began to dance among the moon flowers and the fireflies, which began to fly circles around them. He felt really awkward with his hands around her waist especially now that he knew that he liked her, and was worried about doing something incredibly stupid at the moment - like yelling out a confession or trying to kiss her or something equally idiotic and potentially life threatening. So Alec decided to make some harmless small talk instead.

"Yukino? Tomorrow is the Ghost Master Tournament."

Yukino nodded.

Alec swallowed, "Will you enter it with me?"

Yukino looked surprised, "Of course! I was planning on being your Battle Ghost from the very beginning. Besides, you're going to need me if RedAki manages to get himself another real ghost. You'd simply be lost without me." Yukino finished teasingly.

Alec let out a breath of relief, "Yea, I would be, but together we can win this thing Yukino. Together we can do anything. I just know it."

Yukino smiled back in return. "Yea."

Alec steeled himself for what he wanted to say next, "Um, Yukino? Remember the promise I made you? That I would help you recover your memories and help you cross over?" She nodded. "Well, I want to make you a new promise now that I know you're still alive. I still want to help you. After the tournament I want to devote all my free time to trying to find out where you've been taken in reality. I want to find you and break the curse that's upon you Yukino. I promise to save you."

"*Alec...*" Yukino's voice was moved.

Alec reached out his hand with his pinky finger sticking out and Yukino did the same. "I pinky promise." Yukino wrapped her pinky around Alec's. "Oh and Yukino? When we meet in reality...there's something important I want to tell you." Alec blushed as he thought about how maybe in person he'd be able to scrounge up enough courage to tell Yukino how he really felt about her.

"*Nani?* What is it?" Yukino quirked her head at him.

421

"Now that..." Alec wagged his finger at her, "Is a secret." *Until I fulfill my promise and save you I won't tell you how I feel.* Alec decided to himself.

"Stingy." Yukino pouted at him, but still hadn't let go of his hand.

With their pinkies still intertwined they continued to admire the moon flowers together...

· · · · · · · · · · · · · · · · · · ·

Once Alec had logged out of Yokai World and was back in reality he went to deliver Akira his food tray. The mini-door opened and Alec slid the tray under the door, but then Alec knocked on the door loudly.

"Akira! I need to speak with you!" Alec yelled outside the door.

Akira unlocked the door angrily, and stood in the doorway in a nonchalant pose, "What is it?" He drawled as Alec pushed his way past Akira and strode into the room, acting like he owned the place. "*Oi!* Hey!" Akira angrily called after him as he followed.

Alec spun around to face Akira and glared daggers at him. Akira raised an eyebrow at Alec's strange behavior. "What?"

"Tell me where Yukino is?" Alec demanded.

"Huh? Who?" Akira sneered but then Alec grabbed him by the front of his black shirt and shoved Akira violently backwards.

"Don't play dumb with me - Kaguto has her! He's kidnaped her and she's being held hostage by him. She's in a coma! You have to know about it! You're one of his subordinates aren't you?" Alec demanded as he shook Akira roughly.

Akira blinked back at Alec in shock, "A girl in a coma? I really don't know anything about that...honest." Alec's expression remained skeptical but Akira's expression remained passive as he put his hands up in a surrendering gesture.

Alec continued to glare at him until he finally let go of Akira. He sighed heavily and his anger seemed to deflate like a popped balloon. Alec felt extremely drained all of a sudden as he hung his head in a defeated manner, his white hair shadowing his sad eyes from view. "I'm sorry. But I had to ask...I know he has her..." Alec clenched his fists at his sides.

Akira looked at Alec with a concerned expression on his face now. "Who? Kaguto?"

Alec nodded.

Akira looked at his only friend worriedly - Alec looked so fragile and broken in that moment that it unnerved Akira who felt that Alec was one of the strongest people he had ever met. "Why is it so important to you that you find her, anyways?"

Alec looked up, a stricken expression on his face. "Because Yukino is my friend. And I made her a promise."

"A promise *ka?*" Akira sighed and ran a hand through his spiked up, black hair, "You know, I suppose I could try and find something out about her. But I make no promises..."

Alec's expression brightened dramatically. "*Honto?* Really!"

Akira shifted awkwardly on his feet surprised at how fast Alec's mood was able to change. Hope was a powerful thing. "Yea, if it's really so important to you. I'll find out where she is."

Alec grasped Akira's hand in his two hands and looked at him with large, shimmering, puppy-dog eyes. "*Tomodachi!* My friend!"

"*Hai?*" Akira looked back at Alec quizzically.

"Thanks so much Akira! You're a great friend. I knew I could count on you." Alec insisted as he shook Akira's hand up and down excitedly.

Akira coughed to hide his discomfort before snatching his hand away. "Yea, right." The corner of his mouth twitched.

Alec was still smiling happily apparently on cloud nine, "So, tomorrow is the Ghost Master Tournament, you know."

"So?" Akira became instantly suspicious.

"So...are you going to enter? Did you find yourself another real ghost?" Alec questioned curiously.

"That's none of your business." Akira crossed his arms in front of his chest. "But yea I'm entering alright. I'm also going to win. The title of Ultimate Ghost Master will be mine. I won't lose to you again. I've been training hard for this chance to get to utterly defeat you, Alec. You're *so* going to get your butt kicked. And don't expect me to go easy on you because we're friends. *Keh.*"

Alec just smiled back serenely, "I've been training pretty hard too. I've also been looking forward to this chance at a rematch with you. I also don't want to lose. And I also don't want you going easy on me. Let's give it our all. Kay?" Alec reached out his fist.

"Be careful what you ask for, punk brat." Akira drawled.

"Bring it on Akira." A cocky grin formed on Alec's face.

The two rivals both bumped their fists together in agreement.

Chapter 17:
THE GHOST MASTER TOURNAMENT

Alec, Yukino, Junpei, LadyV and Dr. M all teleported from 'Home Town' to the special area which had been specifically created for the Ghost Master Tournament called 'Battle Dome Area'. When they arrived to the special area Alec saw a huge domed stadium before them. Junpei whistled through his teeth. Dr. M (a.k.a Neji) eyed it through his glasses looking impressed as he pushed his glasses up his nose. LadyV was looking a little wide-eyed. And Alec's jaw had simply dropped in awe. Yukino just eyed the battle dome with a serene expression on her face, not in the least intimidated or unnerved.

They entered the battle dome and saw that is was packed with players, who had logged on to Yokai World just to watch the event. The elimination rounds had already taken place and now it was finally the finals. The inside of the stadium, which had been created for the tournament, was HUGE and in the center of the stadium was a large raised battle stage where each of the Ghostly Duels would soon be taking place.

Alec caught sight of RedAki, Catara, Kiba, and Smoker as they were about to pass Alec and his friends - apparently the Renegade Reapers had also made it to the finals. Funny, Alec thought, how the only two guilds to make it to the finals for the Ghost Master Tournament turned out to be a group of players from the Guardian Knights guild and a group from the Renegade Reapers guild. *This is turning out to be more of a guild war than a tournament,* Alec decided.

RedAki seemed to sneer as he caught sight of Alec and his 'little friends' as he liked to think of them. "I don't know how you and your little friends managed to make it to the finals." RedAki drawled, curling his upper lip.

"It's the Renegade Reapers." Dr. M narrowed his eyes at them.

The two groups glared at each other, lightning seeming to flash between their locked gazes - their guild rivalry running deep.

Alec nodded stonily, "And I see your 'friends' made it as well. But I assure you someone from *our* guild will hold the title of Ultimate Ghost Master at the end of this tournament."

"I doubt it." RedAki tucked a stray hair behind his ear in a careless gesture. "Where's Night?" RedAki suddenly looked around for any signs of the *Shinigami*. "Isn't he going to participate? Surely, he made it to the finals? Or is he too much of a coward to face me?" RedAki's lips twisted into a dark grin. "Darn, I was looking forward to challenging him for the title of Ultimate Ghost Master."

Alec clenched his fists at his sides, so that his knuckles were turning white. Akira had just insulted his *sensei* and mentor and that really pissed him off. He may not agree with all of Night's beliefs but he still highly respected and admired Night's strength - and he would always see Night as a kind of hero. "Night is no coward. *Shinigami* Squad business called him away so he couldn't make it. By the way, now that I think about it where's Kaguto? Opps, I mean your beloved Reaper-*sama*?" Alec said that last part with a note of sarcasm in his voice.

RedAki frowned thoughtfully. "I guess you could say he also couldn't be here today due to *Shinigami* business."

"Maybe they're working together on a case then?" Alec shrugged.

RedAki snorted. "Together? I highly doubt that. You still don't know enough about Night to serve him so loyally like you do-"

"And you still think Reaper's some kind of saint and he's far from it." Alec shot back cutting RedAki off.

The two boys both glared at each other and electricity seemed to crackle between their eyes. Alec shook his head. He decided they shouldn't be behaving like that. They were friends weren't they? *Neh?* "Whatever. Let's all do our best out there today." Alec put out his hand to shake RedAki's.

RedAki pointedly ignored Alec's hand and looked down at it with a disgusted expression on his face as if Alec had picked his nose before holding his hand out to him. "We intend to." RedAki said before turning around and stalking off. Catara and Kiba both snickered at Alec's hurt and bewildered expression as they followed close behind RedAki. Smoker remained his usual silent self, RedAki's second shadow, as he followed after his guild mates.

Alec frowned as he watched them go. He noted that RedAki was acting strangely that day...or was *that* the real RedAki? Junpei, Dr. M, and LadyV's eyes were all glaring at the RR's backs with eyes full of hate and Alec sighed and put his head in his hand. *Can't we all just get along?* He wondered wistfully.

"That guy's a total jerk. You were just trying to be nice." Junpei started.

Dr. M pushed his glasses up his nose knowingly. "When have we ever known the RRs to be *nice*?"

"I don't intend to lose to the likes of them." LadyV flipped her hair in a careless gesture. "I have a reputation to uphold after all. I don't want to lose my #4 ranking as Ghost Mistress."

A sudden hush fell over the crowd of players as everyone caught sight of an emcee making her way up onto the battle stage. The emcee was a *Shinigami* PC with a *dango*-bun hair style and a short, hot pink *kimono* dress on. She also had a matching pink microphone in her hand. The emcee began to explain how the tournament was an elimination round tournament. The Ghost Masters, who had made it to the finals, would fight each other in randomly selected one on one duels until only two Ghost Masters remained, who would then fight each other for the title of Ultimate Ghost Master.

"My name is Kiki and I will be your emcee for this tournament. Now let's get this Ghostly Tournament started shall we?" Emcee Kiki began enthusiastically. "Will Ghost Masters LadyV and Catara come up to the stage please?"

LadyV and Catara got up on the battle stage from different sides and both stood facing each other.

"Ghost Masters are you ready? Let the Ghostly Duel begin!" Emcee Kiki brought her hand down with a flourish signaling the start of the duel.

LadyV raised her hand in the air so that her control ring glowed. "Noppera-bo! I summon you!" LadyV's Noppera-bo Battle Ghost sprang out of her ring and materialized next to her - its long, flowing, black *kimono* robes swirling in a nonexistent wind. It's face blank and eerie looking.

Catara followed suit and raised her right hand into the air so that her own control ring glowed. "Oiwa! Come forth!" Materializing next to Catara was a different Battle Ghost from her usual Nekomata ghost, Alec noticed. As the mysterious new ghost materialized next to Catara the crowd of players all gasped at Oiwa's appearance. Oiwa was wearing a white, traditional, 'burial *kimono*'- the type that was traditionally worn when someone died. She had long, wild black hair covering parts of her face, but when she raised her head to reveal her face, Alec sucked in a breath. She was partially bald on one side of her head and her face was horribly disfigured - her left eye was drooping and her left eyeball was partially hanging down out of the socket in a rather grotesque manner.

Alec could feel an aura of anger and hatred swirling around her and was surprised to *smell* a putrid stench coming from Oiwa. He gagged and covered his mouth as an intense feeling of nausea came over him and he swayed on his feet. There was this reek of death and decay that Alec couldn't explain that

427

seemed to surround the Battle Ghost. He also sensed an evil spiritual presence and powerful energy coming from Oiwa.

Junpei put a hand on Alec's shoulder in concern. "Alec? What is it?"

"That ghost she's...*real.*" Alec was trembling slightly from the overwhelming feeling of Oiwa's spiritual power.

Junpei swore. "Dang it. I knew the RRs were going to cheat during this thing - using real ghosts again. Those jerks. I wonder if that's really the real Oiwa but that seems impossible."

"Real Oiwa?" Alec gave Junpei a questioning look.

Junpei stared at Alec in disbelief. "You've never heard of the ghost story of Oiwa? It's pretty famous. Here's the PG censored version of the tale for you Alec. There was a *ronin* named Ieymon, who was married to a beautiful but sickly woman named Oiwa. In order to support his sickly wife and child the prideful *ronin* was forced to work as an oilpaper umbrella maker, and because of this he began to resent Oiwa for having to do such menial work. However, a well-to-do neighbor of Iyemon's happened to have a pretty granddaughter that was in love with him and together they plotted to get married. In order for that to happen Iyemon planned to kill his wife Oiwa. Iyemon bought a deadly poison, which he gave to his wife saying it was in fact 'blood-road medicine' and that it would supposedly help her with her weak constitution.

"Instead of helping her however it was a poison that caused her face to become deformed, her hair to fall out, and her left eye to droop. When one of her servants held a mirror up to Oiwa to show her her unnatural and horrible disfigurement she died on the spot from the shock of her husband's betrayal. Iyemon then cast Oiwa's body into the river and was happy to finally be rid of her. However, when he went to see his bride-to-be on their wedding day and lifted her veil he saw Oiwa's disfigured face instead of his bride-to-be's. He instantly beheaded her only to find that he had accidently killed his bride-to-be.

"Horrified Iyemon went to confess the crime to his would-be father in law but encountered the ghost of Oiwa instead. Again, he tried to slay her ghost and this time he found that he had accidently slain his would-be father in law. Iyemon continued to try and escape the ghost of Oiwa which was now haunting him wherever he went and fled deep in the mountains thinking he'd be safe from her there. When one day he went fishing and ended up fishing out Oiwa's dead body from the river. Iyemon rushed back to his mountain home screaming and locked himself up inside. That night the vines around his house all turned into snakes, the hanging paper lanterns inside his house eerily turned into Oiwa's face and the smoke from the fire in his hearth oddly seemed to resemble Oiwa's hair. Iyemon fled his mountain home in a fit of madness and unexpectedly encountered his brother-in-law, who killed Iyemon on the spot, and so avenged all the murders. Oiwa appeared to her brother-in-law and smiled thankfully before disappearing."

Alec's eyes widened in horror as Junpei completed the tale. He looked back at Oiwa realizing she was an *onryo*, or vengeful ghost. Alec also knew that this type of ghost was the worst kind to face since they were usually the most powerful.

"Oh my god, we can't let LadyV fight Oiwa. She's no match for her! We have to stop the Ghostly Duel!" Alec blurted out frantic.

Junpei frowned and watched as LadyV eyed Oiwa apprehensively, his expression turning to concern. "You're right Alec. We have to stop the match."

Dr. M cleared his throat and stopped them. "No." He said and gave them a pointed look. "This is LadyV's fight. She wants to be the next Ultimate Ghost Master of Yokai World just as much as either of you do. This is her battle. You can't interfere. Alec, all you can do is believe in her."

Alec and Junpei exchanged a 'look' before grudgingly agreeing to let LadyV continue her duel.

The hairs on LadyV's arms stood on end and she had goose bumps running up and down her arms as she looked at Oiwa. Was her spirit sense trying to tell her something? But LadyV swallowed her fear and prepared to duel.

"Noppera-bo use Delete Attack!" LadyV commanded waving her arm forward.

Noppera-bo flew forward in attack, her sleeves extending and shooting outwards to attack Oiwa. They quickly wrapped around Oiwa's body and the front of one sleeve latched on and covered the whole of Oiwa's disfigured face. Oiwa raised a hand to place it on Noppera-bo's sleeve...

Catara summoned two *katana* swords from her inventory and got into a fighting stance before LadyV, one sword held slightly forward and the other was held slightly backwards. That day, Catara had chosen to dress as a female *Shinigami* in a short purple *kimono* dress and without her usual *ninja* claws.

LadyV followed suit and summoned a *katana* instead of her usual *naginata* to face Catara in close combat more easily. Sword vs. sword worked much better after all, LadyV decided.

"LadyV...or rather Lady Virus. I never did like you. You think you're so special don't you? Being a Game Idol and everything. You and all your stupid fans make me sick. I hate people like you who think they're better than everyone else. You must think you're perfect or something. But I can see through your mask and I'll reveal your true face to everyone here when I rip off that pretty face of yours!"

LadyV's confident expression faltered for a moment as she was caught off guard by Catara's words that seemed to cut a little too close to home, but she quickly managed to regain her composure. "I'd like to see you try."

Catara rushed forward in attack, spinning like a top, her swords flashing through the air in a deadly manner. LadyV raised her own sword to block the attacks which came again and again in rapid succession as Catara spun so fast that LadyV never had a chance to move on the offensive and was kept on the defensive. *She's good.* LadyV admitted to herself as their swords continued to clash. Catara was smirking and laughing as she pressed her advantage against LadyV, pushing her back.

Meanwhile, Oiwa's mere touch suddenly began to eat away at the sleeve which held her captive, and it appeared as though the material of Noppera-bo's *kimono* sleeve was being eaten away as if by acid. Oiwa put her other hand on the other sleeve and the same thing began to happen. Noppera-bo pulled back her sleeves and leapt backwards away from Oiwa to put distance between them, but Oiwa eerily floated forward with her hand raised and before Noppera-bo could move in time she stroked Noppera-bo's blank face leaving a trail of destructed data in the wake of that deadly caress. Then Oiwa leaned forward and placed a kiss on Noppera-bo's blank face and the effect from the poisoned kiss was immediate -

Green veins appeared on Noppera-bo's blank face like a spider's web and moved outwards pulsing with the green poison from Oiwa's lips. The green spider's web of poison began to cover the whole of Noppera-bo's PC body until she was completely infected by Oiwa's poison. Then Noppera-bo's data and body began to be eaten away, disappearing into little dots of data as if a virus had suddenly attacked the Virus Mistress' pawn herself! Noppera-bo fell backwards as all her data was being deleted and she slowly disappeared into cyber space.

LadyV turned in shock to see that her Noppera-bo was being deleted. "Noppera-bo! Return!" She tried to summon Noppera-bo back into her control ring but it failed to work. LadyV watched in horror as Noppera-bo simply disappeared - she had been completely deleted. The Battle Ghost that cyber hacker LadyV had designed, created, and programmed herself had just been deleted.

"*Noppera-bo...*" LadyV said sadly as she watched her Noppera-bo completely disappear into nothingness.

Catara grinned gleefully, "Oiwa! Burn the mask that is LadyV's face to reveal her true ugliness! NOW!" Catara appeared to need to yell 'Now' at the end as Oiwa seemed to hesitate on Catara's orders, and Catara noticeably clenched her hand tightly around her control ring.

From the stands, Alec noticed that as Oiwa floated forward and moaned pitifully that the control collar around her neck was glowing, which meant that Oiwa was being controlled against her will, and was even then fighting against Catara's hold upon her. Alec realized that Oiwa was yet another victim of the RRs. Oiwa eerily had her hand reached outwards as she approached LadyV.

LadyV shook her head and pulled herself together. Holding her *katana* out before her in a two-handed grip LadyV charged froward, her sword raised, and then LadyV quickly leapt up into the air so that she was able to bring her sword down hard upon Oiwa in a high downwards slash. However - Oiwa caught the sword's blade with a single hand, stopping its descent. And as Oiwa's grip tightened around the steel of the blade her mere touch began to eat away at the sword like acid.

LadyV struggled to pull her sword free from Oiwa's grasp but it was too late. When she did manage to pull back her sword, half of it was already melted away and the rest of it was still melting off in drips of liquid metal. LadyV was forced to toss her ruined sword aside. LadyV stumbled away from Oiwa in shock at her uncanny abilities, but then Oiwa teleported so that she was suddenly standing directly in front of LadyV and reached out to stroke LadyV's cheek, which began to burn painfully at Oiwa's touch. The face of LadyV was then being eaten away by the poisonous, acid touch of Oiwa's hand.

LadyV cried out in pain as Oiwa continued to touch her and then Oiwa was pressing her lips hard against LadyV's. The poison of Oiwa's lips began to go into LadyV's mouth and Alec could see the green poison as it traveled through LadyV's PC body showing up in veins that had suddenly appeared on LadyV's face around her mouth and on then her arms and legs. The poison was quickly traveling throughout her body and LadyV found herself paralyzed and unable to move from Oiwa's deadly clutches.

Oiwa then pulled away and unsupported LadyV simply began to fall backwards onto the battle stage, and to Alec, who was watching, it all seemed to happen in slow motion...

And the fact that LadyV had cried out in true, real pain, made Alec's heart stop as he realized just what that meant. It might not have been a true physical wound that LadyV had just suffered, but it was indeed a mental and spiritual one.

"LadyV!" Alec cried out.

"LadyV no!" Junpei echoed at his side and with such feeling that Alec shot his friend a surprised look. Had Junpei liked Rika *all* this time and *that* much? Why hadn't Alec noticed before? Alec was suddenly sure of it and that Junpei had stepped aside for Alec since they were friends.

Junpei...Alec shook his head of such thoughts since there were more important things to be worrying about right then. Alec could feel it - the presence of a curse. A curse had just been placed on LadyV! *Oh no! LadyV's just been cursed by Oiwa! I have to do something! I have to save her*! Alec rushed off towards the battle stage.

Yukino looked startled as Alec suddenly ran off, "Alec!"

The emcee Kiki didn't seem too concerned that LadyV had just fallen down onto the stage and lay there unmoving. She assumed LadyV would soon turn into a PC ghost after all. Little did she know that a real curse had just been placed on LadyV and that if it reached her body back in reality LadyV a.k.a. Rika would end up in a coma. Emcee Kiki strode to the center of the battle stage and waved a hand towards Catara. "And the winner is Ghost Master Catara! And her Battle Ghost Oiwa!"

A loud applause went up for Catara.

Catara grinned triumphantly and looked down her nose with a haughty expression on her face at the unmoving form of LadyV, thinking the Game Idol had just gotten what she deserved.

However, Alec had climbed his way up onto the battle stage and was rushing towards the fallen LadyV now.

"Hey! You! You're not allowed up here!" Emcee Kiki complained as Alec rushed over to LadyV's still form and cradled her gently in his arms. He didn't hesitate as he pressed his lips fiercely to hers.

Yukino, who was watching all this from the stands, was in shock. Mixed feelings were rushing through her at the sight. Anger. Sadness. Confusion. *Oh, so that's the girl that Alec likes. I see...of course he likes her.* Yukino's fists clenched at her sides until her knuckles had turned white.

Dr. M noticed Yukino's odd behavior out of the corner of his eye. "Yukino? Is something wrong?"

Yukino seemed equally surprised at herself - she wasn't possibly *jealous* was she? Like Tamamo-no-mae had accused her of being? Naw. Yukino shook her head and then tossed her long hair back casually. "Of course not. Why would there be?"

Dr. M however didn't look too convinced and he eyed Yukino curiously from then on.

Alec began to summon his curse breaking power and a golden aura glowed around him. He concentrated hard as he began to send his power into LadyV's mind to purge the curse before it could infect Rika's body back in reality through the HMD and then put her in a coma. The golden light passed from Alec's kiss and to LadyV's body. The golden light turned into a golden liquid that was seen spreading through the veins in LadyV's body that had once been filled with Oiwa's green colored poison. The golden liquid began to replace all of the green poison that was flowing in LadyV's veins before in seconds the poison was purged completely.

LadyV's eyes fluttered open and Alec pulled back, letting out a sigh of relief.

"Alec?" She blinked back at him in surprise.

Junpei had waited patiently for Alec to finish his curse breaking but couldn't wait any longer. He quickly hurried over to the battle stage and scrambled up before he was running towards Alec and LadyV. "LadyV!"

LadyV turned to see a concerned expression on Junpei's face as he approached them. "What happened? You both look like you just saw a ghost." LadyV smirked at the irony of that statement.

"You were almost cursed (again). But Alec saved you *again*." Junpei smirked and ruffled Alec's hair in thanks. "Way to go buddy."

"Junpei! *Mou!*" Alec blushed.

LadyV looked over to Alec and blushing slightly she gave him a small smile. Alec smiled back and a silent communication passed between them. They forgave each other. And Alec found himself oddly unaffected by LadyV's pretty blush, which at one time would have caused butterflies to flutter in his stomach.

Meanwhile, Yukino was reading more into that exchanged look between Alec and LadyV and that blush that was on LadyV's face. She failed to notice how Alec was acting aloof and appeared to be unaffected by LadyV. She also didn't notice when Alec backed away from LadyV so that Junpei could be the one to help LadyV up and support her off the stage. Yukino was blind sided and just saw LadyV with both Alec and Junpei at her sides, and both boys smiling broadly that LadyV was alright and that the curse had been broken.

Catara frowned and bit her thumbnail angrily. She was incredibly pissed that LadyV had been saved by that meddling brat.

"LadyV, how is your face back in reality?" Alec asked concernedly.

LadyV put a hand to one side of her face, "It's a little sore. I'll do some first aid on it later after the tournament." Alec raised an eyebrow as he noticed that Junpei's arm had somehow been slung casually over LadyV's shoulders and shook his head ruefully. He had a feeling this had somehow all happened right under his nose and he hadn't even noticed it. Talk about clueless. Alec wasn't arguing.

Alec let out a breath of relief though, glad that his friend hadn't been hurt. "Good." He told LadyV in response.

However, an angry Catara approached the trio.

"You think you're going to get away that easily? Do you!" Catara cried with a maniac gleam in her magenta colored eyes, and suddenly materialized a holographic keyboard in front of her using her own hacker skills and began to type away rapidly on the keys. Alec wondered if she was also a cyber hacker like LadyV. "LadyV, I shall reveal your true form!" Catara declared.

And then LadyV's PC body was bathed in a green-tinged light before suddenly her body began to change from the '15-year-old hottie' that LadyV had programmed herself to look like back into her 13-year-old girl body instead. Her chest becoming dramatically smaller and her legs becoming a little shorter.

"This is what LadyV really looks like! Take a good look at your beloved Game Idol everyone! She's just a hack!" Catara declared waving her hand at the new LadyV.

Junpei shook his head at the loss of LadyV's assets, "That should be a crime." He pouted regretfully. "Stealing my eye candy away like that."

LadyV shot him a venomous look and Junpei flinched. The crowd of players seemed baffled about how to react to this sudden development or rather lack thereof. Their beloved Game Idol, LadyV, was no longer the 'hot babe' they thought she was but instead a young girl. And then that's when the laughter started and rose until the entire stadium was laughing at LadyV.

LadyV groaned and put her face in her hands. "This is so embarrassing... damn that Catara..."

Junpei patted her back sympathetically, "Well, that's what you get when you deceive people LadyV but...you shouldn't have to deceive them anyways because the real you is just fine in my book."

LadyV looked back at Junpei in surprise.

Alec let them have a moment alone together and walked back to the stands alone where he encountered Yukino, who was eyeing him strangely. "What? Do I have something on my face?" Alec asked her.

Yukino just looked away from him with a *Hmph!*

Alec just shrugged off her strange behavior, *Girls.* Who knew what they were thinking.

* * *

Emcee Kiki waited for Catara and the others to leave the battle stage before she called up the next duelists. "Will Ghost Masters Junpei and Smoker please take your places up on stage!"

Junpei, with his arms behind his head nonchalantly, and a goofy grin plastered on his face, made his way up on the stage. He'd been itching for a fight with the Renegade Reapers. The stoic *ninja*, Smoker, also made his way up onto the battle stage. Alec saw that he was still wearing that face mask of his which covered the lower half of his face and also that his messy gray-colored hair still hid one side of his face revealing only his almost solid-black eye. As usual he was dressed all in black.

Junpei threw a wink at Kiki. "Hey, how about a kiss on my cheek for luck?" He pointed to his cheek in an exaggerated fashion.

"Ewww!" Kiki declared, "Like I want to get cooties from you! Anyways, Ghost Masters are you ready? Begin!" Kiki waved her hand down signaling the beginning of the match.

Junpei wasted no time in acting and raised his control ring so that it flashed with power. "Goku! I summon you!" The Monkey King, Battle Ghost, Goku immediately materialized besides Junpei with his long red *bo* staff in hand, and he was spinning it before him impressively.

Smoker calmly raised his control ring hand. "Enenra!" He called and the strange Battle Ghost which was made up entirely of smoke materialized next to Smoker. The Enenra had a head, torso, and arms made of smoke but its face had no real facial features just a gaping, grinning, black hole of a mouth. Its body wasn't really solid and its lower half was curled like a wisp of smoke and ghost-like.

Earlier Junpei and Alec had decided on a few hand signals so that they could communicate to each other once Junpei was up on the battle stage. Alec had been worried for the safety of his friends after LadyV had ended up facing a real ghost and had decided on this precaution. This way Junpei would be able to know if Alec, with his incredible sixth sense when it came to ghosts and spirits, sensed that Smoker was using a real ghost or not. And so Junpei would be able to know what to expect during his Ghostly Duel and not underestimate his opponent. Junpei glanced over in Alec's direction to see what the verdict was.

Alec rubbed his nose and tucked a stray hair behind his ear, which meant - *It's a real ghost.*

Junpei frowned and put a finger to his chin, which meant - *What?*

Alec frowned, rubbed his nose, tucked a stray hair behind his ear and then scratched his cheek. *It's a real ghost, baka!*

Junpei just scratched his chin - *Huh?*

Alec began to pick his nose vigorously - *Reallll!*

Yukino raised an eyebrow at both Alec and Junpei's strange behavior and shook her head at them. Boys. Alec really was still so immature after all.

Junpei snickered and motioned back. *I gotcha.*

Alec frowned realizing Junpei had just been playing with him and had made him pick his nose like a total idiot in front of Yukino to boot! *Aw man!* Alec's face was bright red as he turned to see if Yukino had been watching him and groaned when he saw Yukino's disgusted look directed his way.

"Enenra! Go!" Smoker directed in his serious tone.

"Goku, go get 'em!" Junpei smirked as he commanded his Battle Ghost to move forward. Junpei eyed the Enenra curiously since Smoker had used an

AI Enenra Battle Ghost the last time they had faced each other, so he hadn't been too surprised to see the ghost. But Junpei now realized it had looked a little different from before and now thanks to Alec he knew that the ghost was actually real. But that still didn't explain how in the blazes did Smoker and the others get their hands on real *yokai* and ghosts in the first place. Junpei found this mystery to be very unsettling.

Goku attacked Enenra with his *bo* staff, causing it to extend forward at the smoke *yokai*, but Enenra quickly dematerialized and then reappeared further to Goku's right. Goku attacked again but Enenra simply vanished and reappeared now far to Goku's left. Goku spun and tried to attack it again but when he finally managed to land a blow upon Enenra his *bo* staff simply passed straight through Enenra's smoky body.

Meanwhile, Smoker had moved into attack Junpei, and was throwing razor sharp *shuriken* at the martial artist, who was forced to dodge out of the way. Junpei kept trying to get into a fighting stance but was once again forced to jump out of the way as a flurry of *shuriken* flew towards him, spinning in a deadly fashion. The *shuriken* instead hit the battle stage floor and were imbedded there, all in a row. Smoker reached into his *ninja* outfit again and found that he was out of *shuriken*.

Junpei shot Smoker a cocky grin. "Out of *shuriken* eh? Let's settle this like real men shall we?"

Emcee Kiki snorted loudly at the word 'men' that Junpei had used as she continued to watch the two boys fighting.

Smoker arched a single eyebrow at Junpei.

Junpei got into a fighting stance and Smoker did the same, however, as they both began to attack each other in a mind blowing, flurry of kicks and punches Alec noticed that their fists were glowing with a blue-tinged light, which could only mean -

Whoa. They're using their spirit energy here in the game to make themselves more powerful.

Meanwhile, Goku was unable to get a hit on the elusive Enenra and then suddenly Enenra was wrapping its body around Goku like a snake. Goku struggled in Enenra's grasp but it was no use. Soon Goku's arms were pinned to his sides as Enenra wound its body tighter and tighter around him. The smoke *yokai* was already covering half of Goku's face and it appeared as though Enenra planned to simply consume Goku's entire body in smoke completely. Goku was being constricted, suffocated. His body made of data flickering like a dying hologram -

Alec noticed a look of fear on Goku's face and it seemed much too real for a primitive AI program to express an emotion like fear so realistically. And weren't mere AI Battle Ghosts supposed to be unable to exhibit any sort of emotion at all? Except for his AI Ghost Ryuu there shouldn't be any other Battle Ghosts in the game world that were able to express themselves like that. Alec had a bad feeling about this as the hairs on the back of his neck prickled in warning, and he called out a warning to Junpei. "Junpei!"

Junpei quickly turned to see that Goku was in trouble. "Goku!" Junpei turned to Smoker and just as the *ninja* was charging him Junpei used an *aikido* move to use Smoker's forward momentum against him, and grabbed Smoker's arm causing him to fly forward as he then managed to throw Smoker so that he hit the battle stage landing on his back with a hard thud. Smoker lay stunned and unmoving on the battle stage's floor.

Junpei then quickly turned to Goku and using both hands started to form a ball of spirit energy while at the same time he was running towards the dueling Battle Ghosts. Junpei then released the energy blast at Enenra. At the same time Goku rammed his *bo* staff into the battle stage to embed it there and to keep Enenra from being able to escape as the energy blast hit Enenra dead on, and instantly exorcized the *yokai* so that it vanished into thin air. A golden control collar fell to the battle stage with a clatter.

Smoker, who was back on his feet, a *kunai* knife now in his hand was trying to take Junpei by surprise and stab him in the back from behind. Luckily, Goku noticed this just in time and elongated his *bo* staff so that it shot out and hit Smoker square on the chest. He was sent flying backwards where he landed on the battle stage with an *Oof!* He was a bit dizzy-eyed and did not get up again as he fell backwards.

Kiki ran up to Junpei and Goku smiling, "The winner - Junpei and his Battle Ghost Goku!" She declared in her perky manner.

"*Yatta!* Alright!" Junpei punched the air enthusiastically, "I couldn't have done it without you buddy." Junpei said turning to face his Battle Ghost, Goku. "Give me five!" Junpei held up his hand for Goku to slap.

Goku blinked confusedly before giving Junpei a high five. Junpei gave Goku a lopsided grin, and then gave Goku a thumbs up, which Goku mimicked right back at him.

Alec shook his head at Goku's odd behavior in disbelief. There was definitely more than meets the eye to that Battle Ghost, Alec decided.

"That was impressive, Ghost Master." Kiki leaned in and surprised Junpei by giving him that kiss on his cheek that he had wanted. Junpei blushed and the crowd cheered in response.

Once Junpei had stumbled his way off the stage (since he was still in a bit of a daze after that unexpected kiss) and the RRs had dragged Smoker unceremoniously off the stage, Kiki coughed and prepared herself to start the next duel.

"Alrighty then! Will Ghost Masters Dr. M and RedAki please take your positions up on the stage!" Emcee Kiki began to announce.

Alec paled considerably at this match up - if RedAki's Battle Ghost was real then Dr. M would be in serious danger. *Epp!* "No." Alec shook his head and then repeated himself with more force. "*No.* You have to forfeit the duel Dr. M. If RedAki got his hands on a real ghost he could end up cursing you and you'll end up in a coma! You don't even have any spiritual power to go up against a *real* Ghost Master. You're not like us Dr. M."

Dr. M frowned and shot Alec a disapproving look. He then pushed his glasses up his nose and a haughty expression formed on his face. "I am ranked #5 Ghost Master of Yokai World. I will do everything it takes to protect my rank. This is my fight - I won't run away from it, Alec." A flash of hurt crossed Dr. M's face as he remembered Alec's last words. It hurt that one of his closest friends didn't believe in him but Dr. M quickly schooled his expression into a neutral mask. Dr. M sighed heavily. "You should try believing in me a little more Alec. We're friends aren't we? And I think you're forgetting just who I am in *this* world. I may be a geek and a dork in the real world but here I'm Dr. M. Let's just say, I have a few tricks up my sleeves even if RedAki does turn out to have a real ghost."

Dr. M gave Alec a small smirk before he walked away from Alec without a backwards glance and made his way up onto the battle stage. RedAki was acting bored and appeared unconcerned as he also took his place up on stage. He was eyeing Dr. M critically with a look that Alec recognized as one someone gives to a bug they're about to squash under their shoe.

RedAki had this confident, insolent sort of smirk on his face.

Dr. M wore a grim smile.

"Ghost Masters are you ready?" Kiki looked back and forth between Dr. M and RedAki. "Let the Ghostly Duel begin!" Kiki waved her hand through the air enthusiastically. "This is a match we've all been waiting for folks. RedAki is ranked #3 Ghost Master in this world and Dr. M is currently ranked #5...how will the rankings end up? We'll have to watch and find out." Kiki began her commentary.

Dr. M raised his hand and the control ring there glowed. "Tanuki! Come forth." Tanuki, the racoon dog, *yokai* ghost, materialized next to Neji, boxing gloves on his paws that were held out before him ready for action.

Alec sucked in his breath and held it - this was it. The moment he had been waiting for. To see what ghost RedAki now had in his possession.

RedAki smirked and raised his hand carelessly so that his control ring also took on a faint glow. "Yoshitsune! I summon you!" A majestic looking *samurai* materialized next to RedAki, a gleaming *katana* in his hand. Yoshitsune looked like one of those ancient *samurai* from Japan's Feudal Era that Alec had seen in the history books back at Izanagi Academy. He was wearing traditional, red *samurai* armor with a menacing looking, golden horned, helmet on his head.

Alec reached out his senses to feel that Yoshitsune was not only very real but he was also super powerful. Yoshitsune's spirit energy signature alone was unbelievably high - perhaps the highest that Alec had ever felt.

"Yoshitsune? I think I've heard of that *samurai* before." Alec said thoughtfully.

Junpei gave Alec a noogie, "Of course you've heard of him! Yoshitsune is one of the most famous and legendary *samurai* of Japan's history. He's a rather popular, tragic sort of hero. You know, they say that Yoshitsune was trained in his martial arts and swordsmanship by powerful *tengu* up in the mountains near Kyoto. I wonder how someone like RedAki managed to capture the ghost of Yoshitsune anyways? Dude, that's just crazy." Junpei shook his head in wonder.

Alec struggled out of Junpei's clingy grasp and straightened his outfit. "What else do you know about Yoshitsune?" After all, Alec decided it was a good idea to be well informed of one's enemies.

Junpei took a long breath before he began to tell Alec a bit of background info and history on Yoshitsune. "Yoshitsune was a famous general of the Minamoto Clan. When he was little his father and oldest two brothers were killed, but his life was spared and he was sent to Kurama Temple, which was a Buddhist temple that was close to Kyoto and where some say he encountered the *tengu*, which trained him in military tactics. Yoshitsune was also rumored to have learned great and powerful, secret sword techniques from the *tengu*, which enabled him to be able to cut falling tree leaves in half with ease.

"Later on in his life Yoshitsune heard stories of his older brother who was still alive, Yoritomo, and who was head of the Minamoto clan at that point, and so decided to join his brother. His brother was in the middle of a conflict between the Minamoto clan and the Taira *samurai* clan. The war between the two clans was known as the Genpei War. Yoshitsune became a great asset to the Minamoto clan and it was due to his great skill that they were able to defeat the Taira at the Battle of Ichi-no-Tani and then again in the Battle of Yashima in Shikoki, and finally they were able to completely destroy the clan in the Battle of Dan-no-ura.

"After the Genpei War, due to his brother having schemes against the current emperor, Emperor Go-Shirakawa, Yoshitsune decided to go to the emperor's aid and move against his brother even though he knew he didn't have much of a chance. However, Yoshitsune was betrayed and defeated at the Battle of Koromogawa and forced to commit *seppuku*, ritual suicide, along with his wife and daughter. They say because of this betrayal his soul has not yet found peace and so roams the battlefields of Japan in unrest." Junpei finished.

Alec had found the tale of Yoshitsune to be quite interesting and decided he'd look more into the tragic hero's past, thinking that if he knew more about the *samurai* perhaps he could help Yoshitsune with his unfinished business and help him to cross over some day.

Alec gave Dr. M the sign which meant that the ghost Dr. M was about to face was indeed real. Dr. M caught Alec's eye and nodded. The message had been received. Dr. M had suspected this might happen during the Ultimate Ghost Master Tournament that day since a lot of the RRs had made it to the finals and so he had come prepared.

"Tanuki. Shapeshift!" Dr. M commanded his Battle Ghost.

Tanuki glowed with a green light before he began to shapeshift until he became an exact mirror image of Yoshitsune, who was standing before him. Although the copy's appearance was somewhat darker and more malevolent looking since the copy's *samurai* armor was black and gold versus Yoshitsune's armor that was red and gold.

"Tanuki attack!" Dr. M continued to direct his ghost.

CopyYoshi unsheathed his *katana* and charged forward. Dr. M then faced RedAki and from his game inventory selected a special gun he had invented before it suddenly appeared in his hand materializing there. It was a rather large gun with a long gun barrel and rather large opening. As Dr. M aimed the gun at RedAki and slowly pressed down on the trigger the gun appeared to be charging up. The gun was glowing with a red-tinged light that was swirling around the gun. Dr. M then pressed down on the trigger all the way and shot his ASEG (Artificial Spirit Energy Gun) at RedAki so that a ball of concentrated red light shot out towards the unsuspecting player killer.

As Dr. M fired consecutively at RedAki, the *KuroShinigami* was forced to block the shots with his black-bladed *katana* but then the spirit energy bullet began pushing against RedAki's blade as he held it up before him, and RedAki was surprisingly being pushed back! Skidding across the arena stage RedAki dug his heels into the floor while trying not to be moved back by the force of Dr. M's bullets but was finding that to be impossible. The sheer power behind that single shot of red light was surprisingly strong.

RedAki had a stunned expression on his face. He eyed Dr. M curiously trying to figure out what the hell was going on. "According to my information Dr. M you don't possess any spiritual abilities. And yet those bullets you just shot at me *feel* like they're made out of pure spirit energy, care to explain? I'm curious to know just what that red light is?"

Dr. M frowned and pushed his glasses up his nose. "It's artificial spirit energy. It's my very own invention. I discovered how to create it by researching the particles of real spirit energy and replicating its effects in other particles, so that I managed to create an energy with the same ability to exorcize ghosts or purify *yokai*."

RedAki nodded looking somewhat impressed, "I see, you're a very dangerous person to leave alive, Dr. M. Prepare to die!"

Meanwhile, CopyYoshi was charging forward in attack at Yoshitsune, and his body was surrounded by a fiery, flaring, red aura of artificial spirit energy. CopyYoshi moved his sword forward and then sideways so that a blast of artificial spirit energy was released upon Yoshitsune. Yoshitsune raised his *katana* but was pushed back as he tried to block the sudden and unexpected energy attack. Unexpectedly, Yoshitsune lost control and was flung backwards so that he landed on his backside.

RedAki caught this out of the corner of his eye in disbelief - "He pushed back Yoshitsune? *Bakana.* Impossible." RedAki's jaw dropped.

The crowd of players, emcee Kiki, and Alec were also all very impressed and wore a variety of equally shocked and surprised expressions.

"Wow! It seems like Dr. M isn't holding anything back and appears to have the upper hand in this duel! He's definitely pulling out all stops! I wonder what he'll do next!" Kiki commentated.

Alec blinked in disbelief at Dr. M. Dr. M had just managed to actually push RedAki back and Dr. M's Tanuki Battle Ghost had managed to knock Yoshitsune off his feet! *Uso! No way!* Did Dr. M really have the upper hand in this duel? Could he truly win? Alec's mind was spinning.

However, RedAki pulled himself together and suddenly shrugged appearing unfazed. "I didn't think I'd have to get serious while facing someone who doesn't even have any spirit powers. Consider this an honor Dr. M - getting to see me get serious. It's time for me to kick things up a notch. Yoshitsune! It's time for you to get serious as well! Our opponents are not to be underestimated after all."

Yoshitsune stood and nodded. "Yes Master." He pointed his sword at his copy and began to gather his spirit energy around himself so that he glowed with a blue-tinged aura.

CopyYoshi followed suit and summoned his own artificial spirit energy so that a red aura flared to life around him.

Then both *samurai* charged each other. Yoshitsune waved his sword forward - CopyYoshi doing the same and then both *samurai* unleashed energy attacks at each other. The red and blue energies collided in midair but then Yoshitsune added more power to his attack and suddenly CopyYoshi's attack was quickly overpowered. CopyYoshi was flung backwards as the attack hit him dead on and he landed on the floor of the stage where he was flickering in and out of existence. His data had been heavily damaged.

"Tanuki!" Dr. M cried out, concerned for his Battle Ghost.

RedAki feigned boredom as he picked his ear and flicked his fingers off into the air to show just how unconcerned he was with everything that had to do with the battle at hand. "All too easy - prepare to be defeated once and for all, Dr. M. I have to admit that your inventions and especially your Tanuki Battle Ghost were most impressive, but what it all boils down to is they just weren't good enough."

RedAki charged forward, this time summoning his spirit energy to increase his speed. Dr. M raised his ASEG and fired. But RedAki was too fast and easily blocked the bullets with his sword as he continued to charge forward. And then RedAki was suddenly standing in front of Dr. M and using his sword to cut through Dr. M's Spirit Gun as easily as a knife through butter.

Alec was closely watching as RedAki continued to move his sword elegantly through the air and noticed that it was glowing with his real spirit energy, a blue aura surrounding the blade of his black sword. Alec held his breath as he watched and didn't want to believe that RedAki would stab Neji through while using such a truly dangerous attack.

Didn't RedAki realize that if Dr. M sustained a wound in the game that contained real spirit energy behind it that Neji would suffer a true spiritual or mental wound back in reality? Was RedAki really trying to kill Dr. M! Alec shook his head vigorously. It couldn't be true. *This can't be happening.* If Alec didn't do anything Dr. M could end up falling into a coma or worse he could really die this time.

"No! Dr. M!" Alec called out in concern, "RedAki! Don't! *Please!*" Alec's voice was tinged with desperation.

RedAki flinched at the sound of Alec's broken voice and hesitated before removing his spirit energy from his sword at the last second, but still stabbed Dr. M through the gut anyways. RedAki leaned in to whisper in Dr. M's ear - "I could care less if you lived or died, hacker scum. You're lucky you're *his* friend..." RedAki pulled back his sword and Dr. M fell backwards onto the stage floor. RedAki then turned his attention to the fallen form of the CopyYoshi and its flickering image. "Yoshitsune, finish the copy off. It's too risky to leave that kind of anti-ghost technology intact right now."

Yoshitsune nodded, "Yes Master." Yoshitsune walked over to CopyYoshi and raised his *katana* in a two-handed grip before bringing it down through the air to stab the CopyYoshi in his stomach.

"No! Tanuki!" Dr. M called weakly from his position on the floor.

Yoshitsune sent a blast of real spirit energy into his sword and thereby into CopyYoshi's body so that it broke apart and exploded into little dots of light and data. CopyYoshi a.k.a. Tanuki had been effectively deleted.

Dr. M's PC body died and Alec let out a breath of relief as Dr. M's PC body became a PC ghost, which meant RedAki hadn't used his spirit energy to harm Neji back in the real world. *Phew.*

Emcee Kiki hurried up on stage. "What a surprising turn of events! Well, that just shows you that RedAki is a Ghost Master to be reckoned with once he gets serious! The winner is RedAki!"

A cheer went up from the crowd of players. RedAki bowed in a flashy manner, cocky grin on his face, before he strode off the battle stage without a backwards glance.

Alec scrambled up the stage to quickly resurrect Dr. M.

"*Oi Kimi!* Hey you! Not again - you're not allowed up here!" Kiki complained as Alec ignored her and ran across the stage.

As soon as Alec had reached Dr. M's side he clicked on a red potion in his inventory to use on Dr. M's PC ghost. "Red Potion! Resurrect!"

Dr. M's PC ghost glowed with a green light before it was restored to his normal PC body. Dr. M gave Alec a lopsided smile. "Thanks Alec...looks like you were right after all. I lost."

Alec shook his head vigorously "No Dr. M I was wrong. You were incredible out there. I had no idea - you're a total genius dude! To have come up with a way to combat real ghosts with technology - that's incredible. Why didn't you tell me you'd completed your research?" Alec's eyes sparkled with admiration.

Dr. M looked pleasantly surprised before he puffed up his chest and laughed. "I am a genius aren't I? Ha!"

Junpei shook his head ruefully at the geek's cocky behavior. LadyV smiled and Yukino looked amused.

Kiki was doing a shooing motion towards Dr. M. "Alright already. Get off the stage would you? The next duel is about to begin. And as for you." She turned to Alec and pointed at him. "You might as well stay since you're in the next duel anyways. Ghost Master Kiba please come up on stage and take your position!"

Kiba sauntered up on stage, the monk's pose haughty as he looked down his nose at the shorter Alec. Alec simply met his stare and didn't look away. Yukino hopped up on to the stage and joined Alec by his side. Kiba raised an eyebrow at this but made no comment.

Kiki eyed Yukino curiously, "Dranarch you are not allowed to summon your Battle Ghost before the duel has started. You know that right?"

"Uh, yea, about that...I'm having a technical problem summoning her back into my control ring...is that going to be a problem?" Alec asked scratching his cheek bashfully.

Kiki turned to Kiba, "That depends...if your opponent will allow this?"

Kiba shrugged. "I don't mind. He's going to need some handicaps if he expects to win against me, anyways." He shot Alec and Yukino a challenging glare.

Kiki shrugged, "Alright then - Ghost Masters let the duel begin! STARTO!"

Alec waited patiently for Kiba to summon his Battle Ghost and watched as Kiba raised his hand into the air, his control ring glowing before he yelled out - "Kiyohime!"

Alec gasped as he recognized the name from a ghost story his 'father' Mori had once told him. So, apparently Kiba had also gotten his hands on another legendary ghost - this time Kiyohime. From what Alec could remember the story was of a beautiful waitress named Kiyohime, who worked at a teahouse by a river. She was happy working there but also very lonely. When one day, a traveling priest stopped by the teahouse and fell in love with Kiyohime as soon as he laid eyes upon her and she also fell in love with him. They spent many wonderful days together, enjoying each other's company. However, his love for her soon faded and he ended up leaving her without even saying goodbye.

Angry and broken-hearted Kiyohime fled to an ancient religious temple, the Temple of Kompera to learn the art of magic and shapeshifting in order to get her revenge upon Anchin. There after lots of difficult training, she learned how to turn herself into a dragon. In her dragon form she flew to the Buddhist temple where he lived. Anchin was outside when he saw Kiyohime approach and tried to hide under the temple bell, however Kiyohime opened her mouth and unleashed her fiery breath upon the bell melting it and killing Anchin at the same time.

Alec shook his head as he cleared his mind of the story and turned to watch as Kiyohime materialized next to Kiba. She was wearing a beautiful *kimono* in greens, silvers, and blues. On her sleeves there seemed to be a pattern which mimicked reptilian scales of some kind. She had long black hair and sparkling, emerald colored eyes.

Alec reached out his spirit sense to confirm that Kiyohime was real and could sense a powerful spiritual presence coming from her. He also felt a great sadness coming off of her in crashing waves and spotted the glowing collar that was around her neck. *Ghost control tech.* She was a victim of the RRs, who wanted to use her broken heart and her demonic powers for their own ends. Alec knew from the tale and others how a woman could become a demon when she was betrayed by the man she loved. There was a fine line between love and hate.

Alec pointed his silvery *katana* at Kiba - "Release Kiyohime now! Or else!"

Yukino shot Alec a surprised sideways glance and hissed through her teeth, *"Alec? What do you think you're doing...?"*

Kiba raised an eyebrow at Alec's chivalrous attitude before he burst out laughing. "Yea, I think *not*. Kiyohime attack him!"

Kiyohime appeared to take a deep breath and her cheeks puffed up with air before she suddenly released a blast of fiery breath towards Alec unexpectedly. Alec raised his sword prepared to block the fire blast attack, however, Yukino suddenly stepped in his path and waving her fan let loose a powerful icy wind which easily blocked and countered the fiery breath.

"Yukino..." Alec knew he had to defeat Kiba in order to get his control ring and then use it to free Kiyohime. "Take care of Kiyohime for me while I attack Kiba okay?"

Yukino nodded, "Right, you just leave her to me!"

Yukino and Kiyohime moved to attack each other and began to battle. Yukino waved her fan and a barrage of icy daggers went flying towards Kiyohime. Kiyohime countered by unleashing her fire breath on Yukino and melting all of the ice daggers.

Meanwhile, Alec charged Kiba with his *katana* and it clashed with Kiba's monk staff. Both boys summoned their spirit power and a blue aura formed around them as they continued to fight, sparks flying up into the air as their weapons clashed again and again until Alec managed to disarm Kiba suddenly with a twist of his blade. Kiba's ringed staff flew up into the air and then fell to the stage's floor with a clatter.

Alec pointed his sword at Kiba confidently, "You lose, Kiba."

But Kiba let out a cackling laugh that made Alec furrow his brows in confusion. "Did you really think it was going to be that easy? Silly rabbit tricks are for kids. Kiyohime transform! I said - TRANSFORM NOW!" Kiba's control ring glowed and Alec noticed that the control collar which was around Kiyohime's neck also glowed and seemed to slightly constrict in response.

Kiyohime screamed and then she began to glow with a bright golden light. Alec was blinded by the light and had to shield his eyes and so didn't see the transformation, but when he opened his eyes again instead of Kiyohime standing there before him he now saw instead a huge, fire breathing dragon! The creature had a combination of silver and green scales going down its long, serpentine body and it stared at him with fierce looking, dark green eyes with slanted pupils.

"Kiyohime kill them!" Kiba directed waving his arm at Alec and Yukino.

The she-dragon slashed her tail at Alec who raised his sword to block. He continued to block slash after slash from her powerful tail but then he was painfully knocked backwards, tripped off his feet. The she-dragon then brought her tail down hard upon Alec's back, so hard that he cried out in pain -

"Alec!" Yukino yelled out in concern and formed her ice sword and charged Kiyohime with it. "Get away from him, you monster!" Yukino slashed her ice sword at the dragon's tail and tried to find a weak spot. Seeing the softer looking scales beneath her tail Yukino aimed for those and managed to wound Kiyohime. The she-dragon cried out in pain and rage.

Alec pushed himself up off the floor and stood again.

Yukino was eyeing the soft underbelly of the she-dragon as she reared up in pain and realized this was the opportunity she had been waiting for. Yukino knew the underbelly of a dragon was always their weak point. Chance! Yukino aimed her deadly ice sword and prepared to launch an attack against the she-dragon - aiming for the creature's heart.

Alec saw what Yukino was intending to do. "No! Yukino! Don't kill her!"

Yukino leapt up into the air and lunged her sword at the she-dragon's heart but just as she would have pierced it Alec was suddenly in front of her and parrying her blow with his own *katana*. Yukino was startled but jumped backwards landing on her feet as Alec landed on the floor before her.

Yukino eyed Alec in disbelief, "Alec *no baka*! Just what do you think you're doing? Why are you protecting Kiyohime? We have to kill her - there's no other way. Do you want to die?"

Alec shook his head at Yukino, a mixture of stubbornness and sadness on his face. "No, Yukino, there's always another way."

The she-dragon Kiyohime cried out in rage at Yukino for almost having stabbed her through the heart and opened her large jaw lined with sharp teeth to unleash her fiery breath upon Yukino - her lungs filling up with air and her chest enlarging as she prepared her fire breathing attack.

"Yukino! Look out!" Alec yelled and pushed Yukino out of the way and was suddenly engulfed in the spiritual flames of Kiyohime's breath. Alec cried out in pain as the pain he felt from the attack seemed to burn his mind and body.

Yukino looked up from her place on the floor at Alec, utterly shocked and horrified, "*BAKA!*"

The she-dragon also seemed confused by his actions as she continued to stare down at Alec apparently too stunned to resume her attack.

"Kiyohime! What are you doing? Finish him!" Kiba demanded. But when Kiyohime made no immediate response Kiba decided to use the power of the ring against her. "I *said* finish him!"

The collar glowed with a golden light and the she-dragon cried out in pain but still she didn't move to attack Alec.

Alec pushed himself unsteadily to his feet and looked at Kiyohime in awe and smiled timidly at her. Their eyes met - silver gray clashing with emerald green. He raised his sword before him. "Don't worry Kiyohime, I won't kill you - I'll save you! Trust me. Open your heart to me Kiyohime!" Alec leapt up into the air, his *katana* glowing with a blue-tinged light and then he pierced through the she-dragon's heart.

The she-dragon cried out in a roaring, bestial yell that then changed to sound more like a woman's pained scream. She began to return to her human form with Alec's sword still imbedded in her heart. Then an evil spirit that was in the shape of a shadowy dragon rose up and out of her body. Alec's sword didn't appear to have been in its normal material form as Alec began to slowly take his sword out from Kiyohime's heart. And from the looks of things strangely Alec's sword hadn't harmed Kiyohime. What Alec didn't know was that his will not to harm Kiyohime had caused his sword to become a sword that could only harm the evil spirit presence that had been trapped deep within Kiyohime's soul, and had been able to leave Kiyohime's spirit untouched.

Alec then turned his attention to the evil dragon spirit and leapt up into the air to exorcize the spirit by slashing his sword through the air and the shadowy dragon was instantly destroyed.

Kiyohime had been freed from the incarnation of her own anger, hatred and jealousy.

Kiba was in shock. "Kiyohime! You *will* obey me! Kill him!"

Kiyohime grasped her head in pain as she fought against Kiba's control. She looked straight at Alec with a pleading expression on her face. "Hurry... kill me...I can not resist him much longer. Thank you...for trying to help me..."

Alec nodded but then turned to attack the defenseless Kiba instead, making sure to kill him without using his spirit energy. Alec rushed forward and stabbed Kiba unexpectedly through the chest. Kiba looked down in a mixture of shock and disbelief at Alec's protruding sword. Alec pulled his sword out of Kiba and the monk fell back and died turning into a PC ghost. The control ring clattered to the battle stage floor. Alec went over to pick it up and quickly put it on his finger.

Yukino had a pretty good idea of what foolish thing Alec was intending to do next. But that didn't mean she had to like it. "Alec - no way." Yukino stalked up to him, and glared straight into his gray eyes. "You can't seriously be thinking of freeing Kiyohime? She'll kill you!"

Alec shook his head and looked at Kiyohime, directly into her green eyes that were now shimmering with new emotion, "No, she won't. I trust her." Alec raised his hand and the control ring there glowed. "I release you, Kiyohime!"

The collar around Kiyohime's neck glowed golden before it opened and fell off and landed on the battle stage with a resounding clang. Kiyohime put a hand to her neck in surprise and then smiled kindly at Alec. "Thank you, *hoshi-sama*, Sir Monk, I can finally rest in peace..." Kiyohime's body burst into dots of light which floated upwards all the way until they disappeared through the domed ceiling.

Alec smiled as he watched her go. *Phew.* Glad that he was able to save her.

Kiki quickly hurried up onto the battle stage. "Wow...that was some duel wasn't it folks? The winner is Dranarch! And his Battle Ghost Yukino!" Kiki declared.

The cheers that went up from the crowd were incredibly loud due to Alec's impressive duel. Alec took a step forward to leave the stage, but then found himself sinking to one knee in pain. He put a hand to his forehead when he found that his head was spinning and gritted his teeth against the pain not wanting it to show on his face and alert and therefore worry Yukino. Apparently, that last fire attack that Alec had had to endure had affected him a bit more than he had originally thought and now that the adrenaline from the battle had left his system he was able to feel the pain he hadn't known was there before. He could tell his body was even trembling slightly from the attack his mind had just suffered and hoped Yukino wouldn't notice.

Unfortunately, she seemed to anyways. Yukino was at Alec's side in an instant, placing a hand on his shoulder. "Alec-*kun*?" Her voice was laced with worry.

Alec couldn't help but feel flattered that Yukino seemed to care about him. "I'm alright Yukino - just a little tired." He tried to give her a warm smile which came out more as a lopsided grin.

Yukino frowned darkly, "Liar."

Alec just continued to smile at her, much too tired to argue as he let Yukino help him off the stage with his arm around her shoulders.

Kiki watched the Ghost Master and Battle Ghost walk off the battle stage together with a curious expression on her face. She shrugged off her thoughts on how advanced Battle Ghost Yukino was and finished her commentating. "Alright, well, there we have it. That was the end of the third round. We're going to let our Ghost Masters have a small break before we begin the second and next to last round of this tournament!" Kiki informed the crowd of players. "You won't want to miss it!"

Chapter 18:
YOSHITSUNE: THE LEGENDARY SAMURAI

Junpei looked at Alec's pale, sweat-soaked face worriedly as he and Yukino approached everyone back in the stands. "Alec, buddy, you okay?"

Alec simply nodded.

Dr. M frowned and pushed his glasses up his nose as he eyed Alec critically. "You look far from okay to me."

Alec sighed, beginning to feel a bit exasperated, and ran a hand through his snow-white hair. Really, his friends were *way* too overprotective. "I'm alright guys, *really*."

They all gave Alec skeptical looks.

"Alec...I just wanted to thank you for saving my life back there." LadyV began hesitantly, "And I wanted to apologize-"

But Alec held a hand up to stop her, "Apology *not* necessary LadyV. There's nothing to forgive."

LadyV's eyes were wide, "Oh Alec."

Junpei ruffled Alec's hair affectionately, "You're just too nice for your own good Alec, *neh* LadyV?"

Yukino nodded sagely.

Alec suddenly remembered something. "Junpei." Alec leaned in a conspiratorial fashion, "Can I talk to you alone for a minute?"

Junpei raised an eyebrow but nodded, "Sure."

Alec and Junpei walked off a little ways from their friends so they could talk in private.

Alec scratched the back of his neck nervously, the kind of conversation he was about to begin really wasn't his forte. "Junpei, I know you like Rika."

Junpei's jaw dropped but then he quickly shook his head. "Huh? Who me? Like Rika? I think you must have had one too many hits to the head Alec. I think that last attack must have fried your brain like an egg or something. Yep, you've got it all wrong. I don't like her-"

Alec held up a hand and smiled knowingly. "It's okay Junpei. I don't like Rika anymore, at least not in the way I used to. You don't have to keep being supportive of us or trying to push us together either. It's actually beginning to get a bit bothersome really."

Junpei was shocked that little Alec had noticed all this and raked a hand through his spiky orange hair thoroughly messing it up. "Whoa - I'm surprised you figured all that out on your own Alec, let alone noticed it. Maybe you're not as clueless about girls as I thought?" He narrowed his eyes at Alec suspiciously.

Alec put both his hands up before him in a mock gesture of surrender. "No, I'm still clueless but I'd have to be blind not to see you and Rika have 'something' going on. And I just wanted you to know that I'm perfectly okay with it."

Junpei looked thoughtful for a moment before he seemed to hit the nail on the head. "Aha! You like someone else now don't you?"

Alec immediately began to freak out and wave his hands before him frantically. "Huh? What? No way! I don't like anyone! What makes you say that?"

Junpei chuckled at Alec's overreaction. "You do! You *do* like someone. Tell me who the lucky girl is." Junpei's lips twisted into an amused grin.

Alec kept his mouth stubbornly shut. "I really don't know what you're talking about, Junpei."

Junpei reached over and grabbed Alec putting him in a painful headlock. "Come on, tell me!"

"No!" Alec choked out.

Junpei reluctantly let Alec go, pouting, "Stingy." But then he seemed to get an idea. "Is it someone we know?" Alec stiffened and Junpei was quick to notice. He quickly went down the list of girls that they knew. "Aha! I know! It's Yukino isn't it...?" Junpei said the last part in a low voice.

Alec instantly freaked out and slapped a hand over Junpei's mouth. "*Shhh!*" Alec looked over in Yukino's direction hoping she hadn't heard anything amiss and sighed with relief when it seemed she was in deep conversation with LadyV and Dr. M.

Junpei nodded, his lips smirking against Alec's hand, and Alec took his hand away. "Aha, I knew it. But Alec...she's in a coma somewhere. What if we never find her?"

"I will find her Junpei." Junpei noticed the steely look that was suddenly in Alec's silver gray eyes. "I made a promise."

"Does she know that you...?" Junpei kept his voice low.

Alec shook his head. "No, and for now I'd like to keep it that way please. Understand Junpei? You can't tell her. This is very important."

Junpei frowned but then nodded understandingly. "I won't." Junpei spit into his hand and held it out to Alec for him to take. "Scout's honor."

Alec spit into his own hand and clasped Junpei's. "Dude, that's disgusting." Alec grinned and Junpei smirked back.

"Hey guys! What's with all the secrets? Get your butts back over here!" Dr. M called over to them.

"Coming!" Alec called, and turned to Junpei. "Thanks for understanding, Junpei."

Junpei was still frowning however, "I just don't want to see you get hurt Alec..."

Alec just smiled sadly back. He already knew Yukino didn't like him like *that* - that she only saw him as some kind of little brother and that she only liked older, more mature guys. He basically didn't have a chance in hell. But maybe one day he'd change Yukino's mind about that.

But until then there was no point in confessing his feelings to her, he decided, since he already knew what her answer was. Pout. And he really didn't want to lose Yukino's friendship either over something like a confession. His friends...Alec looked back at them as he walked over to them. He realized suddenly he couldn't live without them now.

● ● ● ● ● ● ● ● ● ● ● ● ● ● ● ●

After the short 30 minute break the emcee Kiki made her way back up onto the battle stage to announce the next duel. "Ghost Masters Junpei and RedAki, come and take your places!"

RedAki sauntered up on stage, confidence in his step.

Junpei was about to go when Alec grabbed his wrist stopping him. "Be careful Junpei, RedAki he's...dangerous. And so is Yoshitsune - they haven't even begun to show their true power yet."

Junpei nodded, a serious expression on his face, and then turned to go.

LadyV called after him as she watched him leave. "Junpei!"

Junpei turned around to face her. "G-good luck." She offered, stuttering slightly.

Junpei gave her a thumbs up and then made his way up onto the battle stage to face the cocky RedAki. Though Alec noticed both Ghost Masters were looking pretty confident.

Kiki threw a wink at Junpei before starting the match. "Ghost Masters begin!"

Junpei raised his hand and his control ring glowed. "Goku! I summon you!" Goku materialized next to Junpei, *bo* staff in hand.

RedAki, in an almost bored manner, followed suit. "Yoshitsune come forth." Yoshitsune materialized next to RedAki.

RedAki looked over at Goku and raised an eyebrow. "A normal AI Battle Ghost...not special like Dr. M's or...real like my own. Tell me Junpei-*kun*, do you really think you have a chance of beating me? I thought you were smarter than that." RedAki shook his head at Junpei. "I assumed if you were going to actually face me you must have something up your sleeve like Dr. M had, but I guess I was wrong." RedAki shrugged and looked at Goku curiously when he noticed that Goku was strangely glaring at him. RedAki arched an eyebrow in surprise at the realistic feeling portrayed in that glare. "Yes, well, Yoshitsune destroy his Battle Ghost - there's no need to waste your spirit energy on that one though." RedAki directed his Battle Ghost.

Yoshitsune got into a fighting stance, his *katana* held out before him, "Yes, Master."

Yoshitsune charged forward and brought his sword down upon Goku. Goku however leapt backwards and where Goku had been standing moments before Yoshitsune's sword came down to hit the floor of the stage, causing it to crack, a small crater forming there, and pieces of the stage flew up into the air.

"Goku!" Junpei called out worriedly.

RedAki charged Junpei next, sword raised, "I think you should be more worried about yourself Junpei-*kun*. I am your opponent after all!" RedAki's body and sword glowed with the familiar blue-tinged light as he gathered his spirit energy.

Junpei barely avoided getting sliced in half but back flipped to put distance between himself and RedAki and then summoned his own spirit energy to try and go on the attack, but he was forced to instead dodge and evade deadly swings from RedAki's sword by moving his body from side to side as RedAki continued to come at him mercilessly.

"Impressive - you were able to dodge my attacks but it won't be good enough! HA!" RedAki charged forward and brought his sword down upon Junpei in a high downwards slash, however, Junpei caught RedAki's blade with his two glowing hands. Junpei was shielding and protecting his hands by covering them with his spirit energy. RedAki tried to move his sword but to no avail.

Junpei smirked. "I have you now, RedAki!"

"Who has who?" RedAki kept one hand around his sword's hilt but released his other hand and immediately summoned a dagger from his inventory so that it materialized there. He then quickly jabbed his dagger forward, stabbing Junpei through the chest, but without using his spirit energy.

Junpei looked down in shock. "No fair...you cheated..."

RedAki's smirk simply broadened. "Cheated? Yea, well, that's my style *neh*? I'm a player killer remember? We don't' fight fair." RedAki removed his dagger from Junpei's chest.

Meanwhile, Goku and Yoshitsune were still locked in deadly combat, Goku's *bo* staff clashing against the metal of Yoshitsune's sword. Then they attacked each other, both passing the other as they attacked while both using their finishing moves. Yoshitsune turned around to face Goku whose back was still turned to him, but then Goku suddenly fell forward as he was destroyed and then the ghost turned into a small ball of light that zoomed back into Junpei's control ring as he was defeated.

From the stands, Alec noticed that when RedAki had knifed Junpei he had done so without summoning his spirit energy and how RedAki had told Yoshitsune not to use his spirit energy when he took out Goku - if Alec didn't know any better he'd say that RedAki was being merciful? Naw. Or maybe, just maybe...because RedAki knew Junpei and Goku were Alec's friends he was going easy on them? Hmm. It made Alec wonder and perhaps hope that he hadn't been wrong about RedAki after all.

Junpei fell back and 'died' and became a PC ghost.

Emcee Kiki pouted at Junpei's loss, "Aw, that's too bad. I mean - the winner is RedAki!"

A cheer went up from the crowd of players, though most of them were RRs. Alec, followed close behind by Yukino, rushed up on to the battle stage to resurrect Junpei.

"Red Potion! Resurrect!" Alec cried as he activated a red potion.

Junpei's PC body restored itself, and he put a bashful hand behind his head. "I lost..."

"RedAki's just that strong." Alec murmured.

"Yea, I guess. I'm lucky he didn't destroy Goku. I've gotten kinda attached to my Battle Ghost." Junpei put a hand over his ring thoughtfully.

"Yea, you are." Alec agreed looking over at RedAki as he walked off the stage. Though Alec had a feeling that luck had nothing to do with it.

Junpei followed suit and also left the battle stage. Kiki frowned at Alec and Yukino, who had remained up on stage, and simply shook her head at them, being used to their antics of saving their friends by now "Why do I

453

even bother. You guys are up next anyways. Ghost Master Catara please join Dranarch on stage and take your position."

Catara climbed up on to the battle stage and faced Alec, hands on her hips and gave them both a condescending look.

Alec stared back at Catara and raised an eyebrow at her behavior. Catara had hurt LadyV...and had Oiwa at her mercy. Catara was also a girl and Alec had never really had to fight a girl before. Could he really do it? And he needed to save Oiwa somehow. But he also realized that Oiwa was not possessed as Kiyohime had been, but was a vengeful spirit herself....so how could he save her? How could he reach her? Alec wondered worriedly, his head spinning.

"Ghost Masters! Are you ready? Let the duel begin!" Kiki lowered her hand, signaling the start of the duel.

Catara raised her control ring and summoned Oiwa. "Oiwa!" Oiwa materialized next to Catara and then Catara materialized her two *katana* from her inventory as she equipped them. She then got into a fighting stance, her sharp blades held out before her and aimed towards Alec in a menacing manner.

Alec materialized his own *Shinigami* sword as well and pointed it towards Catara.

Catara had a haughty smirk on her face. "Bring it on, *Shinigami* boy."

Alec was ready to attack, taking a step forward, but then shook his head frantically. "*Uso.* No way." He turned to Yukino, eyes pleading. "*Yukino,* I can't do this. I can't attack a *girl.*" Alec nearly whined.

Yukino blinked at Alec in disbelief.

"Let me face Oiwa since I have to try and save her anyways. Please?" Alec decided to give Yukino his best puppy dog eyes.

Yukino's jaw dropped at this. "*Nani?* Huh?"

But Alec was already charging Oiwa even as Yukino called after him. "Alec *no baka!*" Yukino sighed heavily as she turned to face a surprised Catara. Yukino sighed heavily. She had to do what she had to do. Yukino decided as she got into a fighting stance prepared to fight Catara.

Yukino reached into her *kimono* sleeve and pulled out her fan and opened it with a flick of her wrist. "Looks like I'm to be your opponent, Lady Catara."

Catara blinked. "I was told you could talk...well, you really must be a real ghost. No matter, I'll still defeat you!"

"We'll see about that." Yukino waved her fan through the air gracefully, "Ice Dagger Attack!" She unleashed a barrage of icy daggers at Catara. Catara spun and used her deadly sword blades to block the daggers that went ricocheting off and into the air. Yukino realized her dagger attack would be useless and so formed her ice sword instead and got into a fighting stance, her sword aimed at Catara and prepared to charge forward.

Meanwhile, Alec was facing Oiwa. He knew he had to protect his sword from her poisonous touch and so had shielded it with his spirit energy. Oiwa was eerily floating towards him with her hand outstretched to touch him. Alec blocked her attempts to touch him with his sword, however, when she suddenly got a bit too close for his liking Alec slashed his sword down through the air haphazardly and accidently sliced her hand off.

Oiwa howled in pain in response.

Alec, was horror-stricken by his own attack and quickly apologized, "I...I'm sorry! Oiwa! I didn't mean to hurt you. I really didn't. In fact, I want to help you. I want to save you somehow Oiwa!" There was a note of desperation in Alec's voice since he didn't even know where to begin with his self appointed task.

Oiwa appeared unfazed however by his attack and ignored his words as she turned to face Alec again and raised her other hand now towards him as she continued to walk towards Alec. Alec took a step back intimidated by Oiwa's frightening presence, but then he looked at her face and noticed the tears falling from Oiwa's drooping eye, as well as the tears falling from her other eye that was on the side of her face that wasn't disfigured. That particular eye Alec noticed was beautiful - it was a golden brown, hazelnut color with long, dark lashes. He gasped in surprise as he focused his vision on just that side of her face. He could almost envision what she had looked like before the poison.

"Oiwa..." Alec murmured in a stunned stupor as he let Oiwa approach him and then she reached out to stroke his cheek. Alec hissed in pain at her hurtful touch, but ignored the pain as he let Oiwa step even closer to him. He then raised his own hand and stroked Oiwa's unmarred cheek-

Yukino turned to notice that Alec was practically in Oiwa's evil clutches - "Alec *no baku!* What does he think he's doing? He's going to get himself killed! Alec!" Yukino tried to charge in his direction but Catara blocked her path, both swords raised in a threatening manner before her.

"Uh, uh, uh." Catara waved a sword back and forth at Yukino. "I don't think so. Your opponent is me. Oiwa finish him!" She called out without taking her eyes off of Yukino.

Oiwa was shocked when Alec reached out his hand to willingly touch her, and Alec tried not to flinch as his finger tips burned. "Oiwa...you're beautiful." Alec kept his gaze upon her one good eye and the unscarred side of her face, so she could hear the sincerity in his voice.

Oiwa's eyes widened in shock and she sucked in a harsh breath. Oiwa, who had been about to press a poisoned kiss to Alec's lips, suddenly pulled

Sophia Hughlette

back. She put a hand to her good cheek where Alec's hand had been only moments before and blushed despite herself - she hadn't felt a *kind* touch from a man in eons.

Catara had noticed that Oiwa had pulled away form Alec - "Oiwa! What are you doing? Finish him! Reaper-*sama* said he must be cursed during the tournament! Oiwa! Gah, she's completely useless. Sometimes to get something done right you have to do it yourself." Catara suddenly abandoned Yukino and charged at Alec instead, who was too busy smiling at Oiwa goofily while feeling glad that he had somehow managed to reach her, to notice Catara's sneak attack.

"Alec!" Yukino cried out, but it was too late.

Oiwa noticed however and just as Catara's swords that were glowing brightly with her spirit energy would have cleaved Alec in two, Oiwa stepped in front of Alec and put her arms out to her sides as she shielded and protected him. And so it was Oiwa who was cleaved in two by Catara's swords instead of Alec.

"Oiwa!" Alec cried out as he realized what was happening.

Oiwa's body fell down in two parts and a green goo appeared to be oozing out from her wounds.

Catara frowned down at Oiwa's broken form. "Useless ghost."

Alec looked up at Catara, his eyes were cold steel. "Useless?" He gathered his spiritual power and then he was suddenly in front of Catara before she could even blink. "How dare you insult her." Catara's eyes widened in fright at Alec's icy glare. Alec stabbed Catara so quickly that her PC body instantly died and turned into a PC ghost. Lucky for her, he had been angry with the RR but not angry enough to use his spirit energy.

Alec then rushed over to the disappearing form of Oiwa. "Oiwa!" He sunk down to his knees beside her and put a hand to cup her good cheek. Alec then used his curse breaking power to purge the rest of the poison that was within Oiwa's body, so that her face and torso began to transform. There was a flash of bright, white light, and then Oiwa's entire body was lying on the floor of the battle stage, whole and beautiful once more, but still rapidly disappearing. Her spirit had been destroyed by Catara's attack, which meant Oiwa would disappear forever.

Oiwa's angelic face peered up at Alec and he whispered down to her. "So beautiful..." Alec gave her a faltering smile, his heart breaking since he was powerless to help her now.

Oiwa smiled back, silvery tears running down her ghostly, translucent face. "Thank you...*Shinigami* boy...you really did save me, you know." And then Oiwa simply vanished in Alec's arms so that he was soon clutching air.

Alec punched the floor of the battle stage in frustration. He had failed to save her in his book. "Dang it!" He swore.

Yukino walked over to stand close to Alec, unsure, hesitating, "Alec - you can't save everyone."

"What good am I if I can't save ghosts?" There was a tinge of bitterness in Alec's voice.

"*Baka.*" Yukino shook her head at Alec's selflessness. "Who's going to save you when you need saving?"

Alec hung his head so that his white bangs shielded his stormy, gray eyes. "I dunno."

"Then you really are an idiot." Yukino frowned, *Doesn't he know that's why I'm here?*

"Winner - Dranarch!" Kiki announced enthusiastically. "Which means folks after we let our Ghost Masters take another short break that the final duel of this tournament is about to take place. Dranarch will be dueling against RedAki for the title of Ultimate Ghost Master!"

Alec picked himself up off the floor somewhat reluctantly and headed off the battle stage ignoring Yukino's concerned look. He walked back towards the stands dragging his feet, zombie-like, completely lost in his own dark thoughts. *What use am I if I can't save ghosts and yokai...?*

* * * * * * * * * * * * * * * * * *

Meanwhile, several hours earlier that day, Yoru was in the middle of training at Izanagi Temple when a message was unexpectedly delivered to him. The letter had a wax seal upon it, which Yoru instantly recognized as the seal of the Izanami Clan. Yoru was sick with dread as he slowly broke the seal and opened the letter to read:

Yoru

Come to the Kuroneko teahouse in Kyoto if you ever want to see your precious Yukino alive and well again.

Kaguto, Headmaster of Izanami Academy

Yoru crumbled the letter in his one hand and nodded to Jin and Junko, who were standing nearby and waiting impatiently to hear what the letter was about. "We're going to Kyoto." He announced and they merely nodded in return not having to question his orders.

Yoru, Jin, and Junko arrived at the Kuroneko teahouse and were startled to find that it had been set on fire. Yoru immediately feared the worst - that Yukino, his beloved sister, was trapped inside.

"Yukino!" Yoru yelled as he rushed in the direction of the teahouse door.

Jin and Junko, however, reacted quickly and grabbed both of Yoru's arms stopping him.

"No Yoru! It's a trap!" Jin declared gruffly.

That was when a *miko* dressed in a black *haori* shirt and *black* hakama pants appeared suddenly before them. She had cascading, black hair that fell around her shoulders. Her narrow, intelligent brown eyes were lined in red and Yoru noticed the strange tattoo of a red eye in the center of her forehead. Her face was painted a stark white and she gave them an appraising smile with her red painted lips while a man, who appeared to be a monk, but was also dressed in blacks and reds, appeared next to her. He gave Yoru and the others an amused look. The *miko* had a bow and arrows with her while the monk had a long, golden staff with a golden ring on the end that had smaller golden rings on the larger ring and which jingled as he moved forward, held in his hand.

"Kaguto said he was stupid." Shino began as she laughed cruelly while observing the struggling Yoru between Jin and Junko. "I just didn't think he'd be *this* stupid."

A merciless smirk formed on Sumi's face. "To think he'd actually fall for it. Poor thing." The monk had pale pink hair (definitely dyed) and Yoru noticed that the monk's lips were painted in black giving him an rather sinister appearance. Sumi almost reminded Yoru of a clown and he had always found clowns to be rather creepy. And was that a leather collar around his neck with spikes on it? Yoru couldn't help but raise an eyebrow at this.

Yoru stopped struggling as he immediately recognized the *miko* and monk. They were a part of the Izanami Clan - *miko* Shino and monk Sumi, Kaguto's minions of a kind. "Where is your Master? Where is Kaguto?" Yoru demanded in a hard voice.

Sumi playfully wagged a finger back and forth in front of Yoru, "Now that..." His smile got even wider and more Cheshire-like. "Is a secret."

"Yes, I wonder where our Lord Kaguto is at this very moment. Really Yoru, do you truly have no idea?" Shino raised an elegant eyebrow at Yoru.

Yoru frowned as realization seemed to hit him like a ton of bricks. The game - Kaguto must be logged onto Yokai World which could only mean - "A trap. I've been so foolish. This was all a trap to keep me away...the Ghost Master Tournament...of course! Yukino! Alec! They're in danger. We must save them!"

Yoru began to rush off, Jin and Junko hot on his heels.

"What's your hurry? Stay and play a while." Shino teased as she shot an arrow at them and which landed in the ground directly in front of Yoru and the others becoming imbedded there and stopping them in their tracks.

"Did you really think we'd let you go so easily?" Sumi tucked a stray hair behind his ear, "Kaguto told us to make sure you stayed here and so that's what we're going to do. We won't let any of you harm our Lord."

"I say we invite some more guests to the party." Shino suggested slyly.

"Why that's a brilliant idea Shino. Why didn't I think of it myself!" Sumi grinned back at her.

And then the monk and the *miko* began to summon a dark-tinged aura of energy around themselves as they then began to chant simultaneously and form hand seals.

"Evil spirits, we summon you!" They both chanted together when they had finished.

From out of thin air several evil spirits began to appear - they were lower level, evil spirits but there were enough of them to be a threat to Yoru and the others. They were strange beings with black, shadowy, cloud-like and smoke-like bodies with large, hairy eyes and gaping black holes for mouths. Most had a single, large eye in the center of the shadowy mass that made up their bodies.

Shino waved her hand elegantly forward. "Spirits! Go get them!"

Junko knocked an arrow to her bow and Jin took out some *o-fuda,* and without taking their eyes off the approaching spirits they addressed Yoru.

"Yoru go now and leave this to us!" Junko declared.

"We can handle them. Believe in us. Yukino's waiting for you! And Alec is too. Go now, Yoru! " Jin insisted when Yoru seemed to hesitate.

Yoru, who had already been moving forward to fight at his friends' sides, was deeply moved by his friends' bravery and kindness. They were going to put themselves in danger for his sake. "*Jin...Junko...*" His voice was thick with emotion. But he nodded, his expression grim. He knew he had to go and help Yukino and Alec after all. It could already be too late... "Alright, but be careful!" Yoru called before rushing off.

Junko and Jin, brother and sister, moved side by side prepared to face the assortment of evil spirits together. They exchanged a look and nodded to each other before letting loose -

* * * * * * * * * * * * * * * *

Yoru ran as fast as he could back into Kyoto and entered the first Internet Café that he caught sight of that allowed 'log ons' to the ever popular Yokai World. Yoru quickly got the needed equipment at the front desk and hooked himself up, placing the VR HMD on his head before logging on...

* * * * * * * * * * * * * * * *

RedAki was walking outside of the battle dome alone to clear his mind and prepare himself for his upcoming duel with Alec since he was feeling somewhat conflicted about where his true loyalties lay when suddenly someone grabbed his shoulder hard and pulled him back into the shadows.

"Ack! Who the hell?" RedAki demanded spinning around to face his attacker. His eyes widened in shock as he turned to see that it was none other than Reaper. "Reaper-*sama*? What are you doing here? I thought you had *Shinigami* business?" RedAki blinked back at him in confusion.

Reaper smiled this chilling smile as he lowered his hood to reveal his blood-red hair and sharp, yellow eyes. "Business was concluded a bit earlier than anticipated." Flames of delight seemed to flicker in Reaper's eyes as he seemed to be remembering something very pleasant or RedAki had the sinking feeling 'unpleasant' would have been more accurate. "Anyways, I wanted to watch your duel against Dranarch. I saw some of your other duels as well. I must say I was impressed."

RedAki flushed with pride at Reaper's unexpected praise. "Reaper-*sama*..."

Reaper suddenly frowned, "However, I noticed how you are going easy on your opponents which is *not* what we discussed. The time is close at hand for Night to make his move. It would have been more convenient if a few of the Guardian Knights had been cursed..." Reaper shrugged, "But no matter, as long as you don't hold back in your next duel RedAki things should turn out satisfactory. To see you win would make me most pleased with you indeed. So do try to not disappoint me. I expect great things from you RedAki, as I always do." Reaper patted RedAki's head affectionately.

RedAki preened from all the lavish attention his beloved Reaper-*sama* was giving him all of a sudden and he couldn't help but smile somewhat goofily before he nodded eagerly in response. A boy having had very little affection in his life RedAki took the few times Reaper showed him interest like a man dying of thirst in the desert acted when he was suddenly handed a bottle of water. "*Hai!* Reaper-*sama*! I won't let you down!"

A sly smile formed on Reaper's lips. "I know."

· · · · · · · · · · · · · · · ·

The last duel of the Ghost Master Tournament was about to begin to determine who would be the Ultimate Ghost Master. Players were coming back into the battle dome and taking their places in the stands as the emcee Kiki made her way back up on to the battle stage and stood in the center of it.

Kiki smiled as she looked over at the huge crowd of players. "Welcome back! We are about to start the final duel of the Ghost Master Tournament!"

A rowdy round of applause ensued. "Which will determine today's champion and the one that will be known in our world as the Ultimate Ghost Master! Now, will Ghost Masters Dranarch and RedAki come up and take their positions on stage please!"

Alec and Yukino walked up onto the battle stage together while RedAki walked up alone, hands behind his head in a cocky pose.

Kiki looked back and forth between the two Ghost Masters, "Ghost Masters are you ready? Then let the final duel of the Ghost Master Tournament begin!"

Alec and RedAki locked eyes with each other and seemed to be sizing each other up. But a smile then formed on RedAki's lips as he raised his hand and the control ring there glowed with an eerie red light. "Yoshitsune! Come forth!"

The *samurai* Yoshitsune materialized next to RedAki and unsheathed his *katana* in one fluid motion before pointing it towards Alec and Yukino.

RedAki unsheathed his own black-bladed *katana* and pointed it at Alec. Alec followed suit and unsheathed his own *katana* and pointed it at RedAki and Yoshitsune.

And then the duel began.

"Yoshitsune!" RedAki called.

"Yukino!" Alec directed.

Yukino took out her fan and waved it through the air at Yoshitsune, who was charging forward at her. "Ice Daggers Attack!" The ice daggers went flying through the air towards Yoshitsune, who stopped running to stand still as the ice daggers were almost upon him, and then he moved his sword from side to side rapidly to block all the ice daggers with extreme speed.

Whoa.

Alec's jaw was dropping as he caught himself watching Yoshitsune out of the corner of his eye.

Even Yukino couldn't help but be a little impressed by the speed of his sword movements for a mere human. Yukino bit her lip, "Not bad. How about this then!" Yukino began to dance and raise her fan towards the dome ceiling of the battle stage. She began to summon her elemental power - the control of ice and snow - so that thick, gray storm clouds suddenly began to form overhead inside of the dome itself. A chill wind began to blow through the battle dome causing the players watching the duel to shiver in their seats. And then a light snow began to fall all around them and the temperature suddenly dropped several degrees on the battle stage. Yukino then made a motion with her fan and yelled - "Icicle Rain Attack!" She brought her fan up and then down, swiftly through the air. From the clouds came a shower of sharp, deadly icicles.

Yoshitsune looked up in surprise - there was no way he'd be able to dodge or block all of those icicles in time.

* * * * * * * * * * * * * * * * *

Alec and RedAki charged each other as their Battle Ghosts fought, their swords clashing. Both of them summoned their spirit power and their spirit energy so that blue-tinged auras of light formed around them and their swords. Their movements had also become much faster with the added energy as the power simply flowed through them.

They leapt backwards from each other to give themselves room to prepare their next energy attacks. They gathered their spirit energy as they began to empower their swords so they began to glow more brightly. Their auras were flaring more and more brilliantly around the boys as they powered up a la *Super Saiyan.*

Alec realized that it didn't seem like RedAki was going to hold back this time and the only thing Alec could do was at least make sure he'd be able to defend himself, but hopefully not do any permanent damage to RedAki in reality if he could help it.

RedAki suddenly waved his sword forward with a battle cry, "Hooryah!" And a large energy blast attack was unleashed in Alec's direction. Alec quickly followed suit though and waved his sword forward as well to unleash his own energy attack upon RedAki. The two energy blast attacks clashed in the middle of the battle stage warring with each other as the two *Shinigami* tried to empower their own attacks in order to overcome the other's attack.

* * * * * * * * * * * * * * * * *

Yoshitsune had been heavily wounded - in the spiritual sense - by Yukino's attack and though he was a little lower on spirit energy than he would have liked he was still able to stand facing Yukino. The attack should have completely defeated him - Yukino frowned. She danced and spun and began to gather her spirit power for another type of attack to use against Yoshitsune and then finally when she was ready she waved her fan forward at him and unleashed a freezing, cutting wind.

Yoshitsune gathered his spirit power as the cutting wind was almost upon him and he used his glowing *katana* to cut through Yukino's attack! The force of his blow cut through the energy of her attack so that it flew past on either side of him, and since the energy of her attack was visible it appeared as if he were cutting through a blue wave of tangible energy.

Yukino was beginning to get frustrated by her failure and formed her Ice Sword - it was in the form of a giant icicle, a bit jagged in shape, and with a very sharp point. She moved in to attack Yoshitsune ready to pit her swordsmanship that her brother had taught her against the sword master, and legendary *samurai* Yoshitsune's skill. Her Ice Sword clashed with Yoshitsune's *katana* and they seemed equally matched, both trying to push the other back -

Yoshitsune rose an eyebrow at her, intrigued, "You chose to face me with a sword, little ice witch? Let me see your skill then, girl."

Their swords continued to clash but Yoshitsune was beginning to push Yukino back using his towering height over her to his advantage along with his brute strength. "Impressive but not good enough to beat *me*. You should always stick with your strengths when in combat against an opponent you don't know if you can truly win against instead of letting your opponent push you into unfamiliar ground. It was a novice mistake. It's time to end this play time."

Yoshitsune moved his sword forward and as it was glowing with his spirit energy he moved it in a sideways slash that clashed with Yukino's Ice Sword. Then he used a burst of his spirit energy to manage to slice straight through it. Yukino's Ice Sword was suddenly shattered. Yoshitsune then brought his sword back and then forward to stab Yukino through the middle of her chest, his sword still glowing with a blue-tinged light. Yukino cried out in pain as she felt his very real attack.

As soon as Alec heard Yukino's cry of pain he became distracted. He quickly turned to see Yoshitsune and Yukino, and watched as Yoshitsune stabbed her through the chest. He also noted in horror how Yoshitsune's sword was glowing blue, which meant he had used his spirit energy during that attack. Yukino's mind was already trapped within the game, so what would become of her if she was killed in the game now? Alec wondered as his panic mounted. Would she simply disappear forever?

"Yukino!" Alec cried out in concern.

Alec's energy attack had weakened because of his distraction, and so RedAki was able to charge forward slicing through Alec's attack as he used his own attack as cover to hide himself behind, so that RedAki was suddenly in front of the unsuspecting Alec in seconds. Before Alec could register what was happening RedAki was in front of him pressing his advantage with his sword flashing through the air and slashing Alec's chest open.

Alec's mouth gaped open in shock, and he put a hand to the bleeding wound on his chest before he fell forward. Alec noted in a daze that RedAki's sword was not glowing blue.

Alec's PC body died and then transformed into a PC ghost. His control rings clattered to the floor of the battle stage. Alec could see that Yukino had fallen backwards and lay frighteningly motionless. Yoshitsune's sword was poised at her throat.

RedAki had won.

"The winner is - RedAki!" Kiki announced loudly into her pink microphone.

While Alec was trapped inside the PC ghost body he was able to observe what was going on and so watched as Yukino continued to lay on the floor of the battle stage defenseless, and with a shining sword blade at her throat. Alec felt himself going slightly mad with worry. "Yukino! RedAki don't hurt her!" Alec growled before his voice turned pleading. "Please don't kill her! You don't understand - she's the girl in the coma I told you about before! If she dies in the game she'll cease to exist in reality too! RedAki *please*!" Alec begged, his eyes beginning to shimmer with unshed tears.

RedAki shot Alec a confused look. He really didn't understand or expect that kind of a reaction from Alec over the welfare of some ghost girl. But then again hadn't Alec just been saying something about how she wasn't a ghost at all but some girl trapped in a coma? RedAki shook his head ruefully. "Huh? That's the girl...? Yoshitsune don't touch her!" RedAki ordered as the pieces of the puzzle slowly began to fall in place.

However -

Reaper suddenly appeared up on the battle stage, mysteriously materializing there out of thin air. He bent over to pick up Yukino's blue stoned, control ring and placed it gingerly on his finger, a gleefully triumphant look on his face. He then strode over to Yukino with fast, purposeful steps before he reached down and scooped her up into his arms.

Alec began to panic as he was forced to witness this but was still maddeningly unable to do anything about it since he was still trapped and unable to move as a PC ghost. "Yukino! Reaper get away from her, you jerk! Don't you dare touch her! Let go of her!"

RedAki watched Reaper's actions in confusion, his brow creasing. "Reaper-*sama*? What are you doing? Do you know who that girl is? Is she the one-"

Reaper raised his hand to cut RedAki off in an imperious gesture. "Night is about to make his move and I need to get this young lady to safety. Don't let anyone interfere RedAki especially *him*. He is not to be trusted." Reaper nodded in Alec's direction.

RedAki bit his lip, still feeling confused, "Reaper-*sama*?"

Junpei, LadyV, and Dr. M had noticed what was going on and had rushed up to the battle stage to help Alec.

"Alec!" Junpei called as he quickly clicked on a red potion in his inventory to resurrect his friend, "Red Potion! Resurrect!"

Alec's PC body glowed before it was restored to its normal state. Alec then picked up Ryuu's control ring and swiftly put it back on his finger before he turned to face Reaper, a steely glint in his eyes.

"I leave things to you here RedAki." Reaper raised his arm. "Teleport! Haunted Mansion Area!"

Alec charged forward his sword raised and pointed at Reaper. "REAPER!" Alec recklessly slashed his sword through the air at Reaper's neck but Reaper managed to teleport using his hacker skills before Alec's sword would have cut him. "Darn it!"

Alec raised his arm to teleport as well. "Teleport-" But he was forced to stop mid-teleport as RedAki was suddenly attacking him and their swords clashed. Alec looked at RedAki in disbelief - hadn't he figured out what was really going on *yet*? "RedAki? What are you doing!"

"Reaper told me not to let you interfere. So, I can't let you teleport." RedAki sneered.

"*Baka*. Idiot. Can't you see yet that you're on the wrong side? Reaper is lying to you. He just teleported to the Haunted Mansion Area to use the tear there to get to Yomi and once there he intends to break the seal on Izanami using Yukino to do so - and unleash the goddess of the underworld upon Japan and then the world! Don't you see RedAki - Reaper's crazy! He wants to destroy the world!"

"Okay, half of that I didn't even understand." RedAki remained stubborn as their swords continued to clash. "But releasing Izanami - that's what Reaper told me Night's after!"

"Argh!" Alec wanted to rip his hair out in frustration. He turned to his friends instead. "Junpei, Dr. M, LadyV, you guys teleport to the Haunted Mansion Area and try and stop Reaper. I kinda have my hands full right now with this moron."

Junpei nodded. "Right." The three of them raised their hands and were about to teleport when suddenly they were attacked by Catara, Smoker and Kiba, who had jumped up on the battle stage to help RedAki.

Catara's two swords were flashing through the air as she attacked LadyV, who summoned her *naginata* to keep Catara at a distance. Smoker, who still had a bone to pick with Junpei, flung several daggers in his direction and Junpei was forced to dive out of the way. Kiba rushed forward with his monk staff and he and Dr. M clashed their weapons together.

"You guys aren't going anywhere!" Catara declared.

"Reaper told us not to let you meddling brats interfere." Kiba informed them.

"We will protect Reaper-*sama*," Smoker agreed in a dull voice.

Alec was feeling incredibly frustrated as even more nuisances seemed to present themselves and just when the damsel in distress desperately needed his help. "GAH!" He didn't have time for this crap - Yukino needed him.

Just then - Night appeared, materializing on to the battle stage, having teleported directly to the Battle Dome Area using his hacker skills.

Alec blinked in disbelief when he caught sight of his mentor. "Night?"

Night turned to Alec and saw that he was currently locked in combat with RedAki and also noticed how the others were busy fighting the rest of the RRs. "*Yare, yare,* my oh my, where's Yukino?" He suddenly asked as he scanned the group and noticed her missing.

The expression on Alec's face became a mixture of guilt and desperation. "Reaper took her! He teleported to the Haunted Mansion Area to get to Yomi! You have to stop him Night. You have to save her!"

Night nodded in understanding. "Right." He raised his arm. "Teleport! Haunted Mansion Area!"

RedAki snarled, bearing his teeth and showing his incisors. "Oh no you don't Night!" He charged at Night but this time Alec stood in his path and blocked RedAki's attack while glaring at him furiously.

Lightning seemed to flash between their eyes. "Get out of my way Alec!" RedAki growled.

"Never!" Alec shot back stubbornly.

Night managed to successfully teleport away and Alec let out a breath of relief. If anyone could save Yukino it was Night. Alec frowned back at RedAki. "I'm sorry RedAki but I don't have time to deal with you right now. Yukino needs me-" Alec began to summon his spirit energy so that his entire body and sword were glowing fiercely in a blue colored light.

RedAki jumped backwards and mimicked Alec's intent also summoning his spirit energy for an attack.

Alec waved his sword forward, "Out of my way RedAki!" His angry eyes were as cold as steel.

RedAki swung his sword forward as well and their energy attacks clashed in midair, but then Alec poured more of his energy into the attack, and RedAki was surprisingly being pushed back until finally Alec's energy attack completely managed to overpower RedAki so that he was sent flying backwards across the battle stage.

Alec wiped the sweat from his brow. Phew. He raised his arm not hesitating for another instant. "Teleport! Haunted Mansion Area!"

* * * * * * * * * * * * * * * * *

Meanwhile, Reaper had carried Yukino, who was still unconscious, to Yomi before using his own unique powers to heal the wound on her chest. He couldn't very well have the only *miko* in Japan to have the ability to break the seal upon his mother die after all, now could he? He then laid her gently on the ground and waited for Yukino to wake. Yukino opened her eyes a few moments later and gasped in a mixture of shock and fear when she saw who it was that had saved her.

"*Reaper...*" Her voice was filled with hate. Yukino stood up and looked around quickly, "Where?" But then she realized in despair that Reaper had brought her close to the entrance of the cave. "I should have known..."

"Come Yukino, your destiny awaits." Reaper grabbed her roughly by the wrist and began to drag her towards the cave.

Yukino struggled against his grasp. "Let me go, Reaper! You're hurting me!"

Night suddenly appeared running out from the line of trees of the forest- "Reaper! Let Yukino go!"

Yukino turned to face Night starry-eyed since her brother had come to save her. "*Onii-sama!* Brother!"

"Keh, I don't think so Night. I will not allow you or anyone to interfere any longer. I tire of your meddlesome ways. This will be the last time though Night. I will finally make you disappear for good." Reaper raised his hand and a red gemmed, control ring glowed. "Tamamo-no-mae! I summon you!"

Tamamo-no-mae suddenly materialized next to Reaper. *Uh oh.*

Night took his huge sword down from his back, ready to face Tamamo-no-mae and give it everything he had however. He had to save his sister after all whatever the cost, even if it cost him his life.

"Tamamo-no-mae, kill him!" Reaper commanded.

Tamamo-no-mae nodded, a somewhat dazed expression on her face, as she formed a fireball and flung it at Night. Night raised his sword, and it was glowing with his spirit energy as he blocked the first fireball attack. But then as Tamamo-no-mae formed more and more fireballs, which she flung at him in quick succession, it was all Night could do to hold up his sword and block these attacks as he was beginning to get pushed back.

"*Onii-sama!*" Yukino cried out worriedly.

"Now, you will break the seal on my beloved mother for me, little girl." Reaper smiled grimly. "And perhaps I will *think* about sparing your brother's life."

Yukino frowned. "I will not."

Reaper held up Yukino's control ring, "Oh yes, you will." Reaper began to activate the power of the ring and it began to glow with a dark aura and so did the necklace that was around Yukino's neck. "Now let the ceremony begin!" The blue sapphire glowed brightly and Yukino was brought to her knees as she tried to resist its power. A magical circle glowed in a golden light as it formed in the parched ground around her. And then in a voice that was truly not her own she began to chant while her body that also wasn't obeying her will anymore began to do a series of complicated hand seals to undo the seal on the cave.

The hanging *o-fuda* began to glow and then the entire cave seemed to glow with a dark, eerie light as well.

Oh yes…that's it…the power…soon I shall be free at last. A silky voice echoed through the air.

Night was still battling Tamamo-no-mae, but even as he tried to move forward Tamamo-no-mae's attacks continued to be relentless. They were becoming too powerful for Night to handle as he was suddenly pushed back when a large burst of fire was sent at him as Tamamo-no-mae used both of her hands to form her attack. This blast of fire sent him stumbling backwards and at the same time Night's sword was flung from his grasp. *Uh oh.* The sword flew into the air and came down to embed itself in the ground not too far away from where Night was.

Reaper smiled gleefully, and Yukino thought he was wearing the kind of cruel expression someone might wear when they were about to stick a needle into the body of a butterfly that was still alive in order to pin it to a display board.

"Tamamo-no-mae! Finish him! Burn him alive! Yes, that's it. I want to watch him *burn*." Reaper declared and then began to laugh maniacally.

"Yes, Master," Tamamo-no-mae replied in her emotionless voice. Tamamo-no-mae then formed a fireball with both her hands and flung it at Night.

Night, who was now weaponless, and completely defenseless stood against the blaze of fire that was almost upon him and found he had no way to block the flames that suddenly consumed him. Night cried out in pain as his mind and spirit were burned. He sunk to his knees from the pain, the flames still surrounding him.

Reaper cackled happily, "Yes! Oh yes! That's it! Beautiful! Lovely! I love your screams Night. Oh yes, let him burn! Burn! Burn! Burn! More Tamamo-no-mae!" Reaper ordered the fox *yokai* in a crazed and hysterical manner. The fire-lust that the pyromaniac suffered from was getting the better of him as it consumed him and his sanity.

"Yes…Master…" Tamamo-no-mae threw more fireballs upon the already wounded Night until he was writhing on the ground in pain as spasms wracked his body.

"His mind will probably break before his body." Reaper's voice had oddly changed from hysterical to calm as he was now making a casual observation with a detached sort of air. "And then Night will no longer be the unbearable thorn in my side that he has always been. You will no longer be in my way Night. I will get what I want. And now Night you will die." Reaper declared as he prepared to tell Tamamo-no-mae to finish him off.

469

Tears were streaming down Yukino's face but she couldn't even cry out her brother's name since her voice was now under Reaper's control.

However, just as Reaper was opening his mouth to speak -

Alec had appeared running out of the forest.

Phew.

Alec immediately realized what had happened as he took in the scene before him. Tamamo-no-mae had once again managed to get herself captured and was being controlled by Reaper like a pawn. He instantly knew what he had to do.

"Tamamo-no-mae! Please, don't kill him!" Alec yelled.

Something within Tamamo-no-mae's lifeless eyes seemed to ignite and there was a flicker of light as recognition formed in them. "Alec...*kun?*" Her voice seemed to echo from someplace far away. But then her hands stilled and she stopped her attacks upon Night.

Reaper gawked at the sudden change in Tamamo-no-mae's behavior in disbelief. "Tamamo-no-mae! What are you doing? Finish him!"

"No." Tamamo-no-mae said simply, the fiery life coming back into her ruby-red eyes as she glared at Reaper defiantly. "I am not your slave."

Reaper blinked back at her stunned, but then his expression quickly shifted to anger. "Tamamo-no-mae you will obey me! Now!" The control ring for Tamamo-no-mae glowed upon Reaper's hand and then the collar around Tamamo-no-mae's neck glowed in response. Tamamo-no-mae cried out in pain as she tried to resist Reaper's control, which resulted in the collar painfully constricting around her neck and sending painful electric shocks into her body.

Alec knew what he had to do to help Tamamo-no-mae. He had to get the control ring away from Reaper somehow.

Alec then looked over at Night's body that was still twitching on the ground and then his eyes went to Yukino, who was still being forced to break the seal, and then he noticed the tears that were streaming down her silent face. And then Alec saw red. Uh oh. Alec could feel his inner demon nature taking over...growling at him to be released. And this time Alec answered it with a 'yes'.

Alec's eyes glowed until the whites of his eyes were no longer visible - his eyes became just one solid, silvery-blue color. Then a fierce aura of spirit energy exploded and burst out from Alec until it surrounded him like flames. Alec quickly moved in to attack Reaper and was in front of Reaper before he could even blink, with Alec's sword at this throat. "You made Yukino cry. You will pay dearly for that Reaper! For hurting the people I care about!" Alec moved his sword away from Reaper's neck before he slashed his sword through the air - it was glowing with a blue-tinged light - and then at the last second Alec aimed for Reaper's wrist instead, so that he sliced the hand that held Yukino's and Tamamo-no-mae's control rings off.

Reaper cried out in a mixture of shock, pain, and disbelief. "My hand! You awful boy you! You cut off my hand! How is that possible? I am Reaper! I am Kaguto son of Izanami! What are you - *demon*? What is your power?"

Reaper's hand fell to the ground and disintegrated so that Yukino and Tamamo-no-mae's control rings fell to the ground. As soon as Yukino was freed from Reaper's control she stood up and rushed over to her brother's side. "*Onii-sama!*"

Alec, his eyes still glowing solid silver and blue, turned his attention back to Reaper. "You will pay Reaper for hurting her. You're *so* dead." He pointed his sword at Reaper and got into a fighting stance.

Reaper took a step away from Alec eyeing him with unexpected fear.

Alec charged forward, sword raised, and prepared to run Reaper through when -

RedAki suddenly stood in Alec's path and blocked the attack meant for Reaper with his own black-bladed sword. "Alec! What do you think you're doing?" RedAki had not failed to notice the great deal of real spirit energy that was behind the attack Alec had been about to deal Reaper.

"He needs to pay for hurting her...for hurting them..." Alec growled in a low voice.

RedAki looked off curiously to see that Night was being cradling in Yukino's arms and he also noticed the tears that were on her face. He turned back to face Alec and was surprised by the look of pure murderous intent that Alec flashed Reaper over his shoulder - it caused a shiver to go down his spine. Was this dangerous person before him now really Alec? "Alec, this isn't like you. Snap out of it. Reaper-*sama* what's going on?"

Reaper, however, had turned his attention to the cave. "You're too late..." He murmured as the rope of *o-fuda* suddenly dissolved away. "It's too late!" He declared triumphantly. "I've done it! Mother will soon be free! The seal has been broken!" Reaper began to laugh maniacally.

The entire cave was glowing in a dark light and then suddenly there was a huge amount of spirit energy that was then released from the mouth of the cave like a fierce wind as it washed over Alec and the others, sending goose bumps down their arms.

RedAki frowned darkly. "Reaper-*sama* what are you talking about? What the hell is going on. I don't get any of this. You told me you wanted to stop Izanami from being reawakened!"

Reaper's expression suddenly turned serious and he stopped laughing as he turned to face RedAki. "I lied."

RedAki sucked in his breath and then his face fell. He jumped away from

471

Alec, confused now about who he should be fighting. Alec's sights seem to narrow and set themselves on Reaper once more.

Alec was acting slightly crazed and disoriented as he approached Reaper. "*Reapperrr...*" He growled.

RedAki shook his head at Alec's strange behavior. Oh well, it looked like it was up to him to do *something*. Sigh. Isn't that what friends were for? Alec would thank him for this later, RedAki decided. RedAki snuck up behind Alec and bonked him hard over the head. "Alec *no baka!* Snap out of it! We have more important things to deal with right now than Reaper! Look!"

Alec shook his head like a dog and blinked at the intense spiritual presence that he was suddenly sensing. *Uh oh.* The power was overwhelming, and incredibly evil. And then from out of the cave stepped Izanami herself. Everyone gasped at her sudden appearance.

Alec thought there was one phrase that could sum up what he thought of Izanami when he first laid eyes upon her - Oreo cookie. Alec quickly shook his head of such juvenile thoughts and was 100% thankful no one could read his mind. He probably would have insulted the goddess of the underworld otherwise and as he eyed the dark goddess before him he knew there was nothing *sweet* about her.

She was the manifestation of good and evil blended together. Her eyes were two different colors - one sun gold, the other blood-red. Her long, wavy, chaotic hair was a golden-blonde color streaked with black highlights. Alec saw that her *kimono* was decorated in swirls of gold and black running across the silk and she wore a black *obi* sash that was tied about her waist, the ends of which were floating behind her, stirring due to her power. Also outstretched behind her were two feathery wings - one angelic white and the other demonic black. Alec's eyes were then drawn to the curved horn that was sticking out of Izanami's head on one side of her face, the side of her face that had the piercing red eye.

Izanami approached Reaper with delicate steps, "My son..." Her voice was filled with obvious affection.

Reaper rushed over to her and kneeled at her feet, kissing her outstretched hand. "*Mother...*" He sounded moved to the point of tears.

Izanami stoked his hair and face affectionately, but then she noticed Reaper's missing hand. "Someone has hurt you, my son. That is...unacceptable." She reached out and easily restored his hand with her power that seemed to bridge the gap between reality and fantasy. "Rise my son...you must be rewarded."

Reaper obediently rose and from out a large black hole that seemed to have appeared from out of nowhere Izanami summoned an incredibly long and deadly looking spear that was at least twice her height and that was forged in a golden metal. The golden pole of the spear was simple until it reached the end where the metal twisted and spiraled to form a deadly point. She placed this impressive and otherworldly weapon in Reaper's hands. "This is the legendary Ame-no-nuboku (heavenly spear). It will make you invincible, and give you both great power and strength."

Reaper's voice cracked. "Mother, thank you."

Izanami looked off towards the trees. "Now, I need to go to the game world, which has become a link to the real world, a tear. Once in the real world I can use my power to guide my army of ghosts, the most powerful warriors in Japan's history, through this world to reality."

Reaper nodded. "Yes, mother."

"Do not let these ones interfere." She continued nodding her head towards Alec and the others. "I sense..." She shook her head instead and left whatever she was about to say unsaid.

Reaper's eyes gleamed as he eyed Alec. "Of course not, mother."

"Left alive they could become a threat. When you're *finished* here I shall see you back in the real world, Kagu-tsuchi, my son. I trust you to take care of things here."

"Oh, yes," Reaper grinned maliciously. "You can count on that."

With a great flap of her large wings, Izanami then took off into the air and flew swiftly in the direction of the dark forest.

Uh oh. "Izanami wants to go to reality! We have to stop her!" Alec exclaimed.

RedAki raised an eyebrow, "We?"

Alec sighed in an exasperated fashion. "She'll destroy the world! That includes your room, you know."

"Good point." RedAki nodded suddenly convinced.

Reaper meanwhile appeared to be going a bit power crazy as he was summoning his spirit power and letting the spear amplify it so that it began to swirl around him. "The power! Such power! With this much power I am invincible! I will take over the world!" Reaper let out a stream of maniac laughter.

"I don't think so Reaper, you egomaniac!" Alec charged forward and attacked, slashing his sword through the air at Reaper. Reaper raised his spear to block easily, and then smiled viciously at Alec before he sent out a blast of his spirit energy that went up through his spear and then straight out at Alec, who was instantly blasted back. Alec was swatted away as easily as a fly. But Reaper didn't stop there and pointed the Ame-no-nuboku at him, prepared to unleash another attack upon Alec. Reaper gathered his power and swung his spear forward so that a large crackling electric attack was sent Alec's way.

Alec didn't have time to move out of the way and was instantly engulfed in the painful attack, crying out in pain before he then collapsed to the ground.

Yukino, who still had the barely conscious Night in her arms, yelled out in concern, "Alec!"

RedAki turned to frown at Reaper. "You jerk!" RedAki turned to face Reaper with his sword raised in a two-handed grip.

Reaper raised an eyebrow at RedAki. "RedAki you would raise your sword against me? I'm the one who saved you from the loneliness in your heart and soul! The one who trained you! You would really turn against me?"

"Hmm let me think about that..." RedAki tapped his chin in thought before he then glared at Reaper, "Hell yea. I never knew how crazy you were, Reaper! I won't forgive what you just did to my friend, Alec, either." And at Reaper's look of disbelief he continued. "Yea, you heard me right. He's my friend. More of a friend than you ever were to me." RedAki raised his hand. "Yoshitsune!" Yoshitsune instantly materialized next to RedAki.

Reaper blinked and then began to laugh mercilessly. "You intend to use a ghost against me? I'm the one who gave you the power to control ghosts in the first place. And since I'm the one who bestowed that power upon you I can just as easily take it away! Ring break!" Reaper declared suddenly.

RedAki's hand burned as the control ring on it suddenly cracked and the control collar that was around Yoshitsune's neck shattered simultaneously. Yoshitsune was now free.

"Now Yoshitsune will no longer obey you! Ha! You are truly *alone* again RedAki!" Reaper mocked. "Who after all, would help the likes of you! Isn't that why your own parents abandoned you? Left you here at this school and ran away? Because they knew you were useless, cursed, that you would never amount to anything?"

"Alone...all alone..." RedAki choked, on the verge of a nervous breakdown - the suffocating world that he tried to escape from in his *hikikomori* lifestyle seemed to press in around him from all sides. Kaguto's words - the truths RedAki had been trying to escape from suddenly being brought to the surface.

Yoshitsune's calm voice cut through RedAki's tumultuous thoughts. "Master? Your orders."

RedAki spun to face Yoshitsune in disbelief, eyes wide - "Yoshitsune!"

Yoshitsune gave RedAki a small smile back.

"*Yosha!* Let's get 'em Yoshitsune!" RedAki pointed his sword at Reaper again. Yoshitsune and RedAki attacked Reaper from both sides, using their spirit energy in their slashes and blows, but Reaper's spiritual power and the combined power of the spear was just too much. Reaper waved his spear almost carelessly to block all their most powerful attacks. And then they were both blasted back painfully as Reaper gave them a taste of his true power.

RedAki sunk to his knees, totally spent, "Dang it...I can't fight anymore..."

Reaper grinned and aimed his spear directly at RedAki, prepared to unleash a deadly attack upon the now defenseless boy. RedAki was too tried and low on spirit energy to care or move and just shut his eyes waiting for the attack to hit him as it flew towards him.

"Master!" He heard Yoshitsune cry out but knew his ghost was too far away to help him in time. That Yoshitsune really was quite the honorable *samurai*, RedAki thought to himself vaguely as he prepared himself to meet his fate.

However -

Alec suddenly appeared in front of RedAki and with a wave of his sword Alec cut through Reaper's energy attack. He looked back at RedAki, a smirk on his face. "You alright there RedAki?"

"Yea," RedAki said, thoroughly surprised that it was true.

Alec reached his hand out to RedAki and helped him up. "Let's do this, together."

RedAki nodded. "Right." Before he seemed to change his mind. "You sure about this?" Alec just glared at him and RedAki raised his hands before him in a defensive gesture. "Alright already, geez, I get it. Together then. Man, this is *so* going to hurt...oh well." RedAki shrugged. "That's what I get for being friends with a boy that has a hero-complex."

Alec just gave the *KuroShinigami* a half-smirk before turning his attention back to Reaper.

However, Tamamo-no-mae took that moment to appear next to them. "Alec, you need to get back to reality *neh?* Just leave Reaper to me!"

"Tamamo-no-mae?" Alec blinked.

"Whew...saved by the *yokai* lady..." RedAki murmured under his breath.

"I *am* one of the four Demon Lords of the Makai after all. I can handle him - now go!" Tamamo-no-mae turned to face Reaper with a confident expression on her face.

Alec nodded. "Alright, let's go RedAki." Alec took off running towards Yukino and Night.

"Yoshitsune, stay and help Tamamo-no-mae!" RedAki called behind him as he took off after Alec.

"Yes, Young Master - I mean Master." Yoshitsune corrected himself.

"Young Master is fine by me!" RedAki called back in an amused tone.

"We need to get back to the game world and then log out and try and stop

Izanami in reality. If only I knew where Yukino was being held captive - we could use a priestess' power." Alec mused as he ran.

"I know where Yukino is." RedAki suddenly informed Alec as they continued to run. "I found out when you asked me before to investigate. She's being kept in one of the lower level labs of Izanami Academy back in Kyoto."

Alec turned to blink back at RedAki in awe. "RedAki, I could kiss you!"

RedAki grimaced in response. "If you want to live long enough to see the end of the world I suggest you don't."

They had finally reached Yukino and Night, who were close to the edge of the dark forest. Yukino was standing and supporting the now semi-conscious Night with his arm around her shoulders.

"Yukino, how's Night?" Alec looked over at Night worriedly. "We need to get back to the game world as soon as possible. And Night needs to log out as well and meet us back in reality. Then me and RedAki are going to come and find you in reality."

Yukino's eyes widened at this statement.

"*Chottomatteo!* Whoa, wait just a minute. I never agreed I'd come anywhere with you in reality. I'm a *hikikomori* remember?" RedAki shot Alec a death glare.

Alec gave RedAki a serious look in return. "I need your help RedAki... the world needs your help."

"Keh," RedAki looked away awkwardly feeling a bit overwhelmed that anyone needed *him*, "I guess there's no way around it. I mean, if the world needs me and everything *neh?* And I bet you are pretty helpless on your own. You'd probably waste time saving cats stuck in trees if I wasn't there to tell you to get a move on."

Alec's eye twitched but he smiled anyways, "You're right, I'd be lost without you RedAki. You're one of my closest friends after all. Now let's go!" Alec finished with sincerity in his voice.

RedAki blushed at Alec's unexpected words and quickly followed. Yukino was supporting Night and following close behind the two boys as the group made their way back into the game world. They first had to pass through the forest, find the well, jump down it, and then they popped up in the Haunted Mansion Area.

"*Yosha*, alright RedAki, Night, we need to log out and meet up in reality. Night where are you currently logged on from?" Alec questioned curiously.

"I'm in an internet café in Kyoto." Night informed them in a weak voice.

Alec nodded. "Good we'll come and get you then since that's where we're going." Alec turned to Yukino. "Yukino...I'm coming to find you at last." He reached out his hand as if he'd stroke her cheek before stopping himself at the last second and taking his hand back.

RedAki looked back and forth between Yukino and Alec and seemed to come to some sort of a conclusion, a sly smile forming on his face. "Come on *Romeo*, we need to go."

Alec and Yukino both blushed at RedAki's words, and jumped away from each other having realized they had been unconsciously getting closer and closer to one another.

Alec, RedAki, and Night all raised their hands at the same time. "Log out!"

* * * * * * * * * * * * * * * * *

When Yoru logged out of Yokai World back at the internet café in Kyoto he instantly collapsed at his computer.

A waitress wearing a french maid outfit along with a pair of cat ears went up to Yoru concernedly, "Sir? Sir!" She began to shake his shoulder, a worried frown forming on her pretty face.

* * * * * * * * * * * * * * * * *

Alec logged out of Yokai World and found himself back in the computer room. He quickly made his way out of the school building, down to the dorm building, and to Akira's dorm room in record time before he was already knocking on Akira's door impatiently.

"*Hai, hai.*" Akira's slightly annoyed voice came through the door as he went over to it and unlocking several locks finally opened it.

Alec wasted no time in grabbing Akira's wrist and dragging him from the room and down the hall as he took off running. "Come on! Let's go! Hurry!" Alec said urgently.

Akira was forced to run behind Alec. "Hey! Wait! This is all just too sudden for me! The light! The light! I think I'm melting!" Akira whined as he and Alec rushed out of the dorm building and across the school grounds.

Alec snorted. "Akira this is serious. We have to hurry and get to Kyoto and find Yukino and get back here *before* Izanami summons her army of ghosts into the real world! Because when she does..." Alec swallowed and trailed off.

Akira ran a hand through his spiky hair. "Alright already, I get it. No need for a recap. We have a lot on our plate besides saving the world, but how the heck are we going to get to Kyoto, genius?"

"Uh..." Alec blinked, he hadn't really thought that far ahead.

Luckily, Jinx appeared at that moment flying towards Alec and Akira. "Alec! It's awful! I sense a malevolent spiritual presence that feels like it's going to swallow up the entire school!"

Alec nodded. "I know Jinx...that's why we need to get to Kyoto pronto. Do you have a way to take us there?"

Jinx tapped his chin thoughtfully. "Yea, I think I do."

Alec gave Jinx a stern look. "This is very important Jinx."

Jinx nodded his head vigorously. "Just leave it to me boss! I know what to do!" Jinx waved his wand through the air so that it sparkled with golden light, "Travel Bubble Charm!" Two soapy, large, translucent bubbles formed around Akira and Alec that were big enough for them to stand up inside.

Akira lost his balance, sunk to his knees, and looked down at his now soapy hands. "Yuck, what *is* this?"

"It's a Travel Bubble *duh*." Jinx gave Akira a strange look before shaking his head at him. "Now off we go!" Jinx declared as he waved his wand at the two Travel Bubbles and they began to rise up into the air and then Jinx flew forward, the bubbles trailing behind him. The group flew on and on until finally they had reached Izanami Academy, which as Alec looked down upon the school grounds, appeared normal enough, but for some reason had an overall creepy feel to it. There was something not quite right about that place, Alec decided. The hairs on the back of his neck were already prickling in warning.

Akira pointed downwards. "Look there it is - Izanami Academy!"

They touched down in the middle of the front lawn before the main school building and the Travel Bubbles popped leaving both Alec and Akira covered in soap suds. Akira rushed to the front doors of the main school building. "Come on, follow me!"

The trio rushed inside, continued their way down a hallway and then stopped in front of an elevator. They slipped inside and Akira pressed his hand to a hand print, sensor pad, which was beneath the normal, numbered elevator buttons. As Akira touched his hand to the touch pad and then removed it a glowing, symbol of two Rs appeared on the touch pad before the elevator began to move downwards.

"What was that?" Alec asked curiously.

"Spirit signature sensor. My spirit signature is authorized to enter the lower levels here even though I've never actually been here before. Catara told me all about how she had to check on this girl who was in a coma from time to time. It was actually really boring to have to listen to. She just went on and on complaining about it, but anyways that's how I know where to go and what to do right now. We'll have to thank Catara for spilling the beans later."

The elevator door opened with a *ping* sound into an enormous laboratory.

On either side of a long aisle there were large, dome-shaped, glass containers. Alec noticed an evil spirit with a giant, hairy eyeball and a shadowy body pressing up against its glass prison. Then as they continued to walk down the center of the aisle Alec noticed another *yokai* in one of those glass containers as well. Though the evil spirit had still been moving the *yokai* had been killed and its body was merely being preserved in some kind of green-tinted, translucent liquid.

Alec was beginning to feel a bit nauseous. "What is this place? Just what kinds of experiments do they do here?"

Akira shook his head. "Trust me, you don't want to know. Come on, it's this way."

They continued to head down the aisle until they reached a single, metal door. Akira put his hand to the Spirit Sensor and the symbol of the double Rs appeared once more before the door slid open. They entered the room and immediately Alec caught sight of a girl, who was lying on a bed with bright white sheets towards the far end of the room. She had an oxygen mask upon her face, there was an IV in her arm, and she also appeared to be hooked up to a heart monitor that was giving off a steady *beep beep* sound that made Alec feel even more sick than before. He had always hated hospitals or medical rooms - although he sure seemed to be ending up in those kinds of places a lot lately.

"Yukino..." Alec's eyes widened and he stood frozen in the doorway.

Jinx looked over at the sleeping girl in the bed with his expression turning to surprise. "*The* Yukino?"

Akira was beginning to get impatient - What? Did Alec's feet get glued to the floor or something? He shoved Alec hard so that he stumbled forward. "Well, what are you waiting for? Go on."

"But I have to break the curse upon her..." Alec trailed off hesitantly as he licked his lips and looked off at Yukino's sleeping form on the far side of the room. He was still in shock that he'd be meeting her in person for the very first time. And that he'd have to kiss her that very first time as well. Gulp...

Akira sighed and messed up his hair with his two hands in a frustrated gesture, "Yea so? You know how to do that don't you?"

Alec nodded and shuffled his feet awkwardly. "Yes, but...I'll have to kiss her..."

Akira blinked. "So? You've done it before to save other people haven't you?"

"Yea, but this time it's different." Alec chewed his bottom lip nervously.

Akira raised an eyebrow at Alec. "How so?"

Silence~

Akira's eyes widened in realization. "Oh, I get it now." A merciless grin

479

formed on his face. "But then why are you hesitating? You want to save her don't you? You care for her right? That much is like totally obvious. Then be a man and kiss her!"

Alec blushed. "I'm only thirteen years old..." Alec muttered to himself.

"Don't worry. I won't watch." Akira spun around and reached out to spin Jinx around too - for good measure.

Alec looked at Akira's back, his throat thick with emotion as he tried to swallow. He then turned to walk towards Yukino's bed with stiff, tin-man steps. He made his way over to the side of her bed and slowly took off her oxygen mask. He gulped as he looked down at Yukino's sleeping face and then her pale pink lips. It was now or never. Alec leaned over and pressed his lips to hers while summoning his curse breaking power so that he was surrounded by a golden aura of light. This light passed through Alec's lips and into Yukino's body.

Then one of her fingers moved, and Yukino opened her eyes. Alec pulled back and looked at her. He noticed that both of her eyes were this deep, sapphire blue and he sucked in a surprised breath at the sight of how endless those eyes appeared in person. Yukino sat up in shock. "Alec?"

Alec simply nodded, his voice having left him momentarily.

Yukino's expression turned to immediate happiness. "Alec-*kun*!" She hugged him warmly and he hugged her back timidly. "Thank you...for keeping your promise."

Alec just hugged her back, lost in his own little world, not daring to believe he was actually there with Yukino in his arms in reality. It was all just too good to be true.

Akira turned around with a smirk on his face and cleared his throat loudly to get their attention. "Plenty of time for that later, love birds. We need to go."

Alec was surprised by the sudden increase in the sound of the beeping coming from Yukino's heart monitor, which had increased in speed since her heart rate had just sped up dramatically. Alec smiled to himself since that had to mean that Yukino was flustered, and though he was by no means confident in himself that he had been the cause of this he liked to think so, and couldn't help but feel pleased at the same time.

"Yukino we have to get you out of here." Alec said as he began to help Yukino unplug herself from the machines and helped her pull back the covers on her bed.

Yukino began to step out of bed, however, her legs unexpectedly seemed unable to hold her weight and she collapsed to her knees.

Alec was at her side in an instant. "Yukino?"

Akira rolled his eyes at the two of them. "Well, of course it'd be difficult for her to walk since she's been in a coma for the entire past year! Just carry her on your back *baka* and let's get the heck out of this creepy place."

Alec nodded with a serious expression on his face that made Akira roll his eyes heavenward, before he helped Yukino onto his back to carry her piggy-back style.

"Yukino can you sense where your brother is?" Alec asked her.

Yukino nodded solemnly. "Yes, I'll take you there."

Chapter 19:
Izanami: Death Goddess

Once outside Jinx conjured Travel Bubbles for the group - one for Akira and one for Alec, who was still carrying Yukino in his arms bridal style. The bubbles rose up off the ground and Yukino began to direct them to their destination.

"That way!" Yukino pointed, still in Alec's arms.

Jinx guided the bubbles with a wave of his wand to float in the direction in which Yukino had pointed.

Yukino directed them to the center of Kyoto and to a modern looking, internet café called *Cyber Cat*. They landed right outside of the establishment receiving several strange looks from people walking past on the sidewalk in front of *Cyber Cat*. Alec left Yukino with a chagrined Akira, so that he could rush inside to find Yoru. Alec skidded to a halt, however, when he caught sight of Yoru, who was collapsed and unconscious in front of a computer while a concerned waitress wearing a french maid outfit and cat ears was trying to shake him awake.

Alec walked up to Yoru's unconscious form and looked down at him. *Epp. Is he cursed? That would mean...Gulp.* Was he going to have to kiss Yoru *again*? There was only so much Alec could take all in one day. He considered just passing out right then from all the strange things he'd been forced to do that day, and save himself the trouble of passing out later.

Alec swallowed as he began to lean over Yoru to place a curse-breaking kiss on his lips with the cat-eared waitress watching him curiously when an amused smirk formed on Yoru's face making Alec blink in surprise. Huh?

Yoru then opened his eyes and his sapphire blue eyes were twinkling.

"Don't worry, Alec, you don't have to kiss me." Yoru stretched his arms over his head and let out a huge yawn. "I was just resting my eyes for a moment."

Alec shook his head ruefully, now was not the time for jokes. "Yoru? Are you really okay then?"

Yoru nodded solemnly, "Yes, I just needed to regain my strength. Let's go."

Yoru and Alec quickly made their way out of the café where Yoru was startled to see Yukino, alive and in the flesh *and* in Akira's arms. Uh oh. Alec hadn't thought about what Yoru would think of that.

Akira was beginning to wonder if he should have let Alec leave Yukino in his care when he caught sight of Mr. Protective Brother striding towards him with purposeful steps. *Gulp.*

"*Yukino...*" Yoru breathed as he approached her, his voice thick with emotion.

"*Onii-sama,*" Yukino smiled back.

He rushed up to her and took both of her hands in his, while ignoring Akira entirely. "Yukino, are you alright?" Akira felt a trickle of sweat form on his brow as he watched the exchange.

Yukino nodded. "Thanks to Alec."

Yoru looked back at Alec and gave Alec a grateful look.. "Alec, we both owe you a great debt."

Alec blushed, and put a hand behind his head in an awkward manner. "Naw..."

Akira coughed and spoke in a highly sarcastic voice. "As much as I hate to interrupt this *touching* moment Izanami has been set free and the end of the world is close at hand - so shouldn't we like get going and you know try and save the world and all that jazz?" Akira finished with a sneer.

Alec blinked.

Yoru nodded. "He's right. Let's go."

Akira practically tossed Yukino back into Alec's arms and Jinx waved his wand to conjure another Travel Bubble for Yoru to use. Then with another wave of Jinx's wand the bubbles were rising up off the ground and with Jinx leading the way the group headed back towards Izanagi Academy.

When they arrived at Izanagi Academy it was to find it in chaos. Izanami was perched on top of the ancient clock tower that was next to the main school building while letting loose an evil cackle that rang through the air as she looked down upon the havoc she had created. Kaguto was on the front lawn directing his star students: Catara, Smoker and Kiba into action in the battle that was currently taking place. Alec saw that from the looks of things Izanami had already managed to create a tear that led from reality directly into Yomi, and from which her ghostly *samurai* army was currently pouring out from.

Izanami had decided to summon only the most powerful of warrior ghosts from Yomi to make up her army and the ghosts of ancient Japanese *samurai* were some of the most powerful ghosts in existence that she had the power to summon. *Samurai* that had fought the very wars that shaped the Japan that Alec had come to know. Kaguto thought it was only fitting that those very same *samurai* would have a hand in the creation of a new Japan - or rather its destruction and then rebirth.

Alec watched as the teachers of Izanagi Academy and monks and *miko* of the Izanagi Buddhist Temple were helping normal students to flee the battlefield that the school grounds had become. Alec saw that those with *Shinigami* or spiritual training like the monks and *miko* were combating the *samurai* ghosts and exorcizing them with a combination of *o-fuda* and sacred arrows.

Alec caught sight of Jin and Junko who were fighting what appeared to be a dark *miko* with long, black hair and a strange, red tattoo of a third eye in the center of her forehead, along with a pink-haired monk, who was wearing black lipstick and a spiked, leather collar. Alec shook his head. The villains they had to face were...weird.

Alec then caught sight of Rika, Junpei, and Neji, who appeared to be fighting three students that Alec didn't recognize right away. As he took a closer look at their faces, however, he realized they had to be Catara, Smoker, and Kiba, but in the *flesh*. Oddly enough, Catara had the same hair style in real life as in the game, this flirty, flipped do, and she was wearing a Japanese high school uniform or sailor outfit now. Smoker also had his hair shielding one side of his face still, and his one eye gleamed. Kiba also still had his short buzz cut and his brown eyes were narrowed fiercely. Both boys were in the Izanami Academy uniform, an all black outfit with a black jacket and pants.

Alec also noticed that they were wearing silver collars around their necks, and which suspiciously reminded him of the ghost control collars from the game Yokai World. Did that perhaps mean that Kaguto was controlling them? Alec wondered if perhaps they had reacted similarly to Akira when he had found out Kaguto had been lying to him all along and had rebelled against him. This would mean Catara, Kiba, and Smoker were not in control of their actions and had been reduced to mere pawns. But how to free them Alec wondered? And then he realized the only way would be to defeat Kaguto and take the control rings...

Alec's mind was working a mile a minute as he tried to formulate a plan to help those in need.

Rika had an easel set up before her and was painting ink-spirit reinforcements for Izanagi Academy. With a quick, elegant movement of her brush she ended up painting a very handsome man, who when he came out of her canvas seemed to possess impressive exorcist abilities as he immediately began combating the ghostly *samurai*. He was tall, gallant, and dressed in full, silver, battle armor - that of a medieval knight. He had long, silvery hair and gray eyes. He was also wielding a giant, Excalibur-like sword in his hands that appeared to have the power to exorcize ghosts with ease as the mysterious knight moved his sword gracefully through the air exorcizing samurai left and right while using his extreme speed and grace.

"*Oi oi oi*! Hey, hey, hey! And just who the hell is that?" Junpei demanded heatedly.

"Oh, who him? He's my dream guy." Rika admitted with a blush.

"Well, then why does he look like a grown up version of Alec dressed in medieval knight armor!" Junpei suddenly pouted.

Rika blinked back at her creation and her face turned bright red, "Now that you mention it..."

"If you're idle enough to participate in ridiculous pre-teen conversation allow me to occupy your time instead." The stoic boy, Smoker, strode forward towards Junpei and got into a fighting stance, a dangerous gleam in his solid black eye.

Junpei mirrored his actions and also took a fighting stance, a cocky smirk on his face. "I'm always up for a good fight. Bring it on, Smoker!"

Junpei and Smoker began to fight each other with a series of quick kicks and punches and complex martial arts moves that were making Alec's head spin as he tried to follow their impossibly fast movements, his eyes becoming all swirly. Alec worriedly noticed that both their hands were glowing with their spirit energy making the fight before him a matter of life or death.

"Hey Rika, you're looking a little lonely over there. How about I give you some company?" Catara's unmistakable haughty voice purred, and Alec turned to see her begin to chant and form hand seals with her two hands before several low level, evil spirits began to be summoned into the air all around them.

"Ewww." Rika complained as she saw the evil spirits, which were mostly made up of hairy eyeballs and floating, shadowy, smoke-like and blob-like bodies. "I'll paint something to take care of that mess." Rika declared as she quickly painted a drawing of that *kappa*-like creature Alec had seen her use once before. Once finished the kappa-like creature leapt off the canvas and into Rika's waiting arms. She then turned around with the small creature in her arms towards the mass of evil spirits. "Dinner time, K-*chan*!"

"*Idatakimasu*!" The creature exclaimed gleefully as it opened its mouth

485

and used a vacuum-like suction to begin to suck all of the ghosts and evil spirits into its mouth until it had devoured them all in mere seconds. The creature burped loudly as he finished his meal, which had easily been of at least 50 evil spirits all together. *"Gochisousama."*

Catara looked utterly put out and disgusted by this turn of events.

Alec had to hold back a laugh at the funny way Catara's nose scrunched up. Alec's eyes quickly scanned the battlefield to see how his friend Neji was doing and saw him close by wielding a giant, high tech looking gun, which he was using to shoot at the *samurai* ghosts. Alec's jaw dropped as he thought that for a second there Neji was looking pretty darned cool. Large balls of red light shot out from Neji's ASE gun and the *samurai* ghosts that were hit were instantly exorcized into nothingness.

That's when Alec noticed that standing next to Neji was a girl, who seemed a bit out of place given the current circumstances and made Alec do a double take. Alec realized she resembled one of the magical girls that Neji had posters of back in his room. She was wearing a pink, sailor outfit with lots of ribbons and lace. Her long, blonde hair was done in pigtails *a la Sailor Moon* and she had a pink, sequined, domino mask on her face. She also wore ballet slippers that were laced up to her knees. And in her hands Alec noticed she held one of those things called a 'ribbon dancer' - which was basically a wand stick with a long ribbon attached to it.

Alec's jaw dropped when he watched the magical girl suddenly begin to spin towards the *samurai* ghosts dancing and waving her ribbon dancer through the air so that the ribbon shot out towards the *samurai* ghosts. The ribbon was encased in a red-tinged light and as the magical girl danced and flicked her ribbon towards the *samurai* ghosts they were immediately exorcized. *Whoa.* Alec couldn't help but think. *Girls with pig-tails can seriously kick butt. This is better than a late night anime show.* As soon as Alec saw the magical girl slicing through *samurai* ghosts with her ribbon dancer he knew it was no ordinary ribbon dancer *thing*. Alec noticed the light coming from the ribbon was red and realized it had to be artificial spirit energy. Which could only mean -

"Could she be...Neji's robot? RoboGirl2.0?" Alec blinked as he recognized those dance moves. "That is so *cool*."

Just then Alec noticed Kiba, knocking an arrow to his bow and aiming it right at Neji.

"Neji!" Alec began to call out a warning, and was prepared to go to his friend's aid, however -

RoboGirl2.0 beat him to it. The magical girl robot danced over towards Kiba and stopped the arrow as it whizzed towards her master by simply plucking it out of the air and breaking it in half in her one hand. Her eyes glowed red menacingly as she approached Kiba on tip-toes. Talk about a killer ballerina. Kiba gulped and took a step back.

"No one hurts Master!" The magical girl robot declared as she attacked Kiba with her ribbon dancer, and he took off running while looking like a complete fool with a cute, killer robot hot on his heels.

Alec shrugged since it seemed as though his friends had things under control after all.

That was when Yoru seemed to catch sight of Kaguto somewhere on the battlefield that had become the school grounds. "Kaguto!" Yoru growled and unsheathed his Spirit Sword before empowering it with his spirit energy so that the blade of light was instantly formed.

Alec turned to see where Yoru was looking and saw that Kaguto appeared to be directing some of the *samurai* ghosts while wielding the enormous and threatening *Ame-no-nuboku* spear that had a coil of crackling energy surrounding it.

Kaguto turned and spotted Yoru as well. "Come to me, Yoru!" Kaguto laughed gleefully as he spun his spear, preparing to meet Yoru's attack. "Let us settle this once and for all - our beautiful rivalry!"

Alec noticed that in reality Kaguto had long, black hair, which was pulled back in a ponytail whereas in the game his hair was blood-red, but Alec also noticed he still had those same eerie, golden colored eyes.

"Yoru!" Alec called out, concerned to let Yoru face Kaguto on his own, however, Alec became distracted when he heard a cry for help.

Alec turned to see that the three boys, who were always picking on him: Tatsuya, Ken and Omi, appeared to be cornered by several *samurai* ghosts, who had formed a circle around the boys. They were currently closing in for the kill with their glowing *katana* raised and their eyes glowing red through their horned *samurai* helmets.

"AH! Someone help us!" Tatsuya cried out, his voice cracking.

"I can't believe I'm about to do this." Alec sighed and turned to Akira, "Here take Yukino for a second would ya?"

"Huh?" Akira blinked in surprise as Alec suddenly shoved Yukino into his arms and took off running towards the boys.

"Why me?" Akira sighed as he looked down at the not too pleased Yukino.

Alec unsheathed his Spirit Sword as he ran, and empowered it quickly with his spirit energy so that the blue, spirit blade flared to life. He then charged the *samurai* ghosts and Alec's Spirit Sword clashed with the ghostly warriors' *katana* blades when Alec easily managed to get past their defenses, mostly due to Yoru's great swordsmanship training, and slashed through them. As Alec's sword sliced through the *samurai* ghosts they were instantly exorcized bursting into dots of light that disappeared.

Alec continued to exorcize *samurai* ghosts left and right until there were no longer any left standing around the three boys.

Alec looked back at them, panting for breath, "You guys okay? You should hurry and get to safety."

Tatsuya, and his lackeys Ken and Omi, just blinked at Alec in total shock before Tatsuya stepped forward. "But why? Why would you save us after everything we've put you through?"

Alec just gave them a pitying smile. *Because most of the time I thought I deserved it.* "It's just what I do - I'm a *Shinigami* after all."

The boys continued to blink at Alec in disbelief.

Alec was beginning to feel awkward when their eyes began to turn from confusion to admiration. "Anyways, hurry and get yourselves out of here. It's too dangerous here for people like you guys without any spirit powers."

Tatsuya nodded, "Right." The boys all turned to go, but then Tatsuya seemed to turn around on an afterthought. "Oh and Alec?"

"Yes?" Alec raised an eyebrow at Tatsuya wondering what the boy could have to say to him.

Tatsuya couldn't meet Alec's eyes as he said: "Thanks."

Alec just nodded back and hurried back to where he had left Akira and Yukino. He had forgotten that Akira was RedAki, the very same player killer who had tried to capture Yukino again and again and realized it might have been unwise to leave Yukino so vulnerable and in enemy or rather ex-enemy hands. *Gulp. Yukino...*

Meanwhile, Akira was trying to end the awkward silence that had sprung up between he and Yukino as soon as Alec had left them...alone...together...

"Yo." Akira began in a slightly nonchalant attitude. "Some battle huh?"

Yukino frowned and turned her head away, "Hmph!"

Akira scowled darkly at her response. "Keh! Like I'd want to talk to you anyways..."

Yukino turned back to look at Akira and shot him a dark glare, "I can't believe you just said that. You certainly lack manners. If you knew anything at all about proper etiquette you would be apologizing to me before trying to start some small talk. Or have you forgotten about all those times you tried to capture me? You RRs made my life a living hell back in Yokai World... "

Akira paled in embarrassment as he realized what she said was true. "Yea, well...that was then and this is now. And um..." Akira trailed off wondering why he was finding it so hard to talk to this strange girl.

"Yes?" Yukino arched an eyebrow expectantly.

"*Sorry.*" Akira mumbled under his breath.

Yukino smirked. "What was that? I'm afraid I couldn't hear you."

Akira glared down at her and cleared his throat. "I'm sorry okay?"

"Really, didn't catch that." Yukino was having a little too much fun.

"I'M FRICKIN SORRY! Okay?" Akira bellowed and a few *samurai* ghosts that had been stalking up to the unsuspecting pair decided to back off for the time being.

Alec arrived and skidded to a halt as he heard those words fly out of Akira's mouth and blinked back at the *hikikomori* in disbelief. Apparently, the two had managed to get along a bit better than Alec had thought they would. He smiled and ran up to the pair. "Hey guys, sorry about that."

Akira let out a breath of relief as he thankfully relinquished his hold on Yukino and handed her back to Alec. In Akira's book - girls were scary and were a reason to stay in one's room and certainly not a reason to go out from it.

Yukino suddenly pointed off towards the clock tower. "Hey, look there! It's Izanami!"

Alec followed Yukino's finger to see that it was indeed Izanami that seemed to be perched on the top of the clock tower. Alec could sense her immense spirit energy and could see the dark aura of power that had formed around her. In fact, Alec worriedly noticed that her spirit power seemed to be increasing by the minute for some reason.

"But what's she doing?" Alec narrowed his eyes at her. Suddenly, he began to notice these round balls of white light that were shooting through the air to Izanami and entering her body. The aura of energy around Izanami seemed to become even brighter and more powerful as more of these little balls of light entered her body. "Just what are those?"

Suddenly, Alec, Yukino, and Akira began to see students and teachers collapsing to the ground all around them and for no apparent reason. Then as a few students near to them suddenly fell over Alec was able to watch as small balls of light rose out of the students' bodies and headed towards Izanami.

"It's their souls..." Yukino informed them in a morbid tone. "She's eating students' souls in order to gain more power."

"Oh my god," Alec looked sickened by this and was turning slightly green. "We have to stop her."

Yukino nodded back at him.

Akira looked back and forth between Yukino and Alec in disbelief noticing their fierce expressions, "Whoa, whoa, whoa. *Chottomatteo!* Wait just one minute. You guys can't actually be thinking of going up against Izanami can you? Just what do you expect to be able to do against her? She's the goddess of the underworld - *remember? Bakas!*"

Alec turned to Akira, a steely look in his eyes, "That doesn't matter. We have to do *something*. I can't just stand back and watch as she sucks out the souls of my friends."

Yoshitsune suddenly appeared floating at Akira's side, "Young Master!"

Akira turned to Yoshitsune in surprise. "Yoshitsune? You're here too?"

Yoshitsune nodded, "I was able to pass through the tear Izanami created. Your orders young Master?"

Akira couldn't help but smirk to himself that he had a powerful, ghost *samurai* for a lackey and turned his attention towards the ghostly army of *samurai*. "Let's get those guys. I can't let that punk brat show me up and get all the credit for saving the world now can I? Besides, Alec's been stealing all the fun. Hey...do you know any of these guys?" Akira asked on an afterthought as several *samurai* ghosts in full armor approached them.

"No." Yoshitsune shook his head, "But I do know some *samurai* who can help us. Men!" Yoshitsune called out and several *samurai* ghosts appeared materializing in the air around Akira and Yoshitsune. Akira whistled through his teeth, impressed at the number of Yoshitsune's old comrades.

They all bowed before Yoshitsune, "General."

Yoshitsune nodded at them. "We engage the opposing force and protect this school and it's students. Right Master?" Yoshitsune turned to confirm with Akira.

Akira nodded. "Sounds good to me. Let's do this thing!"

"*Osu!*" The *samurai* cheered.

· · · · · · · · · · · · · · · · ·

Alec, with Yukino on his back piggyback style, ran towards the looming clock tower and stood in front of it looking up at Izanami, who was perched on the very top of the pointed roof.

"How are we going to get up there?" Yukino questioned Alec fretfully.

"Uh..." Alec realized he once again hadn't thought that far ahead.

Just then, Jinx appeared flying towards Alec and Yukino at top speed. "Alec!"

Alec shook his head upon the sudden appearance of Jinx. Was the bad luck fairy psychic or something? He had to wonder. Alec turned towards the fairy, "Hey Jinx, perfect timing. We need a spell that will enable me to fly up there, so Yukino and I can face Izanami, while at the same time I need to be able to use my sword."

Jinx looked thoughtful for a moment before he gave Alec a rather piercing look. "I know a way...but I don't know if you're going to like it very much."

Alec simply nodded with a resigned expression on his face. "Just do it

Jinx. I trust you." Alec was ready to do whatever it took to stop Izanami from absorbing anyone else's soul.

Jinx was frowning slightly but nodded anyways. "Alright boss if you say so. I trust you too. True nature come forth!" Jinx waved his wand at Alec and it glowed brightly before Alec was enveloped in a purple colored light. Then suddenly two leathery, silver-gray, bat-like wings sprouted from Alec's back on either side of Yukino.

Yukino gasped in surprise as she watched the wings appear on Alec's back. Alec suddenly felt funny with all the extra weight on his back. Alec turned his head to peer behind him to see what the heck had happened to him, and stunned blinked back at his own new wings, his mouth gaping open in shock. "Whoa." Alec turned beaming to Jinx. "Thanks Jinx this is perfect! I knew you could do it!" Alec kicked off the ground, stretching out his leathery wings to his sides. He then flapped them hard so that Alec and Yukino shot up into the air.

Alec didn't hear Jinx's hushed words that trailed after him - "I didn't do anything Alec. It's all you."

As they flew up towards the top of the clock tower Alec warned Yukino that he was going to have to unwrap his arms from around her legs, "Yukino keep a tight hold around my neck! I'm going to have to let go of you. I need my hands free in order to use my Spirit Sword alright?" Alec called to her over the sounds of fighting below them.

"Okay!" Yukino yelled back as she tightened her hold around Alec's neck.

Alec and Yukino flew up to the top of the clock tower to see where Izanami was. Alec saw that the dark goddess wore an amused and careless expression on her face and was calmly watching all the chaos she was currently creating as students and teachers were falling over unconscious as she sucked out their souls. Alec was then able to pull out his Spirit Sword, which he had stuck into the back pocket of his uniform, and then he summoned his spirit energy, empowering the sword hilt so that a blade of blue light came forth.

Izanami watched Alec and Yukino approach her with a bored expression on her face, not appearing in the least fazed.

"Izanami! Stop stealing people's souls - RIGHT NOW!" Alec threatened as he flew up past Izanami and then shot back down through the air to bring his sword upon her in a hard downwards slash while he unleashed a battle cry. However, as he brought his sword down it suddenly hit an invisible shield that Alec knew had to be Izanami's pure spirit energy that was radiating off and around her body protectively.

Izanami merely sneered at their futile attempt. "Foolish humans - that amount of power can do nothing to harm me!" Izanami then quirked her head and sniffed the air curiously. "Oh! How absolutely delicious you both smell! I could just eat you up. And I think I will too!" Izanami cackled as her dark silver and black aura suddenly began to expand and glow more brightly. "Allow me to show you pathetic humans my true form, which is all the better to devour you with!"

A bright silver light engulfed Izanami's body and before Alec and Yukino's eyes her body began to shift and transform into an enormous, winged creature. When the blinding light cleared and Alec was able to see again Izanami's transformation was complete and Alec's jaw dropped at the beautiful but deadly creature that was now perched on the top of the clock tower.

The creature had two dragon-like heads, a long serpentine body and tail, which ended in sharp spikes, and two sets of enormous wings emerged from the creature's back. Alec thought the creature looked as though it were part bird and part dragon. One dragon head was covered in shimmering black scales and had piercing red eyes. Along this side of the creature's body black scales covered its entire length and the wings were midnight black. The other dragon head was covered in golden colored scales that gleamed like molten metal and had a pair of yellow eyes. Gold scales trailed down this side of the creature's body and the wings on that side of the creature's length were a brilliant white.

"Uh oh..." Alec didn't like the look of this *yokai* one bit and decided the best thing to do would be to lure the creature away from the school if he and Yukino were going to battle the beast since it could end up breathing fire down upon the school or its students. Decision made, Alec took off flying towards the forest on campus and Izanami quickly gave chase flying after them with an angry roar.

Once Alec thought they were far enough away from the school he turned around in midair prepared to face Izanami.

Izanami wasted no time in attacking them. The black dragon head's mouth opened and let out a breath of fire towards Alec and Yukino. Alec raised his sword and empowered it with a lot of his spirit energy to use it to shield her attack. He slashed his sword through the air while at the same time releasing a blast of spirit energy, so that it was able to cut through the fire attack. However, the golden headed dragon opened its mouth next and unleashed a spray of some kind of green liquid towards Alec and Yukino. Alec dodged the attack but it caught part of the sleeve of his school uniform and a sizzling sound filled the air. Alec looked down in shock to see that the green goo was eating away at the sleeve of his uniform. Alec's eyes widened in realization - acid. Alec flinched as some of the liquid touched his skin burning him there.

Uh oh...I have to make sure none of that gets on Yukino. Alec quickly dodged any more attacks coming from that head while having to block fire attacks from the other head with his sword. He was tiring quickly from all the acrobatic maneuvers he was forced to execute as he blocked and evaded the deadly attacks from both the dragon heads. Dipping, and diving and blocking through the air Alec continued to face Izanami while trying to find an opening with which he could attack her. Alec waved his sword at Izanami again unleashing another blast of spirit energy at her but Alec's attack seemed to harmlessly bounce off the dragon's scales.

"Hang on Yukino!" Alec yelled as he was forced to execute a complex maneuver as both the heads attacked Alec and Yukino simultaneously. "My spirit energy alone doesn't seem to be powerful enough to pierce that dragon's scales. If only we still had Oyuki's power at our disposal. Her command over ice and snow would be really useful right about now. And it may have even been enough to defeat Izanami."

Yukino blinked at Alec in confusion, "Well, why didn't you say so in the first place, *baka* brat?" Yukino closed her eyes and began to chant while at the same time she was moving her hands into complex seals while she was still clinging to Alec's back. "Oyuki! I summon you!"

A bright ball of white light suddenly appeared in the sky overhead and then floated down towards Alec and Yukino. The ball of white then formed into the shape of a woman and then suddenly Oyuki was materializing before them. Alec blinked at the unmistakable presence of the Snow Witch with her flowing ice-blue hair, serene golden eyes, and signature white and blue *kimono*.

"It looks like you two could use a little help." Oyuki started in a calm voice as she eyed the fierce creature they were battling.

Yukino smirked. "Indeed."

Oyuki floated up over Yukino and entered her body. Yukino closed her eyes and when she opened them her eyes were now two different colors - one eye a deep sapphire blue and the other eye a bright gold color. Her clothing also shifted and transformed so that she was now wearing a smaller version of Oyuki's white and blue kimono. Oyuki had successfully possessed Yukino therefore lending her power to Yukino, which Yukino was able to control using her powers as a *miko* and medium.

Alec could feel Yukino's body suddenly become as cold as ice and even the air around him seemed to chill suddenly causing Alec to shiver slightly.

"Oyuki has successfully lent me her power." Yukino informed Alec when the possession had been completed.

"G-great!" Alec's teeth were chattering from the cold and he was surprised he could suddenly see his own breath upon the air. "Please lend me your strength, Yukino. Together I know we can do this."

"Of course, I will. You are not alone Alec." Yukino let her new power flow through Alec's body and his Spirit Sword began to transform as a result, a coil of icy white energy seemed to wrap around the bright blue blade of Alec's sword, so that it turned to solid ice and tripled in size becoming more deadly in appearance.

Alec looked down at his new sword in awe. "Whoa. You really are a cool girl Yukino. You know that? Anyways, let's do this!" Alec fixed his gaze ahead of him on Izanami.

Yukino nodded and Alec didn't get to see the slight blush that was on her face at his spontaneous words.

Dark clouds began to gather high overhead, gray and swirling until a thick snow began to fall through the air all around them and then a fierce, chilling, wind began to blow through the air.

Alec flew off towards Izanami, at top speed, his new and deadly ice sword held out before him in a two-handed grip. "Izanami! Eat this - my and Yukino's Ice Spirit Sword!"

Izanami opened one of her dragon mouths and shot a large fireball at Alec and Yukino, which they easily sliced through with their new sword. Alec then waved his sword forward so that a powerful, icy cutting wind flew forward and hit Izanami's body with such force that she was sent tumbling backwards in the air and howling in pain. Izanami tossed her head and let lose a loud roar into the air as she cried out in pain up at the swirling clouds above them while at the same time exposing her scaly chest and stomach.

Chance! Alec realized as he thought back to his battle with the dragon Kyohime. "Now! Yukino, let's combine our spirit powers into one final attack." Alec directed her and Yukino nodded. Alec flew forward towards Izanami with his giant Spirit Ice Sword raised, while at the same time he was sending his spirit energy into the sword so that it was glowing brightly with a blue light from the inside of the crystal-like ice. Then Yukino began to transfer her own spirit energy into the sword, which began to coil around the sword with a pink-tinged light.

"Pink?" Alec blinked at the color of Yukino's spirit energy in surprise.

"Oh, shut up." Yukino wasn't really mad, however, as she smirked slightly at Alec's comment.

The pink and blue energies swirled around the Spirit Ice Sword as Alec aimed for Izanami's heart. Alec let loose a battle cry of 'Hooryah!' as he lunged the sword forward and managed to pierce through the creature's diamond hard scales.

Izanami cried out in rage and pain as the sword pierced through her scales and to her heart.

Alec and Yukino concentrated on sending their combined spirit energies into Izanami's body, through the sword, and began to purify the *yokai* from the inside out.

Izanami's dragon-like body began to disappear and as this occurred the souls of Alec's fellow classmates began to zoom out of the creature's disintegrating stomach and shot back towards the school, flying through the air.

As the creature's body began to disappear completely, however, Alec noticed a strange ball of swirling, black and silver colored energy. This ball of dark light shot off escaping in the direction of the school and Alec realized it had to be Izanami's soul.

"Izanami's soul! We can't let her get away!" Alec declared as he began to fly off in the direction Izanami had fled.

However, as Alec was flying back towards the school he failed to notice that Yukino was completely exhausted and no longer had the strength to keep her arms wrapped around Alec's neck, and so as he suddenly surged forward it caused her to lose her hold upon Alec's neck, and she began to fall backwards, off of Alec's back, and began to plummet towards the ground headfirst.

Alec was startled to feel Yukino's body unexpectedly slide off this back and turned around startled to see her falling headfirst towards the forest. "YUKINO!"

Alec folded his leathery wings and dived after her.

Yukino looked up at the sound of Alec's panicked yell and weakly reached her hand out towards him as she watched him fly down towards her.

Alec managed to reach her but instead of taking her hand grasped his hand around her wrist and quickly pulled Yukino protectively into his arms. As Alec held Yukino bridal style she looked down at the forest floor far below them and swallowed thickly. She blinked back at Alec disbelieving that he had actually managed to catch her in midair from a free fall like that - therefore saving her life. For a moment there she had really thought she would die but then Alec had unexpectedly saved her. Yukino couldn't help but stare at Alec with a mixture of surprise and awe on her face.

Alec looked down at her with a fierce expression on his face, his eyes as sharp as steel. "Are you alright, Yukino?"

Yukino gasped when she admired Alec in that exact moment and was taken by surprise - his eyes...she had never really noticed before, but they weren't just gray but had flecks of blue and green in their depths. She wondered why she had never noticed this before but realized it was probably because she had never been that close to Alec or so intensely focused on *him*. He had an oddly serious expression on his face compared to his usual careless one. Yukino also noticed his eyes held a fierce determination and purpose both of which were surprisingly directed towards her. And the silky strands of his snow-white hair were blowing wildly in the chill wind that was swirling around them framing his face. His silvery wings were outstretched behind him making him look like some kind of avenging angel.

He looks so different - grown up. Yukino couldn't help but think to herself.

Right then in her eyes Alec didn't seem like the weak-willed, shy boy she had come to know and that she sometimes had to look after and protect. Right then, he seemed like a young man, a hero. He seemed handsome and strong...

"Oh, yes. I'm more than alright." Yukino breathed as she grabbed the back of Alec's neck and unexpectedly pulled Alec into a kiss. If he teased her about it later Yukino decided she could always blame it on Oyuki...and maybe that would explain where these strange *adult* feelings had been coming from anyways.

Alec's eyes widened in surprise as Yukino's soft lips were suddenly pressed up against his own - hadn't Yukino said she'd never kiss a little boy like him? Whatever. Alec shrugged the matter off and closed his eyes and decided it would be wiser to just kiss her back now while he had the chance.

There, flying amidst the snow filled air Alec and Yukino simply kissed each other. Both of them trapped for that single moment in their own little world. A world where things like ghosts and *yokai* and *Shinigami* and the end of the world didn't exist. A world where only the two of them existed. A secret dream of Alec's having come true - if only in that single moment...

But Alec knew he couldn't stay locked away in his dream forever. He couldn't be that selfish - not when the fate of the world was at stake. Alec pulled away from Yukino ending their kiss but with a lopsided grin on his face. Oddly enough it was Yukino who was blushing back at him and eyeing him in confusion. "Yukino we have to go after Izanami's spirit." He explained the reason for suddenly breaking their intense kiss.

Yukino nodded slowly coming to her senses and her expression turned serious. "I think I know where she's headed. She's probably returned to Yomi and to the cave in order to restore her strength. We need to use the tear Izanami has created at the school and enter Yomi. Once there I can restore the seal upon her."

Alec nodded, "Good. You really are something else, Yukino. Now, let's go!"

"Right." Yukino agreed with a nod and a smile.

Alec, with Yukino in his arms bridal style, flew back towards the school as fast as he could. They spotted the giant tear that Izanami had created and from which the *samurai* ghosts were still emerging from. The tear appeared to be centered around the stone statue that was in the center of the school's courtyard. The statue was of the god of creation, Izanagi, who was fighting against what appeared to be a dragon. Around the statue was the glowing red slash mark, which meant that the statue itself had become a tear.

Before Alec and Yukino were about to fly through the tear, however, Yukino formed a hand seal. "*Kai!* Release!"

Oyuki's spirit rose out of Yukino's body and she turned to face Alec and Yukino, floating in the air before them as Yukino's eyes and clothing returned to normal.

"Thank you for your help, Oyuki." Yukino offered.

Oyuki nodded. "Anytime, my lady. Good luck."

No longer hesitating Alec flew through the tear and entered Yomi. Alec flew through the forest with Yukino still in his arms until they reached the break in the trees that opened out onto the barren wasteland area where the cave of Izanami was now before them. Alec could sense an evil presence from within the cave and knew it had to be Izanami. Alec gently set Yukino down on the ground in front of the cave, so that she was kneeling there since she was still too weak from her coma to stand.

"Do you need any help?" Alec asked while frowning down at her in concern.

Yukino shook her head. "No, this is what I do - I am a *miko* after all."

Yukino began to summon her spirit power and a magical circle began to form on the ground beneath her glowing with a golden light. She then started to perform the ritual ceremony that would be necessary to fix the broken seal upon the cave of Izanami. She began to form complex hand seals and then began to chant holy words in a low voice as she concentrated all her energy and power into this task.

However -

Kaguto suddenly appeared out of the forest, having leapt through the tear after Alec and Yukino, having sensed that something was amiss. Kaguto turned to see what Yukino was doing and a horrified expression came over his face. "NO!" Kaguto yelled before he charged towards Yukino with the *Ame-no-nuboku* spear held out before him in his two hands.

Alec deftly stepped in front of Yukino and activated his Spirit Sword, holding it out before him in a two-handed grip, more than ready to protect her. However, Yoru, who had jumped through the tear after Kaguto, managed to get in Kaguto's path first and their weapons clashed.

"Kaguto! I'm not finished with you yet!" Yoru declared as he summoned more of his spirit energy to go into his Spirit Sword to increase the sword's length, so that it would more easily compete with the massive spear that Kaguto was wielding.

Alec then noticed out of the corner of his eye that apparently Akira had also jumped through the tear and as he came out of the forest looked somewhat conflicted by the odd series of events that was occurring before him now.

"You keep getting in my way!" Kaguto growled at Yoru.

"And I always will as long as you're doing things that will put the whole world in danger!" Yoru shot back.

Kaguto's eyes flickered to Yukino, who had almost finished the ritual and his expression turned desperate. "You just don't understand. I *need* this to happen. Things will be better if Izanami is unleashed upon the world. The world is an awful place as it is now - full of hatred, anger, and war. If Izanami is unleashed upon the world she'll destroy everything, cleanse everything so that humanity can be given a blank slate to start again. It's the only way Yoru - don't you see? And then when *they* see Izanami's ghost army *they* will finally have to accept that ghosts and demons actually exist. And *they* won't be able to say that I'm crazy or possessed anymore! Ghosts and *yokai* do exist! I'm *not* crazy!" Kaguto was looking at Yoru with an oddly pleading expression on his face now and this was beginning to unsettle the other *Shinigami*.

"Who's 'they'?" Yoru blinked back furrowing his brows in confusion, "And of course ghosts and demons exist. It's only people without spiritual abilities that cannot see them who have a hard time accepting the truth. And who said you were crazy or possessed?"

"My own parents thought I was crazy when I told them about the things I could see or hear. And when I started exhibiting my awakening power to control fire - my mother became afraid of me and tried to have me exorcized at various shrines and temples, but then when that didn't work - she finally tried to kill me. She called me a demon and said I wasn't her son...But I suppose she was right in a sense. I wasn't truly her son. I was someone else's - Izanami's. I am the reincarnation of Izanami's son Kagu-Tsuchi! Don't you see? It must be my destiny to do her bidding upon this earth! It's the only thing I can think of that will give my worthless life any meaning."

In Yomi, a place of high spiritual power - things like memories could be shared and so Alec and the others began to see flashes of Kaguto's past, perhaps without him even knowing or realizing it -

Flashes of memory of how Kaguto had suffered swirled through Alec's mind. Of how his parents had thought he had been possessed and how one day Kaguto was forced by his mother to go to a shrine to preform an exorcism on her own son. How he was stripped naked and had freezing cold holy water splashed against him until he was trembling from the cold and made to stay in a tub like that for hours. And then there was a flash of memory where Alec got to see when Kaguto's own mother had tried to strangle him out of fear that Kaguto could suddenly set things on fire. Ironically, the fear of dying that Kaguto's mother had given him had caused Kaguto's power to go out of control and he had begun to set the room on fire accidently. The flames began to consume the room, house, his mother, his father - but the flames didn't harm Kaguto.

Alec realized as he watched these flashes of memories that Kaguto killing his parents had been an accident. Did that mean that Kaguto wasn't the heartless murderer he had always assumed him to be? The typical all-evil villain Alec had been expecting Kaguto to be all along and that some hero, namely Yoru in Alec's mind, would have to defeat in the end to save the day? He knew that Yoru was probably thinking something along the same lines.

Then Alec saw more flashes of Kaguto's memories about how he was feared, scorned, and hated by the people he came across later in his life and who found out about his strange ability to see ghosts or his ability to create and control fire until finally he was captured and committed to an insane asylum. Alec then saw flashes of memory from the time Kaguto had been at the asylum and before the time he must have later escaped and returned back to the outside world. Alec knew that once he returned to the outside world he had ended up becoming a *hikikomori* and had shut the world away.

And after having watched his memories Alec could hardly blame Kaguto for having wanted to shut the world away and escape reality. Now there were flashes of memory of the time that Kaguto had told Yukino about - about when he had played Yokai World and then discovered the tear in the game that led to Yomi and how there he had been able to meet his mother, Izanami, who had claimed Kaguto was in fact the reincarnation of her son Kagu-Tsuchi and had given Kaguto's worthless life meaning.

There were also flashes of memory from the time when Izanami had showed Kaguto the first kindness he had received in ages, and how she had trained him to control his power over fire. Then how later he had been guided by her to take control of the Izanami Clan as its rightful leader and how he had become the Headmaster of Izanami Academy in order to gather people under him with spiritual power that could help him fulfill his wish. His wish to free his mother Izanami from her prison in Yomi.

"Yes, Izanami gave me a wish." Kaguto said in a wistful tone, "Not only did I want to free my mother but I also wanted to have her help me destroy this world, so that I could then remake it as I saw fit. I would make the world a better place - one where people like me would be accepted. In fact, a world where people like you, Yoru, or you, Alec, or I who have spiritual powers and who are protecting Japan behind the scenes from spiritual threats will finally be able to come out into the open and finally get the credit and recognition that we rightly deserve!

"For *Shinigami* and people with powers like ours to be glorified...for us to become like gods upon the earth as we should be! Without us they would be doomed - destroyed by demon kind. Without us *Shinigami* the world is already lost don't you see?" Kaguto stretched his arms out to Yoru in a beseeching manner. "Now do you see? Why you can't do this to me? You can't seal my mother away from me again. She's the only one that cares for me. Humanity has come to hate me - people like us. Humanity is evil and deserves to be destroyed - taught a lesson!"

"But aren't you human?" Yoru asked in a serious tone.

Kaguto whirled around to face Akira, "Don't you agree Akira? Your own parents abandoned you when they found out you were different and left you alone at Izanagi Academy. Can you not agree with me that humanity is ugly indeed?"

Akira swallowed and shook his head. "You're right Kaguto I did used to think that all humanity was ugly. But now I know better...After I met Alec I realized not all humans are so ugly or evil after all. He befriended me and helped me to stop being a *hikikomori*. I learned what having a friend means. It means not being alone anymore...it means being accepted by someone."

"*Akira...*" Alec spoke in a moved voice as he looked over at Akira.

"Friendship?" Kaguto shook his head, a frantic look forming on his face, "I don't have any friends. Who would be friends with a monster like me?"

At that moment, as if having heard Kaguto's words, Shino and Sumi came out from the forest and were running towards the cave where Kaguto and the others were.

"Master Kaguto!" Shino called out concernedly.

"Kaguto-*sama*? Are you alright?" Sumi asked, worry etched onto his features.

"I think you're wrong about that Kaguto." Akira smirked at the sight of Kaguto's right hands.

Kaguto blinked at the appearance of Shino and Sumi in a slightly surprised manner.

"I don't care." Yoru spoke up suddenly and all eyes turned to him. Yoru's hands clenched tightly around the hilt of his Spirit Sword until his knuckles had turned white, "I don't care if he's suffered or is a victim of humanity's fear of that which they do not understand. *Boo hoo.*" Yoru's voice was laced with sarcasm. "I'll never forgive him - he killed my parents. I hate him. He *deserves* to be punished - he *deserves* to die! I will have my revenge no matter what!" Yoru charged forward. "I will show you no mercy Kaguto - my revenge is everything to me. It's the only thing that matters. The only thing that has kept me going all this time."

Kaguto's expression was equally grim, "You hate me do you? Well, show me your hate Yoru and I'll show you mine - for having taken my mother away from me! For taking away the meaning of my existence!" Kaguto spun the *Ame-no-nuboku* spear in his hands and prepared to meet Yoru's attack.

Their weapons clashed fiercely as Yoru and Kaguto battled each other. Yoru's large Spirit Sword was glowing brightly and his entire body was surrounded by a blazing blue aura of his spirit energy. Kaguto's body was also surrounded by a large aura of dark energy that had also surrounded his *Ame-no-nuboku* spear. As they battled they sent spirals of energy up into the air. Then they moved in to attack each other preparing to use their most powerful final attacks or finishing moves upon the other -

Red blood spurted into the air as Yoru's Spirit Sword pierced Kaguto's chest at the very same moment that Kaguto's *Ame-no-nuboku* spear managed to pierce Yoru's chest. However, the two *Shinigami* still weren't done with each other yet and began to summon their spirit energy around themselves preparing to finish each other off at the same time.

Blood dribbled down Yoru's chin as he smiled back at Kaguto. "So this is the end huh?"

"I have nothing left to live for anyways," Kaguto smiled grimly back, "Let's end this Yoru."

"Let's." Yoru agreed. "Mother...father...finally you will have your vengeance."

"No! Yoru!" Alec rushed up to the two battling *Shinigami*. "This isn't what your mother would have wanted at all! She wouldn't have wanted her son to become a murderer all for the sake of revenge! Midoriko told me to save you Yoru and now I think I know what she meant for me to do. This isn't what you really want. Do you want to leave Yukino all alone? You jerk! I thought you promised Yukino you would protect her! She needs you Yoru!"

Yoru began to hesitate at Alec's words. "Yukino...my dear sister...I had forgotten. I'm so sorry. But it's too late now..."

"No you're wrong! It's not too late. There's always another way! You guys can just stop fighting now." Alec pleaded with them.

Akira rushed up to Alec's side. "Kaguto! I know you hate Yoru from stopping the revival of your mother but are you sure that's even what you really want? You do realize that if Izanami is allowed to roam free across the world everything will be destroyed along with everyone - if you *live,* if you're alive, you will still have the chance to get to meet someone *nice.* But maybe you already have met people that care for you and you just haven't realized it yet. Are you really okay with Izanami sucking out the souls of Shino and

Sumi? They're your friends Kaguto! Set aside your hatred for humanity long enough to open your eyes and realize a part of humanity has already accepted you. And isn't that what you've really wanted all along?"

"Friends...I have friends?" Kaguto turned to look at the worried faces of Shino and Sumi.

Yoru, however, was still feeling torn as their spirit energies continued to swirl around them. "But he killed them! He used his fire controlling ability to burn down Izanagi Temple while my mother and father were still inside. All because Mother refused to break the seal on Izanami and help him!"

But then, at that moment as Kaguto was also forced to remember that day Kaguto's memory suddenly began to replay in everyone's mind -

FLASHBACK...

Kaguto had been at the Izanagi Temple trying to convince Midoriko to help him break Izanami's seal but when Midoriko refused Kaguto had no choice but to leave empty handed.

Kaguto was stalking down a hallway with furious steps when he suddenly heard a familiar voice in his head -

Kaguto...where do you think you're going, my son? You did very little to convince her to help you. How about you reveal to her who you really are? Perhaps, give her a taste of your true power...

Kaguto shook his head vigorously. "No, there must be some other way to free you, Mother. Don't worry I'll find it or learn it. And when I do I'll do whatever it takes to make it work. I promise."

That's not possible. Only a miko of the Izanagi Clan is able to break the seal that has been placed upon me. That unique ability has been passed down in their clan through the generations as well as the duty to protect that ability from the Izanami Clan. They will do all they can to stop us. That is why you should use your power...

Kaguto's eyes widened in fear. "No! I don't want to use it! I can't control it! What if someone gets hurt? I...the last time I used my powers I ended up killing them....My other mother...my father. She was right about me. I am a demon. A monster."

You have no reason to fear your own power. You must embrace it and who you truly are as the reincarnation of my long lost son Kagu-Tsuchi. Now set your power free!

Kaguto cried out all of a sudden and grasped his head in pain as Izanami tried to take control of his body. "No! Don't!" But Kaguto's fire starting abilities were already being activated and his entire body had spontaneously burst into flames.

Concerned, Midoriko rushed into the hallway upon having heard Kaguto's scream of pain and gasped when she saw that he was covered in flames. "Kaguto? What happened? Let me help you." Midoriko rushed to his side.

"No!" Kaguto screamed, "Stay away form me!" He waved his hand frantically towards her and then watched in horror as he accidently sent a blast of flame in her direction that hit her and sent her collapsing to the floor. "No!"

Midoriko's husband, Heero, came rushing into the hallway to see that his wife was collapsed upon the floor and covered in flames. "Midoriko!" He turned to face Kaguto his eyes burning with hatred. "What have you done?" He growled.

Kaguto backed up a step at the man's frightening expression, "I...I didn't mean..."

"You will pay!" Heero suddenly lunged at Kaguto, who was still covered in an aura flames.

"No! Wait! Don't touch me! You'll-" But it was already too late as Heero knocked Kaguto to the ground and punched him hard across the face. Almost instantly Heero's body began to become enveloped in the demonic flames as well. Kaguto shoved Heero off of him and looked down at his flame-covered hands in shock. Kaguto backed away in horror as he realized he had yet again accidently killed people with his power.

"No...no...this isn't what I wanted..." Kaguto put his face in his hands to block out the sight of the two forms now on the hallway floor covered in flames.

Kaguto heard the sound of fast approaching footsteps before a *shoji* door was quickly slid open and there, standing in the doorway was none other than Yoru. Yoru looked at the burning forms of his parents and hot rage came over his features. "Murderer!" He turned to glare hatefully at Kaguto.

"No!" Kaguto shook his head.

"*Onii-sama!*" Came Yukino's unmistakable scream from somewhere in Izanagi Temple, which had already begun to catch fire all throughout the structure.

"Yukino!" Yoru hesitated a moment before turning around and running down the hallway from Kaguto and towards Yukino's frightened voice instead.

Kaguto ran out of Izanagi Temple to see that he had managed to set the entire place on fire. Kaguto looked down at his hands, which were still on fire and tried to concentrate on putting out the flames but his powers still wouldn't obey him. Kaguto sunk to his knees in despair and continued to look down at his hands morosely. "I'm a murderer...I really am a demon...a monster..." Kaguto's expression suddenly hardened as he stood. "So be it. I can no longer escape my destiny. I am what I am. Isn't that right mother?" Kaguto stood and his eyes seemed to turn dull and lifeless. "There is no other way...than to tread the path of a devil."

Kaguto turned and walked away from Izanagi Temple without looking back.

END OF FLASHBACK

Yoru blinked back at Kaguto in shock after the vision had finished. Yoru realized the although Kaguto had caused his parents deaths he hadn't meant for it to happen. Also, his mother Midoriko had even tried to help Kaguto and had died trying to do so. Yoru stopped the flow of his spirit energy into Kaguto and removed his sword from Kaguto's chest with the last of his strength.

"Kaguto..." Yoru swallowed and Kaguto looked at him in confusion. "I forgive you."

Kaguto gawked back at Yoru, his jaw dropping, "But how? How can you possibly forgive me after all I've done to you and your family...to your sister?"

"Alec has helped me to see there is another way. Another path from the one of revenge that I had chosen. Alec once told me I was trying to best a devil by becoming a devil myself instead of staying an angel and convincing the devil to tread the same path as I." Yoru chuckled and blood dribbled down his chin. "I'm no angel but I think I finally understand what Alec was trying to say. Alec was right and I...was wrong. I also think this is truly what my mother would have wanted. I saw how she had tried to help you, Kaguto. So I think I'll follow in her footsteps."

Kaguto snorted. "I'm no angel either." But Kaguto lowered his spirit energy and also removed his sword from Yoru's chest.

The two *Shinigami* both sunk to their knees from their heavy injuries and their hands on each other's shoulders were the only thing keeping them from merely toppling over onto the blood soaked earth.

"Wow, get a load of us." Yoru shook his head grimly, "We're a mess."

"We definitely did a number on ourselves." Tears of blood had begun to leak out of Kaguto's eyes. "What a way to go huh? At least, we've met our ends in style. That was one hell of a fight Yoru. You're one tough *Shinigami!*"

Yoru chuckled but a gurgling sound was heard in his throat. "You too."

Alec, Akira, Shino, and Sumi rushed over to the fallen pair.

Yoru looked up at Alec. "Alec...thank you for stopping me from doing something I would have regretted. Take care...of Yukino for me." Yoru struggled to speak.

Kaguto turned to speak to Shino and Sumi, "I'm...sorry. I never realized you guys were my friends until now when it's already too late."

Alec and Akira exchanged worried glances. "Yoru, what are you guys talking about?" Alec's brows furrowed in concern.

505

"We're dying Alec...we can both sense each other's spirit energy signatures dropping. There's nothing we can do." Yoru explained.

Alec looked horrified and shook his head vigorously. "No! There must be a way...to save you both..." He trailed off looking at Yoru and Kaguto helplessly.

Kaguto shook his head, "It's too late for me now anyways, Alec. I've done too many evil things. I could never atone for them all no matter what I did."

Yoru frowned and gazed at Kaguto piercingly, "That's not true. You were a victim in all this Kaguto. I see that now. Though I've been a rather stubborn jerk not to notice it earlier."

"I'm no saint." Kaguto sneered in response.

Yoru just smiled. "That may be true but everyone deserves the chance of a new beginning. It's never too late to turn away from the wrong path and chose a new one. That's what it means to be *human* - you make mistakes and learn from them and *grow*. So that way the person you are tomorrow can be different from the person you are today."

"*Yoru...*" Kaguto murmured his voice thick with emotion.

"I won't let either of you die!" Alec declared suddenly, with his fist raised adamantly in the air before him. "Too many people will be devastated if that happens! I'll save you both!" Alec quickly got down on his knees and wrapped his arms around both Yoru and Kaguto. He then summoned his spirit energy so that a bright white light surrounded him and he began to pass this light into Yoru and Kaguto's bodies. This mysterious white light caused Yoru and Kaguto's bodies to glow and pulse with energy before their wounds began to close. The light around Alec, Yoru, and Kaguto increased until Akira and the others were blinded by it.

From very far away, Alec could hear Yukino cry out his name, right before darkness consumed him and he knew no more.

. . . .

Epilogue:

Alec felt someone stroking his hair and it was a slightly familiar touch that made him feel warm and protected. "Mother..."Alec murmured. The hand on his forehead stilled for a moment as if it might be pulled away, but Alec was glad to find that it did not and instead remained there stroking his head tenderly. Alec's eyes fluttered open and he saw Haruna-*sensei*. "Haruna-*sensei*... where am I?" Alec swallowed, his throat felt very dry for some reason.

Haruna-*sensei* frowned down at him. "The infirmary at Izanagi Academy."

Alec yawned broadly. "How long have I been out this time?"

"2 days."

Alec blinked back in surprise and quickly sat up, "2 days! Where is everyone? Is everyone okay? What happened?"

"You are a very kind and brave boy Alec. You used your own life energy to heal and save the lives of Yoru and Kaguto. It must have been instinctual really for you to be able to use your life energy like that though it's not completely uncommon. But that was also a very dangerous thing you did, Alec. Something that you must never do again. We almost lost you, Alec."

Alec plopped back down on the bed with a sigh of relief, "Yea, but they're okay aren't they? That's all that matters. That it worked. Giving them my life energy and all." Alec smirked to himself. "So that's what I did...all I remember is thinking about how sad Yukino would be if Yoru were to die and how there were people who would be sad if Kaguto died as well. I didn't really think about anything else but saving them somehow."

"And it almost cost you your own life." Haruna-*sensei* tucked a stray hair behind her ear, "If they hadn't brought you here in time for me to heal you Alec..."

"It's alright." Alec shrugged. "Even if I had died it would have been okay as long as I had managed to save Yoru and Kaguto because at least then no one would have been sad." *I doubt anyone would be sad for very long to lose me - I'm nothing but trouble after all being a Spirit Magnet and everything. Everyone would be better off without me.*

Haruna frowned. "But...you're wrong about that Alec. Everything would not have been alright if we had lost you. Not at all. I think you're forgetting something very important Alec. Didn't you ever stop to think about the people *you* would be leaving behind and that would be sad if *you* died." Alec blinked at her. "I'm talking about your friends, Alec. And don't be a *baka* and say you don't have any because you have *tons*. They were all here visiting you - about half the school and of course the usual suspects. They've all been extremely worried about you. Alec, you have to realize that even as much as you tried to push people away...it didn't work. You don't belong to only yourself anymore. You belong to your friends. Also...I was very worried about you Alec and I assure you I would have been quite sad if you had died."

Alec blinked back at Haruna-*sensei* in surprise and could feel the familiar sting of tears forming in his eyes. "Haruna-*sensei*..."

"And I was extremely worried as well." A gruff voice echoed through the nurse's office as Takahashi-*sensei* walked into the room.

Haruna-*sensei* eyes seemed to light up. "Takahashi-*san*."

Takahashi-*sensei* stood behind Haruna-*sensei* and put a hand on her shoulder in a natural gesture that perplexed Alec. "Are you two...?" It was like a light bulb had just gone on in his head.

Haruna-*sensei* raised her right hand and showed Alec her diamond engagement ring.

"Whoa." Alec's grinned. "That's so great. Congratulations. I'm really happy for you both."

Haruna-*sensei* and Takahashi-*sensei* both exchanged a look and Haruna-*sensei* smiled knowingly and looked back down at Alec. "He really is a good boy."

Takahashi-*sensei* nodded, "That he is. He helped us get together after all..."

"And that's why we wanted to ask you something Alec," Haruna-*sensei* bit her lower lip nervously, "How would you like it if we were to adopt you?"

Alec blinked back at them in shock before giving them a skeptical look - his teachers couldn't be that crazy after all, "Adopt me? Would you really want to do that? I mean I'm a Spirit Magnet! I'll be nothing but trouble. How could anyone possibly love me?"

Haruna-*sensei* and Takahashi-*sensei* immediately wrapped their arms around Alec in response to his own harsh words. "Who wouldn't want to adopt you? Who couldn't love a strong, brave boy like you? You saved the world Alec. I think you deserve to have a little saving in return." Haruna-*sensei* smiled warmly at him.

"I'd be honored to call you my son. I only wish I could protect you from those darned spirits but you're more powerful than I am in that department." Takahashi-*sensei* shrugged helplessly. "All I can give you is my love and support, but I don't know if that will be enough...?" He gave Alec a hopeful look.

Alec's vision was blurring as tears filled his eyes. "I stopped having dreams a long time ago so that I wouldn't be hurt when they couldn't come true. But now...dreams can't really come true in reality can they?"

"Of course they can Alec. When you wish for them strongly enough and try your hardest to make your dreams come true - they will. I know that you will make your dreams come true, Alec." Haruna-*sensei* assured him.

"What is life without dreams but an empty one?" Takahashi-*sensei* began, as he looked at Haruna-*sensei* fondly. "Haruna was my dream...and because of you it came true. Remember this Alec - sometimes you need someone else to help you make your dream come true. You can't always do things alone and that's why we want to be here for you if you ever need us Alec. To help you on the path to your dreams."

Alec smiled back. "Then my answer is yes but..." Alec's smile faltered. "What about Mori and Laura?"

"We've already contacted them. In fact, when I contacted them both earlier to tell them you were in a coma Mori explained to me how he and Laura had gotten back together. It's still a very delicate situation between the two of them and Mori didn't want to risk upsetting Laura. So he said the two of them would not be coming to see you. This upset me greatly and gave me the idea of perhaps adopting you." Haruna-*sensei* declared, a twinkle in her kind brown eyes. "And when I told Takahashi about how they had been behaving he readily agreed with my idea. Your parents both seemed to be interested with the idea since they both want to start a new life together, but we still had to discuss things with you first before anything becomes official."

"I see..." Alec couldn't help but feel a little sad that his adoptive parents had wanted to get rid of him so easily. But he couldn't say he didn't expect it - Laura was selfish and only concerned with her own hobbies. If Mori expected to make his relationship with Laura work he would have to put her interests first. Mori was not a strong enough man to protect Alec where Laura was concerned. And Mori had been in love with Sarah and Alec was the son of the man Sarah chose over him. That had to have stung - having this constant reminder around that Mori had failed to make Sarah fall in love with him. No wonder Alec had always sensed a sort of conflict within his father. And with Laura's fear of the supernatural - It was no wonder she had hated him. Alec had many times thought he had simply imagined it - that his parents didn't love him, but now it all made sense. Laura wanted nothing but a normal life, centered around her wants and desires. And Mori wanted nothing more than for Alec to be his son and not Lord Ryuuzaki's.

"I bet your friends will be happy to know you're alright. We were worried you might never wake up. Yukino seemed especially worried. She's been here by your bedside all this time, but I finally had to send her away to go and get some rest herself." Haruna-*sensei* gave Alec a knowing smile.

"Yukino was here?" Alec perked up, sitting up in bed again.

"That she was." Takahashi gave Alec a wink.

Alec blushed and put a hand behind his head in a nervous gesture. "Is she alright? Is she able to walk again?" Alec's expression had turned to concern.

Takahashi chuckled. "He really is a good boy, *neh?*"

Haruna giggled and nodded while Alec's blush grew deeper.

• • • • • • • • • • • • • • • •

Alec had received an urgent sounding email from his friends to log on to Yokai World as soon as possible, so wasting no time he logged on from the computer room, and immediately teleported to the Guardian Knights guildhall. As soon as his PC body had materialized a loud cry went up through the hall -

"Surprise!"

Alec blinked in surprise at all the players that were in the guildhall and did a double take when he caught sight of a banner that was hanging down from the ceiling: *Welcome Back Shinigami Boy! PS- Thanks for saving the world!*

"*Minna*....guys..." Alec's voice was thick with emotion as he looked around the room at all the familiar faces of his friends - Junpei, LadyV, Dr. M, Night, Jinx, Midoriko, Jin, and Junko (in their ninja PC bodies as No.1 and No.2), Reaper, RedAki, Catara, Smoker, Kiba, Sumi, and Shino.

Alec also noticed that towards the back of the hall a stage had been set up and a band of NPC dancing skeletons in bow ties and top hats were playing a haunting melody on violins and other instruments. Alec noticed that several players were beginning to form couples and dance.

Alec's closest friends were the first to rush up and greet him.

Junpei ruffled Alec's shaggy white hair, "You alright there, Alec?"

Alec gave Junpei a lopsided grin, "Yea, what is all this?" Alec waved a hand at the large gathering of players and music.

"We wanted to surprise you and have a little party in honor of the boy, who saved the world and all." LadyV's green eyes shimmered with amusement.

Alec noticed that she was back to her more developed self and dressed specially for the occasion in a beautiful dark green *kimono* with a golden flower pattern and a matching golden colored *obi* sash tied about her waist. The *kimono* and sleeves were long and went to the floor.

Alec scratched his cheek bashfully, "But I didn't do it alone..." Alec was really bad at dealing with this type of attention.

"He's quite modest isn't he." Dr. M pushed his glasses up his nose knowingly.

Night walked up to Alec and clapped him hard on the shoulder. "I owe you one, kid. I wouldn't be here right now if it wasn't for you."

Reaper frowned, strolling casually up to the pair, "I guess you could say I owe the boy one too. So..." Reaper gritted his teeth. "Thanks."

Alec's brows rose in surprise at Reaper's words. He knew it must have been hard for Reaper to actually *thank* another human being for something. "Your welcome." Alec gave Reaper a grin.

Shino had walked up next to Reaper and looped an arm through his. She eyed Alec before giving him a surprisingly warm smile. "If it wasn't for you my beloved Reaper-*sama* might be dead. I am also in your debt."

"Same here, kiddo." Sumi declared and gave Alec a playful wink, "You're quite the little hero. It's a good thing you heroes save the bad guys too." Wherever Reaper went Sumi wasn't too far behind.

"No, that's just Alec," RedAki drawled, "Alec is the worst kind of idiot hero - the kind that risks his life to save his enemies. How ridiculous is that?"

"Hey!" Alec pouted.

"Although," RedAki continued as if Alec hadn't interrupted him, "About half of us wouldn't be here right now if it wasn't for the, *baka* brat."

Alec's eye brows rose. "Was that a thank you?"

"You wish," RedAki sneered but then smiled to take the harshness off his words.

Everyone was nodding and smiling in agreement since they knew RedAki's words rang true. Alec had always been a bit too kind-hearted for his own good and rarely thought of his own welfare.

"That's just the type of boy he is." Midoriko smiled serenely, "That's why I knew he could save my Yoru and my Yukino."

"Mother..." Night looked at his mother with eyes swirling with unreadable emotions.

"Anyways, it was all just as I had foreseen." Midoriko nodded confidently. "I knew Alec was the key to saving us all."

Shino frowned, "I foresaw it too, you know. Just not that once Alec and Yukino were reunited they would have the power to destroy and rescal

Izanami. I only foresaw that together they would be able to prevent the unsealing and for our plans to come to fruition it was pivotal to keep them apart."

Alec's jaw dropped at this sudden information.

Meanwhile, Catara, Kiba, and Smoker were all in their own little group chatting to each other.

"Why are we here again? This is enemy territory." Kiba frowned and looked around suspiciously.

"Because, it's a *party*." A cat's paw smile formed on Catara's face, "And I want to get to dance with RedAki. You guys are just here for moral support." Catara informed them in a nonchalant manner. Catara was wearing a pretty pink *kimono* with a magenta *obi* sash tied about her waist.

"Figures." Kiba sighed. "Girls."

Smoker was frowning behind his *ninja* mask, "I don't *do* social gatherings like this. Catara said we had a mission."

"You do have a mission," Catara's eyes sparkled mischievously, "And that's to enjoy yourself. I know..." Catara continued in a low voice. "How much you like LadyV so how about you ask her to dance?"

"I think this may be the first time I fail a mission." Smoker shook his head.

"Don't worry Smoker you can always dance with me," Kiba offered with a playful smirk.

"Pass." Smoker took a few precautionary steps away from Kiba causing both Catara and Kiba to laugh.

Midoriko was looking at Alec with eyes full of admiration - it was beginning to make Alec extremely uncomfortable, "Thank you so much Alec for not only having saved my son, but also my daughter as well..."

"She's been waiting for you, Alec," Jinx nudged Alec's side with his elbow.

Alec turned to look where Jinx had been staring and the crowd of players began to part to reveal Yukino at the other end of the dance hall. She was wearing a stunning, dark blue *kimono* that had a pattern of silver half-moons throughout the thick, silk material, and there was a glistening, silver *obi* tied about her waist. Like LadyV's *kimono* it was long and the sleeves reached the floor as well. The sight very nearly took Alec's breath away.

Alec gulped and walked towards her with awkward, tin-man steps, while she approached Alec as well seeming to glide across the hall floor. Once he was standing directly in front of Yukino he gathered his courage before reaching his hand out to hers, "May I have this dance?" Alec held his breath.

Yukino smirked. "Just this once." She put her hand in his. "*Shinigami* boy."

"Maestro! Better make it a long one then!" Alec dared to request aloud, earning a slight blush on Yukino's cheeks, which made Alec feel quite pleased with himself as he swept Yukino out across the dance floor. He had been practicing waltzing in secret for when he'd have the chance to dance with Yukino again and had become quite good." *I wish this moment could last forever...*

The other players had also broken off into couples and were following Alec and Yukino's lead - Junpei was dancing with LadyV, Night and Junko had paired off, Reaper and Shino were dancing, and Akira and Catara had begun to dance together as well.

Jinx waved his wand and made a bunch of fairy lights and streamers along with a disco ball suddenly appear to adorn the hall with some extra light. Along with the normal dance decorations he managed to summon he had accidently summoned some Halloween decorations as well. Jinx shrugged, Oh well, this was Yokai World after all, the world of ghosts.

Despite all his practicing Alec accidently stepped on Yukino's foot several times due to his nervousness. "You're still such a brat." Yukino teased knowing Alec was trying so hard to impress her.

Alec pouted but then a mischievous glint formed in his eye. "You know, Yukino, all men were once boys. One day I won't be a brat anymore what then?"

Yukino tapped her chin thoughtfully for a moment as Alec held his breath. She then smiled broadly at him. "Guess we'll just have to wait and see to find out. No one knows what the future will bring."

"You're right Yukino," Alec agreed as he spun her, "But I do have a dream for the future..." Alec hesitated in telling Yukino how he felt for her and decided against it. "Hopefully, some day it will come true."

Yukino smiled warmly back, "If you wish for it hard enough Alec, with all your heart and soul. I'm sure your dream will come true. I believe in you, *baka* brat. So...are you going to tell me what this mysterious dream of yours is?"

"Now that..." Alec trailed off as Yukino leaned forward, "Is a secret."

"*Baka.*" Yukino pouted.

Alec just chuckled in response and they continued to dance. *My dream Yukino is to one day become someone special to you...and I don't plan on ever giving up because I am...Shinigami boy.*

END

Alec's saga will continue in

Shinigami Boy Returns

Coming soon!

Questions? Feedback?

You can reach the authoress at her artist webpage:
http://ladymafdet.deviantart.com
or her Facebook page "Sophia Hughlette"

LaVergne, TN USA
26 August 2009
155995LV00004B/6/P